THE DELIAN CYCLE

The Dray Prescot Series

THE DELIAN CYCLE

Kenneth Bulmer

writing as
Alan Burt Akers

Published by
Bladud Books

First published in 2007 by Bladud Books.

Originally published separately by Daw Books, Inc., as:
Transit to Scorpio (1972)
The Suns of Scorpio (1973)
Warrior of Scorpio (1973)
Swordships of Scorpio (1973)
Prince of Scorpio (1974)

This First omnibus edition published in 2007 by
Bladud Books, an imprint of Mushroom Publishing, Bath,
BA1 4EB, United Kingdom

www.bladudbooks.com

ISBN 978-1-84319-553-5

Contents

Transit to Scorpio

A note on the tapes from Africa

In preparing the strange and remarkable story of Dray Prescot for publication I have become overwhelmed at times with the power and presence of his voice.

I have listened to the tapes Geoffrey Dean gave me, over and over again, until I feel I know the man Dray Prescot as much through his voice as by what he reveals in what he says. At times deep and reflective, at others animated and passionate with the fire of his recollections, his voice carries absolute conviction. I cannot vouch for the truth of his story; but if ever a human voice invited belief, then this one does.

How the tapes from Africa came into my possession is soon told. Geoffrey Dean is a childhood friend, a gray, prim, dedicated man of fixed habits, yet for the sake of old friendship when he called me from Washington I was glad to speak with him. He is a government man with one of these shadowy organizations related to the State Department and he told me three years ago he had had occasion to go to West Africa to supervise fieldwork in connection with a famine emergency. Many brilliant young men and women go out with the Foreign Aid programs, and Geoffrey told me of one, an idealistic youngster, Dan Fraser, who had been working harder than a man should up-country.

Fraser told Geoffrey that one day when the situation was almost impossible with horrific numbers of deaths daily a man staggered out of the African forest. Men were dying everywhere around and there was nothing unusual in that. But this man was completely naked, badly wounded, and he was white.

I met Geoffrey Dean for lunch on a flying visit to Washington. We ate well at an exclusive club. Geoffrey brought the conversation around to his telephone call and went on to say that Fraser, who had almost lost control, was shaken and impressed, profoundly impressed, by this stranger.

The famine was killing people by the thousand, massive epidemics were being staved off by daily miracles, aircraft were encountering near-insuperable difficulties flying in supplies; yet in the middle of this chaos and destruction of human life Dan Fraser, an idealistic but seasoned field-worker, was uplifted and strengthened by the character and personality of Dray Prescot. He had given Prescot food and water and bound up his wounds. Prescot could apparently live on next to nothing, his wounds healed rapidly, and when he realized the famine emergency resolutely refused any special treatment. In return Fraser handed across his cassette tape recorder in order that Prescot might record anything he wished. Prescot had a purpose; Fraser said he could see.

"Dan said he was saved by Prescot. They were miles from anywhere and he'd been alone. The strength, the calmness, the vitality of Dray Prescot was amazing. He was a little above middle height with shoulders that made Dan's eyes pop. His hair was brown, and so were his eyes, and they were level and, according to Dan, oddly dominating. Dan sensed an abrasive honesty, a fearless courage, about

3

him. The man was a dynamo, by Dan's account."

Geoffrey pushed the pile of cassettes over to me across that expensive table with the wine glasses and the silver and fine china and the remains of a first-class meal. Outside that exclusive club Washington, the whole of the United States, seemed as far away, suddenly, as the wilderness of Africa from which these tapes had come.

Dray Prescot told Dan Fraser if he did not hear from him inside three years he could do as he saw fit with the tapes. The possibility that they might see publication gave Dray Prescot a deep inner satisfaction, a sense of purpose that Fraser felt held more significance than this mysterious stranger would reveal.

Fraser was extremely busy with the famine — I gathered more from what Geoffrey did not say that the end of the boy's nervous resources was close — and only the appearance of Dray Prescot had saved an ugly situation from sliding into a disaster that would have had international repercussions. Geoffrey Dean speaks little of his work; but I believe a great deal of foreign health and happiness is owed directly to him.

"I promised to abide by the conditions laid down by Dan Fraser, who would, in any case, have absolutely refused me permission to take the tapes back to America had he not known I would respect his wishes and the wishes of Dray Prescot."

Geoffrey, I had always thought and saw nothing to make me change my mind, had little imagination. He went on: "That famine was a bad one, Alan. Dan had too much to do. When I arrived, Dray Prescot had gone. We were both hellishly busy. Dan did say that he'd seen Prescot, at night, beneath those African stars, staring up, and he'd felt an unease at the big man's expression."

He touched the cassettes with the tip of his finger.

"So — here they are. You'll know what to do with them."

And so I present in book form a transcript of the tapes from Africa. The story they tell is remarkable. I have edited as little as possible. I believe you will detect from the textual evidence how Dray Prescot swings from the expressions of one age to that of another, freely, without any feeling of anachronism. I have omitted much that he says of the customs and conditions of Kregen; but it is my hope that one day a fuller transcript will be possible.

The last cassette ends abruptly in mid-sentence.

The tapes are being published in the hope that anyone who may be able to shed some light on their extraordinary contents will come forward. Somehow, and I cannot explain this, I believe that is why Dray Prescot told his story in the midst of famine and epidemic. There is more to learn of that strange and enigmatic figure, I am confident.

Fraser is a young man dedicated to helping the less fortunate of the world, and Geoffrey Dean is a civil servant quite devoid of imagination. I cannot believe that either of them would have faked these tapes. They are presented in the conviction that however much lacking in proof they may be, what they tell is a real story that really did happen to Dray Prescot on a world many millions of miles from Earth.

Alan Burt Akers

One

The Scorpion calls

Although I have had many names and been called many things by the men and beasts of two worlds, I was born plain Dray Prescot.

My parents died when I was young, but I knew them both and loved them deeply. There was no mystery about my birth and I would consider it shameful now to wish that my real father had been a prince, my real mother a princess.

I was born in a small house in the middle of a row of identically similar houses, an only child, and a loved one. Now I find myself often wondering what my parents would make of my strange life and how they would greet with delight or that delicious family mockery my walking with kings and my dealing as an equal with emperors and dictators, and all the palaces and temples and fantastic settings of distant Kregen, that have fashioned me into the man I am today.

My life has been long, incredibly long by any standards, and yet I know I merely stand at the threshold of the many possibilities the future holds. Always, for as long as I can remember, ill-defined dreams and grand and nebulous ambitions enclosed me in a fervent belief that life itself held the answers to everything, and that to understand life was to understand the universe.

Even as a child I would fall into a strange kind of daze in which I would sit back and stare upward sightlessly, my mind blank, receptive of a warm white light that pulsed everywhere. I cannot now say what thoughts passed through my brain for I do not believe I thought at all during those times. If this was the meditation or contemplation so ardently sought by Eastern religions then I had stumbled on secrets far beyond my comprehension.

What is still vividly in my mind of my young days is my mother's apparently continuous letting-out of my clothes as I grew. She would bring out her sewing basket and select a needle and look at me with such an expression of loving helplessness as I stood there, my shirt once more torn across my shoulders. "You'll soon not be able to go through a door, Dray, with those shoulders," she would scold, and then my father would come in, laughing perhaps over my wriggling discomfiture, although we had, as a family, precious little to laugh at in those days.

The sea which boomed and thundered whitely at the mouth of the river had always conveyed to me a siren song; but my father, who carried his certificate of exemption with him day and night, set his face against my going to sea. As the gulls wheeled and called across the marshes and swooped about the old church tower, I would be on the grass and ponder my future. Had anyone then told me of Kregen beneath Antares and of the marvels and mysteries of that wild and savage world I would have run as though from a leper or a madman.

The natural aversion my father held to the sea was founded on deep suspicion of the morality and system of those responsible for manning the ships. He had all his life lived with horses as his chief interest, capable of dealing with all aspects of their care and training, and when I was born in 1775 he was earning our living by horse-doctoring. During the time I spent with the Clansmen of Felschraung on Kregen long after my father's death I felt myself nearer to him than ever before.

Our spotless kitchen was always crammed with greenish bottles of mysterious mixtures, and the smell of liniments and oils struggled with those of cabbage and freshly-baked bread. There was always weighty talk of the staggers, glanders, pinkeye and strangles. I suppose, speaking logically, I could ride a horse and jump him moderately well before I could toddle safely from our kitchen to the front door.

One day an old hag woman with curious eyes and a bent back and dressed in rags stuffed with straw wandered through the street and suddenly it was the craze for our neighbors to have their fortunes told. It was on this day I discovered that my birthday, the Fifth of November, somehow turned me into a Scorpion, and that Mars was my planet of the ascendant. I had no idea of the meanings of these strange words; but the concept of a scorpion intrigued me and possessed me, so that, although I was forced to indulge in the expected fisticuffs with my friends when they dubbed me The Scorpion, I was secretly thrilled and exultant. This even compensated me for not being an Archer, as I longed, or even a Lion, who I conceived would roar more loudly than that Bull of Bashan the school-master loved to imitate. Do not be surprised that I was taught reading and writing, for my mother had set her heart on my being an office clerk or school-teacher and so raise myself from that sunken mass of the people for whom I have always felt the most profound respect and sympathy.

When I was about twelve a group of sailormen stayed at the inn where my fa-ther sometimes helped with the horses, combing them and speaking to them and even finding raggedy lumps of West Indian sugar for them to nibble and slobber from his upturned palm. On this day, though, my father was ill and was carried into the back room of the inn and placed gently on the old settle there. His face dismayed me. He lay there weak and listless and without the strength to sup from the bowl of strong ale the kindly tavern wench brought him. I wan-dered disconsolate into the yard with its piles of straw and dung and the smells of horses and ale filling the air with an almost solid miasma.

The sailors were laughing and drinking around something in a wicker cage and, immediately intrigued like all small boys, I went across and pushed between the burly bodies.

"How d'ye like that abed with ye at nights, lad?"

"See how it scuttles! Like a foul Sallee Rover!"

They let me look into the wicker basket, quaffing their ale and laughing and talking in their uncouth sailor way that was, alas, to be all too familiar to me in the days to come.

In the basket a strange creature scuttled to and fro, swinging its tail in the air like a weapon, rocking its whole body from side to side with the violence of its movements. Its scaly back and the two fierce pincers that opened and shut with such malice repelled me.

"What is it?" I asked, all innocently.

"Why, lad. 'Tis a scorpion."

So this was the creature whose name I bore as a nickname!

I felt the hot shame course through me. I had learned that people like me, Scorpios, are supposed to be secretive; but there was no hiding my reaction. The seamen laughed hugely as at a joke and one clapped me on the back.

"He won't get at you, lad! Tom, here, brought him all the way from India."

I wondered why.

I mumbled out some kind of thank you — politeness was a drudgery of social custom my parents had drummed into me — and took myself off.

How these things happen are secrets well kept by heaven, or by the Star Lords. My father tried to smile at me and I told him Mother would be coming soon and some of the neighbors and we would carry him home on a hurdle. I sat by him for a time and then went to beg another quart of ale. When I returned carrying the pewter tankard my heart seemed to stop.

My father was lying half off the settle, his shoulders on the floor and his legs tangled in the blanket that had been tucked around him. He was glaring in mute horror at the thing on the floor before him; yet that horror was contained within an icy mask of self-control. The scorpion crept toward my father with a hideous lurching roll of its obscenely ugly body. I dashed forward as the thing struck. Filled with horror and revulsion I mashed the tankard down on that vile body. It squashed sickeningly.

Then the room was filled with people, the sailors yelling for their pet, the tavern wenches screaming, ostlers, tap-boys, drinkers, everyone, shouting and crying.

After my father died my mother did not linger long and I stood beside the twin graves, alone and friendless, for I had no cousins or aunts or uncles I knew of, and I determined to shake off altogether the dust of my country. The sea had always called me; now I would answer that summons.

The life of a sailor toward the close of the eighteenth century was particularly arduous and I can claim no personal credit that I survived. Many others survived. Many did not. Had I cherished any romantic notions about the sea and ships they would have been speedily dispelled.

With a tenacity that is of my nature, whether I will it or not, I fought my way up from the lower deck. I found patrons willing to assist me in acquiring the necessary education so that I might pass my examinations, and incidentally I ought to say that in finding navigation and seamanship subjects over which I seemed to have an instinctive command puts into a proper perspective my eventual arrival on the quarterdeck. It seems now, looking back, that I walked as though in a somnambulistic trance through that period of my life. There was the determination to escape the foulness of the lower deck, the desire to wear the gold lace of a ship's officer, the occasional moments of extreme danger and terror, and as though to balance out emotion the nights of calm when all the heavens blazed overhead.

Study of the stars was required of a navigator and continually I found my eyes drawn to that jagged constellation of Scorpio with its tail upflung arrogantly against the conjunction of the Milky Way and the ecliptic. In these days when men have walked upon the moon and probes are speeding out beyond Jupiter never to return to Earth, it is difficult to recall the wonder and inner apprehension with which men of an older generation regarded the stars.

One star — Antares — seemed to glow down with a force and fire of hypnotic power upon me.

I stared up from many a deck as we crossed with the Trades, or beat about in blockade, or dozed along in the long calm nights in the tropic heat, and always that distant speck of fire leered on me from where it jointed that sinisterly upraised scorpion's tail, threatening me with the same fate that had overtaken my father.

We know now that the binary Alpha Scorpii, Antares, is four hundred light-years away from our sun and that it blazes four thousand times as brightly; all I knew then was that it seemed to exercise some mesmeric power over me.

In the year in which Trafalgar was fought, the same year, I ought to mention, in which I had once again been disappointed of gaining my step, we were caught up in one of the most violent gales I had ever experienced. Our ship, *Rockingham*, was thrown about with contemptuous ease by waves that toppled, marbled with foam, to threaten our instant destruction should they poop us. The counter rose soaring against the sky and then, as each successive roller passed away, sank down and down as though it would never rise. Our topgallants had long since been struck down; but the wind wrenched our topmasts away into splintered ruin and slashed into ribbons even the tough canvas of the storm jib. At any second we would broach to, and still those enormous waves pounded and battered us. Somewhere off the lee bow lay the coast of West Africa, and thither we were driven helplessly before the fury of the gale.

To say that I despaired of my life would not be true; for I had as much irrational desire to cling to life as any man; but this was by now only a ritual act in defiance of a malignant fate. Life held little of joy for me; my promotion, my dreams, had all faded away and were gone with the days that had passed. I was weary of going on and on in a meaningless ritual. If those sullen waves closed over my head I would struggle and swim until I was exhausted; but then when I had done everything a man in honor can do and should do, I would bid farewell to life with much regret for what I had failed to achieve, but no regret for a life that was empty to me.

As *Rockingham* lurched and shuddered in that tremendous sea I felt my life had been wasted. I could see no real sense of fate in keeping my spirit still alive. I had fought many times, with many weapons, I had struggled and battled my way through life, roughly, ever quick to avenge a wrong, contemptuous of opposition; but life itself had beaten me in the end.

We struck the sand shoals at the mouth of one of those vast rivers that empty out of the heart of Africa into the Atlantic and we shivered to pieces instantly. I surfaced in that raging sea and caught a balk of timber and was swept resistlessly on and flung half-drowned upon a shore of coarse yellow-gray sand. I just lay there sodden, abandoned, water dribbling from my mouth.

The warriors found me with the first light.

I opened my eyes to a ring of narrow black shanks and splayed feet. Anklets of feathers and beads indicated instantly that these black men were warriors and not slaves. I had never touched the Triangular Trade although tempted many times; but that would not help me now. To these blacks I was not a strange white apparition. As I stood up and looked at them in their feathers and grotesque headdresses, their shields and spears, I thought at first they would treat me as a white man engaged in the Trade on the Coast and take me to the nearest factory where there would be others of my kind.

They jabbered at me and one thrust a tentative spear tip at my stomach. I spoke boldly, asking them to take me to the other white men; but after only a few moments I realized none understood English, and my pidgin had been learned in the East Indies. By this time in my life I had grown into full stature, a little above middle height and with those broad shoulders that had been the despair of my mother developed with ropes of muscle that had stood me in good stead before in the midst of storm or battle.

They did not overpower me easily. They did not attempt to kill me for they used their spears with the flat or the butt and I assumed they intended to sell me into slavery with the Arabs of the interior, or to cut my carcass up slowly over a stinking village fire, delicate in their torture.

When they had beaten me down I awoke to my senses lashed to a tree in an odiferous village set above the eternal mangrove swamps, those notorious swamps where a single false step would mean a slow and agonizing death as the rank water gradually slopped up over the distended mouth. The village was surrounded by a palisade on which bleached skulls added a grim warning to strangers, where cooking fires smoked and cur dogs whined. I was left alone. I could only surmise my fate.

Slavery has always been abhorrent to me and I found a grim irony that I should be the recipient of racial revenge for a crime I had not committed. Again the feeling of destiny urging me on overwhelmed me. If I was to die, then I would fight every last step of the way for no other reason than that I was a man.

The bonds around my wrists cut cruelly and yet, as the day wore on in heat and stench and stifling dampness, by continual rubbing and twisting that left my wrists raw some slack became evident. During the afternoon two other survivors of the wreck of *Rockingham* were dragged into the village. One was the bosun, a large surly individual with reddish hair and beard who had evidently put up a fight, for his red hair was caked with dried blood. The other was the purser, still fat and greasy, a man whom no one liked and, as was to be expected, he was now in a pitiable state. They were lashed to stakes on each side of me.

With flies buzzing around us for company we hung and rotted until at blessed last the sun fell. Fresh hordes of insects then took up the task of sucking our blood. I will not dwell on what happened to my two unfortunate companions, hung one on each side of me on their trees of suffering; but their awful cries of torment forced me to chafe even more savagely at my bonds.

Looking back, it seems now that the reason I was left until the last came about because the blacks wanted to use the utmost of their diabolical arts on me, caused, no doubt, because twice during the day I had bodily lifted my legs and kicked a too-importunate inquirer into my condition forcefully in the stomach. I understood as my two companions died why our feet had not been pinioned.

By now it was pitch-dark with the red firelight flickering from the crude walls of the huts and the palisade and grinning in jagged reflections from the naked jaws of the skulls atop their stakes. The blacks danced around me, shaking their weapons, shuffling and stamping their feet, darting in to prod with a spear, springing back out of reach of my kicking feet. Any tiredness of a normal kind is soon learned to be lived with in any life at sea. My fatigue was of a deeper kind. But, grim and unyielding, I determined, as my Anglo-Saxon forebears would say, to die well.

Despite the horror of my position I bore these blacks no ill will. They merely acted according to their lights. No doubt they had seen many a miserable coffle of slaves trudging down to the factory to be branded and herded like cattle aboard the waiting scows; perhaps I made a grave mistake, and these very men were members of the local tribes who bought slaves from the blacks and Arabs of the interior to sell at a profit to the traders on the Coast. Either way, it did not concern me. My one concern was to break that last reluctant strand binding my wrists. If I did not break free very soon I would never do so, and would die a mutilated hulk on the stake.

Firelight reflected redly from the eyeballs of the savages and darted pinpricks of blinding light from their spear blades. They closed in, and I saw that this was the moment when they would begin their devilish practices on me. I put out a last desperate effort; my muscles bulged and the blood thundered in my head. The last strand parted. My arms were afire with the agony of returning circulation, and for a long moment I could do nothing but stand there feeling as though I had dipped my arms in a vat of boiling water.

Then I jumped forward, seized the spear from the first astonished warrior, clubbed him and his companion down, let out a shrill shriek followed by a deep roaring bellow as we used to do when boarding, and raced as fast as my legs would allow between the huts. The crude palisade gate could not stop me, and in an instant I had ripped away the line lashing it to the upright, flung it ajar and bounded out into the jungle night.

Where I was going I, of course, had no real idea. Escape impelled me on. The warriors would be after me this very moment, their shock overcome, running like hunting dogs and with their spears held ready for the deadly cast that would bury the blade in my back.

The instinct that drove me on was so deeply-buried in my subconscious that I could barely comprehend why I ran. That I would die was obvious. But that I would struggle and seek every means to prolong life, that, too, given the nature of the man I eventually understood myself to be, is equally obvious.

When one can run along the fore-topgallant yardarm in a gale on a pitch-black night, one could cross the footbridge to hell.

I ran. They followed and yet, I fancied, they did not follow as fast or with as much vigor as they might and the idea occurred that they might be more frightened than I was myself of this jungle night. But follow they would and capture was inevitable. Where lay safety in this predatory jungle aprowl with unknown dangers and festering with poison? Reaching a cleared space where a tree had fallen and dragged down some of its neighbors I clambered up onto the rotting trunk, dislodging some of the residents as I felt a trickle across my feet like grains of sand blowing in the wind. I kicked out. Up I climbed and there, above me, riding clear of the surrounding vegetation, shone the stars of heaven.

The stars glowed above me and as the familiar constellations met my eyes I turned instinctively to seek out one well-known shape that among all the rest had insistently drawn me with hypnotic power I could neither understand nor explain.

There sparkled the arrogant constellation of Scorpio, with Alpha Scorpii, Antares, blinding my eyes. All the other stars of heaven seemed to fade. I was feverish, light-headed, weak, knowing my sure death followed on stalking feet through the jungle. I had thought to use the stars to guide my escape as they had guided me over the trackless seas. I had thought to use the stars to navigate my way back to the beach. What I hoped to do there God knows. I stared at Scorpio malevolently.

"You killed my father!" Sweat stung my eyes. I was half off my head. "And you seek to do the same to me!" I have no real, coherent memory of what followed, for sweat blinded me, and my breathing pained. But I was aware of a shape like a giant scorpion limned in blue fire. I shook my fist at the Scorpion Star. "I hate you, Scorpion! I hate you! If only you were a man like myself..."

I was falling.

Blue fire coruscated all around; there was blue fire in the stars and blue fire in my eyes, in my head, blinding me, dazzling me. The blue changed to a brilliant malignant green. I fell. I fell with the blue and green fires changing and pulsing brilliantly into red as the red fires of Antares reached out to engulf me.

Two

Down the River Aph

I awoke lying flat on my back.

With my eyes closed I could feel warmth on my face and the flutter of a tiny breeze, and beneath me a familiar motion told me I was aboard a boat. This information did not seem at all strange; after all, had I not spent the last eighteen years of my life at sea? I opened my eyes.

The boat was simply a very large leaf. I stared like a man staggering from Copley's taproom in Plymouth stares owlishly on wan daylight. The leaf sped along the center of a wide river whose green water shone splashing and rippling very merrily alongside. On either bank extended a plain of greenish-yellow grass

11

whose limits were lost beneath a horizon shimmering in heat. The sky blazed whitely down on me. I levered myself upon my elbows. I was stark naked. My wrists chafed and the irritation plucked untidily at my memory.

Then I became extremely still and silent, frozen.

The leaf was large, being a good eighteen feet in length, and its curved stalk rose in a graceful arc like an ancient Greek galley's sternpost. I sat silent and rigid in the bows. Where the sternsheets would be in an ordinary Earthly boat crouched a scorpion fully five feet in length.

The monstrous thing was of a reddish hue, and it pulsated as it swayed from side to side on its eight hairy legs. Its eyes were set on stalks, round and scarlet, half-covered by a thin membrane, and they moved up and down, up and down, with a hypnotic power I had to force myself to conquer. Its pincers could have crushed a fair-sized dog. The tip of its sting-armed tail rose high in the air in a mocking blasphemy of the graceful arc of the leaf-stem — and that tip dripping a poisonous green liquid aimed directly at my defenseless body.

Around its mouth clumps of feelers trembled and its mandibles ground together. If that mandibular array once seized on my throat...

That macabre tableau held for what seemed a very long time as my heart beat with a lurching thump very distressing to me. Scorpion! It was no blown-up Earthly scorpion. Within that grotesque body covered by its exoskeleton-like plates of armor a real vertebrate skeleton must exist to support the gross bulk. Those ever-moving eyes were no eyes a scorpion would use. But those pincers, those mandibles — that sting!

Scorpion! I remembered. I remembered the African night, and the firelight and the gleaming spears and the mad flight through the jungle. So how could I be here, floating down a river on a giant boat-shaped leaf with only a monstrous scorpion for crew? Antares — that red star that had blazed down so powerfully upon me as I sought to escape — Antares at which I had hurled my puny mortal hatred, without a single doubt I knew that some uncanny force had drawn me from my own Earth and that Antares, Alpha Scorpii, now shone luridly in the sky above my head.

Even the gravity was different, lighter, freer, and this I saw might give me some slender chance of survival against this fearsome monster.

Scorpions feed by night. By day they skulk beneath logs and rocks. Stealthily I drew back first one leg and then the other, lifting myself slowly onto my haunches. And all the time my eyes were fixed on the weaving eye stalks before me. One chance I had. One fragile chance to leap forward, first to avoid the scy-thing gripping blows of the twin pincers, second to duck the downward darting sting, and then with a heave and a twist to topple the thing overboard.

My empty hands clenched. If only I had a weapon! Anything, a stout root, a broken bottle, an oar loom, even a cutlass — a man who has lived as I have lived knows the meaning of personal weapons, respects them for their meaning to him. However smartly I could break a man's back with my bare hands, or gouge out an enemy's eyes, a mortal human's natural weapons are a poor substitute for the weapons of bronze and steel with which mankind has struggled out from the caves and the jungles. I felt my nakedness then, my soft flesh and brittle bones, my puny human muscles, and I hungered for a weapon. Whatever force had brought me here had not with kindly consideration also provided me with a pistol, or a cutlass, a spear or shield, and I would have suspected weakness had that mysterious force done so.

No thought entered my mind then that I might dive overboard and swim to the river bank. I do not know why this thought did not occur to me and I think, sometimes, that it had to do with my reluctance to abandon my ship, to betray my own trust in myself, and the feeling that no animal should be allowed to conquer me and that if we were to battle then the prize was this simple leaf boat.

I drew a long slow breath and let it out and drew another, filling my lungs. The air was fresh and sweet. My eyes never left the scarlet rounded eyes at the ends of their stalks as they moved up and down, up and down.

"Well, old fellow," I said in a soft and soothing voice, still not moving in any way that could be the signal for the monster to pounce. "It looks as though it's you or me." The eye stalks weaved up and down, up and down. "And believe me, you ugly Devil's Spawn, it is not going to be me."

Still speaking in a low soothing voice, as I had often heard my father speak to his beloved horses, I went on: "I'd like to rip your belly up to that fat backbone you've got in there and spill your tripes into the river. Sink me, but you're a misbegotten lump of offal."

The situation was ludicrous and looking back now I marvel at my own insensitiveness, although I realize that much has happened since and I am not the man I then was, fresh from the inferno of life aboard an eighteenth century sailing ship, and no doubt prey to all the superstitious nonsense plaguing honest sailormen.

And, truth to tell, I talked not only to soothe the beast but also because talking delayed the time when I must act. I could see the sharpness and the jagged serrations of the pincers, the crushing power of the mandibles and the oozing greenish liquid dribbling from the poised sting. The frog believed the scorpion and gave him passage across the river, and the scorpion stung the frog, because, said the scorpion, it was in his nature. "Well, scorpion, it is in my nature not to let anyone or anything best me without a struggle and loathsome though you are to me I allow it is in your nature to kill me, therefore you must allow it in mine to prevent you. And, if necessary, to kill you to protect myself."

The thing swayed gently from side to side on its eight legs, and it pulsated, and its eyes on their stalks weaved up and down, up and down.

With the palms of both hands flat on the greenish membrane of the leaf between the darker green of the veins, I prepared to hurl myself forward and risk that formidable armament and heave the thing overboard. I tensed, holding a breath, then thrust with all the power of corded muscles in thigh and arm. I shot forward.

The scorpion heaved itself up, its tail curling and uncurling, its pincers clashing — then in a single giant leap it flung itself end-over-end out of the boat. I rushed to the gunwale of the leaf and looked over. A splash surrounding an eight-pointed outline with a stinging whip of tail — and then the scorpion vanished.

It was gone.

I let out that held breath. For the first time I noticed that the thing had not exuded any smell. Had it been real? Or could it have been an hallucination brought on by the fantastic unreality of my experiences? Was I still chasing madly through the African jungle, demented and doomed? Was I still lashed to the stake and was my mind winging into a fantasy world to escape from the agony being inflicted on me? People always pinched themselves in this kind of situation; but I had no need of that crude analysis. I knew I was here, on some other world than Earth, beneath the giant red sun of Antares. I knew it, without a doubt.

Shielding my eyes I looked up at the sky. The light streamed down from the sun, tinged with a reddish hue, warming and reassuring. But a new color crept across the horizon turning the yellowish-green grass more green. As I watched with streaming eyes and sparks shooting through my brain another sun rose into the sky, glowing a molten green, suffusing the river and the plain with light.

This green star was the companion to the giant red star that made up the star we called Antares — later I understood that the words "red giant" were a misnomer — and the quality of the light did not discommode me as much as I would have expected. And, too, there were more surprises in store for me in this new world that explained the more Earthly-type of lighting we receive from our own yellow sun shining here. The leaf had ceased its rocking now and my little command had shipped very little water. I scooped up a handful and drank and found it clean and refreshing.

The best thing to be done now was to allow the leaf to carry me down the river. There would be habitations along the river, if there were people in this world, and I found it all too easy to drift with the current and let things happen as they would.

The river wound in wide sweeping reaches. Occasional shoals of sand shone yellow. There seemed to be a complete absence of trees of any stature, although tall reeds and rushes grew in many places along the banks. By dint of much splashing with my hands and with a seaman's instincts to take best advantage of the set of the current, I eventually drove my craft ashore onto a shelving beach. I ran her up well above the water mark. I did not much fancy walking when I had a perfectly adequate boat at my command.

The reeds were of many varieties. I selected a tall straight-stemmed specimen and by much levering and cursing managed to break off a ten-foot length. This would serve as a punt-pole in the shallows. One variety attracted my attention because I accidentally nicked my arm on its leaf. Again I cursed. Swearing is an occupational disease at sea. This reed grew in clumps with straight round stems perhaps an inch or an inch and a half in diameter; but the thing that attracted me was the leaf, which sprouted upright from the top of each stem to a length of perhaps eighteen inches. This leaf was sharp. The width was of the order of six inches, and the shape was — not surprisingly — that of a leaf-bladed spear. I broke off a bundle at a softer node some six or eight feet from the leaf, and I then had a bundle of spears that I wished I had had when my boat's crew had been aboard an hour ago.

The reeds rapidly dried into a tough hardness under the sunshine and the edge of the blade was sharp enough to allow me to hack down more samples.

Taking stock, I looked across the shining surface of the river. I had a boat. I had weapons. There was abundant water. And by splitting reeds lengthwise I could fashion lines with which to catch the fish that were undoubtedly swarming in the river, waiting with open mouths to be taken. If I couldn't fabricate a hook from a sharpened reed or thorn, I would have to construct fish traps. The future, with people or without, appeared giddyingly attractive.

What had there been in life for me back on Earth? The endless drudgery of sea-toil without reward. Hardship inconceivable to the mind of scientifically-pampered twentieth century man. An eventual certainty of death and the dread possibility of maiming, of having an arm or leg taken off by a roundshot of grape or langrage smashing into my face, hideously disfiguring me, unmanning me, tipping out my intestines onto the holystoned decks. Yes — whatever force had brought me here had done me no disfavor.

A flutter of white caught my eye. A dove circled around, fluttering inquisitively nearer, then taking fright and circling away. I smiled. I couldn't remember the last time I had made so unusual a grimace.

Above the dove I saw another shape, more ominous, hawk-like, planing in hunting circles. I could see the second bird very clearly. It was immense, and it glowed and sparkled with a scarlet coat of feathers, golden feathers encircled its throat and eyes, its legs were black and extended, their claws rigidly outstretched. That bird flaunted a glorious spectacle of color and power. Although at the time it would have been impossible for me to have recalled the lines, now I can only leap to those magnificent words of Gerard Manley Hopkins as he reacts with all a man's mind and body to the achievement of, the mastery of, the thing that is so essentially a bird in the air. And more particularly, knowing now what I could not know then, Hopkins' words have a deeper meaning as he calls the windhover "Kingdom of Daylight's Dauphin."

I shouted and waved my arms at the white dove.

It merely circled a little way farther off and if it was aware of that blunt-headed, wing-extended shape above it gave no sign. The deadly hawk shape with its broad wings with their aerodynamic fingertip-like extensions, the wedge-shaped tail, the squat heavily-muscled head cried aloud their own warning. The nature of the hunting bird is to kill its prey; but I could at least warn the dove.

A piece of reed tossed at the dove merely made it swerve gracefully in the air. The eagle or hawk — for that magnificent scarlet and golden bird was of no Earthly species — swooped down. It ignored the dove. It swooped straight for me. Instinctively I flung up my left arm; but my right thrust forward one of my spears. The bird in a great cup-shaped fluttering of its wings and a powerful down-draft effect of its tail, braked in the air above my head, hovered, emitted one single shrill squawk, and then zoomed upward with long massively powerful beats from its broad wings.

In a moment it dwindled to a dot and then vanished in the heat haze. I looked for the dove only to discover that it had also vanished.

A strong feeling came over me that the birds were no ordinary birds. The dove was of the size of Earthly doves; but the raptor was far larger even than an albatross whose shape in the sky above our sails had become familiar to me in many southerly voyages. I thought of Sinbad and his magical ride aboard a bird; but this bird was not large enough to carry a man, of that I was sure.

As I had promised myself I caught my dinner and with some difficulty found enough dry wood. By using a reed bow I made fire by friction, and almost in no time at all I was reclining and eating beautifully-cooked fish. I hate fish. But I was hungry, and so I ate, and the meal compared very favorably with salt pork ten years in the barrel, and weevily biscuits. I did miss the pea soup; but one couldn't have everything.

I listened very carefully and for some considerable time.

With no knowledge of what hostile creatures there might be in the vicinity I judged it advisable to sleep aboard the boat; my patient listening had not revealed the distant thunder of a falls which would bring to a premature end this river journey. For I was now convinced that I had been brought here for a purpose. What that purpose was I did not know and, truth to tell with a full belly and a pile of grasses for a bed, I did not much care.

So I slept through the red and green and golden afternoon of this alien planet.

When I awoke the green tinged crimson light still flowed from the sky, deeper now but the color values of objects still true. After a time I came to ignore the pervading redness of the light and could pick out whites and yellows as though beneath the old familiar sun that had shone on me all my life.

The river wound on. I saw many strange creatures on that uncanny journey. One there was, a thin-legged animal with a globe-like body and a comical face set atop it, for all the world — this or the Earth — like that of Humpty Dumpty. But it walked on eight immensely long and thin legs — and it walked on the water. It skimmed by me, its legs pumping up and down in a confusing net-like motion. The thin webs on its feet must each have been three feet across, and there must have been some kind of valvular action to break the suction created as its weight came on each pad in turn. It skittered away from the leaf boat and I laughed — another strange and somewhat painful movement not only of my mouth but also of my abdomen — as it tiptoed over the river surface.

One of the spears made an excellent paddle by which the boat could be steered. Counting days became meaningless. I did not care.

For the first time in many weary years I felt free and relieved of burdens — of care, of fear, of frustration, of all the intangible horrors that beset a man struggling to find his way through a life that has become meaningless to him. If I were to die, either soon or at a more distant date, well — Death had become a companion all too familiar.

Drifting thus in a mellow daze down the river, not bothering to count the turn of days, there occurred times of sudden emergency, of stress and of danger, like the occasion when a great barred water snake attempted to clamber with its stunted forelegs aboard the leaf boat.

The battle was short and incredibly ferocious. The reptile hissed and flicked its forked tongue at me and gaped its barn-door jaws open to reveal the long slimy cavity of its throat down which it intended to dispatch me. I balanced on the leaf, which danced and swayed and tipped in the water, and thrust my spears at the water snake's hooded eyes. My first fierce thrusts were fortunate, for the thing let loose a squeal like swollen sheets shrieking through distorted blocks, and flicked its tongue about and threshed those stumpy forelegs. This creature emitted a smell, unlike that scorpion of my first day in this world.

I stabbed and hacked and the thing, shrieking and squealing, slid back into the water. It made off, curving like a series of giant letter S's laterally in the water.

The encounter filled me only with a fuller awareness of my good fortune.

When the first distant roars of the rapids whispered up the river I was ready. Here the banks rose to a height of between eighteen and twenty feet and were footed with black and red rocks against which the water broke and cascaded, spuming. Ahead the whole surface was broken. Standing braced against a thwart constructed from a number of reeds broken to length and thrust between the sides of the leaf which were amply strong enough, and with my body in a bracket of more reeds attached higher up, I was able to lean out and down and thus gain tremendous leverage with the spear-paddle.

That swirling rush through the rapids exhilarated me. The spray lashed at me, water roared and leaped everywhere, the boat spun and was checked by a thrust of the paddle; the black and crimson rocks rushed past in a smother of foam and the lurching, dipping, twisting progress was like Phaëthon riding his chariot upon the high peaks of the Himalayas.

When the boat reached the foot of the rapids and the river stretched ahead once more, placid and smoothly running, I was almost disappointed. But there were more rapids. Where a prudent man would have beached the boat and then made a porterage, I exulted in the combat between myself and the river; the louder the water roared and smashed against the rocks, the louder I shouted defiance.

Having arrived in this world naked and carrying nothing with me I had no tie for my pigtail and water-drenched as my hair was it now hung freely down my back past my shoulder blades. I promised myself that I would have it cut to a slightly shorter length and never again adopt the required queue and its tie. Some of the men aboard ship had had pigtails that reached to their knees. These they kept coiled up most of the time, only letting them down on Sundays or other special occasions. I had put that life behind me now — along with the pigtail.

Gradually from the horizon into which the great river vanished a range of mountains rose, growing higher day by day. I could see snow on their summits, gleaming cold and distant. The weather remained warm and glorious, the nights balmy, and the skies covered with stars whose constellations remained an enigmatic mystery. The river was now over three miles in width, as best I could judge. There had been no falls for a week — that is, seven appearances and disappearances of the sun — but the sound of thunder now reached my ears in a continuous diapason, swelling in volume perceptibly as the current of the river increased in velocity. The width of the river narrowed sharply; in a morning the banks closed in until they were no more than six cables' length apart, and narrowing all the time.

When the river was two cables' wide I paddled furiously across to the nearer bank, almost deafened by the continuous roaring from ahead. There the river vanished between two vertical faces of rock, crimson as blood, streaked with ebony, harsh, and raking half a mile into the air.

I pulled the boat out of the water and considered. By the smooth humped surface of the river I could tell the enormous power concentrated there. The river was now very deep, the water pent between those frowning precipices. The bank was a mere ledge of rock, above which the cliffs rose towering out of my sight. A bush grew there that I recognized, of a deep green with a profusion of brilliant yellow berries the size of cherries; it was a welcome sight. I picked the yellow cherries and ate them — they tasted like a full-bodied port — while I considered.

After a time I took a spear and set off for the falls.

The sight amazed me. By clinging to a rock at the extreme lip I could look over and down that majestic expanse of water as it slid out and over into nothingness and then arched down until far, far below it battered into the ground once again. A solid sheet of spray sleeted from the outward face of the waterfall and obscured what lay beyond. Below, the pool was like a great white lily spreading in widening circles of foam, with the roaring cataract toppling smoothly downward into its eye.

There was no climbing down the rock.

Again I considered. A force had brought me here. Had it brought me merely to stand and marvel at this waterfall? Must there not be something beyond to which I must go? And if I could not climb down the rock — was there no other way of descent? The sheer volume of noise fashioned itself into words: *"You must! You must!"*

Three

Aphrasöe — City of the Savanti

Still munching those delicious cherries whose delights I had found and often savored higher up the river, I went back to my leaf boat. It was hard with the same kind of tough fibrous hardness the reeds had displayed when cut. But also it had a sinuous suppleness about it that stemmed from its leaf-construction. It would twist and squirm through the rapids, as I had found to my satisfaction.

But would it withstand the battering it was bound to sustain? Would I, a mere mortal human, remain alive under such colossal punishment?

To haul the boat back up the river against that smooth powerful current would be an enormous task. I could not stay here. I ate some of the meat left from the last animal I had brought down with a flung spear higher up the river. On both banks vast herds of various kinds of animals, many of them resembling cattle and deer, had roamed and I had pleasantly varied my diet between them and fish and the other vegetables and berries and cherries — but no animals roamed here.

Thoughtfully I took out of the bottom of the leaf the flat stones I had used as ballast to give better stability. As I did this, as I bundled the spears in a lashing of split reed and secured them to the sides, I knew I had made the only decision fate or whatever other forces involved had decreed.

The leaf boat would float upside-down, this I knew. I strapped myself in with split reeds, flat to the bottom, with the ten-feet long pole to hand. The boat rushed down the current. I knew when we took off and sprang out into thin air.

The boat dipped. The air whistled from my lungs. My ears pained. I was aware of a floating sensation. Just when we hit I must have lost consciousness, for the next thing I remembered was of the boat upside-down, pitching and tossing and going in circles, and of myself hanging in my reed strappings above the greenish gloom of foaming water. It hurt to breathe and I wondered how many ribs I had fractured. But I must get out of the whirlpool. There was not even time to feel thankful I was still alive.

Freeing myself was easy enough with a spear-blade. To right the boat took a little more time; but those broad shoulders of mine did the job and I tumbled in and seized a spear-paddle and, with a series of vigorous thrusts, pushed myself from the dangerous vicinity of the foot of the waterfall. In an instant I was floating free and being whirled away down the river once more.

I breathed in deeply. The pain was not severe. Bruises only.

Only a fool or a madman — or one beloved by the gods — would have dared do what I had done. I looked up at the sheer descending wall of water, at the powerful smooth descent and the foaming caldron where the water struck and bounced in a frothing frenzy, and I knew that luck or no luck, mad or not, beloved of the gods or the prey of the Scorpion, I had come through alive what few men could have survived.

Now I could see what lay on the other side of the mountains.

They extended in a chain all around the horizon, gradually diminishing in size as they trended in a circle until directly before me they were a mere purple thread on the horizon. But obstructing the view directly ahead was a — was a — even now it is difficult to adequately convey that first breathtaking sight of Aphrasöe, the City of the Savants.

The rim wall of mountains formed a crater as vast as a crater on the moon and in the exact center the river flowed into a wide-spreading lake. Rising from the center of the lake grew tall reeds. But their reality dwarfs words. They were each of various thicknesses, ranging from newly-growing specimens of a yard in diameter to mature growths of twenty feet across; at intervals up their stems bulbous swellings grew like Chinese lanterns strung on cords. Up and up soared the reeds, and I was reminded of kelp with its bulges growing up underwater.

From the gracefully arching tops of the reeds long filaments descended again, and I was soon to understand the use to which this multiplicity of lines was put.

I have lived a long life and seen the marvelous steel and concrete towers of New York, have ascended the Eiffel Tower and London's Post Office Tower, have explored the cliff hanging palaces of Inner Tibet; but in no other place in no other world have I found a city quite like Aphrasöe.

The very air was scented as my leaf boat bore me on.

From starboard another river wended across the plain pent between the circular crater walls and joined my river in a wide confluence some three miles from the city and the lake. The lake itself I judged to be five miles across, and the height of the vegetable towers — at that time I could only sit and stare upward, baffled.

How could one call those serene vegetable giants reeds? From the clusters of filaments growing from their tops, down past the protuberances swelling from their stems, many of them the size of an Indian bungalow, many the size of a solid Georgian mansion in old England, right down to the massive girth of their trunks which vanished into the water, they were of themselves, independent, isolate, retaining their own essential nature despite anything that might occur around them. The nearer I approached, the bigger they became. Now I had to crane my head back to stare up at them, and could no longer see their tops for the froth of fronds depending. Those fronds were in perpetual motion, swinging in every direction. I wondered at this.

A boat was approaching me up the river.

Naked as I was, all I could do was smooth my drying hair back and lay hold of a spear, and wait.

Like any sailorman I studied the craft approaching with a critical eye. She was a galley. Long silver-bladed oars rose and fell in a rhythm, feathering perfectly together, giving that short sharp chopping stroke that is the Navy way of driving a boat through water. That was needful in a seaway, where there were waves of consequence; within this landlocked water a longer stroke could have been used. I surmised that the rowing arrangements — to use a landsman's phrase — precluded a long stroke and recovery.

The bows were finely molded and high-raked, with much gilding and silver and gold work. She carried no masts. I waited in silence. Now I could hear, above the sounds of the oars and the bubble of water from her stem, shouted commands; the starboard bank backed water, the larboard continued to pull ahead, and the galley swung around smoothly. Another order was followed by the simultaneous lifting of the oars — how often had I given a similar command! — and the galley drifted gently broadside on as I swung down on the current.

From this angle her lines were clearly apparent; long and low as was to be expected, with that high beak and with a high canopied quarterdeck and poop. People thronged her deck. Some of them were waving. I saw white arms and a multitude of colored clothing. There was even music, wafting gently on the breeze.

Had I wanted to escape there was no escape possible.

As I drifted down, a single oar lowered. My boat ran alongside. Still gripping my spear, I leaped out, onto the blade, and men ran lightly up the loom toward the gunwale. It was a stroke oar. I vaulted the rail to land on the quarterdeck. The canopy overhead rustled in the breeze. The deck was as white as any on a King's Ship. The only person visible here was a man wearing a white tunic and duck trousers who advanced toward me with outstretched hand, smiling, eager.

"Dray Prescot! We are glad to welcome you to Aphrasöe."

Numbly I shook hands.

Above the quarterdeck the poop rose in a splendor of gilt and ornamentation.

Up there would be the quartermasters at the tiller. I turned to look forward. I could see row after row of bronzed upturned faces, all smiling and laughing at me. Brawny arms stretched to the oars and muscles bunched as a girl — a girl! — nodded and beat lightly on a tambourine. In time with her gentle strokes the oars bit into the water and the galley smoothly gathered way.

"You are surprised, Dray? But of course. Allow me to present myself. I am Maspero." He gestured negligently. "We do not take much pride in titles in Aphrasöe; but I am often called the tutor. But you are thirsty, hungry? How remiss of me — please allow me to offer you some refreshment. If you will follow me—"

He led off to the stern cabin and, dazed, I followed.

That girl, with her corn-colored hair and laughing face, banging time with her tambourine — she had not taken the slightest notice of my nakedness. I followed Maspero and once more that sense of foreordained destiny encompassed me. He had known my name. He spoke English. Was I, then, in truth in the grip of a fevered dream, hanging near to death on a torture stake in the African jungle?

The chafe in my wrists had all gone. There was nothing now to chain me to reality.

A last look back over my shoulder at this amazing galley revealed that our prow now pointed at the city. We moved forward with a steady solid motion very strange to a sailor accustomed to the rolling and pitching of a frigate in the great waves of the ocean. A white dove flew down from the bright sky, circled the galley, and alighted on that upthrusting prow. I stared at the dove. I remembered that it had flown into my view many times since that first occasion; but the gorgeous scarlet and golden raptor had not returned. The people I had seen were now drifting back onto the deck and their clothes blazed brilliantly in the sunshine as they laughed and gossiped like merry folk at a fair.

The man called Maspero nodded, smiling and genial. "We attempt always to respect the mores and behavior of the cultures invited to Aphrasöe. In your case we know that nakedness can cause embarrassment."

"I'm used to it," I said. But I took from him the plain white shirt and duck trousers — although as my fingers closed on the material I realized I had never encountered it before. It was not cotton or linen. Now, of course, that Earthmen have discovered the use of artificial fibers for clothing, the garments or their like could be found in any chain store. But at the time I was a simple seaman used to heavy worsteds, coarse cottons, and the most elementary of scientific marvels could astonish me. Maspero wore a pair of light yellow satiny slippers. Most of my life — until I eased my way through the hawsehole — I had gone barefoot. Even then my square-toed shoes had been graced by cut-steel buckles, for I could not even afford pinchbeck. Gold buckles, of course, were waiting on the taking of a prize of real value.

We walked through the aft cabin with its simple tasteful furniture constructed from some light wood like sandalwood and Maspero motioned me to a seat beneath the stern windows.

Now it was possible to take stock of him. The first and immediately dominating impression was one of vivacity, of aliveness, alertness, and of an abiding sense of completeness that underlay all he did or said. He had very dark curly hair and was clean-shaven. My own thick brown hair was in not too conspicuous a disarray; but my beard was now reaching the silky stage and was not, I venture to think, too displeasing to the eye. Later on, when they were invented, the name torpedo would be given to that style of beard.

Food was brought by a young girl clad in a charming if immodestly brief costume of leaf-green. There was fresh-baked bread in long rolls after the French fashion, and a silver bowl of fruit including, I was pleased to see, some of the yellow port-flavored cherries. I selected one and chewed with satisfaction.

Maspero smiled and all the skin around his eyes crinkled up. "You have found our Kregish palines tasteful? They grow wild all over Kregen wherever the climate is suitable." He looked at me quizzically. "You seem to be in a remarkable state of preservation."

I took another cherry — another paline, as I recognized I would have henceforth to call them. I did not understand quite what he meant by the last part of his sentence.

"You see, Dray, there is much to tell you and much you must learn. However, by successfully reaching Aphrasöe, you have passed the first test."

'Test?"

"Of course."

I could become angry now. I could lash out in fury at being wantonly dragged through dangers. There was a single redeeming feature in Maspero's favor. Speaking slowly, I said: "When you brought me here did you know what I was doing, where I was, what was happening to me?"

He shook his head and I was about to let my anger boil.

"But we did not bring you, in that sense, Dray. Only by the free exercise of your will could you contrive the journey. Once you had done that, however, the voyage down the river was a very real test. As I said, I am surprised you look so well."

"I enjoyed the river," I told him.

His eyebrows rose. "But the monsters—"

"The scorpion — I suppose he was a house pet of yours? — gave me a fright. But I doubt if he was really real."

"He was."

"Sink me!" I burst out. "Suppose I'd been killed!"

Maspero laughed. My fists clenched despite the gracious surroundings and the goblet of wine and the food. "Had there been a chance of you losing your life you would not have been entered on the river, Dray. The River Aph is not to be trifled with."

I told Maspero of my circumstances when the red eye of Antares had fallen on me in the jungle of Africa and he nodded sympathetically. He began my education there and then, telling me many things about this planet called Kregen. Kregen. How the name fires my blood! How often I have longed to return to that world beneath the crimson and emerald suns!

From an inlaid cabinet Maspero took a small golden box, much engraved, and from this box he lifted a transparent tube. Inside the tube nestled a number of round pills. I had never had much time for doctors; I had seen too much of their bungling work in the cockpit, and I steadfastly refused to be bled or leeched.

"We of Aphrasöe are the Savanti, Dray. We are an old people and we revere what we consider to be the right ways of wisdom and truth, tempered with kindness and compassion. But we know we are not infallible. It may be you are not the man for us. We have many entrants seeking admittance; many are called but few are chosen."

He lifted the transparent tube. "On this world of Kregen there are many local languages, as is inevitable on any world where growth and expansion is taking place. But there is one language spoken by everyone and this you must know." He extended the tube. "Open your mouth."

I did as he bid. Do not ask me what I thought, if perhaps the idea of poison did not cross my mind. I had been brought here, of my own free will — maybe — but all this effort, like the provision of the leaf boat, would scarcely be wasted the moment they had seen me. Or — might it? Might I not already have failed whatever schemes they had in mind for me? I swallowed down the pill Maspero dispensed.

"Now, Dray, when the pill has dissolved and its genetic constituents habilitate themselves in your brain, you will have a complete understanding, both written and oral, of the chief language of Kregen. That tongue is called Kregish, for clearly it could bear no other name."

To me, a simple sailorman of the late eighteenth century, this was magic. I then knew nothing of the genetic code, and of DNA and the other nucleic acids, and of how imprinted with information they can be absorbed into the brain. I swallowed down the pill and accepted what new marvels there might lie in store.

As to the business of a world having many languages, this was natural and anything else would have been a foolish dream. We on our Earth almost had a common language which might be spoken and understood from the farthest western shores of Ireland across to the eastern frontiers against the Turk. Latin was such a language; but that had vanished with the rise of nationalism and the vernacular.

The galley rocked gently beneath us and Maspero jumped up. "We have docked!" he cried gaily. "Now you must see Aphrasöe, the City of the Savanti!"

Four

Baptism

Aphrasöe was Paradise.

There seems to me now no other way of describing that city. Many times I wondered if in very truth I was dead and this was Heaven. So many impressions, so many wonderful insights, so much beauty. Downriver wide acres of gardens and orchards, dairy farms and open ranges, provided an abundance of plenty.

Everywhere glowed color and brilliance and lightness, and yet there were many cool places of repose and rest and meditation. The people of Aphrasöe were uniformly kind and considerate, laughing and merry, gentle and compassionate, filled with all the noble sentiments so much talked about on our old Earth and so much ignored in everyday life.

Naturally, I looked for the canker in the bud, the dark secret truth of these people that would reveal them to be a sham, a city of hypocrites. I looked for compulsions I suspected and could never find. In all honest sober truth I believe that if Paradise ever existed among mortal men it is to be found in the City of the Savanti, Aphrasöe on the planet Kregen beneath the crimson and emerald suns of Antares.

In all the wonders that each day opened out to me one of the greatest came on that very first day when Maspero led me into the city growing from the lake.

We left the galley and stepped down onto a granite dock festooned with flowers. Many people thronged here, laughing and chattering, and as we passed toward a tall domed archway they called out happily: "Lahal, Maspero! Lahal, Dray Prescot!"

And I understood what Lahal meant — a word of greeting, a word of comradeship. And, too, as the language pill dissolved within me and its genetic components drifted into place within my brain, I understood that the word "Llahal" — pronounced in the Welsh way — was a word of greeting given by strangers, a word of more formal politeness.

Stretching my lips, which are of the forbidding cut of habitual sternness, into the unfamiliar rictus of a smile, I lifted my arm and returned the greetings. "Lahal," I said as I followed Maspero.

The entranceway led into the interior of one of the enormous trunks. Having left the Earth in the year of Trafalgar, I was not prepared for the room in which I now found myself to rise swiftly upward, pressing my feet against the floor and bending my knees.

Maspero chuckled.

"Swallow a couple of times, Dray."

My ears performed the usual antics as the Eustachian tubes cleared. It is unnecessary now to describe lifts or elevators, save to say that to me they were another wonder of the city. During my stay in Aphrasöe I found myself, against my will as the days passed, continually searching for that flaw in the gem, that canker in the bud, that worm in the heart, that I suspected and that I dreaded to find. Then, I knew that ways of compulsion existed that I understood and had used. The press gangs would dump their unsavory human freight at the receiving ships, and from the slopships they would come aboard, miserable, seasick, scared, angry. The cat would tame them and discipline them along with Billy Pitt's Quota Men. The discipline was open and understood, a stark fact of life, given the circumstances a necessary evil. Here I suspected forces that worked in darkness away from the sight of honest men.

Subsequently I have seen and studied many systems of control. On Kregen I have encountered disciplines and methods of enforcing order that make all the notorious brainwashing indoctrinations of Earth's political empires seem as the strictures of a gray-headed mistress at a girls' school.

If any brainwashing system or any other method of indoctrination and compulsion existed in Aphrasöe I was not then, and never since as my knowledge has expanded, aware of any secret controls.

When the elevator stopped and the door opened by itself I jumped. I knew nothing of selenium cells and solenoids and their application to self-opening doors. It now sounds droll that among the vagaries of my memory I knew that there existed a thing — whether substance, liquid, fluid or what I knew not and nor did anyone else — called *vis electrica*, named by the English physician Gilbert, obtaining his derivation from the Greek word for amber — electron; and that also I knew that Hauksbee had produced sparks. I had heard of the men Volta and Galvani and their work had excited me — and then the thoughts of making a frog's leg twitch abruptly reminded me of that froggy thought I had had on my leaf boat as that damned great scorpion had sat staring at me with his eyes going up and down, up and down, rather like the elevators within the tree trunks.

I stepped out into fresh scented air. All about me stretched the city. The city! Such a sight no man could see and possibly forget. At this height the lake revealed its almost circular shape, cut into by the many tall trunks — I found myself calling them tree trunks; but they were surely of an incredibly more ancient order of vegetable life than trees. From their tops the massed bunches of tendrils drooped. I admit to a shaming thought then, for the appearance of these dangling lines was faintly similar to those of a cat-o'-nine-tails as it lifts in the fist of the bosun's mate at the gratings.

In the railing of the platform before us a gateway led out onto thin air. Maspero started forward confidently. He touched one of a number of colored buttons set in a small desk with, inscribed above it, the name *Aisle South. Ten.* A platform large enough to accommodate four people within an encircling railing flew toward us through the air and notched itself against the opening in the platform on which we stood. It had come swinging up toward us. I noticed a line extending from a cradle in the center of the aerial platform leading aloft — and guessed at once that this line was really a tendril of the great plants. Maspero politely motioned me aboard. I stepped on and felt the resilience as the line took my weight. Maspero jumped on, released the locking device and at once we swung out and down and gained a tremendous acceleration like a child on the downward arc seated in a playground's swing.

We swung through the air, the line arcing under the wind-pressure above us, flying between the tall trunks and their bulbous houses, and as we swung so I saw many other people swinging past in all directions. Maspero had sat down so that his head was below the transparent windshield and he could speak to me. I stood, letting the wind hurtle past my ears and stream my hair out behind me like a mane.

He explained that a central system prevented tangling; it was complicated but they had machines capable of the task. Computers were unknown — except in their most basic ancient forms — to sailing ship officers. The experience of standing on that platform and swinging dizzily through the air was one of the greatest liberating moments of my life. We curved up in a great graceful arc and docked ourselves against another high platform. At perigee we had skimmed the surface of the lake. We transferred to another platform. This time Maspero had to manipulate the translucent vane, rather like a vertical bird's-tail, that trailed away from the line above our heads. He corrected our course so that we passed in a flash another flying platform. I heard a delighted shriek of girlish laughter as we hurtled by.

"They will play their pranks," Maspero sighed. "She well knew I would give way, the minx."

"Isn't it dangerous?" was my foolish question.

We swooped down on our line, swinging grandly toward the lake, and then up and up we climbed dizzily until once again we notched into a platform around a trunk. Here other people were climbing aboard platforms, pushing off to swoop down like playful children. We covered perhaps a mile in this fashion, and all without a single error or tangle. There was a pattern observable in the line of swinging so that right-angle confrontations were obviated. I could have gone on swinging all day. Swingers, the flying platforms were called, and Aphrasöe was often referred to as The Swinging City.

On one high railed platform a party waited for our swinger and one of them, after the greeting: "Lahal, Maspero," and a quiet, polite word to me, said: "Three graints came through Loti's Pass yesterday. Will you be there?"

"Alas, no. I have matters to attend to. But soon— soon—" The party boarded the swinger and then for the first time I heard the words of farewell that came to mean so much to me. "Happy Swinging, Maspero," called his friend.

"Happy Swinging," replied Maspero, with a smile and a wave.

Happy Swinging. How right those words are to express the delight and joy in life in The Swinging City!

Among the many people swinging from place to place I saw youngsters sitting astride a simple bar, holding in one hand the downward-pointing handle of their guiding vane and with the other waving to everyone they passed as they twisted and turned. It looked so free, so fine, so much a part of the air and the wind, this rushing arcing swinging that I yearned to try my skill.

"We have to sort out the tangles they make from time to time," said Maspero. "But although we age but slowly, age we do. We are not immortals."

When we reached our destination Maspero ushered me into his house fashioned from a gigantic bulbous swelling. It must have been five hundred feet from the lake. Up the center went the trunk containing its elevator, and around it extended a ring of rooms with wide windows overlooking the city and the plants and the lake glinting through the traceries of trunks and swingers.

The place was furnished with impeccable taste and luxury. For a man whose ideas of comfort had been formed by moving from the lower deck into the wardroom I gasped. Maspero made me at home very kindly. There was much to be learned. During the days that followed I learned of this planet Kregen, and dimly sensed the mission the Savanti had set themselves. Put into simple terms I could grasp it was their task to civilize this world but coercion could not be used, it must be done by precept and example, and there were very few of them. They recruited — as far as I could understand — from other worlds of which they seemed to know, to my great surprise, and I was a candidate. I wanted no other future.

The Savanti possessed a driving obligation to help all humanity — they still do — but they needed help to fulfill this self-imposed task. Only certain people would be capable and it was hoped I would be one of them. I find it painfully difficult to detail all the wonderful events of my life in Aphrasöe, The Swinging City, the City of the Savanti. I met many delightful people and was absorbed into their life and culture. On excursions I saw the extent of their cut-off little world within that giant crater. Here they were fashioning the instrument that would bring a similar level of happiness and comfort to all the world.

I saw their papermills and watched as the pulp gradually changed through their whining spinning machinery into smooth velvety paper, beautiful stock, fit to commemorate the loftiest words in the language. But there was a mystery attached to their paper manufacture. I gathered that on certain times during the year they dispatched caravans of paper which would find its way all over Kregen. But the paper was blank, virginal, waiting to be written on. I sensed the secret here; but could not fathom it.

Very soon I was told to prepare for the baptism. I use the English word as the nearest equivalent to the Kregish, intending no blasphemy. Very early we set out, Maspero, four other tutors whom I now knew and liked, and their four candidates. We took a galley which pulled steadily up the other river, not the Aph but the Zelph. The oarsmen laughed and joked as their brawny arms pulled. I had discussed slavery with Maspero and found in him the same deep hatred of that ignoble institution as burned in me. Among the oarsmen I recognized the man who had asked Maspero if he were hunting the graint. I had myself taken my turn at the oars, feeling the muscles across my back slipping into familiar power lines as I pulled. Slavery was one of the institutions of Kregen that the Savanti must needs change if they were to fulfill their mission.

We pulled as far up the River Zelph as we could and then transferred to a long-boat pulled by all of us in turn. I had seen no old men or women, no sick or crippled, in Aphrasöe, and everyone took a cheerful hand at the most menial of tasks. The galley turned back, with the girls at the tiller waving until we were out of sight between craggy gray walls. The water rushed past. It was of a deep plum color, quite unlike that of its sister river Aph. The ten of us pulled against the current.

We then went through rapids, portering the boat, and pressed on. Maspero and the other tutors held instruments that revealed themselves to be of potent power. A giant spider-like beast leaped from a rock to bar our way. I stared rigidly at it — and Maspero calmly leveled his weapon; a silvery light issued from the muzzle that quietened the monster until we were past. It clicked its jaws at us, its great eyes blank and hostile; but it could not move. I do not think even the science of Earth can yet reproduce that peaceful victory over brute force.

One of the candidates was a girl, of a clear cast of feature with long dark hair, not unprepossessing but in no way a great beauty. We pushed on, passing many horrific dangers that were quelled by the silvery fire of the tutors.

At last we reached a natural amphitheater in the rock where the river plunged down in a cataract that was a miserable imitation of the one over which I had plunged on the Aph; but which was nevertheless of considerable size.

Here we entered a cave. This was the first underground place I had been on Kregen. The light streamed in with its usual warm pink glow; but it gradually faded as we advanced and that pinkness was slowly replaced by an effulgent blueness — a blueness that reminded me vividly of the blue fires that had limned my impression of the Scorpion as I had stared upward from the African jungle.

We gathered at the brink of what seemed a simple pool in the rocky floor of the cave. The water stirred gently, like heating milk, and wisps of vapor arose from its surface. The solemnness of the occasion impressed me. A flight of stairs was cut leading down into the pool. Maspero took me to one side, politely allowing the others to go first.

The candidates, one after the other, removed their clothes. Then, with uplifted faces and firm tread, we all walked down the steps into the water. I felt the warmness enclosing me and a sensation like a warm mouth kissing me all over, a sensation like a billion tiny needles pricking my skin, a sensation that penetrated to the inmost fibers of what I was, myself, unique and isolate. I walked down the rocky steps until my head sank beneath the surface.

A great body moved in the milky fluid before me.

When I could hold my breath no longer I returned up the steps. I am a good swimmer — some have said I must have been spawned from a mermaid (and when he got up with a black eye and apologized, for I admit of no reflection upon my father and mother, I had to admit he meant nothing ill; that in truth what he said could be proved by the facts of my swimming ability). Now I can see they were joking; but in my young days jokes and I were rough bedfellows.

I was the last out. I saw the three young men and they seemed to me strong and healthy and fine-looking. The girl — surely she was not the same girl who had walked with us into the pool? For now she was a resplendent creature, firm of body, with bright eyes and laughing face and red lips ripe for the kissing. She saw me and laughed and then her face changed expression and even Maspero said: "By the Great Savant Himself! Dray Prescot — you must be of the chosen!"

I must admit I felt in better health than I could ever remember. My muscles felt toned up and limber; I could have run ten miles, I could have lifted a ton weight, I could have gone without sleep for a week. Maspero laughed again and handed me my clothes and clapped me on the back.

"Welcome, again, Dray Prescot! Lahal and Lahal!" He chuckled, and then, casually, said: "When you have lived for a thousand years you may return here to be baptized again."

Five

Delia of the Blue Mountains

A thousand years!

I stammered in confusion. We were back in Maspero's house. I could not believe it. I only knew I felt as fit and healthy as I ever had. But a thousand years of life!

"We are not immortals, Dray; but we have work to do and that work will not allow us to die off after three score years and ten."

The wonder of that stayed with me for a long time; and then I pushed it away. Life was still lived from one day to the next.

Maspero apologized for the Savant's atavistic attitudes when we went hunting the graint. From time to time huge wild animals would wander through the few passes into the inner world of the crater and because they would damage the crops and kill the people, they must be caught and returned. But the Savanti had once been warlike and fierce like any Kregan of the outer world. They joyed in the dangers of physical combat; but they would not allow of any danger to their quarry. The dangers where they existed were to the Savanti.

So, like a Kregan war party we went forth onto the plains upriver to hunt the graint. I should mention that Kregen, the planet, Kregish, the language, and Kregan, for the inhabitants of Kregen, is pronounced as though there were an acute accent on the letter "e" in the French fashion. I wore hunting leathers. Soft leather cinctured my waist and was drawn up between my legs. On my left arm a stout leather arm guard might prevent slavering jaws from ripping that arm off. My hair was bound back by a leather fillet. There were no feathers in that band, although Maspero, had he wished, could have filled his fillet with feathers — what the Indians called calling coup — and he joyed and delighted in the hunt, and at the same time woefully deplored his savage and primitive behavior.

I carried the sword Maspero had given me. This sword was not designed to kill. The Savanti delighted in meeting the monsters with various weapons; but their chief joy lay in the Savanti sword, a beautifully balanced arm, straight, not a shortsword, not a broadsword and not a rapier; but a subtle combination that I, for one, would not have believed possible had I not seen and wielded one. I felt it to be an extension of my arm. Of course I did not then know how many men I had killed with cutlass, tomahawk or boarding pike. Pistols at sea almost always became wetted or damp and refused to fire; it was not until two years after my translation to Kregen that, on Earth, the Scottish Reverend Alexander Forsyth perfected his percussion caps. I knew how to use a sword and I had used them in action among the smoke of broadsides in the wild plunge to an enemy's deck. I was not one of those fancy university fencers with a foil like a maid's feather duster; but that old Spaniard, Don Hurtado de Oquendo, had taught me well how to use a rapier, and he had been broad-minded enough to allow me the

29

French as well as the Spanish grip and system. I took no pride in the number of men I had spitted as I took no pride in the numbers whose skulls I had cleft through with a cruder Navy cutlass.

We hunted the graint. The beasts somewhat resembled an Earthly bear with eight legs and jaws that extended for over eighteen inches like a crocodile's. Our only chance against them was speed. We would take turns to dart in and parry those wide-sweeping vicious paws armed with razor-sharp claws. We would parry and duck and then cut or thrust and the Savanti sword would inflict a psychic wound that was directly proportional to the power of our blow. When a graint was subdued the poor beast would be carefully tended and taken back over the hills. To accomplish this the Savanti used what was to me then another miracle.

They possessed a small fleet of flying petal-shaped craft powered in a way that I was not to understand for some time. The graint was strapped down and with a plentiful supply of food and water would be flown back over the passes and deposited in a favored place. If he was stubborn enough to retrace his steps then the Savanti could logically accept his decision and once more we would don our hunting leathers and sally forth.

On one such bright day of summer we sallied out ready for a day's sport that would not injure our quarry and would not harm ourselves if we were quick and lithe enough. I had seen a man brought back with a badly slashed side from which the bright blood poured; he was up and about the next day none the worse. But one could be killed at this game, and this the Savanti accepted as a spice to life. They recognized their own weakness in this desire; but they accepted it as a phenomenon of their human character.

We had subdued two graint and I had wandered a little off on my own seeking the spoor of a third. My friends were resting and eating at our little camp. A shadow passed over my head and, looking up, I saw one of the petal-shaped flying boats skimming close. I ducked and it continued on and hit the ground, bounced, lurched, and skidded askew. Thinking that the Savanti taking a monster back would need help, I ran across.

At that moment the graint I hunted bounded from a low hillock and charged the airboat.

Aboard the airboat were three dead men clad in strange coarse garments of some yellow stuff, hooded, and girdled with a scarlet rope with tassels. Their feet were sandaled. There was also a girl, who cried out in terror.

She was blindfolded.

Her hands were bound behind her and she struggled in a silvery tissue gown. Her hair was of the auburn-tinged brown I have always found attractive. I had no time to look further at her for the graint was clearly intent on eating her for his dinner. I shouted, high and hard, and leaped forward.

Somehow, by continuous struggling, the girl had managed to slide the blindfold down from her eyes. As I charged I cast her a single swift glance. Her large brown eyes were terrified; but as soon as she saw me an entirely different expression filled them. She stopped her screaming at once. She shouted something in a fierce excited tone, a word that sounded like: "Jikai!"

I did not understand; but her meaning was plain.

The graint was a large fellow, a good eight feet tall as he reared back on his hind two pairs of legs and pawed at me with the upper two pairs. His long crocodilian snout gaped and the teeth looked extraordinarily hard and sharp.

I might be playing a game; but he was not, and he was hungry, and the soft flesh of the girl represented a nice juicy dinner to him.

I darted in and instantly leaped back so that his responding blow sliced the air where my head had been. I thrust quickly; but he turned and I had to dive forward and roll over as his other paws clapped together in an attempt to imprison my body. I scrambled up and faced him again. He grunted and snuffled, put all his paws to the ground, and charged at me. I skipped aside at the last moment and slashed down as he passed. The blow would, had the Savanti sword not been charged with its miraculous powers, have lopped off his forequarter. As it was the stun lost him the use of that paw. It was erroneous to call his parts quarters, they were eighths; but my father's horse-training died hard. A damned sight harder than this pesky graint. I jumped in again, ducked the gaping fangs, and thrust. This time his other foreleg went out of action. He roared. He swiped at me and I met the blow with a parry; the edge did not cut into him but again that stunning power drained the strength from that limb.

But I had been slow. His fourth upper limb raked down my side and I felt the blood spurting down my flesh. I also felt the pain; but that had to be pushed aside.

"Jikai!" shouted the girl again.

A blow had to be landed on his head. I had scorned to use the superior leaping ability the slightly lessened gravity of Kregen afforded my Earthly muscles as unsporting. These beasts were only doing what was in their nature. But now this girl's life was at stake. I had no choice. As the graint charged in again I leaped up, a good ten feet, and slashed him across the eyes and snout. He went down as though a thirty-two pounder had caught him between wind and water. He rolled over and stuck his eight clawed paws in the air. I felt rather sorry for him.

"Jikai!" the girl said again, and now I realized that the three times she had used the word had been with a different inflection. It was a Kregish word, I was sure, yet, for some reason, it had not been dissolved into my neural net along with all the other words of Kregish I had acquired.

Now Maspero and our friends ran up. They looked concerned.

"You are unharmed, Dray?"

"Of course. But let us see to the girl — she is bound—"

As we untied her Maspero grumbled away to himself sotto voce. The others of the Savanti looked with as much ill will as that people ever could look at the bodies of the three men clad in the yellow gowns.

"They will try," Maspero said, helping the girl up. "They believe it, and it is true; but they will take such risks."

I stared at the girl. She was a cripple. Her left leg was twisted and bent, and she walked with an effort, gasping at each painful hobble. I stepped forward and took her up in my arms, cradling her against my naked chest.

"I will carry you," I said.

31

"I cannot thank you, warrior, for I hate anyone who despises me for my crippling. But I can thank you for my life — Hai, Jikai!"

Maspero looked remarkably distressed.

She was remarkably beautiful. Her body was warm and firm in my arms. Her long silky brown hair with that enraging tint of auburn hung down like a smoky waterfall. I could plunge over that waterfall with great joy. Her brown eyes regarded me with gravity. Her lips were soft, yet firm and beautifully molded, and of such a scarlet as must have existed only in the Garden of Eden.

Of her nose I can only say that its pertness demanded from me the utmost exertion not to lean down and kiss it.

I could not dare to dream of kissing those red lips; for I knew that were I to do so I would drown and sink and succumb and I would not answer for what would happen then.

An airboat flew out from the city. It was a pure white, which surprised me, for all the airboats used to carry the animals back through the passes were brown or red or black. Savanti came from the flier and gently took the girl from me.

"Happy Swinging," I said, unthinking.

She looked at me, obviously not understanding.

"Remberee, Jikai," she said.

Remberee, I knew instantly, was Kregish for *au revoir* or *so long,* or *I'll be seeing you.* But Jikai?

I forced my smile and found to my amazement that to smile on her was easy — too easy.

"Am I not to know your name? I am Dray Prescot."

The white clad Savanti were carrying her to the airboat.

Her grave brown eyes regarded me. She hesitated.

"I am Delia — Delia of Delphond — Delia of the Blue Mountains."

I made a leg, as though I were in my admiral's drawing room in Plymouth among his great ladies.

"I shall see you again, Delia of the Blue Mountains."

The airboat was lifting.

"Yes," she said. "Yes, Dray Prescot. I think you will."

The airboat soared away to the City of the Savanti.

Six

Testing time in Paradise

Much I was learning about the planet Kregen as it swung beneath its emerald and crimson suns, and this I feel would best be related when occasion arises, for I must speak of many wild and terrible things, and deeds for which to find a name is difficult. I would stand on the balcony of Maspero's house when the twin suns had gone from the sky and stare upward. Kregen has seven moons, the largest almost twice the size of our own, the smallest a hurtling speck of light low over the landscape. Beneath the seven moons of Kregen I brooded long on the girl Delia of the Blue Mountains.

Maspero was continuing to run his long series of tests on me. I had passed the first by successfully arriving at the city; and he still found amusement that I had enjoyed that voyage down the River Aph. I gathered that many had failed to arrive; they had been defeated by the very conditions that had delighted me.

He carried out what I now realize to be a comprehensive analysis of my brain wave patterns. I began to gather the impression that all was not well.

A great deal of my time was spent indulging in the sports of the Savanti. I have spoken of their uniformly powerful physique and their aptitude for all manner of sport. All I can say is that I did not disgrace myself. I could usually manage to find that extra inch, that last spurt, that final explosive thrust that would bring me victory. They were all hollow victories, of course; for until I was accepted as one of the Savanti, and there were other applicants as I well knew, my life would be incomplete.

When I questioned Maspero about Delia — as I now called her to myself without any self-consciousness — he was unusually evasive. I saw her occasionally, for she had been quartered on the other side of the city, and she still hobbled about on her twisted leg. She refused to tell me where she came from, whether by her own design or by express orders of the Savanti I did not know. There was no government that I could determine; a kind of benevolent anarchy prevailed demanding that when a task needed to be done there would always be willing volunteers. Myself I helped gather crops, work in the paper mills, sweep and clean. Whatever chained Delia's confidences was a force I did not as yet know. And Maspero would shake his head when I questioned him.

When I demanded to know why she had not been cured of her crippled leg, which the Savanti could so easily do, he replied to the effect that she was not one who had, like myself, been called.

"Do you mean because she has not taken the journey down the River Aph?"

"No, no, Dray." He spread his hands helplessly. "She is not as far as we can tell one of the people we need to fulfill our destiny. She came here uninvited."

"But you can cure her."

"Maybe."

He would say no more. A chill gripped me. Was this the canker in the bud that I had suspected and then put aside from me as an unworthy thought?

Strangely enough I had never mentioned the glorious scarlet and golden bird to Maspero. Just how the subject came up was trifling; but as soon as I told him that I had seen the raptor he turned with a quick motion to face me, his eyes fierce, his whole body tense. I was surprised.

"The Gdoinye!" He wiped his forehead. "Why you, Dray?" He whispered the words. "My tests indicate that you are not what we expected. You do not scan aright, and my tests refute all that I know, of you and your ways."

"The dove was from the city?"

"Yes. It was necessary."

I was forcibly reminded how little I knew of the Savanti.

Maspero went out, to confer with his associates, I had no doubt. When he returned his expression was graver than at any time I had known him.

"There may be a chance for you yet, Dray. We do not wish to lose you. If we are to fulfill our mission — and you do not yet understand what that is, despite what you have learned, we must have men of your stamp."

We ate our evening meal in a heavy atmosphere as the moons of Kregen spun past overhead in all their different phases. There were five on view tonight. I munched palines and studied Maspero. He remained withdrawn. At last he raised his head.

"The Gdoinye comes from the Star Lords, the Everoinye. Do not ask me of them, Dray, for I cannot tell you."

I did not ask.

I sensed the chill. I knew that in some way unknown to myself I had failed. I felt the first faint onset of regret.

"What will you do?" I asked.

He moved his hand. "No matter that the Star Lords have an interest in you. That has been known before. It is in your brain patterns. Dray—" He did not go on. At last he said: "Are you happy here, Dray?"

"More happy than I have ever been in my life — with perhaps the exception of when I was very young with my mother and father. But I do not think that applies in this situation."

He shook his head. "I am doing all I can, Dray. I want you to become one of the Savanti, to belong to the city, to join us in what we must do, when you understand fully what that is. It is not easy."

"Maspero," I said. "This is Paradise for me."

"Happy Swinging," he said, and went toward his own apartments in his house.

"Maspero," I called after him. "The girl. Delia of the Blue Mountains. Will you make her well?"

But he did not answer. He went out and the door closed softly.

On the following evening I saw the crippled girl at one of the parties that could be found all over the city. Always there were singing and laughing and dancing, formal entertainments, musical contests, poetic seminars, art displays, a whole gamut of real vivid life. Anything the heart desired could be found in the Swinging City. Perhaps twenty people circulated in the relaxed atmosphere of this quiet party given by Golda, the flame-haired beauty with the bold eyes and the lush figure, a woman with whom I had spent a number of pleasant evenings. She greeted me bearing a book, a thick tome of many pages and thin paper, and she smiled tilting her cheek for me to kiss that smooth rosy skin.

"You'll love this one, Dray. It was published in Marlimor, a reasonably civilized city some long way off in another of the seven continents and nine islands, and its legends are really most beautiful."

"Thank you, Golda. You are very kind."

She laughed, holding out the book. Her gown of some silvery lamé glistened. I wore my usual simple white shirt and trousers and was barefoot. My hair had

34

been, as I had promised myself aboard the leaf boat, cut to a neat shoulder length and, in honor of Golda's party, I wore a jeweled fillet in my hair, one of the many presents I had received from friends in the city, among the trophies I had won.

"You were telling me about Gah," said Maspero, walking up with a wine goblet for me. He drank from his own.

Again Golda laughed; but this time a different note crept into her deep voice. "Gah is really an offense in men's nostrils, Maspero, my dear. They delight so in their primitiveness."

Gah was one of the seven continents of Kregen, one where slavery was an established institution, where, so the men claimed, a woman's highest ambition was to be chained up and grovel at a man's feet, to be stripped, to be loaded with symbols of servitude. They even had iron bars at the foot of their beds where a woman might be shackled, naked, to shiver all night. The men claimed this made the girls love them.

"That sort of behavior appeals to some men," said Maspero. He was looking at me as he spoke.

"It's really sick," said Golda.

"They claim it is a deep significant truth, this need of a woman to be subjugated by a man, and dates right back to our primitive past when we were cavemen."

I said: "But we no longer tear flesh from our kill and eat it smoking and raw. We no longer believe that the wind brings babies. Thunder and lightning and storm and flood are no longer mysterious gods with malevolent designs on us. Individuals are individuals. The human spirit festers and grows cankerous and corrupt if one individual enslaves another, whatever the sex, whatever specious arguments about sexuality may be instanced."

Golda nodded. Maspero said: "You are right, Dray, where a civilized people is concerned. But, in Gah, the women subscribe also to this barbaric code."

"More fools them," said Golda. And then, quickly: "No — that is not what I really mean. A man and a woman are alike yet different. So very many men are frightened clean through at the thought of a woman. They overreact. They have no conception in Gah of how a woman is — what she is as a person."

Maspero chuckled. "I've always said that women were people as well."

We talked on, about the latest fashions that had, in some mysterious way, reached Aphrasöe from the outside world. The city contained a pitifully few people to lead a planet. Everyone was needed. Maspero, later on, told me that he was now beginning to feel that I would be really the right fiber — as he put it — one of the privileged few who could shoulder the responsibilities of the Savanti. It would be hard, he said. "Don't think the life will be easy; for you will be worked harder than you have ever worked in your life before—" He held up a hand. "Oh, I know of what you have told me of the conditions aboard your seventy-fours. But you will look back to those days and think them paradise compared with what you, as a Savanti, will have to undergo."

"Aphrasöe is Paradise," I said simply, meaning it.

Then Delia of Delphond hobbled across, her face as twisted as her leg at the effort of walking, her gasps loud and separate, a series of explosive blasts of pain.

I frowned.

Frowning was easy, habitual.

"And in Paradise," I asked Maspero, "what of—?"

"I cannot talk about it, Dray, so please do not ask me."

To have spoken at that moment to Delia would have been a mistake.

As the party was breaking up and the guests were calling "Happy Swinging!" to one another and leaping out into space aboard their swingers, I found Delia and, without a word, put my hand beneath her armpit and so helped her along toward the landing platform where Maspero stood talking gaily with Golda. Delia, after a single angry wrench, allowed me to assist her. She did not speak and I guessed her contempt for her own condition, and her furious resentment of me chained her tongue.

"Delia and I," I said to Maspero, "are engaged to take a boating trip downriver tomorrow. I notice my old leaf boat is still moored at your jetty."

Golda laughed with her tinkly shiver of amusement. She looked with a very kindly eye on Delia. "Surely you don't have to prove anything, Dray? If only Delia could be—" And then she caught Maspero's eye and stopped and my heart warmed toward Golda. There was much I did not yet understand, not least what was the real mission of the Savanti with all their powers on a savage planet like Kregen.

I kissed Golda on the cheek and bowed quietly to Delia, who looked at me with an expression quite amazing, compounded of bafflement, annoyance, pique and — could that be amused affection? For me, plain Dray Prescot hot from the reeking battlesmoke swathing the bloody quarterdecks of my life on Earth?

That she might not meet me at the jetty was an outcome I was prepared to meet when it came. But she was there, dressed in a plain green tunic and short skirt, with silver slippers — one piteously twisted — on her feet and a reed bag in her hand filled with goodies like a flask of wine and fresh bread and palines.

"Lahal, Dray Prescot."

"Lahal, Delia of the Blue Mountains."

Maspero watched us cast off. I had provided a pair of oars and I pulled with that old familiar rhythm. "I thought you might care to see the vineyards this morning," I said, loudly, for Maspero's benefit. I headed downstream.

"Remberee!" called Maspero.

Delia turned to face him from the sternsheets and, together, we called back: "Remberee, Maspero!"

I suddenly shivered in the warm pink sunshine of Antares.

We did not see the vineyards. I circled back along the extreme edge of the lake, and the green sun, which because of its own orbital movement around the red sun rose and set with an independent cycle, cast a deeper glow upon the waters.

I entered the mouth of the River Zelph.

We had not spoken much. She had told me when I asked that her accident had resulted in a fall from an animal — she called it a zorca and I gathered it was a kind of horse — some two years ago. She had no explanation of how she had come to the City of Savanti. When I mentioned the three men, now dead, in the yellow robes, her brow furrowed in puzzlement. "My father," she said, "moved worlds to find a cure for me."

Waiting until we were far enough up the river to be out of range of prying eyes I pulled in for the bank. Here we ate our lunch — and very good it was, to sit in my old leaf boat under the emerald and crimson suns of Antares with a girl who intrigued me and tugged at me and yet who regarded me as merely a warrior; to quaff rich ruby wine and to eat freshly-baked bread and nibble scented cheese and to chew on the ever-luscious palines.

Upon the bank I threw off my white shirt and trousers and donned my hunting leathers that I had earlier concealed beneath a fold of blanket in the bottom of my craft. The soft leather encircled my waist and was drawn up through my legs and looped, the whole being held in position with a wide black leather belt, its gold buckle a trophy won in the arena. My leather baldric went over my shoulder so that the Savanti sword hung at my left side. On my left arm the strong leather straps were belted up. I had also brought with me a pair of leather Savanti hunting gloves, flexible yet strong, thonging to the wrist, and these I now drew on. The leather Savanti hunting boots would remain in my boat until we were forced to walk; I do not like wearing footwear aboard a boat, even though I had been forced to do so when walking the quarterdeck.

The only item of equipment not belonging to a Savanti hunting accouterment was the dagger. Of course, it was of the city; but it was cold steel; it did not possess that miraculous power of stunning without killing. Many times had I saved my own life, and killed quickly, with a knife or dagger in my left hand — I understood that in the old days such a weapon was called a main gauche — in the melee of boarding or storming. It would serve me again now in what I purposed.

Delia cried out in surprise when she saw me, but instantly recovered her habitual poise. Mockingly, she called out: "And who are you hunting today, Dray Prescot? Surely not me?"

Had I been of a more insensitive character I would have felt a fool, dressed up like an idiot; as it was I was too well aware of what lay ahead to allow petty distractions to deflect me.

"We will go now," I said, and settled in the boat and took up the oars and gave way.

If Delia felt any fears at being alone with a man in a boat she did not show them. I believe she had already sized up some, at least, of the character of the Savanti, and knew that the behavior of the people of Gah, for instance, would not be tolerated in the city. Outside, yes, within the precincts of others' cities, yes, for what they did was for the nonce their business. And, too, in her own Delphond a lazy afternoon's pulling on the river with a man meant exactly no more and no less than what the two involved wished.

When I beached the boat at the foot of the first rapids and helped Delia ashore she turned a questioning face to me.

"You must go with me, Delia."

She jerked her head back as I used her name without the rest; but there was no time then to consider what that automatic flinching meant. Certainly, it had to do with my use of her name, not the path on which we now set out.

37

I had to carry her. She must have guessed at something of what I intended; and I am quite sure she felt no fear, or, feeling it, would allow me to see.

To look back on that wild and harrowing journey up the River Zelph to the cataract and the pool is to marvel at my own foolhardiness. Here I was carrying the most precious object in two worlds, and walking calmly into dangers that would have sent any man screaming in panic, without the protection of the silvery light weapons of the Savanti. I do not remember — I do not want to remember — the number of times I set Delia hastily down and snatched out my sword and met the furious charge of some enraged monster.

There was continuous effort, and cunning, and brute strength. I hacked down the spider-beasts, and the worm-beasts, and all the beetle-beasts that crept and leaped and writhed upon me. I knew that I would get through. I knew that clearly. Delia through it all remained calm, as though in a trance, hobbling along with painful gasps of effort when she could to free me to fight unimpeded. My sword arm did not tire easily. My left hand, wrist and arm were red and running with blood right to the armpit. That cold steel did not stun.

It killed.

They were clever and ferocious, those guardian monsters.

But I was more clever and more ferocious, not because I was in any way intrinsically better than they; but because I guarded Delia of the Blue Mountains.

We reached the little sandy amphitheater among the rocks and plunged into the cave.

I lifted Delia as the pink glow faded and that uncanny blue luminescence grew, and I laughed — I laughed!

Delia could no longer hobble along, and her lips were tightly compressed to keep back her gasps of pain, so I had to carry her into that milky pool. Wisps of vapor curled from the surface. I strode down the wide flight of steps. The liquid lapped my feet, my legs, my chest. I bent my lips to Delia.

"Take a deep breath and hold it. I will bring you out."

She nodded and her chest swelled against me.

I descended the last few steps and stood with my head beneath that milky liquid that was never simple water and felt once more that lapping mouthlike kissing, that million-fold needle-pricking all over my body. I judged when Delia's breath would be failing, for she could not remain as long underwater as I could, and then walked back up the steps.

All our garments, my sword, my belt, everything, had melted away. Naked we emerged from the pool, as, naked, we ought to have entered it.

Delia craned her head around and looked up into my eyes.

"I feel—" she said. Then: "Put me down, Dray Prescot."

Gently I put Delia of Delphond down on the rocky floor.

Her crippled leg was now rounded, firm, as graceful as any leg that had ever existed in any world of the universe. She radiated a glory. She arched her back and breathed in deeply and pushed her glorious hair up and back from beneath and smiled upon me in a dazzlement of wonder.

"Oh, Dray!" she said.

But I was conscious only of her, of her smile, the luminous depths in her eyes; in all the worlds only the face of Delia of the Blue Mountains existed for me; all the rest vanished in an unimportant haze.

"Delia," I breathed. I trembled uncontrollably.

A voice whispered through the still air.

"Oh, unfortunate is the city! Now must occur that which is ordained—"

Beyond Delia, from the milky pool, a vast body lifted. Liquid ran from smooth skin. Pink flesh showed through the whiteness. The size of the body dwarfed us. Delia gasped and huddled close and I closed both my arms about her and stared up defiantly. And, too, now I could feel a strange sensation within me. If my first dip in the pool of baptism had made a new man of me, then this second baptism had rejuvenated me beyond all reason. If I had felt strong before, now I felt ten times as powerful. I bounded with vigor and health and energy, defiant, savage, exultant.

"The cripple is cured!" I shouted.

"Begone, Dray Prescot!" The voice from that vast body soughed with sorrow. "You would have been acceptable, and sorely do the Savanti need men like yourself! But you have failed! Begone and begone and never Rembaree!"

Delia was a naked soft shape in my arms. I bent my head and pressed my lips on hers and she responded with a joyous love that shocked me through and through.

"Begone!"

I felt the blue luminosity crowding close about me. I was slipping away from this world of Kregen. I shouted.

"I will return!"

"If you can," sighed the voice. "If you can!"

Seven

The Star Lords intervene

"Hey! Jock!" a coarse voice shouted. "Here's some poor devil crawled outta the jungle!"

I opened my eyes. I knew where I was. A wooden palisade crowned with skulls. Thatched huts. The smoke from cooking-pot fires. A coffle of black slaves being herded to the beach and the waiting canoes of the Kroomen. Moored in midstream, on a brown and stinking flood, was a brig. The place stank. Oh, yes, I knew where I was.

The harsh sunlight blazed yellow, stinging my eyes.

I do not believe it necessary or even wise to speak of the next few years. I was able to ship out from the slave factory, nauseatingly aboard the slaver brig, and then in some fashion resume my old life. Promotion to post rank still eluded me; but now I did not care. I hungered for Kregen. I bore the Savanti no ill will. I recognized their essential goodness and I acknowledged that I did not understand all the answers to my questions. I failed to comprehend why they had refused to treat Delia — my Delia! Delia of Delphond, Delia of the Blue Mountains — how many nights I stood by the quarterdeck rail and stared up at the stars and ever and ever my eyes sought that red star that was Antares, and there, I knew, lay all of hope or happiness I wanted in all the universe.

I knew what had happened to me. I had been flung out of Paradise.

Paradise. I had found my heaven and had been debarred from entering.

After my life of hardship and struggle Aphrasöe was Paradise.

Now that I have lived so long and have visited Earth many times, always, in some strange way it seems, during times of stress or crisis, I can speak more calmly of my feelings then. So that you may better understand the kind of man I am now, speaking into your little recording apparatus, I should say that on Earth I have amassed a considerable fortune over the years in the normal course of business investment. Had I possessed a hundred times that sum in those days when I once more walked the quarterdeck and plunged into the battlesmoke on Earth I would have given it all, over and over, to be returned once more to Kregen of Antares.

When Lloyd's Patriotic Fund voted me a fifty pound sword of honor I grasped the gaudy thing with its gilt and its seed pearls and I longed to feel once again the firm grip of a Savanti sword in my fist.

I do not believe it possible for anyone of Earth to imagine my state of mind as I thought of the crimson and emerald suns of Kregen, of the seven moons glowing in the night sky against those constellations so alien to Earth and yet so familiar to me. The tortured regrets impelled me to a strange step, for I obtained a scorpion and kept the thing in a cage. I would stare at its ugliness for many minutes on end, and hope that some familiar drowsiness would overtake me. The thing was cursed at by the men when we had to clear for action, and as bulkheads and cabin partitions were removed and struck down, I would have my pet scorpion sent down with the rest.

The Peninsular War opened and I was appointed first lieutenant aboard *Roscommon,* a leaky old tub of a seventy-four whose captain was one of the famous mad captains of the Navy List. Clearly, before me lay a career as a lieutenant until my hairs were gray and I was at last discarded on half pay to rot on the beach. Except that — my hair would not turn gray for a thousand years.

We carried out a number of interesting operations, interesting only in that they provided a strong anodyne for the ache in my soul. We took a French eighty gun ship and were thereby cheered. I heard the officers remarking on the astounding ferocity of my conduct during the boarding. I did not care. After the battle, drained of emotion, I stood on the quarterdeck, gripping the rail, and as always my eyes lifted to the heavens. Alpha Scorpii blazed its mocking ruby fires into my eyes.

Was that a hint of blueness limning Antares? Was that a blue shape leering down on me? The shape of a scorpion?

I reached up my arms.

I heard a cry from the quartermaster, and the midshipman of the watch yelled to the master's mate. I ignored them. The blueness grew. It was. It was!

I reached out and felt that blueness expand and take my consciousness into itself and I shouted, loudly and exultantly: "Kregen!" And: "Delia — Delia of Delphond, my Delia of the Blue Mountains! I return, I return!"

I opened my eyes on a sandy beach with the sound of great waves.

Sick despair clogged my mind. Standing up, I looked around upon a vast heaving sea, a sandy beach, a line of bushes inland and beyond that a prairie vast and wide, extending to the farthest horizon.

The gravity — the sun — the suns! — the feel of the air — yes. Yes, this was the world of Kregen beneath Antares. But — but where was the city? Where the River Aph? Where was Aphrasöe, the City of the Savanti, the Swinging City?

My eyes adjusted quickly to the warm pink sunshine; but I could not see what I wanted to see. I hammered a fist into the sand. Where could I be on the surface of an unknown world? Was I in Loh, that continent of mysteries and veils and hidden walled gardens? Or in Gah, that pathetic semblance of a man's sick dreams where women were chained to bedposts? There were Havilfar and Turismond, continents of which I knew nothing — and there were the other continents and the nine islands and all the seas between.

How I cursed my inadequate knowledge of Kregen!

A shadow fleeted between me and that great bloated red sun. I saw a scarlet feathered bird, with golden feathers about its neck and head, its black legs extended with wicked claws wide, its broad wings stiff and stately as it wheeled in hunting circles above me. I stood up and shook my fist at the Gdoinye. It uttered a harsh croak. After a time of surveillance it began to wheel higher and higher with a lazily powerful wingstroke. When it was but a dot in the sky I heard along the beach a sudden shrill chopped-off cry. A woman's cry.

A girl ran toward me along the beach.

It could only be Delia.

With a great shout of joy I ran toward her.

The devil might take me if I cared where in the whole world of Kregen I was if I could have Delia of the Blue Mountains at my side.

A group of riders burst from the dunes beyond Delia. They rode strange beasts, extremely short-coupled with four long narrow legs poising their bodies more hands high than any horse had any right to be. Each had a single curled horn rising from its forehead. The men wore high helmets of blazing gold. They were clad in purplish-colored jerkins studded with brass nails, a color made into vivid bruise-shine by the light. They carried weapons. And they were gaining on Delia far faster than I could reach her.

She, like myself, was completely naked.

The air in my lungs scorched like fire. I bounded in fantastic leaps, my Earthly muscles scorning the pull of gravity. Once before I had let all my Earthly muscle-power leap out in defense of this girl; now my bounds were truly of fantastic distance. Sand sheeted away at each footstep. But the riders gained on Delia, and now I could see they were not men, although possessing two arms and two legs, for their faces were like nothing so much as the big tabby cat's bewhiskered face I remembered from home. Their slit eyes blazed. I shouted, and then saved my breath for running.

41

Delia flung both arms up as her foot caught in some driftwood discarded on the beach and she fell. I heard her scream: "Dray Prescot!"

A rider leaned one furred arm down and caught her up around the waist, flicked her over to lie facedown across his saddle. I lunged forward like a demented man. I could not lose her after all, not now, not so soon after finding her again!

The lead rider reined up, those enormously long legs of his mount spindling with muscled power. Sand cascaded, his mount slid backward, then, with a snickering shrill, it had regained its balance. But in those few vital moments I had reached a stirrup. I grasped the booted foot and jerked and pulled as though I could tear the thing's leg clean off.

He screamed and something thwacked down on my shoulders. I glared up. Delia moaned. The rider threw away his crop in fury and drew a long curved sword and lifted it high. I reached up, took his elbow between my fingers, twisted, and heard the bones grind and snap. The thing shrieked again.

Delia's eyes opened; horror clouded them. "Behind you—"

I whirled and ducked and the curved sword sliced air. Now they were all about me. Swords lifted in a net of steel. I reached again for him whose arm I had mangled. He let out a keening shriek and hauled desperately at his mount's reins. The beast reared, throwing me off. Ducking a swiping sword, silently, I leaped again. I was on the thing's haunches, and so short were they that I half hung over nothingness with my left arm clamped around the rider's waist and my right dragging his head back in that arrogant golden helmet. I heard his neck snap and cast him from me. I slid forward into the saddle, seized the reins and kicked my heels into the flanks of the beast. It shivered and snorted and bounded forward.

Then the world spun around in a blaze of sparks and I saw the sand rising up toward me and, for only a fractional moment of time, felt the hardness of the sandy ground smash all along my face.

They must have left me for dead.

When I recovered, sick and groggy, and looked about, the beach was silent and deserted and only the pitiful humped shape of the dead beast, and the sprawled rider beyond, told of the tragedy that had unfolded here.

At the instant of my success, on the point of escape, I had had my mount shot from under me. The weapon still protruded from the poor thing's flank. It was an eight-foot long spear, the head fashioned from bronze and heavy although not particularly sharp. It was an unhandy weapon.

Beneath the rider — I subsequently learned that these feline-like semi-humans were called Fristles — I found his curved scimitar-like sword. Despite his broken elbow he had retained grasp of his sword hilt. When I had flung him from the high saddle he had fallen so that the point of the blade had entered his stomach with the hilt jammed against the ground. That blade had gone clean through his body and the stained point protruded eight inches past his backbone. The blood was blackened and caked and a few flies — for they exist everywhere — rose as I approached.

I turned him over with my foot, freed his hand from the hilt, put a foot on his body and dragged the sword clear. I cleaned it thoroughly with the sand all about me. I was not thinking at all clearly. I did not care to use this creature's clothes, so I cut up the purple leather and fashioned myself a breechclout after the fashion of Savanti hunting leathers; and I cut from his tunic enough to wind about my left arm. His boots fit me well enough. I slung the sword over my shoulder, its scabbard suspended from a leather baldric, and I felt that when I ran across these cat-people again I would kill very many of them before they could once again wrest Delia of Delphond from me.

The sound of hooves would be muffled to a succession of steady thumps in the sand. At the sound I drew the sword and turned to face the rider who approached. The wind blew grains of sand across the hoof prints; there had been no chance of tracking those who had taken Delia.

"Lahal," the rider called when he was fairly up with me. "Lahal, Jikai."

"Lahal," I likewise replied. I had learned what Jikai could mean in the various inflexions put upon the word. It could mean simply "Kill!" It could mean "Warrior" or "A noble feat of arms" or a number of other related concepts, to do with honor and pride and warrior-status and, inevitably, slaying. It had been used in admiration by Delia of the Blue Mountains, as it had been used by her as a command. I studied the stranger, as I said: "Lahal, Jikai."

For, clearly, he was a warrior.

I had made a mistake in custom and usage; for he made a face and pointed to the dead rider and his mount. "Indeed, it is for me to call you Jikai; what have I done that you know of?"

"As to that," I said, "I doubt not that you are a mighty warrior. But I seek a girl these — things — took."

He had an open, frank face, burned brown by the suns of Antares, with light-colored hair bleached by those suns. He carried a steel helmet at his saddle bow, and his mount was of the same strange high-stepping breed as the dead one at my feet. He wore Leathers, russet-brown, tasseled and fringed after the fashion in New England, and he sat his saddle with the alert carriage yet relaxed air I knew bespoke a master rider. I could not say horseman, although no doubt from sheer familiar usage the word crosses my lips from time to time.

"I am Hap Loder, Jiktar of the First Division of the Clan of Felschraung." The last word, as you can hear, was pronounced deeply with a great sound as of clearing the throat. The way Hap Loder said it, made it sound menacing, prideful, arrogant.

"I am Dray Prescot."

"Now that we have made pappattu, I will fight you at once."

Very little would startle me now. Any other time I'd have been pleased to fight him, if he so desired; but at this imperative time I must find Delia. He dismounted.

"You have not told me if you have seen a girl—" I began. His lance flashed before my eyes.

"Uncouth barbarian! Know you not we cannot speak of anything save obi until we have fought and given or taken obi?"

43

Furious anger flooded me. Pappattu, I understood, meant introduction. The formalities had been observed; but now this idiot would not tell me of Delia until he had fought me! Well — my captured blade flashed. I would not take long over this.

He went back to that tall-legged animal, stuck the slender willowy lance in its boot, came back with two swords. One was long, heavy, straight, a swashbuckling broadsword. The other was short, straight, simple of construction, a stabbing short sword like a gladius. "I have challenged. Which sword, since that is what you have, will you choose?"

I looked him in the eye. Impatient or not to have the thing done, I recognized honor when I met it. This young man, Hap Loder, was offering me a chance of life, and of death for himself. The powerful broadsword, of course, would not stand against my scimitar, except perhaps on sand. I nodded toward the shortsword. He smiled. "It matters not to me," I said. "But make haste." Then, for he was a fine-looking young man and, as I was to discover, Hap Loder was steel-true honest and fearless, I added: "But I think you would do well to choose the shortsword."

"Yes," he said, and took it up by its grip, replacing the long broadsword in its scabbard strapped to his mount's saddle. "Should you win I do not mind giving obi; but I have no wish to die unnecessarily."

On which fine point of logic we fell to.

He was a fine swordsman, yet the very advantages of the quick and deadly shortsword were lost to him now. The shortsword is at its best when used with a shield, packed with room to play in the long ranks of a disciplined army, each man relying on his neighbor. Or in the close and sweaty melee of the press, when the elbow has room only to move within the compass of the body, does the shortsword rule. The great broadsword, too, can be outfought by a wily and nimble opponent, and I think he had made the better choice. But he could not match the demon-driven needs that obsessed me.

"Jikai!" he shouted, and lunged.

I made a few quick passes, left his blade short and faltering, and then, with the old over-underhand loop, sent his blade flying. My point hovered at his throat. He stared up, his eyes suddenly wide.

"Now, Hap Loder, tell me, quick! Have you seen a girl carried off by such carrion as this dead thing?"

"No, Dray Prescot. I speak truth. I have not."

He scrambled up, backing away from my point. He drew himself up in the position of attention. He put his palms to his eyes, his ears, his mouth, and then clasped them over his heart.

"I make obi to you, Dray Prescot. With my eyes I will see only good of you, with my ears I will hear only good of you and with my mouth will I speak only good of you. And my heart is yours to feast upon."

"I don't want your bloody heart," I told him. "I want to know where Delia of the Blue Mountains is!"

"Had I that knowledge it would be yours."

44

I stood looking at him, at a loss. He was a young man, proud and upstanding, and a fine swordsman. If he got into many fights he'd be taking obi all the time.

He stirred awkwardly and then bent and retrieved his sword. I watched, alert, but he fingered the weapon and then walked across to his animal. He spoke to it for a moment, soothing it, and a pang of remembrance touched me.

Then he came back leading it by the reins.

"My zorca is yours, Dray Prescot, seeing that you are afoot, which no clansman may be."

A zorca! So this was the type of animal from which Delia had fallen.

"Are you not a clansman? Would you then not have to walk?"

"Yes. But I have made obi to you."

"Hmm." Then the obvious question asserted itself. "Which way lies Aphrasöe, the City of the Savanti?"

He looked blank.

"There is only one city. I have never heard of any other."

This was the answer I had feared to hear. I must be stranded in some remote and forgotten region of Kregen. Then the truth presented itself painfully. It was Aphrasöe that was isolate and hidden; these people were of the planet Kregen, living a natural human life. I thought of the cat-people — or as natural as their customs and environment allowed.

All I could do was go along with Hap Loder and learn all I could from him. I would find Delia, I would! And to find her I must learn, and quickly, damn quickly, everything I could.

I studied the zorca with its twisted single horn. The saddle was richly decorated, but it was functional, comfortable, and the stirrups were long so that there was nothing here of the bent-legged crouch of the Rotten Row jigger up-and-down. One could ride a long way in that saddle. I fancied I would.

Besides the pair of swords and the willowy lance, Hap Loder owned an ax of a peculiar and deadly character, double-bitted, daggered with six inches of flat-bladed steel. Also he had a short compound bow. I looked at his arsenal with amusement; then again at the bow, with respect. He could have shot me down with that long before I could reach him. I cocked an eye at him.

"Show me your skill with the bow, Hap."

He responded willingly. He strung it with a quick practiced jerk, looking up apologetically. "This is a light hunting bow, Dray Prescot. It has no great power. But I joy to show my skill to you, obi-brother."

A piece of driftwood lay in the sand fifty yards off.

Hap Loder put four arrows into the wood — *thunk! thunk! thunk! thunk!* — as fast as he could draw back the string, and loose. I was impressed.

Maybe that was all the weapon he needed, after all.

Also strapped to the saddle in the confined space allowed to so short-coupled an animal were a number of pieces of armor. Most were steel, although some were of bronze, and it looked as though Hap had built up his harness at different times and from different sources. He told me that a Jiktar commanded a thousand men, and my respect for him increased. The Clan of Felschraung was less than ten miles distant. I have for the moment spoken of distances in Earthly terms; when the time is ripe I will tell you more fully of Kregan methods of mensuration and numerology and of time. With two suns and seven moons the later is complex and fascinating.

I had yearned for years to return to Kregen; now I was here and I must not waste time.

"Wait here, Hap," I said. I leaped up to the saddle. The feeling was at once strange and familiar, but altogether exhilarating. It was not the same as swooping down and zooming up in an Aphrasöean swinger; but as I pounded along with the wind in my hair I felt much the same feelings of freedom and exultation. I would find Delia — I would!

I skidded to a halt before Hap Loder and jumped down.

"We will walk together, Hap."

So we started off toward the Clan of Felschraung.

Loder pulled the Fristle spear from the dead zorca. "It is not good to waste a weapon," he said.

"Where do they come from, Hap? Where would they have taken Delia?"

"I do not know. The wise men may answer you. We have but lately come into this area, for we cover many miles in a year. We wander forever on the great plains."

We left the sea far behind us and I realized I had not seen one sail on all that vast expanse.

I learned that there were many clans wandering the prairies of this continent, whose name, according to Hap Loder, was Segesthes, and that between them was continual conflict as one vast conglomeration of people and animals moved from grazing area to grazing area. The city, which was the only city he knew of and which he had never seen, was called Zenicce. There was in his demeanor when he spoke of Zenicce not only hatred but a certain contempt.

Some few miles inland we ran across the hunting party from which Hap Loder had parted in chase — a chase, incidentally, he had lost — and I was introduced. The moment we had made pappattu, the necessary preliminary to the challenge, Hap cried out that he had made obi to me.

On the bronzed faces of the clansmen I saw a dawning respect. There were a dozen of them, and two looked as though they would challenge me, anyway, for the custom was that any man may challenge any other to take obi; but the others recognized that if I had beaten Hap Loder I would also beat them. Hap looked down haughtily. Among the clansmen honor and fierce pride ruled. Weakness would be instantly singled out and uprooted. I was to learn of the complicated rituals that governed a clansman's life, and of how by a system of duel and election their leaders were chosen. But at this time I looked about ready to fight them all if needs be. And, according to their custom, had I chosen to do so, then Hap would have fought at my side until either we had been killed or they had all made obi to me.

That they had all made obi to Hap was in abeyance at a time of new pappattu; whenever a new challenge was made to take obi, all old obis died. In effect this would never work in practice, and the challenge and the giving and taking of obi would be left to the two contestants.

One of the men, a surly giant, decided. There seems always such a one in a group, resentful of his defeat at the hands of him who has taken obi from him, putting it down to chance or ill luck, and vengefully always on the lookout to reclaim what he considers is rightfully his. This one was a deposed Jiktar. He leaped from his zorca, immediately pappattu was over, and said to me, sneeringly: "I will fight you at once."

Hap stiffened and then said: "According to custom, so be it." He drew his own sword. "This sword is in the service of Dray Prescot. Remember that."

The fellow, one Lart, stood balanced on the balls of his feet, a steel-headed spear out-thrust. I caught Hap's eye. He nodded at the spear across the zorca that was ours.

"It is spears, Dray."

"So be it," I answered, and took the spear, and poised it.

As I had known it would be, it was heavy as to blade and light as to haft, ill-balanced and clumsy. It would throw reasonably well, and no doubt that was its primary function. But if Lart threw his, and I dodged, I would break his neck.

As we circled each other warily I understood that Hap had challenged me with his sword because that was the weapon I had been wearing. This must be another of their customs.

Lart darted in, thrusting and slashing as he came, hoping to bewilder me with his speed and ferocity. I leaped aside nimbly, not letting the spears touch. The same desperate urgency was on me now as had spurred me on when I had fought Hap Loder. I had to find Delia, not prance about at spear-play with a hulking vengeful lout. But I would not wantonly kill him. The Savanti had taught me that, at the least.

But it was not to be. In a quick flurry of the bronze blade I feinted left, swirled right and thrust and there was Lart, a stupid expression on his face, clutching the haft of my spear which had gone clean through his body. Thick blood oozed along the shaft from the wound. When, with a savage jerk, I wrested the spear out, blood spouted.

"He should not have challenged me," I said.

"Well," said Hap, clapping me on the shoulder. "One thing is sure. He has gone to the Plains of Mist. He cannot make obi to you now."

The others laughed at the witticism.

I did not. The fool had asked for it; but I had vowed never to kill unless there was no other way. Then I remembered my more binding vows, and I said to them curtly: "If any of you have seen a girl captured by Fristles, or any of their loathsome kind, tell me now, quickly and with truth."

But none had heard or seen anything of Delia.

I took Lart's zorca, as was proper, and I understood that all his property, after the clan leaders had made their judgment, would be mine. Surrounded by clansmen I rode out for the tents of the Clan of Felschraung. Delia seemed enormously remote to me.

Eight

I take obi of the Clansmen of Felschraung

I, Dray Prescot of Earth, sat miserably hunched in the skin tent of a man I had killed and felt all the impotent anger and the frustrations and the agony and the hell of total remorse and sorrow.

Delia was dead.

I had been told this by the clan leaders themselves, who had heard from scouting parties who had seen the Fristles set upon by, as they phrased it, "strange beasts riding stranger beasts" and there was no doubt. But there had to be doubt. How could Delia be dead? It was unthinkable, impossible. There must be a mistake. I questioned the scouts myself, impatient of pappattu and of the challenges that sometimes came. All the camp knew that Hap Loder, a Jiktar of a thousand men, had made obi to Dray Prescot, and there were few challenges. I learned the customs and how it was that ten thousand men could live together without a continual round of challenges. On first meeting, obi could be given or taken. Subsequently, it was a matter for jurisdiction of the wise men and the clan leaders, of custom and of necessity, and of elections when a leader died or fell in battle. I was impatient of it all. I searched the camp for the men, and asked my questions easily enough after I had killed the first three and taken obi from the rest, all of them, to the number of twenty-six. Their stories tallied. Strange beasts riding beasts had set upon the Fristles and all the party had been slain.

So I, Dray Prescot of Earth, sat in my skin tent surrounded by the trophies my search had brought me, and brooded long and agonizingly on what had been lost.

Even then, even then I doubted. Surely no man would be foolish enough to slay such glorious beauty as Delia of Delphond? But — but it had been beasts who had attacked. I shuddered. Would they not see beauty in Delia? And then, came the horrific thought, perhaps if they did it were better she were dead.

I believe you, who listen to the tapes spinning between the heads of your recorder, will forgive me if I do not dwell on my life among the clansmen of Felschraung. I spent five years with them. I did not age. By challenge, by election and duel, I rose in the hierarchy, although this was not of my seeking. It is an amazing and sobering fact to realize the power of ten thousand men who have made obi to one man. By the end of the five years every single one of the clansmen of Felschraung had made obi to me, either directly as the result of a victory in combat or through the indirect method of acknowledging me, with all the ceremony demanded by obi, as being their lord and master.

It all meant nothing, of course.

Mainly, it was forced upon me by circumstances and my saving my own skin. I knew why I wanted to live. Quite apart from my abhorrence of suicide, despite the dejection into which I can fall, if I surrendered my life abjectly and Delia of the Blue Mountains still lived and needed me — how would I acquit myself on the Plain of Mists then?

Some days of sunshine and rushing winds as we rode our zorcas across the wide prairies I would think Delia truly dead. And then on other days as the rains lashed down and the pack animals and the endless lines of wagons rolled across the plains, sinking axle-deep into the mud, I would begin to think that perhaps she still lived. Often I found myself believing she had in some miraculous way been transported back to Aphrasöe, the City of the Savants. If so, that was a happening I could understand and applaud. I had been discharged from Paradise for helping her, as being unworthy. Perhaps the Savanti had reconsidered their verdict. Could I look forward once more to seeing the Swinging City?

That I had under my direct command ten thousand of the fiercest fighters I had ever led was an accident.

Their chief weapon was the laminated reflex bow. I, too, learned the knack of sending five shafts out of five into the chunkrah's eye. The chunkrah, as the reference suggests, was the cattle animal, deep-chested, horned, fierce, superb eating roasted. I had need of this expertise with the bow, for more than once or twice when elections had selected the combatants I fought men who wished to take obi from me with bows. I found a primitive pleasure astride zorca or vove in stalking my opponent, clad in hunting leathers like myself, bow to bow, slipping his arrows and sending my own shafts deep into his breast.

The clansmen used an ancient and superbly thought-out system of warfare. While they used their earth-shaking herds of chunkrah to break down enemy palisades or wagon circles, they considered this a waste of good chunkrah-flesh. They fought when the need arose from within the tightly-drawn wagon circle, the laager of the plains. But they took their fiercest joy in the two riding animals, the vove and the zorca. As a clansman I shared with them the two entirely different exhilarations to be found in charging knee to knee in the massive vove phalanxes and in pirouetting superbly on the nimble zorcas as the flashing shafts from our bows seethed into the hostile ranks.

For the first shock of vove combat when the earth shuddered to the pounding of the hooves, the clansmen used the long, heavy, couched lance, banded with iron and steel. Then they would take to their axes, with which they were irresistible. The broadsword was used, and often; but normally only when the ax was smashed or lost from its thong. With my experience of wielding a tomahawk in boarding parties on my own Earth I was able to hold my own. But an ax has a relatively short cutting edge; a striking sword will wound down almost its whole sharpened length. Even from their zorcas and voves, perched in their high saddles, they could not with their axes best me. I found that in the melee of mounted combat when the mighty voves struggled head to head and the swinging room was restricted, an ax could crushingly do more damage, biting down solidly through steel and bronze and bone. It was a useful weapon then. But as the press increased and the dust rose choking and blinding and stinging in our sweating eyes and clogging in our riding scarves, the short stabbing sword came into its own, and made short work of opponents against whom axes would clog.

The balanced throwing knife was regarded with some favor by certain of the clans of the great plains, and the terchick, as the form in which it was forged was called by the clansmen — I suspected not from its shape but from the sound it made — was swift and accurate. However, it was essentially the woman's weapon, and the fierce tawny-skinned bright-eyed girls of the clans could hurl their terchicks with unerring skill. In the nuptial ceremony the groom would stand for his bride as she sank a quiver-full of terchicks into the stuffed target sacks at his back. Then, laughing, when all her defenses were gone, he would take her up in his arms and place her tenderly upon his vove for their bridal ride.

The voves were eight-legged, large, savage, horned and tufted, shaggy with a russet color glorious beneath the suns of Antares. Their endurance was legendary. Their hearts would pump loyally for day after day in the long chase if necessary, until the animal dropped dead, still struggling on. They carried the main war divisions of the clansmen, fighting with bulk and strength. The zorcas were lighter, fleeter but without the awe-inspiring stamina of the vove.

After five years it became necessary for me to conquer and take over the Clan of Longuelm. Again there was only a marginal joy in it. Hap Loder, who was now my right-hand man, remarked that I could, if I wished, weld the whole of the clansmen of the great plains into a single mighty fighting force.

"Why, Hap?" I said to him.

"Think of the glory!" His face reflected the shining promises he could see. "A force so powerful nothing could stand in its way. And you could do it, Dray."

"And if I did, whom would we fight?"

His face fell. "I had not thought of that."

"Perhaps," I said to him. "Because there would not then be anyone to fight, it might be worth the doing."

He did not really understand me.

Great wealth reckoned in any terms had been amassed during that five years. I possessed zorcas and voves by the thousand, and chunkrahs by the tens of thousand. I commanded with the rights of life and death the lives of twenty thousand fighting men, and three times as many women and children. The wagons contained chests of jewels, rare silks of Pandahem, spices from Askinard, ivory from the jungles of Chem. A flick of my fingers could bring a dozen of the most beautiful girls one could find to dance for me. Wine, food, music, literature, good talk and the wisdom of the wise men, all were mine without a thought.

But I merely existed through this time, for all I cared about was Delia of the Blue Mountain, and through her for Aphrasöe where all the luxuries and delicacies of the clansmen would taste immeasurably sweeter.

Life, however, was for the living.

If I have given the impression that obi was a mere matter of a challenge, and a relatively brainless combat, then I do the clansmen a disservice. It carried far more ramifications than that. The wise men, for instance, could not in their aged sagacity be expected to be continually leaping up to swing a sword and shoot a bow. The electoral system balanced out in the end to the benefit of the clan, and the clan leader was a fine fighting man, as would be essential given the conditions of life on the great plains of Segesthes.

I knew that I could count on the absolute and fanatical loyalty of every single man of the clans of Felschraung and Longuelm. I had made it my business to weed out men of Lart's type. The first lieutenant of a King's Ship soon learns to handle men. I could find an inverted, ridiculous pride in the fact that my men owed me loyalty without the need of the lash, and if I fancied they also held me in some affection, I would not be a human being had that not pleased me.

These were poor substitutes for what I had lost.

The clansmen kept no slaves.

There was no need for me to do as I would undoubtedly have done, and freed them all with that procedure's consequent tears and confusions and tragedies. Out on the great plains loyalty and affection between man and man and between man and woman would have clogged had slavery obtruded. We rode like the wind, and like the wind were here and gone before oafish mortals could apprehend. Mysticism came easily on the great plains beneath the seven moons of Kregen.

Most obi challenges were fought mounted; only my own flat feet on which I had been standing those first few times had given me an advantage which later I recognized. A clansman lived in the saddle. When a man and maid joined themselves in the simple nuptials recognized by the elders they would ride off together astride their mounts as a natural extension of the lives they had known. They would always contrive to ride off into the red sun's sunset, and not the green sun's. This I understood. Among the many languages of Kregen — and I soon picked up enough of the clansmen's so that I could converse in that tongue as well as Kregish — there were many and various names for the red sun and the green sun and for all the seven moons, and all the phases of the seven moons. Suffice it that if the need arises I will use the most suitable names; for names are important on Kregen, more, if that be possible, than on Earth. With a name a primitive man may conceive he possesses the inner nature of the thing named. Names were not given lightly, and once given were objects of respect. Yes, names are important, and should not be forgotten.

I will speak no more for the moment of the clansmen of Segesthes but pass on to a day of early spring — the Kregan seasons must revolve like our own so that there is a time of planting and a time of growing and a time of harvesting and a time of feasting; but the binary suns make these elementary distinctions gradually change year by year — when I rode out at the head of a hunting party. The men were happy and carefree, for life was good and, as they said, never had they known a greater Warlord, a mightier Vovedeer, a more furious Zorcander, than Dray Prescot.

We had ventured far to the south, leaving that gleaming sea many miles distant — its name was not on record among the clansmen for they were men of the great plains — and we could include in our grazing swing fresh areas opened up to us by the amalgamation with the clan of Longuelm. This had been one reason for my diplomacy of swords.

Even so we had entered areas unknown to the men of Longuelm and this party was as much a scout as a hunt.

Looking back now I can blame myself for bad scouting, or for bad generalship. But had our point not missed what he should have seen before he died, all that followed would not have occurred and you would not be listening to this tape.

The ground was breaking with the green growing burgeon of spring as we trotted down between two rounded hills whereon trees grew. We always welcomed trees as signs that water and a break from the plains was near. The air smelled as sweet and fresh as it always does in the better parts of Kregen. The twin suns shone, their emerald and crimson fires casting the twin shadows that were now so usual to me.

We bestrode high-spirited zorcas, and a string of fierce impatiently following voves trailed in the remuda. A few pack animals, calsanys and Kregen asses, mostly, carried our few belongings for camp. Yes, life was good and free and filled with the zest of high living for all those young men who followed me. The image of Delia of the Blue Mountains remained a constant dull ache within me. Yet I was beginning to accept, at last, that I must go on without her.

The shower of arrows and spears felled four of my men, slew my zorca, and pitched me into the dust. I was up in an instant, sword drawn, and a net closed around my head. I could see weirdly-shaped creatures flinging the nets and I hacked and slashed — and then a club smashed against my head and I went down into unconsciousness.

How could I be surprised when I regained consciousness to find that I was naked, apart from a breechclout, and that my hands were lashed together with cords and that I was yoked to what remained of my men?

We were prodded to our feet and commanded to march.

The beasts who had captured us smelled unpleasantly. They were not above four-foot tall, covered in thick hair of a dun color tending to black at the tips, and each had six limbs. The bottom pair were clad in rough sandals, the upper pair wielded the prodding spears and swords and shields, and the middle pair seemed to serve any other function as it became necessary. They wore slashed tunics of some stuff of brilliant emerald color — the color of the green sun of Antares — and their heads, which were lemon shaped with puffy jaws and lolling chops, were crowned with ridiculous flat caps of emerald velvet. They carried their spears as though they knew how to use them.

"Are you all right, Zorcander?" asked one of my men, and the nearest beast growled like a dog in its throat and beat him over the head. He did not cry out. He was a clansman.

"We must stick together, my clansmen," I shouted, and before the beast could strike me I raised my voice and bellowed: "We will come through yet, my friends."

The spear-blade lashed alongside my head and for a space I stumbled along blinded and weak and dumb.

The camp to which we were brought was resplendent with richly-decorated marquees, and everywhere signs of opulence and luxury indicated clearly that this hunting party believed in making life on the great plains as comfortable as possible. Lines of zorcas tethered together on one side were matched by lines of another riding animal, an eight-legged beast not unlike a vove, except that they were smaller and lighter and without the ferocious aspect of a vove, without the horns and the fangs. Our own captured zorcas had been brought in, I noticed, and tethered with the others. But our captors had not brought in one single vove. Had I been given to empty gestures, I would have smiled.

A man stepped from a tent and stood wide-legged, his hands on his hips, regarding us with a curl to his lips. He was very white-faced, dark-haired, and he wore tight-fitting leathers over all his body. They were of the same brilliant emerald as the garments worn by the things that had caught us.

I decided it would be something to do to snap his neck; something that might lighten the drabness of days.

He turned his face back toward the tent opening. The tent was the most grandiose in all the camp. We stood bedraggled and naked in the dust.

"Ho, my princess!" the man called. "The Ochs have made a capture that may amuse you."

So, I thought to myself, they have princesses hereabouts, do they?

The princess strolled to the entrance to her tent.

Yes, she was beautiful. After all these years, I must admit she was beautiful. One first noticed her hair, like ripe corn with the morning sun shining on it in a field of our own Earth. Her eyes were the cornflower blue of the flowers one might find in that field. These were old and tired clichés before ever they reached Kregen; but I recall her as I first saw her that day long ago as she stood looking down on where we had been flung captive in the dust.

She lifted a white rounded arm that glowed with the warm pink pulse of blood. Her lips were red, red, and soft like a luscious fruit. She wore an emerald green gown that revealed her throat and arms and the lower portion of her legs, and she wore around her neck a string of blazing emeralds that must have ransomed a city. She looked down on us, and her nostrils pinched together as at an offensive smell. Very beautiful and commanding, she looked, on that day so long ago.

I was lifting my face to look at her.

The man walked across and kicked me.

"Turn your eyes to the dirt, rast, when the Princess Natema passes!"

Within my lashings and the yoke I rolled over and still looked up at her although the man had kicked me cruelly hard.

"Does the princess then not desire admiration from a man's eyes?"

The man went mad.

He kicked and kicked. I rolled about; but the bonds interfered. I heard the princess shouting with anger, and heard her say: "Why clean your boots on the rast, Galna? Prod him with a spear and have done. I weary of this hunt."

Well, if I were to die, then this monkey would die with me.

I tripped him and rolled on him and placed my bound wrists on his throat. His face turned purplish. His eyes protruded. I leered at him.

"You kick me, you blagskite, and you die!"

He gargled at me. There was an uproar. The Ochs ran about waving their spears. I surged upright gripping Galna, and my men on the lashings rose with me. I kicked the first Och in the belly and he tumbled away, screeching. A spear flicked past my body. Galna wore a fancy little sword smothered with jewels. I dropped him as though he were a rattler, and as he fell I managed to drag the little jeweled sticker out. The next Och took the small sword through the throat. It broke off as the beast shrieked and struggled and died.

I flung the hilt at the next Och and cut his head open.

I picked up Galna again, my hands and wrists swelling against the lashings, and hurled him full at the princess.

She gave a cry and vanished within her tent.

Then, as it seemed so often when things were becoming interesting, the sky fell in on me.

Neither of us would ever forget my first meeting with the Princess Natema Cydones of the Noble House of Esztercari of the City of Zenicce.

Nine

Black marble of Zenicce

The most recalcitrant of slaves were sent to labor in the Jet Mines of Zenicce's marble quarries. On the surface the quarries lay open to the twin suns whose topaz and opal fires blazed down on the white marble and lit it with a million hues and tones. Quarrying the white marble was hard unremitting labor; where we were, down in the Jet Mines, the work was a continual torture.

How many people realize, when they admire a fine piece of black marble statuary, a graceful vase or magnificent architrave, that agony and revulsion have gone into its production? Marble that is black is black because of the infusion of bituminous material. Whenever the marble splits, at every blow, it sends forth a fetid, filthy, stinking odor.

We were completely naked, for we wrapped our breechclouts around our mouths and noses to try in some ineffectual way to diminish that charnel house breath that gushed up at us each time our chisels struck into the stone.

Greasy wicks burned and sputtered in black marble bowls and pushed back a little of the darkness of the mines. In this mine there were twenty of us, and the guards had shut down the hewn-log doors upon us. Only when we had cut and hauled up the requisite amount of marble would they feed us, and if we did not produce we would not be fed. For a full seven days we would labor in the Jet Mines, continually sick, desperately attempting to adjust to the smells and the fatigue, and then we would be let out to labor for seven days in the white marble mines of the surface, and then for a further seven days we would be employed on dragging and ferrying the stones along the canals of the city.

My clansmen and I often missed that third period of seven days, and would rotate seven days in the black below and seven days in the white above. I could remember little of my journey here. The city had been large, impressive, cut by canals and rivers and broad avenues, massed with fine buildings and arcades and dripping with green and purple plants growing riotously over every wall. Many strange-looking peoples thronged the streets, half-beast, half-human, and all, so I understood, in inferior positions, little better than slaves and functionaries.

The most recalcitrant of Zenicce's slaves labored in the Jet Mines. My resentment at slavery was so great that, I confess now, I failed to use my reasoning powers, and I fought back, and lashed out, and snatched the whips from the guards and broke them over their heads before a measure of wisdom returned.

When young Loki, a fine clansman from whom I felt honored to receive obi, died in my arms in the foul deliquescence of the Jet Mines, and the vile miasma from the broken walls of marble breathed its poisonous fumes over us as he sprawled there with his sightless eyes unable to be blessed by the twin fires of Antares, I knew I was responsible for his death, that I had been selfish in my hatred. But the guards were clever. They had split my clansmen into three sections, each laboring on a different shift, so that when aloft in the white quarries and escape a mere matter of planning and execution, I could not take that escape route because the rest of my men were not with me, a third of them down in the Jet Mines where no man would leave a friend.

The guards were recruited from a number of races. There were Ochs, and Fristles, and other beast-humans, notably the Rapas, human monsters who might have been the blasphemous spawn of gray vultures and gray men. Very quick with their whips, were the Rapas, quick and finicky and cutting.

Of all the many foolhardy actions I have made in my life, what I did that day in the Jet Mines of Zenicce must rank as one of the most stupid, for I know it cost me a great deal to make the decision. At the end of our seven days in that filth and stink when we were let out to go aloft to work the white quarries, I secreted myself behind a stinking rock and waited for the new shift. One of my clansmen in the shuffle of passing slaves caught a friend from the newcomers and hurried him out in my place, so that numbers would tally.

When the massive log doors clashed shut on us I stood up in the lamplight.

"Lahal, Rov Kovno," I said.

Rov Kovno looked at me silently. He was a Jiktar of a thousand, a mighty warrior, barrel-bodied, fair-headed and with a squashed broken nose and an arrogant jut to his chin. He was of the clansmen of Longuelm. I thought I had made a mistake, that I had miscalculated. I thought as I stood there in the lamp-splashed darkness with the stink of that infernal black marble choking my nostrils and mouth that he blamed me for our capture. I waited, standing, silently.

Rov Kovno moved forward. He held the hammer and chisel of our trade. He dropped them into the chippings and dirt of the floor. He put both arms out to me.

"Vovedeer!" he said, and his voice choked. "Zorcander!"

One of the men of his gang, not a clansman but just one more of the unfortunates enslaved by the city of Zenicce, looked at me and spat. "He stayed in here after his shift was up!" he said. He could not believe it. "The man is a fool — or mad! Mad!"

"Speak with respect, cramph, or do not speak at all," growled Rov Kovno. He put the palms of his hands to his ears and his eyes and his mouth, and then over his heart. He had no need to speak, and I was pleased, for it meant my plan could go ahead and free me from that worry.

I grasped his hand. "I cannot escape without taking all my clansmen," I told him. "There is a plan. As soon as you make your escape with your men, Ark Atvar will then make his. My shift will go last."

"Does Ark Atvar know of the plan, Dray Prescot?"

"Not yet."

"Then I will remain here, in the Jet Mines, for the next shift to tell him."

I laughed. There, in the Jet Mines of Zenicce, I, a man not given to empty gestures, laughed.

"Not so, Rov Kovno. That is a task laid on your Vovedeer."

He inclined his head. He knew, as did I, the responsibilities of leadership, of the taking of obi.

We all knew that the first escape would be relatively easy, a clean break from the wherries carrying the blocks of marble from the quarries through the canals to whatever building site in the city had need of them. The second escape would be a little more difficult; but it should be done. The third escape would be the most difficult, and that would fall to my shift. I knew my men would not have it any other way.

I had to give Rov Kovno an agreement that I would order Ark Atvar to make the first escape.

The fanatical loyalty of the clansmen of the great plains of Segesthes is legendary.

On the seventh day of that unremitting shift cutting and moving the huge black stones, Rov Kovno begged me to allow him to remain in that hell to pass on the instructions to Ark Atvar. I may take a foolish pride in thinking he would not have thought any the less of me had I succumbed to his earnest pleas. And, truth to tell, the idea of climbing up out of that pit and seeing once more the daylight and smelling the sweet air of Kregen affected me powerfully.

I said to Rov Kovno, rather harshly: "I have taken obi from you, and I know what obligations the taker of obi owes to the giver. Ask me no more."

And he did not ask me any more.

When Rov Kovno whisked an incoming clansman back out to join his shift and make the numbers up I gagged on the stench of the place and almost broke free. But I restrained myself, and was able to speak almost normally as I said: "Lahal, Ark Atvar."

The ensuing scene was almost a repetition of that before.

No time would be wasted. From the week in the white quarries on the surface the slaves would go for their week transporting the blocks. Then Rov Kovno would escape. That week passed as slowly as any week ever has for me — and it was my third consecutive week in the Jet Mines. No one before, I was told, had survived three weeks in that nauseous hell. All that kept me alive and moving was the thought that I had taken obi from these men, and that I owed them their lives and liberty. I confess that the image of Delia of the Blue Mountains faded then, shaming me, to a thin and distant dream, the stuff of fantasy.

When the logs rolled back and the beast-guards prodded the fresh batch of slaves down I looked at the newcomers with a trembling expectancy. From the looks on the faces of my men I knew — they had never expected me to survive, they had not expected ever to see me again.

Now began the fourth consecutive week in the Jet Mines.

By the last day I was very weak. The abominable stench coiled around my head, reached down with vile tendrils into my stomach, caused me a continuous blinding headache, made it impossible for me to keep anything down. My men worked like demons cutting and loading so that my uselessness would not prevent them from receiving our miserable quota of food and drink let down on ropes. The other slaves with us, not clansmen, grumbled; but a rough kind of comradeship had of necessity grown up and we worked together, well enough.

On that last day as the great black blocks swung up in their cradles, gleaming against the lamplight, we waited for our relief. At last the logs rolled back and the fresh shift of slaves began to descend. I saw shaven-headed Gons, and redheaded men from Loh, and some of the half-human, half-beast men driven as slaves; but not a single clansman was herded down into the pit.

Rov Kovno and his men had escaped!

There could not be any doubt of it.

As we rose up into the marble quarries with the glinting rock cut in gigantic steps all about us, and we saw the tiny dots of slaves and guards working everywhere on the faces, the great mastodon-like beasts hauling cut blocks, the wherries lying in the docks slowly loading as the derricks swung, I began to think life could begin again.

Parties from the other cells of the Jet Mines were joining our band of twenty as we were marched off. There were thousands of slaves employed here. If twenty or so escaped, the overseers would be blamed; but the work would go on. But those twenty men meant more to me than all the other thousands put together.

"By Diproo the Nimble-fingered!" wheezed a weasel-faced runty little man, blinking and squinting. "How the blessed sunlight stings my eyes!"

His name was Nath, a wiry, furtive little townsman with sparse sandy hair and whiskers, with old scars upon his scrawny body, his ribs a cage upon his flat chest. I had marked him out as of use. By his language I guessed him to be a thief of the city, and consequently one of use to me and my clansmen.

In the air above the quarries hung a constant cloud of dust, rock and marble dust, stirred up by continual activity, and this irritated eyes and nostrils, so that we all cut a piece of our breechclouts to wear across our faces, making the garment briefer than ever. Across from the huddle of swaybacked huts enclosed by a marble palisade where we barracked during our period of seven days in the white quarries I saw a band of slave women chipping marble blocks. Their backs gleamed with sweat and the sweat caught and held a patina of marble chips and dust. They too wore simply the slave breechclout. Around their ankles and joining them in coffles stretched heavy iron chains. There was no romance of slavery here, within the marble quarries of Zenicce.

There were more guards in evidence than usual.

One of my men, young Loku, a Hikdar of a hundred, who was poor dead Loki's brother, reported to me. His fierce warrior's face with its sheen of dust-covered sweat looked gray and sunken; but the vicious look in his eyes reassured me.

"The women told me, Dray Prescot," he said. He had taken a risk, talking to the slave women in broad daylight. "There have been two escapes. One from the marble wherries, the other from these very quarries, last night."

"Good," I said.

Nath, the thief, cleared his throat and spat dust.

"Good for them, bad for us. Now the Rapas, for sure, will strike twice as hard."

Loku would have struck Nath for the disrespect he showed a Vovedeer; but I restrained him. I had need of Nath.

"Find out whose turn it is to feed the vosks," I told Loku, "and arrange for one of us to do that unsavory task."

The vosks were almost completely devoid of intelligence, great fat pig-like animals standing some six feet at the shoulders, with six legs, a smooth oily skin of a whitish-yellow color, and atrophied tusks; their uses were to turn waterwheels, to draw burdens, to operate the lifting cages, and also to furnish remarkably good juicy steaks and crisp rashers. We, as slaves, saw them only as work animals. We ate the same slop as the vosks.

The mastodons which did the really heavy work fed cheaply on a special kind of grass imported from the island of Strye.

As well as Rapa guards there were many Rapa slaves working with us, gray vulturine beings with scrawny necks and beaked faces, whose gray bodies reeked with their own unpleasant sweat. They were more restless than most in the quarries that night as the twin suns sank beneath the marble rim and the first of the seven moons glided across the sky.

I made Nath tell me what he knew of this city of Zenicce.

The city contained approximately one million inhabitants, about the same number as the London of my own time, but in Zenicce there were uncounted numbers of slaves, hideously suppressed and manipulated. By means of the delta arms of the River Nicce and artificially constructed canals as well as by extraordinarily broad avenues, the city was partitioned into independent enclaves. The pride of House rode very high in Zenicce. Either one belonged to a House or one was nothing. I learned with an expression I kept as hard as the marble all about us beneath the glowing spheres of the first three moons of Kregen that the House color of the Esztercari Family was the emerald of the green sun of Kregen. So the cramph Galna whom I had hurled at the Princess Natema was of her House. I wondered how he would die, shackled to the horns of a vove and released across the broad plains of Segesthes? He would not, I fancied, die well — in which as I discovered later I did him an injustice.

Across the outer compound a Rapa slave was being beaten by a pair of Rapa guards. They used their whips with skill and cunning, and the gray vulture-like being shrieked and jerked in his chains. He had lost, so the whisper went around, his hammer and chisel, and if the overseer so willed it, that was a mortal offense. The vosks in their patient turning of the capstan bars would haul his broken body to the topmost step of the marble quarries, and then he would be flung out and down, to crash a bloody heap on the dust and chippings of the floor a thousand feet below.

In the moon-shadowed dimness of the marble walls Loku crept to my side. His face was just as gray and lined; but a fiercer jut to his chin lifted my spirits.

"We feed the vosks for this sennight," he said, his eyes gleaming in the moonlight.

"And?" I asked.

He drew from his breechclout a hammer and chisel. I nodded. It was death to be found with these tools in the barracks, when not working on the marble faces, or down in the Jet Mines. Down there, shut in by the logs for seven days and seven nights, slaves did not wear their chains. Now, back on the surface, we were heavily chained and shackled. "You have done well, Loku," I said. Then, I added: "We shall not forget Loki, we clansmen of Felschraung."

"May Diproo of the fleet feet aid me now!" moaned Nath. His wizened body shrank back. Loku cuffed him idly, sent him keening to a corner of the marble hut.

I did not think that Nath, the thief, would betray us.

We waited that seven days in the white quarries until it was our turn to take the huge marble slabs in their straw balings onto the wherries and transport them into the city. Somewhere in the city, or better yet out on the open plains, my men would be waiting for us. They had not been recaptured. What was done to recaptured slaves was ugly and obvious, given the circumstances.

All that week extra guards were posted, many of them men in the crimson and emerald livery of the city wardens, men supplied by all Houses as a kind of police force. The Rapas made very free with their whips. The Rapa slaves seethed. My men and I were model slaves.

The glint of marble chippings in the air, the eternal tink-tink-tink of the women trimming stones, the heavier thuds of the hammers on chisels all over the quarry faces, the deeper slicing roars as vosk-powered saws bit in clouds of flying chips and dust, all these sounds frayed at our nerves day after day; but we remained quiet and attentive and docile in our chains.

We took turns to feed the vosks, swilling the remnants of our slops into their troughs, pent between priceless marble walls. The places stank almost as much as the Jet Mines. They would put their pig-like snouts down and grunt and gulp and waves of the nauseating liquid would pulsate out around our legs, filling our noses with the stench. Those whose duty it was, and whom we had relieved of that duty, thought we were mad. Many guards patrolled, on the alert; but few cared to venture too near the vosk pens, as none ventured into the Jet Mines. One shift had refused to send up the stinking black marble, and had simply been shut in there to die. When other slaves had brought the twisted, ghastly bodies out, the guards paraded them through the workings so that none should miss the lesson.

Gradually, on my orders, we cut down the vosk swill.

On the second to last day the vosks were hungry; but we fed them sufficient to quieten the immediate rumblings of their stomachs. On the penultimate day we did not feed them at all, and they were as recalcitrant as an unpunished slave so that, for a time as I labored at the marble, with the sunshine lancing back from the brilliant surface and dazzling my eyes, I feared I had miscalculated. But the vosks are stupid creatures. At the end of the day they grunted and squealed and fairly broke into ungainly waddles on their way back to their pens. We tempted them with morsels of food, sparingly, and so quietened their uproar.

But they received no more food.

On the last day they were surly, puzzled, drawing their loads and turning their wheels with a stupid pugnacity that made me feel heartily sorry for them and what we were being forced to do to them. The slaves, mostly lads and girls, whose task was to prod them along, gave them a wider berth than usual, and stood well out of their way at evening when the twin suns sank in floods of gold and crimson and emerald.

We carried the great slopping vats of swill to the pens and I managed to spill a quantity of the vile stuff near the boots of a Rapa guard, who croaked his guttural obscenities at me, and I stood the flick of his whip in a good cause, for the guards moved away. We poured the slop down outside the marble walls of the pens. The vosks went hungry on the last night — and in the morning when we should have fed them for the last time before punting our loaded wherries from the docks. They squealed and grunted and some, finding hunger a stimulus to a more primitive action, butted their atrophied tusks against the walls of their pens.

That morning the twin suns of Antares rose with a more resplendent brilliance. We ate hugely of the slop the vosks had not seen. Nath was under the eye of Loku. All our chains had been cut through in stealth and with muffled hammers, and now were lapped about us, ready to be cast off. Nath shivered and called on his pagan god of thieves.

We went aboard the wherry for which we would be responsible, clambering about among the gigantic blocks of marble the women had trimmed clean and square, following the slave masons' chalked marks, and I took the greatest chance of all and went swiftly and quietly in that morning radiance to the vosk pens. I threw open all the gates. With a vosk goad I urged the stupid beasts out, and I joyed to see the idiot ugliness of their faces, the pig-like malice in their tiny eyes. They were hungry. They were loose.

The vosks began to roam the quarries, looking for food.

Guards ran yelling angrily, prodding with spears and swords. I saw one Och, his six limbs agitated, attempt to prod a stupid vosk back and rejoiced at his dumbfounded surprise when the usually docile beast turned on him and knocked him end over end with a resounding thump of those two tiny tusks. Had I been inclined, I would have laughed.

I jumped from the jetty onto our wherry and joined the rest of my men, my chains wrapped about me, as the Rapa guards stalked aboard. There would have been ten of them, I knew, for the citizens of Zenicce were naturally touchy about insufficiently guarded slaves in their city. This morning, because for some unfathomable reason the vosks had gone mad and were overrunning the quarries, there were only six guards.

We pushed off and with the long poles punted slowly along the canal between marble banks.

Soon the banks became brick, and then the first of the houses passed. Mere hovels, these, of people without a House, living on the outskirts of the city, free only in name.

I admit now it was a strange sensation to me to be riding water again.

We passed beneath an ornate granite arch over which passed the morning procession of market vendors and peddlers and housewives and riffraff and thieves, and all that smell and bustle and morning talk and laughter awoke a thrilling in my veins. The sky grew pinker with that pellucid liquid rose-glow of Kregen on a fine morning. The air as we approached nearer the city grew sweeter, and this alone indicates the putrid atmosphere of the mines in which we had sweated and slaved. The canal debouched into a larger channel whose brick walls rose to a height of some ten feet above the water. On each side the blank walls of houses, each joined to the other, frowned down, their roofs at different heights and forms of architecture so that the skyline formed an attractive frieze against the light.

Sentinels in the colors of their Houses were to be seen at vantage points along those walls. Between enclave and enclave on the perimeter of the city lies always an armed truce.

Close now to our destination we swung out of the broad canal which had steadily increased its freight of traffic. There were light swift double-ended craft which, given the niceties of canal navigation, would be almost certainly some form or model of gondola. There were deep-laden barges, like ours, punted by slaves. There were stately pulling barges gay with awnings and silks, the oarsmen, sometimes men, as often as not some outlandish creatures decked out in weird finery, all gold or silver lace with cocked hats gay with plumes. I watched all these strange craft with as strange a hunger in my belly, for I had not seen a boat for years, let alone a ship billowing under full canvas to the royals, heeling to the Trades.

Ahead a truly enormous arch towered over the canal. One side of the bridge laid atop the arch was festooned with ocher and purple trappings; the other side gleamed all in emerald green. We turned up a perimeter canal past the bridge, turning toward the green hand, and soon a more open aspect made itself felt in the architecture. We had entered an enclave. From the colors I knew it to be the enclave of the House of Esztercari and a fierce and unholy joy threatened for a moment to sway me from my purpose.

The building site lay to the rear of a stone jetty. We poled in slowly and more slowly toward the jetty, the water pooling and swirling from the wherry's blunt bows. I nodded to two of my men. They slid their poles inboard and ducked down in the center of the spaces we had left between the carefully-stacked marble blocks. I heard short sharp sounds, as of iron on iron.

A Rapa guard swung around from the bows, looking back, his vulturine face questioning. I, from my position in the stern, also looked back as though seeking, like the guard, for the noise astern. I saw another wherry following ours, loaded with marbles, its crew Rapas, its guards Ochs. It was coming in very fast, due to our loss of way, and would collide very soon. I did not mind. Now I could hear the fresh gurgle of water, bright and cheerful and inspiriting, welling from inside our wherry.

"What's that racket?" demanded the Rapa in his croaking voice.

I lifted my shoulders to indicate I did not know, and then jumped down from the high stern and went forward, as though he had called me, trailing my pole. The wherry was appreciably lower in the water. A Rapa guard in the waist made as though to stop me. Him, I struck full force and knocked down and into the marble blocks where two of my men seized him and silenced him. Two more Rapa guards had vanished. Water sloshed and gurgled almost to the gunwale. Another Rapa guard vanished. I saw Loku, with Nath at his side, loop a coil of chain about the fifth guard's bird-like ankles in the big boots and drag him down out of sight. His beginning shriek chopped off short, as though a bight of chain had snared his windpipe.

The following wherry had avoided us and was poling past. No one aboard seemed to be taking any notice of us — and then I saw why. Instantly fury and outrageous indignant anger spurted up in me.

The Rapa slaves on the second wherry were slaying their Och guards with their chains, were flinging the small six-limbed puffy-faced people overboard in bright splashes of water.

We were now sinking. Within seconds the canal water slopped inboard. Now the plan was for us to dive and swim for the bank, covered by the confusion of the sinking wherry. But guards were rushing from every direction. The Rapa revolt had sparked an instant reaction, so clumsy, so violent had it been. Our own escape could not avoid detection now. The Rapas' wherry touched the jetty and they boiled ashore, shrieking, inflamed, their grisly chains whirling in their fists.

Ten

"Dray Prescot, you may incline to me!"

The Princess Natema Cydones of the Noble House of Esztercari had come early that morning to the stone masons' jetty of her enclave to select new marble for the walls of a summer palace she was having built on the eastern side of her estate. That she would be taking marble destined for the building of the new water-rates building did not concern her in the slightest. As far as the princess knew there was nothing she might not have if she wanted it.

As I watched in dumb fury those idiotic Rapa slaves destroy the fruits of my planning, I did not know, then, that among the knot of brilliantly attired nobles on the jetty stood the Princess Natema impatiently stamping her jeweled foot on the stone, waiting to have the coverings ripped from the marble so that she might choose the exact stones she coveted.

All I saw was the charging mob of Rapas and the sudden wink and flame of weapons in the sunshine and the ugly whirling of the iron chains.

The Rapas were not so stupid, after all. They had successfully smuggled many more of their fellows aboard the wherry. They had been aided in this, without a doubt, by my ruse with the vosks. They were a formidable scarecrow crew in their rags and chains who roared onto the landing. Almost at once brilliant emerald green uniforms were flying through the air and splashing into the waters of the canal.

There was a chance for us, after all...

"Loku!" I cried. "Now! Nath — it is up to you to show the way through the city. We depend on you — if you fail us you know what your fate will be."

"Auee!" he cried, and he grasped his left arm with his right fist, as though it were broken. "By the Great Diproo Himself, I won't fail! I dare not!" And he dived over the side. Those of my men who could not swim, and the clansmen often practiced the art in the lonely tarns of the moorlands far to the north, were equipped with balks of timber. They now all took to the water and began swimming for the far bank. There everything would be up to Nath.

I waited, as a Vovedeer, as a Zorcander, should. A leader of a clan is called that, a leader. When two or more clans are joined together under one leader he is then entitled to take the name of Vovedeer, Zorcander, the derivations of these names being obvious. The taking of obi becomes then that much more of a responsibility. So I waited until all my men were safely away.

They had thrown off their chains; I still gripped a bight of mine between my fists, ready.

The wherry had ceased its last drifting and was now nuzzled bows up against the larboard quarter of the Rapa wherry. The canal here was shallow, and the wherry with its marble freight had sunk until its bottom touched the silt and mud. Now about four feet of marble blocks stood above the water. I crouched on a block between two others, watching.

From the shrieks and screams, the pandemonium and the fierce clash of sword and spear on iron chain I guessed more guardsmen had run up and were engaged in the task, no doubt not entirely unenjoyable to the soldiery, of butchering the last of the slaves. I could take no part in that. My duty lay with my men.

A new timbre arose in the din. Perhaps the slaves were not being dismissed so easily. I chanced a peek around a block and saw the sunshine lying athwart the jetty, with the guards and the Rapa slaves battling in a savage and unholy conflict. Iron chains whirled with reckless and desperate courage make fearsome weapons.

I saw three men bundling a woman into a small low skiff by the jetty wall. Evidently they had been caught by the slaves' first onslaught and were unable to escape. Now the canal was their only chance. The skiff cast off and swung and collided with the first wherry and a flung chain fairly took the head from the man at the oars so that he lolled all dripping and bloody over the side. The woman screamed. The second man seized the oars; but the body cumbered him.

The skiff bounced down the side of the wherry. Now a group of slaves seized their chance.

With shrill vulturine shrieks they leaped onto the marble blocks of the wherry, bounded to the stern and leaped down into the skiff. It plunged wildly in the water. The two men, and their dead companion, were tipped overboard without ceremony. Two Rapas seized the oars. Another pair sprawled in the sternsheets, their chains still whirling in reflexive violence. A fifth jumped forward and seized the woman about the waist and pressed her to him, twisting and holding her up so that she could be clearly seen from the jetty.

His intentions were plain.

"Let us go!" he shrilled. "Or the woman dies!"

A confused shouting rose above the battle din.

The woman's screams knifed through the uproar, and unsettled me. I thought of my men, waiting for me. I thought of Delia. I do not know what I thought.

I only know I could not see a woman killed this way, so uselessly. If you ask me if it had been human slaves escaping and using the despised body of an aristocratic woman to shield them, I do not know how I would answer.

Without a sound I jumped from the sunken wherry into the skiff. I tried not to kill. I toppled the two oarsmen overboard. The two men in the bows reared up, their chains chirring with ugly menace.

"Slave — die!" and "Human — perish!" they shouted.

Had they not shouted that, perhaps I would not have fought as I did. But I did fight. My chain blurred through the air and sliced a vulturine beak; the thing gargled and toppled. I ducked the second chain and then brought my own back so fast I nearly overbalanced. It looped around that incredibly thin and long neck, doubled on itself. I yanked and the Rapa staggered forward so that I could land a solid blow. He collapsed. I heard a shout behind me and ducked again and the chain smashed a huge chunk from the wooden side of the skiff. I sprang to face the last Rapa.

He poised, the chain circling.

His beaked face leered on me; he knew all must be over for him — and yet, could he dispose of me and row for the main canal he would be away, and with a human woman as a hostage. He had all to play for. I feinted and the chain hissed. I pulled back and he leered at me again.

"Human offal!" His gobbling croak harsh in my ears stilled the mad thumping of my heart. I sized him up. That chain could break an arm, a leg, could throttle me, long before I could reach him. I flexed my legs, braced against the bottom boards where water slopped. He had not, perhaps, the experience in boats I had. I began to rock from side to side.

His arms flew up. The chain circled crazily. The woman was clutching the transom in both hands. I could not see her face for she wore a heavy veil of emerald silk. I rocked furiously. The Rapa staggered and lurched, recovered his balance, toppled the other way. The gunwales of the fragile skiff were slopping water at each roll.

With a shriek of mingled fury and despair the Rapa dropped his chain and lurched down to grab at the gunwale and with a last savage rocking motion of my leg I tipped him clean out of the boat. He flew across the water and went in face first, spread-eagled. His splash was a magnificent flower of foam. I did not laugh.

I quietened the skiff in the water and seized the oars. The Rapa drifted away. I turned to the woman.

"Well, my girl," I said harshly. "You're all right. No harm has come to you."

I did not want her to panic, lest she upset the skiff.

She regarded me through the eyeslits of her veil. She sat very still and straight. I towered above her, my naked chest heaving from the slight exertion of the fight, water and sweat riveting down my thighs where the ridged muscle shone hard, like iron.

She wore a long gown of emerald green, unrelieved by ornament. Above the green veil she wore a tricorn hat of black silk, with a curled emerald green feather. Her hands were cased in white gloves, and on three of her fingers, outside the gloves, she wore rings: one emerald, one ruby and one sapphire.

I began to pull back to the jetty.

A story to account for my broken slave chains rose in my mind.

The woman had not said anything. She sat so still, so silent, that I thought she must be in shock.

When we reached the jetty she stood up and held out a foot in its jeweled strappings. I reached out my palm and she put her foot in that brown and powerful hand and I lifted her up onto the jetty as an elevator lifts one up through the giant trunks of the plant-houses in distant Aphrasöe.

A certain concern was removed from my mind as I saw floating in the water the form of a Rapa guard with a slave chain wrapped around his neck, his great beaked face twisted sideways and loose from his trunk. He was a Deldar, a commander of ten, and he had been the sixth guard aboard our wherry.

Slowly I climbed onto the jetty.

The woman was surrounded by a clamoring mob of guards and nobles in gaudy finery. Of slaves there was no sign save the blood that stained the stones beneath their feet.

"Princess!" they were calling. And: "We thought your precious light had been removed from us!" And: "Praise be to mighty Zim and to thrice-powerful Genodras that you are safe!"

She turned to face me, her head high, her gown stiff and tent-like about her, her jeweled feet invisible. She lifted a white-gloved hand and the babble fell silent.

"Dray Prescot," she said, and, saying, astonished me beyond words. "You may incline to me."

I stood there in the light of the twin suns, a reddish shadow from my heels lying north-northwest and a greenish shadow lying northwest by north, give or take a point. Nowadays, of course, a ship can be steered to a degree; it is wonderful what a difference steam and diesel and nuclear power have made to navigation of the oceans — I gaped at her.

The man I remembered as Galna thrust forward. His face was at once ugly and vengeful and gloating. His all-over green leathers glistened in that Antarean sunshine.

65

"I shall run him through now, my Princess, as you desire."

He drew a rapier from a velvet lined sheath. I hardly noticed the thing. I stared at the woman. Incline to her? I did not want to die. I bowed, a stiffly formal making of a leg, my right hand elegantly waving in the air before my breast and then finishing up, fingers gracefully curled; before me, my leg stuck forward, the other back, my left arm outstretched behind me, my head bowed over low — low!

If this absurd posture, so carefully taught in the scented drawing rooms of Europe, should be taken as an insult — I heard a light laugh.

"Do not kill the rast now, Galna. He will make better sport — later."

I straightened up. "I was freed from my chains by the Rapa guard so as to help better with the marble—" I began to say. Galna struck me viciously across the face with the flat of his rapier. At least, he would have done, had I not jerked my head back. Men jumped forward.

"Down, rast, when the princess addresses you."

An arm laid across my back, a foot twitched my ankles, and I was down, spine bent, rear high, nose thrust painfully into the stones of the jetty where marble dust irritated my eyes and nostrils. Four men held me.

"Incline, rast!"

Perforce, I inclined. I had learned something a slave of the Esztercari Household must know in order to stay alive.

Even then, as my nose bumped painfully in the marble dust of the jetty, I contrasted this barbarous posture with the graceful gestures of the ceremony of obi.

I knew that death was very near.

Princess Natema Cydones stirred me with her jeweled foot. Her toes were lacquered that same brilliant green.

"You may crouch, slave."

Assuming this meant exactly what it sounded like I sat up in a crouching position, like a fawning dog. No one struck me, so I guessed I had learned a little more. There had been some sharp words, and muttering, and acid commands from the group and now I heard the clink of chains. A short stout man clad in a pale gray tunic-like garment bound with emerald green borders, and with two large green key-shaped devices stitched to his breast and back, now strutted forward. Under the fuming eyes and pointed rapiers of Galna and the other nobles, this man loaded me with chains. He snapped an iron ring about my neck, an iron band about my waist, wristlets and anklets, and from loops on all of these weighty objects he strung what seemed to me more than a cable's length of harsh iron chain.

"See that he is transferred to my opal palace, Nijni," ordered the princess, casually, as though discussing the delivery of a new pair of gloves. No — as I was prodded along by the slave-master Nijni's sturm-wood wand of office, I knew I was wrong. She would give more concern, much more concern, to the choosing of a new pair of gloves.

I had escaped from one kind of slavery to that of another.

The future loomed as dark and perilous as ever. Only one ray of hope in all this I could see — my men, my loyal clansmen, my brothers in obi, had been set free from their slavery and their chains.

Eleven

The Princess Natema Cydones of the Noble House of Esztercari

How my brothers in obi would have laughed to see me now! How those fierce fa-natical clansmen would have roared their mirth to see their Zorcander, their Vovedeer, dressed like a popinjay! Three days had passed since my futile attempt at escape. I knew I had been bought from the marble quarries. When the Prin-cess Natema wanted anything men trembled for their lives until that thing was brought her. Now I strode the tiny wooden box in the attic of the opal palace I had been given as my room — strange, I had thought when a gray-clad slave girl had shown me in with a furtive, scared look — and stared at myself in contempt.

I had refused to don the garments; but Nijni, the fat, dour, ever-cham-chewing slave-master had whistled up three immense fellows — scarcely human with their bristle bullet-heads, their massively rolling shoulders, their thick dun-colored hides mantled with muscles of near-armor thickness and toughness, their short sinewy legs and splayed feet — two to hold me and the third to strike me painfully across the back and buttocks with a thin cane. This was so remark-ably like the rattans carried by our warrant officers of the King's Ships on which I had served that I received three strokes before I had sense enough to cry out that I would don the garments, for, after all, what did foolish fancy dress signify in so much of squalor and misery?

The man who had struck me, and I must think of him as a man although from what pot of incestuous and savage genes he sprang I do not care to contemplate, leaned close as he went out.

"I am Gloag," he said. "Do not despair. The day will come." He spoke in a voice throttled in his throat, a whisper from lungs and voice box used to a stentorian bellow as a normal method of conversation.

I gave no sign I had heard.

So now I looked in dissatisfaction at myself. I wore a fancy shirt of emerald and white lozenges, with scarlet embroidery. A silk pair of breeches of yellow and white, with a great embroidered cummerbund of eye-watering colors. On my head perched a great white and golden turban, ablaze with glass stones, and gay feathers, and dangling beads. I felt not only a fool, I felt a nincompoop.

If my savage brethren of the plains of Segesthes saw me now what would they not make in jest and ribald comment of their feared and respected Vovedeer?

Nijni came for me with Gloag and his men, and three lithe lissom young slave girls. The girls were clad in strings of pearls and precious little else. Gloag and his men were from Mehzta, one of the nine islands of Kregen. They wore the usual simple gray breechclout of the slave, but they each had an emerald green waist-belt, from which dangled the slim rattan cane. I went with them. In my naïveté I had no idea of where I was going, or of why I was dressed as I was, or even why I had been forced, not unpleasantly, to go through the baths of the nine. This was simply a process of proceeding from lukewarm water where the grime washed off me in sooty clouds into the liquid, through nine rooms where the water grew at each step hotter and hotter until the sweat rolled from me, and then colder and colder until I shouted and shivered and bounded as though from ice floes. I did feel invigorated, though.

Nijni paused before an ornate gold and silver door set with emeralds. From a side table he took a box and from the box a paper-wrapped bundle. Carefully he pared back the tissue. Within, virginal, white, gleaming, lay a pair of incredibly thin white silk gloves.

The slave girls with exquisite delicacy helped me don the gloves. Nijni looked at me, chewing endlessly on his wad of cham, his head cocked on one side.

"For every rip or tear in the gloves," he said, "you will receive three strokes of the rattan. For every soil mark, one stroke. Do not forget." Then he threw open the doors.

The room was small, sumptuous, refined past elegance, decadent. It was, I suppose, what one would expect of a princess who had been brought up from birth to have every whim instantly gratified, to have every luxury heaped on her as a right, and who had never felt the restraining touch of an older or wiser hand, or the sound common sense of a person to whom everything is not possible.

She reclined on a chaise longue beneath a golden lamp carved in the semblance of one of the graceful flightless birds of the plains of Segesthes that the clansmen love to hunt and catch to give their bright feathers to the girls of the vast chunkrah herds. She wore a short gown of emerald green — that eternal hateful color — relieved by a silken vest of silver tissue. Her arms were bare, round and rosy in the light. Her ankles were neat, her calves fine, but I thought her thighs a fraction heavy, firm and round and delightful; but that infinitesimal fraction too thick for a man of my finicky tastes. Her lush yellow hair was piled atop her head and held in place by pins with emerald gems. The sweetness of her mouth shone red and warm and inviting.

Beyond her, in an alcove, I could see the lower body and feet of a gigantic man clad in mesh steel. His chest and head were hidden from view by two carved ivory swing doors. By his side, its point resting on the floor, he held a long rapier. I did not need to be told that a single command from the Princess Natema would bring him in a single bound into the room, that deadly point at my throat or buried in my heart.

"You may incline," she said.

I did so. She had not called me a rast. A rast, I knew now, was a disgusting six-legged rodent that infested dunghills. Maybe she was wrong. Maybe, apart from my four limbs and my larger size I, in this palace, was no better than a rast in his dunghill. At least, that was his nature.

"You may crouch."

I did so.

"Look at me."

I did so. In all truth, that was not a hard command to obey.

Slowly, languorously, she rose from the couch. Her white arms, rounded and rosy in the lamplight, reached up and, artfully, lasciviously, she pulled the emerald pins from her hair so that it fell in a glory around her. She moved about the room, lightly, gracefully, scarcely seeming to touch the scented rugs of far Pandahem with those pink feet with their emerald-lacquered toenails that shone so wantonly. The green gown drooped about her shoulders and I caught my breath as those two firm rounds appeared beneath the silk; lower down her arms dropped the gown, lower, sliding with a kind of breathless hiss, so that at last she stood before me clad only in the white tissue vest that ended in a scalloped edge across her thighs. Silver threads glittered through the tissue. Her form glowed within like some sacred flame within the holy precincts of a temple.

She stared down on me, insolently, taunting me, knowing full well the power and the drug of her body. Her red lips pouted at me, and the lamplight caught on them and shot a dazzling star of lust into my eyes.

"Am I not a woman, Dray Prescot?"

"Aye," I said. "You are a woman."

"Am I of all women not the most fair?"

She had not touched me — yet.

I considered.

Her face tightened on me. Her breathing came, sharper, with a gasp. She stood before me, head thrown back, hair a shining curtain about her, her whole body instinct with all the weapons of a woman.

"Dray Prescot! I said — am I of all women not the most fair?"

"You are fair," I said.

She drew in her breath. Her small white hands clenched.

She stared down on me and I became closely aware of that grim mailed swordsman half-hidden in the alcove.

Now her contempt flowed over me like sweetened honey.

"You, perhaps, know one who is fairer than I?"

I stared up at her, levelly, eye to eye. "Aye. I did, once. But she, I think, is dead."

She laughed, cruelly, mockingly, hatefully. "Of what use a dead woman to a live man, Dray Prescot! I pardon your offense—" She halted herself, and put one hand to her heart, pressing. "I pardon you," she said, again, wonderingly. Then: "Of all women living, am I not the most fair?"

I acknowledged that I saw no reason to get myself killed for the sake of a spoiled brat's pride. My Delia, my Delia of the Blue Mountains — I thought of her then and a pang of agony touched me so that I nearly forgot where I was and groaned aloud. Could Delia be dead? Or could she have been taken by the Savanti back to Aphrasöe? There was no way I could find that out except by finding the City of the Savanti — and that seemed impossible even if I were free.

As though suddenly wearying of this petty taunting, although, heaven knew, she was prideful enough of her beauty, she flung herself wantonly on the chaise longue, her head back, her arms flung casually out, her golden hair cascading down to the rugs from far Pandahem. "Bring me wine," she said, indolently, pointing with her jeweled foot.

Obediently I arose and filled the crystal goblet with a golden, light wine I did not recognize, from the great amber flask. It did not smell particularly good to me. She did not offer me any to drink; I did not care.

"My father," she said, as though her mind had turned ninety degrees into the wind, "has a mind I should marry the Prince Pracek, of the House of Ponthieu." I did not answer. "The Houses of Esztercari and of Ponthieu are at the moment aligned and in control of the Great Assembly. I speak of these matters to you, dolt, so that you may realize I am not just a beautiful woman." Still I did not reply. She went on, dreamily: "Between us we have fifty seats. With the other Houses, both Noble and Lay, who are aligned with us, we form a powerful enough party to control all that matters. I shall be the most powerful woman in all Zenicce."

If she expected a reply she received none.

"My father," she said, sitting up and propping her rounded chin on her fist and regarding me with those luminous cornflower blue eyes. "My father, because he holds the power of the alignment, is the city's Kodifex, its emperor. You should feel extremely fortunate, Dray Prescot, to be slave in the Noble House of Esztercari."

I lowered my head.

"I think," she said, in that dreamy voice, "I will have you hung from a beam and whipped. Discipline is a good item in the agenda for you to learn."

I said: "May I speak, Princess?"

She lifted her breast in a sudden deep intake of breath. Her eyes glowed molten on me. Then: "Speak, slave!"

"I have not been a slave long. I am growing uncomfortable in this ridiculous position. If you do not allow me to stand up I shall probably fall over."

She flinched back, her brows drawing down, her lips trembling. I am not sure, even now, even after all these long years, if she truly realized she was being made fun of. Such a thing had never happened to her before — so how could she know? But she knew I had not responded as a slave should. In that disastrous moment for her she lost the semblance of a haughty princess beneath whose jeweled feet all men were rasts. Her silver vest crinkled with the violence of her breathing. Then she snatched up her green gown and swathed it carelessly about her body and struck with her polished fingernails upon a golden gong hung on cords within arm's reach of the chaise longue.

At once Nijni and the slave girls and Gloag and his men entered.

'Take the slave back to his room.'

Nijni cringed, making the half-incline.

"Is he to be punished, oh Princess?"

I waited.

"No, no — take him back. I will call for him again."

Gloag, as it seemed to me, very roughly bundled me out.

The three slave girls in their scanty strings of pearls were laughing and giggling and looking at me slyly from the corners of their slanting blue eyes. I wondered what the devil they were finding to chatter about; and then bethought me of my ludicrous clothing. I thought what Rov Kovno, or Loku, or Hap Loder, would make of them, on the backs of voves riding into the red sunset of Antares on the great plains of Segesthes.

Gloag clapped me on the back.

"At least, you still live, Dray Prescot."

We left that scented powdered corridor where Nijni removed the silken gloves from my hands. The wine had stained my right thumb. He looked up, crowing, chewing his chain-cud.

"One stroke of the rattan!" he said, annoyed it was not more. A slave girl in the drab gray breechclout of all slave menials walked around the corner before us carrying a huge earthenware jar of water. A lamp swung from golden chains beyond her head suddenly aureoled her hair and shone into my eyes. I turned my face away, glowering at Nijni.

I heard a desperate gasp. I heard the jar of water smash into a thousand pieces and the water splash and leap in that hidden corridor of a decadent palace. I looked up, moving my eyes away from the light so I could see.

Clad in the gray breechclout, her head high and face frozen, her eyes filled with tears, Delia of the Blue Mountains looked hard and long at me, Dray Prescot, clad in those foolish and betraying clothes.

Then, with a sob of anger and despair, she rushed from my sight.

Twelve

The Jiktar and the Hikdar

Was it truly Delia of Delphond, Delia of the Blue Mountains?

How could it be? A slave, in the gray breechclout, was that my Delia? I was back in my little wooden room behind the ornate facade lining one of the tilting roofs of Princess Natema's opal palace. I groaned. Delia, Delia, Delia...

It must have been a girl who in that sudden lamplit illumination had reminded me of Delia. Then why had she turned from me with tear-filled eyes, why had she run from me, sobbing with anguish — or choking back her anger and scorn? In truth I did not know, so tumbled were my thoughts, just how this girl had reacted.

An over-man-size statue of a Talu, one of those mythical, as I thought, eight-armed people of the sloe-eyes and the bangles and the dances, carved all in the ivory of the mastodon trunk, had been standing on the corner beyond the lamp. It had gleamed palely ivory at me as I leaped forward. I collided with the thing and, instinctively catching it and supporting it, its eight arms a wagon wheel of wanton display about me, fingertips touching in erotic meaning, I lost sight of the girl who vanished between the mazes of colored pillars supporting the roof. A giant gong note sounded.

Nijni was puffing and chewing furiously.

"She will not escape!" he shouted, gobbling the words, beside himself. "I shall have her whipped on that fair skin—"

I took his gray tunic between my fingers, and gripped, and lifted him until the curled toes of his slippers left the carpet and he dangled in my fist. I thrust my ugly face into his.

"Rast!" I roared at him. "If you so much as have one hair of her head injured I shall break your back!"

He gobbled to speak, and could not, although his meaning was plain.

"Though you flog me a thousand and a thousand times," I snarled at him, shaking him, "I shall break your back."

I dumped him down onto the carpet where he staggered back into the arms of the slave girls who had huddled, staring at me in terror. I noticed how slowly Gloag and his men had come to the assistance of the slave-master. Now they stepped forward, whistling their rattans about their heads, and I was prepared to be taken back to my room. Here Gloag administered the single stroke I had earned by spilling wine on my silk glove. I thought his stroke oddly fierce. He whispered to me as they left.

"The time is not yet. Do not arouse their suspicions, or by Father Mehzta-Makku I'll break your back myself!"

Then he was gone.

Of course I tried to find out about the slave who had smashed and spilled the water jar; but no one would tell me anything and I fumed and fretted in that stifling room. Occasionally, wearing those infernally idiotic clothes, I would be taken out into a tree-shaded courtyard for exercise, and twice I saw the green-gowned and veiled form of a woman I surmised to be Natema watching me. No noble woman of Zenicce would venture beyond the confines of her enclave unveiled.

There were three more interviews with her, as unsatisfactory as the first, and on the last occasion she made me strip for her, a proceeding I found extraordinarily unpleasant and degrading; but necessary in light of the swordsman in the alcove and the rattans of the beings of Mehzta on guard outside the door. I gathered from the laughing comments of the pearl-strung slave girls that the princess was sizing me up and taking stock of my points as she might a zorca or a half-vove. The half-voves were the smaller and lighter and far less-fierce animals, like small voves, these people used.

Her contempt blazed on me, her scorn dripped on me, her complete disregard of me as a human being showed me how utterly she despised me. I did not care. I craved news of Delia. How Natema loved to flaunt her insolent rosy curves in my face! I sensed she was attempting to arouse me to some grand act of folly. I was not to be so lightly gulled.

Once she had Gloag and his men flog me with their rattans for no reason other, I supposed, than a girlish desire to impress me with her power. This time Gloag took it easy on me, and my skin was not broken, although it hurt damnably enough. All the time Natema stood with her lower lip caught between her teeth, her cornflower blue eyes enormous and shining, her hands clasped convulsively to her breast.

"Understand, rast, that I am your mistress, your divine lord and master! You are as nothing beneath my feet!" She stamped her jeweled foot at me, her breast heaving with the tumult of her passion. I did not smile at her, although it would have been treacherously easy a thing to do, for I thought the gesture meaningless. Nevertheless, I did say: "I trust you sleep well tonight, Princess."

She stepped forward and struck me with her dainty white hand. A blow across the face I scarcely felt, so intense were the pains from my back. I looked at her, brows lowered, chin lifted, broodingly.

"You would make an interesting slave," I said.

She whirled away, shaking with a passion that Gloag, for one, did not want to try. He and his men hustled me out and a crone with a withered face and one eye doctored my back. I'd been used to flogging as part of naval discipline and four days, with the help of ointments and rest, saw me completely recovered. Gloag had proved a friend.

"Can you use a spear?" he asked me as the crone worked on my back.

"Yes."

"Will you use one, when the time is here?"

"Yes."

He bent down to me as I lay face down on the bed of my room. His blunt, square, powerful face studied mine quizzically. Then he nodded, as though finding something that satisfied him.

"Good," he said.

The Noble House of Esztercari employed no Rapa slaves. According to the other slaves it was because the Rapas stank in the nostrils of their mistress. This would be true. They employed no Rapa guards. There were Ochs, and the Mehztas, who were slaves but with petty powers involving the use of the rattan, and other fearsome creatures I occasionally glimpsed about the opal palace. And still I could find no word of Delia — or the girl who might be Delia of Delphond.

The palace was a warren in the manner of these immense structures built by slave-labor and accreting through the years under the varying whims of successive dynasties. I had a limited run of those corridors and halls beneath the roof; but all exits were guarded by strong detachments of Chuliks, who were born with two arms and two legs like men and who possessed faces which, apart from the three-inch long upward-reaching tusks, might have been human; but who in all else knew nothing of humanity. Their skin was a smooth oily yellow and their skulls were shaved except for a green-dyed rope of hair that fell to their waists. Their eyes were small and round and black and habitually fixed in a gaze of hypnotic rigidity. They were strong, bodies well-fleshed with fat, and they were quick. The House of Esztercari uniformed them in a dove-gray tunic with emerald green bands. Their weapons were the same as gentlemen and nobles of Zenicce — the rapier and the dagger.

The rapier is known generally as the Jiktar — commander of a thousand — and its inseparable companion the dagger as the Hikdar — commander of a hundred. Of the throwing knife men will often say, dismissingly, that it is the Deldar — the commander of ten. In this I think they make a mistake. For some strange reason the men — and the quasi-human beasts — of Segesthes are absolutely contemptuous of the shield. It is known and scorned. They seem to regard the shield as a weakling's weapon, as cowardly, sly, deceitful. Given their skill with arms, an undoubted skill as you shall hear, it is amazing to me that the manifold advantages of the aggressively-used shield are not obvious to them. Perhaps they are, and their code of honor forbids its use. Long have I argued the point, almost until my friends looked at me askance, and wondered if I were not like the shield myself, weak, cowardly, deceitful — until I have thumped them a buffet and proved them wrong in friendly combat.

By now it was clear to me what my intended role would be as a pampered slave in the House of Esztercari. From hints and whispers, and forthright counsels of scorn from Gloag, I gathered that never before had the Princess Natema been faced with a man who was not overawed and unmanned by her beauty. She could make men crawl on their knees to kiss her jeweled feet. She could make me do this, too, of course, by threat of torture and flogging. But she had always gloried in her womanly power over men without need of other coercion.

More and more she grew tired that I would not break to her of my own free will. I suspected if I did the mailed swordsman would be summoned from the alcove to make an end of me and Natema would look for her next plaything.

No one, not even Nijni, knew how many slaves there were in the House of Esztercari. There were books of account, kept by slave scribes; but slaves died, were sold, fresh slaves were bought or exchanged and the accounts were never up-to-date. To add to the confusion, within the Noble House itself there were many families — that of Cydones being the Premier Family — and one might sell a slave within the House and cross him or her off the lists; but he was still slaving in the stables or she was fetching water in the kitchens of one of the palaces on the Enclave of Esztercari.

During this period the news of an encounter flew about the slave rooms and halls. The Lay House of Parang had been attacked across the canal separating its enclave from that of the Noble House of Eward. Those of Eward hotly denied their guilt, blaming others unknown. Gloag winked at me.

"That's the work of the Ponthieu, by Father Mehzta-Makku! They hate Eward like poison, and our House backs them."

I remembered what Natema had said of the alignment of power.

This petty political chicanery and bravo-fighting meant nothing to me. I hungered for Delia. And yet, I had to face the unpalatable fact that I had no proof Delia cared for me. How could I aspire to her, after what had happened? Had I not interfered in Aphrasöe, she might have been cured, have been safely home with her people in far Delphond — wherever that was. The name was known — and I had thrilled to that information — but no slave could tell me where it was, or if it was a continent, an island, a city.

Undoubtedly, I reasoned, Delia had every cause to hate me.

The next evening I was sent for by Natema and instead of Gloag and his Mehztas the escort consisted of yellow-skinned Chuliks, their gray tunics bright with emerald bands, and their rapiers swinging with an insolent swagger. They wore black leather boots that clashed on the floor. A fresh consignment of Chulik mercenaries had recently arrived in Zenicce and the House of Esztercari had taken the major proportion to serve her devious ends.

The first thing I noticed as I entered that scented room with the white silk gloves upon my hands was that the steel-meshed swordsman no longer stood half-concealed in his alcove.

Steel-mesh was a rare and valuable armor in Segesthes; men habitually wore arm and leg clasps, and breasts and backs, with dwarf pauldrons, mostly of bronze, sometimes of steel. Always, the ideal of the Segesthan fighting man was attack — always, attack.

The Princess Natema looked incredibly lovely this evening as the first of Kregen's seven moons floated into the paling topaz sky. Her long emerald gown was gone, and she wore a sparkling golden vestment that limned her form breathtakingly. She smiled on me and held out her arms.

"Dray Prescot!" She stamped her jeweled foot; but not in rage. A subtle transformation had turned her domineering ways aside, so that she seemed to me almost more lovely than she had been. She bade me rise from the incline — and amazingly she made me sit down at her side. She poured wine for me.

"You said I would prove an interesting slave," she whispered. Her eyes lowered. Her breast moved with the violence of her breathing. I felt most uneasy. That damned swordsman was missing, and I'd come to regard him, incredible though it may sound, as a kind of chaperon.

Our relationship, Natema's and mine, had flowered almost unnoticed by me; but clearly she believed that I was passionately drugged by her beauty and frightened only of being killed, and ready, now, to overlook that blemish in my pure regard for her. Many men had died for her, I knew. Her seduction of me progressed with a steady sure possessiveness like that of a python swallowing down its kill. I resisted, for although she was a flower of women, and immensely subtle in her dispensation of pleasure, I could think only of Delia. I do not claim any great powers of self-control; many men would regard me as a fool not to sip the honey while the blooms are open. But the more her passionate advances continued the more she, contrariwise, repelled me.

How it would have ended I do not like to think.

Strings of emeralds twined about her white throat and draggled along her naked arms as she lay on the floor at my feet, pleading unashamedly now, turning her tear-stained face up to me. Her face was flushed, hectic, passionate.

"Dray! Dray Prescot! I cannot speak your name without trembling! I want you — only you! I would be your slave girl if I could — all you want, Dray Prescot, is yours for the mere asking!"

"There is nothing between us, Natema," I said roughly.

Sink me, if I were to be killed for it I wanted nothing of this scented, evil, beautiful woman!

She ripped the golden tissue vestments from her glorious body and stretched up her arms to me, pleading, sobbing.

"Am I not beautiful, Dray Prescot? Is there a woman in all Zenicce so fair? I need you — I want you! I am a woman, you are a man — Dray Prescot!"

I backed away, and I knew then, I admit it, that I was weakening. All the passionate loveliness of her lay at my feet, all her contempt, her scorn, her taunting gone, and in their places only a beautiful distraught girl with disheveled hair and tear-streaked face begging me to love her. Oh, yes, I nearly succumbed — I was, still, at heart only a simple sailorman.

"I have watched you, Dray, many and many a time! Oh, yes! I have struggled against my desires, against my passion for you. It has torn my heart. But I cannot resist any longer." She crawled after me, begging. "Please, Dray, please!"

Could I believe her? Her words sounded like rote, like phrases learned against a need, as though she repeated them with a set purpose. And yet — naked, jewel-entwined, her rosy flesh glowing, she lay there at my feet in supplication. I did not know if this was one more damnable trick, or if she truly fancied she loved me.

She rose to her feet, her arms outstretched, her breast rising and falling with the tumult of her passion, her red lips shining, her eyes ardent with love, all her emotions rich and full and aroused—

The door smashed open and a Chulik staggered through with a thick and clumsy spear transfixing his body from which the bright blood spouted.

Natema screamed like one caught in red-hot pincers.

I leaped. I snatched up the Chulik's fallen rapier in my right hand and scooped up in the same movement his dagger in my left. I sprang before Natema and faced the broken door.

Another Chulik collapsed inward, trying to hold together the slit edges of his throat. Men and half-men boiled outside.

"Quick!" Natema grabbed my arm. Naked, she raced to the alcove where the steel-meshed warrior had once stood. A panel slid aside. We passed through and Natema gave a quick and vicious laugh of vengeful triumph at our escape — and a spear lanced through to embed itself quivering in the wood and block the closure of the secret panel.

The sound of fierce yells and the clash of steel spurred us on and we ran bounding down stone stairs in dim lamplight until we reached a landing from which many doors opened. Feet clattered down the stone stairs after us. Before one of the doors lay the body of the man in mail. He had simply been battered to death with clubs. His body was broken and pulped within the mesh. Around him lay piled bodies of slaves, both men and beast. He had died well. A door had banged as we descended and I surmised the slaves trying to pass the mailed man had heard us descending and thought we were guards come to reinforce this lone warrior. I saluted him as he deserved.

Then I bent and took off his broad leather belt with its plain steel buckle. On the belt were hung his rapier and dagger scabbards. Those two superb weapons I picked up — one from the body of an Och slave, the other from a plug-ugly with black hair all over him and a nose ten degrees to port.

"Hurry, you fool!" screamed Natema.

I ran after her, clutching my arsenal of weapons.

We passed through a door and along passageways within the palace dimly-lit with oil lamps. Shadows swung wildly about us. I heard the noise of feet ahead and halted. Natema clung to me, soft and firm and panting, her hair dangling before her face. Angrily she thrust it back. I took the opportunity to buckle the

76

warrior's broad leather belt about my waist. The fancy clothes came in useful to wipe the blades clean; then I wadded them and tossed them aside and stood only in my breechclout.

"Nijni will not be pleased," I whispered.

"What?" She was startled.

"His white silk gloves are ruined."

"You idiot!" Her nostrils whitened. "There are killers ahead of us, and you prate of white silk gloves!"

Natema still wore emerald earrings and a single chain of gems about her neck, depending to her waist. These I took in my fingers and removed, and she stared at me with her blue eyes wide and drugged with the emotions of the moment. I threw the stones away.

"Come," I said. I looked at her. I bent, rubbed my hand in the dust of the floor and then smeared that filth all over her face and hair and body as she struggled and twisted, cursing. "Remember," I said harshly. "You are slave."

She slew me with her eyes. Then we padded on, furtively, toward the sounds of conflict and killing, and I made very sure that the Princess Natema hung her head and dragged her heels as a docile slave should.

Thirteen

The fight in the passage

There were five of them in a narrow passageway that led between the slave's domestic workrooms and the noble portion of the palace on the floor immediately below that containing the princess' private boudoir. They had three slave girls for their sport and they wanted another. Natema and I had worked our way through the chaos of the palace, passing furious isolated fights, dodging aside as slaves ran and were killed by Ochs or Chuliks, and as guards ran and were slain by slaves. I had picked up a gray breechclout for Natema, and she had grimaced at the filth and bloodstains upon it; but I had spanked her where it stung and she donned the dismal garment. We insinuated ourselves through the slave-dominated areas, ever-watchful for guards; but it would have been madness to have declared Natema for who she was here. To my satisfaction, I must admit, the slaying of guards was far more in evidence than the killing of slaves and we must, perforce, wait. Although I itched to get into the fight and battle alongside my fellow slaves, I felt a curious inverted responsibility for Natema.

She could not be all evil; she might truly love me, as she said, and that at once placed a responsibility in my hands. And, even if she did not, I did not relish the thought of her radiant loveliness despoiled by the frantic army of carousing, slaying, singing slaves everywhere on the rampage.

So we worked our way through to where she promised me there would be safety, and here we were, our way barred by five Chuliks with three human girls for their sport, not joining the fighting as, being paid mercenaries, they should.

They saw Natema and laughed, their tusks gleaming, and called out.

"Let her go, slave, and you can return." And: "Give her to us and you will not be killed." And: "By Likshu the Treacherous! She is a beauty!"

I put Natema behind me. We must go ahead, to the safety of the noble apartments. The Chuliks stopped laughing. They looked puzzled. Three of them drew their rapiers and daggers.

"What, slave, would you dispute an order from your masters?"

I said softly: "You may not have this girl. She is mine."

I heard a low gasp from Natema.

The three huddled slave girls scarcely merited a glance; all my attention was on the mercenaries. Had they been Ochs the odds would have been more even. I advanced a foot and brandished the rapier and dagger as my old Spanish master had taught me so long ago.

"The French system is neat and precise," he had said. "And the Italian, also." He had taught me fine arts of fencing with the small sword, often erroneously called a rapier. With that nimble little sticker one can thrust and parry with the same blade. With the heavier, stiffer Elizabethan rapier, such a blade as I now grasped, one needed to dodge or duck a thrust, or to interpose the dagger, the rapier's lieutenant, the Hikdar to the Jiktar. Even so, I could fence well with the rapier without a main gauche. I hold no great pride in this thing; it was all of a oneness with my ability to run out along the topgallant yard in a storm, or to swim incredible distances underwater without coming to the surface for a breath. One is what one is, what is in one's nature.

Nowadays, that is in the twentieth century, foil fencing, foil-play, such as one learns at a university, is as far removed from the art of sword fighting to kill as is Earth from Kregen. *La jeu du terrain* also bears little relation to the ferocious and deadly sword combats of Kregen. Given the featherweight lightness of modern foils, the parry which avoids an electric light and bell recording a hit would be passed scarcely noticed by the rapier wielded by a duelist of Zenicce. No young cockscomb who foil-plays at a university could hope to survive on savage Kregen without a sharp and salutary alteration of his ways.

At the time of which I speak, however, most of my sword fighting had been done with cutlass aboard ship and with the broadsword or shortsword from the backs of zorca or vove. I had not fenced or used a rapier in years. All sword fighting tends from the complicated to the simple. These Chuliks, because of the narrowness of the corridor, further narrowed in one place by an enormous Pandahem jar, could come at me only two at a time. Very well, then. They could die two at a time.

The blades clashed and rang between the walls. I took the first one on my dagger, twirled, twisted at the same time, the second Chulik's rapier on my own, rolled my wrist, thrust, drew out the stained blade and immediately took the renewed first's attack once more on the dagger. It was all very slow. Slow, yes — but deadly.

My rapier was caught on the third opponent's blade — he stepped most gallantly over the twitching body of his companion to get at me — but before he could fairly engage I had spitted the first one through the throat, and then, springing aside, let the long lunge of the new antagonist go swishing past my side. I closed in rapidly, inside his guard, and thrust my dagger into his belly. Instantly I dragged my blades clear and sprang to meet the last two — and at the first onset my captured Chulik rapier snapped clean across with a devastating pinging.

I heard the women screaming.

Blood made the floor slippery. I hurled the broken hilt at a Chulik, who dodged nimbly. His yellow face slicked under the lamplight. The fray was close and deadly for a moment as my dagger held them at bay, and then I had drawn the rapier I had taken from the mailed warrior — he who had fought so nobly and died so well.

Indeed, and his blade was a marvel! The balance, the deftness of it, the suppleness as the gleaming steel whickered between the ribs of the penultimate antagonist!

The last one stared in appalled horror on the four dead bodies of his carousing-companions. He tried to escape. I would have let him go. I stepped aside for him in the corridor and raised my blood-stained blade in ironic salute. My eye caught a movement to the side and I glanced quickly to see the three slave girls rising. Two were still partly draped in strings of pearls. Trust these mercenary ruffians to select the prettiest and most pleasure-skilled of slave girls. Then I saw the third — naked, trembling, but with eyes filled with a fire I knew and remembered and loved — Delia, my Delia...

Natema shouted, shrilly, her voice filled with terror.

I flicked my glance back. The Chulik whom I had been about to let go, with the honors of battle, had seen my involuntary look toward the girls, and he had stepped in and was in the act of thrusting his rapier between my ribs. My opinion of him as a fighting man went down. He should, in those close quarters, have used his dagger. Had he done so I would not now be telling you this. I flicked the long blade away with my own dagger and sank my rapier into his belly. He writhed for a moment on the brand; then I withdrew it and he slumped, vomiting, to the floor.

Natema rushed to me and clasped me, shaking and sobbing.

"Oh, Dray! Dray! A true fighting man of Zenicce, worthy of the Noble House of Esztercari!"

I tried to shake her off.

I stared at Delia of the Blue Mountains, who drew herself up, naked and grimed, her hair dusty and bedraggled, her body taut and firm in the lamplight. She looked at me with those limpid brown eyes and — was it anguish, I saw? Or was it contempt, and anger, and a sudden cold indifference?

I was standing by that great jar of Pandahem porcelain.

We were abruptly surrounded by green clad nobles who surged into the corridor, chief among them Galna, whose hard white face ridged and planed as he saw Natema. He cried out in horror and whisked a fellow-noble's gaudy cape about her glowing nakedness. The slave girls were hustled back with the rest of us as the princess was placed within a solid palisade of noble living flesh. There was some confusion.

Galna saw me.

His eyes were always mean; but now they narrowed and the hardness and meanness drilled me. He lifted his rapier.

"Galna! Dray Prescot is—" Natema stopped. Her voice lifted again, once more arrogant, once more assured, the mistress of the utmost marvels of Kregen. "He is to be treated well, Galna. See to it."

"Yes, my Princess." Galna swung back to me. "Give me your sword."

Obediently I handed across the nearest Chulik sword I had already picked up against this moment. I also handed across the Chulik dagger that had not, like its Jiktar, failed me. Now my breechclout concealed the broad belt, and the scabbard flapped against my legs, empty. Galna let me keep those, as he supposed, tawdry souvenirs of my struggle.

I tried to hurry after Delia; but there was much coming and going in the barricaded nobles' quarters as arrogant young men, gentlemen, officers, bravos, from Esztercari and from Ponthieu and many of the Houses who were aligned with those two Houses' axis, congregated for the great hunt and slaying of slaves that was to ensue. I lost Delia. I was ordered by Natema to take the baths of nine and then to go to my room. As though I were some infant midshipman caught in a childish prank, banished to the masthead!

"I will send for you, slave," were her farewell words to me. I didn't give a tinker's cuss for her. Delia... Delia!

Natema for the sake of her dignity and position must display her pride and arrogance before all men. She could not own to anyone the love for a slave she had only recently been so ardently displaying to me, naked and begging on her knees. But when she would send for me — what could I do, say?

A knock sounded on my door, rather, a furtive scratching that lacked the courage to knock loudly. When I opened it Gloag stumbled in, his body blood-stained, his face ghastly, his fist still gripping the stump of a spear. He looked at me.

"Was this the day, Gloag?"

He shook his head. "They brought their airboats, flying to the roof, they brought men onto our rear, men and beasts and mercenaries — swords and spears and bows — we did not have a chance." He sagged, exhausted.

"Let me bathe your wounds."

He wrenched his lips back. "This is mostly accursed guards' blood."

"I am pleased to hear it."

He did not say what had brought him here. He did not need to. This man had struck me with the rattan. I fetched water in a bowl, and salves left by the old crone for his wounds and bruises, and fresh towels, and I cleaned him up. Then I pulled my trundle bed away from the wall and pointed to the space beneath it, between wall and floor.

He grasped my hand. His great booming voice husked.

"Mehzta-Makku, Father of all, shine down in mercy upon you!"

I said nothing but pushed the bed back, concealing him.

The killing of slaves went on for three days in the opal palace of the Princess Natema Cydones of the Noble House of Esztercari. Many were the brilliantly-colored liveries of the different Houses in alignment with Esztercari as they came hurrying to suppress this slave revolt. The city wardens in their crimson and emerald also acted with vigor, for this was a matter that touched the security of the whole city of Zenicce.

During this period I brought food and wine for Gloag, hidden beneath my bed, and saw to his toilet needs, and talked to him, so that we came to understand each other better.

"I hear you are a great swordsman with rapier and dagger," he said, licking his bowl with a crust.

"I could show you a style of fence with a smaller sword than a rapier, without a dagger, that would astonish these rufflers."

"You would teach me swordplay?"

"Do you know the layout of the palace?"

Gloag did; he might know little of the city, but he could find his way about the opal palace readily enough by its secret warrens and runnels. He had not escaped before because his duty lay with the slaves; now he was trapped in my room. I promised him.

I believe that only Delia and the two slave girls in their strings of pearls, Gloag and myself, and one other, escaped the dreadful retribution wrought upon the slaves. When all had been killed the Noble House spent of their fortune to buy more slaves. That hurt them — the sheer financial loss on the slave revolt.

Natema sent for me and, once more dressed in my offensive clothes, a new set even more luxurious than the last with a great deal of brilliant scarlet, I went with guards and Nijni — who as slave-master held a post of some authority and had hidden during the revolt — up to a high roof overlooking the broad arm of the delta on its seaward side. Wide-winged gulls circled overhead. The suns sparkled off the water, and the air smelled fresh and sharp with sea-tang after the close sickly confinement of the palace. I opened my lungs and drew in that old familiar odor.

Landward of us lay the city, a blaze of color and light, with tall spires, domes, towers, battlements, creating a haphazard jumble of perspectives. Across the canal the purple and ocher trappings of the House of Ponthieu flamed from a hundred flagstaffs. Beyond their walls there were other enclaves built upon the islands of the delta. Seaward I could see — and how my heart leaped — the masts of ships moored to jetties hidden by the walls and the intervening roofs.

This hidden roof garden rioted in a thousand perfumed blooms, shady trees bowed in the breeze, marble statuary stood in niches of the walls where vines looped, water fountains tinkled. Natema waited for me reclining in a swinging hammock-type seat facing a rail overlooking a sheer drop of a thousand feet. Gulls whirled there, shrieking.

Delia of Delphond, clad in pearls and feathers, crouched by her jeweled feet.

I kept my face expressionless. I had sized up the situation instantly, and the danger made me tremble for Delia.

For Delia had uttered a low gasp at sight of me, and Natema's proud patrician face had turned to her, a tiny frown indenting her forehead above her haughty nose.

The interview wended its way as I had expected. My refusal astonished Natema. She bade her slaves retire out of earshot. She regarded me tempestuously, her hair ruffling in the breeze, her cornflower blue eyes hot and languorous, together, so that she seemed very lovely and desirable.

"Why do you refuse, Dray Prescot? Have I not offered you everything?"

"I think," I said carefully, "you would have me killed."

"No!" She clasped her hands together. "Why, Dray Prescot, why? You fought for me! You were my champion!"

"You are too beautiful to die in that way, Princess."

"Oh!"

"Would you offer me all this if I were not your slave?"

"You are my slave, to do with as I will!"

I did not answer. She looked back to where Delia sat, idly sewing a silken bit of tapestry, and pretending not to look at us. Her cheeks were flushed. Natema's ripe red mouth drew down. "I know!" she said, and her voice hissed between her white teeth. "I know! That slave wench — Here! Guards — bring me that wench!"

When the Chuliks stood grasping Delia before us, she lifted her little chin and regarded Natema with a look so proud and disdainful all my blood coursed and sang through my body. Delia did not look at me.

"This is the reason, Dray Prescot! I saw, in the corridor where you slew the five treacherous guards! I saw."

She gave an order that froze me where I stood. A Chulik drew his dagger and placed it to Delia's breast, over her heart. He looked with his oily yellow face to Natema, stolidly awaiting the next order.

"Does this girl mean anything to you, Dray Prescot?"

I stared at Delia, whose eyes now remained firmly fixed on me, her head lifted, her whole beautiful body taut and desirable and infinitely lovely. Queen among women is Delia of the Blue Mountains! Immeasurably the most beautiful woman in all Kregen and all Earth, incomparable, radiant, near-divine. I shook my head. I spoke roughly, contemptuously.

"A slave girl? No — she means nothing to me."

I saw Delia swallow and her eyelids blinked, once.

Natema smiled, like one of those she-leem of the plains, furred, feline, vicious, against which the clansmen wage continual war in protection of the chunkrah herds. She gestured and Delia returned once more to her tapestry. I noticed her fingers were not quite steady as she guided the needle; but her back was erect, her body taut, the pearls faking all their luster from the glowing glory of her skin.

"For the last time, Dray Prescot — will you?"

I shook my head, thankful that, at least for the time, Delia had been spared from immediate danger. What happened next was quick, brutal and, given the circumstances, expected.

The Chuliks at Natema's fierce, broken-voice command, seized me, ran me to the rail, thrust me half-over where I hung suspended over that gulf. Below me the water curled away from the long sandspit tailing at the end of the island. The air smelled very sweet and fresh, tanged with salt.

"Now, Dray Prescot! One word! One word is all I ask!"

I was not such a fool as to imagine I might easily survive such a dive; it would be a gamble with the odds heavily against me. I could easily throw these Chuliks off, snatch a rapier, fight my way through them and hope to escape into the warrens of the palace. But I did not think Natema would have me tossed into eternity. And, thinking that, I realized I was a fool, that she had been accustomed to doing anything at all and having anything she wanted from birth. But, if she did fancy she loved me, would she destroy me?

I braced myself, ready to twist like a zorca and fling these two yellow-bellies into space.

"One word, Natema, one word I spare you! *No!*"

I heard Delia screaming, and the scuffling sounds of a struggle. I dragged up one arm and the Chulik gasped and tried to hold me down. I was ready to turn and rend them...

"What is going on here?"

The voice was harsh, strong with the tone of habitual absolute authority. The Chuliks hauled me back inboard. A tableau was frozen on that scented roof garden.

All the slaves were at the incline. Delia was held down by two Chuliks. Natema was gracefully inclining her head in a semblance of a curtsey. The man to whom these obvious and immediate marks of servile respect were addressed must be Natema's father, the Head of the House, the Cydones Esztercari, the Kodifex of the city himself.

He was tall, gaunt, with a grim pucker in the lines around his mouth, an arrogant black light in his eyes. His hair and beard were iron-gray. He stood tall, clad all in the Esztercari emerald, a jeweled rapier and dagger at his side, and I wondered how many slaves he had had killed, how many men he had spitted in duel and bravo-fight. In his face showed clearly the fanatical obsession of power, the greed to possess power and to exercise it ruthlessly.

"It is nothing, Father."

"Nothing! Do not seek to fob me off, daughter. Has the slave interfered with your girl? Tell me, Natema, by the blood of your mother."

"No, Father." Natema resumed her natural arrogant stance. "The girl means nothing to him. He has said so."

The hooded black eyes pierced into me, into Delia, into his daughter. His hands, gloved, gripped the weapon hilts.

"You are pledged to the Prince Pracek of Ponthieu. He is here to speak to you of the wedding arrangements. I have, as is proper, attended to the financial bokkertu."

A man stepped forward from the mass of emerald green clothing in the rear of the Kodifex. I saw Galna there, his face as white and mean as ever. This young man wore the purple and ocher of Ponthieu. His rapier was over-ornate. He took Natema's hand and raised it to his forehead. He had a sharp-featured face, with that kind of lopsidedness to it that offends some people; but he was most polite.

"Princess Natema, star of heaven, beloved of Zim and Genodras, the crimson and emerald wonders of the sky — I am as dust beneath your feet."

She made some formal icy reply. She was looking at me. The Kodifex saw that look. He gestured and men — human men — seized me and Delia. They hustled us to stand before the Kodifex. Natema cried out. He silenced her.

"Do not think I am not aware of what the frippery this slave wears means, daughter! By your mother's blood, do you think I am a fool! You will obey! All else is nothing!" He gestured, a familiar, habitual movement. "Kill the man, and the girl, kill both the slaves. *Now!*"

Fourteen

Delia, Gloag and I eat palines together

"Kill both the slaves. *Now!*"

I kicked the noble Kodifex in the place where it would do him the least good, dragged the two guards around before me and hurled them staggering into the emerald green knot of nobles, snatched the Kodifex's rapier from its scabbard, slew the two guards holding Delia with two quick and savage thrusts, and seized her hand in my free left hand and dragged her running toward the stairs at the end of the roof garden.

"Dray!" she said, sobbing. "*Dray!*"

"Run, Delia of the Blue Mountains," I said. "*Run!*"

At the foot of the stairs where the doorway, ornate this side, plain the other, separated the noble area from the slave quarters beneath the roof, two Ochs tried to stop me and died for their pains. I slammed the door shut after us. We ran.

Slaves moving about their business stared at us with lackluster eyes. The buyers of the new slaves and the slave-masters like Nijni had beaten many backs right from the start so as to instill from the outset that fear and despair that is the necessary condition of the slave. We were not molested, scarcely remarked. I hoped that in a month or so the slaves would have found some semblance of the usual slavish chatter and hubbub and quick interest.

"Where are we going, Dray? What are we to do?"

I wanted to fall on my knees before this radiant girl and beg her forgiveness. But for me she would be home in Delphond, happy in the bosom of her family. How she must regard me with contempt and loathing! And, even worse, because I had been suspected of loving her she would have been killed! How often can that be said of a man's unwanted attentions to a girl on Earth?

"Hurry," I said, not trusting myself to say more.

In my room I rolled the trundle bed away. Gloag stared up. He saw Delia. His eyes went big. He saw the rapier. He whistled.

"Come, Gloag, my friend," I said, speaking with a harsh ruthlessness that made him jump up and Delia flinch.

Out we sped into the warren of passageways and halls. In an alcove far from my room I ripped off the stupid finery and between us with the rapier we cut it up and fashioned breechclouts for Gloag and myself and a tunic shift for Delia. I felt a warm admiration for the way in which she had completely accepted her nakedness in our presence. On matters as desperate as those on which we were engaged the sight of a few inches of pink skin mattered little.

We stood ready to venture forth. Delia went to hurl the strings of pearls away in disgust; but I restrained her. I put them to my teeth.

"They're real. They will serve a purpose."

Then a thought of shocking impropriety hit me. Natema as a proud princess would not clothe her slave girls in imitation pearls; it would be tasteless and loutish behavior. Would, then, she likewise clothe the man she hoped to make her paramour in imitation gems? I fancy my fingers shook a trifle as I rummaged through the pile of discarded clothing, the immense turban, the jeweled sash and slippers.

The gems were real.

I knew. I had not boarded prizes among the battlesmoke for the glory of it. I had been to a London jeweler and had handled the gems, precisely against that need.

I held a fortune in my hands.

"Hurry," I said, and thrust the gems in a fold of cloth within my breechclout. Around my waist was buckled the broad leather belt of the steel-meshed warrior. We padded down corridors known to Gloag. He carried a billet of wood. I would not much like to stop that with my cranium.

On Gloag's tough dun-colored hide, over his left shoulder blade, I had noticed a brand-mark, the solid block-lettered outlines of the Kregish letters for "C.E." Natema would not disfigure the slave maidens who attended her and whom she would see every day, and to my infinite relief Delia, having been in the kitchens only for a day, she told me, had not been branded. As the princess' potential lover and then a corpse, I, too, had not been branded.

We made sure that not a scrap of emerald green cloth remained of the fancy clothes in the material we chose for our new clothing. I slung a short scarlet square from my shoulders as a cape, and I forced Gloag to do likewise.

He knew his way with unerring accuracy, and I had navigated my way from the roof garden to my room, and so now I navigated my way alongside Gloag until we reached a narrow, dusty, cobwebby, flang-infested corridor low in the palace where water seeped oozing through the cracks between the massive basalt blocks of the walls on one hand. We would have a better chance at night, when the twin suns have set in their riot of topaz and ruby and, if we were lucky, with a little cloud to drift between the first of the seven moons. Like any sailor, once I knew the state of tide or moon I kept that information continually turning in my head, ready at any moment to bring forth the exact state of either. On Kregen, there were seven moons with their phases to consider; but I was automatically sure that I could tell when the darkest period of the night would occur.

Accustomed to long periods on duty without food, I was concerned over Delia; but then Gloag astonished us all by producing a length of loaf, somewhat limp and bent, and a handful of palines he had kept over from the previous meal I had smuggled to him. We ate with a gusty hunger, not leaving a crumb.

Given the circumstances the rest of our escape was not overly difficult. We crawled through a stinking conduit and postern. Gloag was a superb scout. We swam the canal, stole a skiff, rowed in the dim light of three of the smaller moons passing low overhead. The nearer moons of Kregen have an appreciable motion. To escape from the city would be out of the question without an airboat, and even then the city wardens would patrol the air lanes. I asked directions, discreetly, of slaves, and Gloag it was who discovered the exact whereabouts among the islands of the enclave of Eward. I was taking a desperate gamble; but I had a card to play.

The city would be up over the escape of slaves, particularly from the ruling House, and we might simply be handed straight back. But I did not think so. Eward and Esztercari were at daggers drawn. We rowed quietly up to the stone jetty where men in the powder blue livery of Eward escorted us to an interview with the Head of their House. I had acted with arrogant authority, letting the guards see the tangible reality of my presence. A Vovedeer can be as autocratic and dictatorial as any other man who commands men, when the need arises.

Our interview was informal and pleasant. Wanek of the family of Wanek of the Noble House of Eward reminded me of no one more vividly than Cydones of Esztercari. Both men contained that gaunt obsessive drive for power. He sat in his powder blue robes, hand on fist, listening. When I had finished he called for wine, and slave girls to care for Delia.

"I welcome you to Eward, Dray Prescot," Wanek said, as we sat down to the wine and a meal. The suns were breaking in golden and crimson glory patinaed with a paler green fire in the dawn above the rooftops. "My son, the Prince Varden, is away at this time. But I shall be honored to help you. We are not as the rasts of Esztercari." His fingers gripped his chin, whitening about the knuckles. "This union between their princess and the puppy Pracek you speak of is serious." And then he began a long discourse on the tangled power politics of the city.

The General Assembly sat continuously. Never was there a break in their deliberations and debates and legislation. There were four hundred and eighty seats in the Assembly. In the city there were twenty-four Houses, both Noble and Lay, so that the average number of seats per House was twenty. Some, like Esztercari, boasted more, twenty-five, the same number as Eward. But the pressures came from alignments of power, alliances and pacts between House and House so that a party might always have the majority vote. When I marveled at the stamina of the Assemblymen Wanek laughed, and explained that only the seats counted. Anyone from a House could sit in the seats reserved to his House in the Assembly. Only the number of seats conferred the power; the men who sat in them came and went, continuously, often on a rota basis, like our system of watches at sea.

"And the Esztercari carry the weight, the alignments, and Cydones Esztercari is Kodifex of all Zenicce!"

Clearly, this was the source of the rancor in Wanek of Eward. Clearly, in his eyes, he should be Kodifex, the acknowledged leader of the most powerful coalition.

Then I saw another of the interesting facts of life in Zenicce. A bent, wizened, bearded fellow in the gray breechclout of the slave was summoned and he, with a delicacy marvelous to see, removed the brand-mark from Gloag's shoulder. He would have heated his irons and branded Gloag afresh, with the entwined "W.E." but I prevented him.

"Gloag is free," I said.

Wanek nodded. "Evidently, you and Delia of the Blue Mountains are free, Dray Prescot, for you are not branded. And so therefore must be your friend, Gloag." He motioned the brand-remover away. "I will have his skin doctored. The scar will not show." He chuckled, an unlikely sound, and yet fitting in context. "We are old hands at removing brands and substituting our own, in Zenicce."

His wife, upright, stern, yet still bearing an unmistakable aura of vanished beauty shining about her motherly virtue, said gently: "There are about three hundred thousand free people in Zenicce, compared with seven hundred thousand in the great Houses. Of course" — she gestured with one ivory-white hand — "they have no seats in the Assembly."

"They live on islands and enclaves split by avenues," said Wanek. "They ape our ways. But they are merchants and tradesmen, like ourselves, and sometimes they are useful."

I had the sense not to remark that from his words one might assume those in the Houses might not be free. Within the Houses all those not slaves were free with a freedom denied to those independent free outside.

Toward the center of the city the river Nicce divided once more in its serpentine windings to the sea and left a larger island than any other in the complex of land and water. On this island was situated the heart of the city — the buildings of the General Assembly, the city wardens' quarters, administrative buildings, and a mind-confusing maze of small alleyways and canals off which opened the souks where anything might be bought or sold. The noise was deafening, the colors superb, the sights astounding and the smells prodigious.

After a time when it seemed that Wanek and his wife had nothing better to do than talk to me, Wanek asked, most politely, if he might inspect my rapier. I did not tell him I had taken it from Cydones Esztercari. He took it with a reverence strange to me — he could have bought and discarded a thousand like it — and then his mouth drooped.

"Inferior work," he said, looking across at his wife with a small smile. She tut-tutted, interested in her husband's occupation.

"Krasny work. But the hilt is fashionable although too cluttered with gems for a fighting man." He shot a look at me as he spoke. I rubbed my fingers.

"I had noticed," I said.

"We Ewards are the best and most renowned sword-smiths in all the world," he said, matter-of-factly.

I nodded.

"My clansmen obtain their weapons from the city, as needs they must; we do not care who fashions them provided they are the best we can buy — or take."

He rubbed his chin and handed the rapier back. "The weapons we make for sale to the butchers and tanners, who sell them to you for meat and hides, are never rapiers. Shortswords, broadswords, axes — rapiers, no."

"The man who owned this is not dead," I said. "But he is probably still doubled-up and vomiting."

"Ah," said Wanek of Eward, wisely, and asked no more.

The talk drifted. I suppose they, like a number of persons in authority, did not realize that other people were tired when they were not. The hated name of Esztercari cropped up again, and I learned they were the leading shipowners of the city. That figured. Then Wanek's wife said something almost below her breath, about the damned butchers stealing what was not theirs, and murder, and then I heard a name spring out, hard and strong and resounding.

Strombor was the name.

I believe, now, that then, when I first heard that name it rang and thundered in my ears with a clarion call — or do I deceive myself and am I influenced by all the intervening years? I do not know; but the name seemed to soar and echo and resound in my skull.

At last I managed to make my leave — the question of payment for their hospitality had delicately been raised and as delicately dropped — and I was conducted to a chamber where Gloag snored away in the corner. I dropped on the bed and sank into sleep and my last thought was, inevitably, of Delia of the Blue Mountains. As it was on every night of my life.

We roused in the late afternoon and satisfied our hunger with the fresh light crispy bread of Kregen, loaves as long as rapiers, and thin rashers of vosk-back, and palines, with the Kregen tea — full-bodied, aromatic, pungent — to finish. When we saw Wanek again he greeted us kindly. I asked for Delia.

"I will ask her to join us," said Wanek, and a slave departed — only to come back with the word that Delia was not in her room and the slave who had with such kind care and attention insisted on attending to her was also missing. I sat up. My hand fell to the hilt of the rapier.

"Please!" Wanek looked upset. A search was instituted; but Delia was not to be found. I raged. Wanek was beside himself at the insult he was thus forced to endure — the insult to him in that he insulted an honored guest.

Delia of the Blue Mountains and I had exchanged only a few words during our escape, for Gloag was near and, at least on my part, I felt a constraint, sure that she hated and detested me for what I had done to her. She had said something that puzzled me mightily. When we had both vanished from the pool of baptism in far Aphrasöe she had opened her eyes to find herself on the beach with the Fristles bearing down upon her, so that she had not been surprised to see me. When I had, in the moment of victory, been tumbled from the zorca, she had been taken to the city and straight to the House of Esztercari. Because of their shipping interests the Esztercari did a thriving business in slaves, and they could also command those caught in other ways. Then Delia had shaken me. For, she said, *the very next day*, she had seen me in that corridor, dressed in those accursed clothes, and had spilled and broken the water jar.

She also told me that on each of those occasions when she had been captured or enslaved she had seen a white dove flying high, with a great scarlet and golden raptor far above.

A messenger was announced. A bluff, moustached bulky man looking oddly out-of-place in the powder blue of the Ewards stalked in, his rapier clamped to his side, his face alive with wrath and baffled fury. He was, I understood, the House Champion, a position occupied in Esztercari by Galna of the white face and mean eyes.

"Well, Encar?"

"A message, my leader, from — from the Esztercari. A slave whom we trusted — how they mock us for that! — has abducted the Lady Delia of the Blue Mountains—"

I leaped to my feet, my blade half out of its scabbard, my hands trembling, and I know my face, ugly as it is, must have seemed diabolical to those around me.

It was true. The slave wench with her blandishments had arranged it all. She was a spy for Natema. She had got a message out, it seemed clear, and men had been waiting in that damned emerald livery at a tiny postern. There they had snatched my Delia, thrown a hood over her head, carried her swiftly aboard a gondola and poled away to the enclave of Esztercari. It was all true, heartbreakingly true.

But there was more.

"Unless the man called Dray Prescot freely surrenders himself to the Kodifex," Encar went on, his bluff honest face reflecting the distaste he felt at his words, "the Lady Delia of the Blue Mountains will meet a fate such as is meted out to recalcitrant slaves, to slaves who escape—" He faltered and looked at me.

"Go on."

"She will be stripped and turned loose into the Rapa court."

I heard gasps. I did not know — but I could guess.

"Dray Prescot — what can you do?" asked Gloag. He had risen to stand by me, splayfooted, incredibly tough, intelligent, a friend despite his dun bristly hide.

As I may have indicated, I do not laugh easily. I threw back my head, I, Dray Prescot, and laughed, there in the Great Hall of the House of Esztercari.

"I will go," I said. "I will go. And if a hair of her head is injured I will raze their House to the ground and slay them all, every last one."

Fifteen

In the leem pit

Gloag wanted to fight for me.

"No," I said.

"Give me a spear," he growled in that rumbling voice.

"It is my business."

"Your business is my business. At least, a spear."

"You will be killed."

"I know the warrens. Without me, you will be killed."

"I know," I said.

"Then we will both be killed. Give me a spear."

I turned to Wanek, leader of the Noble House of Eward.

"Give my friend a spear."

"Now may the light of Father Mehzta-Makku shine on us both."

From Wanek I obtained a high-quality rapier and dagger, and in return told him who had been the last owner of the rapier I bore.

His delight at holding the trophy wrested from his hated enemy was keen.

"You said the hilt has value," I said. "And, here, will you keep these gems in trust for me?" I handed over the cloth-enfolded gems. Gloag insisted his share, also, should be handed over, and then I knew he meant business, for with that wealth he could have set himself up in a small way in business in the free section of the city and lived out his life in prosperity and respect.

When I told Wanek what further I requested of him he slapped his thigh in merriment, and called Encar to ready a skiff in which would go one of his men disguised to look as much like me as possible. We then went up to the roof and not without a tremor I lay down on an airboat. This was the first time I had been in one; the first time I had ever flown. Such a thing was a marvel to me. It was petal-shaped, with a transparent windshield in front, and straps to retain one in place and pelts and silks to cover the rider. Gloag and I strapped down. The driver — the word pilot was unknown to me then — except in the connotation of a ship's pilot — sent the little craft leaping into the air into the floods of sunset light from the crimson sun. The green sun would soon follow. In the course of time, after the suns' eclipse, the green sun would precede the red in order of rising and setting. The Kregan calendar is based on the suns' mutual rotations to a great extent. I braced myself as we skimmed through that ruddy falling light.

I had planned to descend on the roof garden before the skiff bearing the pseudo-me reached the Esztercari landing stage. We slanted down and, thankfully, I saw the garden empty beneath us. Gloag and I leaped off and the airboat withdrew to a discreet distance. We raced for that stairway and so into the slave quarters. Wearing the slave breechclout of grimy gray we would still attract attention by reason of our weapons, so I had elected to retain my scarlet breechclout and scarlet cape, and Gloag had done likewise. Often I have been able to pass in disguise suddenly devised where, say, a man with red or green hair would find it impossible to go, although in the House of Esztercari green dyed hair, where it was not shaved off, was common.

We found a slave girl who under the threat of Gloag's spear was only too anxious to tell us that the prisoner, whom she remembered well, was shut in the cage above the leem pit. I shuddered. Bad enough it had been to plunge once again into that towering pile of the opal palace; but far worse was it to know that we must venture down into the depths, below the water level, where the leems slunk, furry and feline and vicious, around the damp walls of their pit. Many human bones moldered there. The leem is eight-legged, sinuous like a ferret or a weasel, but leopard-size, with wedge-shaped head and fangs that can strike through oak.

We killed them without compunction on the great plains as they sought to raid the chunkrah herds, going for preference for the young; for a grown chunkrah will impale them on his horns and hurl them a hundred yards, spitting and mewling through the air.

I have seen a blow from a leem paw with claws extended rip a warrior's head from his body and squash it like a rotten pumpkin.

Yet the leems would be far more preferable a fate for my Delia of the Blue Mountains than to be tossed nude into the Rapa court.

Our only chance was the speed and audacity of our venture.

I hoped that Cydones Esztercari and his evil daughter, the Princess Natema, would be awaiting with Galna at the landing stage the arrival of the skiff that would surely be reported to them. Yet — was Natema evil? If she truly loved me, and given the circumstances of her birth and upbringing so unfortunate as to character, would she not have acted exactly as she had done? A woman scorned is not a person to turn one's back upon, especially when she wields a dagger or can hurl a terchick.

We circled warily around the high ledge above the leem pit. The walls exuded moisture cloudy with nitrates. The place stank of leem, that close, furry, throat-clogging stench that is so noticeable in confined spaces and that is dispersed on the plains by the wind, to be scented by the savage chunkrah and warn them it is time to tail-lock, and with infants in the center, to face horn outward.

A large fully-grown leem can pull down a zorca.

A vove and two leems present so frightful a picture of mutual destruction in combat that its hideousness is best left to the imagination. I have witnessed it, and testify that truth. A vove will win, for a vove is a terrible machine of destruction; but he will need careful nursing for days thereafter, if the leems fought well.

These were the creatures who circled the walls of the pit beneath us. In the center, hanging suspended, was the cage in which Delia slumped, her wrists bound. Lines led to the cage through blocks by which means it could be pulled in and out. When Delia saw us she cried out, and the leems below hissed and spat and leaped in graceful vicious arcs up the walls of the pit.

There were six cords and I laid my hands on the one I could see would haul in the cage.

Gloag laid his spear across my arms.

"No," he said. I looked at him. "My Lady!" he called to Delia. "You must stand up and lock your arms in the bars of the cage. Hold on tightly — for your life!"

I hesitated no longer. "Do as Gloag says!"

Stumbling, her hair falling across her face, Delia stood and wedged her bound arms between two bars, hung onto a crossbar. "I am ready, Gloag," she said. Her voice did not falter.

I hauled in.

The instant the line tautened the bottom of the cage parted along the center and flapped down in two halves. Had Delia been meekly standing there she would have been pitched out like coal from a dumper, to plummet down to the fangs and claws of the leems.

I hauled her in and caught her in my arms and lowered her to the ledge. She still wore the scarlet breechclout. She trembled, suddenly, uncontrollably, and I lifted her up and a single slice of the rapier freed her from her bonds. Then we were hurrying and slipping and sliding around the ledge and out of that infernal pit.

Lamplight streaked across the sweat slicked on Delia's smooth long back and cupped in the hollows at the base of her spine. We reached the roof and the green sun had sunk; now the largest moon of Kregen, the maiden with the many smiles sailed above us drenching the garden in a cool pink haze. The airboat driver was on the alert and came slanting in. Another airboat was approaching; the two were on converging courses. The night breeze rustled the blooms which had closed their petals at sunset and were now opening their larger outer rim of petals to the moonlight, and there were footsteps on the stairs, and voices, and harsh torchlight and the flicker of swords and daggers.

Our airboat touched. The second dropped beside it and Chuliks bounded out, their gray and emerald a weird sheen under the light. Men boiled out onto the roof behind us.

I pushed Delia toward the airboat and Gloag with his spear low made a dead run for the Chuliks.

Men behind, Chuliks before; we were outnumbered and trapped; but we would fight.

I slew three with quick simple passes, backing toward the airboats. Chuliks were attempting to get at Gloag, who passed his spear, and lunged and returned, with a wild exultant precision; but he was bringing their life's blood out to stain the flowers a more sinister color. I caught Delia around the waist with my left arm, the dagger dabbling her breast with blood.

"Up into the airboat, Gloag!" I yelled. "Hold them off from there with that damn long implement of yours!"

With a shout he leaped. The driver was now in action, his sword a glitter of fire beneath the moon. We were being pressed. Chuliks slid before me, and I battled on. Delia squirmed against my arm. "Let me go, you great ninny!"

I released her and she scooped a dropped dagger, plunged it into the heart of a Chulik who would have taken that opportunity to do the same to me, and sprang for the Chulik airboat. The next Chulik was dispatched by me with a single thrust. I jumped for the airboat, bundling in alongside Delia, turning like a leem to slice my blade down on an upturned face, beating down his rapier guard and biting deep into his skull. An arrow caromed from the windshield. I yelled, deep and fierce, and Gloag's driver sent his craft swinging upward. The driver of the Chulik airboat, a soft-looking young man in Esztercari green, stared at my blade, gulped, and passed his hands over his controls. We began to rise. Pink moonlight fell about us. The breeze caught at my scarlet cape.

A hand grasped the gunwale of the craft, tipping it. A Chulik rose into view, his dagger between his teeth, his rapier leaping for Delia. I brought my blade down overhand onto his head, splitting it, and he shrieked once; his hand flung up and the dagger spun away, and he fell back and wrenched the rapier, wedged in the bones of his skull, from my hand.

A long soft groan like a small explosion sounded from the airboat and it whirled and all the world jumped into my throat. Delia...?

An arrow had struck the driver, passing through him, and a shower more, passing where my head had been, tinkled and feathered into his controls. The airboat leaped wildly.

It rose like a cork, swinging, the wind catching it and driving it under the moonlight.

Faintly, far below, I could hear shouts.

I tipped the dead driver out of his reclining seat, and flung him overboard.

Then I stared helplessly at the controls.

"They are smashed, Dray Prescot," said Delia of Delphond. "The airboat cannot be controlled."

The wind thrust us over the city faster and faster. In an instant the mammoth buildings fell away to the dimensions of toy blocks on a nursery floor. They vanished in moon haze and we were alone, drifting helplessly over the face of the plains beneath the moons of Kregen.

Sixteen

On the Great Plains of Segesthes

If you say to me that, in view of her two suns, Kregen was provided with an inordinate, not to say excessive, number of moons, I can only reply that nature is by nature prolific. That is Kregen. Wild and savage and beautiful, merciless to the incompetent and weak, tolerant of the ambitious and mercenary, positively rewarding to the stouthearted and unscrupulous, Kregen is a planet where the virtues take different forms from those of our Earth.

And, too, as I understand it, Earth's moon and the planet Mars, which is relatively small, were both fashioned from the molten crust of the Earth flung off in primeval days when the solar system was in process of formation. Something like two-thirds of the Earth's crust was thus lost to space, and the floating plates of the Earth's crust, on some of which lie continents, and on some seas, now slip and slide over the molten magma beneath, bereft of the building materials that would have given us a greater area of land surface and consequently deeper seas. On Kregen, so I believe, only about a half of the original molten surface was flung off, to form not one moon and a planet but seven moons. It is all astronomically apposite.

Of the nine islands of Kregen not one is lesser in area than Australia. There are, of course, uncounted numbers of smaller islands scattered about, and who, still, can say who or what lives there?

We floated, Delia of the Blue Mountains, and I, Dray Prescot, in our crippled airboat far out onto the Great Plains of the continent of Segesthes.

We talked but little. I, because I felt the hurt in this girl against me, the natural feelings of disgust and contempt she must have for me, despite that I worshiped her as no man has worshiped a girl in all Earth or Kregen, for she did not know, must not know, of that selfish passion.

At first she refused my offer of the scarlet cape; but before dawn when the Maiden with Many Faces paled in the sky she accepted, with a shiver. The red sun rose. This was the sun which was called Zim in Zenicce. The green sun was called Genodras. I doubt if any scribe knew the numbers of names there were all over the planet for the suns and the moons of Kregen.

"Lahal, Dray Prescot," said Delia of Delphond when the sun's rim broke free of the horizon.

"Lahal, Delia of the Blue Mountains," I replied. I spoke gravely, and my ugly face must have oppressed her, for she turned away, sharply, and I saw she was sobbing.

"If you look in that black box under the control column," she said after a time, her voice still choked, "you may find a pair of silver boxes. If you can move them apart, just a little, just a fraction—"

I did as she bid, and there were the two silver boxes, almost touching, and I forced them apart with a grunt, and the airboat began gently to descend.

My surprise was genuine. "Why did you not—" I began.

But she turned that gloriously-rounded shoulder on me, and pulled the scarlet cape higher, and so I desisted.

We touched down at last and once more I stood on the prairie where I had spent five eventful years of my life. I was a clansman once again. Except — I had no clan about me.

Our only weapons were my dagger, our hands and our brains.

Soon I had caught a prairie fox, good eating if rolled in mud and roasted to remove the spines, and we drank from a bright clear spring, and sat before the fire, and I stared at the beauty that was Delia's and I found it in my heart to be content.

We had passed over the wide fertile cultivated strip of land that borders this sea — the sea into which the River Nicce flows, the sea men hereabouts call the Sunset Sea, for it is to the western edge of the continent. It reminds me, nowadays, of the sea into which the sun of San Francisco descends in those fantastic evening displays. We were in the outskirts of the Great Plains proper. Zenicce draws her revenues, and her slaves, the minerals from her mines and the produce from her fields, from all the coast and for far inland. There are settlements of small size all along the coast and for some way inland. I had hopes that if we were lucky we would run across a caravan before we decided to walk back to the city.

I had decided to wait a week. The chances of clansmen finding us were grave; for I could not hope that the Clans of Felschraung and of Longuelm would happen by. Any other clan might well be hostile to us. The girl, then, would be a burden in negotiations. We waited six days before we saw the caravan. During that time I had found a dawning break in the granite barrier that separated Delia and myself. She was beginning to lose that reserve and to be the impulsive, lovely, wayward girl she really was. She would not speak to me of Delphond, or of her family or her history. The only people who might have told me where Delphond was I had not asked — the House of Eward — and the slaves were ignorant of it.

We had made our little camp and Delia helped willingly about the chores. I had fashioned a stout sharpened stave from a sturm tree, and would twirl this about, remembering. Once I had to fight an outraged she-ling. It had crept from a bush and sought to snatch Delia away. The ling lives between the bushes and rocks of the small-prairie, where there are trees and streams, and is as large as a dog of the collie variety; but it has six legs, a long silky coat, and claws it can extend to four inches in length and open a rip in chunkrah-hide. From the pelt, I fashioned Delia a magnificent furred cape. It suited her well. She looked gorgeous and feminine in the furs.

Our first intimation that the caravan was near was not the tinkle of caravan bells, or the thud of calsany pads, or the shouts of the drivers; but the shrill yammer of men in combat and the gong-like notes of steel on steel.

I leaped for the fringe of bushes above our camp, the sharpened stake gripped in my fist. This period with Delia had become very precious to me. Had I deluded myself, or had there been a softening in her attitude to me? Always, she was correct, polite, meek and obliging about the camp in the small matters of domestic chores. When we avoided the agreed taboo subjects we could talk, lazily, for hours on topics ranging from that vexed question as to who was the first creature on Kregen, to the best way of dressing the silky white ling furs, and all manner of delicious speculations in between. Yes, very precious to me was that time beneath the moons of Kregen around our campfire at night. These thoughts rushed through my head as I saw a small caravan under attack by clansmen. Why should I embroil myself? Far better to wait until it was over and the clansmen had taken their booty and such prisoners as would bring a ransom and had ridden off, singing the wild boisterous clan songs. Any interference on my part might well result in an ax-blade through my thick skull, and would certainly destroy this too short sweet period of growing friendship between Delia and myself.

"Look, Dray Prescot," said Delia from where she lay at my side, peering down through the bushes. "Powder blue! Eward — a caravan of the Noble House of Eward."

"I can see," I grunted.

The clansmen were from a clan I did not recognize. When I rode the Great Plains as a clansman, had we met, there would have been bloodshed between us, perhaps; if we lived, the giving and taking of obi. They meant no more to me than the men of Eward. But Delia compressed her lips, and looked at me, and her eyes sparkled dangerously — at least, that is how they appeared to me, for whom, in two worlds, there was no other woman fit to hold the hem of her dress.

"Very well," I said. Lately I had been speaking a very great deal. Naturally taciturn except when a subject excites me, with Delia lately I had, as a newer time would have it, been shooting my mouth off. Having decided, I wasted no time. I stood up, hefted my hunk of timber, and charged down into the fracas.

Men in powder blue were riding their half-voves in furious combat with zorca-mounted clansmen. That gave the men from the city some chance. Rapiers sliced past clumsy guards and pierced brawny chests; axes whirled high and descended to split skulls and spill brains. It was a small raiding party of clansmen — the zorcas told me that — and they must have stumbled on the caravan unexpectedly. I was down and among them before anyone realized a new force had been added to the conflict. I did not utter a sound.

In an instant I had dismounted two clansmen, seized an ax, swung violently against a group of three who sought to rip the hangings from a sumptuously appointed palanquin. I had discarded the notion of making a noise as though I were the forerunner of an army. I was not dressed as a clansman, nor as a city man — I was dressed as a hunter of Aphrasöe — and both sides would immediately have seen through the ruse and all surprise would have been lost.

The ax parted a neck from its trunk, sliced back to sever a cheek and knock the man from the saddle. The third man reined up his zorca, its hooves flashing, ready to swipe down on me, fully extended. I convulsed back and his blow swept through empty air. The hangings parted and a head crowned in a wide flat cap poked unsteadily out. Beyond the man about to attack me again I saw a man in powder blue sink his rapier into the throat of a clansman, the blade caught, and he jerked for a moment unavailingly. To his side a clansman lifted a bow string drawn to his ear. The next instant would see that iron bird buried in the man of Eward's back.

I hurled the ax high and hard, in the old clansman's cunning, and the daggered six inches of bladed steel sank into the zorca rider's breast. He looked down stupidly and then fell off.

Then the man facing me was spurring forward and bringing his ax down. I went in under the sweep of the blow, avoided the zorca's mouth — with a vove I would have been already a dead man — and sprang upward and took him about the waist. We both toppled to the ground. When I arose and looked alertly about my dagger was brightly-stained.

"Well done, Jikai!" I heard a croaking voice call.

The zorca riders had had enough. What should have been a nice leisurely killing and plundering had turned into a bloodbath. With wild and baffled shrieks they rode off. We avoided their last Parthian discharges as the bolts thunked into the ground. If they stood off, we had bows enough to give them a spirited return to their shooting.

Often these days I am forced to smile when reading the ill-informed and ignorant usage of words when Earthmen speak of barbaric weapons. How often one reads that arrows are "fired" in combat. I have used flint and steel to fire a musket, and a percussion cap to fire a pistol, and have fired a high-velocity rifle many and many a time — I have even used a lighted match wound around a linstock to fire a thirty-two pounder in the pitching gundeck of a three-decker — but in all this smoke and flame I have never "fired" an arrow. One does not "fire" bow and arrows. Except, perhaps, if you allow that term to those occasions when we clansmen set blazing rags to our shafts and used them to set fire to the wagons and the roofs of our foemen, as we did that wild day in the Pass of Trampled Leaves.

The half-vove rider had freed his rapier. He looked at me with curiosity all over his bronzed, keen face, with the black eyes and the cropped hair beneath the steel cap, and he sized me up as I sized him up. Lithe and strong, he rode well, and I had seen his swordplay — with the last exception of those neck-bones, and they can be lubbers at letting a blade free — and he handled himself superbly well.

He rode over.

He passed me with an intent, anxious look on his face, bent to the palanquin.

"Great-Aunt Shusha! Are you all right?"

The old head in its wide flat hat poked out again. This time more of the old woman appeared; I saw she carried a dinky little dagger in her gloved right hand. Her face was old — old — and lined and pouched with the record of her years; but her eyes were lively enough, bright and malicious on her nephew.

"Don't prattle so, young Varden! Of course I'm all right! You don't think I'd let myself be fretted by a miserable bunch of scallywags like these pesky clansmen, do you?"

She was thrashing about now in attempting to alight, and men ran to let down the steps of the palanquin from its height, slung between two calsanys. She stepped down, small, incredibly vital, dressed in a powder blue gown that had scarlet stitching threaded all over it like sunshine on water.

"Great-Aunt Shusha!" The young man, whom I knew now to be the Prince Varden Wanek of the House of Eward, protested in mock horror and despair. "You mustn't keep tiring yourself."

"Tush and bottlecock! And you haven't even said Lahal to this young man—" She peered up at me with her faded eyes. "Look at him, walking about half-naked, and killing men as easily as I push a needle through a tapestry." She hobbled over to me. "Lahal, young man, and thank you for what you have done. And, it minds me—" She broke off, and Varden leaped from his high saddle and caught her to support her. "The color — the color! It reminds me so vividly..."

"Lahal, my lady," I said. I made my voice as gentle as I could; but it still came out in the old forbidding growl.

Varden, holding his great aunt, stared at me. His eyes were frank on mine. "Lahal, Jikai," he said. "I own to a fault, it was remiss of me not to thank you seemly. But my great-aunt — she is aged—"

She tapped his bronzed hand with her gloved finger. "That is enough of that, you young razzle-dazzle, insulting me. I'm no older than I should be."

I knew that on Kregen men and women could look forward, if they were not killed or fell sick, to a life considerably longer than that on Earth, and this old lady, I judged, must be nearer two hundred than one hundred years old.

All this time I had not smiled. "Lahal, Prince Varden Wanek of Eward. I am Dray Prescot."

"Lahal, Dray Prescot"

"You did not see Dray Prescot save your hide, did you, nephew?" She explained how I had thrown my ax to save Varden as the man about to kill me charged. "It was true Jikai," she finished, a trifle breathlessly.

"I had my Hikdar, my lady," I said, holding up the dagger.

She chuckled and coughed. "As I had my little Deldar."

I looked, and, it was true, the dagger was a terchick.

A shout of surprise brought our attention back to the scene around us. Delia of the Blue Mountains walked down the little slope toward us. Clad in the scarlet breech-clout and with the white furs swinging, swinging in time to the sway of her lithe body, her long lissom legs very splendid in the suns' light, she brought a gasp of awe and wonder to the lips of the men. I caught my breath. She was magnificent.

After the introductions were made it only remained for us to ride back to the city with the Eward caravan. It had been to fetch Great-Aunt Shusha from her annual pilgrimage to the hot springs of Benga Deste. Benga, I should hasten to say, is the Kregish word most corresponding to "saint" in English. Beng is the male form and Benga the female, the suffix letter "a" playing a similar part in Kregish as it does in Italian.

I cannot explain why, but when I asked my habitual question of fresh acquaintances on this occasion I felt a taut sense of expectancy. A vague look came over Great-Aunt Shusha's wrinkled face.

"Aphrasöe? The City of the Savanti? It seems I *have* heard of such a place, once; but it is long ago, so long ago and my poor head cannot remember."

Seventeen

A bravo-fighter of Zenicce

Now life took a completely fresh turn for me, Dray Prescot.

If I had missed companionship before, finding that rare commodity at last on Kregen among the tents and wagons of the clansmen with Hap Loder and his like — for Maspero and those, as I thought godlike beings, of Aphrasöe created always in me a breath of awe — I found it once again with Prince Varden and his drinking companions in the House of Eward of the city of Zenicce. And, too, most strangely, I found a compelling sense of friendship, warm and human and very luxurious to me, in the wise companionship of old Great-Aunt Shusha. I owned she might one day recall what she knew of Aphrasöe; but I did not need that hope to make me respect and admire her, and I admit my fondness for her grew almost foolish, if affection can ever be called foolish.

Airboats are rare and precious objects in Segesthes and Wanek sent a party to repair and bring back the one Delia and I had escaped in, regarding it as another trophy wrested from the hated Esztercari. Delia said that she was familiar with airboats, and added that they were not manufactured in her land. That ruled out Havilfar, where I understood the mining was done on which the airboats depended for their lifting force.

I had entered with some spirit into the plans of the House of Eward to take down more than one peg the House of Esztercari. Dressed in the powder blue of Eward, I would ruffle it with the other young blades as we strolled through the arcades, patronized the drinking taverns, watched the varied amusements in the Barbary Coast area of Zenicce. I went to the impressive Grand Assembly buildings, and watched as the never-ending debates took place, with men and women walking in and out to leave or resume the seats allotted to their Houses. We even got into one or two bravo-fights, all flurrying cloaks and the clink and rattle of rapier and dagger, and shouting and laughing, and hurried retreat as the crimson-and-emerald of the city wardens was espied, hurrying to break up the fracas.

Once across the canal and within the cincturing walls of our enclave, of course, we were absolutely safe. To break into a House enclave would take an army and although many sporadic raids took place — often, I learned with an amusement so grimly ironic Prince Varden was surprised, to steal a girl — no House felt strong enough alone to challenge another directly. The Esztercaris had by chicanery, murder, corruption and then naked force, ousted the previous House from the enclave and further estates in which they had now settled some hundred and fifty years ago. Some of Great-Aunt Shusha's venomous hatred for the emerald green was explained when I learned she had been a Strombor, a girl of the previous House and recently married into the Eward's, when her family, her friends, her retainers were killed and scattered. Some had been sold as slaves, some had gone to the clans, some had vanished in their ships over the curve of the world and never returned.

By the twin forces of law and custom all the rights, ranks and privileges of the House of Strombor had passed to the House of Esztercari.

Each House enclave was a city in itself: tessellated pavement, marble, granite and brick walls, domed roofs, colonnades, towers and spires, all the whole gorgeous jumble of splendid architecture enclosed and supported a living entity within the greater entity of the city. The Eward beer was extremely good; Zenicce was famous for its beers, although its lagers, as all are, were weak and dispirited. We young blades would go ruffling a long way to sup a new brew of beer, commenting wisely and with many hiccups on its quality and strength. Zenicce claret, too, is very fine. I looked very kindly upon being a citizen of Zenicce, and of having the undisputed run of the enclave-city of the Ewards with its own canals, avenues and plazas.

There were temples throughout the city, of course, mostly erected to Zim and Genodras; but each House also maintained its own temples and churches to its own personal House deity.

In all this frenzied pleasure-seeking I indulged in at that time I could see, even then, that it was merely a hollow scrabbling at an anodyne. The problem of Delia remained forever with me, and nothing would remove it. I hugged my ache to myself, hating it and yet incapable of cauterizing it. Delia must be returned to her own land; yet to find that land was the difficulty.

We pored over the maps and charts in the library, and I saw with a nostalgic pang how similar and yet how different were the charts of these people. There were portolanos in the great library of the Esztercaris; we could not study those. The globes were so like those of Medieval Europe, the confident coastlines of countries near at hand, the gradual loss of definition as distance threw a pall of ignorance across knowledge until, on the opposite sides of the globes, only the most general outlines of those of the seven continents and nine islands thought to lie there were represented. Aphrasöe was never shown; neither was Delphond.

Looking at the maps, Delia shook her head.

"My country is not shaped like any of these."

I had shared the gems three ways, and Gloag had smiled his wolfish smile, and taken them; but he remained with me as a raffish drinking companion. Delia had pushed the gems back to me across the shining sturm-wood table, her face disdainful, her mouth prim.

"I would not take anything from *that* woman."

I kept in a chest those gems, promising myself they were in trust for Delia of the Blue Mountains.

Wanek and his son, Varden, insisted that we regard the captured airboat as our own. Delia took me flying and showed me how to operate the controls, which I found magical and wonderful, and of which I will speak at another time.

During this period I talked long into the night with Great-Aunt Shusha, for she needed little sleep, and I have grown accustomed to doing without all my life. She had witnessed that terrible attack on her House, and had seen the young girls carried off and the men killed. She did not, I noticed, maintain a great retinue of slaves, and, indeed, the Ewards were as humane as they could be, given the circumstances and the nature of the thing, in all their dealings with their slaves.

At last we had fomented our plan and it was time for me to play my part. I had more or less given my word to Varden that I would assist him. The Esztercaris, we had discovered, planned a great rising against the Ewards, and the Reinmans and the Wickens, Houses in alignment with the Ewards. The stroke was audacious; but it could be accomplished, and we must get in our blow first, or we would be lost. Almost inevitably, whichever way the contest went, the city would be up. The stakes at risk were enormous.

From the zorcas and the equipment we had taken on the day I'd helped beat off the clansmen's attack on the caravan, I had selected a fine beast and set of equipment. I donned my scarlet breechclout and then over it pulled on a clansman's russet leathers with the fringings. I would say a brief farewell to Delia and then be on my way. It was on this day, strangely enough, that I learned just which girl it was that Prince Varden mooned after, and had told me of during our tavern-times and ruffling strolls through the city. Varden, it seems — and I felt a jolt of incongruous guilt strike through me — had lost his heart to the Princess Natema. He had seen her many times, always with a powerful bodyguard, and his hopeless passion festered in his breast.

"She is promised to another, to that oaf Pracek of Ponthieu. And, anyway, how could our two Houses consent to such an alliance?" I felt very sorry for the prince; for I would have you know he was a true and gallant friend.

"Strange things have happened, Varden," I told him.

"Aye, Dray Prescot. But none as strange as the chance I shall ever hold Natema in my arms!"

I said: "Does she know?"

He nodded. "I have had word taken to her. She scorns me. She sent back insulting— It is enough that she refuses."

"That is her father's doing. It may not be hers."

"Ha, Dray! You seek to cheer me and mock me more!"

If I told my friend Prince Varden that I had come from the planet Earth which I now know is four hundred light-years from Kregen under Alpha Scorpii, Antares, and that the strangeness of that must surely outweigh the strangeness that a girl would change her mind, he would have gaped at me. I thought again of Natema, of her willful obstinacy, her complete lack of understanding that others besides herself had any desires that should be fulfilled. Her obstinacy, I knew, was a pliant reed beside the steely obduracy of Delia of the Blue Mountains. Delia had stood at my side as we fought hostile men, Chuliks and wild animals. Delia had even smiled at me over the smoke of our camp fire as we ate the meat from my kill she had cooked. Delia wore the white furs I had stripped from the fresh kill I had made for her in protecting her life.

I noticed that Delia of the Blue Mountains wore those white furs I had given her when she might have had the choice of a hundred furs far more magnificent.

She must do that, I thought in my ignorance, to mock and humiliate me, and I could not blame her for that, seeing to what distress I had brought her, and I feel nowadays the shame of my worthless thoughts; but then I was in agony for Delia of Delphond, knowing, as I thought, that she hated me, despising and scorning me for my clumsiness and high-handed actions toward her.

If Varden had had the same experience with his Natema as I had had, and if he had gone through what I had with Delia, I wondered, very bitterly, how he would regard her then.

Delia was always kind to Varden and, it seemed to me, went out of her way to be pleasant to him. He would be a good match, if the Esztercaris did not slit his throat. But I refused to allow jealousy to foul our friendship.

And so I went that morning in the turn of the year to see Delia and bid her what I hoped would be a brief farewell. She was sitting in a powder blue gown reading an old book, its pages browned and crumbling. On the low seat at her side the white ling furs glowed silkily.

"What!" She started up as I finished telling her. "You're going away! But — but I think—"

"It will not be long, Delia. In any case, I do not think my absence would displease you."

"Dray!" She bit her lip, then thrust the book toward me, her pink and shining nail, perfectly trimmed, pointing out a smudgy woodcut.

The art of printing varies widely as to quality and technique throughout Kregen; but this was an old book, and the woodcuts messy, the print heavy.

"I believe, Dray, that that is a map of my country."

At once I felt the flare of interest.

"Can we reach it — in an airboat, say?"

"I believe so — but I must compare this with the more modern charts. And, they do not compare. So—"

Then I remembered why I had come to see her, and my promise to Varden. I felt my eyebrows pulling down and my lips thinning, and knew my ugly face wore its ruthlessly forbidding look. "I have promised Varden. I must go."

"But— Dray—"

"I know with what contempt you must regard me, Delia of the Blue Mountains. It was my selfishness that has dragged you through all the dangers you have undergone. I am sorry, truly sorry, and I wish you were back with your family."

I make it a rule never to apologize — but I would say I was sorry a million times to Delia of the Blue Mountains. She started up from the seat, and her face flushed painfully, her eyes bright and brown and glorious upon me. She grasped the white ling furs convulsively.

"If you think that, Dray Prescot, you had best be gone on your mission." She turned away from me, holding the book in one small hand limply at her side. "And when you are successful and have conquered the Esztercaris, the Princess Natema will be freed from her father's domination. I think perhaps you welcome that."

Delia had seen me in that ridiculous emerald, white, scarlet and golden turban and robes, coming out of Natema's boudoir. She had seen me fighting desperately for the princess' life. She had seen and scarcely understood the drama on that high rooftop of the opal palace, when I had scorned her for the sake of the dagger at her heart, and Natema had had me held over nothingness. What did she think of that? How could I explain? I looked at her and I felt as low as a man has any right to be in his life.

Then I swung away with a clash of my swords — for I wore clansman's gear — and stamped out, seething, furious, sad and empty, all at the same time.

The powder blue of the Ewards escorted me until I was safely well away from the city, and then astride my zorca. With three more in a following string, I galloped headlong out toward the Great Plains and my clansmen.

Eighteen

I feast with my clansmen

Hap Loder was overjoyed to see me.

Truth to tell I had expected some stiffness about this reunion.

But Hap danced about, shouted, thumped me on the back, grabbed my hand and threatened to wring it off, bellowed for wine, hugged me, roaring and hullabalooing so that all the wide camp of the clan came arunning.

They were all there, Rov Kovno, Ark Atvar, Loku, all my faithful clansmen. There was no business to be transacted that night. Immense fires blazed; chunkrah were slaughtered and the meat roasted to its gourmand's delight of tastiness, the flesh perfect, the fat brown and crisp, the juices more heaven-savory than all the sauces of Paris and New York put together.

The girls danced in their veils and silks and furs, their golden bells and chains ringing and tinkling, their white teeth flashing, their eyes ablaze with excitement, their tawny skin painted exotically by the firelight. The wine goblets and wineskins and wine jugs passed and repassed; the fruits of the plains lay heaped in enormous piles on golden platters, the stars shone and no less than six of the seven hurtling moons of Kregen beamed down on our feasting.

Oh, yes, I had come home!

In the morning Hap rolled into my tent declaiming he had a head like the hoof of a zorca, thump, thump, thump across the stone-hard plains during the drought.

I threw him a branch from a paline bush and he began to chew down the cherry-like berries. They were near-miraculous when it came to hangover time.

The awkwardness I had expected arose from my presumed death. Hap Loder would now be Zorcander, Vovedeer. There was a step in rank between the two, the Vovedeer being the higher; but my clansmen of Felschraung and Longuelm regarded me as a Vovedeer, anyway, even though strictly speaking the name applied to the leader of four or more clans. But Hap was explaining that they were not sure I was dead, that they believed I would return, that he was a Half-Zorcander. I put a hand on his shoulder.

"I want you to be Zorcander of the clans, Hap. If I ask the people to help me in this it is as one of them; not as their Zorcander and commanding them."

He would have been insulted if I'd given him the chance.

"I know you will help, Hap; but I want you to know that I do not order it, and I do not take it for granted. I am truly grateful."

"But you are our Zorcander, Dray Prescot. Always and forever."

"So be it." I told him the plan and then the others came in, my Jiktars, and I was pleased to see Loku among their number. A Jiktar does not necessarily command a thousand men, or the other ranks their multiples of ten; the names are names of ranks and, like the centurions of ancient Rome, command whatever numbers the current military organization demands.

Loud were the shouts of glee when the plan was spread out for inspection. It was childishly simple, as most good plans are, and depended on surprise, stealth and the awesome fighting prowess of the clansmen for success.

Loku jumped up, laughing. "We can find that little thief, Nath. He will help, for he knows the city like a louse knows an armpit."

"Nath?" I said. "Why, Loku, you mean you didn't slit his throat?"

Loku roared with merriment.

"It will be very good," said Rov Kovno with fierce meaning, "to return there with weapons in our hands."

"Bows, mainly," I told them, once more their Vovedeer. "And axes. I feel you would be at a disadvantage if you opposed your broadswords to the citizens' rapiers and daggers. The shortswords, though..."

There were wise nods. These men well understood the difference in techniques required for fighting astride a vove in the massive cavalry charges of the plains, and those required by close fighting in the streets of a city. They possessed the sheer speed and striking ability to beat down a rapier and dagger man, and I knew, because I had insisted on the art being continued, that they could wield a shortsword in the left hand as they used broadsword or ax in the right; but they would be slow. Maybe it would be best to rely on the techniques they knew, and so I did not suggest that each man carry a main gauche. I did, say, however, tentatively: "Of course, a particularly long broadsword wielded as a two-hander might tickle a rapier man before he got at you." I freely admit I was desperately worried at the thought of my nomadic warriors going up against the sophisticated rapier men of the city.

After all, a rapier is a hefty weapon, quite unlike the small sword with which the French style of fencing is done. Maybe sheer weight and muscle would carry my men through.

"If only you'd consider carrying shields, then your shortswords would be deadly," I began; but their reaction choked the idea off. I sighed. In a clash of cultures the newer usually wins; but then, the clansmen were no babes-in-arms, no novices. I can see now, what I could not see then, the comical reactions of myself to the coming conflict when so much was at stake, that my main concern was with the well-being of as rough and tough and fearsome a bunch of fighting men as I've ever had the good fortune to meet.

Originally I had intended only to spend a single night and day with my clansmen. Already I had seen how effective was the control exercised by Hap Loder, and if a great deal of his success in handling the clans sprang from the tuition he had imbibed as my right-hand man, I took little credit for that, for Hap is a marvelous man at absorbing obi. As a matter of interest he absorbs it like he absorbs the clan wines. He can drink from a flagon with his left hand and swing his razor-sharp ax with his right, in the midst of a battle. I have seen it. I've done it myself, of course; but I doubt if I do it quite with the panache of Hap Loder.

So it was that I spent the next night with my clansmen also, wherein we drank hugely, cheered and clapped the girls as they danced for us — they were never dancing girls, and the man who made that mistake would have a terchick in him before he'd finished the last syllable of his mistake — and roared the clan songs to the hurtling moons above.

"Remember," I said, pulling out the suit of powder blue from my saddle bag. "This color is for us. If you see emerald green — stain it crimson with its owner's blood."

"Aye!" they roared. "The sky colors were ever in mortal combat."

At last, and not without a last ten or eleven stirrup-cups pressed on me by my Jiktars and the crowding clansmen, I bade them all farewell and began my ride back to Zenicce. The plan was for me, some miles from the city, to find a caravan and change into my powder blue and thus enter the gates without notice. As a clansman, of course, I would have been an object of deepest suspicion.

The caravan was large and slow and colorful and ablaze with the panoply of Kregen. It had come safely through the prairie limits of the clans, and as well as Chulik guards, there were mercenary clansmen serving in the long lines of pack animals. My powder blue mingled easily with the chiaroscuro of colors.

As well as the indefatigable calsanys, and long strings of the plains asses, there were many pack mastodons. These goliaths could each carry two-ton loads, slung a ton each side, and they lolloped along like true ships of the plains. I admired their rolling muscles and massive tread. I hoped that when they reached their destination they would not be slaughtered for their ivory and hides, as often happened, and would once more be able to plod so tirelessly along the untracked pathways of the Great Plains.

The discovery by chance that much of the pack mastodons' burdens consisted of paper — reams and reams of it all beautifully packed — excited my intense curiosity. I recalled the mystery surrounding the manufacture and distribution of paper from Aphrasöe. Coins had, since I had taken up residence in the House of Eward, now formed part of my transactions with life. The Savanti used no form of monetary exchange and the clansmen cared for coins only as booty from plundered caravans, which they might melt down for the metal, or use to barter with the city. As a slave, there had been no time for me to acquire the small copper coins that often came the way of slaves. Now by the suitable distribution of some silver coins with the face of Wanek finely executed upon one side, and the Kregish symbol for twelve on the other, plus a bottle of the fiendish drink called Dopa, I was able to make an inspection of the paper.

It was fine, smooth-textured from super-calendering, tough with a rag fiber base, and, I judged with a rush of blood to the head, milled in Aphrasöe. Questions elicited the dismaying information that it had come already packed and wrapped in these very bundles, from ships plying into Port Paros, over across the peninsula three hundred miles away, the last port of call before Zenicce. I had heard of Port Paros, a minor seaport serving a hinterland remote enough from Zenicce not to bother that great city. Port Paros was not a great city and did not count; but I wondered why the paper-carrying ships had docked there and not Zenicce. The merchants winked their bright eyes and laid fingers alongside their noses. They would by this means avoid the iniquitous port taxes levied by the House of Esztercari on foreign ships. Paper, particularly, was ruinously taxed. Alas, no, they had no idea from which land ships had sailed.

Also, they bought the paper at ridiculously low prices and could look forward to a thumping one thousand percent profit in Zenicce.

One unsettling event took place as we made the last few miles to the city. I do not count the cutthroat who tried to stab me that night having seen the silver Eward coins I had disbursed. I rolled away from his blade and took him by the throat and throttled him a little and then broke his blade over his head, lifted him up and kicked his rump with some force, and sent him stumbling, yelling, into the lines of calsanys, which did what they always did when excited all over him. I did not feel inclined to stain my steel on him.

The event was simply the sight of a gorgeous scarlet and golden raptor, floating high in hunting circles above the caravan. That magnificent bird, I felt sure, must come as a sign that the Star Lords were taking a further interest in me. Undoubtedly, they had been instrumental in bringing me to Kregen for the second time, and, I surmised, with a complete faith in my own reasoning, they had not consulted the Savanti as to their action. The Savanti, I often had to remind myself with surprise, the memory of their warm goodness and fellowship so strong upon me, had kicked me out of Paradise. The Star Lords, I reasoned, would regard me as a very suitable tool if they wished to work against the Savanti.

The caravan-master, a lean, chisel-faced black man from the island of Xuntal, an experienced and honest farer of the plains, looked up with me. He dressed in amber-colored gear and cloak, and carried a falchion, and his name was Xoltemb. "Had I a bow with me now," he said in his slow voice, "I would not lift it. I think perhaps I might cut down a man who lifted a bow against that bird."

Questions convinced me he knew nothing of the bird; that only its scarlet magnificence awed him, and the stories told around the campfires about that serene and lofty apparition.

I paid him the fees he had earned by the protection, as he supposed, his caravan had extended to me and my four zorcas. The fee was reasonable and I had not traveled far with them. He did say, as we saluted and parted: "I would welcome your company if you travel the Great Plains again. I am always in need of a good blade. Remberee."

"I will bear that in mind, Xoltemb," I said. "Remberee."

Prince Varden, and his father Wanek and his mother and Great-Aunt Shusha were most pleased and relieved to see me returned safely.

"The plains are never safe," scolded Shusha. "Every year I must make my pilgrimage to take the hot springs of Benga Deste, I sometimes wonder if I do not fret away all the good they do me on that frightful journey."

"Why," I said, "do you not take an airboat?"

"What?" Her old eyebrows shot up. "Risk my poor old hide on one of those flimsy, scary things!"

Then they all suddenly looked extraordinarily grave. Varden stepped forward and put a hand on my shoulder.

"Dray Prescot," he said — and I knew.

I can remember that moment as vividly as though it were but this morning, when — but never mind now. Then — then I knew what he was going to say and I believe my heart turned to ice within me.

"Dray Prescot. Delia of the Blue Mountains took your airboat and left us. She did not say she was going, or where. But she is gone."

Nineteen

The Lord of Strombor

The next day I had a little recovered.

Wanek was distressed, and his wife even cried a little until Great-Aunt Shusha shushed her and then drove them all away. Varden stood before me, all his friendship glowing in his face. He lifted his chin.

"Dray Prescot. You may strike me, as you will."

"No," I said. "I am the one to blame. Only me." I could not say how much I raged and scathed myself with deep biting contempt. Delia had been dragged into all these miseries because of me, and I had failed her when she had almost found the answer to her way home. If only I had listened to her! If only I had done as she asked! But my stupid pride had blinded me; I conceived it my duty to stand by my promise freely given to Varden when, I felt sure, by a word he would have freed me from it. I had felt we owed much to the Ewards and I owed them my loyalty. How much more I owed all my loyalty, my life, to Delia of the Blue Mountains!

When a retainer reported that the airboat, the one we had captured from the Esztercari, had been only temporarily repaired and that more work was needed on it to make it really airworthy, I felt no more crosses need be hung upon me. Delia could be adrift over the face of Kregen, a prey to any of the many and various ferocious men and beasts, and half-men, half-beasts, loose upon the planet. She could have fallen from the air in a wild swooping plunge that would end with her body broken and lifeless upon the rocks beneath. She could have drifted out to sea and be starving and driven to desperation by thirst — I knew it, I knew it! I do not like, at any time, to recall my frame of mind in those days.

Great-Aunt Shusha tried in her own guileful ways to comfort me. She told me of the old days of the Strombors, and I found some sort of surcease from agony with her. Many of the girls and some of the young men had gone to the clans, and most, I gathered, had gone to Felschraung.

"My clan," I said. "Of which they will not let me loose the reins of leader — of Zorcander and Vovedeer, with Longuelm."

She nodded, bright-eyed, and I guessed she was turning over ripe schemes in that devious mind of hers.

"I am an Eward by nuptial vows, and they are a goodhearted House, and the family of Wanek is very dear to me. It was Wanek's uncle whom I married. But they are not Strombors! Only by treachery were we conquered. I think it is time a new House of Strombor arose in Zenicce."

"You would be its Head," I said, feeling my affection for her make me reach out and touch her wrinkled hand. "If that were so, then I agree. You would make a superb Head."

"Tush and flabber-mouth!" Then she turned her bird-bright old eyes up at me, so woebegone and miserable with worry over Delia. "And if I were, and it were so, I could delegate, could I not? That would be my right by law and custom."

"Varden," I said. "He would be a good choice."

"Yes. He would make a fine leader for a House. I am glad you are friends with my great-nephew. He has need of friends."

I thought of the great Noble House of Esztercari, and of a certain enameled porcelain jar of Pandahem style over-man-height standing in that corridor between the slave quarters and the noble, and I sighed. Varden and Natema would make a splendid couple. I had fought for her there, against the Chulik guards, and Varden would have done the same.

Varden had something else on his mind.

We were standing in an immense bay window overlooking an interior avenue of the enclave filled with the bustle of morning market and the cries of street vendors and the passage of asses and the squawking of birds and the grunting of vosks, with the slaves purchasing food and clothes and drink and all the busy hustle and bustle of everyday life. Varden tried to open the subject of conversation a number of times, and at last I had to make him speak.

"I know you fought for Natema," he said. "For Delia told me of it. I do not know how to thank you for saving her life."

I spread my hands. If this was all! But he went on.

"Delia told me, and she was angry — how superb she is when she is angry! — that you were in love with Natema." Varden rushed on now, ignoring my sudden start and the glowering look of fury I knew had flashed into my face. "I believe that was the true reason for her leaving us. She knew you did not care for her, that you regarded her as an encumbrance, for she told me all this, Dray, and she was very near to tears. I do not know whether to believe it or not, for from all I have seen I had thought you loved Delia, not Natema."

I managed to blurt out: "Why should my not caring for Delia make her leave, Varden?"

He looked astonished.

"Why, man, she loves you! Surely, you knew that! She showed it in so many ways — the ling furs, the scarlet breechclout, her refusal to take Natema's gems — and the way she looked at you. By Great Zim, you don't mean to say you didn't know!"

How can I say how I felt, then? Everything lost, and now, when it was too late, to be told I had had everything within my grasp and thrown it away!

I rushed from that sunshine-filled bow window and found a dark corner and heard only the stamp of my heart and the crash of blood through my head. Fool! Fool! *Fool!*

They left me alone for three days. Then Great-Aunt Shusha wheedled me into returning to life once more.

For their sake, for pride's sake, for the sake of my bonds of obi-brotherhood with my clansmen, who were riding over the plains toward the city, I paraded a facsimile of normal living. But I was a husk, hollow and dead, within.

Varden told me, with a smile he tried to hide in face of my agony, that Prince Pracek of Ponthieu had contracted with a most brilliant bride-to-be, a princess from the powerful island of Vallia; that the Esztercaris had, however unwillingly, agreed to this match, for it would strengthen their alignment — and this meant, as I saw at once, that Natema was freed. Varden bubbled with the hope that in some fantastic way he would claim her. I told him I was pleased for him. I even ventured out into the public places of Zenicce once more. I had to live now only for my life with the clansmen.

An unpleasant scene developed one day as storm clouds rolled in from the Sunset Sea over the city. We had gone to the Assembly Hall and, leaving, were met by a crowd of the Esztercaris entering, and with them the purple and ocher of the Ponthieu. In the animated crowds always to be found talking and lobbying in the corridors and halls surrounding the Great Hall there were the silver and black of the Reinmans and the crimson and gold of the Wickens, so we were not alone.

Among the Ponthieus walked a tall and burly man clad in a fashion strange to me. He wore a wide-brimmed hat, curled at the edges, and with two strange slots in the brim above his eyes. His clothes were of buff leather, short to his thigh, belted in at the waist so the small skirt flared, and immensely wide across the shoulders. The shoulders were padded and artificially broadened, I saw; but the effect was in no wise incongruous. He wore long black boots reaching over his knees. He wore no single item of jewelry. His face was wind-beaten, bluff, with a fair moustache that curled upward.

"The consul of Vallia," remarked Varden. I knew that in the city there were many consular offices, their functions more mercantile than diplomatic, for the niceties of foreign protocol are not too highly developed on Kregen, and a Noble House would have no hesitation in smashing down a consul's door should they desire for some reason to do so.

The man struck me as a seafaring man, and his manner, quiet, relaxed, reminded me of the calm that deceives before the gale. "They're discussing the bokkertu, I suppose," said Varden gleefully. Vallia was unusual among the land masses of Kregen in that the whole island was under one government. It lay some hundreds of miles away between this continent of Segesthes and the next continent of Loh. Vallia, as a consequence, was extremely powerful, with an invincible fleet. Such an alliance would make the Esztercari-Ponthieu axis so formidable nothing could stand against it. We must strike first, before their plans to attack us matured.

It was on that day, I remember, that for some reason I went to the chest where I had stored the gems I held in trust for Delia. They were gone. Upset, miserable with my own worries, I had no stomach for further upsets and slave beatings, so I did not mention the matter. There was my portion that Delia might have — Delia, wherever she was now!

Now we glowered on the Esztercaris and rapiers were fingered and half-drawn and someone had the sense to send for the city wardens, and no blood was spilled. But the storm clouds above Zenicce were no blacker than our faces, and portended no greater hurricanes and whirlwinds.

A day later Gloag at last reported he had found Nath, the thief, and that Nath would help, for — how I relished the irony — he regarded himself as an obi-brother of the clansmen with whom he had escaped and shared dangers.

The simplicity of the plan was its strength.

No walls girded Zenicce with a ring of granite. Each enclave was a fortress in its own right. An attacking army might swirl along the canals and open avenues; they would swirl as the French cavalry swirled about the British squares at Waterloo — a scene I witnessed for myself. Even the three hundred thousand free people without the Houses maintained their own fortress-like enclaves into which they could retire from their souks and alleys.

Great-Aunt Shusha gave me a surprise. She called me into the long room of her private apartments, and smiled and cackled at me as I gaped at a dozen of her personal retainers. They were clad not in the Eward powder blue but in a glorious, flashing, brilliant scarlet. They looked pleased.

"Strombor!" she said. She spoke the name proudly. "I have made up my mind." She motioned and a slave girl brought forward two sets of scarlet gear for Gloag and myself. "Varden will have need of your strength, Dray Prescot. Will you wear the Strombor scarlet for me, and aid him?"

"I will, Great-Aunt Shusha," I said.

She picked me up sharply. "I am not your great-aunt, Dray Prescot. Never think it."

The affection I believed existed between us made me smother my surprise, for, of course, she was right. I was simply a wandering warrior, a clansman, with no claims to relationship with a great noble of the House of Eward or of Strombor. I took the scarlet gear and nodded.

"I will remember, my Lady."

"Now," she said, her bird-like eyes bright on me. "Go, Dray Prescot. Jikai!"

That evening as the storm clouds roiled and burst above the city the final plans were made. Clad in the gray slave breechclouts and carrying our magnificent scarlet gear and our weapons rolled in bundles, Gloag and I and the men we had chosen, twenty of us, swam the canal toward the island of Esztercari that had once been the island of Strombor. We entered through that low conduit from which Gloag, Delia and I had escaped — it seemed so long ago — and secreted ourselves.

The messenger from Hap Loder had arrived; in the dawn light the clansmen would reach us. Nath would see to that.

We waited, Gloag and my men and I, in the pouring rain, waiting for the first sign of the lumbering wherries easing through the canal water, dimpled with raindrops, from the marble quarries. The waiting was fretting.

So far I have deliberately made no mention of the Kregan system of time-keeping. But that wait was kept in counting the slow passage of the leaden-footed burs. A bur is forty Earth minutes long, and there are forty-eight of them in a Kregan day and night cycle. The discrepancies in the year caused by Kregen's orbit of a binary were smoothed out by the addition or subtraction of burs during the festive seasons, and a similar calculation with regard to days at those times. Each bur contains fifty murs, or minutes. Seconds, although known and used by astronomers and mathematicians, are generally unnecessary in the daily commerce of Kregen. The position of the two suns by day, or any of the seven moons by night, can tell a Kregan the time instantly.

An uproar broke out far above our heads. It was clearly extraordinarily loud for us to hear it, with the rain splashing down into the canal by our ears. I knew what it was. Up there on the bewildering profusion of roofs the powder blue of the Ewards would be spiraling down in their fliers, the men would be leaping out with rapiers aflame. They had not waited! They had gone into the attack early — and I could half-guess that the pride of the Eward House could not stomach waiting for my tough clansmen to strike the first blow. The fliers would be swirling away to bring more fighting men. The emerald green would be surging back, now. There would be death, violent, ugly death, sprawling all over the rooftops and down the stairways of the Esztercari enclave.

And I was waiting here, helpless, in the rain.

By the nearness or the distance of the noise of combat we could tell how went the fray. And soon it was clear the Esztercaris were smashing back the men of Eward. Our allies in the Houses aligned with us and contracted to keep in play the Ponthieu and the others of their enemies. It was between Esztercari and Eward.

The Houses varied in numbers of population and a Great House, whether Noble or Lay, might contain as many as forty thousand persons. Because of the practice of hiring guards, mercenaries, either men or half-men or half-beasts, the actual number of fighting men available to a House was more than a normal breakdown of population would yield. We had estimated there would be about twenty thousand fighting men against whom we must strike in the Esztercari House. I had told Hap Loder he must leave ten thousand of our clansmen with the tents and wagons and chunkrah. If we failed and disaster overtook us, the clans must have a cadre on which to build afresh. Hap was bringing about ten thousand warriors.

"They have struck too soon," Gloag was saying from where he lay at my side in the rain. "Where are the clansmen?"

Through the veils of rain we stared down the canal until our eyes stung.

Was that a wherry? Shadows moved through the rain as it hissed into the water. Gray shapes, moving vaguely, like pack mastodons, through the mist-veils? The suns were up now and trying to strike through the sodden cloud masses. Was that a harder shape, a long broad shape in the water, with the figures of men like ants poling it along? I stared — and—

"Time!" I said, and stood up and took my sword.

Without a second glance for the first wherry, which now showed its blunt snout over the rippled water, I led my men through the postern to the conduit and, clad in our slave gray, we hurried up the winding stair. The Chulik guards had split, half remained at their posts, the other half had gone to repel the rooftop attack. We cut them down instantly.

Then we flung our shoulders to the windlass and gradually the deadweight of the portcullis over the entrance canal lifted. We strained and struggled and puffed. Through an arrow slit I could look down from the masonry onto the mouth of the canal. The portcullis rose, dripping. And the snout of the wherry ghosted under it, heading into the Esztercari fortress, and in the bows, standing with bow in hand, was Hap Loder. Cheekily, he looked up, and waved.

We left the windlass dogged so that all the remaining wherries Nath had arranged to steal from the marble quarries and which had been packed overnight with clansmen could pass. Then we hurried through ways known to Gloag, down dim corridors and flang-infested crannies, until we reached the slaves' cess-pit door. We flung it open, cutting down the Och guards, let in Hap and my men. Other clansmen led by Rov Kovno branched away at once. Loku would be bringing his men in through the postern conduit opening we had used. Now my clansmen were loose within the fortress of the Esztercari!

Once my men had solid roofs above their heads they dried their hands and then brought out the carefully coiled bowstrings from their waterproof pouches, strung their bows with quick practiced jerks. Their plains-capes were thrown off with the rain slick and shining upon them. The feathers of their arrows bristled from the quivers over their right shoulders, dry and perfect. We went hunting emerald green.

I believe I do not want, at this time, to dwell on the taking of the Esztercari enclave. We killed the enemy, of course; we drove them in a wave of shafts and steel from wall to wall and corner to corner; we linked hands with the exultant ranks of men in powder blue; but we sought to win the victory and not just simply to kill. Where that was necessary we did so, for that is the nature of warfare. But hundreds of emerald green sets of clothing floated in the canals as the mercenaries fled, and gray tunics with the green bands, and we did not pursue. We did not set flame anywhere, for I had told my men that this great House was the home of a noble lady, Shusha of Strombor.

I wore my old scarlet breechclout; and over it the brave scarlet gear of Strombor, as I had promised Shusha. Like my clansmen I did not disdain the wearing of armor, and had strapped on a breast and back, a pauldron over my left shoulder, and arm and wrist bands on my left arm. But my right arm and shoulder were naked, as they had been when I hunted in my Savanti leathers. In the press the blow that kills comes so often unseen, from the blind side, from the back. Armor can save a man's life then. It saved mine.

The final stand was made around the noble quarters in the opal palace.

I raged through that old fighting ground where I had defended Natema, my clan ax biting into skulls and lopping arms. Now it was the nobles of Esztercari we faced. The corridor now presented the same problems. Two by two we fought. I knew everywhere else was in our hands. I leaped forward and hacked down a noble and my ax split along its sturm-wood handle so that the leather thongs sprang spiraling out. Galna, he of the white face and mean eyes, roared hugely and lunged with his glinting rapier. I dodged aside. For a moment, we stood in a cleared space, our men at our backs. There sometimes falls in battle a strange kind of hush as all the combatants pause to take breath and renew their strength before continuing. Such a hush fell now as Galna stalked me. One of my men, it was Loku, shouted and hurled an ax. I took the handle in my fist as it sailed through the air.

Galna smiled toothily. "My rapier will spit you, Dray Prescot, before you can lift that ax."

He was the Champion of Esztercari. A master swordsman.

"I know," I said, wasting breath, and turned, and smashed that gorgeous jar of Pandahem porcelain into a thousand shards. From the wrecked interior of the vase I snatched the mailed man's rapier I had hidden there at the close of that epic fight, and swung up, and stood, facing Galna. I know now my face must have daunted him. But he faced me bravely, his blade a living streak of light in the lanternglow. Our blades crossed. He was very good.

But I live and he is dead, dead and gone these many years.

He fought well and with great cunning; but I took him with a simple developed attack against which his return faltered at the last instant; my dagger twisted his blade and then my brand passed between his ribs and through his lungs and protruded all blood-smeared beyond.

No further resistance was offered as my wolves of the plains surged forward.

We stood in the Great Hall beneath that wonderful ceiling with the lamplight and the torches adding to the crimson and topaz glory of the suns' light through the tall windows. My men crowded about me, their russet clan leathers grim beside the powder blue and, even, beside the Strombor scarlet I wore. Their swords and axes lifted high, in salute.

"Hai, Jikai!" they roared.

A figure in emerald green, lost and drowned now in the surge of newer colors, was flung forward to the foot of the steps of the dais on which we stood. Wanek, Varden, great nobles of Eward, and my Jiktars, crowded the dais. We looked down on that crumpled figure in emerald green, with the rosy limbs and white body, the corn-yellow hair.

The Princess Natema of Esztercari lay there, at our feet.

Someone had loaded her with chains. Her gown was ripped. Her cornflower blue eyes were wild with baffled fury; she could not comprehend what had happened, or, believing, refused.

Prince Varden, at my side, started to rush down the steps.

I held him back.

"Let me go to her, Dray Prescot!"

He lifted his rapier, all bloodied.

"Wait, my friend."

He stared in my face, and what he saw there I do not know; but he hesitated. A man of Eward stepped forward and stripped off the emerald green gown and cast it underfoot so that Natema groveled at our feet, naked. But Natema would never grovel. She stared up, beautiful, disheveled, naked, but prideful and arrogant and demanding.

"I am the Princess Natema, of Esztercari, and this is my House!"

Wanek spoke to her, gravely but with iron resolve that bewildered her. "Not so, girl. You are no longer a princess. For you no longer have a noble House. You own nothing, you are nothing. If you are not slain, hope and pray that some man will take kindly to you, and may buy you. For you have no other hope in all Kregen."

"I — am — a princess!" She forced the words out, gasping, her hands clenched and her vivid scarlet lips curved and passionate. She stared up at us on the dais — and she saw me.

Her cornflower blue eyes clouded and she jerked back in her chains as though I had stepped down and struck her.

"Dray Prescot!" She spoke like a child. She shook her head. At my side Varden jerked like a goaded zorca.

I spoke to the Princess Natema. "Natema. You may be permitted to retain that name; your new master — if you are not slain, as the Lord Wanek has suggested — may give you a new one, like rast or vosk. You have been evil, you have cared

113

nothing for other people; but I cannot find it in my heart to condemn you for what your upbringing made you."

"Dray Prescot!" she whispered again. How different now were the circumstances of our meeting! How changed her fortunes. With my clansmen about me with their weapons raised I looked down on Natema.

"You may live, girl, if you are lucky. Who would want a naked ragbag like you now? For you have nothing but an evil temper and a violent tongue and know nothing of laboring to make a man happy. But, maybe, there is to be found a man who can see something in you, who can find it in his heart to take you in and lift you up and clothe your nakedness and learn to school your tongue and temper. If there is such a man in all Kregen, he needs must love you very greatly to saddle himself with such a burden."

To this day I do not truly know if Natema really loved me or was merely gratifying a lustful whim when she proposed herself to me. But my words struck through to her. She looked bewilderedly upon the pressing men in hostile dress all about her, at the steel of their weapons, at Wanek's iron-masked face of hatred, and then she looked at her own naked body with the heavy chain pressing the white skin — and she screamed.

No longer could I hold back Prince Varden Wanek of Eward.

He cradled her in his arms, smoothing back the lush yellow hair, calling for smiths to strike off the chains. He was whispering in her ear, and slowly her sobs and wild despair eased and her body relaxed from its rigid grip of hysteria. She looked at him, and, indeed, he was a fine and handsome sight. I saw those ripe red luscious lips curve.

I heard what she said.

She raised those luminous cornflower blue eyes to Varden, who was staring down at her with a foolish, happy, devoted and unbelieving look on his face.

"I think," said the Princess Natema, "that blue will go with my eyes very well."

I almost smiled, then.

A press circled in the hall and I saw a stately palanquin swing and sway in between the towering columns of the main entrance, slowly move toward the dais as the solidly packed masses of men whirlpooled away to give it passage. I also saw a sharp, weasel-faced little man dressed incongruously in clansman's russet and with a long knife stuck through his belt, standing truculently, as though he had conquered everything himself, at the foot of the dais. Beneath the tunic of Nath the thief there were a number of highly suspicious bulges, and I remarked to myself that Shusha would be missing a few choice items when she installed herself in her new home.

"Hai, Nath, Jikai!" I called down to him, and he looked up with his furtive weasel face as proud as though he had stolen all three eyes from the great statue of Hrunchuk in the temple gardens across the forbidden canal.

The palanquin swayed to a halt and scarlet-liveried men helped Great-Aunt Shusha — who was not my great-aunt — up the dais steps. More men provided an ornate throne she must have had carried from some dusty and long-forgotten attic. She sat in it with a thankful gasp after climbing the dais steps. She was so covered with gems that scarcely a square inch was to be seen of her scarlet gown. Her bright eyes fixed on Varden, who had flung a great blue cape about Natema, and who now stood with his bride-to-be to one side.

All the noise of shuffling feet, of laughing, of hugely-excited men, fell silent. There was in the Great Hall of Strombor, that had once been Esztercari, an overwhelming tenseness of feeling, a current of thrilling excitement, a sense that history was being made, here and now, before all our eyes. The light fell from the tall windows and burned upon the colors and the weapons. The torches smoked and their streamers lofted into a high haze in which darting colored motes weaved endlessly. Even the very air smelled differently, tangy, tingling, bracing.

Here was a nodal point of history. Here was where a Noble House vanished, and another took its place, where the rightful House once more claimed its old rewards. The vague thought that I had been brought to Zenicce to encompass just this result flashed upon my mind, to be instantly dispelled.

I knew that Shusha might wish to administer the House of Strombor herself, for her Eward husband and sons and daughters were all dead and she was herself alone — but that she would certainly wish to unite the two Houses in the person of her great-nephew Varden. I felt this to be a most happy outcome. She would will him everything, and this friendship between the Houses would be assured. I smiled at Varden where he clasped Natema, and surprised myself at the curve in my lips. His response a little surprised me, for he laughed widely, his eyes alight with merriment as he clasped Natema, and he bowed to me, a stately half-incline. I wondered what he meant.

Shusha of Strombor began to speak.

She was heard out in utter silence.

What she said shook and dumbfounded me, and explained Varden's laugh and bow, for he must have known and approved.

Shusha of Strombor had made me her legitimate heir, given me suzerainty over all the House of Strombor, with all ranks, privileges and dues thereto entailed in law; all the bokkertu — that is to say, the legal work — had been concluded. I was to assume at once the lawful title of Lord Strombor of Strombor. The House of Strombor was mine.

I stood there like a loon, stunned, not believing, thinking myself the victim of some kind of insane practical joke. But my men did not doubt. My wild wolves of the plains lifted their weapons on high and amidst a forest of flashing blades the cheers rang out. "Zorcander! Vovedeer! Strombor!" Among the russet and the powder blue there was now to be seen more color. The black and silver of Reinman, the crimson and gold of Wicken, others of our allies; they crowded in and lifted their weapons and shouted and roared.

"Dray Prescot of Strombor! Hai, Jikai!" My slave clansmen knew I would not desert them for a soft city life; was I not their Zorcander and was I not sworn in obi-brotherhood with them? So they bellowed with the best. That great and glorious hall rang to the repeated cheers as the swords lifted high.

I looked at Shusha.

Her wizened face and bright eyes reminded me of a wise old squirrel who has stored her nuts and seeds for the winter to come. That stiff slit in my lips twitched again. I smiled at Shusha.

"You cunning—" I said. And as she laughed I went to her and knelt. She put her ring-loaded hand on my shoulder. That hand trembled; but not with age.

"You will do what is right, Dray Prescot. We have talked long into the night and I have seen you in action and I believe I know your heart."

"Strombor will be a mighty House once more," I told her, and I took her other hand in mine. "But, there is one thing — slavery. I will not tolerate slavery whether it be a kitchen drudge or a pearl-strung dancing girl. I will pay wages and the House of Strombor will maintain only free retainers."

"You do not surprise me, Dray Prescot." She pressed my hand. "It will seem a little strange, an old woman like me, going through life without a slave at my beck and call."

I looked at her on her great throne. "My Lady of Strombor," I said, sincerely. "You will never be without a slave at your feet."

"Why, you great big slobber-mouth lap-lollied chunkrah! Get along with you!" But she was pleased. The noise in the Great Hall bellowed and racketed to that wonderful ceiling and I could look down from the dais again.

A man in black and silver was talking to Varden, who had been about to leap up to congratulate me as had the others on the dais, clasping my hand, the first of whom had been Hap Loder. Varden, holding Natema in the crook of his left arm, seized the man by his silver cords, staring into his face. My attention was instantly arrested. Then, the man's laughing having ceased abruptly, he was pushed back by Varden, who came roaring and raging up the dais steps to me. Shusha regarded him with a lift of her old eyebrows. He came straight to me.

I stood up and held out my hand in affection.

"You knew of this, Varden, my friend?"

"Yes, yes — Dray! Hanam of Reinman has just brought news. He was laughing at our good fortune that the Prince Pracek of Ponthieu did not intervene in the fighting, and that they had had no need to cover us in that quarter, for the prince was celebrating his nuptials this day."

"I had heard," I said, surprised at his manner, at once agitated and nervous. "He is marrying a princess of Vallia, is he not?"

"A great match," put in Wanek, with an odd look at the form of Natema shrouded in her blue cloak. I guessed he wished Varden, his son, had made a match that brought with it a whole island under one government, an invincible fleet, and trade contacts firm for ten thousand miles of Kregen. Plus a fleet of air-boats hardly seen outside Havilfar.

"A great match, indeed, Dray Prescot!" burst out Prince Varden. "A match such as a Jikai would not suffer to go on! Know, Dray Prescot, that the Prince Pracek is marrying the Princess Delia of Vallia."

Twenty

The Scorpion again

There is little more to tell.

There is little left to say about that time, my second sojourn on the planet Kregen beneath Antares.

I cared nothing for honor, for glory, for the colors of pride, I cared nothing for the bokkertu, for what might have been written down and signed and sealed. My wild clansmen would follow me across the Plains of Mist if needs be. With that marvelous rapier gripped in my fist, with my battle-stained scarlet gear flaming beneath the twin suns, and with my clansmen at my back, I paid a call on the wedding of Prince Pracek and his exotic foreign bride.

The Ponthieu enclave lay just across the canal. There would be trouble there in the future. I might have to raze or capture the whole complex. On that day, so long ago, I and my men roared across in fliers, in skiffs, in the wherries that had ghosted up from the marble quarries with my men packed within. We smashed in with unceremonious power when the place was decked in purple and ocher, and wreaths of flowers hung everywhere and the scents of costly perfumes wafted in the corridors and halls, where slave girls danced in their silks and bangles, where music sounded on every hand. At the head of my men I burst into the Ponthieu Great Hall and a guard of Ochs and Rapas and Chuliks fell away before the ranked menace of our clan bows. Grim and terrible to see, as I know I must have looked by the way the women shrank away from me and the men in their purple and ocher fingered their rapier hilts and would not look at me, I strode down the central aisle. Gloag, Hap Loder, Rov Kovno, Ark Atvar, Loku — and Prince Varden — were with me, but they kept at a distance, silent and watchful.

So sudden, so violent, so vicious had been our descent that nothing could stop us. The first Ponthieu to reach for crossbow or rapier would have died with a dozen arrows feathered in his purple and ocher trappings. I halted before the great dais as the music faltered and died away.

Absolute silence hung in that Great Hall as it had hung in the Great Hall of Strombor — my Great Hall! — only, it seemed, moments ago when Shusha proclaimed my inheritance.

Prince Pracek, with his lopsided face and sallow visage, stood there, his hand gripping his rapier hilt, gorgeously clad in his wedding trappings. Priests were there, shaven-headed, long-bearded, sandaled. Incense smoke coiled, stinking. A crimson and green carpet led to the altar.

And there, standing with lowered head, stood the bride-to-be. Clad all in white, with a white veil concealing her face, she waited quietly and patiently to be united to this twisted man at her side. Bride-to-be! Could I be too late! Then — then I promised, she would be a widow within the second.

Pracek tried to bluster the thing out.

"What is the meaning of this outrage! We have no fight with you — clansmen, a scarlet trapped foe! I know you not!"

"Know, Prince Pracek, that I am the Lord of Strombor!"

"Strombor?" I heard the name taken up and repeated in a buzz of speculation about the great chamber.

But my voice had betrayed me.

The white-crowned head lifted; the veil was torn away.

"Dray Prescot!" cried my Delia of the Blue Mountains.

"Delia!" I shouted, high, in answer.

And then, before them all, I took her in my arms and kissed her as I had kissed her once before in the pool of baptism in far Aphrasöe.

When I released her and she released me she still clung to me and her eyes were shining wonders. She trembled and held onto me and would not let go — and I would not have let her go for all the two worlds of Earth or Kregen.

There was nothing Pracek could do. The papers relating to the bokkertu were brought and ceremoniously burned. I took Delia of the Blue Mountains — this strange new Delia of Vallia — away with me back to my enclave, to my House of Strombor. Any man who had tried to lift a finger to stop us would have been cut down in an instant.

Laughing, sighing, kissing, we went back to the Great Hall where I showed Delia of Delphond to everyone and announced she was the Queen of Strombor.

There is little left to tell.

How brave she had been! How foolhardy, how noble, how self-sacrificing! Believing I regarded her as an encumbrance, as a hindrance, that I was doing what I was doing out of love for Princess Natema, she vowed to aid me in every way she could. If she could not have me, then she would help me to obtain the woman she thought I wanted, if that would make me happy. I chided her, then, accusing her of weakness and of giving in; but she only said: "Oh, Dray, my dearest! If only you could see your own face at times!"

She had taken Natema's gems, glad now to use them to aid me, and slipped away in the airboat so that I might think she had returned home. Of course, she had known where Vallia was all along. At first she had been reluctant to tell me she was the daughter of the Emperor of Vallia for fear I would demand an immense ransom — which would have been paid, I knew. Then, when she had known she could not live without me — I believe she might have done something brave and foolish immediately after the wedding ceremony with Pracek — she did not tell me because then she thought I would simply see her home and leave, or just send her home, away from me. And she could not bear that.

But when her poor confused thoughts had tangled Natema with me she had gone to her father's consul in Zenicce, that bluff, robust, booted man with the buff gear, using the gems to ease her way in the city and setting the airboat to drift far out over the sea, and told him she wished to be betrothed to Pracek. He had tried to dissuade her, for the match was too far beneath her; but with her own imperious will so different from that of Natema, she had insisted.

I hugged her to me. "Poor foolish Delia of the Blue Mountains! But — I must call you Delia of Vallia now." She laughed up at me, holding me close.

"No, dearest Dray. I do not think Delia of Vallia an euphonious name and never use it. Delphond is a tiny estate my grandmother willed me. And the Blue Mountains of Vallia are magnificent! You will see them, Dray — we will see them together."

"Yes, my Delia of the brown eyes, we will!"

"But I wish to be called Delia of Strombor — for are you not Lord of Strombor?"

"Aye — and you will be Queen of Felschraung and Longuelm, Zorcandera and Vovedeera!"

"Oh, Dray!"

There is not much more to tell.

We were sitting in a room with the sunshine from Zim flooding crimson all about us waiting for Genodras to pour its topaz fires into the room. At the far end were all my friends, laughing and talking and already the bokkertu for our betrothal was taking place. Life had come to be suddenly a precious and golden wonder to me.

As the green sunshine slanted in through the window and mingled with the crimson I saw a scorpion scuttle out from under the table. I had never before seen one on Kregen.

I jumped up, filled with a frenzied, sick loathing, a foreboding, even a knowledge. I remembered my father lying white and helpless as the scorpion scuttled so loathsomely away. I leaped forward and lifted my foot to bring it down squashing on the ugly creature — and I felt a blue tingling of fire limning my eyes and penetrating into my inmost being — I was falling — and Delia was no longer a warm and wonderful presence. I opened my eyes to a harsh and yellow sunshine and I knew I had lost everything.

I was on the coast of Portugal, and Lisbon was not far off and there was some trouble before I, naked and with no explanation of my appearance, could break free and try to make some kind of a life at the beginning of the nineteenth century on Earth.

The scorpion had stung once more.

For hours I would stand, gazing up at the stars, picking out Scorpio. There, four hundred light-years away, on the wild and beautiful and savage planet of Kregen, beneath the crimson and emerald suns of Antares, was all I wanted on any world, denied, it seemed to me, forever.

"I will return!" I shouted, over and over, as I had shouted once before. Would the Savanti hear and take pity on me, return me to Paradise? Would the Star Lords once again pluck me across the interstellar gulf to be used once more as a pawn in their inscrutable plans? I could only hope.

So much — so much — and all lost, all lost.

"I will return," I said fiercely. "I will never give up my Delia of the Blue Mountains, my Delia of Strombor!"

I would return, one day, to Kregen beneath Antares.

I would return.

I would return.

The Suns of Scorpio

A note on the tapes from Africa

Some of the strange and remarkable story of Dray Prescot, which I have by a fortunate chance been privileged to edit, has already seen publication (*Transit to Scorpio*). Yet still as I listen to my little cassette tape recorder the power of Prescot's sure calm voice haunts me. There is much in the incredibly long life of this man yet to learn and we must be thankful that we have been given what we do have available to us.

The cassettes my friend Geoffrey Dean handed me that day in Washington, cassettes he had received in Africa from Dan Fraser who, alone of us, has actually seen and talked with Dray Prescot, are incalculably valuable. Yet some cassettes are missing. This is quite clear from the textual evidence. That this is a tragedy goes without saying and I have urgently contacted Geoffrey to discover if he can trace any way in which the loss might have occurred. So far he has been unable to offer any explanation. It is too much to imagine that by some miraculous stroke of good fortune someone might stumble upon these missing cassettes — say in the baggage room of an airline terminal or a lost property office. If, as I fear, they are lying abandoned in some pestiferous West African village, unrecognized and forgotten, someone may use them to record the latest ephemeral pop tunes...

Dray Prescot, as described by Dan Fraser, is a man a little above medium height, with straight brown hair and brown eyes that are level and oddly dominating. His shoulders made Dan's eyes pop. Dan sensed an abrasive honesty, a fearless courage, about him. He moves, Dan says, like a great hunting cat, quiet and deadly.

Dray Prescot, born in 1775, insists on calling himself a plain sailor, yet already his story indicates that even during his time on this Earth when he was attempting with little success to make his way he was destined for some vast and almost unimaginable fate. I believe he always expected something great and mysterious to happen to him. When he was transplanted from Earth to Kregen beneath Antares by the Savanti, those semi-divine men of Aphrasöe, the Swinging City, he positively reveled in the experiences designed to test him. Something about his makeup, perhaps his mental independence, his quick resentment of unjust authority, and most particularly his defiant determination to cure in the pool of baptism the crippled leg sustained by his beloved Delia in a fall from a zorca, made the Savanti cast him out of his paradise.

Subsequently, after he had been transported back to Kregen beneath the Suns of Scorpio by the Star Lords, he fought his way up to be Zorcander of the Clan of Felschraung. Then, after his enslavement in the marble quarries of Zenicce, he graced himself — in that same enclave city of Zenicce — in the eyes of Great Aunt Shusha, who bestowed upon him the title of Lord of Strombor, giving him possession of all her family's holdings. All these experiences seem, to judge by what he says himself in the following narrative, to have touched him lightly. I cannot believe that to be true. During these early periods on Kregen Dray Prescot was maturing in ways that perhaps we on this Earth do not understand.

As to the editing of the tapes, I have abridged certain portions, and tried to bring some order out of the confusion of names and dates and places. For instance, Prescot is inconsistent in his usage of names. Sometimes he will spell out the word, and this makes transcription easy; at other times I have tried to spell the name phonetically, following what I hope are the guidelines he indicates. "Jikai," for instance, which he spells out, he pronounces as "Jickeye." He uses the word "na" between proper names, and I take it to mean the English "of" used rather in the French fashion of "*de*". But he also uses "nal." He says: "Mangar na Arkasson" but: "The Savanti nal Aphrasöe." I feel the usage bears no relation to the double vowel. Clearly there are grammatical rules on Kregen that diverge from those with which we are familiar on this Earth. Generally I have substituted "of" in these circumstances.

Prescot speaks with the characteristic lack of calculated forethought to be expected from a man recollecting past events. He will wander from one point to another as various enticing memories recur to him; but I feel this lends a certain lightness and vigor to his narrative and, at some risk of displeasure from the purists of the language among us, I have in most cases merely amended the punctuation and left the train of thought as Prescot spoke it.

So far he has said nothing of note about the seasons, and he uses that word as a rule, hardly ever "year." I suspect the seasonal cycles to be far more complicated astronomical, meteorological and agricultural affairs than we here are accustomed to.

Geoffrey Dean said to me: "Here are the tapes from Africa. I promised Dan Fraser I would honor what he had promised Dray Prescot, for I truly believe, Alan, there is a purpose behind Prescot's desire to have his story read by people on Earth."

I believe that, too.

Alan Burt Akers

One

Summons of the Scorpion

Once before I had been flung out of paradise.

Now as I tried to gather up the broken threads of my life on this Earth, I, Dray Prescot, realized how useless mere pretense was. Everything I held dear, all I wanted of hope or happiness, still existed on Kregen under the Suns of Scorpio. There, I knew, my Delia waited for me. Delia! My Delia of the Blue Mountains, my Delia of Delphond — for the Star Lords had contemptuously thrust me back to Earth before Delia could become Delia of Strombor. There on Kregen beneath Antares all I desired was denied to me here on Earth.

My return to this Earth brought me one unexpected experience.

Peace had broken out.

Since the age of eighteen I had known nothing but war, apart from that brief and abortive period of the Peace of Amiens, and even then I had not been completely free. What the new peace meant to me was simple and unpleasant.

The details of my wanderings after I managed to escape the inquiries after my arrival, naked, on that beach in Portugal are not important, for I confess I must have been living in shock. I had vanished overboard as far as the deck watch was concerned, that night seven years ago, disappearing forever from Roscommon's quarterdeck the night after we had taken that French eighty-gun ship. Had I, as far as the navy was concerned, still been alive I would in the normal course of events have expected to be promoted to commander. Now, with the peace, with a seven-year lapse of life to explain, with ships being laid up and men cast adrift to rot on shore, what chance had I, plain Dray Prescot, of achieving the giddy heights of command?

Through chance I was in Brussels when the Corsican escaped from Elba and aroused France for the final dying glory of the Hundred Days.

I imagined I knew how Bonaparte felt.

He had had the world at his feet, and then he had nothing but a tiny island. He had been rejected, deposed, his friends had turned against him — he, too, in a way, had been kicked out of his paradise.

It had been my duty to fight Bonaparte and his fleets; so it was without any sense of incongruity that I found myself at Waterloo on that fateful day of the eighteenth of June, 1815.

The names are all familiar now — La Belle Alliance, La Haye Sainte, Hougoumont; the sunken road, the charges, the squares, the cavalry defeats, the onslaught of the Old Guard — all have been talked about and written about as no other battle in all this Earthly world. Somehow in the smashing avalanches of the British volleys as the Foot Guards hurled back the elite Old Guard, and I charged down with Colborne's 52nd, and we saw the sway and the recoil of the

Guard and then were haring after the ruined wreck of the French army, I found a powder-tasting, bitter, unpleasant anodyne for my hopeless longings.

In the aftermath of battle I was able to render some assistance to an English gentleman who, being inopportunely pressed by a swearing group of moustached grenadiers of the Old Guard, was happy to allow me to drive them off. This meeting proved of no little importance; indeed, had my life been led as are ordinary people's lives — that is, decently, on the planet of their birth until their death — it would have marked a most momentous day. Our friendship ripened during the days he was nursed back to full health and on our return to London he insisted I partake of his hospitality. You will notice I do not mention his name, and this I do for very good and sound reasons. Suffice it to say that through his friendship and influence I was able to place my little store of money into good hands, and I mark the beginning of my present Earthly fortune as originating on the field of Waterloo.

But it is not of my days on Earth that I would tell you.

Feeling the need once more of wide horizons and the heel of a ship beneath my feet I shipped out — as a passenger — and traveled slowly in the general direction of India, where I hoped to find something, anything, I knew not what, to dull the ever-present ache that made of all I did on this Earth pointless and plodding and mere routine existence.

There seemed to me then little rhyme or reason for the malicious pranks played on me by the Star Lords. I had no clear conception of who or what they were — I didn't give a damn then, either, just so long as they returned me to Kregen beneath Antares. I had seen that gorgeous scarlet and golden-feathered hunting bird, greater than either hawk or eagle, the Gdoinye, circling above me during moments of crisis. And, too, I had seen the white dove that had up to then ignored the scarlet and golden raptor. There were forces in play I did not and didn't want to understand as the Star Lords battled for what they desired in their mysterious unhuman ways with whatever forces opposed them; and the Savanti — mere human men after all — looked on appalled and attempted to move the pieces of destiny in ways that would benefit mere mortal humanity.

The forces that moved destiny chose to transport me to Kregen under the Suns of Scorpio during my first night ashore in Bombay.

The heat, stifling and intense, the smells, the flies, the cacophony of noise, all these things meant nothing to me. I had experienced far worse. And on that night, so long ago now, the stars above my head flung down a sheening light that coalesced and fused into a burning patina mocking me and closing me in. I had reached that point of despair in which I believed that never again would I tread the fields of Kregen, never again look out from the walls of my palace of Strombor in Zenicce, never again hold in my arms Delia of Delphond.

From the balcony, I looked up at the stars, with the night breeze susurrating great jagged leaves and the insects buzzing in their millions, and picked out, not without some difficulty, that familiar red fire of Antares, the arrogant upflung tail of the constellation of Scorpio. I stared longingly, sick with that inner crumbling of spirit that recognized with loathing that I did, indeed, despair.

126

In my agony and my desperation I had thought that India might provide a scorpion — as it had bred the one that killed my father.

Clearly, that long-ago night, I was light-headed. When I looked up at the stars, at the red fire of Antares, and the familiar blue lambency grew, swelling and bloating into the blue-limned outlines of a giant scorpion, I was drained of all the exultation that had uplifted me the last time this had happened.

I simply lifted up my arms and let myself be carried wherever the Star Lords willed, happy only that I should once again tread the earth of Kregen, under the Suns of Scorpio.

Without opening my eyes I knew I was on Kregen.

The stinking heat of a sweltering Bombay night was gone. I felt a cooling breeze on my forehead. Also, I felt a peculiar scrabbling tickling sensation on my chest. Slowly, almost languorously, I opened my eyes.

As I had half expected to be, I was naked.

But, sitting on my chest and waving its tail at me, a large, reddish, armor-glinting scorpion poised on its squat legs.

Without being able to help myself, moving with a violence entirely beyond my control, I leaped to my feet with a single bound. I yelled. The scorpion, dislodged, was flung out and away. It fell among a rocky outcrop and, regaining its legs with an ungraceful waddle, vanished into a crack among the rocks.

I took a deep breath. I remembered the scorpion that had killed my father. I remembered the phantom scorpion who had crewed for me aboard the leaf boat on that original journey down the sacred River Aph. I remembered too the scorpion that had appeared as my friends laughed and I had sat with Delia, my Delia of the Blue Mountains, with the red sunshine of Zim flooding the chamber and the greenish light of Genodras just creeping into the corner of the window, as we made the bokkertu for our betrothal, just before I had been flung out of Kregen. I remembered these times of terror and despair when I had previously seen a scorpion — and I laughed.

Yes, I, Dray Prescot, who seldom smiled, laughed!

For I knew I was back on Kregen. I could tell by the feeling of lightness about my body, the scent on the wind, the mingled shards of light falling about me in an opaline glory from the twin suns of Antares.

So I laughed.

I felt free, rejuvenated, alive, gloriously alive, the blood singing through my body and ready for anything this savage, beautiful, vicious, and beloved world of Kregen might offer. With a strange exalted kind of curiosity, I looked about me.

That blessed familiar pink sunshine bathed the landscape in glory. A grove of trees before me, bending in the wind, showed the white and pink blossoms of the missal. Grass as green and luscious as any that ever grew on Earth spread beneath my feet. Far away on the horizon, so far that I knew I stood upon a lofty eminence, the line of the sea cut cleanly into the brilliant sky. I breathed in deeply, expanding my chest. I felt more alive than at any time since I had been snatched away from my palace of Strombor in Zenicce. Once again I was on Kregen. I was home!

I walked slowly toward the demarcated edge of the grass near to me on my left hand, at right angles to that distant prospect of the sea. I was naked. If it had been the Star Lords who had brought me here this time, or the Savanti, those dispassionate, near-perfect men of the Swinging City of Aphrasöe, then I would not expect otherwise. Truth to tell, I think they understood how less in my estimation they would stand had they thought to provide me with clothing, with weapons, a sword, a helmet, a shield, or spear. I was brought to this planet of Kregen beneath Antares, as I believed, for a purpose, even though as yet I might not divine what that purpose might be. I understood something of the way of those forces that had snatched me across four hundred light-years of interstellar space.

The grass felt soft and springy beneath my feet and the wind blew through my hair. At the lip of the precipice I stood looking out and down on a sight at once incredible and beautiful in its insolent power. However beautiful that sight might be and however incredible, I did not care. I was back on Kregen. Just whereabouts on the surface of the planet I had been placed I had no way of knowing, and I didn't care. I knew only that whatever faced me in the days ahead I would find my way back to Strombor in Zenicce, that proud city of the continent of Segesthes, find my way back to clasp Delia in my arms once more. If she had left Strombor, where she would still regard herself as in a foreign land, and had returned to her home by the Blue Mountains in Vallia and to her father, the emperor of the unified island empire, then I would follow her there too. I would go to the ends of this world as I would my own to find Delia of the Blue Mountains.

Below me extended a rocky shelf cut from the side of the cliff. Below that another extended. Each shelf was about a hundred yards wide. They descended like a dizzyingly disorienting giant's staircase, down and down, until the last shelf vanished beneath the calm surface of a narrow ribbon of water. Opposite me the shelves rose again from the water, up and up, stepped up and back and back, rising until I could look across five miles of clear air to the opposite lip. Here and there smaller stairways threaded the rock faces. I turned and looked inland. The perspectives dwindled away and were lost in the distance.

The supposition appeared extraordinary — ridiculous, even — but from the order of the level steps, the block facings, and the uniformity of appearance, I judged this Grand Canal to be man-made. Or, if not entirely man-made, then certainly the hand of man had been laid on what was originally a canal linking the outer wave-tossed ocean with the calmer and smoother waters of an inland sea.

I could see no sign of any living thing. However, I felt that a projecting mass perched on the topmost level directly opposite me, a rocky edifice squared and minutely distinct in the clean air, must be some form of habitation. A tremor of smoke arose from its summit, black and thin at the distance, trailing away in the wind.

The last time I had arrived on Kregen I had heard Delia's scream ringing in my ears. This time, also, I heard a scream; but I knew instantly that it was not Delia's.

Running toward the bluff from which the breeze blew and the gentle sound of the sea could now be heard susurrating murmurously in the warm air, I saw a figure break through a screen of trees and, staggering a few steps forward, fall full-length on the sward.

As I reached him I saw he was not a man.

He was a Chulik, one of those beast-humans born like men with two arms and legs, with a face that might also have been human but for the twin three-inch long upward-reaching tusks, and who in nothing else resembled humanity. His skin was a smooth oily yellow. His eyes small, black, and round like currants. He was strong and powerful, a mercenary warrior, with his mail coif from which the ventail hung open, and a hauberk that reached down to mid-thigh. He carried no weapons that I could see. His strength and power was attested to by the fact that he had screamed at all, with the red pudding that was his face all pulpy, lacerated, and bloody.

A silence descended.

I had no idea as yet which one of the many hostile and savagely ferocious predators of Kregen might have so ravaged his face. But I felt a familiar thrill of blood thump along my veins — and then I truly knew I had returned to Kregen beneath the Suns of Scorpio.

The only previous occasion on Kregen I had seen mail had been when the Princess Natema Cydones had tempted me. In an alcove a giant mail-clad man had stood, silent and motionless, bearing a rapier of such marvelous workmanship and balance, that same rapier I had captured and used in that final victorious fight in Strombor. Armor of any kind was a useful sort of clothing to wear on Kregen. Around the Chulik's waist was a white garment striped with green.

At sight of the green-striped material I frowned.

However, as you will have gathered by now, I am not overly squeamish about the small things of life, and so I stripped off the garment of green-striped white cloth and wrapped it about myself into a kind of breechclout.

Infinitely more important than clothes on Kregen are weapons, more important even than armor. This Chulik carried no weapon. This was exceedingly strange. Carefully, walking with that light springy tread that carried me soundlessly over the grass, I approached the edge of the cliff overlooking the sea.

The wind sported in my hair. I looked over and down.

The sea heaved gently a long way down the jagged cliffs. I could barely make out a curving beach of yellow sand where waves broke which I could barely hear. A few gulls and other seabirds wheeled; but they were strangely silent. That sea shone a refulgent blue. The seas that washed the shores of the continent of Segesthes were green, or gray, sometimes blue with a hardness and coldness about that blueness; this sea moved languidly, smoothly, and its blueness struck back at the eye. I had seen that blueness of water in the Mediterranean. With a sailor's eye I studied the scene, and I took particular notice of a vessel half-drawn up on that narrow curve of yellow sand.

She was a galley. Her ram beak, her pencil-thin lines, the oars now drawn inboard, all proclaimed that clearly. But she was not like that galley that had welcomed me to Aphrasöe, the Swinging City, after my inaugural journey down the sacred River Aph.

I looked about the edge of the cliff, rooting among the bushes that lined the crest. I did not find any weapon the Chulik might have dropped.

I looked further along the cliff edge, seeking the probable path the mercenary would have ascended. I became very still.

A group of creatures squatted there half-hidden by the bushes. The bushes were thorn-ivy, thickets to be avoided by those with tender skin. These creatures snuggled within the thick thorn-encrusted loops, squatting on all sixes, their coarse gray pelts matted with dirt, leaves, and excrement, their heads all turned to look down the ascending pathway up the face of the cliff.

Now I knew what manner of creature it was who had torn out the Chulik's face.

They were not unlike the Segesthan rock-ape, the grundal, some five feet in height when standing erect, with thin spiderish limbs that in their agility could take them swinging with nonchalant ease across rocks that would defeat a mountain goat. I had seen them on occasion among the distant mountains bordering the Great Plains of Segesthes, when I had hunted with my Clansmen; these fellows were of a land: vicious, cowardly, deadly when hunting in packs. Their heads were all turned away from me, yet I knew what they would be like from a frontal view. Their mouths were incredibly large, closing in folds of flesh, and when open round and armed with concentric rows of needle-like teeth. They looked not unlike some of those single-minded predatory fish dredged up from the deep seas, all mouth and fangs.

Something like ten or a dozen waited in the bushes.

Sounds broke on the still air. The scuffle of feet, the rattle of stones, the quick chatter of people in animated careless conversation. Listening with ears trained as a warrior with the Clansmen of Felschraung, I did not hear the sound I wanted to hear. I could hear no chink of weapons.

Now the voices were close enough for me to understand what was being said. The language was a form of Kregish so close to what I knew that I was convinced Segesthes could not be far removed from wherever I was now.

"When I catch you, Valima," puffed a light eager boy's voice, "you know what to expect, I trust?"

"Catch me?" The girl's voice was filled with laughter, clear, trilling, carefree, hugely enjoying herself and the moment. "Why, I declare, Gahan Gannius, you could not catch a fat greasy merchant at his prayers!"

"You will be at your prayers in a moment!"

Now I could see them as they laughed, puffing and toiling up the slope. The explanation for their words and the young man's clear exasperation was simple. He pursued the girl up the trail zigzagging in the cliff face, and she, a laughing sprite, danced on ahead. She carried a twisted bundle of clothing over her head. From the bundle loops of pearls hung down over her ears, a leather belt, a corner of a green and white cloth, a golden buckle. Both she and the boy were naked; and despite her burden she was able to keep him at any distance she desired. She bounded ahead with a gay laugh that sounded by far too reckless for a young naked girl on a cliff face with a dozen grundals lying in wait.

Their guard, the Chulik, lay with his face ripped out.

I picked up the first stone. It lay near the edge, a large, jagged stone, satisfactorily heavy in my hand.

A man, weaponless among a world of predators, must find what he can to defend himself. It is in his nature not to let himself die easily. I had proved that, many times.

I stood up.

"Hai!" I shouted. And, again, "Hai!"

I threw the stone. I did not stop to check its flight but bent immediately, seized another from the crumpled outcrop, and hurled it. The first stone, as I threw the second, cracked into the head of the nearest grundal. When the third was on its way I saw the second smite the next grundal a glancing blow, upon that round teeth-filled muzzle so like that of a deep sea fish.

"Beware!" I took breath to yell. "Grundal!"

Six stones I threw, six hard jagged bolts of pulverizing rock, before the grundals were on me.

They were not like the Segesthan rock-apes I had known before. Each one ran on his lower pair of limbs, claws scrabbling, and his upper pair reached out to grasp me and draw my face into that grinning orbit of teeth so that it might be bitten off. But, surprising me, each one carried in his middle limbs' hands a stout stick, a cudgel perhaps three feet long.

Had they known it, that was their mistake.

Claws and cudgels and needle-sharp teeth raked for me. I sprang sideways, took the first upraised cudgel, turned, and twisted and bent, and the cudgel was mine.

A grundal screeched and leaped in from the side and I in my turn leaped and kicked him alongside his head, feeling the needle-fangs' pressure through those folds of skin. The cudgel broke the skull of the one in front.

"Your back!" a voice screamed from somewhere.

I bent and rolled and the lunging grundal went over me and the cudgel helped him on his way. I could not dispatch him for the next two who attacked; these I treated separately thus: the first was caught by his cudgel and pulled forward, the second was beaten over the shoulders and, also, stumbled forward and I, with a gliding motion at once graceful and very unpleasant to them in its consequences, removed my body from the point of impact. They smashed into each other and went down screeching.

I took two quick strokes to beat in their skulls and was facing the next when a Chulik, his yellow skin extraordinarily sweaty and shiny from the run up, smote downward with a sword and split a grundal down to his shoulders.

The rest turned, screeching, beginning to drop their cudgels and to dance on their four lower limbs, a dance of rage and frustration, a reversion to their near-savage ancestry.

Not many of them were left.

Another Chulik appeared and the two semi-humans charged the grundals. The rock-apes spat defiance, but retreated and then dived over the cliff edge, swinging in fantastic overhand leaps across the rock face, disappearing into cracks and crannies and shadow-shrouded holes.

As a welcome to Kregen, I decided, staring at the girl and boy who were now hurriedly clothing themselves, at the sweaty Chuliks, and the dead grundals, this had been a fair old party. The boy, as soon as he was dressed, was cursing the Chulik guard commander. I took little notice, letting the old, familiar, hated tones of harsh authority flow over my head. Truth to tell, the Chuliks should have done their job better. They were regarded as among the best of mercenary semi-human guards, and they charged a higher premium for their services as a result. The dead one beyond the trees was no advertisement for them.

Looking at the girl was a much more rewarding occupation. She had very dark hair, not quite black, and a pleasant, open face with dark eyes. She was somewhat full about the jaw and her figure, for I had seen that whether I wished it or not, had been full, too, plump, almost; but this I suspected was merely youth and would trim off in a few years. The boy was slender, strong in his movements and gestures, with dark hair and eyes; but there was in his face a certain expression, a cast of character, a shadow I coldly felt upon me. At that time I did not brood upon him, this Gahan Gannius, for I had just come to Kregen and needed information.

He was giving orders now, harshly, meanly, the horror of what might have occurred to him still fresh in his mind. The girl, Valima, looked at me. I remained standing, the cudgel still grasped in my hand. No one had spoken to me since that swift warning shout that a grundal was about to attack my back.

"We cannot picnic here, that is certain," Gahan Gannius was saying, very disgruntled, almost sulky. "I suppose we had best go back to the shore."

"If you command, Gahan."

"I do so command! Is there any doubt?"

The Chuliks, a few more had now appeared, puffing, stood stolidly by. Their place as hired mercenaries obviated any form of inhibition from these young people, the master and the mistress. And still they had taken no notice of me.

The young master shouted at the servants who had been struggling up laden with food and wines, with tables and tablecloths, with chairs, with awnings, with rugs. Now they turned back to shore again, these men and women clad in brief gray garments with broad green borders. With the contents of a ship's stateroom upon their shoulders, they trudged up the cliff and now down, so as to fulfill the whim of these insensitive young people for a foolhardy picnic.

When they had all gone down again I was left alone.

I stood at the summit of the cliff, abandoned, and I marveled. I marveled that I had done nothing about their bad manners.

Two

The Todalpheme of Akhram

From the summit of the opposite side of the canal I could look up and see the structure rising a half mile away. I had arrived here by the simple expedient of climbing down the myriads of stairs cut into the giant rock shelves, swimming the half mile stretch of water, and then climbing up again. The twin suns were low in the sky now and their light, still mingled, would gradually fade and turn into a purer greenish glow as the green sun, the one called Genodras, lingered a while after the larger red sun, Zim, had vanished.

Then the stars would come out and I might have a better idea of just where I was on the surface of Kregen beneath Antares.

The structure appeared a solidly constructed castle or hotel with stoppered windows; its many turrets covered a roof I felt sure was more than a simple closure of halls behind curtain walls. There were domes, minaret-like spires, and the gable-ends of lofty buildings. The opaline shadows fell across its gray walls. I wondered if it had been built at the same time the canal had been straightened and faced with stone, or if its builders had, like those of Medieval Rome, plundered the ancient edifice for their own materials.

I walked slowly up toward the structure in the gathering green light.

From the dead body of the Chulik I had taken his mail coif, hauberk, and leather gear. The boy and girl, Gahan Gannius and Valima, evidently had not bothered to inquire into the fate of their guard, and his companions were under constraint. I had met the Chuliks before. I knew it was their custom to adopt the uniforms, accouterments, and weapons of those by whom they were hired. In Zenicce, where for a time I had been a bravo-fighter, the Chuliks carried the long rapier and the dagger; here, they carried the weapons suitable to mail-clad men.

The long sword had turned up at last, in my search, skewered into the ground beyond a clump of the ivy-thorn. It must have flung up, somersaulting, from the dead Chulik hand. I picked it up and studied it. Much may be learned of a people by a diligent study of their weapons.

The first object of scrutiny was the point. This was a true point, yet its wedge-shaped flanks, although reasonably sharp, were not those of a thrusting weapon. The point was known here, but, confirming the mail-clad armored Chuliks, was not favored. There exists the well-known fallacy that the point and thrusting were unknown during the European Middle Ages; the truth is simply that thrusting is not the most effective way of disposing of a mail-clad opponent. So the long sword — I turned it over in my hands. It was straight, cheaply-made, well-sharpened, as I would expect of a Chulik mercenary, with a simple iron cross-guard and wooden grip, ridged and notched. On the flat of the blade, below the guard, was etched a monogram that I took to be the Kregish letters for G.G.M. There was no maker's name.

So. A cheap, mass-produced weapon, a trifle clumsy as to balance and swing; it would serve me until a better came along.

Now I stood before the strange structure with its many domes and cupolas, its square-cut walls, in the dying light of Genodras, the green sun of Kregen.

They came out to me. I was ready. If they came to greet me, all well and good. If they came to slay me or take me captive I would swing this new sword until I had made good my escape in the shadows.

"Lahal!" they called in the universal greeting of Kregen. "Lahal."

"Lahal," I replied.

I stood waiting for them to approach. They carried torches and in the evening breeze that would strengthen with the dying suns the torches streamed like scarlet and golden hair. I saw yellow robes, and sandals, and shaven heads in flung-back hoods. I looked at these men's waists and I saw ropes wound about them, with tassels that swung as they walked.

The ropes and the tassels were blue.

I let out my breath.

I had hoped they would be scarlet ropes and tassels.

"Lahal, stranger. If you seek rest for this night, then come quickly, for night draws on rapidly."

The speaker lifted his torch as he spoke. His voice was peculiar, high and shrill, almost feminine. I saw his face. Smooth, that face, beardless yet old, with wrinkled skin about the eyes and puckering beside the mouth. He was smiling. Here, I thought then, and was proved right, is a man who thinks he has nothing to fear.

We walked back to the structure and entered through a great masonry archway which was immediately closed by a bronze-bound lenken door. I recognized the wood by its color, an ashy color with a close-textured grain; I suppose the lenk tree and lenken wood is the Kregan equivalent of our Terrestrial oak. If there were grundals out there, with jaws waiting to bite our faces off, the closing of that bronze-bound lenken door gave a comforting feel to our backs.

Conducted to a small chamber where I was offered warmed water for washing and a change of clothing — a robe similar to the yellow robes worn by the men here — and then invited to join the men for dinner in the refectory, I found everything well-ordered and calm. Everything proceeded as though governed by a routine so well established nothing would overturn it. A feeling of pleasure, quite unmistakably pleasure, began to steal over me. This might not be Aphrasöe, the City of the Savanti, but the people here knew something of that art of making everything seem important and part of a ritual of life that would go on everlastingly.

The food was good. Simple food, and I had expected that; fish, some meat I suspected was vosk cooked in a new way, fruits including the essential and beneficial palines, all accompanied by a fine bland wine of a transparent yellow color and a low alcohol content, as I judged.

All the men gathered in the refectory were dressed in the same way and they all spoke in the same high-pitched voices. There were about a hundred of them. The men who brought in the food were dressed exactly in the same way, and when they had finished serving they joined us at the long sturm-wood tables. Many lanterns shed a golden light on the scene. Halfway through the meal a youngish man mounted a kind of stand, scarcely a pulpit, and began to recite a poem. It was a long rigmarole about a ship that had sailed into a whirlpool and been caught up to one of Kregen's seven moons. I do not smile easily and I seldom laugh. I neither laughed nor smiled at the story; but it interested me.

I did not think I was in a Kregan equivalent of a monastery. Such things did exist, I knew, and there had been the order of the purple monks in Zenicce. However, something about these people, their lack of fuss or ceremony, convinced me their lives were dedicated to something other than the disciplines of the convent.

I imagine that you who are listening to my story, as you play the recordings I make in this African famine area, will guess at my thoughts. Was this the reason I had been brought back to Kregen? Had the Star Lords brought me, or the Savanti? Tantalizingly, I had not seen either a scarlet-feathered raptor or a white dove to give me any clues.

One of the men spoke directly to me as I drained the last of my wine. He appeared older than the others, although there were many elderly men as well as middle-aged ones. The lines and wrinkles in his face belied the otherwise smoothness of his skin.

"You should retire now, stranger, for it is clear you have traveled much and are tired."

Could he have known just how far I had traveled!

I nodded and rose. "I would like to thank you for your hospitality—" I began.

He raised a hand. "We will talk in the morning, stranger."

I was quite prepared to accept this dismissal. I was tired. The bed was not too soft for comfortable sleep, and I slept; if I dreamed I no longer recollect what phantoms filled my mind. In the morning, after a fine breakfast, I went for a stroll along the battlements with the old man, whose name was Akhram. The name of the building too, he told me, was Akhram.

"When I die, which may occur in perhaps fifty years or so, then there will be a new Akhram in Akhram."

I nodded, understanding.

Over the high parapet I could see, stretching out on all sides except for those where the Grand Canal and the sea cliffs hemmed us in, broad fields, orchards, tilled land, carefully tended agricultural holdings. This place would be rich. In the fields people labored, mere ants at this distance. Were they slaves, I wondered, or free?

I asked my usual questions.

No, he had never heard of Aphrasöe, the City of the Savanti. I forced down the pang of disappointment.

"I once saw," I said, "three men dressed as you are, except that they wore scarlet ropes around their waists, with scarlet tassels."

Akhram shook his head.

"That may be so. I know of the pink-roped Todalpheme of Loh, and we are the blue-roped Todalpheme of Turismond; but of scarlet-roped, alas, my friend, I know nothing."

Turismond. I was on the continent of Turismond. I had heard of Turismond. Surely, then, Segesthes could not be far?

"And Segesthes?" I asked. "The city of Zenicce?"

He regarded me. "Did you not ask these scarlet-roped Todalpheme, yourself, what of Aphrasöe?"

"They were dead, the three, dead."

"I see."

We walked for a space in that wonderful streaming opaline radiance.

Then: "I have heard of the continent of Segesthes, of course. Zenicce, as I am given to understand, is a not too popular city with the seafarers of the outer ocean."

I made myself walk sedately at his side as we patrolled the battlements in the early morning suns-shine.

"And of Vallia?"

He nodded quickly. "Of Vallia we know well, for their world-encompassing ships bring us strange and wonderful things from far lands."

I was as good as back with my Delia of the Blue Mountains. For a moment I felt faint. What of the Star Lords' intentions now — if in truth it had been the Star Lords, the Everoinye?

Akhram was talking on and out of politeness, that which had been so earnestly drummed into my head by my parents, I forced myself to listen. He was talking about the tide they expected that afternoon. As he spoke, I understood what went on here and what was the service in which these Todalpheme were engaged. The Todalpheme, in brief, calculated the tides of Kregen, kept accounts, and reckoned up with all the old familiar sailor lore I had learned back on Earth. I felt a wonder at the kind of calculations they must do. For Kregen has, besides the twin suns, the red and the green, her seven moons, the largest almost twice the size of Earth's moon. I knew that with so many heavenly bodies circling the tidal motions would to a very large extent be canceled out, the very multiplicity of forces creating not more and higher tides but fewer and less. Except when bodies were in line, when they spread evenly; then the spring or neap tides would be marvelous in their extent. Back in Zenicce I had seen the tidal defenses, and the way in which the houses along the canals had been built well above the mean water level. When tides ravaged through Zenicce tragedy could result, so the barrages, defenses, and gates were kept always in good repair, a charge on the Assembly.

Akhram told me that a great dam stood at the seaward end of the Grand Canal that connected this inner sea with the outer ocean. There were closable channels through the dam. The dam faced both ways. It had been constructed, so Akhram said, by those men of the sunrise — he said sunrise, not suns-rise — in the distant past as they had faced and leveled the canal itself, so as to control the tidal influx and efflux from the inner sea.

"We are an inward-facing people, here on the inner sea," he said. "We know that outside, in the stormy outer ocean, there are other continents and islands. Sometimes ships sail through the regulated openings in the Dam of Days. Vallia, Wloclef from whence come thick fleeces of the curly ponsho, Loh from whence come fabulous, superbly cut gems and glassware of incredible fineness: these places we know as they trade with us. Donengil, also, in South Turismond. There are a few others; otherwise, we remain willingly confined to our inner sea."

Later I was allowed to visit the observatories and watch the Todalpheme at work. Much of what they did with ephemeris and celestial observation was familiar to me; but much was strange, beyond my comprehension, for they used what seemed almost a different kind of logic. They were as devoted to their work as monks to theirs. But they laughed and were free and easy.

They showed a certain respect for my own understanding of the movements of heavenly bodies and the predictable movements of bodies of water, with tides and currents and winds and all the hazards thereto attached.

This inner sea was practically tideless. There was little wonder in this, of course (the Mediterranean tides never exceed two feet), and these dedicated men spent their lives calculating tide tables so that they might warn the custodians at the gates of the dam to be ready when the outer ocean boiled and seethed and roared in with all its power. I gathered there was no other navigable exit from the inner sea.

"Why do you live here, on the inward end of the Grand Canal?" I asked.

Akhram smiled in a vague way and swung his arm in a gesture that encompassed the fertile soil, the orchards, the smooth sea. "We are an inward-facing people. We love the Eye of the World."

When Akhram referred to the dam he called it the "Dam of Days." I realized how much it meant. If the outer ocean got up into a real big tide and swept in through the narrow gut of the Grand Canal, it would sweep like a great broom across the inner sea.

That great Dam of Days had been built in the long-ago by a people now scattered and forgotten, known only by the monuments in stone they had built and which time had overthrown, all except the Grand Canal and the Dam of Days.

I saw a stir in the fields. People were running. Faintly, cries reached up. Akhram looked over and his face drew down into a stern-lined visage of agony and frustrated anger.

"Again they raid us," he whispered.

Now I could see mail-clad men riding beasts, swooping after the running farm people. I saw a man stagger and go down with a great net enveloping him. Girls were snatched up to saddlebows. Little children, toddlers even, were plucked up and flung screaming into ready sacks.

The long sword I had found by the thorn-ivy was below, in the room I had been assigned. I started off along the parapet. When I emerged by the massive lenken door it was just closing. A frightened rabble crowded in, the last just squeezing through the little postern cut in the main doors. I lifted the sword.

"Let me out," I said to the men bolting and barring the doors.

I wore the green-striped material taken from the dead Chulik. I had been unable to don the hauberk or coif; my shoulders are broader than most. I held the sword so the men at the doors could see it.

"Do not go out," they said. "You will be killed or captured—"

"Open the door."

Akhram was there. He put a hand on my arm.

"We do not ask visitors for their names or their allegiances, friend," he said. He stared up at me, for I am above middle height. "If they are your hereditary foes, you may go freely forth and be killed for your convictions. But I take you for a stranger. You do not know our ways—"

"I know slaving when I see it."

He sighed. "They are gone by now. They sweep in, when we do not expect them, not at dawn or sunset, and take our people. We, the Todalpheme, are inviolate by nature, law, and mutual agreement; for, if we were killed, then who would give warning when the great tides were coming? But our people, our loyal people who care for us, are not inviolate."

"Who are they?" I asked. "The slavers?"

Akhram looked about him on the frightened mob of peasant folk in their simple clothing, some with the pitchforks still in their hands, some with infants clinging to their skirts, some with blood upon their faces. "Who?" asked Akhram.

The man who answered, a full-bodied man with a brown beard to his waist and a seamed and agricultural face, spoke in a tongue I had difficulty in following. It was not Kregish, the universal Latin of Kregen, and it was not the language of Segesthes, spoken by my Clansmen of Felschraung and Longuelm, and by the Houses and free men and slaves of Zenicce.

"Followers of Grodno," Akhram said. He looked weary, like a civilized man who sees things with which civilization should be done. Then, quickly, as he saw me open my mouth to ask, he spoke. "Grodno, the green-sun deity, the counterpart to Zair, the red-sun deity. They are, as all men can tell, locked in mortal combat."

I nodded. I remembered how men said the sky colors were always in opposition.

"And the city of these people, these slavers, these followers of Grodno?"

"Grodno lies all to the northern side of the inner sea; Zair to the south. Their cities are many and scattered, each free and independent. I do not know from which city these raiders came.

I said, lifting the sword again: "I shall go to the cities of Grodno, for I believe—"

I did not say any more.

Suddenly I saw, planing high in the air and descending in wide hunting circles, the gorgeous scarlet plumage of a great bird of prey, a raptor with golden feathers encircling its neck and its black feet and talons outstretched in wide menace. I knew that bird, the Gdoinye, the messenger or spy of the Star Lords. As I saw it so I felt that familiar lassitude, that sickening sense of falling, overpower me, and I felt my knees give way, my sword arm fall, my every sense reel and shiver with the shock of dissociation.

"No!" I managed to cry out. "No! I will not return to Earth! I will not...I will stay on Kregen...I will not return!"

But the blue mist encompassed me and I was falling...

Three

Into the Eye of the World

North or south... Grodno or Zair... green or red... Genodras or Zim... Somewhere a conflict was being fought out. I did not know then and even now I must in the nature of things be unaware of all that passed as I sank down in a stupor in the courtyard of the tidal buildings of Akhram with the frightened rabble of peasantry about me and the massive lenken door fast shut with its bronze bolts and bars. I was aware of a vast hollow roaring in my head. This perturbed me, for on my previous transplantations from Kregen to Earth, or from Earth to Kregen, the thing had been done and over with in mere heartbeats.

I seemed detached from myself. I was there, in that courtyard with the kindly concerned face of Akhram bending over me. And, also, I was looking down on the scene from a goodly height and the scene eddied around like a whirlpool, like that whirlpool into which I had plunged in my leaf boat going down the River Aph. I shuddered at the thought that I might be seeing that scene from the viewpoint of the Gdoinye, the scarlet and golden bird of prey.

As I looked, both upward and downward, simultaneously, I saw a white dove moving smoothly through the level air.

I thought I understood, then.

I thought the Star Lords, who I imagined had brought me here to Kregen on this occasion, did not want me to go to the north shore cities of the followers of Grodno, the cities of the green sun; but maybe the Savanti, whose messenger and observer the white dove was, would prefer it if I did go.

I hung as it were in a kind of limbo.

With a hoarse scream the scarlet bird swung toward the white dove.

This was the first occasion on which I had seen either bird take any notice of the other.

The white dove moved with that deceptively smooth wing-beat and climbed away, slipping past the stooping bird of prey.

Both birds turned and rose in the air. I followed them into the opaline radiance of the sky where the twin suns shed their mingled light fusing into a golden pinkish glory whose edges shone lambently with a tinged green. Then I could see them no longer and I sank back and fell, and so opened my eyes again on the dust of the courtyard.

Sandaled feet shuffled by my nose. Hoarse breathing sounded in my ears and hands reached down to lift me. I guessed I had not lain on the ground for half a minute. The friendly and concerned peasants were trying to carry me. I hauled out an arm and waved it and then, still groggy, stood up. I do not smile often, but I looked not without pleasure on the courtyard of Akhram, on the peasants, on the great lenken door, and on Akhram himself, who was staring at me as though, truly, I had risen from the dead.

There remains little to tell of the rest of my stay in Akhram, the astronomical observatory of the Todalpheme.

I learned what I needed of the local language with a fierce obsessive drive that disconcerted my teacher, a Todalpheme with a gentle face and mournful eyes. His voice, as high-pitched as the others, and his face, as smooth as those of the younger brethren, unsettled me. I learned quickly.

Also, I learned that if I wished to cross the wide outer ocean to reach Vallia, it would be necessary to take a ship from one of the ports of the inner sea. Few ships ventured past the Dam of Days, and it would serve my purpose to go to a city rather than wait meekly here for a ship from the outside world to pass on her way home.

Finally, Akhram spoke gently to me, pointing out my knowledge of the sea, tides, and calculations over which we had amicably pored together. Navigation has always come easily to me, and by this time I had fixed in my head the geographical outlines of the inner sea as well as Akhram could teach me with the aid of maps and globes kept in his own private study. I was also able to give him some sage advice on the higher mathematics, and his grasp of calculus also was thereby strengthened.

What he proposed was obvious, given the context of our relationship.

He now knew my name, Dray Prescot, and used it with some affection. Because of my somewhat stupid and vainglorious attempt to rush outside and deal with the raiders, alone, with my sword, I understood he felt that he owed me gratitude. I owned no particular loyalty to any set of codes; codes, in a general sense, are for the weaklings who rely on ritual and formula; but I granted their use at the right times and places; that had not been one of them. Had I got outside I would have been killed or captured and, very probably, only further annoyed the mail-clad men of Grodno.

"You are at heart one of us, Dray," said Akhram, then. "Your knowledge is already far advanced over that normal for one of your years in our disciplines. Join us! Join us, Dray Prescot; become a Todalpheme. You would enjoy the life here."

In other days, in other climes, I might have been tempted. But — there was Delia of Delphond.

There were the Star Lords; there were the Savanti; but most of all there was Delia of the Blue Mountains, my Delia.

"I thank you for your gracious offer, Akhram. But it cannot be. I have other destinies—"

"If it is because we are all castrati, and you would of necessity have to be castrated likewise, I can assure you that is of little importance beside the knowledge gained—"

I shook my head. "It is not that, Akhram."

He turned away.

"It is difficult to find the right young men. But, if the Todalpheme were no more, who, then, would warn the fisher folk, the sailors in their gallant ships, the people of the shore cities? For the inner sea is a calm sea. It is flat, placid, smooth. When storms come a man may see the clouds gather and sense the change in the wind, and sniff the breeze, and say to himself a storm is due and so seek harbor. But — who can warn him when the tides will come sweeping in to smash and crush and destroy if the gates are not closed on the Dam of Days?"

"The Todalpheme will not die, Akhram. There will always be young men ready to take up the challenge. Do not fear."

When it was time to go I promised the Todalpheme that I would halt on my journey to the outer ocean and give them Lahal. I also promised myself the sight of this wonderful Dam of Days and its gates and locks, for judging by the Grand Canal it must be an engineering work of colossal scale.

They gave me a decent tunic of white cloth, and a satchel in which were placed, lovingly wrapped in leaves, a supply of the long loaves of bread, some dried meat, and fruit. Over my back I slung a profusely berried branch of palines. Then, with the hauberk and coif rolled up around my middle and the long sword depending from a pair of straps at my side, sandals on my feet, I set off.

They all crowded to see me go.

"Remberee!" they called. "Remberee, Dray Prescot."

"Remberee!" I called back.

I knew that had I tried, now, to take any other course I would have been flung back to Earth. Much though I wanted to rush to Delia, much though I yearned to hold her in my arms again, I dare not take a single step overtly in her direction.

I was trapped in the schemes of the Star Lords, or the Savanti — although I suspected that those calm grave men wished me well, even though they had turned me out of paradise. If I tried to board a ship for Vallia, I felt sure I would find myself engulfed by that enveloping blueness and awake on some remote part of the Earth where I had been born.

Being unprovided with either a zorca or a vove, those riding animals of the great plains of Segesthes, I walked. I walked for the better part of six burs.[i]

I had absolutely no concern over the future. This time was different from all the other times I had gone forward into danger and adventure. I might seek to hire myself out as a mercenary. I might seek employment on a ship. It did not matter. I knew that the forces that toyed with me and drove me on would turn my hand to what they had planned for me.

Do not blame me. If you believe that I welcomed this turn of events, then you are woefully wrong. I was being forced away from all that I held dear in two worlds. I had more or less resigned myself to the truth that I would never again return — or be permitted to return — to Aphrasöe, the City of the Savanti; and all that I wanted on Earth or Kregen was my Delia of the Blue Mountains. Yet if I took a single step in her direction I felt sure the forces that manipulated my destiny would contemptuously toss me back to Earth. I felt mean and vengeful. I was not a happy man as I walked out in the mingled suns-shine to seek the city of Grodno; the man or beast who crossed my path had best beware and walk with a small tread when I passed by.

The shoreline presented a strangely dead appearance.

I passed no habitations, no small fishing villages, no towns or hamlets bowered in the trees that grew profusely everywhere. Trees and grass and flowers grew lushly all along my way; the air tanged with that exciting sting of the sea, salty and zestful; the green sun and the red sun shed their opaline rays across the landscape and over the gleaming expanse of smooth blue sea. But I met no single living soul in all that journey.

When the provisions given me by the Todalpheme were exhausted I used my acquired Clansman's skills and hunted more. The water in the streams and rills tasted as sweet as Eward wine from Zenicce. I was slowly working on the hauberk, unfixing the linked mesh along the spine and the sides and lacing it up again to a broader fit with leather thongs. I did not hurry the work; I did not hurry in my walk. If those dung-bellied Star Lords wanted me to do their dirty work for them, then I would do it in my own time.

I could not be sure it was the Star Lords who had arranged this. I did feel sure, though, that if they did not wish me to travel where I was traveling they would stop me. I had the idea that the Savanti, powerful and mysterious though they were, could not, when all was said and done, overmaster the Everoinye, the Star Lords.

No matter who was forcing me to take this course (I did not discount the emergence of yet a third force into the arena where actions and conflicts were being battled out quite beyond my comprehension), I was being used on Kregen. I had been used in Zenicce to overthrow the Most Noble House of Esztercari. I had done so, and in the doing of it had become the Lord of Strombor. Then, in my moment of victory when I was about to be betrothed to my Delia, I had been whisked back to Earth. Oh, yes, I was being used, like a cunning and shiftless captain will use his first lieutenant quite beyond the bounds of duty. So. I can remember the moment well, as I walked along a low cliff line above the sea, that smooth inner sea of Turismond, with the breeze in my face and the twin suns shining brilliantly down. If I were to be used in a fashion that the modern world, the world of the twentieth century, would call a troubleshooter, then I would be a troubleshooter for the Star Lords, or the Savanti, or anyone else, on my own terms.

Nothing I did must interfere with my set purpose to find Delia. But, equally, I could do nothing to seek her until I had settled the matter in hand. Accordingly, then, I walked along with a heart if not lighter, at least less oppressed. Still, I hungered for some tangible opponent to face with steel in my hand.

I had not led a particularly happy life. Happiness, I tended to think in those far-off days, was a kind of mirage a man dying of thirst sees in the desert. I had found great wonder and pleasure among my Clansmen, and had striven for the achievement of Delia of Delphond only to lose her in the moment of gaining; I wondered if I would ever be able to say with Mr Valiant-for-Truth, out of Bunyan's *Pilgrim's Progress*: "With great difficulty I am got hither, yet now I do not repent me of all the trouble I have been at to arrive where I am."

The days passed and I had seen no human life, only avoided a pack of grundals. I had looked out on an empty sea and walked through an empty countryside.

What I had seen at Akhram and my knowledge mainly gained from long hours reading during off-watch periods made me take a long swing inland. The Todalphemes' maps had shown the inner sea, the *Eye of the World*; it was marked down in the cursive script on the ancient parchment, as being bean-shaped, humped to the north, and something over five hundred dwaburs[ii] long from west to east. Because of its indented coastlines, it was studded with bays, peninsulas, islands, and the river deltas. Its width was difficult to measure accurately although proportionally a bean-shape gives a good impression.

The average width might be something in the order of a hundred dwaburs; however, that would not take into account the two smaller but still sizable seas opening off the southern shore, reached through narrow channels. I was in the northern hemisphere of Kregen still, and I had gathered that Vallia lay across the outer ocean, the sea that in Zenicce we called the Sunset Sea, east with a touch of northing in it from here. Between the eastern end of the inner sea and the eastern end of the continent of Turismond lay vast and craggy mountains; beyond were areas inhabited by inhospitable peoples around whom had gathered all the chilling and horrific legends to be expected from a land of mystery. I gathered also that these people of the inner sea, the Eye of the World, relished a tall story as much as the folk of Segesthes.

So I struck a little inland, away from that shining sea.

On the third day I was rewarded by finding myself among cultivated rows of sah-lah bushes, their blossom incredibly sweet, bright like the missal I had seen by the Grand Canal. This particular season was burgeoning with the promise of a rich, ripe harvest and every chance of a successful second crop.

I watched carefully, for I had enough experience of savage Kregen now not to rush in headlong without a surveillance; alas, a stricture I was continually forgetting in the stress of one emergency after another. Here, however, there seemed to be no emergency; in fact I would then have hazarded a guess that stress and danger were unknown. I would have been wrong; but not for the reasons I advanced to myself as I crouched in the bushes and stared out on the orderly rows of huts, the busy men and women in the fields, the sense of discipline and order everywhere.

When I had satisfied myself that this must be some kind of farm on a colossal scale, with all the usual muddle and filth inseparable from farm life removed in some magical way, I decided I had best wash myself before making an appearance. I found a stream and stripped off and thus, all naked and streaming water, I saw the mailed man ride into sight over the bank. I was to be caught more than once swimming, naked, to mutual misunderstandings, for men shed more than clothes when they strip. On this occasion I was given no chance at explanations, no chance to talk, no chance to prove myself a stranger here, not one of their people.

A man clad in steel mesh leaned from his mount and swung his sword down toward my head.

I ducked and turned, but the water stinging my eyes had betrayed my accuracy of vision, the water around my waist hampered me, and the blade caught me flatly across the back of the skull.

I have a thick skull, I think, and it has taken enough knocks to prove it tough and durable and obstinate, too, I admit. All my poor old head bone could do on this occasion was to save my life. I could not stop the sudden black swoop of darkness and unconsciousness.

Four

Magdag

"I have persuaded Holly," said Genal, looking up with a squint from where he slapped and shaped a mud brick, "to bring us an extra portion of cheese when the suns are overhead."

"You'll ask that poor girl to do too much one day, Genal," I told him with a severity that was only half a mockery. "Then the guards will find out, and—"

"She is clever, is Holly," said Genal, slapping his brick with a hard and competent hand. The sounds of bricks being slapped and patted and the splash of water, the hard breathing of hundreds of work people making bricks, floated up into the stifling air.

"Too clever — and too beautiful — for the likes of you, Genal, you hollow-bricker, you."

He laughed.

Oh, yes. The work people here in the city of Magdag could laugh. We were not slaves; not, that is, in the meaning of that foul word. We worked for wages that were paid in kind. We were supplied from the massive produce farms kept up by the overlords, the mailed men of Magdag. Of course we were whipped to keep up our production quota of bricks. We would not receive our food if we fell behind in output. But the workers were allowed to leave their miserable little hovels, crowded against the sides of the magnificent buildings they were erecting, to travel the short distance to their more permanent homes in the warrens for weekends.

I made a scratch with my wooden stylus on the soft clay tablet I held in its wooden bracket.

"You had best move at a more rapid rate, Genal," I told him.

He seized another mass of the brick mud and began to slap and bang at it with the wooden spatula, sprinkling it with water as he did so. The earthenware jar was almost empty and he cried out in exasperation.

"Water! Water, you useless cramph! Water for bricks!"

A young lad came running with a water skin with which to replenish the jar. I took the opportunity to have a long swig. The suns were hot, close together, shining down in glory.

All about me stretched the city of Magdag.

I have seen the Pyramids; I have seen Angkor; I have seen Chichen Itza, or what is left of it; I have seen Versailles and, more particularly, I have seen the fabled city of Zenicce. None can rival in sheer size and bulk the massive complexes of Magdag. Mile after mile the enormous blocks of architecture stretched. They rose from the plain in a kind of insensate hunger for growth. Countless thousands of men, women, and children worked on them. Always, in Magdag, there was building.

As for the styles of that architecture, it had changed over the generations and the centuries, so that forever a new shape, a fresh skyline, would lift and reveal a new facet in this craze for megalithic building obsessing the overlords of Magdag.

At that time I was a plain sailor lightly touched by my experiences on Kregen, still unaware of what being the Lord of Strombor would truly mean. For years my home had been the pitching, rolling, noisy timbers of ships, both on the lower deck and in the wardroom. To me, building in brick and stone meant permanence. Yet these overlords continued to build. They continued to erect enormous structures which glowered across the plain and frowned down over the inner sea and the many harbors they had constructed as part and parcel of their craze. What of the permanence of these colossal erections? They were mostly empty. Dust and spiders inhabited them, along with the darkness and the gorgeous decorations, the countless images, the shrines, the naves, and chancels.

The overlords of Magdag frenziedly built their gigantic monuments and mercilessly drove on their work people and their slaves; the end results were simply more enormous empty buildings, devoted to dark ends I could not fathom then.

Genal, whose dark and animated face showed only half the concentration of a quick and agile mind needful in the never-ending task of making bricks, cast a look upward.

"It is almost noon. Where is Holly? I'm hungry."

Many other brick makers were standing up, some knuckling their backs; the sounds of slapping and shaping dwindled on the hot air.

An Och guard hawked and spat.

Now women were bringing the midday food for their men.

The food was prepared at the little cabins and shacks erected in the shadows of the great walls and mighty upflung edifices. They clung like limpets to rocks. The women walked gracefully among the piles of building materials, the bricks, the ladders, the masonry, the long lengths of lumber.

"You are fortunate, Stylor, to be stylor to our gang," said Genal as Holly approached.

I nodded.

"I agree. None cook as well as Holly."

She shot me a quick and suspicious look, this young girl whose task was to cook and clean for a brick-making gang, and then to take her turn with the wooden spatula of sturm-wood. The sight of my ugly face, I suppose, gave her pause. Because I had been discovered to possess the relatively rare art of reading and writing — all a gift of that pill of genetically-coded language instruction given to me so long ago by Maspero, my tutor in the fabulous city of Aphrasöe — I had automatically been enrolled as a stylor, one who kept accounts of bricks made, of work done, of quotas filled. Stylors stood everywhere among the buildings, as they stood at seed time and harvest in the Magdag-owned field farms, keeping accounts.

For that simple skill of reading and writing I had been spared much of the horror of the real slaves, those who labored in the mines cutting stone, or bringing out great double-handfuls of gems, or rowed chained to galley oar benches.

Magdag, despite its grandiose building program that dominated the lives of everyone within fifty dwaburs, was essentially a seaport, a city of the inner sea.

And here was I, a sailor, condemned to count bricks when the sea washed the jetties within hearing and the ships waited rocking on the waves. How I hungered for the sea, then! The sea breeze in my nostrils made me itch for the feel of a deck beneath my feet, the wind in my hair, the creak of ropes and block, the very lifeblood of the sea!

We all sat down to our meal and, as she had promised, Holly portioned out a double-helping to Genal, who motioned to her to do likewise for me. We were all wearing the plain gray breechclout, or loincloth, of the worker. Some of the women also wore a gray tunic; many did not bother, wanting their arms free for the never-ending work. As Holly bent before me I looked into her young face. Naïve, she looked, dark-haired, serious-eyed, with a soft and seemingly scarcely-formed mouth.

"And since when has a stylor deserved extra rations, stolen at expense and danger?" she asked Genal.

He started up hotly, but I put a hand on his shoulder and he went down with some force.

"It is no matter."

"But I think it is a matter—"

I made no answer. A man was running toward us through the gangs of workers eating their midday meal. He thwacked a long balass stick down on shoulders as he ran, his face angry.

"Up, you lazy rasts! There is work. Up!"

With a snarled yelp of indignant anger Genal rose, his young face flushed, his eyes bright. Holly took a quick step to stand beside him. Her head came just to his shoulder. Both of them had to look up if they wished to stare into my face.

"Pugnarses," said Genal disgustedly. He would have said more, but Holly laid her slender hand upon his arm.

The man was an overseer, a worker like ourselves but selected out from our miserable ranks to be given his tithe of petty authority, a balass stick — balass is similar to Earthly ebony — and a gray tunic with the green and black badges of his authority stitched to breast and back. He was a tall man, almost as tall as me, burly, with unkempt black hair and pinched nostrils, his eyebrows shaggy and frowning above his malice-bright eyes. He was the gang-boss of ten gangs, and he would never tolerate underproduction or skimped work. Always, the threat of the whip hung over Pugnarses as it dominated our lives.

We all rose, grumbling and stretching and bolting the last mouthfuls of our food.

Pugnarses thwacked his stick down with a ferocity I clearly saw came from his own simmering anger at what he did. He was a man born into the wrong area of life. He should have been a son to some high overlord, to strut about wearing his mail armor, his long sword at his side, giving orders in the midst of battle rather than orders as to quantities and qualities of mud bricks.

We could now hear the high yells of other overseers and the long moaning chants of hundreds of workers and slaves. As we ran down among the scattered confusion of the brick works and out past where the masons were looking up from their midday meal, we could see the winged statue fully three hundred feet tall, being dragged by hundreds of men and women. The colossal statue towered above us, magnificent in its barbarity of inspiration and cultural attainment. Many days had been spent carving those immobile features, that cliff-like forehead, the feathered crown, the folded arms with their implements of semi-divine authority, those spreading wings of minutely carved feathers. Beneath its footed pedestal massive rollers of lenk creaked with the weight. As the slaves pulled and hauled and struggled in the heat, dragging that whole awful mass by long ropes, other workers lifted their rearmost roller in turn and carried it to the front. There the great overseer — with the blaze of color on his white tunic and a coiled whip in his right hand — could direct its accurate placing for the forward rolling weight.

We were hurriedly positioned onto a rope and we toiled on as Pugnarses, sweating, shouted and lifted his balass stick. In time with the convulsive heavings of the other slaves we dragged the monstrous statue up the gentle incline that had been the cause of its momentary hesitation and the consequent calling out of fresh draft-animals — us — men and women, workers of Magdag.

Between us, with much breath wasted on cursing and swearing and the calling on Grakki-Grodno, the sky god of the draft-beasts, and with the balass sticks and the whips of the guards falling upon our sweating naked backs, we hauled that divine effigy up the slope. We dragged it clear of the incline and halfway toward the shadow-darkened gateway, four hundred feet high, into which it must pass to be set against the wall and serve as just one more reminder of the majesty and power of Magdag.

In the long lines toiling on the ropes alongside I saw numbers of the half-humans of Kregen. There were Ochs; and Rapas, those vulturine-like people whose smell was so offensive in the nostrils of men; there was even a handful of Fristles. I saw no Chuliks among the slaves, although there were other beast-humans whose forms were new to me.

Other men and Ochs and Rapas with swords and whips guarded and goaded on men and Ochs and Rapas. Truly, creation on Kregen had leveled the species. Humanity, although apparently everywhere in the ascendant here in this section of Kregen, was not the only Lord of Creation. I saw a number of men greasing the ropes near their fastenings, and inspecting each roller in turn as it was dragged clear for cracks and weaknesses. Many of these men had red hair, and so might well have come from Loh, that continent of hidden walled gardens and veils, that lay southeast of Turismond in the Sunset Sea, nearer to Vallia than the eastern tip of Turismond, where only isolated cities flourished in a sea of barbarity. The thought of Vallia with its island empire I had never seen brought unbidden other memories from which I could never shake free, and I bent to the rope with a curse.

"By Zim-Zair," panted a burly slave, entirely naked, next to me on the adjoining rope. "I'd have this accursed heathen statue topple and split into a thousand fragments!"

"Silence, slave!" A Chulik flicked a cunning whip in a welting blow down the man's back. "Pull!"

The slave, his mass of curly black hair wet and glittering in the suns-shine, cursed but had no spittle to express his contempt. "Loathsome beasts," he grunted, low, as he hauled with cracking muscles. His skin was tanned and healthy, his nose an arrogant beak, his lips thin. "By Zantristar the Merciful! If I had my blade at my side now—"

On and on we hauled and heaved that mighty colossus into its appointed resting place. It would make, I knew, another fine haunt for spiders.

As we crowded out through that towering opening, jumbled together, the workers talking and laughing now the work was done, the slaves moody and silent, I made it my business to get alongside the curly-haired man.

"You mentioned Zim," I said.

He drew a brawny forearm across his bearded lips. He looked at me cautiously. "And if I had, would that surprise a heretic?"

I shook my head. We moved into the light. "I am no heretic. I thought Zair—"

"Grodno is the sky deity these poor deluded fools worship when all men living in the light know it is to Zair we must look for our salvation." His eyes had measured me. "You have not been a slave long? Are you a stranger?"

"From Segesthes."

"We know nothing of the outer ocean here in the Eye of the World. If you are a stranger, then in peril of your immortal soul I counsel you to have no truck with Grodno. Only to Zair can men look for salvation. They took me from my galley, the overlords of Magdag; they branded me and made me a slave. But I shall escape, and return across the inner sea to Holy Sanurkazz."

We were thrust apart in the throng, but I caught his arm. Here was information for which I hungered. The name of Sanurkazz caught at my imagination. I have mentioned how, when I first heard the name Strombor, my blood thumped and I felt a golden splendor unfolding. Here, now, was an echo of that feeling as the name Sanurkazz fell for the first time on my ears.

"Can you tell me, friend—" I began.

He interrupted me. He looked down at my hand on his arm.

"I am a slave, stranger. I suffer the whip and the irons and the balass. But no slave or worker lays a hand on me."

I took my hand away. I did not remove it swiftly. I did not express an apology, for I have made it a rule never to apologize, but I nodded, and my face must have given him pause.

"What is your name, stranger?"

"Men call me Stylor, but—"

"Stylor. I am Zorg — Zorg of Felteraz."

We would have gone on speaking, but the overseers whipped the slaves away and shouted at the workers, and so we parted. I had been impressed by this man. He might be a slave; he was not broken.

By the time we had returned to the brick works, a temporary site among the colossal buildings all around, the time for our midday meal break had long passed and we were put immediately onto brick making again. As I checked the production and made the neat marks in the Kregish cursive, for there was always a strict accounting, I pondered on this man, Zorg of Felteraz. He, most clearly, did not share in the worship of the green-sun deity, Grodno. He was a follower of Zair. So, that was why he was a slave and not a worker. The differences between the two conditions were small; they existed and were either resented or proudly proclaimed; but for a free man the pride involved was a pitiful thing.

My days among the megalithic buildings of Magdag passed.

The sheer scope of the complexes amazed me. Men would be perched atop crazy scaffoldings of wood executing marvelous friezes along the architraves, five hundred feet in the air. The statuary varied from life size to enormous creations of many artificially interlocked masses of stone. So much art, so much skill, so much painstaking labor, and all to decorate and beautify vast and empty halls. Some of these buildings were truly gigantic. I heard odd comments about the time of dying, the time of the Great Death and the Great Birth, but little added up beyond what might be a simple agricultural death and re-creation cycle.

I was sure of one thing. These were not giant mausoleum sacrifices of the living to the dead: they were not tombs; they were not Kregan Pyramids.

Most of life aboard ship is occupied in waiting, and so I slipped easily into that life among the megaliths of Magdag, having been well-schooled in waiting. I knew that if I tried to break away without the permission of the Star Lords — I had by now convinced myself they must be the instruments of my present position — I would be punished by transferral back to Earth.

As a stylor I could move among the buildings with some freedom, and I spent some time searching for the man of Zair, Zorg of Felteraz, but I did not find him. However, I will speak only of those things immediately touching on what followed, leaving out most of the unpleasant punishments; the starvings that followed low production or the lack of height in a wall by a certain date; the sporadic revolts ruthlessly put down by the half-beast, half-human guards; the infrequent days of feasting; the fights and quarrels and thievery of the warrens. They made a life savage, bizarre, demanding: a life that no man or woman should have to endure.

I said to Genal: "Why do you and your people slave and suffer for the overlords simply so as to build them more empty monuments? Don't you wish to live your own life?"

To which he would reply, his fists knotted: "Aye, Stylor, I do! But revolt — that must be carefully planned — carefully planned—" He looked about him uneasily.

Many men and women talked of revolt. Slave and worker, all spoke of the time when they could become free men through rebellion. At this time I do not think one of them thought beyond a rebellion to a true revolution.

Maybe I do the Prophet a disservice in saying this.

Perhaps, even then, he had a glimmering of the true ideals of revolution over the bloody gut-reaction of rebellion, for afterward he proved himself nobly. He was called only the Prophet; he must have had a name, but it was forgotten. Slaves might be called what their master wished; in my case I had been called Stylor for the task I performed without my even being aware of that until the name was in habitual use. Among the close-packed warrens on the landward edge of the city, outside the gay and noble sections where the overlords lived in luxury with the sea breeze to cool them in the heat of the day, the Prophet moved with a sure tread, preaching. He spoke simply that no man should own another in slavery, that no man should cringe to the whip, whether slave, worker, or free, that men should have some say in what happened to them in life.

I met him from time to time wandering the warrens among the slaves and the workers, speaking in words of fire, to be met with lackluster eyes and disillusioned shrugs, the sloughing away of all hope. He was constantly on the run from the guards. He was an object of pity and some affection to the workers, like a blind dog they would not see killed, and so they hid him and fed him and passed him along from hideout to hideout. In those runnels of ancient brick and mud walls, of crazy roofs and toppling walls and towers, an army could have been lost. The guards ventured into the ulterior at their peril, only in force.

For two days in every twelve the workers might return to their homes in the warrens, although often they contrived to spend more time there than that, until roused out by guards. Then the Prophet would speak to them, trying to inflame them, trying to arouse them.

Because he was an old man, even by Kregan standards, being, I suppose, about a hundred and eighty, his hair was white. His white mass of hair, his white beard, his white moustache, were merely the ordinary features of an old man, and their remarkable similarity to what one conceives of as a prophet's appearance was merely coincidental. His old eyes fairly snapped at me like a barracuda as he spoke, his voice a hoarse resounding trumpet easily audible a quarter of a dwabur away. Such men are known on our own Earth.

The guards, whether human or beast, seldom ventured into the slave warrens. Holly, Genal, and I were standing in a doorway listening to the Prophet, and both young people's faces were alight with their inner passions. They, at least, saw sense in what the Prophet said. Beneath scattered torchlight the mass of workers and slaves before us listened as at an entertainment; their spirits had been whip-broken. Then the shouts and shrieks broke out, the trample of iron-shod hooves, the clash of arms.

A party of mail-clad men rode in heavily from a side street, deploying instantly, yodeling and shouting, to come smashing into the mass of people. They were using their swords' edges. Blood spouted. The Prophet disappeared. Holly screamed. I grabbed her arm and Genal took her other hand and we dived back into the doorway. Even as the warped boards closed on us the mounted men hammered past.

"They're not after the Prophet," said Holly, her breast heaving, her eyes wide and wild. "This is sport for them, a great Jikai!"

I winced to hear that word in this contemptible context.

"Yes," said Genal viciously. "It is time for them to come hunting for fun." His eager voice broke. "For fun!"

"There is work for me tonight," said Holly. I stared at her. I had no idea what she meant. I was to find out.

Five

Bait for overlords

The Maiden with the Many Smiles, the largest moon of Kregen, floated free of cloud. Brilliant pink moonlight flooded down over the deserted square on the outskirts of the warrens. In many doorways human bright-eyed maidens waited. Given the size of the moon, almost twice that of Earth's satellite, the fullness and the brilliance of the night, the square was lit as brightly as many a daytime on Earth. In the shadows between the moonlight the girls waited. Presently, the soldiers, the mercenaries, the guards came. They carried money, presents, eager smiles, and manifold lusts.

In one shadowed doorway, only the long limber length of one shapely leg showing in moonlight, waited Holly.

"Are you sure?" I whispered to Genal.

"Yes. We have done this before."

"Quiet, you stupid calsanys!" Pugnarses spoke with venom and ill-concealed impatience. His balass stick was gone; now he clutched a cudgel made from homely sturm-wood. Genal also held a cudgel. We watched as the men in their ornate robes, their hair coiffed and perfumed, the rings glittering on their fingers, walked along the arcades and past the doorways of the square, gradually filling it as more and more appeared after the arduous day's tasks. Holly's leg looked almost indecently exposed and alluring, there in that streaming pink moonlight. Two other moons, also at the full, hurtled past low over the crazy rooflines of the warrens.

The men at arms were not wearing their mesh steel now. It would interfere in their delights of love.

One approached Holly. He was tall and saturnine, with a black down-drooping moustache and a mouth like a rast. He wore a gorgeous green robe, much bedecked with silver embroidery. His coin purse chinked as he walked. He had a long dagger belted at his waist.

Holly said: "Do I please you, master?"

His eyes appraised her boldly.

"You please me, wench, by your looks. But can you perform?"

"Come with me, master, and you shall taste delights such as the voluptuous Gyphimedes the immortal mistress herself never vouchsafed the beloved of Grodno."

The man's eyes brightened and his tongue-tip moistened his narrow lips. "You interest me, wench. Two silver oars."

I could guess Holly would be pouting, twisting her hips so as more excitingly to strain the thin material of the shush-chiff, the sarong-like garment worn by girls on festive occasions. "Three silver oars, master," she wheedled.

"Two."

Genal was fidgeting next to me, and Pugnarses rumbled thickly: "May Makku-Grodno take the girl! What does the money matter? Let her make haste!"

Genal said quickly: "She must act her part."

The bargain was struck at two silver oars and two copper oars — those tarnished coins of Magdag with the crossed oars on their reverses, a variety of vapid faces of Magdag overlords on their obverses. The man bent his head to follow Holly into the doorway, with a lascivious chuckle on his lips, his hands already reaching to strip away the shush-chiff. Genal and Pugnarses, one on each side of the door, struck the man over the head and as he collapsed soundlessly forward into my arms I dragged him bodily inside. Not one of us said a word. I stared at Holly in her shush-chiff and, indeed, she was exceedingly beautiful, young and fresh and soft, sweet with the promise of youth.

Then she went to stand once more flaunting her beauty insolently in the pink moonshine, as human bait.

That night, my first at the task, we picked up six men who wished to sample Holly's wares. We bound them and gagged them and took their finery, personal jewelry, money, and weapons. This facet of Holly amazed me; I saw she could act with all the sure purpose of a mature woman. The men would be sent into the warrens by certain paths Holly knew. From there, naked and bound, they would find their way into distant slave gangs over the other side of the building complex. It would be impossible to prove their identities when confronting the immediate response from the overlords and the guards, which was usually a blow to the head. Holly, however, seldom took even that risk. She usually insisted the men be sent to the galleys; who would not tremble at that simple phrase? Sent to the galleys.

When I asked why the hated overlords and guards were not killed out of hand, Genal looked at me as though I were mad.

"What?" he exclaimed. "Send them straight up to Genodras, to sit in glory at the right hand of Grodno, before they have suffered here on earth? I want to know they suffer, first, before they die and are received into the Green Glory."

I did not say anything.

What had impressed me as a vital element in the structure of the Eye of the World was that while the slaves believed in the red-sun deity, Zair, in general, the workers, whose allegiance should have wholeheartedly belonged to Grodno, were most lax and loose in their beliefs. This feeling that death would release them to go to their hopes of glory in the green sun was perhaps the strongest religious tenet they tolerated.

The surrounding countryside was terrorized by the mailed men. They took anything they wanted outside the immediate bounds of their city limits and the enormous machine-run, factory-type farms. By galley and by their mounted cavalry, they dominated the northern littoral. There were other cities on the northern shores, but none approached Magdag in size, power, or magnificence.

So far I had seen no zorcas or voves, those magnificent riding animals of Segesthes. The overlords rode a six-legged beast rather like a skittish mule, blunt-headed, wicked-eyed, pricked of ear, with slatey-blue hide covered with a scanty coarse hair that overlords trimmed and oiled. I wondered at their suitability as mounts; the six-legged gait is often awkward and uncomfortable for a rider. The riders did not wield lances, relying on their long swords. I saw little evidence of bows, and those I did see were the standard short, straight bow; neither the reflex compound bow of my Clansmen nor the long English yew bow were in evidence in Magdag. The riding beasts, the sectrixes, seemed to me good sturdy animals, although I doubted their hardiness; they did not, in my estimation, stand enough hands high to give a Clansman all the room he would like in which to swing his ax or broadsword.

More and more I was coming to see Magdag as a great builder's yard. The slaves and the workers, and occasionally the free artificers, lived in their tiny shacks of straw or lathe or mud brick tucked against the sides of the mighty buildings they were constructing or ornamenting. There was great richness in the buildings, masses of gold leaf and encrustation, acres of precious stones, porphyry, chemzite, chalcedony, ivory, kalasbrune, slabs of marble veined and pure, flashing in the suns. Inside the labyrinthine areas where the slaves gathered in the shadows, filth, and the smells there was only mud brick and clay and harsh stone, and miserly quantities of sturm-wood. The imbalances were great and terrible, greater, even, than my own Earth's at the close of the eighteenth century.

Inside these warrens was a kind of no-man's-land. The guards did not care to venture in unless in such force as to smash the slightest opposition. They did so enter, from time to time, to rout out skulkers, for there were many who sought to take sanctuary in the slaves' warrens.

It was Genal who apprised me of the latest plot.

In the maze of alleys and courts linking and separating the hovels and the slave compounds, we walked after a period of a two-day rest. We had disposed of a goodly number of guards, and the reaction was, as usual, brusque. A new guard commander for our gangs, those of Pugnarses and the other slave overseers, had been appointed. He was a man whose meanness was a byword. Already he had had Naghan's woman flogged to death, the bright blood spouting as her back was ripped down to bone, the flesh and blood hanging in striped ringlets of agony. The plan was to kill this overseer, this overlord of the second class, one Wengard, and his whole platoon, and then to make an escape and seize a galley from a harbor — any galley, any harbor.

"I do not like it, Genal," I said.

"Neither do I." He hunched his shoulders as we walked toward the brick works, surrounded by slaves and workers. I was aware that I knew little of the inner conspiracies that must fester continually in a situation like this. There must be gangs, clans, sects, mobsters and criminals, perverts and blackmailers, by the thousand in these sinks. The person who wished to lead this latest revolt was a Fristle, one called Follon. I had no love for Fristles. They were not true men. They had two arms and two legs, true; but their faces were like those of cats, bewhiskered, furred, slit-eyed, and fang-mouthed. Fristles had carried my Delia off to her captivity in Zenicce when I had been transplanted to that beach in far Segesthes.

"There are Chulik guards, now, under Wengard, the overlord of the second class," I said.

"Yes," agreed Genal. "But Fristles are hereditary foes of Chuliks, except when hired as mercenaries by the same employer."

"Who is not a foe of Chuliks?" I said carelessly, not wishing to continue the conversation. I felt sure the Star Lords did not wish me to become embroiled with a plan of rebellion that had almost no chance of succeeding.

"Follon, the Fristle, had told me, now he has asked me outright. Do we join — more particularly, as a stranger here, do you join?"

"No," I said.

I thought that would be an end to it.

All about us the noise, the buzz, the stink, the never-ending toil went on. Work and work and more work, under the lash and the knout, under the balass stick. We worked, we workers and slaves. We worked.

Follon approached me during the single break of the day when the suns stood overhead. His cat-face looked mean, the whiskers stiff and spiked.

"You, Stylor. We have seen you fight. We need you."

There were always fights and scrimmages in the warrens and as a stranger I had had to impress on my unwilling comrades that I was not a man to be trifled with. I had broken in a few heads in the proving of that, and Follon, the Fristle, had not missed that significance.

"No," I said. "You must find help elsewhere."

"We want you, Stylor."

"No."

He puffed himself up at me. He reached up to my chest. His cat-face showed an expression I could clearly read — anger, resentment, blind fury that I had denied what he asked, and, too, fear. Why fear? He thrust at me. I moved back two steps, not a stagger, a deliberate disengagement. He jumped in, hands raking. I sidestepped, and chopped down on the back of his neck. He went on going forward, forward and down. He stayed down.

A whip cracked agonizingly across my back and I turned to stare at Wengard, the overlord of the second class. His mail-clad arm was raised and the whip about to lash down again.

"Cramph! I will not tolerate fighting! Pugnarses! This is your man... Have him disciplined." As Pugnarses, sweating, ran up, Wengard said: "Stripe him with your balass, Pugnarses. No, you calsany, not now! After work, so that he may lie and suffer all night. I will inspect his back. I want to see blood, Pugnarses, blood and bone! And, tomorrow, I want to see him back at work."

The overlord prodded his foot into Follon's prone body.

"Take this stupid calsany away and when he awakes treat him in the same way. You hear, slave?"

"I hear, master," said Pugnarses. I saw his right fist contract on his balass stick, white like tallow, his knuckles like skulls. He dared not tell this mighty overlord that he was not a slave. The whip was poised, ready, hungry.

I rose to my feet and straggled off, prepared to endure a thrashing, of which I have had more than my share in life, rather than do anything that would upset the plans of the Star Lords and so hinder my eventual return to Strombor.

The mighty overlords could not be expected to know what slavery was like. Wengard, now, was serving as a slave-master because he must have committed some misdemeanor. Usually the overlords themselves only came to the workers' and slaves' warrens for sport — blood sport. I felt it would be very good to have Wengard and his ilk for a full day's work in the megaliths of Magdag.

As the twin suns dropped to the horizon, I prepared for my unpleasant interview with Pugnarses. He would not spare me for the fragile friendship we shared with Genal and Holly, for he was ambitious. One day he might, given luck, ruthlessness, and continuing health, become an overseer of overseers himself and wield a whip, clad in a white garment like the overlords themselves, giving his orders to the overseers of the balass. Pugnarses resented the fact that he had not been born an overlord.

Follon waited for me in the lath hut with its straw roof where I expected to find Pugnarses. I put down my clay tablet and laid the wooden implement carefully beside it. I moved gently, cautiously. A Fristle, suddenly appearing at the door, slammed it against the laths. In the sudden dimness I felt a thick net fall and envelop me. I heard a quickly-stifled uproar as Fristles jumped me.

"Pin his legs!"

"Smash his head in!"

"Kick him in the face!"

I lashed out, but the hampering net blunted my blows.

I saw the gleam of a dagger, a dagger like the one we had taken from the guard who had tried to sample Holly's fresh beauty. I tensed myself and then relaxed, ready to concentrate all my energy on that dagger. The door opened.

"Hold!"

I did not recognize the voice. Someone out of my vision was now giving quick, hissing instructions. I heard fragments. "Would you have him go straight to Genodras, to sit on the right hand of Grodno, in glory? Think, fools! Let him suffer for betraying us. Let him repent and repent again as he labors at the oars. To the galleys with him!"

I did not feel too grateful. Death — what was death to a man such as me? I had gained a thousand years of life by my baptism in the pool in the River Zelph that flows into the lake from which Aphrasöe, the Swinging City, grows. I had quivered at the thought, until I had found Delia of the Blue Mountains, and recognized that twice a thousand years would not be long enough to consume all the love I had for her.

It was my duty not to die while she lived. But, the galleys! I did not think much more. The sack in which they tied me was coarse and stinking and oppressive so that I struggled and gasped to breathe. Ignominiously, I was bundled down the secret slave ways from the warrens to the wharves and jetties of the harbor of Magdag.

After much bumping and stealthy movement I was flung down onto a wooden floor which moved with a swinging, familiar lilt. I was lying on a deck. Once more I was aboard a ship. I felt then the movement of the Star Lords — or the Savanti, those one-time friends of Aphrasöe — a movement I could neither understand nor explain.

Six

Zorg and I share an onion

The two onions balanced on Zorg's calloused palm were not the same size. One was, to speak in Earthly measurements, something over three inches in diameter, plump and round, its orange-brown outer skins shining, crisp, and flaky. We both knew its insides would be sweet and succulent, tangy and rich. The second onion looked like a slave beside a master: smaller, about two inches in diameter, with hard stringy outer skins already extending up into a growing neck of unpleasant yellow-green. It was scrawny. But it, too, would contain food to sustain us within its unlikely-looking skin.

We studied the onions, Zorg and I, as the fortyswifter *Grace of Grodno* heaved forward on the swell with that blessed quartering breeze filling the sail above us. Sounds of shipboard life rose all about us, with the smells as well. The twin suns of Scorpio blazed mercilessly down on our shaved heads. Our crude, round conical hats fashioned of straw gave pitiful protection. Of course, up on the poop — *Grace of Grodno* was of that class of galley not provided with a quarterdeck — the overlords of Magdag lolled at their ease in deck chairs beneath striped awnings of silk and mashcera, sipping long cool drinks and toying with fresh fruits and juicy meats. Our two naked companions on the bench had already shared their onions between them, onions of the same size.

"The choice is onerous, Stylor," said Zorg of Felteraz.

"Indeed, a weighty problem."

We would receive no more food until breakfast the next morning; we were only reasonably provided with water, and that was simply because *Grace of Grodno*, with her single square sail and arrogantly jutting beak, had caught a favoring breeze. We would make port in Gansk that evening, and sail again the next morning. The galleys of Magdag would venture on a cruise that would take them across the inner sea out of the sight of land for as much as four days at a stretch, but they did not like that. They preferred to hug the coast.

"If, my friend, we possessed a knife…"

Zorg had lost a lot of weight since I had first seen him, as a slave, in the colossal, empty hall of Magdag, dragging the idol of stone with me. The moment I had seen him again, after I had been transferred from the training liburna, I had made it my business to be near him when the oar-masters sorted us into benches. We had been oar companions now for a season — I had lost all count of days. On the inner sea, the Eye of the World, navigation even for galleys is possible for almost all of the season.

Zorg lifted the larger of the onions to his mouth. I simply looked at him. We had come to understand each other in these days. He regarded me with an expression that, for a galley slave, was as near to a reassuring smile as can be. He started to bite.

He bit swiftly and cleanly around the onion, his strong, yellow, uneven teeth chomping like a beaver's. He parted the onion into two not quite equal halves. Without hesitation he handed me the larger of the two.

I took it.

Then I handed him the smaller onion.

"If you value my friendship, Zorg of Felteraz," I said, with a ferociousness I had not intended, "you will eat this onion. Without argument."

"But, Stylor—"

"Eat!"

I do not pretend I enjoyed giving up part of my rations, but this man was clearly not as fit as he had been, or as he should be. And this was strange. It is well-known that if a man can survive as a galley slave for the first week he stands a chance of eventual existence; once he had become, as it were, pickled to the galley slave's life, he can endure unimaginable hardships and indescribable tortures. Once one has proved a galley slave, one can overcome obstacles of monstrous proportions. Zorg had come through the first terrible weeks when men were flogged to death daily at the benches and tossed overboard, when men's hands ran red with blood with no scrap of skin left on their palms or fingers, when they tore crazily at their ankles implacably fastened by the rings and chains, so that the blood and flesh oozed and scraped away to the bone.

The terrors of the galley slaves' lives are well known in the abstract. I lived through them.

Zorg made that peculiar grimace that in a galley slave passes for a smile and idly, automatically, nipped a nit that crept upon his weather-beaten and salt-crusted skin. The coarse sacks stuffed with straw were alive with vermin. We cursed the nits and all the other bloodsucking parasites, but we endured them because while they lived we had the sacking bundles of straw with their mangy coverings of ponsho skins upon which to fling ourselves. The idea of galley slaves rowing as we were, four to an oar with the whole bodily movement thrust and pulled and flung into the stroke, without some form of bench covering is ludicrous. Our buttocks would have been lacerated within the space of three burs; even the cruel oar-masters of Magdag recognized that. The ponsho skins, which covered the sacks and fell to the decks, were not there because we were loved; they were provided because without them the galley would not function.

I admit, I had become used to the smells — almost.

Life aboard a two-decker beating about in blockade gave one a flying start in enduring discomfort, dampness, stink, and short rations. I enjoyed advantages that Zorg, for all that he was a powerful man and had been galley captain, did not share.

Now his face held a shrunken look that worried me.

Nath, next along on the loom of the oar, burped and cocked an ear. Nath is a common name on Kregen; this Nath was big and had once been burly, for galley slaves tend to fine down. I had wondered how that other Nath, Nath the Thief in far Zenicce, would have fared in the galleys.

"Wind's changing," Nath said, now.

This was bad news to Zorg and to Zolta, the fourth on our oar. As an experienced sailor I had known the wind shift for perhaps ten murs, but I had wished to keep that unpleasant news from Zorg as he finished the onion.

Almost immediately, the silver whistles were heard.

The oar-master took his position in a kind of tabernacle midway in the break of the poop. The whip-deldars ran along the central gangway, ready to lay into the naked backs of the slaves if they were slow in readying themselves. We were not slow. More whistles sounded. A group of sailors handled the sheets, bracing the single sail around. They were an unhandy bunch, and I had time to relish the thought of how my petty officers would like to teach them the ways of the Navy aboard a frigate or a seventy-four. Clumsily, with a great deal of billowing and cracking of sheets, the sail came down. Long before it had been mastered and brailed we were all at the ready, one foot pressed on the stretcher, the other pressed against the back of the bench in front, our arms out, and our calloused hands grasping our oar looms. All the loop-ropes holding the oars clear of the water still outboard, a neat custom of the galley captains of the inner sea, had been removed by the outboard men, in our case Zolta, whose task that was.

Now *Grace of Grodno* rocked before the gentle swell, her forty oars all parallel, in perfect alignment above the water. She must have looked like some great waterwalking beast, light and graceful with her slender lines burgeoning into a richly decorated stern with its upflung gallery, lowering down into the ram and beak low over the water.

Grace of Grodno was a galley that, here in the Eye of the World, men called a four-fortyswifter: forty oars, four men to an oar. The clumsy system sometimes used on Earth of rating a galley by men to a bench was not used in the inner sea. The oars poised, ready. The drum-deldar beat once, a single, admonitory boom. I could see the oar-master as he looked up to where an officer leaned over the poop rail, all white and green and golden finery. No doubt they were savoring a little of our smell back there on the poop now. The officer had a handkerchief to his face. The oar-master lifted his silver whistle, and I collected myself, ready.

The whistle sounded, the drum boomed, all in a practiced series of sounds and orders, and every oar went down as one.

We pulled smoothly through the stroke. The drum-deldar beat out a steady rhythm, a double-beat of his two drums, one tenor and one bass, a smooth steady long-haul stroke. Our backs moved through the rhythm, forward so that our hands and the looms of our oars thrust above the bent backs of the slaves on the benches before us, then a steady — oh, so steady — pull.

Grace of Grodno moved through the water. She moved with the same feeling which had been so strange to me at the time I had stepped aboard that galley in the lake from which the City of Aphrasöe grows. Now, in this smooth inner sea, the galley surged ahead as though on tracks. She scarcely rolled at all, and she drove forward over the calm sea like a monstrous beetle with forty legs.

She was a relatively small galley. Only twenty oars on a side meant that her length was much below those of the fleet galleys I had seen in the arsenal harbor of Magdag, and, at a guess, I would say she was not above a hundred feet on the waterline. Again at a guess, for I never saw her broadside on from a distance, over-all she would not have exceeded a hundred and forty. I admit now that I had been puzzled by these swifters' possession of both ram and beak, thinking them mutu-ally exclusive, but I had learned just how the galleys of the inner sea were fought.

She was, of course, outrageously unseaworthy.

We labored at the oars with a smooth, short, economical stroke that would give us some two knots speed.

I, of course, had no idea what our mission was. I was merely a chained galley slave. As my body went through the unending mechanical motions of rowing, I pondered on that "chained slave" label. Between us, Zorg and I, we had been cau-tiously and carefully rubbing the link of the chain that bound us to the bench against a metal bracket-strut. Sweat-molded filth crammed into the growing breach concealed against discovery. As we bent forward and flung ourselves backward, over and over again, and the galley drove forward through the calm water, I could not help worrying over Zorg.

"Ease up, Zorg," I whispered to him when the whip-deldar had passed, vigilant in his patrolling of the gangway, his whip flicking, seemingly alive, hungry. The galley slaves called the whip "old snake." I knew the expression had been used on Earth. One could easily understand why.

"I — will — bear my part, Stylor—"

"I will push and pull that much more, Zorg." I was annoyed. He was a friend. I was worried about him. Yet he insisted stubbornly on pushing and pulling with the best, all out of his pride. Oh, yes, I knew the pride that burned in my friend Zorg of Felteraz.

"I am Zorg." He spoke in a low mumble. We could speak while rowing this easy stroke. "I am Zorg," he said again as though seeking to hold onto that, and then: "I am Zorg, Krozair! Krozair! I will never yield!"

I did not know what he meant by Krozair. I had not heard the word before. Nath rowed at the oar with a blind convulsion, his lean naked body panting for breath in the hot air. But Zolta looked across with a quick and rhythm-breaking suddenness. His face showed shock. I fought the oar back into rhythm, cursing in a lurid mixture of English, Kregish, and Magdag warren-filth.

We rowed.

I heard a hail.

Looking back toward the poop as I surfaced from each stroke I could see a turmoil up there. The awnings were coming down. That was good. Now their damnable surfaces would not catch wind and slow our progress. Men were running about up there. *Grace of Grodno*, I had been told, was more than a moderately fast galley for a four-fortyswifter, and in our cutting across a gulf in order to reach Gansk we had dropped the nearest land below the horizon.

It seemed to me as I rowed that I had been rowing all my life. Memories were faint around the edges, other worlds and other lives away. Only Delia of the Blue Mountains remained clear and beautiful to me in that time of inexpressible misery. I had been engaged as a galley slave in battles, when the galley of Magdag on which I served had captured a fat merchantman from one of the cities of Zair, and twice we had been involved in a real battle with a galley from Sanurkazz. But, so far, I had not been in action aboard *Grace of Grodno*. I did not know the ways of her captain or her oar-master, her whip-deldars or her drum-deldar in moments of emergency. Zorg and I had been through a lot together on the calm waters of the Eye of the World. Now, the signs were clear: *Grace of Grodno* was clearing for action.

The drum-deldar increased his beat.

We pulled into it, keeping time, hauling the heavy looms through their prescribed arcs as delimited by the rowing frames guiding and controlling the movements of the extreme inboard ends of the looms. As the inboard man I had the most space to move through, and we were graded downward and outward as to size, where Zolta, the smallest, perched almost over the water on the projecting deck-platform behind the parados.

Soon it became clear, from the way in which the officers, soldiers, and sailors were continually looking aft, that we were being pursued. There would therefore be little chance of the ram being brought into action. As though confirming that, a party of sailors appeared on the low foredeck — it was too small to be called a forecastle — and began to rig the forward extension of the beak. I heard shouting from the aftercastle at the extreme aft end of the poop. Soon an officer ran forward and the sailors began to unship the extension, amid a great deal of acrid comment.

Nath, his eyes upturned, his lungs pumping, spat out:

"So the Grodno-gasta thinks he'll fight! Ha!"

Grodno-gasta, I knew, was a blasphemous and extremely indelicate remark.

"Zair rot him!" snarled out Zolta, pulling.

We were now pulling at a back-breaking pace and still the drum-deldar stepped up the rate. Zorg was heaving now, not using his body as a good oarsman, but trying to do the work with his biceps. His face was a color that appalled me, slatey blue-green, something like the hide of a sectrix. He was gasping with a convulsive effort at each stroke.

"Sink me, Zorg!" I said viciously. "Roll with the stroke, you stupid man of Zair!"

He choked and did not have the spittle to hawk. His eyes rolled. He managed to croak out words: "I will never yield! Krozair! My vows — I am — Zorg! Zorg of — of Felteraz. Krozair!" He was rambling now, his body going up and down with the oar, hardly pulling a quarter of his weight. Then he used another name I had not heard before, and I knew that he was no longer with us aboard this foul galley of Magdag but far away: in delirium, yes, but not here with us. "Mayfwy," he said and, again, in a long sobbing groan: "Mayfwy."

He could not escape the observation of the whip-deldar much longer. Nath, Zolta, and I were pulling now with all the dead weight of Zorg hanging on the oar. Sweat reeked down our naked bodies. Then the green conical straw hat fell from Zorg's head and tumbled down.

Bareheaded, Zorg was the object of instant attention.

The whip-deldar lashed him. He laid the whip unerringly across my friend Zorg's back. Old snake talked to him.

Zorg's tanned skin split and blood oozed, then spouted out as the whip fell again and again. I, alongside, was splattered with the blood of my friend as the whip-deldar of Magdag flogged him to death.

"Get back to your oar!" roared the whip-deldar. "Pull!"

But Zorg of Felteraz was past all the pulling he would ever do in this life on this world of Kregen beneath Antares.

The confusion attendant upon freeing a dead slave from his shackles and throwing him overboard and replacing him with one of the oarsmen at the moment luxuriating in a spare capacity and chained deep in the hold, a luxury we all tasted in turn, was as nothing compared with the confusion evident on the poop. As the body of my friend Zorg, all naked and limp, with the blood dripping from his butchered back, was dragged out from the bench and hefted up to be thrown overboard, soldiers ran up to the aftercastle carrying bows. Others manned the ballistae. The sailors were readying their cutlasses. The confusion was abhorrent to me, as a man trained aboard a king's ship, but all my attention was required for the eternal rowing. Pull, pull, pull — and continue to pull. Once again the drum-deldar, under the shrilled commands from the poop, upped the rate.

I did not see Zorg consigned to the deep.

I did not see the splash his mutilated body made as it broke the surface of the water and vanished from mortal men's sight. I knew he believed that, after his death, he would go up to Zim to sit at the right hand of Zair, in all his glory. Suicides did not achieve this resurrection, either to the green or to the red, otherwise many of my fellow galley slaves would have found that shortcut to paradise.

I acted, I believe, out of pure animal instinct, out of hatred, out of sheer lust to kill and kill yet more of those wolves of Magdag. Yet I was a trained seaman, accustomed to handling ships, cunning in the use of wind and weather, and I knew that wolves of greater power than those of Magdag chased *Grace of Grodno*. If I say that instincts impelled me to foolhardy action that professional expertise would approve, that will perhaps best sum up what I then did.

As Zorg was taken from me, his shackles released, I put all my strength into breaking the last web of metal still joining the rubbed-through link. I surged up with such force that the loom of the oar cracked against the rowing frame. Nath and Zolta looked at me with numb faces, their bodies and arms going through the rowing motions that were ingrained into their muscles.

I felt stiff, tight about muscles abruptly trying to perform some different series of actions from those they had been forced into for hour after hour. The whip-deldar heard the crack of loom against rowing frame and came running, his whip high, his face vicious. I caught the lash in my left hand and jerked it and with my right hand I choked him around the throat. I threw him down among the slaves at the oars.

Then I was on the gangway.

So quick, so sudden, I stood there. I had once before seen a slave break from his oar. He had tried to dive overboard and sailors had caught him and held him, so that, later, the whip-deldar could cut him up with old snake.

I moved to the side, above the gawking faces of the slaves.

Four soldiers, in mail, their long swords swinging free, ran down the gangway toward me. My movement to the side convinced them I was going to dive and they hesitated, ready to let me go, willing to be rid of a fool slave who might, just might, be picked up by the following ship. Or so I read their hesitation. If I was picked up, the pursuer would have to slow his pursuit. I think they came to the decision that the pursuer would not stop, would not be fobbed off by a screaming face in the water. They started toward me again — and I was on them. My balled fist smashed in the face of the first. He had no time to scream. I grasped his long sword. It hissed in the air. I clove the second through his ventail and he toppled backward, horror on his face, blood staining the mesh.

"Grab him, you fools!" screamed a voice from aft.

I leaped and swung and my blade hewed into the side of the face of the third even as I avoided the fourth's blow. This was more like the sword fighting to which I had been accustomed aboard Earthly ships, boarding in the battle-smoke. It was very little like the rapier and dagger work of Zenicce.

I bunched my left hand into the fourth man, smashed my hilt down into his face, then I cast him from me.

Now the slaves were yelling.

They were making a hideous row, like vosks in swill, snorting and roaring and screaming. I raced aft down the gangway.

The oar-master in his tabernacle saw what I intended.

He leaped up, shrieking: "Bows! Strike him down!"

I hauled myself up one-handed to the tabernacle and even as he tried to clamber out I cut him down. The drum-deldar had even less chance. The passion of my blow rolled his head down along the gangway for several yards before it toppled off into the rowing benches.

Soldiers were milling, running down the ladders from the poop.

So far I had not uttered a word.

Now, as the soldiers came running, I raced before them along the gangway. The first whip-deldar lay dead, but his mates were flogging the slaves on in an attempt, a desperate attempt, to keep the rhythm of the stroke. But the rhythm had been lost with the death of the drum-deldar.

Their whips were no defense against the long sword. Both whip-deldars went down, the one from amidships and the other from the bows. The mail-clad men were roaring now, pouring toward me. I lifted my voice.

"Men!" I roared. "Galley slaves! Stop rowing! Ease oars! The day of judgment is at hand!"

It was a melodramatic way of putting it, yet I knew the type of man I was dealing with in those whip-beaten galley slaves of Magdag. Some banks of oars faltered, the rhythm went wild, and then, because oars must of necessity swing together or they can do nothing, the larboard and the starboard wings of *Grace of Grodno* fluttered uncontrollably and clashed and fell silent. The looms went inboard. The slaves were now making so much noise I felt convinced the men of the pursuing galley, men and galley I had not yet seen, must hear them and take heart and know their time was near.

An arrow feathered into the gangway near me. I started aft again. I had not had a sword in my fist for too long. I am no believer in the joy of battle, the uplifting surge of blood, the way some men speak of their exaltation in battle. I do not enjoy killing; that, at least, the Savanti had had no need to teach me. But now — something about my whole series of experiences since reaching this inner sea, this Eye of the World, impelled me to a stereotyped reaction. Hatred, revulsion, anger, all were there and mixed in my motives. I felt a savage exultation as my long sword bit into the heads and bodies and limbs of my opponents.

I was young then, a sailor with a grievance, and I swung a mean sword. I roared at them, smiting and striking and lopping. It was necessary to strike with great force to cut through the mail, or so to smash it in as to pulverize what lay beneath. Mail-clad men fight slowly when they hack and slash. They must put extra weight and power behind each blow.

Because of my galley slave training, because of that baptism in the sacred pool of lost Aphrasöe, because my arm was nerved by dark impulses of hatred and revenge, I struck each blow with swift force, smiting and smiting the enemies of Zair who had killed my friend Zorg of Felteraz.

I do not know how long it went on. I only know that I felt a wave of resentment, of disappointment, when the galley lurched and rolled, the harsh grating bump from aft shocked us all forward, and men in mail with gleaming long swords poured over the poop. They wore red plumes in their helmets. They struck down with quick and cunning skill and swamped across *Grace of Grodno*. In the bedlam I heard the fresh and horrific screams from the galley slaves.

I felt a treacherous lurch beneath my feet and a soggy feel of the deck.

The galley was sinking. The men of Magdag had opened her sides in some way, opening them to the sea, willing all to death in their final defeat.

Now there were no men left of Magdag between me and the men of Zair, the red-sun deity, the men from the south.

"The galley is sinking," I said, to one who stepped toward me, his long sword reeking, yet not so befouled with blood as mine. "The slaves must be freed — now!"

"It will be done," he said. He looked at me. He stood as tall as I did, broad and limber, with a bronzed open face with that same set of arrogance to his beak of a nose that my friend Zorg had possessed. His thick dark moustache was brushed upward. The men of Magdag wore down-drooping, hangdog moustaches.

"I am Pur Zenkiren of Sanurkazz, captain of *Lilac Bird*." On the white loose garment he wore over his mail a great blazing device coruscated in my eyes. A circle, it seemed, a hubless spoked wheel within the circle, embroidered with silks of brilliant orange, yellow, and blue. "And you, a galley slave, I assume?"

"Yes," I said. I remembered things I had almost forgotten. "A galley slave. I am the Lord of Strombor."

He looked at me keenly. "Strombor. It seems, I think, I have heard — but no matter. It is not of the Eye of the World."

"No. It is not."

Slaves were being cut free from their shackles, were leaping up, screaming and weeping in their joy, scrambling over the ornate poop to the beak of *Lilac Bird*. Pur Zenkiren made a motion with his long sword, all bloody as it was, a kind of salute.

"You, the Lord of Strombor, a stranger. How is it you came to be fighting the heretics of Magdag, and taking their galley?"

The twin suns of Antares were less hot now, the emerald and the ruby, sinking to the sea horizon. I looked at the long sword, at the blood, at the dead men, at the slaves in all their wretched nakedness leaping for joy as they scrambled across the poop.

"I had a friend," I said. "Zorg of Felteraz."

Seven

A blow makes and breaks

If I seem to you to have passed somewhat lightly over my experiences working in the building complexes of Magdag or to have been less than open in what I have said about my life as a galley slave on the swifters of Magdag, I feel I owe no explanation. Of misery and pain and despair we all know there is enough and to spare, both on our own Earth and on the world of Kregen that I made my own. The long periods I spent under duress passed. That is all. Like black clouds passing away before the face of Zim, the times of agony and humiliation passed.

The hatred I bore the men of Magdag was perfectly natural, given the circumstances of my birth and upbringing, for the Navy does not tolerate weaklings and my training had been harsh and uncompromising. Only in later years have I attained to any little maturity of outlook I may possess, and this, I confess freely, has been brought about in large measure by the liberating influences breaking out on this Earth, for Kregen remains as savage, demanding, and merciless as always.

I have experienced great joy in my life, and Delia of Delphond has been my great and consoling power of the spirit; I owe most of what humanity I possess to her. Now, released from mind-killing and body-exhausting toil, I was free once again and I can remember with what wonder and the light of fresh eyes I looked about me on the deck of *Lilac Bird* as *Grace of Grodno* sank, bubbling, beneath the blue waters of the Eye of the World.

No, it is not necessary to detail my feelings about the men of Magdag, the men of Grodno. If I say that little Wincie, a cherry-lipped, impish-eyed, tousle-headed slip of a girl of whom I was very fond, had been killed in a most barbarous fashion, it conveys little. Her task was to bring the skins of water for the brick making and to slake our thirsts; the mailed men on one of their sporting sorties had caught her and had, as you twentieth century moralists would phrase it, gang-raped her. These are words. The reality in agony, blood, and filth is a part of the mosaic of life. It does not need to be dwelled on to make my position — the young man I then was, harsh, relentless, vicious to those I hated, malignant in my cherished feelings of injustice — clear enough to the dullest of minds.

Now they had flogged to death my friend, Zorg of Felteraz.

Not all the slaves had come weeping with joy aboard the swifter from Holy Sanurkazz. Some had wailed and resisted. These were prisoners of Magdag, men sentenced to the galleys for some crime and with the eventual prospect of freedom before them. Now they would become the galley slaves of their hereditary enemies. Life was stark and brutal on the inner sea.

Lilac Bird interested me. She was a larger galley than *Grace of Grodno*, although not of the largest size that plowed these waters. I gathered her speed had given her captain, Pur Zenkiren, some concern, as she was new and he had had high hopes of her. She was a seven-six-hundred swifter. Simply, this means she had a hundred oars, arranged in two banks with seven men on the upper bank at each oar and six on the lower, two banks of twenty-five oars a side. I thought her length insufficient in proportion to her beam, given the ridiculous shapes of galleys, anyway; her draft was still too deep, caused by the weights, than was desirable for the swiftest of galleys. I caught myself. Here I was, starting to think like a sailor again.

"You are feeling fit in yourself, my Lord of Strombor?" Pur Zenkiren spoke pleasantly as we sat in his plain after quarters, with the arms in their racks, the charts upon the table, the wine glasses and bottle between us. They did not use beckets or swinging tables; they wouldn't venture out if a storm was brewing.

"Fit, thank you, Pur Zenkiren. I owe you my liberty — I had some concern that you might return me, a stranger, to the benches."

He smiled. His face was weather-beaten, his eyes dark and penetrating, and that arrogant beak nose lifted at times so that, for a heartbreaking moment, I would catch that glimpse of Zorg. Zenkiren, like Zorg, had a mass of black curly hair, shining and oiled and remarkably romantic, I have no doubt.

"We followers of Zair have a respect for a man, my Lord of Strombor."

A single chart, of remarkably poor quality, hopeless accuracy, and miniscule scale, had been found in the locker, which showed Strombor. The whole coastlines outside the inner sea were incorrect, but the names were marked down: Loh, Vallia, Pandahem, Segesthes, with Zenicce marked and, alongside in a panel, the names of the twenty-four Houses of Zenicce, both noble and lay. The fascinating thing here was that Strombor was marked and Esztercari was not, proving the map to have been drawn well over a hundred and fifty years before.

"We have a little contact with the outside world, mainly with Vallia and Donengil, but we are an inward-looking people. The main effort to which we are all dedicated is defiance and resistance to the power of Grodno, no matter when, how, and where such a resistance shall be made."

I looked at him. He spoke as though out of rote. Then he smiled at me again, lifted his glass, and said: 'To the ice floes of Sicce with Magdag and all her evil spawn!"

"I'll drink to that," I said, and did so.

They had given me a decent white loincloth and I had washed and rubbed scented oils on my body, and I had eaten real food again. Now, sitting drinking with the captain of the swifter, I felt human once more — or, I reminded myself, as human as I would ever feel while the canker of Grodno and Magdag continued to exist.

My feelings were made very plain to Zenkiren, who had sized me up to his satisfaction, as he thought.

The many parallels of the red-green situation in the Eye of the World to that old battle between Esztercari and Strombor had occurred to me; although I found greater contrast and interest in the Catholic and Islamic conflicts of the late Renaissance, or the bitterness between Guelf and Ghibelline. I was aware, too, that the greater malice seemed always to exist between those whose beliefs

165

had diverged from a single origin. The people of the sunset, the old original in-habitants of the Eye of the World, had built well and industriously to produce the Grand Canal and the Dam of Days, that terrifying structure I had not yet seen. They had also built fine cities, some ruined and lost, some ruined and partially rebuilt, now inhabited by the newer men who had split from the old red-green comradeship.

"Those vile cramphs of Magdag," Zenkiren said to me as we voyaged back to Sanurkazz. "We know how they build. They are obsessed by building, diseased by it."

"It is destroying their culture, their life," I said.

"Yes! They think to find favor in the sight of their evil master, the false deity Grodno the Green, by every act of building, every new construction of mon-strous proportions. They bleed their countryside dry for workers and wealth. So, then they must raid and ravage us in order to replenish their stock."

"I saw a farm, a massive affair, very well-run and producing—"

"Oh, yes!" Zenkiren waved a dismissive arm. "Of course! They have millions to feed; they must produce food, as we must. But they raid us continually and take our young men and our girls and children for their consuming buildings."

"You raid them."

"Yes! It is the glory of Zair laid upon us." He looked at me and hesitated; it sur-prised me, for he was a fine captain and a man who knew his mind. "You were the friend of Zorg of Felteraz. I have heard from Zolta of that. You are a Lord. I think—" Again he hesitated, and then, in a slower and softer voice, asked: "Did Zorg speak to you of the Krozairs of Zy?"

"No," I said. "He used the word Krozair when he was dying. He seemed — proud, then."

Zenkiren changed the flow of conversation, then, and we spoke of many things as *Lilac Bird* rowed steadily toward the south. She was followed by two other swifters, smaller galleys in this swift raiding squadron under Zenkiren's command. They had snapped up three plump merchantmen as well sinking *Grace of Grodno*, and the merchantmen wallowed along aft.

In all honesty I must admit I did not even think it strange that Zenkiren should take my word that I was the Lord of Strombor. I was beginning to adopt the attitudes of mind of the leader of a House of Zenicce, and my years as Vove-deer and Zorcander with the Clansmen had given me the air of habitual authority. But I believe Zenkiren would not have cared had I been the lowliest of foot soldiers, for he did everything merely because he knew that I had been the friend of Zorg of Felteraz and had avenged his death.

I was convinced the word Krozair linked these attitudes. I had seen, as *Grace of Grodno* finally sank, the air bubbling out and the timbers breaking free and shooting up, a white dove circling *Lilac Bird*. That dove heartened me. Could it be, I wondered, that the Savanti were taking a hand again? Could they be con-firming my continued existence on Kregen even though I had been forced away from Magdag? I looked for the Gdoinye, the scarlet and golden raptor; I did not see it.

166

Zenkiren had been taking a considerable risk in sailing so close to the north-ern shore. He had been on the lookout for choice tidbits in the way of Magdaggian merchantmen and the fortyswifter had been a delectable item to snap up. We did not know why she had been en route to Gansk, and perhaps we never would learn. Zenkiren's concern had been for *Lilac Bird*'s disturbing lack of speed. Only my intervention with the consequent interruption in the pulling of the fortyswifter had given him the chance to overhaul her, and then the Sanurka-zzan galley had reached up so swiftly there had been no need to use the ballistae mounted in her bows.

The ballista used on the ships of the Eye of the World was called a varter, and it was a true ballista, in that its propulsive energy came from two half-bows whose butts were clamped in perpendicular thongs twisted many times. The cord was drawn by a simple windlass. The varter could be adapted to shoot arrows, or bolts, large iron-tipped monstrous balks of timber, or to hurl stones. It could achieve a considerable degree of accuracy.

Every sixth day on ships of Sanurkazz the religious observances connected with Zair were solemnly undertaken with due rites and prayers. Religion, I had thought, was the sop for the masses, along with bloodthirsty broadsheets detail-ing the latest murders and hangings, cockfights, prizefights, and the occasional tankard of ale at the local alehouse. Religion kept the masses in order. These men of Sanurkazz, however, well though I might mock them in the privacy of my own thoughts, were very splendid in their best clothes, the ship-priest in his vest-ments, the silver and gold vessels, the blazing embroidery of the banners and flags, the shrilling notes of the silver and ebony trumpets, all conspiring to se-duce any solid man into an euphoric haze of belief.

Naturally, the day on which the rites of Zair were performed was not the same day as that on which Grodno was similarly honored.

I say similarly; I had seen the religious services of the men of Magdag, and they were different in a way that, looking back, I can see was no different at all. Then, I considered them depraved and evil.

It seems obvious that there was only one color which the men of Magdag could paint the hulls of their swifters. The ancient pirates of Greece, who roamed the Aegean, used to paint their hulls green. The men of Sanurkazz had struck a compromise. Green was of some use as a camouflage color; not much, a little. Red would have been some degrees more visible, so the galleys of the men of Zair of the southern shore of the inner sea were painted blue.

They carried three sets of sails in more or less regular use: white for daytime cruising, black for night sailing, and blue for raiding.

On this voyage back to Holy Sanurkazz, a voyage which was something in the nature of a victory triumph, we wore white sails.

Magdag stood upon the northern shore of the inner sea over to the western end; her power and law ran for many dwaburs toward the east until it tended to diminish a little as cities with their own marine wished to flex their own muscles of independence. All, however, were in some way tributary to Magdag, and all, naturally, were partisans of the green.

Holy Sanurkazz stood upon the southern shore of the inner sea over toward the eastern end, at the narrow neck of one of the dependent seas that extended southward. Her hegemony stretched in somewhat different ways from her opponent's toward the west, where cities flourished which grew steadily weaker and less assured the farther west they had been sited. All, however, owed a single burning allegiance to the red.

It seemed clear that the strategy dominating the inner sea would be that of raiding to keep the opponent occupied, and a series of direct and violent blows against the chief hostile city. With either Magdag or Sanurkazz reduced, the other cities of the losing side would, like children deprived of parents, quickly succumb. This was a strategy that had not found favor with either the men of Magdag or Sanurkazz. The answer was obvious enough and human enough not to surprise me. Booty was for the taking upon the seas, and to strike against a smaller city was infinitely safer than any direct assault against the master citadel.

Stretching my legs on the tiny extent of quarterdeck boasted by *Lilac Bird*, I saw Zolta below me thoroughly enjoying himself on the central gangway. He strode up and down, clad like myself in a clean white loincloth, flourishing a whip and every now and then laying into the galley slaves. We were bucking a nasty little wind, and I had cocked my eyes at the clouds more than once.

"Hai, Zolta!" I called down.

He stared back and up, his face brown and cheerful, his black eyes glittering. He cracked the whip with a snap.

"I am collecting interest, Stylor!" he shouted up.

The drum-deldar quickened his beat. The bass and the tenor drums boomed closer together. On the ships of Zair the drum-deldar sits forward of the rowers, in the belief, I gathered, that the sounds would carry more speedily to the oarsmen on the benches. Above the heads of this top bank of oarsmen a light, fighting platform ran around above the bulwarks of the galley where fighting-men could stand in action. Below them, the lower bank of oarsmen were tugging at their shorter and more sharply angled oars. With seven men to a loom, monstrous oars could be wielded. Zolta, with his borrowed whip, intended to see the oars were moved, and sharply. The whip-deldar, from whom Zolta had so unofficially taken over, was standing talking to the oar-master in his tabernacle just below me, and laughing at the antics of Zolta.

So my friends who owed allegiance to the red-sun deity, Zair, used slaves too. Could I have expected anything else? I did know that slavery was practiced mostly aboard their swifters. In their cities normal citizens carried out work, in a way that made sense to an Earthman with a European heritage, and the few slaves were mostly for personal body service.

I looked out over the larboard beam and the clouds there lowered, more black and ominous than they had been half a bur before. I had no wish to interfere with Zenkiren in his handling of his ship. Aft of us the two trailing galleys plunged heavily, and spume broke and burst from their prows. The merchantmen were riding the seas more easily and I saw they had reduced canvas.

Zenkiren stepped out on deck.

The oar-master popped up his little ladder from the tabernacle with its solidly-bolted door. He gestured to larboard.

"I see, Nath," said Zenkiren. "We must weather this out."

This Nath, again, was another of that common name, and not my Nath the Thief, or my oar-mate Nath, who was spending his time playing any one of the many gambling games of Kregen with the released slaves below decks.

Lilac Bird was beginning to roll now in a devilishly uncomfortable corkscrew fashion. Long and thin galleys are no sea boats. Some of the oars faltered as white water broke. The oar-master dived back to his place as the drum-deldar thumped a slower rate, and the whip-deldar jumped along the central gangway below the parados and took the whip from Zolta.

We were in for a blow.

Storms, hurricanes, typhoons, cyclones — gales of all descriptions are no news to me. The gale that overtook us now was such as to give me no cause for alarm at first. Why, snug aboard a seventy-four, or even a thirty-eight frigate, on blockade, we would scarcely have bothered over this blow. However, the swifters of the inland sea were primitive fighting machines, not the sophisticated sailing machines on Nelson's Navy, and *Lilac Bird* behaved like a bitch of the sea. She twisted, she hogged, she sagged, she pitched and yawed and rolled and when she did roll she sent thrills through me I'd forgotten existed.

We smashed ten oars before they were all safely inboard and stowed. That operation — I had had to carry it out myself as a galley slave — is a miserable proceeding. Then covers were dragged out by the sailors and lashed over all the openings in the upperworks. *Lilac Bird* stuck her nose down and heaved like a rooting ferret. I snatched a glance aft and saw the two galleys like matchsticks in the sea, foaming up and down, great spouts of white water crashing upward from their slim bows.

The merchantmen were out of sight. The clouds lowered down and the sky grew black; rain began to fall. That cheered me up a little, but the way this broomstick of a craft was behaving was enough to alarm any sailor. And I had considered she should be longer!

The two rudder-deldars were yelling for help and reliefs rushed high upon the poop to grasp the rudder handles, to control the two paddle-shaped rudders, one on each quarter. Even as they reached the poop the galley rolled and squiggled in her snakelike fashion. To a groaning of timbers and sheets of spray flying inboard the starboard rudder snapped across.

Lilac Bird lurched to starboard, her larboard rudder almost out of the water. She spun around and water and wind smote her without mercy. Zenkiren had been standing near me, shouting to his men. As his ship lurched it caught him unexpectedly so that he staggered, tottered across the deck, and hit his head hard against the break of the poop. He dropped to the deck, senseless.

His second in command, a certain Rophren, jumped up, his face an unhealthy color. He stood shaking.

Now, through the sleeting smash of the spray and the whine of the wind, we could hear, clear and close and ominous, the roaring sound of great waves battering rocks.

"It is all finished!" shouted Rophren. "We must jump for it — we must abandon the swifter!"

I went up to him quickly. I hit him alongside the jaw and I did not bother to catch him as he fell.

The galley heaved up and down beneath me as I ran back.

"Keep on that rudder!" I shouted at the deldars there. "Hold her when she comes around."

Then I ran forward, pushing past the spray-drenched whip-deldars who stared upon me with frightened, puzzled faces. At the main mast I collared some of the sailors skulking there and kicked them into hoisting a scrap of the sail, the yard braced hard up diagonally across the deck. Wind filled that bit of sail at once, pouting it out, hard and drumming. But the galley responded, impossible sea boat though she was. The foremast yard I had likewise braced hard around. We were drifting away to leeward like a bit of driftwood. Down there, iron-fanged rocks awaited us. Now, through the gloom, I could just make out the spout and leap of spray.

I had a moment of doubt that we could weather that fanged pile of rock.

We were being carried broadside on downwind.

"Keep that rudder hard down!" I bellowed into the wind.

Slowly, slowly, we were forereaching on the rocks. But, I thought, too slowly, too slowly.

Spray stung my eyes and I brushed it impatiently away.

I dared not hoist any more canvas; the galley would simply spring away like an arrow and impale herself on the rocks if she did not simply roll over in the first few moments before her head came around. Water broke over her in torrential sheets.

I clung on and hoped.

Rophren had regained consciousness. He had a group of officers with him as he approached me. Their faces showed the fear of the sea corroding within them, the hatred of me.

"You — the Lord of Strombor! You are under arrest!" Rophren spoke flatly, his fear shrieking at the end into his words so that he stammered over them. "We are all doomed — because you stopped me giving the order! We could all have jumped when I said and been saved — now we are too close to the rocks! Cramph! You have killed us all!"

A youngster with a florid face and close-set eyes whipped out his long sword.

"He won't go under arrest! For I shall cut him down — now!"

The long sword glimmered silver in the spray, high over my head. It slashed down.

Eight

Nath, Zolta, and I carouse in Sanurkazz

I moved sideways and I kicked that florid-faced young man where I had kicked Cydones Esztercari, neatly, making him double up and retch all over the sea-wet deck. I took the long sword away. I held it so that Rophren and his friends could see it.

"Countermand a single order I have given," I said, "and you die."

Their hands bunched on their sword hilts. They were proud, arrogant men, used to command. They lurched on the decks as the galley surged and bucked and fought the sea. I stood there, limber and straight, balanced, and the sword in my fist maintained a steady arc upon them.

Whether they would have charged me, desperate in their ill-founded belief that I was consigning them all to a watery grave, whether they would have remained, like chained leems, snarling and impotent, I do not know. I rather suspect the latter, for I have been told that when I, Dray Prescot, challenge a man with a sword in my fist I present a most daunting and unhealthy spectacle.

As they stood there, wet, miserable, and frightened, facing the boiling sea or the bright menace of my sword, a sharp hail lifted from the bows.

Up there Nath, my Nath of the galley bench, perched. He pointed and waved a dripping arm.

"Clear, Stylor!" he screamed. "We're clear!"

We looked, those men like chained leems, and I. The rocks were moving astern of us, their spouting white-fanged venom dropping astern as we pulled away. Slowly, struggling for every inch, *Lilac Bird* labored her way past that cruel point of rock and so weathered the cape and we could run more comfortably into the gulf beyond.

After that it was merely a matter of a routine court of inquiry when Zenkiren regained consciousness. Rophren was placed under arrest. The florid-faced young man, Hezron of High Heysh, also was placed under arrest; but in his presence I spoke for him, knowing this had been his first cruise as an officer aboard a swifter and this his first storm.

"The dangers of the sea vary in proportion as one comes to know them," I said. "I do not hold it against Hezron that his untutored fear impelled him to seek to kill me. Perhaps he may hold it against me that I kicked him between wind and water."

Zenkiren did not smile; but I was watching his face as he sat in the seat of judgment at his table, with the other officers present and the glowering, pasty-faced Rophren between two men-at-arms, and I thought he might have smiled at another time. Zenkiren was a jolly man who loved a good belly laugh despite his ascetic brilliance.

"What do you say to that, Hezron?"

171

Hezron of High Heysh lifted his head. He was a boy who was used to throwing his weight about, that was clear, a member of a rich and powerful family in Sanurkazz.

"I do not forget an injury," he said, and his words splintered in the cabin as *Lilac Bird* pulled toward the harbor. "I shall hold it against you that you demeaned me, that you dared lay a hand on me. I, Hezron of High Heysh. You will not forget that lightly, barbarian."

I looked at him. I had heard the opprobrious epithet barbarian applied to me, as a stranger from the outer seas, more than once, but never like this, never with so much venom. I thought of the galleys of the inner sea, I thought of their fighting qualities, and I wondered. Those ships of Zenicce, which city was not popular on the outer oceans, and the wide-ranging fleets of Vallia, were they fashioned by barbarians? Was the gorgeous enclave city of Zenicce barbarous? If it was, it was of a form and style of barbarity these swifter-men of the Eye of the World could not understand.

"If you wish to make an issue of that," I said, and I know I spoke in a harsh and barbaric voice, "you are welcome to meet me at any time with weapons in our hands."

"That is enough of that!" said Zenkiren. He looked annoyed. "Only through the courage and skill of the Lord of Strombor was *Lilac Bird* saved." He made a face. "Both our consorts were lost." This was true. Their timbers were washed up over the days that followed, with dead bodies. The slaves, where they floated ashore on balks of timber, were still chained to those timbers.

Rophren was remanded to await judgment by the court of the high admiral. That was what, in effect, he was, although his Kregish title ran for five lines of purple prose.

Hezron of High Heysh was reprimanded, and then released, on the authority of Pur Zenkiren, and at my behest. It made no difference to Hezron's attitude to me. I knew I would have to guard my back where he was concerned.

We ran into the outer harbor of Holy Sanurkazz.

I have, as I have said, seen many cities, and I was looking forward to the view of the chief city of the followers of Zair. I expected — looking back, it is foolish, I can see, to expect anything until the reality is there before you, living and real.

Sanurkazz had been sited on the narrow neck of land stretching between the inner sea and the smaller dependent sea, the Sea of Marshes, which formed a kind of blunt arrowhead, the two sharp faces washed by the waters and the base walled off by a girdling wall of six curtains. There were many buildings, some of noble proportions and in a kind of columnar architecture I found pleasant enough. A great deal of warm yellow stone was used that was quarried some few dwaburs along the shore. The tiled roofs were red. Much lush vegetation grew riotously among the houses and along the avenues and streets. There were also many flat walled roofs made into bright gardens, and water mills pumped water to flow into fountains that tinkled tirelessly throughout the city. The markets were exuberant, noisily filled with the clink of coins, the sounds of calsanys, the cries of vendors. In the streets of the crafts there was the eternal noise of the craftsmen's hammers as they beat out bronze, gold, or silver, or the whir of wheels as they fashioned the pots with the bold red designs, or worked the leather which glistened with strength and suppleness and which was famed throughout the inner sea.

Oh, yes, Sanurkazz was a marvelous city, filled with life, ardor, and animation. The harbors were cunningly sited so as to obtain perfect protection from the weather and from any corsair attack by sea. The arsenals were cleverly placed so as to be mutually protected. The domes and spires of the temples pierced the brilliant air.

Oh, yes, Sanurkazz was delightful. It was a city in which to be alive. Magdag was a city of colossuses, of towering buildings marching endlessly into the plain, of work, toil, and a demanding discipline, machinelike, obsessed. Sanurkazz was a city of individuals.

But — there was not a single central fact about Sanurkazz. It was a collection of individuals. It charmed. It had marvelous byways, courts, and tree-shaded bowers where flowers bloomed in brilliance and perfume; it had marvelous inns, pot houses, and roistering spots. I enjoyed myself in Sanurkazz. But I sensed that it lacked that obsessive single-minded purpose of Magdag.

The conflict between red and green was not a clear-cut contest between good and bad. Although at that time I was willing to credit all evil to Magdag, I believe I do not flatter myself if I say that I was capable of perceiving that there were grave flaws in Sanurkazz. It was an intensely human place. I suppose the best way to sum up Holy Sanurkazz would be to say that it roistered in the sun. Carousing was a devotedly followed occupation. Then, every sixth day, the whole city gave itself over to the intensely religious observances connected with the worship of Zair, the red-sun deity.

The women of Sanurkazz were a luscious lot, full-breasted, lithe, sensuous of lip and saucy of eye. To them the idea that a woman should veil herself before venturing on the streets would have smacked of perversion. With Zenkiren's promise that he would employ me aboard *Lilac Bird* — in a capacity on which we would agree — I had money to jingle in my purse, a white apron to wear, and a long sword at my side slung from a belt and harness fashioned from that wonderful Sanurkazz leather.

Out on the fertile fields south of the city and alongside the Sea of Marshes agriculture proceeded on the basis of small farming, with estates of the nobles dotting the countryside. Beyond them, further south, the plains began and here herds of chunkrah roamed. I promised myself I would ride out one day and spend some time with the chunkrah and think of my Clansmen of the Great Plains of Segesthes. Southward again and the climate grew drier and the deserts extended, bleak and orange and harsh. I understood that beyond the deserts lay the coastal lands of Donengil, but almost invariably these would be reached by ship through the Great Canal. Donengil, I guessed, would have a climate very much like the West Indies, on a vaster scale.

Industry of an essential hand-worked kind existed on a surprisingly large scale. There were iron works, and bronze works, manufactories for the production of swords and the supple mesh steel, mining and logging and weaving, all the necessary facilities to maintain a city-state like Sanurkazz. I visited the extensive forests, and saw lenk and sturm growing, saw the cedars and the pines on the uplands to the southwest, saw the way in which the shipwrights selected timbers from the living tree, and placed forms around them so that they would grow into the required shapes for keel arches, or stern-posts, or any other of the necessary ship shapes.

The people of Kregen are not all in the same stage of evolutionary industrial or social or political growth, of course. Steam bending of wood was known: indeed, for the building of galleys such as *Lilac Bird*, it would be essential. The ancients of Earth without knowledge of steam bending were forced to use green wood with the sap in so that they could bend the timbers to shape. The wood warped and very soon the ships leaked and became useless. The galleys of the Greeks were essentially light craft, with one man to an oar, designed to ram. The Romans with the corvus, the studded gangplank for boarding, attempted to bring land-fighting techniques to the sea, but their ships were still slightly built. With Earth's Renaissance and the galleys of the Catholic powers against those of the Muslims, the galley reached a new development. It is hardly correct to say, as so many do, that these last galleys were the direct descendants of those of ancient Greece and Rome.

With one man to one oar, as was universal among the ancients, with the trireme's sets of seats in threes, slanting back toward the stern, with oars of from about fifteen feet in length to about eight feet, with the thranites, the zygites, and the thalamites pulling those oars, with their everlasting baling caused through warping timbers consequent on the use of green wood, and with all their early effort concentrated on quick ramming, rolling the sinking galley off the ram and a smart backwater, the ancient Greek triremes must have been finely tuned instruments. The confusion attendant upon a single oarsman losing his stroke must have worried the trierarch as much as anything else. One man to one oar set a very definite upper limit to the power it was possible to transmit. These sailors of the Eye of the World had gone for the later system, the arrangement *alla scaloccio*; but, with a daring I found admirable, had concentrated their propulsive power into two or three banks. While technically correct to call *Lilac Bird* a bireme, and the other large galleys of the inner sea triremes, I shall stick to what the Kregans themselves called them — swifters.

Wind scoops of a pattern I was familiar with directed fresh air below decks, and many gratings and openings gave free ingress for ventilation. Despite that, the lower rowing deck, where the thalamites sat and sweated, presented a spectacle of hell on Kregen I had no wish to suffer again. If I have not made it clear that for Zorg, Nath, Zolta, and I, fresh out of the thalamite deck of a Magdag swifter, the open pulling benches of *Grace of Grodno* came as a taste of reprieve, I can assure you this was so.

At that time and for some time to come, I was still unsatisfied that the best arrangements for oarsmen had been found.

With my head full of galleys and swifters and triremes I accompanied Nath and Zolta to their favorite drinking haunt, The Fleeced Ponsho — Kregans sometimes have a warped sense of humor — where buxom Sisi apparently was prepared to favor these two unlikely cutthroats without overpayment merely because they happened to have escaped from the Magdag galleys.

"With one man one oar," Zolta was saying, rubbing his chin where his black beard was growing enough to itch, "even with the apostis — for which we must give credit to the Archbolds of Zair—"

"Huh!" interrupted Nath, as we swung into the low doorway of the tavern, out of the pink moonlight from the two second moons of Kregen. "Those rasts of Grodno-gasta claim the credit for inventing the apostis!"

"May Zair rot them!" rumbled Zolta. He pitched his body onto a bench and yelled for Sisi. "Anyway, friend Strombor" — they had taken to calling me that, now, and both could not really stomach the "lord" bit — "as I was saying before Nath opened his black-fanged wine-spout — Sisi! Hurry up, you lecher's delight! I'm as dry as the Southern Desert! As I was saying, one man one oar, even with the apostis, is fine for small handy craft. I'd not care to be aboard when a hundred-and-eighty swifter got on her tail! Ho! She'd be hoicked clear out of the water!"

They still had to convince me.

Sisi's arrival with three leather tankards brimming with wine from Zond, rich and dark and potent, silenced our argument as we quaffed. Then Nath belched and leaned back, brushing the back of his hand across his lips.

"Mother Zinzu the Blessed! I needed that!"

We talked and drank and argued, and got into a gambling game with some ponsho farmers up from the country, and with Nath's uncanny ability to manipulate the dice we were doing very well indeed, when a fight broke out — there always seemed to be fights following Nath's dice manipulation. Laughing and roaring and throwing tousle-headed ponsho farmers from us, left and right, we roistered from the tavern. When I say that Zolta being the smallest of those four of us who had labored on the oar took the outboard, do not infer he was a small man. He could pick up his groundling and hurl him into the bar display with the best.

Sisi came yelling and running, the bodice above her red gown billowing with her outraged anger, but Zolta swept her up in his arms and bestowed on her a wet and bristly kiss and then we went whooping out of The Fleeced Ponsho. The mobiles, the Sanurkazz equivalent to a police force, fat and jolly men with swords at their sides rusted into their sheathes, hallooed into the flower-draped little square before the tavern as we went dancing out at the other side. Nath had a bottle of wine in his hand and he was laughing and dancing, and Zolta was grinning a great big foolish grin and obviously thinking of Sisi. I had to laugh at my two ruffian companions. But we had pulled an oar together in the galleys. That made us comrades with inseparable bonds. We had been four. Now we were three. I believe my laugh was no laugh a civilized man would recognize.

We scampered up the moon-drenched alley.

"We must find another tavern, and that right soon," declared Zolta. "I am primed."

"And what of Sisi, oh man of little faith?" demanded Nath. He pulled the cork out of the bottle with a single jerk.

"She will keep, fat and juicy. I am primed, I tell you, Nath, you nit that crawls upon a calsany."

"As to that—" said Nath, and then paused to upend the bottle and down four hefty slugs: glug, glug, glug — and glug. "Nits are of a size more suitable to he who pulls nearest the parados — yes?"

He yelped as Zolta's toe caught him, and then they were both roaring and yelling and running up the alley, the bottle brandished in Nath's hand, and the great contagious roaring laughter welling up from Zolta to inflame the fire. I sighed. They were ruffians, true, but they were oar comrades.

From the direction of The Fleeced Ponsho came the measured tread of booted feet. There was a ring about those footsteps, four men at least, and clad in mail. Men in Sanurkazz did not wear mail with the same habitual ferocity as the men of Magdag. The mobiles only wore half-mail. Mind you, they were so fat and indolent a lot, preferring a bottle of wine to a fracas any time, that I was surprised they'd even arrived when they did.

The footsteps approached and I stepped back into the shadows of a balcony from which great blossoms glowed, their inner petals shut, their outer petals open to the moonlight.

"The rast went this way," a grating voice said. I remained very still. I did not even make an attempt to free the long sword at my side. The time would come for that.

"Hark at those two cramphs—" Nath and Zolta were certainly making a hullabaloo enough to awaken the whole district. "We had best hurry."

Four men in mail pressed on along the alleyway. They entered a patch of the pink moonlight that moved only slowly with the gentle orbital movement of the two second moons. Their faces showed pink blobs, barred by ferocious upthrust moustaches. The mail glittered where it was not fully covered by the loose-fitting white surcoats. Those surcoats looked odd, and then I saw that they were bereft of the usual sizable badge, worn breast and back, that marked a man for his allegiances.

I think I knew then what all this was about. But I wanted to know for sure. After all, I, Dray Prescot, had more important things to do on Kregen than to engage in a petty feud with a spoiled boy, no matter that he might be the scion of a wealthy and noble family.

The men's swords glittered in the moonlight.

They would have passed me by, hidden in the shadows beneath the balcony. I remember there was a sweet scented odor on the air from the great moon-drinking blooms.

I stepped out into the alleyway.

The long sword lay still in the scabbard.

"You wanted to speak with me?"

It was a challenge.

"You are he whom men call the Lord of Strombor?"

"I am."

"Then you are a dead man."

The fight did not last long. They were fair swordsmen, nothing of note, nothing that my wild Clansmen could not have dealt with. Hap Loder, for example, would have been yelling for a drink as he finished them off, with all his panache.

When I returned to *Lilac Bird* I said to Zenkiren: "I wish to see the father of Hezron."

"Oh?"

We understood each other a little better now, Zenkiren and I. I had asked Zolta what Krozair might mean, and he had shuffled and hedged and then said to ask Zenkiren. His reply had been, simply: "Wait."

When I had pressed him, he said: "It is an Order. It is not something discussed lightly in taprooms." He gestured around his cabin, so plain, so severe, and I had not understood.

Now he looked at me and put a finger to his lips as I told him what had occurred in the alley outside The Fleeced Ponsho.

"This might be serious, my Lord of Strombor. Harknel of High Heysh, Hezron's father, is a powerful man, wealthy and influential. There are intrigues in Sanurkazz, as you may well believe."

I made an impatient movement. Zenkiren spoke more forcefully.

"The boy hired killers and they bungled the job. If you tell the father he will have to deny all knowledge of it, and then discipline his son — for failing, mind, for failing! After that, you will have not that young puppy Hezron out for your blood, but old Harknel himself. Think on, Strombor — and, there is something else."

"I have thought," I said instantly. I couldn't have assassination threats hanging over me if I had work to do for the Star Lords — or the Savanti — or, and more especially, if I was to find my way out of the Eye of the World back to Vallia or Strombor and to my Delia of Delphond. "I will see whoever it takes to have this puppy restrained. That is all."

He pursed his lips. He tried to be fair, did Pur Zenkiren, captain of *Lilac Bird*. He held up a piece of paper — paper of a kind I did not recognize, and my instant alertness relaxed.

"I have had a letter, Strombor. I would like you to go on a little journey — to Felteraz."

"Felteraz!"

"Yes, my Lord of Strombor. You are to see my Lady Mayfwy. The Lady Mayfwy — wife of Zorg of Felteraz."

Nine

Of Mayfwy and of swifters

Two disgusting specimens of some abhorrent species of water vermin were hoisted aboard next morning, swinging groaning and complaining over *Lilac Bird*'s parados to be dumped all squishy and green of face onto the deck.

The mobiles in their gaudy clothes and rusty swords who had brought them home stood on the jetty, guffawing, their hands on their hips, their heads thrown back, emptying their stalwart lungs into the early morning suns-shine. Both the suns of Kregen were close together. The genial sounds of work in the harbor floated up, cries and calls, the clink of tools, the slop of water, the screams of gulls. The lighthouse men were going off watch, rubbing their eyes and yawning. The tall pharos reared up from the far end of the jetty past the first of the seaward defense walls, its immense lantern mirrors dark and motionless. Down by the fishmarket the catch was being landed and the wives were arguing and fighting and more than one silvery-scaled fat fish went *slap!* across the cheeks of a beldame. The scene was one I could half close my eyes and absorb and imagine I was back in Plymouth — well, almost.

Zolta and Nath lay on the deck, two pitiful objects.

Sharntaz, the new second in command, rolled across to inspect them with the toe of his boot.

I, Dray Prescot, who seldom laugh, felt the strange bubbling inside me, straining my ribs. Nath held his head and groaned. Zolta held his stomach and moaned. As objects of pity they aroused only the most violent hilarity in the rough seafolk of Sanurkazz.

When Zenkiren appeared and everyone immediately straightened up ready for morning inspection, he cast a single glance at the two culprits, who attempted to stand up, their faces the color of that interesting cheese sometimes discovered abandoned in the buildings of Magdag.

"You two," he said. He jerked a hand. "With the Lord of Strombor. *Move!*"

"Aye, Captain," they stuttered, and shambled off after me.

It was hardly fair on them, but I knew they would not forgive me if I traveled to Felteraz without them. As I had explained to Zenkiren, they were oar comrades of Zorg also.

We made the journey in a two-wheeled cart drawn by a docile ass, a somewhat different variety from that of the Plains of Segesthes but with the same patient obstinacy, and as I handled the reins those two lay in the back and groaned with every jolt of the wheels.

"My head! Mother Zinzu the Blessed! For a little wine to moisten these cracked lips!"

"You drank it all last night," said Zolta disagreeably.

"And that wench you found me! Aie! How she—"

"You have no stomach for the finer arts, Nath, and that is the truth, by Zim-Zair."

"Ha! Since when have you used Krozair oaths, my fat tallowed sea snake?"

Then we were all silent, for a space, for we remembered our friend Zorg of Felteraz, to whose widow we now traveled.

The way was not far but we did not hurry in the warm sunshine. The weather continued fine and mild. For Zolta and Nath this was a holiday as well as a pilgrimage; for me it was a digression from my set course I had to make, a task laid on me, a task I knew without a single hesitation Delia of the Blue Mountains would approve and applaud.

Felteraz, a town and an estate and a small fishing harbor, lay a little over three dwaburs to the east and we had to be ferried over the neck of the Sea of Marshes to pick up our asscart. The gut there was about a mile or so broad and no bridges spanned it, but the shining water was always alive with small craft, oared wherries, pulling barges, dinghies, ferries, and the occasional stately passage of a swifter, every oar in line and rising and falling as one to the beat of the drum-deldar.

Now we ambled along the dusty path, for the suns had quickly dried the overnight dew. We passed cultivated fields, and small farms and a tiny village or two nestled into the rocks. Here there could be habitation near the shore. For the frowning walls of the citadel of Sanurkazz to the west and the much lesser citadel of Felteraz to the east provided protection and a powerful deterrent to a swift raiding descent on the coast. In general the coasts of the inner sea, the Eye of the World, lie barren beneath the suns.

I wondered what Mayfwy would be like. Zorg had never mentioned her, save that once, when he had been unable any longer to keep bottled within him the passions of his life, for he had been dying. He had said "Krozair" and "Mayfwy" in a breath, a dying breath. I had formed an image of her, of a serene and calm grand dame, straight, with the management of the estate and the overlordship of the town and harbor and citadel a burden she was capable of bearing with dignity and composure, a charge she accepted with all the loyalty I had come to know and admire in Zorg, her husband.

We stopped to eat in one of the villages, and Nath quickly bargained for a bottle of Zond wine, and Zolta had an apple-cheeked girl perched on his knee and screaming with laughter in almost no time at all. I ate bread, soft, fluffy bread torn in chunks from the long loaves of Kregen, and smeared with honey from the innkeeper's hives. A heaping dish of palines in the center of the table completed Nath's hangover cure; there is nothing as sovereign as palines to pick a man up from the floor.

There are many things I know I have forgotten in my long life. I sincerely believe I shall never forget that ambling ride on an asscart from Sanurkazz to Felteraz along the dusty coast road of the Eye of the World with the warm sunshine golden and glorious upon us, streaming in opaline radiance upon the vineyards and orange groves, and upon the browned and smiling faces of the people we passed. It is a simple memory, but a long one. And those two lusty rogues, Nath and Zolta, rollicked and sang in the cart as we rolled creaking and lurching along the road.

Felteraz came in sight. I shall say little about the place. The town was charming, high-banked along the terraced side of a hill, trending up to where a great dike cut off the frowning mass of the citadel. I have seen the incomparable view along the brilliant cliffs of Sorrento. Felteraz is something like that. The harbor lay cinctured by a solid granite wall and there was also a lighthouse as there was in Sanurkazz. From the high loft of the citadel I could look out and down along those cliffs which the setting suns crimsoned and opaled in breathtaking radiance, smothered in profuse vegetation, with blooms of gorgeous color and scents of delight breaking the patterns of greenery and rock.

We rolled along behind our ass up to the drawbridge over the dike, and the bridge was down and a friendly man-at-arms clad in mail let us through. His white surcoat bore a symbol I was to come to know well: two galley oars, crossed, divided upright by a long sword, so that the whole looked something like the letter X with a center upright. The symbol was stitched in red and gold, surrounded by a lenk-leaf border. The man-at-arms lifted his long sword in salute as we passed, and, gravely, I acknowledged it.

A smiling maid in a white apron, with naked flashing legs, with a sprightly eye that sized up Zolta in a moment, led us into a spacious antechamber hung with tapestry and with solid tables and chairs positioned about. She was gone only five minutes or so and I knew Zenkiren had sent a message, that we were expected.

Mayfwy, widow to Zorg of Felteraz, entered the room.

I knew what I had expected. A grand dame, solid, filled with the virtues of her exalted office, wearing stiff robes, brocade, girdled with a golden belt from which hung suspended bunches of iron keys of her responsibilities as chatelaine.

Of all the inward expectation, Mayfwy possessed only the glittering golden belt.

From the belt, the chatelaine itself, hung a silver key.

Mayfwy danced lightly into the room, smiling, brimming over with joy and goodwill. She was young, incredibly young to be what she was. Her mass of dark and curly hair glistened with health and oils and ministrations. Her pert face with its saucy eyes appraised us. Her small and sensuous mouth broke into a smile as she advanced, more sedately, her hand extended.

"My Lord of Strombor. I am heartily pleased to welcome you to Felteraz." She beamed on Zolta and Nath. "And to Nath and Zolta, my dear husband's friends, and therefore my friends. You are heartily welcome." She laughed, rushing on, giving us no time to speak. "Come. You must be hungry — surely you must be thirsty? Nath, deny it if you can! And you, Zolta, the name of the morsel who showed you in is Sinkle."

She went dancing out on her satin slippers and we, like three calsanys, followed her onto a terrace from which the whole breathtaking view of the cliffs and the bay and the harbor below the town spread out below us. I could spare time later to see the view. I studied this girl, this impish sprite, this Mayfwy, who was a widow.

She wore white, a sheer white linen dress that was held in place over her shoulders by golden pins encrusted with rubies. Her golden belt circled her waist and hung low in the front and to one side, emphasizing the long curves of her. Her figure was lithe and feminine and seductive in an artless way, as though no matter what she did she could never fail to be attractive. In her curled dark hair posies of small forget-me-nots clustered.

I have little idea of what we talked about, there on that sun-drenched terrace over the blue sea. Nath took himself off to organize a wine delivery system, and Zolta was taken off by Sinkle, who had the grace to giggle as she led him out.

"Zorg," I said, and plunged brusquely and brutally into an account of our lives as slaves. She quieted down, and listened attentively. She did not cry, and as I talked and felt the response flowing so gently from her, I knew she had cried all the tears she could shed. Captivity and slavery had worn Zorg down. This elfin sprite had once been his match. Her dark days of agony had passed when news came that Zorg's galley had been captured. "He was sent to the galleys as a punishment for breaking the heads of those evil men of Magdag. They sought to discipline him. I tell you, Mayfwy, Zorg's spirit was never broken." And then I told her of what Zorg had said as he died, but I did not tell her of the manner of his death.

"He was a proud man, my Lord of Strombor. Proud. I thank you for your goodness in coming to see me." She gestured, a half helpless little movement of one slender naked arm. She wore no jewelry apart from those blazing rubies in the golden pins clasping the shoulders of her deeply-cut gown. The scent of her perfume came very sweetly as she moved.

I thought of the Princess Natema Cydones, of the Noble House of Esztercari, in far Zenicce, and then I did not think of Natema, who must by now be married to my friend Prince Varden Wanek of the Noble House of Eward, for some considerable time.

"You are not drinking your wine, my Lord of Strombor."

I reached for the crystal goblet.

Truth to tell I always preferred the rich and fragrant Kregan tea I had become used to on the Plains of Segesthes with my Clansmen, but this Felteraz wine was light, golden, and sweet, and cloyed not unpleasantly on the tongue.

"I drink to your eternal happiness, my Lady of Felteraz."

It was polite, a formula; it was also clumsy.

Her face moved toward me, her eyes immense and luminous, dark with remembered pain. "Ah! My Lord of Strombor!"

I rose and walked to the marble balustrade hanging above the tremendous view. I could see three galleys, hundred-swifters, tucked in the inner harbor, their yards and masts struck down, their awnings up, their oar ports leathered over. Gulls wheeled over the sheer drop. The perfume of the flowers was overpowering.

We took time, Nath and Zolta and me, to make ourselves as respectable as three ruffianly fighting-men might for the lavish meal Mayfwy provided that evening. The dishes passed before us, served on platters of beaten gold — which always let the food go cold too fast for a real gourmet — and the goblets of wine consumed were beyond counting. Mayfwy laughed and my two companions roared and sang and told stories that brought a sparkle to my Lady of Felteraz's eyes. Zorg was dead. He now sat in glory on the right hand of Zair in the paradise of Zim. He would not begrudge his old oar comrades some fun and relish from life, nor would he begrudge the girl he had loved the same human needs. We had seen Zorg's and Mayfwy's son and daughter: a fine, upright youngster with the features we had come to recognize in Zorg, and a winning little girl who at first was shy until Zolta perched her on his shoulders and pretended to be a sectrix, the while she belabored him with a stick, at which Nath cried out: "That's the idea, my little darling! Beat him like a calsany! He can only improve!"

The evening meal which in truth was more like a banquet — and I fancied, not without a twinge of shame, a banquet in our honor — passed. Also present were the guard commander and a number of the chief men of the estates and their ladies, all good kindly folk with country ways that came as refreshing as a cool westerly after days of sweltering in southerlies.

I was left at last with Mayfwy in a small retiring room, with only three rose-colored lamps for light, with a soft sofa on which she half reclined, her linen dress changed for one in much the same style but created all from shimmering silk, with a side table on which delicate wines waited our attention.

"Now, my Lord of Strombor," she said to me, her smooth and elfin face serious, that sensuous little mouth trying to be firm, her hands clasped. "I want you to tell me the truth about Zorg. I can stand it. But I must know the truth!"

I felt genuine distress.

How could I explain to her what her man had endured?

Such a thing was barely possible.

I could feel my heart thumping. The wine rose to cloud my vision and coiled thickly in my head. The rosy light of the lamps shed gleams on her curled gleaming hair. Her silken dress clung here and there to her body. She half reclined and gazed at me, and her ripe red mouth trembled so that I could think of nothing save obeying her commands; and yet, to speak of what I knew of the horrors of a Magdaggian galley to this girl?

"My Lord of Strombor," she said softly, and now her breathing was as unsteady as mine. She leaned toward me, her lips half parted, yet clinging still, her eyelids half closed, her breast rising and falling. "Please — my Lord?"

I leaned toward her.[iii]

The Magdaggian hundredswifter had turned now, reached around, her oars a smother of foam in the sea. Again a hurtling mass of rock from her aft varter skimmed over our heads. Men were yelling as arrows feathered into them. The Magdag galley turned, her oars churning, and still Zolta had not sorted out the horrible confusion on our rowing benches amidships.

"Throw them overboard, if you have to, Zolta!" I roared at him. A man at my side screamed and started back with an arrow pierced clean through his eye. "Cut them loose! Get the oars into action!" The hundredswifter was swinging around and her ugly bronze beak was building a comb of white water as she picked up speed.

In only minutes that bronze rostrum would smash into us, her beak would rend over our parados and men would come leaping like sea-leem down among us. My thinned crew couldn't stop that strength in boarding.

Zolta's sword flashed and flashed again as he cut down the frenzied slaves. Nath was there, down from his place at our forward varters. The whip-deldars were unchaining the dead slaves. The mass of rock from the Magdaggian varter had pulped their naked bodies like nits beneath a thumbnail.

Slaves toppled over the sides. The splashes as they hit were lost in the uproar. As in the many fights I had been in, some of which I have mentioned, on the Eye of the World, once again I was struck by the absence of the smashing concussion of gunfire, the choking clouds of smoke. I could see, all right. I could hear. Both senses brought me tales of destruction.

Now our after varter could come into action and the men there let fly and at once began their frenzied efforts to wind up the windlass. The ballista was cocked again. The hundred-swifter was bearing down on us now, gathering speed, the bronze ram cutting the water, the metal gleaming and bright. Where the strengthening wales along the sides met forward at the proembolion the Magdaggian usually covered the junction with a sectrix head of bronze. Above that and beneath the beak the wales met in a bronze risslaca-head, a mythical lizard monster. After the ram had pierced and crushed us below water, the proembolion would push us back off the ram and upright so that the boarders could leap down from their gangways along the beak.

"Hurry it up, Zolta!" I roared.

My decks were covered with dead men. Arrows stood everywhere. My own archers were shooting, but I could not see the results of their handiwork past the erected palisade across the low foredeck of the hundredswifter. Her twin banks of oars rose and fell now in a quicker beat. Each blade hit the water as one, in two straight and parallel lines, churning her forward like a runaway train on tracks. I yelled at Nath again and he charged back up to the forward varter and hounded his men there into making a final fling.

My sword was in my fist.

If we were captured it would be the galleys of Magdag for us. I had tasted the freedom of the inner sea. I would not willingly go back to slavery again.

Zolta was beating all the fresh slaves we had up from the hold, herding them onto the benches. Here was one time when a single-banked swifter had advantages. Four slaves to an oar, then huddled down, lifting the looms, preparing for the stroke.

Even then the whip-deldars were chaining them down. I nodded. That was good. The oarsmen must respond at once to every order. If they were unchained they would be unsettled, thinking of seizing the chance to jump overboard. More of my men fell on the gangways as arrows flew down.

Zolta waved his sword. His face was as wrathful as a whiter storm.

"Clear," he bellowed. "Clear, Captain!"

I yelled down to the oar-master, but old Rizil was up to the job and at once his silver whistle shrilled, the drum-deldar smashed out the first booming beat, the bass and the tenor drumming in turn. The oars swooped down, hauled water, feathered and lifted in that short but incredibly powerful motion of oars arranged *alla scaloccio*. I felt *Zorg* leap through the water.

All our artillery was shooting as we turned, and then the after varter fell silent and it was up to Nath as we swung around, bringing our bow against that of the green galley.

Bronze ram against bronze ram, now, we hurtled across the narrowing space of water.

The foe was a hundredswifter, two banked with probably five or six men to an oar. *Zorg* was a sixtyswifter, single-banked, with four men to an oar. We would be slugged solidly backward at the point of impact.

Both captains, that man I fought and I, knew what to do in this situation.

Amid the shrill of wounded men, the clang of the ballistae, and the plunging swoop of the iron birds of the air, we both stood as I stood, on the quarterdeck, waiting, judging, estimating, ready to choose the exact time.

But — which way would he go?

He would surely try to ram. As surely he would know I would seek to avoid collision and seek to shave down his side, smashing his cat head, rend away his whole double-bank of oars. But — which side, larboard or starboard?

I found my face twisting and realized I must be smiling at that Magdaggian captain's dilemma. He wished to strike me; then he must make the decision. I must needs turn first; he would think. Yes, he surely must think that.

Zolta was at my side, his sword bloody, panting.

"If they set foot aboard, Captain, they'll have to wade over my blood!"

"Yes, Zolta," I said.

My men were crowding forward now, their white surcoats with that brave blazon of Felteraz heartening us all, their long swords ready. They crouched like leems, ready. I spoke quietly to the rudder-deldars.

I had observed a slight incline in our passage, a slender movement with some current and the gentle breeze.

"When I give the order," I told the rudder-deldars, hard-voiced, "turn instantly to starboard. To starboard. When you hear my order. Understood?"

"Yes, Captain," they said, sturdily handling their rudders with a skill I had thrashed into them. "We hear."

"Come on, Zolta," I said. I spoke with a false cheeriness. "Let us go forward. Our blades are dry and thirsty."

"By Zair the all-merciful!" said Zolta. "No Grodno-gasta will stop me enjoying a maiden tonight on Isteria!"

Now the hundredswifter was half-hidden before us by our own palisade stretching across the foredeck aft of the outreaching beak. We ran forward and waved a quick encouragement to Nath, who was keeping his two varters on the bows clanging away with a speed and precision his crews never reached in all the practice I made them sweat through.

I was in command of my own ship; I had been in command now long enough just to have reached a time when organization was beginning to go as I wanted; no mangy Grodno-worshiping sea-leem would cheat me of that now!

Then Nath, high on the varter platform, let out a shrilling shriek of triumph.

"May Mother Zinzu the Blessed be praised! Their drum-deldar lies like a squashed paline!"

Immediately the beat of the hundredswifter's oars faltered. Even as the thought: *Lack of training!* flashed through my mind I turned and, funneling my hands, yelled aft: "*Now!*"

Zorg swung viciously to starboard.

Our larboard side oars went in with a speed that clearly told of the slaves' knowledge of what would happen if they were caught with their blades extended.

I saw the cruel beak of the Magdag galley lurch away. It opened out a glimpse of her bows where the varter crew labored at the windlass. I saw the cat head disappear beneath our beak and felt the jolting crunch as our bronze-clad proembolion, fashioned into the head of a charging chunkrah, ripped it away.

Then we were roaring down the larboard side of the galley, tearing away the oars in a vast and horrible splintering of wood, shaving her side as clean as a Magdaggian harbor barber shaves the head of a slave.

I knew what was happening to those two banks of slaves aboard the hundredswifter. They were men of Zair, fellows, comrades: they would understand what we were doing now, and regret it, and feel the bitterness, but their acrid hate would be for Magdag.

We shot past the upflung stern of the galley and not a single mailed man of Magdag had got aboard us.

After that we lay off on our oars and shot the galley to pieces.

When we boarded, the shambles, blood, and filth had no power to sicken me. After that it was like any other successful action on the inner sea.

Of the eight hundred slaves aboard some three hundred and twenty-nine were either dead or so badly wounded, crushed, as to surely die. Of the Magdaggians we were able to chain to our oar benches a paltry twenty-two. But we outfitted the captured hundredswifter and, with all our reserve of oars used up and many splintered together, we set course for Holy Sanurkazz.

I did all that was necessary in the burial of the slaves at sea. Our decks were scrubbed, our wounded cared for, the rescued slaves happy, now, to labor for just a little while longer at the oars to take us into home waters — and this time with the threat of the whip on their naked backs removed.

We sailed past the pharos over by the outer wall of the sea defenses of Sanurkazz. Zolta had, indeed, enjoyed his maiden on the island of Isteria, where we had passed the night. How often I have spent in that snug anchorage, the last before Sanurkazz herself, a night thinking of my return to Felteraz!

The people of Zair welcomed our return, as they always welcomed the return of a successful venture against Magdag. The four fat merchantmen we had taken would provide me with a substantial increase to my fortune. I had my eye on a gown all of gold and silver thread, silk lined, that I felt sure Mayfwy would admire. And, too, after this Zenkiren could no longer keep from me the command of a double-banked swifter, a hundred-and-twentyswifter! She would be called *Zorg*, of course, the moment I assumed command.

I knew the very ship. She had been reaching completion as we had set sail. Now, she must be ready, brand-new from the shipwrights and fitters, lying waiting for me in the arsenal. Zo, the new king, a man whom I quite liked, would surely not refuse a request from Zenkiren that one of his sea captains should take the command. The high admiral might grumble and Harknel of High Heysh would be sure to interfere and try to prevent me from any success, but intrigue would be met with intrigue. I, too, now had powerful friends in Holy Sanurkazz.

Was I not, after all, the Lord of Strombor, the most successful corsair captain of the Eye of the World?

The formalities were quickly over. The freed slaves, with many expressions of thanks, went to recuperate in Sanurkazz.

My crew was paid off and roaring for a well-earned leave. All the flags of gold, silver, and scarlet floated in the bright air above Sanurkazz and carpets of brilliant color and weave hung from hundreds of balconies smothered in flowers. My agent, wily old Shallan, with his wisp of beard, lined cheeks, and merry eyes, who would charge fifteen percent on a loan and chuckle with merriment as he did so, would see to the disposal of the prizes after the required dues had been paid to Zo, the king, the high admiral, Zenkiren, and to Felteraz.

I sat in the stern sheets of my personal barge, with a crew of sixteen free men to row, Zolta at my side, Zolta's girl acting as drum-deldar, and Nath steering a precarious course as he upended a bottle at the rudder, as we rounded the curve of coast from Sanurkazz to Felteraz. As we glided into the harbor I contrasted this arrival with that first time when we had rolled up roaring on the asscart.

Zenkiren was waiting for me in a tall cool room of tapestries and solid furniture with another man, a man who might have served as a model of what Zenkiren would be like in another hundred years. Mayfwy kissed me on the cheek as her maids brought in wine in chased silver goblets.

"Mayfwy!" I said. Then, "I have a cedar wood chest for you—"

"Dray!" she said, her eyes dancing, her cheeks flushed with my return. "Another present!"

"As I recall," said Zenkiren dryly, "he can never keep his hands off Magdag gold and silver. If he didn't bring you a present I would think my Lord of Strombor had sailed a lonely sea."

"As for you, Zenkiren," I said, unwrapping the blue-etched and gold-mounted Fristle scimitar I had picked up off the deck of that damned Magdag pirate, "I thought this toy might amuse you."

"It is magnificent!" said Zenkiren, running his fingers along the curved blade. "I thank you."

"And now," he said, and a note of solemn seriousness entered his voice, "I wish to present you." He turned to the other man, who had remained calm and cool, his old strong-featured face composed, his simple white apron and tunic immaculate, the long sword at his side scabbarded in the fighting-man's style.

"May I present the Lord of Strombor." He turned then to me. "I have the honor to present to you, my Lord of Strombor, Pur Zazz, Grand Archbold of the Krozairs of Zy."

Ten

The Krozairs of Zy point the path

I can remember, even now, vividly, unforgettably, the zephyr of anticipation that blew through my whole being.

In the seasons I had been hunting with the corsairs of Sanurkazz I had heard a hint dropped here, a casual snatch of conversation there, and I had picked up information that must have been the sum total, or nearly that, of what the ordinary idle, happy, careless folk of Sanurkazz knew of the Krozairs of Zy.

Now this tall, aloof, calm-faced man was here, in the familiar room of the citadel of Felteraz, at the express desire, as it seemed to me, of Zenkiren — and he was the Grand Arch-bold of the Krozairs!

What followed must have been very familiar to him, for he had been master of the Order for a very long time. From hints I picked up I gathered that Zenkiren himself was in line for the succession, that my friend Zenkiren would become Grand Archbold. Pur Zazz sized me up with a cold and level stare. Instinctively I straightened up and squared those inordinately broad shoulders of mine. He looked me over. I felt that he was stripping my flesh away, was paring my very self down to the essence beneath. I had been roistering and going pirating on the inner sea, I had been living life to the full, I had been amassing wealth, and I had made friends. All that seemed to me in that moment to be petty, a mere preliminary to what this man would require of me.

If I do not go too deeply into what happened to me in the year that followed on that interview it is because I am bound by vows of silence I do not wish to break, even to an audience four hundred light-years distant from the scenes of that rigorous training and selection and adherence to the principles of dedication to Zair and to the Krozairs of Zy.

The Order maintained an island stronghold in the narrowing strait between the inner sea and the Sea of Swords, that other smaller dependent sea opening off southward from the Eye of the World. Like the Sea of Marshes it covered an extensive area, but it lay westward, something less than halfway along the curved southern shore. The island had once been a volcano, but through the geological aeons its crater had smoothed and filled, the subterranean fires stilled, and fresh water had found its way up to rill out in pleasant springs. The outer jagged scarps rose harsh and rocky beneath the suns; within a habitation had been built very little less harsh. The Order took its vows seriously. They kept themselves aloof from other orders of lesser chivalry like The Red Brethren of Lizz; they were dedicated to the succor of destitute people of Zair, to the greater glory of Zim-Zair, and to the implacable resistance to Grodno the Green and all his works.

After the novice had served his novitiate he was ranked Krozair, given the titles and insignia of his station, a man fit to stand in the forefront of the ranks of Zim-Zair in the eternal struggle against the heretic. Only men of worth were ever approached. Many refused, for the disciplines were harsh. Many fell by the wayside and never reached into the inner knowledge.

Once a candidate had become a Krozair, he was entitled, as other orders also conferred the privilege, of prefixing his name with the honorific Pur. Pur was not a rank or a title: it was a badge of chivalry and honor, a pledge that the man holding it was a true Krozair. Then the newly-fledged Krozair might choose a number of paths that opened before him. If he chose to become a contemplative, that was his privilege. If he chose to become a Bold, one of the select brethren who manned the fortress isle of Zy and other of the citadels maintained by the Order throughout the red sections of the inner sea, he would be welcomed. Should he desire to return to the ordinary ways of life, he might do that also, for the Order recognized its mission in the world. But a stricture was laid upon that man, that proved Krozair.

Whenever he received the summons to join the Krozairs, wherever they happened to be in need of his aid, then, wherever he happened to be, and whenever it might occur in his life, he was bound by all that he held most holy and dear to hasten as fast as sectrix or swifter might take him to join his brothers of the Order.

"There have been a number of famous and immortal calls in the past, Pur Dray," Pur Zenkiren told me one time as we came from the salle d'armes where we had been knocking the stuffing out of each other with morning stars. "I have been privileged to answer one such summons, some thirty years ago, when the devils of Magdag came knocking on the very doors of Zy itself. From all over the inner sea the brothers gathered." He laughed, a faraway look in his bright eyes. "I tell you, Pur Dray: we had quite a fight of it until the Order gathered and the long swords sang above the hated green."

I had been on Zy long enough to answer, with sincere meaning: "I pray that the summons will come again, and soon, Pur Zenkiren, for the Order to go up against Magdag itself."

He made a face. "Unlikely." He smiled and clapped me on the shoulder. "We are few. Finding men, as it is phrased in the Discipline, of the right caliber, is difficult. We have our eye on men as soon as they don sword and coat of mail. We are a lazy sun-loving lot, we men of Sanurkazz."

"Agreed."

The disciplines were strenuous, difficult, and extremely demanding. The use of weapons had become of itself almost a religion. Sword practice was carried out as a religious observance. Every move was sanctified by religious ardor. Like the Samurai, we dedicated our wills and our bodies to the pursuit of perfection, the facing of an opponent without seeing him as though he were there. We tried to make our opponents transparent, as though they were far off. We could sense a blow, the direction of a cut, the movement of a slash, by an intuitive process beyond reason, allied to our sixth sense. We could move into a parry almost before our foe instigated his attack.

Always, even as a young seaman aboard a seventy-four, I was accounted a good cutlass man. I have spoken of the need for such physical prowess, such good healthy cut-and-thrust, to enable me to survive when I first entered Kregen. Since then I have been in many situations where swordsmanship was vital, and I have been accounted a good man with a blade. But I freely admit that I learned from the disciplines of Zy a dexterity in swordplay that turned me into a different kind of swordsman entirely.

Only in my own inner feelings about the superiority of the point to the edge could I teach the Krozairs much; and the knowledge was unnecessary, for they fought armored men in mesh iron, where the thrust from a sword would be stopped, where the way to dispose of your man was to slash his head off, or lop a limb, or break in his ribs. The disciplines were, in their way, too far advanced for the style of sword fighting practiced on the inner sea. Breathing, isometrics, arduous and prolonged exercises, continuous dedication, long hours of contemplation, hours of drawing on the will and making of the will itself a single central instrument whereby a man might know himself and thus see his enemy as transparent and removed, a foe he could outwit and outmaneuver and eventually triumph over, endless hours of instruction and devotion — all these were my daily portion during that year on the Krozairs' lair, the isle of Zy.

I will not speak of the mysticism.

Then came the day when the Grand Archbold put me through the final ceremonies, and, purified, uplifted, I was pronounced a fit Krozair, worthy to hold the honor of Pur prefixed to my name.

"And now, Pur Dray, what will you do?"

I believe they knew what my decision would be. The Order maintained its own small fleet of galleys, and I had now made up my mind that I would aim for the command of the finest of these. This would take time. In the meanwhile, I intended to return to Felteraz, to a swifter command under the aegis of Zenkiren, who was now commodore in the king's fleet, and to my previous life. I did not want to give up Felteraz.

Any thoughts of becoming a contemplative, or one who actually tended the succored, was, I knew, to my shame, perhaps, not for me. Equally I did not wish to become a Bold, even though this was a sure way to the Grand Archbold's position. But Zenkiren, a roving brother, was to become Grand Archbold. And, perhaps, the greatest reason for my decision to go again into the inner sea — I had almost said outside world, thinking of my young self in those days, so gullible, so (if Zair will pardon) so green — was that I had never forgotten the Star Lords and the Savanti. I knew they still had plans for me. I knew they would manipulate me whenever it suited them.

And — my Delia, my Delia of the Blue Mountains.

Could I forget her?

"I have sent for *Zorg*," said Zenkiren to me as we stood on one of the lookout posts near the crest of one of the long steep slopes of the island. A surprise.

"It has meant a lot to me, Zenkiren, to know that he was here, in these halls, these chapels, these salles d'armes. I sometimes think I can sense his presence here, as we perform the same observances as he performed."

"They have been observed by the Order, not here, necessarily, but in our many abodes, for hundreds of years. And they will go on, through the years, being thus observed."

When *Zorg* made landfall and nosed under the colossal rock arch that led into the inner harbor under the island, I was waiting. I donned my white surcoat with its circled emblem with the hubless wheel within. I saw Nath and Zolta on the beak, perched like gulls on a rock face, ready to jump ashore at the first practical moment. As it was, Nath jumped too soon and would have fallen with a splash had I not hauled him up.

They were all grins and grimaces, dancing around me, prodding me to see if I

189

could still withstand a gut-punch, like in the old days. To them the idea that I was now a Krozair, and they must call me Pur — on top of the "lord" bit they had been unable to swallow — came as ludicrous nonsense with which I thoroughly agreed.

"Nath! Zolta! You disgusting ruffians! Why, Nath, your gut is so swelled with wine a season on the benches would trim you down to man-size again! And you, Zolta — I could scabbard my long sword in those pouches under your eyes!"

"Stylor!" they crowed and we wrestled affectionately.

Zenkiren stood to one side, his arms folded and one hand stroking his chin. The Grand Archbold, Pur Zazz, made a sound that might have been "harrumph" if that silly way of speaking had penetrated here. There were five other newly-fledged Krozairs, and we were all to go back together on *Zorg*, which was now under the command of Sharntaz. They, too, didn't quite know what to make of these two bearded rapscallions in the dedicated, austere enclave of Zy, even if the two specimens of hardy and iconoclastic inner sea sailors were only standing on the outer jetty wall.

But the essential dignity and purpose and a breath of that mystery overawed even Nath and Zolta eventually, so that they quieted down. The laymen kept to the outer courts, those opening off the harbor, of course; only Krozairs and lay brothers, the so-called Zimen, were allowed past the iron doors into the interior of the island. Not all of Zy was austere and given over to the pursuit of the inner light; there was great beauty there, for the Krozairs of Zy believed that Zair was just as approachable through beauty as through devotion and dedication in war.

When the time came for our departure, Zenkiren told me he would be staying on in Zy for a time.

"Pur Zazz is old. There are many weighty matters to be discussed, chapter by chapter, langue by langue, in council. You will come to these in your turn, Pur Dray, one of these fine days."

I knew that the Order was in general maintained by Krozair contributions from all the free cities of Zair along the southern shore, and they therefore would have their say in council. Back along the Sea of Swords lay large salt pans, as there were off the Sea of Marshes, and Zy gathered much of its revenue from the salt as did Sanurkazz. But without the continuous support of the brothers of the Order scattered throughout the Zair portions of the Eye of the World, the Krozairs of Zy would be in parlous state.

Sharntaz greeted me with a kindly word and the necessary formality as one captain going aboard another's vessel, and also with the sign — I hesitate to call it a secret sign, it was so obvious and lucid a greeting — that identified a Krozair brother.

He smiled. "I have no idea what swifter you will be given, Pur Dray. But I rather imagine you will want to call her *Zorg*."

"That is my intention."

"So be it. We now stand on the swifter *Lagaz-el-Buzro*.

I nodded. "Also, I shall take those two useless hands, Nath and Zolta."

He chuckled. "And very welcome to them you are, for their drinking and their wenching. But useless? I would rather have a crew like them than one composed of the spoiled brats of Sanurkazz nobility."

I nodded again. I agreed. There was no need of more words.

Zorg that was now *Lagaz-el-Buzro* pushed off. Everything that had to be done had been done. I was going back to report to the high admiral, with a strong recommendation from Zenkiren, and my future in the Eye of the World looked bright. Also, I wanted to see Mayfwy again, and the children, Zorg and Fwymay.

We drew into Sanurkazz. I reported to the high admiral, who did not like me and knew the feeling was reciprocated. But Zo, the king, was disposed toward me, for I had never caused him any offense, and, besides, I had brought him during the course of my last season's activities more gold, jewels, and the precious commodities that are the lifeblood of the inner sea's trading than any other of his captains.

I got my ship.

I have already given some explanation of the controversy then raging in the inner sea over the relative merits of what were called, for convenience, the long keel and the short keel theories.[iv] Long keels, that is, a long narrow swifter, are necessary for speed. But the short keel men, those who argued for the same oar-power packed tighter, claimed that a shorter craft for the same beam might lose a knot or so of speed but gave immeasurably greater maneuverability and turning capacity. I had not yet made up my mind. Zo, the king, appointed me to a five-hundredswifter of the short keel construction. Immediately I set about devising ways of improving the speed of my new *Zorg*. I had two banks of twenty-five oars a side. I carried six hundred slaves, allowing me a reasonable turnover in use and rest periods.

"I thank you, Light of Zim," I said formally. "Rest assured. I shall bring you in a tail of accursed Magdag broad ships and swifters." It was a rote speech, but I meant it with all my heart.

I went raiding on the Eye of the World.

The seasons slipped by; Felteraz remained as beautiful as ever. Nath grew ever more corpulent. Zolta had a number of narrow escapes from the form of marriage that would have clipped his wings. We sailed and we pulled and we crisscrossed the inner sea with burning wrecks and floating corpses; the totals of our prizes steadily mounted as we pulled in past the pharos of Sanurkazz.

Clever distribution of the weights was always the problem in trimming a swifter. A galley that depends on oar propulsion must possess a shallow draft, yet we were packing as many as a thousand or twelve hundred oarsmen in, besides the crew, soldiers, and varters. Sometimes shipwrights went to dangerous lengths to conserve weight. Although all the enormous deadweight of the guns aboard a ship of the line did not have to be carried, the weights were still considerable. *Victory*'s longest deck measures a hundred and eighty-six feet in length, and the width is fifty-two feet. She is built of wood. A swifter of that length would measure something like twenty feet beam. The differences make for cranky, unwieldy, and extremely unseaworthy craft. But then, no galley could live in a sea that *Victory*, or her sisters of my old Navy, could sail with ease.

Galleys are useless on the open ocean. I know.

I had seen the Spaniards out of Cartagena wallowing as we flashed past with our royals set.

I could never sail back home to Strombor in Zenicce, or to Vallia, that island hub of an ocean empire, aboard a galley.

Equally, I would not relish the journey aboard a broad ship, what the ancients also called a round ship, of the inner sea.

All my growing fortune, my success, the luxury with which I might surround myself if I so wished, the good friends I was making — to my continual surprise, for I think I have indicated sufficiently that I am a loner in life — meant little. I felt more and more restless as the long days of raiding, cruising, and carousing passed. I hungered for something I was not clearly conscious of desiring.

That cunning and politely vicious man, the noble Harknel of High Heysh, continued his attempts at persecution, but I held him off, contemptuously, almost with boredom. He did not pose the kind of problem I was in the mood to deal with. Because he had not been born with the all-important Z either in his name or his place of abode, by which he was known, his resentment of that further embittered him. He had seen that his son possessed the Z in his name. I had found, not without amusement, that my name was taken as Prezcot. It had helped. A man had to have the antecedents or the newly-won right to name either himself or his son with the Z. I often wondered what Zolta's history was, but he would never tell me. Nath, now, was the son of an illiterate ponsho farmer, who had taken to the sea in revolt against fleeces, dips, and eternal flock-tending.

At the beginning of a new raiding season, when the twin suns of Scorpio were so close they appeared almost to touch as they rose in the sky, we had returned from our first cruise, happy and successful. Isteria had witnessed some carousing the night before and we had left a trail of mayhem at our many ports of call. I had taken my last cruise aboard this swifter, and was due to shift to a new six-six-hundred-and-twentyswifter, one built on long keel lines, as an experiment. She would be *Zorg*, of course.

Nath wore a bandage around his head.

A Magdag oar blade had welted him nastily during our last fight and he could still hear the bells of Beng-Kishi ringing in his head.

"He's all right," scoffed Zolta. "He wouldn't know it if the tower of Zim-Zair fell on him. He has the skull of a vosk."

Vosks notoriously had exceptionally thick skull bones, so I laughed, and said: "Maybe, Zolta. He should be thankful. He kept the varters going all through—"

"Vosk skull!" said Zolta, and then Nath threw a wet mop at him and I took myself off to my aft state room. It is not seemly for the captain of a king's swifter to be seen romping with the crew. But again that nag of dissatisfaction came to me.

I have mentioned the single occasion on which I attempted to alleviate the lot of the slaves aboard my galley, and of how they rose as one man and attempted to cut the throats of all my crew.[v] Both red and green kept slaves: the red only for gallery work and a few personal body servants, the green for every aspect of menial labor they required. I had conceived it that my duty lay with the men of Zair

— and I heartily loathed and hated the men of Magdag — but also I tried to remember that perhaps the Savanti had sent me here to the Eye of the World to do something positive about this abhorrent slavery. If they had, if the Star Lords also had their own requirements, I must obey, but I would do so with the clear understanding that I would make for Vallia or Zenicce just as soon as I could.

The Proconia, those fair-haired people who dominated all the eastern shoreline of the inner sea, were involved in another of their internecine wars. As I have said, we always kept out of it, for we had enough to do with Magdag. This time Magdag herself had taken a hand in an attempt to dominate the only area of the Eye of the World where neither Grodno nor Zair were worshipped.[vi] My new *Zorg* was directed to join a squadron outfitted for an expedition toward the east. This would be entirely new sea for me. I found a fresh interest in life again and Mayfwy had had made for me a new coat of mail of a fineness almost as supple as the mail worn by that mailed man in the Princess Natema's alcove. That mesh steel had come from Havilfar, I had learned. The mesh of the inner sea was practical, lumpy, and unsophisticated by contrast.

The Victorian antiquaries who, to do them justice, revived an interest in Medieval artifacts, persisted in their odd usage, a quite erroneous nomenclature, of "chain" mail for the mesh iron coat, or hauberk, for far too long. One even still sees this silly word used of a coat of mail. I sat, I remember, in the stern sheets of my barge, feeling the iron links between my fingers, and thinking deep and powerful thoughts of nothing at all as we rowed back from Felteraz to Sanurkazz. The suns, very close together, were sinking into the sea ahead of us. The water shimmered and sparkled with the most wonderful colors. We drowned in sparkling light. The lighthouse men were climbing up the winding stairs to the pharos. A few fishing craft were sailing out. Some birds flitted against the cliffs. The glow of lamps and torches were lighting all over the city.

Perhaps I was dull, tired, maybe stale. Whatever the cause I was scarcely aware of the abrupt rush of men with dark cloaks swathed over their mail. We had just touched and bow oar had hauled us in with his boat hook and I, as was proper, was first out of the boat onto the steps. The men smashed into us in a fierce and silent onslaught. At once Nath's long sword cleared his sheath and he was fighting for his life. Zolta, cursing, hurled himself into the fray. My men tumbled up from the barge.

We would have had a hard time of it; maybe I would not have survived, had it not been for two men who appeared unexpectedly at the side of the jetty. I heard two whirring thuds, and as two men pitched screaming to the stones of the jetty I knew I was again seeing and hearing the terchick, the balanced throwing knife of Segesthes, in action.

Both victims had been struck in the face where their mail did not protect them.

Zolta was yelling like a crazy man. My long sword cleared its scabbard in time to cut down the attacker who pounced on me like a mad graint. I could see the two newcomers and they were going to their work with a will. Swords flashed in the dying light. Men yelled and bodies made heavy splashes as they toppled from the stones. The attackers had been caught flat-footed by that unexpected flank onslaught; and as more of my men came racing up the stairs, green and slippery with weed, Zolta, Nath, and I with reinforcements drove them off. We had been lucky; without those two on the flank, they might have overwhelmed us by sheer numbers. Nath was puffing with his mouth open, his bulk heaving.

Zolta, to my surprise, was not making rude comments. He was looking at the newcomers.

"By Zim-Zair!" he said, in wonder. "Is that a sword? Or is it a toothpick?" I knew, then.

A light, arrogant, and yet pleasant voice answered. "They don't like it through their eyes, friend. They don't like it."

The man who bent to retrieve his terchick from the bloodied face of a dead man wore buff clothes, short to the thigh and belted in; his legs were encased in long black boots. However, the item that truly identified him for me was the jaunty broad-brimmed hat, with the gay feather, and with those two strange slots cut in the brim above his forehead.

He straightened, the cleaned terchick in his hand. In a single rapid motion it vanished into the sheath behind his neck.

"The little Deldar," he said, "has his uses, like the Hikdar," and he slapped the long left-handed dagger at his right side. "And the Jiktar, my toothpick, as you so disrespectfully called the queen of weapons."

His rapier was long, thin, and elegant, rather too ornate about the hilt, and there were spots of blood about the hilt he had not cleaned off.

Nath and Zolta were over their surprise, now. They had seafared long enough around the inner sea to have learned of the men of Vallia.

The other Vallian, who was older and stouter and whose square-cut face showed a trace of displeasure as he slapped his rapier hilt, said a few words beneath his breath that halted his young companion in his tracks.

The older man scanned us in that streaming dying light, with the dead men and the blood between us. He took a step forward. He did not remove his hat, whose feather was black.

"Which of you," he said in a harsh voice, at once metallic and flat, "is the man known as Dray Prescot?"

Eleven

"Remberee, Pur Dray! Remberee!"

I was going home.

I was going home to a place I had never seen.

What was this Vallia like? This Vallia of the island empire, of the fabled opulence: the ocean-spanning shipping, the fleets of airboats, the wealth and power and beauty. What did it mean to me apart from my Delia, Delia of Delphond, Delia of the Blue Mountains?

I did not forget that my Delia was known as the Princess Majestrix of Vallia.

Tharu of Vindelka, Kov, the older of the two Vallians, treated me with a grim distant courtesy that puzzled me. He was icily polite. When I asked him about Delia's father, the emperor of Vallia, he rubbed a reflective thumbnail along a narrow scar on his jaw. "He is a mighty man, sudden, all-powerful unpredictable. His word is law."

Tharu had made all the arrangements. Vomanus, his aide, was volatile in his enthusiasm for life with a fetching kind of swaggering arrogance. I gathered from Zolta that Vomanus had a love of love also, for my two rascals, Nath and Zolta, took Vomanus out on the town as a kind of way of saying thank you. Tharu of Vindelka ripped into Vomanus on the following morning. I had insisted that they stay at my villa in the best part of Sanurkazz, and I heard the grim rumbling tones rolling on remorselessly, and the dispirited replies from Vomanus, who badly needed a hatful of palines.

We got down to business that very first morning.

Delia, Princess of Vallia had returned home immediately after an exhaustive search of the enclave of Strombor, all the rest of Zenicce that could be searched by parties of allied Houses, the Eward, the Reinmans, the Wickens, and the speediest airboats' messages and inquiries to the Clansmen of Felschraung and Longuelm. Of course I could not be found. By that time I was trying to explain why I was walking naked on a beach in Portugal, some four hundred light-years away.

"Now that we have found you, my Lord of Strombor," said Tharu in his metallic voice, "we will sail at once for Pattelonia on the southeast coast of Proconia. I have an airboat waiting there. You know whereof I speak?"

I nodded. I could feel my pulses jumping, the blood surging through my veins. Delia had gone home to Vallia and had started a search operation to find me that had turned her world upside down.

She had known — for how could she not so well understand? — that a mystery surrounded me. I had not told her of my origin, although I fully intended to. But she had shared with me that eerie experience of being flung in a gesture of contemptuous dismissal out of the sacred pool of baptism in far Aphrasöe, to find herself running on a beach in Segesthes. She must have reasoned that something similar had occurred again, and this time to me alone. So she had set herself to finding me. I heard from young Vomanus of the efforts that had been undertaken. He was very apologetic that he and Tharu had missed me before. I gathered that they had searched Magdag but in all that festering confusion of slaves and workers the discovery of a single man, who bore a name different from the one they sought, was well-nigh impossible and had defeated them. Chance had dictated that they had visited Sanurkazz when I was away at Zy. They had thought they had at last found the man their princess had instructed them to find, and they awaited my arrival, for they would not venture to the Grand Archboldship of the Order. They were thanked by me for waiting; they had almost certainly saved our necks.

"A message must be got back to Vallia as soon as is practicable," said Tharu.

"Then the Princess Majestrix may graciously consent to recalling all the hundreds of other envoys she has sent chasing all over the world in search of you."

I didn't much care for his tone.

I saw Vomanus casting an anxious look between us, and as I was conscious of my position vis-à-vis Vallia, I thought it expedient to say nothing. I told Nath and Zolta to take care of Vomanus: I thought he was a friend.

The coldness of Tharu of Vindelka's attitude quickly made itself understandable as I talked with the Vallians. There, as everywhere, it seemed, intrigues flourished. There were parties of various shades of political opinion, for religion in Vallia was undergoing some kind of psychic upheaval and no one seemed anxious to talk on the subject, and the emperor was acting with his usual autocratic hauteur. I would have to face that man, Delia's father, and tell him that I intended to marry his daughter no matter what he said or did. Tharu raged with anger that his party had not made the vital match with Delia, and he was forced to bottle all that frustrated resentment, for he acted under the orders, as he put it, of the Majestrix that no man may disobey. At that Vomanus pointed out that many men did disobey, and Tharu retired into that hard cold shell. He didn't like me. He considered not only had he lost the chance to marry off his favorite son or nephew to Delia but that Delia was marrying far below her station.

He was right, of course.

A broad ship had been found by Shallan, my agent, that was sailing to Pattelonia with supplies for the upcoming expedition. I had a nasty interview with Zo, the king, and quite unable to explain why I was suddenly leaving my command, Sanurkazz, and him, I went out in what was in reality disgrace. It did not matter. I was shaking the water of the inner sea from my boots.

I will not dwell on the interview with Mayfwy. She had heard the news and had been crying, but she dried her tears and put up a brave front. I kissed her gently, kissed Fwymay, who was turning into a beauty like her mother, clasped hands with young Zorg.

The problem of Harknel of High Heysh I must, perforce, leave unfinished. My natural inclinations after his last attempt to kill me on the jetty had been to take my men, march to his villa and burn it to the ground, and to hell with the high admiral and Zo, the king. Those jolly fat men of the mobiles would no doubt have gathered round, bottles in hand, and might conceivably have helped toss a torch or two.

But I could not do it. I could not risk a vile retribution from Harknel upon Felteraz. Felteraz was important. Very. I had to leave all this ferment in mid-boil. But I was glad to go. I understood what canker had been eating away at me as I went corsairing on the Eye of the World.

Nath and Zolta were a problem — a pair of problems.

I asked them to stay with Mayfwy. She would have need of their long swords.

"What, Stylor? Leave you now, our oar comrade! Never!"

Tharu of Vindelka grumbled, but agreed that there would be room on the airboat for the two. Vomanus was openly delighted.

"Anyway," said Zolta, "the Krozairs will never let harm befall Felteraz. And the king will also protect the citadel, for it holds his eastern flank. Do not fret, old vosk head."

My good-bye to Pur Zazz, the Grand Archbold of the Krozairs of Zy was formal, and then warmly fraternal. He did not seem at all perturbed that I was traveling better than a thousand dwaburs away.

"When the Krozairs have need of you, Pur Dray, and the brothers receive the summons, no matter where you are, I know you will come."

I gripped the hilt of my long sword. I nodded. It was true.

"You will be traveling beyond Proconia, which commands all the eastern seaboard of the Eye of the World and extends her varied powers as far to the east as The Stratemsk. Those mountains are said to have no summits, they extend clear to the orange glory of Zim, and form a pathway for the spirit to the majesty of Zair." He smiled and poured me more wine. "That is nonsense, of course, Pur Dray. But it tells eloquently of the fear and veneration in which men hold the Mountains of The Stratemsk."

I was aware, of course, that educated men knew that both the green and the red suns were suns and not thinking beings. But many of the illiterate folk of all shades of opinion held that the suns in their majesties were entities in their own rights quite apart from being the abode of the deities of Grodno and Zair. Astronomy was a strange art, on Kregen, twisted by its special circumstances into byways unknown to astronomers on Earth. The astrological lore and amazingly accurate predictions achieved by the wizards of Loh astonished even me at a later date.

"Over the mountains you are going where no man can say." Pur Zazz was as cultured and refined and intelligent a man as the inner sea might produce. Now he said: "Men say that beyond the mountains, in the hostile territory, there are whole tribes who fly on the backs of great beasts of the air." He smiled at me again, not ironically, but with the seriousness these subjects merited in an oar-powered geography. "I would welcome news, Pur Dray, of your adventures, and the sights you encounter."

"I will regard that as a first charge upon me, Pur Zazz."

When I left him, straight and commanding in his white tunic and apron, with that blazing emblem of the hubless wheel within the circle upon his breast, and the long sword belted in the fighting-man's way at his side, I half knew, then, I would never see him again.

"Remberee, Pur Dray."

"Remberee, Pur Zazz."

Saying good-bye to Zenkiren was not as easy. But I told him that a message to Strombor would always find me, and my vows to return would remain for as long as I lived.

I did not say that if the Star Lords or the Savanti decided otherwise I might not be in a position to return.

"Remberee, Pur Dray, Lord of Strombor."

"Remberee, Pur Zenkiren."

We clasped hands the final time, and I went down to my barge.

Nath and Zolta, very subdued, saw to getting us under way.

The hurt looks on the faces of my friends, looks they had tried to conceal, would haunt me for a very long time to come.

Two men had arrived from another world, another place across the outer oceans, mysterious and strange and with nothing to do with the Eye of the World, and I had upped and run panting like a dog running to its master. Who was this strange remote Princess Majestrix who called the foremost corsair captain of the inner sea? This is what they were saying.

But — they did not know Delia, my Delia of Delphond.

The broad ship sailed like a bathtub. I endured. I would far rather have preferred to make this little voyage into seas I had never scoured before aboard a swifter, but I was no longer in the employment of the king, no longer in his service.

The Magdaggian caught us as the twin suns, very close together, were sinking in the west and setting long shadows across the placid sea. She pulled toward us, all oars in neat parallel lines, churning the sea, and we could not escape.

"By Zantristar!" I yelled, hauling out my long sword. "They won't take us without a fight!"

The sailors were running, milling. Nath and Zolta, their long swords flaming brands in the dying light, tried to beat them into a resistance. But the merchantman stood no chance. She carried perhaps thirty crew, with little stomach for a fight they knew they could not win. They were launching a longboat and clearly they anticipated rowing to a nearby island, where we had intended to lay up for the night, and from which the Magdag corsair, lying in wait, had pulled with such sudden ferocity.

"My orders, from the Princess Majestrix herself," Tharu told me in his flat voice, "are to bring you safely back to Vallia. Put up your sword."

"You fool!" I said. "I am Pur Dray, the Lord of Strombor, the man the heretics from Magdag will give most to have in their clutches. There is no captivity for me!"

"It is a fight you cannot win," said Vomanus. He was fingering his rapier, and the look on his lean reckless face told me he would dearly love to join in.

"We are neutral." Tharu spoke impatiently, abruptly. "The barbarians from Magdag would not dare to harm us. They may kill all their enemies from Sanurkazz, but they will not touch me, nor Vomanus here — nor you, Dray Prescot."

"Why?"

The galley's long bronze ram curled the seas away in a long creaming bow wave that roiled down her sides where her oars flashed down and up, down and up, like the white wings of a gull. She was a hundred-and-twenty swifter, double-banked, fast. I could see the men on her beak ready to board us and others at her bow varters. Her sails had been furled, but her single mast had not been struck.

Tharu of Vindelka moved to the rail so that I turned to face him. Nath and Zolta below were frantic in their despairing efforts to rouse the crew. Vomanus walked quietly aft. The longboat was in the water and an oar splintered against the broad ship's side in the panicky haste.

"They will not take you, Dray Prescot."

"Why? What will it matter to them that I know the Princess Delia of Delphond? That my every thought is of her? I have never seen Delphond, Tharu, nor the Blue Mountains. But I regard them as my home."

He let that square, hard face of his relax. I did not think he was smiling.

"My duty is clear, Dray Prescot, who is intended to be Prince of Delphond." A grimace clouded his face with his inner resentments. "Rather, I think you had best be a Chuktar — no, on reflection, the dignity of a Kov is better suited. It will impress the Magdaggians more. I am, you should know, a Kov myself, although of a somewhat more ancient lineage."

I stared at him. I as yet did not know quite what he was talking about or where he was driving. Then I heard a light scrape of foot on the deck to my rear. I am quick. The blow almost missed. But it sledged down on the back of my head and dazed me and drove me down, and the second blow put out the lights.

When I regained consciousness I was aboard a Magdag swifter and I was dressed in the buff coat and black boots of a Vallian, a rapier swinging at my side was complemented by a dagger, and I was, so I gathered, an honored guest of Magdag. My name, I was told by Tharu, was Drak, the Kov of Delphond.

Twelve

The Princess Susheeng meets Drak, Kov of Delphond

Because the vessels of the inner sea almost invariably put either into port or were dragged up onto a convenient beach at night they were seldom provided with bunks or hammocks. I was lying on a kind of hard wooden settle covered with a ponsho fleece dyed green.

Green.

It is difficult for me, even now, to recollect anything coherent out of my thoughts then.

Suffice it to say that I simply lay there for a space while the whirling thoughts crowded, mocking and vicious, through my still-dazed head. My skull rang with the blow.

Tharu, Kov of Vindelka, leaned over me so that his stiff beard bristled against my cheek.

"Remember who you are, Drak, Kov of Delphond! It is our heads as well as yours that depend on your memory."

"I have a good memory," I said. I spoke dryly. I was thinking of Nath and Zolta. "I remember faces and names and what people say."

"Good."

He straightened up and I could see a little of the cabin, that of the first lieutenant as I judged, having some skill in reading the infinitesimal touches that mark rank from rank upon the sea — any sea — and despising the lot of them.

"Wait." I caught his sleeve. He thought I wanted assistance to rise and began to draw haughtily away, but I looked him in the eye. Vomanus came into view, his lively face now sadly apprehensive. "Tharu — Delphond I understand, and Kov, because you told me. But Drak? Where did that come from?"

Tharu's square face darkened and he cast a malevolent glance up toward Vomanus.

Vomanus said: "I called you that, Dray — ah, Drak — as the first name that popped into my head."

"Once this young fool had named you, I could do nothing less than accept it. The Magdaggians are not fools."

It seemed that Vomanus was lying, judging by his face.

Tharu went on speaking as I let him go and levered myself up. My head rang like those bells of Beng-Kishi.

"Drak was the name of the emperor's father when he ascended the throne. Also it is the name of a being half-legendary, half-historical, part human, part god, that we may read of in the old myths, those from the Canticles of the Rose City, at least three thousand years old." He spoke impatiently, a cultured man telling a peasant.

Well, and wasn't he right?

I stood up.

Beng-Kishi clanged a trifle less discordantly.

"You've done it now," I told them. "If these devils from Magdag find out who I am, they'll fry you over a fire, chip you into kindling, and feed you to the chanks." Vomanus looked a trifle sick. Mention of the chanks, the sharks of the seas of Kregen, made me think of Nath and Zolta again.

"We saw them pulling for the shore in the longboat," said Vomanus, swallowing.

"They either drowned or were saved," said Tharu. "It is no matter. They were unimportant."

He made a mistake, saying that to me, their oar comrade.

I brushed past him and, ducking my head, went out onto the deck. We were drawn up in the lee of the island; fires blazed as the watches kept a vigilant lookout. The stars of the Kregan night sky blazed down, forming those convoluted patterns the wizards of Loh can read and understand, or so they say. A cooling breeze blew and stirred the leaves ashore. Sentries stood on the quarterdeck and I caught the flash of gold as an officer moved. Only two of the lesser moons were up, and they would soon be gone in their helter-skelter hurtling around the planet.

The thought of conversation with a man of Magdag was nauseating to me. I looked hungrily out to the shore. Perhaps Nath and Zolta were out there, waiting to pounce. But what chance would we stand, three against a swifter crew? I knew an arrow would feather into me if I dived overboard; I decided that I would chance that. I would dive and swim to the island, and the devil take the chanks. If I was to walk the length of the central gangway and try to jump down to the beach I would be stopped. I knew the habits of Magdag captains, as I knew those of Sanurkazz. I knew what I would do were I the swifter captain.

Vomanus joined me, and then a Magdaggian Hikdar, who turned out to be the man whose cabin we had taken. He didn't seem to show his annoyance. I made an excuse, and went below again. The stink of the slaves and their eternal and infernal moaning and clanking of shackles and fetters made me irritable.

I believe, now, looking back, that I had not lost my nerve. There have been times in my life when I have followed a course of action that the casual onlooker would feel smacks of cowardice. I answer to no one, of course, for my actions — except to Delia. If I got myself killed, Delia would be alone, and more and more I was coming to the conclusion that she would need me by her side in the days to come. There were great forces moving implacably and with incredible cunning, somewhere...

We sailed with the rising sun and headed west.

The news was bad. Pattelonia, the city of the Proconia where the flier had been left, had been raided and left in flames. The men of Sanurkazz had suffered a defeat. This swifter, *My Lady of Garles*, a five-five-hundred-and-twentyswifter, had sustained some damage and lost some oarsmen. She had been entrusted with dispatches for the admiralty in Magdag and her smart capture of the old broad ship on which we had been traveling had come as a pleasant diversionary tidbit. Tharu, bowing to the inevitable, had consented to be taken back to Magdag. Without a flier, travel across The Stratemsk and over the hostile lands beyond to the place where we could pick up a ship for Vallia, Port Tavetus, was impossible. Ergo, we must go to Magdag and wait for a ship from Vallia, which was due, so Tharu told me, sometime soon.

The impression I gained was that Tharu, Kov or not, was mighty grateful not to have to fly back over The Stratemsk and that weary length of hostile territory to the Vallian empire port city. The realization made me tremble. I acknowledged something I had not even allowed myself to think from the moment I had arrived, naked and despairing, on the beach of that Portuguese shore.

I felt a profound sense of thankfulness and gratitude. My Delia still loved me! How often I had almost allowed myself to think that she had forgotten me! I knew how unworthy I was, and how I had dismayed and disappointed her in our brief dealings. But she had not forgotten me. She had summoned the strength of her island empire, the only important area of land on this planet that was under the sway of one government, to search for me and seek me out and bring me home to her. Also I felt a strange kind of humbleness in my pride. How puffed up I was, how vaunting in my ambitions, how comical in my aspirations!

Delia's orders had sent this harsh, proud noble, the Kov of Vindelka, to seek me, had caused him to fly over uncharted realms of savages and mythical beings, to risk a neck he must consider the next most-important neck in the whole world. I had him summed up now. He was a king's man. In this case, an emperor's man. For the emperor of Vallia he had an obsessive drive to duty, and that extended to the emperor's daughter, and, *faute de mieux*, to the daughter's betrothed, much though he might dislike and feel contempt for her choice.

If I had been a vain man, a proud man in the evil sense of pride, how I would have rocked with glee!

As it was, and I would ask you to believe me in this, I felt like falling to my knees and thanking the god of my childhood, and also throw in a kind word or two to Zair, the red-sun deity, just to be on the safe side. With that comically impious thought I knew that I was finding my old self again.

While medicine and surgery and knowledge of the proper care for the sick were in a state far advanced of what I had been used to on Earth, the doctors of Kregen were a bunch one did well to give a wide berth to. They had not, and still have not, reached anywhere near the recent achievements of Earthly medicine and surgery — in the matter of heart transplants, for instance. They leaned heavily on herbal drugs, which could obtain seemingly miraculous cures, and their surgery also had developed techniques of acupuncture I found nothing short of miraculous. It was nothing for a patient undergoing a serious operation with his head, or his insides, exposed to the knife — his earlobes or the web between his thumb and first finger quilted with needles — to be given a mouthful of palines to munch, and to keep up a bright conversation with the surgeon. I admit, the first time I saw that, I had a vivid mental picture of the cockpits I was used to, with the aprons caked with blood, their saws, their tubs of boiling tar.

So I did not have the slightest desire to consult a doctor when I began to feel a little of that impatient drive to go to Vallia making me feverish. Since that dip in the sacred pool of baptism in the River Zelph in far Aphrasöe I had never had a day's illness. I did not intend to succumb now.

Pulling into Magdag was, as you may readily imagine, a disorienting experience for me, ex-Magdag galley slave.

My first impression was that the walls did not rear as I remembered them. This came because of the low freeboard, a necessity on an efficient galley, bringing my oarsman's viewpoint down much below that where I now stood on the quarterdeck.

Magdag reared her piles of stone heavily into the bright air. Gulls wheeled and shrieked, but with all my Krozair training I heard them only as croaking magbirds against the tuneful sounds of our own gulls in Sanurkazz. Flags and banners floated on the breeze. The twin suns shone mingled upon the smooth water. *My Lady of Garles* pulled steadily in past the outer breakwater, past the forts with their bristling varters, past the inner breakwater with the forts where always a Sacred Guard, composed on five days of the week of Chuliks and on the sixth of young and high-spirited Magdag nobles, were ready to vent their warrior-like high spirits on anything weak and unable to resist that might come their way. Many a fisherman went back to his quarters with a broken head and his fish baskets full of holes and cuts, having been used by the Magdag nobles for sword targets in their fun.

We rounded to in an inner basin, one of the many harbors of Magdag into which I had never previously been.

Vallia kept no consuls in the cities of the inner sea, presumably, I thought at the time, so as not to become embroiled in the politics of the area. The Vallians are above all, even above their warlike proclivities, a trading nation. But Tharu was quickly able to arrange accommodation for us, through a contact, in what I regarded as a senselessly luxurious palace.

His comment was frosty.

"You are now moving in areas somewhat removed from your usual purlieus."
I liked that word even when he used it, but I had gone past the period of wanting
to bait this Tharu for all he said in his pompous aristocratic way. If all the nobles
of Vallia were like him I was in for a boring or headily exciting time, depending
on how much I was prepared to put up with them. "I am a Kov of Vallia — as are
you, for my sins — and we demand style in our living. Anything less than this
would be unthinkable; in itself it is barely good enough, as I have told Glycas in
no uncertain terms."

"Glycas?"

We slaves of Magdag knew little of the upper crust "A most powerful force, a
man who has the king's ear. We are renting this palace from him—" If he was
about to say words to the effect that I should be careful how I comported myself
in case I damaged the furnishings, he thought better of it.

Vomanus had taken off his buff coat with a sigh of relief and now wore only a
white silk shirt with his breeches and black boots, a shirt, however, whose overlong sleeves were wristed by a mass of ruffles which he liked to flourish up and
down his brown and muscular arms as he gesticulated in his talk.

"The place is well enough, Tharu," he said. Tharu glared at him, but let the
matter drop. We were all anxious to leave and return to Vallia, and soon news
came that a Vallian ship had been signaled. I guessed the Todalpheme of
Akhram would have a hand in that business.

We passed the days in walking about the city, patronizing wineshops and taverns in the evening, watching the dancing girls and the various varieties of sports
available. The girls were slaves, dancing girls clad in bangles, beads, and precious
little else. They were totally unlike the girls who danced so gaily for us among the
wagon circles of my Clansmen.

I was back in the snuffle of slavery, with beasts half-human, half-animal for
guards, and I didn't like any of it.

I scarcely used the suite of rooms assigned to me in the palace rented from
Glycas. When I had been taken unconscious aboard *My Lady of Garles* with a
glib explanation, Tharu, with his accustomed harsh authority, had quickly persuaded the Magdag captain to take aboard our baggage also. Tharu's own
iron-bound chests stood in his rooms. So it was that, with the exception of deviced clothing, I had all that I had brought from Sanurkazz — silks and furs,
jewels, coins, weapons, my own long sword, and the coat of mail Mayfwy had
had made for me. I could clearly see the danger these represented. They were
soaked with the traditions of Zair. They would make me a marked man if discovered.

So I had them hidden away beneath my bed, the three bronze-bound chests of
lenken planks a nail in thickness. Then I took pains to explain to my Magdaggian hosts how I had picked up a long sword and a coat of mail as mementoes of
a pleasant visit to their city, and when comments were made that the hauberk
was unmistakably of Sanurkazzian cut I forced myself to laugh and said that no
doubt this was the booty of a prize made to the greater glory of Grodno. That
pleased those men of the green sun.

Mind you, it was refreshing once more to stroll about with a long rapier at my side.

Glycas was a dark-visaged man on the threshold of middle age, which on Kregen meant he must be turning a hundred or so, and his black hair was still crisp and fashionably cut, his hands and arms white, his fingers loaded with rings. But he was not a fop. His long sword was hilted plainly, with a bone grip that I, personally, would not have tolerated but which I knew was much favored on the inner sea. He was short and squarely built and he possessed a temper that had made him notorious. He was, truly, a dangerous man.

His sister, the princess Susheeng — plus a score of other pretentious names denoting her exalted rank and the broad acres of her estates, the thousands of slaves she owned — was lithe, lovely, and dark-haired, with eyes that tried to devour me with amorous glances from the moment we met. I was forced to contrast her with the gay reckless simplicity of Mayfwy, and had to acknowledge the animal vitality of this woman, her burning gaze, the intensity of the passion with which she took anything she wanted. All her noble honorifics amused me, through their pomposity. I realized afresh how lightly my Delia carried all the ringing brave titles to which she was heir, how subtly and how surely, with what courtesy and quiet gravity — shot through with her own elfin irony at life — she fitted the role of Princess Majestrix of Vallia.

The Princess Susheeng made a dead set at me. I was aware of this, and it annoyed me, through the complications that inevitably must ensue. Vomanus openly envied what he called my good fortune. Tharu, with a darker vision, contained his own resentment and annoyance.

I told her, one day as we stood on the third-level ramparts overlooking one of the harbors that opened out below the palace in which we were lodging, that I was looking forward earnestly to returning home.

"But, my Kov of Delphond, what has your vaulted Vallia to offer you that you cannot find in far greater quantity and quality here in Sacred Magdag?"

I winced, covered that lapse, and said: "I am homesick, Susheeng. Surely you understand that?"

With incongruous pride, she said: "I have traveled not for one single mur outside the lands of Magdag!"

I made some empty reply. That a person would boast of that kind of chauvinism appalled me.

"Well, Princess," I said, and saying it realized how incautious I was, "I intend to return home as soon as possible."

The woman nauseated me.

I had my mind on other women. Put this Princess Susheeng in the starkness of the gray slave breechclout, teach her the humility that is the only sure path to serenity, and she would turn out well. Slaves had no chance to reach to anything beyond their slavery, except those who escaped physically, by running or by death, and the humility a slave learns is corrosive and corrupting; but this girl might profit from it, if she knew she was to learn by her experience.

I wanted to travel to Vallia — and at once.

She saw all that in me; she saw my utter rejection of her.

The next day Vomanus and I were wandering through one of the high-class jewelry streets, a kind of open-air market, when we bumped into the Princess Susheeng with her body of retainers, blank-faced Chulik guards and a group of swaggering popinjay show-off Magdag nobility all fawning on her. She treated them all like dirt, of course.

"And what is that trinket you are buying, Kov Drak?"

She used the familiar tone of address to infuriate her attendants, of course.

I held up the jewelry. It was a beautiful piece of cut chemzite, blazing in the suns' light. It was work of Sanurkazz style and skill.

"I think it a pleasant piece," I said.

"It is of Zair," she said, her mouth drawn down. "It and all like it should be broken up and refashioned into more seemly work of Grodno."

"Maybe. But it is here." I forced myself to go on. "No doubt it is the booty of some successful swifter captain."

She smiled at me. Her mouth was ripely red, a trifle too large, soft, and rapacious with overfed passion.

"And is it for me, a parting gift, Kov Drak?"

"No," I said. I spoke too sharply. "I intend to take it to Vallia as a keepsake of the Eye of the World." That was half of the truth, as you will readily perceive.

She pouted, and laughed gaily, as at a joke, and made some flighty and, in truth, slighting, remark, so as to retain her composure before her toadies. Then she walked swiftly from the market to her sectrix, which she rode well enough, I grant you.

I know, now, that that scene saved my life.

That evening the Vallian ship was sighted rounding the point. She would tie up in Magdag this night. So far I had not set eyes on a ship of Vallia, for they were rare enough in the inner sea, tending to make armadas of their voyages to take advantage of the prevailing seasonal winds, and I had always been raiding when they had called at Sanurkazz. I had once tried to set course to intercept a Vallian I knew to be due off Isteria; however, for a reason that I did not then comprehend, I missed her.

I looked forward to the encounter.

Vomanus took himself off to the harbor to greet the Vallian captain, and then he was back cursing and swearing, to saddle up a sectrix and ride off to a more distant anchorage to which the Vallian vessel had unaccountably been assigned by the port captain. I shouted some jovial remark after him. I had wanted to ride myself, but Tharu had sternly vetoed that.

"A Kov does not ride down to the jetty to greet the mere captain of a ship," he said, and that was that.

I had gathered that a Kov was what we on this Earth would call a duke; the information depressed me. I had often found that empty titles mean nothing, and that intermediary ranks are stifling and frustrating.

There is a board game played a great deal on Kregen called Jikaida. As the name implies it has to do with combat. The squared board is, in shape, like an elongated chessboard, and with a touch of Halma about the moves, as one army of Jikaida men clash with the others. If you expect the colors of the men to be red and green, you are wrong. They are blue and yellow, or white and black. The red and the green, it seems, are reserved for real battle. So to take my mind off waiting, Tharu and I settled to a game of Jikaida.

I make it a practice whenever it is practicable never to sit with my back to a door.

When the door to our room smashed open and the mailed men burst in, their faces covered with red scarves, I jumped up. Tharu, whose back was to the door, was knocked flying across the table. Jikaida men went flying in a shower of blue and yellow. The table tangled my legs. My rapier was lying on the floor at my side, casually in reach but scabbarded — for this was a great city and who would expect attack within a palace? — and by the time I had the blade free a poniard stuck its tip into my throat and a single move would mean my instant death.

At that moment I felt that I was growing old — I, Dray Prescot, who had bathed in the sacred pool of Aphrasöe and would live a thousand years!

I was trussed up like a vosk and between two of the burly thugs was carried like a roll of carpet out and through a secret passage behind a full-length portrait of some arrogant Magdag swifter captain in the midst of a hypothetical destruction of a Sanurkazz fleet. Naturally, I had had no idea of the passage's existence. Far below I was carried out and flung into a dung cart which reminded me of the galley slaves' benches. We bumped along cobbles. I had had no sight of my attackers. I could hear no sound from them. I was gagged, and so I did not expect to hear from Tharu.

They threw me down in a stone cellar where green slime ran on the walls. I looked at their red scarves concealing their faces. Only their eyes, bright and quick, like rasts', shining at me over the red cloths, were visible.

Afterward I learned I spent five days in that cellar, bound loosely but sufficiently to prevent escape, fed on slops, without exercise and with a bucket for toilet purposes, and with two men on guard at all times. Tharu was not with me.

On the sixth day I was rescued. My guards stood up with a casual air as mailed men entered; then they stiffened and although I could not see their faces I could imagine the sudden terror there as they scrabbled to draw their weapons. The newcomers cut them down without mercy, even though the last man attempted to surrender. As he sank onto the floor, his blood oozing from the deep gash smashed through his mail, his killer snatched up the red scarf.

He held it up, and spat on it.

"See!" he cried. "It is the work of those vile heretics of Sanurkazz! The stinking vosks of Zair have done this—"

He bent quickly and slashed my bonds free. Others of his men helped me rise. "But now you are safe, Kov of Delphond!"

Thirteen

I return to the megaliths

"My Lord Kov," said Glycas to me, formally. "I make the most profound apologies. It is unthinkable that such indignities should happen to an honored guest in Magdag. But—" He spread his hands. His dark eyes were most bright upon me. "These are troublous times. The vermin of the red swarm everywhere—"

"Drak should be thankful we saved his life," said the Princess Susheeng. She lolled in a hammock-type chair of silk and fringing tassels of gold thread; one of her arms was thrown back over her head, drawing up her body into a sensuous curve. "Those sea-leem of Sanurkazz will all be destroyed and put down one day. But I am happy that we saved you from them, Drak."

The high balcony overlooking the harbor received a cooling breeze for which we were grateful, the heat being excessive at this time. Magdag, being north of Sanurkazz, is somewhat cooler, but neither basks in the strong bracing breezes that sweep in over the Sunset Sea to cool Zenicce, far to the east. A long and powerful warm current, the so-called Zim-Stream, sweeps up from the south past the coasts of Donengil, the southernmost portion of Turismond. Driving in an arc toward the northeast it pushes in a clearly demarcated line of differently colored water through the Cyphren Sea between Turismond and Loh and so washes all the western and southern shores of Vallia. Its southern branch retains enough energy on occasions to reach Zenicce on the western coast of Segesthes.

"I do thank you," I said. Then, holding myself tightly under control, I said: "It seems they took everything I possess."

Glycas nodded. "Everything you had with you. Strange things, I have no doubt."

"From Vallia," said Susheeng.

I quivered alert.

"Hardly any," I said, offhandedly. "I have been collecting curios from the Eye of the World, artifacts of Magdag — and of Sanurkazz."

"Ah — of course," said Glycas, in a silky murmur I didn't trust.

"Had your Vallian ship captain not taken his ship to so distant a berth, no doubt your gallant companion, Vomanus, would have been here." Vomanus had been enraged to a purple fury when he had at last seen me safe. Tharu, that harsh, stern man, Kov of Vindelka, had not been seen since the attack. Everyone considered him to be dead. I felt that if he was not dead, then he might look upon that state as something to be desired if he had been sent to the rowing benches of a Magdag galley.

"These stupid uprisings continue to occur," Glycas said smoothly. "The slaves on the buildings to the greater glory of Grodno seek to invoke the vile heretical worship of Zair, the misbegotten one. We shall make inquiries and punish the guilty."

"And meanwhile?"

The Princess Susheeng rose like a graceful and deadly leem from the hammock-chair. She smiled on me and her red lips were moistly sensuous. "Oh, we shall, of course, accept entire responsibility for you, my dear Drak, until another Vallian ship calls."

"It will not be wise for you to continue on in this palace, alone," said Glycas briskly. "We hope you will do us the honor of taking apartments in our own palace — it is the Emerald Eye Palace, after all. Only the king, above whom no man dare seek to lift himself, has a finer palace in all Magdag."

"So be it," I said, accepting the inevitable. Then I had the wit to add: "I thank you most sincerely."

So it was that I moved in with Glycas and his rapacious sister Susheeng into the Emerald Eye Palace. The place was large, ornate, not particularly comfortable, noisy — and it had been built with slave labor.

At every opportunity I would clear out of the place and stroll about the city. Although Vallia was my objective, I still looked at the defenses of the city with the eye of a raiding Krozair from Sanurkazz. Glycas had insisted that I take with me an escort of half a dozen Chuliks. I had protested, but the manner of his insistence indicated that he would not have me say no. I thought of that scorpion I had seen on the rocks of the Grand Canal; that was how this man Glycas appeared to me: quick, sudden, and deadly.

The city smoldered under the lambent fires of the twin suns. I walked about the paved streets and avenues, studied the architecture, patronized a few drinking dens and amusement arcades. I even forced myself to look in on a small arena where groups of drug-inflamed slaves fought each other for the shrieking enjoyment of the Magdag nobility. Sickened, I left. Sectrix racing, I thought, might tempt me. But horse racing as it is practiced on Earth has never appealed to me — the degradation of man and beast and the motives thus revealed do no credit to Homo sapiens — and the men of Magdag had evolved no different method. I yearned, then, for the free ranging races with my Clansmen as we sped over the Great Plains, joyous in the race, astride our zorcas or voves.

So it was natural that, saddling up a sectrix and with my bodyguard similarly mounted, I rode out from the Magdag city gate on the landward side and headed for the megalithic complex of obsessive building.

On several occasions I had spoken to architects, often at one of the many intimate dinner parties Susheeng delighted in arranging, hurling shrill abuse at her slaves as they scurried about doing the actual work of preparation. These scented and elaborately coifed men had assured me that the buildings were essential for the soul and spirit of Magdag. Only through this continual erection of stupendous monuments of stone and brick could Magdag find a purpose in life. I heard talk of the Great Death, of the time of dying, and now I knew this to mean the period of eclipse, when the green sun was eclipsed by the red. This astronomical event would in the very nature of things have a tremendous significance for the men who worshiped the green-sun deity Grodno. It would, in truth, be a death. When the green sun passed before the red, and being smaller

208

it did not thus create an eclipse but rather a transit, was the time for the Magdag-gians to break out in another of their surges of violence and upheavals of conquest. During those times the men of Zair looked to their defenses, sharp-ened their swords, and sailed the inner sea in strength.

What the men of Magdag did during the green sun's eclipse, during the time of the Great Death, I was to learn...

The massive buildings were as I remembered them.

I felt my heart move with pity and anger as I saw the slaves in their thousands laboring beneath the suns.

Progress had been made on the buildings that I recalled as being half finished. I saw gang overseers lashing on the slaves to faster and faster work. The Chuliks would not let me approach too close. They had their long swords half un-sheathed. They were not happy. I could smell the tension on the hot air.

"They are behind their schedules," I was told by a rast-faced guard com-mander, an overlord of the second class. He was the first I had met since my second arrival in Magdag. I had been moving in the company of overlords of the first class and of nobles — Zair forgive me.

"The time of the Great Death approaches," he said. He seemed happy to spend the time talking to a noble. "We must have at least one new hall finished by then."

"Assuredly," I said.

He nodded with his own driving conviction. "We will," he said. He held a whip and ran the thongs through his blunt fingers. "We will."

Choked by the redolent memories of the slaves and workers, with sudden bril-liant images of Genal, Holly, and Pugnarses in my mind, I looked over the fantastic scene. I could see it with a new eye, now, from a different perspective. The place swarmed with men and women. In their gray garments, or naked, they moved over the buildings on their scaffolds like a confused army of insects. Huge masses of stone were hoisted into the air as the shrieked commands of the whip-masters cut through the air as their whips cut through the sweating skins of the slaves. The piles of bricks grew under the sun, and were carried away by endless streams of slave children. The shouts, the bedlam, the smoke of dust and chips that hung over everything, the stinks of the thousands of people, rose like an evil miasma. This was what Babel might have been; although here everyone could understand his neighbor. This convulsion of perverted energy smoked to high heaven upon the plain of Magdag, there on my adopted world of Kregen.

Making it my business to inspect every part of the work, I visited places I had never seen before. There were the smiths, working miracles of beauty in scrolled iron and brass. There were the masons cutting stone to delicate perfection. The artists painted their frescoes, their friezes, working with the sure speed that had painted this figure in this position in these colors a hundred times before. A strict and formal routine held the decoration into ritual patterns. Inside some of the lofty halls with their plethora of columns and innumerable images and paintings, I sometimes felt I had reentered the hall I had left only moments be-fore.

The production lines stunned me with their expertise set up or the development of some of the artifacts used. Earth did not reach that state of expertise until the automobile assembly line indicated what mechanical effectiveness might be obtained from this breaking-down of function into separate work-quanta.

Men in long lines labored to produce, for example, barrel after barrel of the iron nails used in fixing wooden fasciae. They worked with a kind of numb professionalism, slaves chained to their benches, the only sounds the eternal clinking of the hammers, the bellow of the forges.

I saw the way masses of slaves were yoked to the gigantic stones ferried down from the mountains of the interior. They could sort themselves out into their gangs and tail onto ropes and haul away under the lash with a skill I remembered.

Down by the sludgy banks of the sluggish stream that bore the ferried stone from the interior — a blackish-gray basaltic stone and quite unlike the yellow stone used in the construction of the city's noble houses — I saw the wide extent of the kitchens. Holly had cooked for the workers on a small scale, by the gang. The slaves had mass cooking. The place stank and crawled with flies and vermin. Down by the river, which ran red here, I saw immense piles of bones, and tall stacks of vosk skulls, too thick and strong to be easily disposed of. The rubbish dumps stretched, it seemed, for miles. Pollution, something I had hardly expected to experience on Kregen, had come to Magdag with a vengeance.

My Chulik guards made no effort to show me the warrens, and I had enough sense to know I could never enter there dressed as I was and with a mere six Chuliks. Glycas had invited me to what he termed a hunting party. When I had gathered that this meant that a group of his friends would be riding, mailed and with long swords in their hands, into the warrens to chase, and cut down and rape what fell in their path, I declined, pleading a fever.

My life had become, again as it had so often done in the past, intolerable to me.

Something must be done, something could be done, and if I, Dray Prescot, thought anything at all of myself and what I was here for at the express command of the Star Lords, then I would have to do it.

I would have to do it

I wanted to do it.

The Princess Susheeng was becoming tiresome. My door was kept locked at night, but she scratched on it two or three times. I knew it was her, for I could smell her perfume, thick and odoriferous and liberally applied. I fancied she would begin a more obvious attack soon and, remembering the Princess Natema, I put in hand a little scheme. Away inland, to the north, beyond the chain of factory farms similar to that one where I had been captured by the men of Magdag, lay broad pastures, lush plains covered with head-high grasses. Here big game hunts were a pastime I might welcome. I recalled with a pang the Savanti, and of how Maspero had apologized for the atavistic behavior of himself and his friends as they had led me out on a graint hunt that would lead, if any danger and harm there was, to them alone.

Away beyond the plains of Turismond lay lands that were colder and colder until at last they vanished beneath the mist and ice. So the Magdaggians said. They never cared to venture there, seldom went other than a few dwaburs into the plains. They were essentially an inward-looking people: the Eye of the World aptly named for them.

Arrangements for my expedition were made and Vomanus, who I thought had a permanent girl waiting for him in some palace or other of the city, was dug out to accompany me. I managed to avoid asking either Glycas or his sister. We had a few Chulik guards, a safari of slaves for porterage, and mounted aboard our sectrixes we set off. Very quickly I lost the safari. I had told Vomanus to carry on as though expecting to meet me out on the plains. I dumped the sectrix and my gear, and donned the gray breechclout I had stolen from a slave of the palace. I crept by night into the workers' areas by the buildings.

I was not home, but I felt a queasy sensation of homely familiarity grip me. At that point I almost called the whole stupid venture off. But I went on. This, I remember thinking, is a part and parcel of what the Star Lords wish me to accomplish.

As the familiar odor of the warrens rose about me and I saw again that crazy skyline of tumbling walls and leaning towers, the sacking-draped flat roofs where the workers would lie out in the heat of the night, the dark mouths of alleys where the streaming pink moonlight fell aslant the dust and the cobbles, I had to restrain myself from picking up my heels and running. Even then I could not be sure which way I would run.

The old familiar hovel looked the same.

A worker who had found a bottle of Dopa lay propped against the wall snoring lustily. I could hear the restless sounds of thousands of people all about me, people crammed into hovels compressed into narrow streets of tumbledown buildings. I pushed open the familiar door. Genal sat up on his sacking bed, blinking like an owl.

"Who—?" He squinted in the parallelogram of pink moonlight. "No — Stylor? Stylor!"

I moved in fast and gripped his hand.

"Lahal, Genal. You are well?"

He looked at me, swallowed, closed his mouth.

"Lahal, Stylor." Suddenly he jumped up and ran across the packed earth floor with its bit of sacking carpet, knocking over an earthenware pot on the way. He bent over another pallet that I had not noticed. He shook the sleeper.

"Pugnarses — wake up, wake up! It is Stylor, returned from the green radiance of Genodras!"

I chilled.

Pugnarses awoke in a foul temper, cursing by Grakki-Grodno, the sky deity of beasts of haulage, and looked blearily at me. He tumbled up from the pallet. His shaggy hair and eyebrows, his malevolent look, all coalesced and I put out my hand to cover my feelings, and I said: "Lahal, Pugnarses."

"Lahal, Stylor."

211

I felt out of place. They both stood looking at me as though I were a ghost. In a way, I was.

But they were both acting in a natural way, both cursing by and calling on Grodno, the green-sun deity of Genodras.

What, I wondered then with a dizzying feeling of helplessness, would Pur Zenkiren, or Pur Zazz, make of this situation?

I pulled myself together.

"I cannot stay long," I said. "And I cannot venture outside the warren."

Genal said, at once, hotly: "You may stay here as long as you wish, Stylor. Here, you are safe."

He bent and picked up a gray tunic. I saw the green and black badges of a worker overseer, he of the balass stick. "I wield the balass now, as well as Pugnarses. We can offer you help, Stylor." He eyed me keenly, looking at my shoulders and biceps. "Was it the galleys?"

"Aye, Genal, it was."

"And you escaped!" Pugnarses whistled. I suspected he was annoyed that Genal had aspired to the balass while he, Pugnarses, still stayed as a worker overseer, and had not yet reached his coveted ambition, the white loincloth and the whip of the overseer of overseers.

"What of Follon the Fristle?" I asked. It would be as well at first to let these two believe what they willed.

Pugnarses let rip with a disgusting sound. Genal made a face and an obscene sign. I had forgotten the manners of slaves; this was a salutary reminder. I had best not forget...

"He, too, is of the balass. He gave information about an escape — when you disappeared — he was rewarded."

"I'm glad you had the sense not to become involved, Genal."

"But we will rise, one day—"

"Yes," I said.

Their heads lifted as I spoke.

"And — Holly?"

Their reactions were interesting. Both cast a swift look at each other, then away, and their faces went blank.

"She is well, Stylor," said Genal.

"She is more fair than all the painted women of the palaces of Magdag," said Pugnarses with some vehemence.

So that was how it was.

I had not come to the slave and worker warrens to see Holly, although I hoped I would see her soon. I had to establish an identity with these men. Already they believed I was an escaped galley slave, coming to them for help. That was a start.

"I may have to ask your help in concealing me," I said. "From time to time. For I have great plans." I broke off. A slim shadow broke the parallelogram of pink moonlight. Soon, that moonlight would silver as the night wore on, but the shadow now hesitating in the doorway was surrounded by a pink halo.

A low voice breathed a single word.

"Stylor!"

Holly was still incredibly lovely. She had matured, but I knew those innocent lines of naïveté concealed an iron resolve. Beside her the Princess Susheeng was an overblown, raddled bloom of autumn.

"Lahal, Holly—" I began.

But she rushed toward me and flung her arms about my neck. Her slender lissome body pressed all nakedly to mine. Her lips, hot and moist and overpowering with a passionate ardor that shocked through me, crushed down on my mouth. And as she kissed me with such abandon I saw over her shoulder the faces of Genal and Pugnarses, staring at me, stricken.

Fourteen

The plans of Stylor

Life thereafter became exciting and interesting and extraordinarily rewarding.

I spent many nights out among the warrens. After I had rejoined the safari and had then returned after a quick hunting trip to Magdag with a few leem as trophies, I arranged a cache near the warrens, adjacent to the river, where I could reach by sectrix easily from the Emerald Eye Palace. I had a cache there of weapons, clothes, and money. I would ride out from the palace without the Chulik escort, having disposed of them by a straight deception, change into my gray breech-clout, and glide silently into the maze of alleyways and courts. Long before dawn I would return.

On the sixth day I could often manage to spend the entire time with the slaves and workers, as Glycas and Susheeng were devoted in their observations of the rites of worship owing to Grodno. Particularly at this time, when the time of the Great Death approached, everyone of Magdag was punctilious in their religious life.

The business of Follon the Fristle was completed in a strange way that turned out to my advantage.

To say that all Fristles looked alike to me would not be true. I could recognize individuals when necessary. One evening as the last of the suns vanished in the sky and the Maiden with the Many Smiles sailed clear above clouds I rode down to the river and hitched my sectrix to a tree branch. Away beyond the bank the warrens stretched, orange in that ruddy reflected light, and I took heart from that.

In only a few moments I had stashed my Vallian gear, wrapped the gray breechclout around me, drawing the ends up between my legs and tucking them in. In the belt that held the clout was a sharp and gently-curving knife snug in its sheath. As I padded toward the first sprawling line of shacks and mud-brick dwellings, I heard a scream, muffled but close.

Screams were common in the slave warrens of Magdag.

Then, forcing itself on my attention, a struggle reeled out into the moonlight:

two Fristles locked together. It took me a moment or two to decide that this was a male Fristle attempting to rape a female. She couldn't scream anymore for the man had his arm locked around her throat. I could see her slit eyes, painfully twisted, and the way the blunted fangs of her mouth champed against her thin dark lips.

Then I saw the male Fristle was Follon.

I recognized him well enough.

I loped over and took him around the throat. Fristles habitually wear a kind of leather jack, brass-studded. Those employed by Magdag had dyed theirs green. It was with some considerable force that I kicked that green color. Follon tried to yell and my fingers clamped on his windpipe. He couldn't get his curved scimitar-like sword out. I bore down on him.

The female Fristle sagged to the ground, whimpering. She wore no clothes. Her body, with its light dusting of fur, gleamed golden in the pink rays of moonlight. Another Fristle, older, with a dun-colored hide, slipped to the fallen female's side, held her head, and began to croon strange half-hissing, half-sobbing words in native Fristle. Then:

"He would have used my Sheemiff, and discarded her, killed her!"

It suddenly became easy to think of these half-human, half-cat people in fully human terms. The old woman glared up with a lift of her narrow chin and her slit eyes blazed red. The girl Fristle moaned again. I saw blood on the fur of her legs.

Follon gave a tremendous wrench, but I held him and leaned back and then, as Zair is my witness, whether it was his own lunge, or my impassioned grip, or my subconscious desire, I do not know.

But, audibly, I heard his backbone snap.

I had been given a thousand years of life without consultation or request and now I could see a long, dark, and exceedingly narrow tunnel before me, delimiting a life in which it seemed my fate would go on facing up to the consequences not only of my own actions but also the reverberations from the natures of other peoples and other beings. It was in the nature of that scorpion to try to kill me; it was in my nature to defend myself. What was natural about this Fristle trying to rape a young girl of his own kind, and was it natural for me to prevent him? I think it was then, as I let the dead limp form of Follon slip through my hands to the ground, that I first began to sense the dim and awful doom that overhung me. I was doomed. Oh, yes, everyone is doomed in the sense that everyone will eventually die. But I began then to feel the clinging strands of a doom outside of time and space drawing about me, and with every step I took, every decision I made, I would merely encompass my own destruction the more securely.

I cursed the Star Lords, then, hating them and all their works.

Follon's body had to be disposed of and so I carried him down to the river that flowed so sluggishly through its retaining banks of granite through Magdag to the sea. Here the banks were of mud, and in the shadow of a toppling tower of vosk skulls, I hoisted the dead Fristle, ready to cast him into the flood.

The old Fristle woman, with a cry, darted forward. She made her intentions plain. I stopped most of the mutilation, but she divested the body of all its clothes and money and she took the curved sword.

"These I will keep," she said, looking up at me. She was crouched, bent with age. "My Sheemiff is yours for the asking, for you are a great Jikai."

I shuddered, and the two women Fristles eyed me speculatively. Jikai! How often, lately, had that great word been debased!

With some formal rote of acknowledgment, I bade them farewell and took myself off. Truth to tell, the sleek furred body of the girl Fristle, with its human outlines, stirred me. I half ran through the pink-tinged shadows into the warren.

As I had asked during my last visit, the Prophet had been found. Now he was waiting for me.

It seems fairly clear that Delia's loving actions in setting her whole empire in action to seek me out had upset the plans of the Star Lords. I had no way of knowing just what problems Delia had overcome in instigating this search: Tharu would not broach the subject and Vomanus shied away from it. He was a good and likely lad and, with a little discipline of the sort that gives a man an eye to survival, would turn out well. But the Star Lords — for, as I have said, I had by this time convinced myself that my presence this time in Magdag was of their fashioning — had drawn me here from Earth, four hundred light-years away, and here must lie the labors to which I must put my hands.

What those labors were blazed painfully obviously to me.

The Prophet looked just the same, with his white hair and beard fierce in his righteous rebellious ardor.

"The workers will rise, Stylor," he said in his rolling sonorous voice. "Too long have we suffered. The time is ripe and we know the secrets of the overlords' hearts." He stared at the assembled workers with an exalted look, an expression of dazed fanaticism on his face, drawing the gaunt lines into sharper and more hungry wedges of skin and muscle.

"We know!" said Genal, with a reflection of that dedicated fanaticism uplifting him.

"Yes, we know the time," said Pugnarses, and the hunger on his face glared bleakly out upon the gathering of those men and half-men who would lead the revolt.

We made plans. I listened. They had accepted me as one who had proved himself, and when I had promised to secure them weapons as proof of my intentions, I was a brother rebel.

But the talk consisted of high-flown sentiments, of passion, hatred, and anger, of long detailed descriptions of what the rebels would do to the overlords once they had them in their power. I fretted.

At last I stood up. They fell silent.

"You chatter," I told them. They reacted angrily to this but I quieted them. "You talk of chaining the overlords in the gangs and making them haul stone, and of the whips you will wield. Have you forgotten? The overlords wear mail, and they carry long swords! They are trained fighting men. What are you?"

Genal leaped to his feet, his dark face flushed and furious.

"We are workers, slaves, but we can fight—"

"I can bring you swords, spears, some coats of mail, but not enough. How, my gallant Genal, will you fight the overlords?"

Such were the dark torments, the passions of frustration twisting in that hovel as I faced them with the truth, that they had no time or energy to spare to wonder — then — where I would find weapons for them. I had brought food, so as not to be a burden on them, and already half a dozen long swords lay hidden in a pit beneath straw, closely wrapped in oiled sacks, below the beaten earth of Genal's and Pugnarses' hovel.

The talk buzzed, coiling, endlessly repeating itself. I let them talk this out. They had to face the truth of themselves.

At last, a silence fell. Pugnarses was knotting his fists together, and every now and again he would smash his fist into the earth of the floor. Genal, I saw, was close to tears, but he did not break down. He was looking at me. I saw that look. I knew the time for hard facts was near. Bolan, a giant man with a head that gleamed all naked and shining in the light, grunted. He had been shaved as a slave once, and his hair had never grown back. He could lift stone blocks that took three other men to shift.

"What do you say, Stylor?" he asked me directly, without artifice, like a charging chunkrah. "You have only dismay and doom for us — can you prophesy to any more effect?"

"Yes, Stylor," cried Genal and one or two of the others. "Tell us a plan." I noticed that Pugnarses did not join in.

Well, he would confirm and conform, for this was the only way he could achieve his heart's desire as to an overlordship. I told them.

There was nothing clever about the plan. It's only dreamers who believe they can develop something so entirely new that the suns of Kregen have not shone down on it before — always excepting, of course, the men of science and art.

"The merits of the plan are obvious," I said eventually. "And its drawbacks, too. It will take longer than we would wish."

Pugnarses started up. "Long! Yes, too long! Give us the weapons and we will kill the overlords and all their beast guards!"

"But, Pugnarses," Bolan said, rubbing his naked skull. "Stylor has just told us, and I believe what he says is true. You cannot beat the overlords and the mercenaries by a mob of workers and slaves with a few swords and balass sticks!"

"You must train," I said, and I put force into my words. "We will forge an army from the workers and slaves of Magdag so that slavery can be abolished from Magdag."

They nodded, still only half convinced. I enlarged on what I wanted to do, and I admit that it is all elementary and obvious, but to a man who slaves in the sun the thought of a single extra day under the lash between him and freedom is intolerable.

"Give me your help and backing; bestow on me your authority so that I may so order and organize that the workers will rise as a strong and keen weapon." I stared challengingly at them. I was beginning to feel alive again, and the shame of

216

that reawakening as to its means may not be mitigated as to its ends; but it is in my nature to rise to a challenge and to strike down first he who would seek to kill me.

"I will fashion you a cadre of men who will use the weapons I shall bring, and the weapons we will make. I want production of certain weapons that I shall designate, and no others. I value freedom and liberty more than most men, for I have been deprived of freedom — in ways you cannot comprehend — but if I tell you that a galley slave knows about slavery, you will not argue with me, I know." I was jumbled, garbled in what I said, but I convinced them. I obtained total authority over the fashioning of this military weapon from the slaves. I had to. I could see this struggle only in military terms, now; for that was the only way to keep a sense of sanity and proportion. I wanted a small well-trained little army that could blitzkrieg the overlords so that the great mass of slaves and workers might follow and devour the struck-down carcass.

Sentiment had gone. I had seen the misery of the slaves; I had experienced it. I knew of the aspirations of the laborers and artificers — and I was well aware of possible conflicts of interest between slave and worker. I was born, you will recall, in 1775 and this year, I venture to believe, has a certain significance on Earth. On Kregen there were more complex antagonisms even than those surrounding, say, the combatants and theorists caught up in the French Revolution. I determined now to look at the revolt of the slaves of Magdag in purely military terms. Then, I would see that they turned their successful rebellion into a true revolution. That, as I conceived it, was what the Star Lords desired.

Also — my Krozairs of Zy and all of Sanurkazz would benefit.

In the days and nights that followed I took greater and greater risks in sneaking out of the Emerald Eye Palace. I would climb out of my high window and use the ropy vines of the ivy-like plants that clothed the walls to clamber down and so over the wall and astride the waiting sectrix. Vomanus, of course, had to be a party to my mysterious disappearances, and he sweated out many a sleepless night waiting for my return. He thought I had a girl somewhere in the city. While cursing me for my stupidity in not sipping from the flower under my lips, he had a grudging admiration for my foolhardiness in taking wing to sip elsewhere.

The cadre began to train with wooden staves. I had them cut to a modest twelve-foot length. A number of soldiers slaving on the buildings were spirited away by Holly, who used her underground route to good purpose, and these men were only too happy to join us. Their vacancies had to be explained. A death of a slave was a common event in Magdag, and even though the overlords were aware, as Glycas often complained to me, that there were slaves hiding in the workers' warrens, the expeditions to rout them out had to be undertaken with due military care. Glycas loved to ride into the outskirts of the ghetto warrens. He and his sectrix-mounted friends would cut down the workers and slaves not clever enough to run at the first sounds. I suppose between them they killed a thousand or so slaves a season; this was a number scarcely missed in the hundreds of thousands who labored on the buildings of Magdag.

Then the overlords would ride out in their mail and their glory and raid adjacent cities who owed them suzerainty. They had a jolly old life of it, the overlords of Magdag.

The slave soldiers we took in were sworn to secrecy with vows that made their hair curl and their bowels turn to water. They were set to work to drill and discipline the volunteer workers. I personally scrutinized every man at this stage. The soldiers — men of Zair mostly, but there was a sprinkling of the fair-haired men of Proconia, and a number of Ochs, Fristles, Rapas — could make little of the twelve-foot staves. They called them staves, thinking that was their function. I did not disillusion them at this stage. That would come later, and as staves they would also serve a purpose.

Soon a small group gathered around me, men I ventured to think would stick to the last.

"You have an overlord of Magdag charging down on you," I said to them as we sat around the hovel, on the beaten-earth floor in the flickering light of the candle. "He is clad in mail. He sits upon a sectrix, which means he towers over you, on foot. And he is bringing his damned great long sword down to cleave your skull to your neck bones." I stared at them, these dozen or so men on whom I must rely. "I don't want the answer, 'Run,' when I ask you the question, 'What do you do?'" We weren't past the joking stage yet. Genal, for sure, would have said "Run."

They coughed and shuffled, and Bolan said viciously: "Leap on the sectrix's back and jab your dagger into the vosk's eyes."

"Fine. How do you get past the sword?"

We argued on. I saw that Genal had the right idea when he said sturdily: "Throw something — a rope weighted with lead — around the sectrix's legs." He laughed nastily. "That should bring the overlord to earth."

"Fine. You'll have to get close to do that with any accuracy. The overlords will be in squadrons and platoons. The ones following will cut you down—"

"So?"

I spread my hands. "Talking in military terms there are two methods of dealing with armored men, and these overlords wear hauberks of mesh iron, link mail. Some wear leg mesh; most do not. Some wear solid helmets; some rely on their coif. There are still two main methods of dealing with them, of dismounting them."

"Kill them," grunted Bolan.

"Yes. You can drive a relatively small hole through the mail, or you can bash a great wedge of it in, cutting it or not according to the opposed strengths." I thrust my rigidly outstretched forefinger at Bolan. He flinched back, but not by very much. He would be a useful man. "To punch a hole you need an arrow, a dart, a javelin or—" I hesitated, found Maspero's genetic language pill had failed me, and so used the English word. "Or a pike."

I opened out my other three fingers rigidly alongside the first finger and I slashed down in a quasi-karate blow at Bolan. This time he did not move a muscle — but, of course, he blinked. "To slash a man's guts in half you need a long sword, an ax, a—" Again the pill failed me in the exact meaning I required. I went on: "You can bash with a mace or, if you have the requisite skill, with a morning star." Again I used English for the elusive words. "To slash, you can also use a species of bill, a halberd, a glaive, a fauchard. And these weapons are those on which we will concentrate our production."

We spent the rest of that session going over and over the weapons which, to these men, were new.

Just before it was time for me to leave, and these men had no idea where I went when I disappeared from their sight in the warrens, I put the final indignity to them.

I have mentioned that the men of Segesthes considered the shield as the cowards' article, a weak, treacherous, miserable item of warfare, one to which they would not deign to give the name of weapon. They had never seen an offensively-used shield. So I took a break and then, when we had drunk a little wine, I said: "Finally, the production lines will make shields."

I quieted them. The men of the inner sea, also, disregarded shields. Only Ochs used shields, a tiny round targe clasped in one of their six limbs with which they attempted to counter aggression. Men derided the Ochs for their little shields. I spent some time arguing; finally I said: "It is settled. When I give you the patterns for the pikes, the glaives, and halberds, you will also receive patterns for shields. These will be manufactured. It is ended for now." I stood up, looking down on them.

"I will see you tomorrow night. Rembereee." I left them.

Fifteen

Vomanus takes a message to Delia of the Blue Mountains

The Princess Susheeng of Magdag was a vibrant, alluring, sensual creature. There was no doubt of that at all. It was all too clearly apparent as she reclined on a low divan covered in ornate green silk, the lighter green of the silks partially covering her white body seductive in their flowing curves and hidden shadows. Poor Vomanus in his buff coat and black boots looked gauche and out of place; essentially I felt the same way, no matter that I wore a lounging robe of that detested green. I had felt it politic to do so; now, clearly, it had been a mistake. The intimate little supper party was over and now Susheeng was devising ways of getting rid of Vomanus. I was countering them with a suaveness I had to admire in myself.

"Oh, Vomanus, my pet," said Susheeng in a dripping-honey voice. "I wish to speak with Drak alone."

She could have said, simply: "Vomanus, clear out." Since she had not, it was obvious that her brother Glycas' warning of the importance of Vallia had got through to her.

Vomanus, casting me a dirty look, rose and, with a graceful farewell speech, left. Susheeng turned her bright eyes on me. Her breast rose and fell beneath the scrap of green silk.

"Why do you always avoid me, Drak? Time after time I seek you out — and you are not there. Why?"

I was astonished. This proud and haughty woman, a beauty in any man's eyes, was in effect begging me. She leaned gracefully toward me, and the green silk moved again tumultuously.

"I keep myself busy, Princess."

"You do not like me!"

"Of course I do!"

"Well, then…? If you knew how lonely I am. Glycas is forever busy about matters of state. The campaign in Proconia does not go well." I had to keep from shouting aloud my joy. She went on, slumping back now, her feelings of neglect beginning to stir different emotions. "All he can talk about are the pirates from Sanurkazz. Everyone is wondering when that arch pirate, that evil devil's spawn, that cramph, the Lord of Strombor, will strike again. He cost me a cool three merchantmen last season. Money of mine, lost to me, in his filthy hands. This Pur Dray, this Lord of Strombor, why, he is a worse Krozair than that mangy Pur Zenkiren."

I felt drunk.

I had quaffed but little wine, for I had to keep my wits about me. But — this was how the enemies I had sworn to oppose talked about me, about Zenkiren, about the Krozairs of Zy! I felt suddenly strong and liberated, rejoicing in the powers that Sanurkazz extended across the Eye of the World.

"I feel sorry for you, Princess," I said. "But I believe you also raid the men of the southern shore. Is this not so?"

"Of course! They deserve it; they are rasts before Grodno."

Then, shaking those creamy shoulders, she reached for her goblet and drank deeply. Her face was more flushed than usual. I thought of Natema. I tensed myself, ready for what might come. There would be no ghetto warrens for me this night.

The work of preparations was going well, and already the production lines were turning out long, beautifully shaped shafts of pikes and halberds, and the smiths were forging the heads to fit. Grindstones were being stolen and if a Rapa guard was found with his throat slit, wasn't that what they hired themselves out to expect?

"My dear Drak," said Susheeng. "I swear you are thinking of something else."

A naturally gallant man might have mumbled that no man could think of anything in the presence of Susheeng except her; that way lay dragons. I said: "Yes."

"Oh?" Her eyebrows lifted. That cruel look flashed over her face.

"I was thinking how strange it is that neither you nor your brother, the noble Glycas, are married."

Her breath caught in her throat. "You — would—?"

"Not me, Princess Susheeng." I took a breath. "I am spoken for in Vallia."

"*Ah!*"

I thought that would finish the matter. She had known that my urgent desire to return to Vallia — as she thought of it as a return — had cooled lately. She had thought it was on her account and now she knew otherwise. I made a big mistake then.

The next night I was able to slip into the warrens with the pattern I had worked out for the shields. They were large, rectangular, curved into a semi-cylinder, and I insisted that they be built to withstand an arrow from the short straight bows of the overlords' mercenary guards. If this meant they must be backed with metal, then the metal must be stolen from the building sites where it was being fashioned into masks and wall-coverings to the greater glory of Grodno. I overrode all obstacles. The weight of the shields thus produced, I said, was not important. I had in mind their use as a kind of pavise. I showed how they might be used in the testudo. I got through to my men in command.

Susheeng was waiting for me as I climbed back in through my window.

"I have been waiting for you all night, Drak."

I kept my composure.

"I was restless, Susheeng. I have been walking — to clear my head."

"You lie!" She flamed at me then, passionately. "You lie! You have a girl out there in the city, a whore for whom you deny me! I'll kill her, I'll kill her!"

"No, no, Princess! There is no other girl in Magdag."

"You swear by Grodno that what you say is true?"

I'd swear anything by Grodno; false deities mean nothing. But there was no girl — and then I thought of Holly. I said, harshly and with an acrid contempt: "I do not need to swear, Princess. There is no other girl in Magdag."

"I do not believe you! Swear, you rast! Swear!"

She lifted her white hand on which the green rings flashed. I caught her wrist and so for a space we stood, locked, looking into each other's eyes. Then she moaned softly and sagged against me, all the rigidity gone from her body. She leaned into me and I could feel her softness. "Tell me true, Drak. There is no other?"

"There is no other, Princess."

"Well, then — am I not beautiful? Am I not desirable? Am I not fair above all other women in Magdag?"

What had Natema said, and what had I said, when I thought Delia was dead? Now I was by that span of years more mature.

"You are indeed the finest flower of Magdag, Susheeng," I said, and felt shame at the vicious irony of my words.

A crisp knock at the door followed by a Vomanus who concealed his chagrin at sight of Susheeng, who was smoothing down her hair now, effectively chopped off that scene.

When Susheeng had left with a long lingering glance at me, Vomanus said enviously: "Well, you lecherous old devil! So you managed it in the end!"

"Not so, good Vomanus." I looked at him, and I found he ranked favorably with those other young men who had followed me to death. "And aren't you supposed to treat a Kov with some kind of respect, hey, young lad?"

He laughed delightedly.

"Of course. But I told poor old Tharu not to tell you who I was, and I don't intend that you should find out now. Just take it from me, Drak, my friend, Kovs are Kovs and Kovs to me."

I glowered at him from under lowered eyelids and he, despite that he had known me for a little while now, started back and I knew I wore that corrosive look of pure authority and domination on my ugly face that I despair so much of.

"And are you going to tell me you aspire to the Princess Delia yourself, good Vomanus? That I am a rival?"

"Drak — Dray! What are you saying?"

I never apologize. I turned from him. Then: "Vomanus — I thank you for your help and comradeship. But I fancy that she-leem Susheeng will set spies on me. I am going to have to disappear."

"What!"

"There is work waiting for my hand. I love the Princess Delia as no man ever loved a woman before in all this world of Kregen, aye! and all of Earth—" He stared then, thinking me going off my head, I shouldn't wonder. "But before I can return to her and clasp her in my arms again I must discharge the obligations laid on me. A Vallian ship was signaled last night — you did not know?" For he had started and his face had lighted up. "Listen carefully, Vomanus. I take a great comfort from your comradeship and your ready wit and help — now, hear me out! I want you to return on the ship, go to Delia, and tell her I am well and dying for her and that I shall return just as soon as certain business has been conducted here. She will understand, I know. I know she will!"

"But, Drak — I dare not return without you!"

"Dare not? When your Princess Majestrix awaits news of me, thinking me dead, perchance, suffering. Go back to Vallia, good Vomanus. Give the good news to your princess. Tell her I shall return just as soon as I am allowed. She will understand."

"But what keeps you here? Not Susheeng of a surety."

"Not Susheeng, nor any other girl. I cannot explain. But you will return to Vallia and give my message and my undying love to Delia of the Blue Mountains."

Besides, I wanted him well out of the way when my slave army struck. I didn't want his head stuck on a pike and paraded along the harbor wall.

He shook his handsome head, and thrust his fist down on his rapier hilt so that the scabbard stuck up into the air, arrogantly. "But, Drak, to return without you!"

"Go! For the sake of Zair, go now! Tell Delia I long to clasp her in my arms — and I will, I will, but go, now, before it is too late!"

He stared at me as though, at last, I had taken leave of my senses.

I calmed myself. "All will be explained. And, too, you could return with an air-boat to Proconia. I know Vallia does not like using the airboats in the inner sea. I can join you there."

He frowned. Then: "Very well, Kov Drak. I will do as you ask."

We made the final arrangements and then I said "Remberee" to Vomanus and went back to my room that evening to collect all that I might need. I was about to leap onto the windowsill when Susheeng called. It was weak of me, I know. But I felt I could not leave without a kind of warning. After all, she was acting of her nature, like them all. So I went to the door and let her in.

She was magnificent.

She was dressed as barbaric murals showed Gyphimedes, the divine mistress of the beloved of Grodno, to be dressed in the old legends. Kregen is a maze of myth and legend, some of it beautiful, some horrible, all of absorbing interest. Storytellers weave their fantasies in every marketplace and on favorite street corners beneath the sturm trees. The very air of the world breathes a scented miasma of romance and wonder. Now Susheeng stood gracefully before me dressed as a living mistress from one of those old legends.

Her hair was coifed and ablaze with jewels. A thick rope of it had been left free and this hung down, coiling lushly over one rounded shoulder. Her body was clad in strings and ropes of emeralds. A priceless fortune glowed against her white skin. The rosy hue in her cheeks was not entirely artificial. Her eyes gleamed and sparkled from lotions. Barbarically bedecked, more nude than if she had been naked, she glided toward me, the golden ankle bells chiming. The breath clogged in my throat.

"Drak — my Prince — do I not find favor in your sight?"

It was a rote question, as old as man and woman.

"You are exceedingly beautiful, Susheeng."

She swayed toward me. My mind was a jumbled amalgam of Holly, and Natema, and Mayfwy — and then, swamping them all and clearing my head and setting my whole being blazing, came the vivid memory of my Delia of the Blue Mountains stepping so lithely down the rocks clad in those magnificent white ling furs, her figure perfection, her eyes glowing on me, her every aspect so far more beautiful — so — words fail me here. I thrust Susheeng from me so that she staggered.

She dropped to her knees. She amazed me even more. In one hand she had hidden a crumpled gray cloth. Now, moving with a frenzy I found fascinating and appalling, she stripped the emeralds from her so that the strings broke and the gems rolled and scattered wildly about the room. Stark naked she stood, her hair down and the jewels shaken from it. Then — then she wrapped the gray cloth about her thighs, drew it up between her legs, and knelt before me clad in the gray breechclout of the slave!

I didn't want to touch her.

But I didn't want her crouching there at my feet, dressed up as a slave girl, demanding from me what she must know I would not give.

"Get up, Susheeng!" I said. I made my voice harsh and she jumped and flinched, and her naked shoulders shook. "You look ridiculous!"

It was, of course, the end.

Slowly, she stood up. Her breast heaved and she gulped to control herself. She succeeded. Calm, icy, deadly, she stood before me, naked in the gray breechclout.

"I have offered you everything, Kov Drak of Delphond. You have seen fit in your folly to refuse me. Now—" Her eyes glowed molten on me in the lamplight. She was incredibly beautiful and evil now that her pretensions had been stripped away. On Kregen there is an expression which means roughly what "my dear" means on Earth, with all the sinister, hating, murderous connotations involved. She used that now, as she turned like a she-leem and glided toward the door.

"You will be sorry, ma faril Drak. Oh, so sorry!"

I knew I had less than a handful of murs to get clear. The mailed men she was even now whistling up would not know I had a sectrix saddled and waiting; and so I stood a chance. But it was a near thing. As I clattered out of that secret court where a sleepy slave padded his way back to his quarters, I heard the sounds of the hunt rising behind me.

As it was, I got clear away. I belted hard for the warrens and, with the die cast, felt a great lightening of my spirits. Susheeng would no longer enter my calculations to ruin all that I was attempting. So I thought as I reentered the ghetto.

The first person I met as I ducked into the familiar hovel was Holly.

She stood up as I went in and her slight figure in the rustling light from the candle sent a quick pulse of futile anger through me. She smiled. We had scarcely seen each other alone since that first greeting. Now she came toward me shyly, but with the firmness of character and resolve I knew she possessed.

"You've been avoiding me, Stylor!"

The incongruity of it all hit me. I gaped at her.

"Stylor! What—?"

"Holly, dear Holly. I have work to do here. The plans must go on—"

"Oh, fiddle the plans! Can't you see—" She stopped herself. The direct approach was not, in general, Holly's way.

Then, thankfully, Genal, Pugnarses, and Bolan stalked in. They were annoyed because a good smith had been whipped since his production of iron nails was down — because he had been forging pike heads for us.

"We will have to spread the load," I said. "There are, after all, enough slaves to make production light enough—"

"But he was *good!*"

"All the more reason to use him carefully, Pugnarses!" I spoke sharply. Pugnarses gave me an ugly look, but I stared him down. "We are a band of brothers, Pugnarses. We must fight together, or go to the galleys together!"

"We will never do that!" flared Genal.

"Very well, then. Now, listen. We come now to the single most important weapon in our armory." I held their attention; even Holly stood, her hands pressed into her breast, listening.

I told them, then, what the sleeting hail of the arrow storm could do.

"We have a few archers," Pugnarses said. "But few men know the bow. We can make them easily enough, and arrows."

"That is the small straight bow," I said. And I laughed. You who listen to these tapes will know I do not laugh lightly.

It is not exactly true to say that the long English yew bow is the peasants' weapon. Of the famous longbows, only about one in five were made from yew, the others being mostly ash or elm or witch hazel, and only the best and most experienced archers were issued with yew bows. I wished I had the men to use those bows. Their deadly accuracy, their armor-piercing piles, would have laid low the overlords in great droves. As it was, I must make do with what a slave economy could provide.

224

"It takes years and years of training to make a longbow-man. You must start almost before you can walk to pull a bow, to draw it to the ear, to attain that instinctive accuracy and that uncanny speed. Do not think of the longbow, my friends, unless there are men of Loh among you."

"We have a few — some are redheaded, most are not."

"Good, Bolan. We will make longbows for them. But for the main archery strength I shall use crossbows."

My wild Clansmen with their own curved compound reflex bows had some respect for the powerful crossbows of the citizens of Zenicce. I would not be making bows quite like that, not yet, here in the slave warrens of Magdag. I had handled and used the crossbows of Zenicce many times. I knew their virtues and their weaknesses.

"Crossbows?" said Bolan, wonderingly.

"Crossbows," I said. I spoke firmly, decisively. "We will make crossbows and with them we will smash the overlords of Magdag into the dust!"

Sixteen

Of pikes and crossbows

The mere manufacture of crossbows and the quarrels they would shoot would not, of course, as with any other weapon, settle the overlords of Magdag.

The men who would use them must be trained.

I insisted that the training be carried out with a great deal of the efficiency and spirit of emulation and success, if without the rewards for failure, that I had applied training my guns' crews aboard the seventy-fours and frigates that sailed other seas four hundred light-years away from Kregen. Volley shooting would be a necessity. Sufficient accuracy should be obtained from individual marksmen so that a wide swathe of the bolts would fall upon the charging overlords' cavalry.

Production was begun as soon as the first crossbow I had designed and seen through its development stages, helped by the slave and worker craftsmen without whom the venture would have been impossible, had been tested and had passed. We began with a simple hand-spanned bow. Once those whom we selected for training had grasped its essential principles, and could put a group of bolts into the targets set up in the alleys of the warrens, we progressed at a jump to bows spanned by windlasses. As a sailor I could handle the simple calculations necessary to arrive at a satisfactory ratio series. The biggest innovation, and one I felt some pride in developing, was what I called the sextet.

One of the main problems with the crossbow is its slow rate of discharge. I have previously mentioned that bows do not fire their arrows or bolts. In every respect the crossbow is inferior to the expertly handled longbow. So men believe. I had so to arrange my crossbowmen as to nullify as many of the disadvantages as possible. We would be fighting from behind barricades. That was essential, as

I saw it. So I took a group of six people. The sharp end was the shooter, he who actually loosed the bolt at the foe. To his rear stood or knelt the hander. He took the discharged bow from the shooter and handed him a loaded bow. To his rear were stationed two loaders. They took the spanned bows and loaded them with the bolts, ready for the hander, alternately. Finally, in the rear, were placed the spanners whose task it was to hook on the windlasses and wind like fury until the bows were spanned, when they would hand them to the loaders.

Six men would use six crossbows — and the end result of their labors would be the discharge of a single quarrel. The big difference between that and having the whole six discharge at once was that the rate of discharge could be kept up. And I would naturally place the best shots as shooters. When necessary, say at the final moment of a charge, the entire six could rise and shoot what would be a devastating broadside.

I say men — there were women and girls and young boys in the ranks of handers, loaders, and spanners. Holly, with her tenacious obduracy, insisted on being taught how to handle a bow through all its phases, and she turned into a fine shot.

With the arme blanche I felt we could not expect even a solid phalanx of pikemen to meet and beat down an overlord charge. But once the slaves and workers understood the problems they insisted that they be trained as though they would have to face the overlords in the open. Accordingly, in the inner squares and plazas of the warrens, where overlords and beast guards ventured only in overwhelming mailed strength, and that only when they chased runaway slaves, we drilled and marched and pointed and lifted pikes. The front ranks contained halberdiers on the Swiss model. When I first saw that forest of eighteen-foot long pikes moving steadily across the square I own to a pang of pride and despair and choked affection.

Those men out there, marching with a swing and a tramp through the dust, their throats parched, their lips dry, were slaves and workers, beaten men, whipped cramphs, despised and derided by the scented overlords of Magdag. And here they were marching in ranks and columns together, brothers in arms, shoulder to shoulder, disciplined and dedicated to a freedom that depended on their discipline. And once they had obtained their freedom — what of their so hardly-won and proudly-vaunted discipline then?

That was a problem for revolution, not rebellion. It must come later.

It would come — I had vowed myself that — quite apart from the duty I conceived the Star Lords demanded from me.

We forged a weapon, there in the miasmic odors and the odoriferous mud of the ghetto. We drilled and trained. We built barricades from which we practiced hurling a sleeting storm of crossbow bolts. We devised tricks and traps, things like loops of rope hung between houses, balks of timber to be thrust hock-high across from door to door — for I believed we would have to call down the wrath of the overlords upon us and meet them in the confines of our warrens.

In this, I found to my surprise, I stood alone.

"Soon," said Genal with the lust for battle kindling unpleasantly in his eyes,

"Genodras will disappear. The accursed Zim will, for a short space, prevent us seeing the true light of the sky."

I had to stand and take all this without a murmur.

"The overlords retire into their great halls during this time of the Great Death as they await the Great Birth. We workers must grovel in our shacks and hovels, condemned to the warrens. We are not permitted in the halls during their times of use, when all they stand for becomes revealed."

"Aye!" growled the listeners, rough, bearded men, their hands horny with labor.

"Then is the time to strike!" declared Genal. "We are debarred from the great rituals of Grodno, when sacrifices are made so that Genodras, the all-mighty green sun, will reappear. We may never witness the sacred ceremonies. Then, my brothers, then is the time to rise up in our justified wrath and strike down the oppressors!"

Genal, it was clear, had been spending a lot of time with the Prophet. He had caught the intonation as well as the words.

It was a good plan, in the sense that we could sweep up into the city in a great wave of iron, steel, and bronze, and find no overlords to bar our path. I felt sure we could deal with the mercenary guards in the confident strength of our newly-won military skill. Then it would be a matter of driving from one great hall of mystery to another, routing out the occupants at their rituals and slaying them piecemeal. I had no objection in principle to this wholesale killing of the overlords of Magdag; you must remember that at that time I was, besides being very young, thoroughly steeped in the precepts of Zair who hated and detested all things of Grodno. I felt it my binding duty to the Krozairs of Zy to destroy everything green on the inner sea, no less than my more nebulous demands from the Star Lords.

If I have given the impression that I am an easy person to live with, then the impression is false. I know I am an exceedingly difficult person to get along with. I know this. I have been told. Poor Holly and Genal found that out, and Mayfwy had been marvelously understanding and undemanding. My Clansmen, chief among them Hap Loder, had of course other reasons for submitting to my ill humors. Sometimes I felt a sensation I knew must be a cold terror as I contemplated what I would do to my Delia, my gentle, fierce Delia of the Blue Mountains when at last we settled down to a form of married life in distant Vallia.

As far as killing the overlords of Magdag was concerned I was again brushed by that feeling of doom spreading shadowy wings over me. I had to shrug it off. Didn't I hate everything green about the inner sea, about Magdag and its slavers? I rallied to the plan. It was good. We would catch the overlords with, as the saying goes, their pants down.

"This means we must wait even longer," Holly pointed out.

"Yes." Genal eyed her and, as I had noticed whenever he looked more than casually at Holly — which was almost always — he became hot and most un-Genal like in his reactions. Now he said: "We must wait just that little longer beneath the lash; old snake will cut our backs open for just that little longer. But the waiting will be more than worth the pain! For we will squeeze these Grodno forsaken overlords, we will crush them, hall by hall we will tear them apart, sweeping over them like the rashoon of Grodno himself!"

Holly looked at me. Pugnarses looked at Holly, and then swung to glare at me. Genal stared. "Well, Stylor?"

"It is a good plan," I said. "We will wait."

There would be more time to train my little cadre and begin to show them what tactical fighting was all about. I thought of my projected barricades with a twinge of regret, but I have always been, like the men of Segesthes, an attacking fighter except when I may gain an advantage by fighting in defense.

Genal had mentioned the rashoon, the sudden treacherous storm wind that blows up on the Eye of the World, and for some reason this reminded me of Nath and Zolta, my old oar comrades. Were they even now, perhaps, battling a rashoon on the heaving decks of a swifter? I felt a stifling choking in the warrens of Magdag. How I longed to stand once more on the quarterdeck of a swifter — that huge swifter to whose command I had never reached!

Then I saw the solid phalanx of my friends, the slaves and workers of the warrens of Magdag, marching steadily across the plaza. The pikes all slanted at a single angle. They marched solidly, close-packed, yet there was about those men a swing, a lilt, almost, that lifted me back to reality again. Bolan roared a command and the pikes swung down into their hedgehog of points, neatly, swiftly, as the men had been trained. Once the philosophy of the pike has been shown a man who must fight on foot, and once he grasps the thick haft with its iron bands in his fists and stands shoulder to shoulder with his comrades, he rapidly understands why he is there packed into the pike phalanx.

Bolan's bald head gleamed in the twin suns' light. Some of the men had fashioned caps of leather. Most were bareheaded and their shaggy manes troubled me. Leather — there is no leather so highly prized as the leather of Sanurkazz, the Magdag efforts being quite inferior; but the Magdaggians have the knack of beautifying leather, of adorning it with stampings and colors that make it beautiful and valuable. A lucrative two-way commerce was viable, there, if the red and the green were not opposed.

Sheemiff, the girl Fristle, strolled onto the plaza and stood idly watching the parade. She had, I knew, become a fast hand at loading and handing and was now training hard to become a first-class shooter. In military matters hierarchies of command and order are perhaps at their loosest in a rebellious army whose men all subscribe to the fight with everything they possess. But I had instituted ranks, for I wanted orders given in the heat of combat to be passed rapidly and to be obeyed instantly. Mind you, even then I believe I would far rather have been sitting on a sun-drenched terrace, with Delia by my side, munching a handful of palines and laughing in the fresh air.

But a stricture had been laid on me.

Bare heads and Sheemiff mingled in my mind. I saw myself once more down by the muddy, bloody banks of the river, where the piles of vosk skulls lay hard and obstinate in the sun. "Old vosk skull!" Zolta would call Nath. Yes.

"Sheemiff!" I called. She ran to me eagerly, her slit eyes lighting up, her golden fur sleek and brushed.

"What does my Jikai desire?"

When I told her she looked surprised and disappointed, but she ran off willingly enough. There were some men who swore that a Fristle virgin knew more about the arts of love than a temple maiden from Loh. I wouldn't know about that — then — and dismissed the idea. When she returned, Holly, Genal, Pugnarses, and Bolan, who had dismissed the phalanx, with some of the other leaders, were talking about all the plans we were maturing. Sheemiff walked up to me in the center of the group and held out the vosk skull on her hands.

The uproar around me, as you may imagine, was comical in the still center of the tragic situation brewing. Vosk skulls! What had they to do with the glorious revolution?

I showed those slaves and workers of Magdag just what the skull of the vosk did have to do for us.

I lifted it high in the air. Then, having seen that Sheemiff had washed it thoroughly in the river, and cleaned it, and dried it, I brought it down over my head. I felt the weight come on my own skull. I stared out through those two blank orbits. The nose bone joined them and projected down like a nosepiece of a helmet.

"The overlords call us vosks!" I shouted. "They call us fools and mangy cramphs, and calsanys — and vosks — stupid, obstinate vosks. Very well. The vosk has a skull of a thickness, my friends. Of a redoubtable thickness, as everyone knows, for the piles of skulls by the river attest this and the broken grindstones in the bone mills. So! We take on with pride all the stubborn thickheadedness of the vosk!" I banged the flat of my long sword against the skull. "We are the vosk-helmets, my friends! Vosk-helmets who will smash into the green halls of Magdag and destroy every last overlord!"

They took it very well. Even as some debated and others ran to the river for their own skull-helmets, I felt the ringing in my head. These vosk-helmets would have to be well-padded, with grass and rags and moss.

We set up a vosk skull on a rock and took turns in smashing at it with a variety of weapons. Even I, who had surmised that nature would take care of so stubborn and stupid a creature as the vosk, was surprised at the resistance offered by the skulls. I remembered when we had let loose the vosks in the Marble Quarries of Zenicce — they had been Segesthan vosks, larger than these of the inner sea. These vosk skulls fitted a man's head like a tailored helmet, and they thrust two upcurving horns forward, arrogant now that all the flesh and skin had been stripped away.

Holly grabbed my arm.

"Oh, Stylor — you are clever! They will save many a poor man's life—"

Genal and Pugnarses looked on.

I said: "We are downtrodden, Holly, like the vosk, considered stupid. So we take as our badge of pride the old vosk skull; we are the Vosk-Helmets! From the lowly comes forth the victory."

The Prophet was standing nearby and I had not been able to resist the magniloquence. Afterward, I felt ridiculous. But the people responded, as they do, and the work went on.

Most of the crossbows were fashioned with a bow of horn and wood; some we made of steel. But quantity, for the moment, had to take priority over quality. I put the steel bows into a corps and made sure the best shots were assigned there. We colored our vosk-helmets yellow, purloining the paint from the paint masters on the great friezes. I gave colored scraps of cloth as badges of rank. We drilled. Gradually we were turning into an army.

And all the time the slaves and workers continued their labors on the great halls. Now work was concentrated on just finishing the nearest-completed hall. It was necessary, as I understood, that at least one new hall be finished for this time of the Great Death. It took season after season to complete a hall, of course, within the complex of the massive buildings that could have swallowed all the pyramids at a gulp.

Having discussed the question of overlord spies among us, I had been reassured by my group leaders. We could carry on our work within the complexes of the warrens and lookouts would warn us of any onslaught from the overlords. Of spies, the slaves had experience. A man, acting the slave, acts differently from one who had felt old snake on his naked back, or so the men said. I was not so sure, but in this had to trust those on the spot.

I was aware that despite their willingness to drill and march the slaves were irked by the enforced discipline. Their ideas of rebellion consisted of snatching up a sword and a torch and running like crazy through the streets. Clearly, they became more difficult to hold in check as the time for the Great Death approached. It was also apparent that Pugnarses and Genal were irked. They had drawn closer together of late, and this pleased me. They were often in long, involved, passionate discussions, which would break up as soon as I appeared. I was glad they were more friendly now than they had seemed to be.

Bolan was a tower of strength, his bald head covered by a massive yellow-painted vosk skull. He was manipulating the pikemen into a force I considered might just have a chance against the overlord cavalry. Just a chance, before they were cut to pieces, but that single chance would be all we would have.

Although I had felt it desirable not to use either red or green as colors for the slave army — yellow and blue and black were the symbols and badges we used — the aspect of a religious war was fading. I did not see this clearly then. Zair forgive me — I actually thought I was extraordinarily clever in thus turning the Grodno-worshiping workers against their Grodno-worshiping masters. As the majority of the slaves were for Zair I had even further vague and nebulous plans I could not even acknowledge to myself, and as a consequence I completely overlooked the character of class war that had taken over. I was for Sanurkazz and Zair and the Krozairs of Zy. In that, I failed. I should have taken the longer view...

One night, returning after a crossbow session with the sextets handling the steel bows, I halted on the threshold of the hovel. Genal was grasping Holly in his arms, pushing the shush-chiff she wore down over her shoulders, his lips seeking her soft flesh. Why she should wear a shush-chiff at this time I did not know, but apparently it had inflamed Genal. Holly was gasping.

"No, no, Genal! Leave off! Please—"

"But I love you, Holly! You know that — you've always known it. I'll do anything, anything at all, for you, Holly—"

"You're tearing my shush-chiff!"

Genal's voice broke into an impassioned sob. "And was it for Pugnarses—"

"No — no! How can you say it! I don't love either of you!"

I made a noise outside, and shuffled and dropped my long sword — a thing a warrior only does if he is troubled or scheming or dead — and then went in. We all acted as though nothing had happened. I am sure they did not know I had eavesdropped on their pitiful little scene.

If I had taken more notice…But I considered this affair none of my business. They were both adult; they should be able to handle their amorous problems like adults. Perhaps I was too concerned over trivia like steel crossbows instead of looking at the springs of motivation of those around me, on whom the success of the revolution would depend.

We were all waiting now with a heightened expectation, for daily the green sun Genodras dropped lower and lower toward the red sun Zim, and the time of the Great Death was at hand.

Each day brought the two closer together with an almost visible rate of closing.

The moment Genodras dropped out of sight behind Zim would be the time we would rise. The workers had no care, now, in their passion, that they, too, were thought to own allegiance to Grodno. For them the seasons of oppression at last were to be broken. The whip and the chain were to be banished. No superstition would prevent that.

On what we all knew was the last night, Holly came to me. She had donned her shush-chiff, and oiled her body and hair, and she looked very delectable. She laughed at me in her own seemingly modest way, and all the blood surged into her innocent face.

"Why, Holly," I said rashly. "You look charming."

"Is that all, Stylor? Just — charming?"

The hovel did not seem to stink quite so badly in the sputtering, fluttering light of the candle. Genal and Pugnarses were out somewhere. I knew we were making last-minute attempts to create a line of underground communication with the slaves in the dock areas, where the bagnios would provide stalwart fighting-men once the initial attack had begun.

I felt uneasy and put that down to Holly's presence.

A foot scraped at the door, but Holly did not hear, for she came to me, pouting, forcing herself to declare something that her nature made of tremendous difficulty and tremendous significance for her. I moved away, as though casually. I had no desire for Genal or Pugnarses — or Bolan, for that matter — to stand in the role of eavesdropper on me as I had on Genal and Holly.

"Oh, Stylor — why are you so blind?"

Her gentle birdlike movements made me step back again, away from the bed

231

where my mail coat and my long sword were hidden beneath the straw, but with the hilt of the long sword ready to instant hand.

"It will soon be time, Holly," I said.

"Time for war, yes, Stylor. But is war all that obsesses you?"

"I should hope not!" I said.

I looked at her, at her bright eyes, the soft and supple figure beneath the shush-chiff, and the men who entered almost had me. They wore the slave gray, but they had fierce faces of overlords with the down-drooping Mongol moustaches, and they carried swords in their hands. There were four who had wrapped gray cloths about their faces so that only their eyes showed.

My lunge for the long sword was made — I was on my way when the first arrow thunked into the wood — and I did not stop then. I whirled with the long sword — and froze.

"That is better, cramph." The overlord sneered the words.

The bent bow, the nocked arrow, the barbed head — they did not stop me, for the Krozairs make religious sport of striking flying arrows from the air with their swords. No — the arrow aimed directly at the heart of Holly, who shrank back, her hands to her mouth, her eyes enormous, choked with horror.

I dropped the long sword, kicked it under the straw. They took me then, without a struggle, and all the time that merciless arrow remained pointing at Holly's heart.

Seventeen

"A Krozair! You — the Lord of Strombor!"

I have sojourned for a spell in many prisons in my long life and the one beneath the colossal Magdag Hall na Priags was no worse than most and a lot better than some.

Stripped naked, spread-eagled out against a damp wall, my wrists and ankles clamped in rusty iron rings, chains dangling infuriatingly from the iron hoop about my waist, I waited in the half-darkness partly lit by a ruddy radiance streaming in through the iron-barred grille.

All thought of the rebellion had fled from my mind. This was not because I despaired, but because I had seen a jumbled pile of my group commanders outside my hovel, dead, hideously dead. Bolan, I had seen, running shrieking into the warrens, his bald head glistening in the streaming radiance of the fourth moon, She of the Veils, and with the arrow striking through his left shoulder. All revolt, surely, would be crushed when the green sun reappeared.

The jailers took me up to judgment. They were men, for no half-human, half-beast mercenaries were allowed in the sacred halls of Magdag during the time of the Great Death and the Great Birth. Overlords of the second class, they were of a kind with that Wengard who had so viciously ordered me a touch of old snake.

The room into which I was conducted — pushed and shoved and pummeled — was walled and roofed in uncut stone. A sturm-wood table crossed an angle. Behind this the guard commander sat, all in mail, his long sword at his side. He stroked that ugly drooping Magdag moustache as he spoke.

"You will tell us of the final plans for the rebellion, rast. Otherwise you will die unpleasantly."

I suppose he saw that this did not convince me; he knew as well as I that they would kill me out of hand. In this, as you shall hear, I was wrong.

"We know of your schemes, you whom the slaves call Stylor. We have samples of your pitiful slave-made weapons. But we would be more exact."

They had been incautious enough to leave me with a bight of chain between my ankles. The chains around my bound wrists would, of course, serve as a weapon. I did not bother to kick the guards next to me. I went straight over the table, wrapped my wrist-chains around the guard commander's neck, and hauled back.

"I will leave you enough air to tell these cramphs what to do," I said, in his ear, low and venomous. He gobbled out a shrieked order to his men to stay back. Impasse.

The door opened and Glycas walked in.

He was speaking in his abrupt, authoritarian way before he was fairly through the opening.

"Send for the prisoner, Stylor. There is a mystery about this slave I would—" Then he saw me. His breath hissed in his throat. His long sword flashed clear of his scabbard.

"I shall cut you down, slave, whether you strangle that miserable guard commander or not." He laughed, his silky, snakelike laugh. "Perhaps I will have him strangled, anyway, for allowing you this much effrontery." He glared around at the paralyzed jailers. "Seize him!"

The death of this Magdag overlord of the second class would benefit no one. I let him go, regretfully, to be sure.

My brown hair had grown long, my trim moustache and beard a trifle shaggy, I was filthy, grimed and mucky with sweat. I stood clear before the table. Glycas kept his sword pointed.

"I am Stylor," I said.

"Your friends have told me a great deal. But they know little of you, slave. You will tell me all I want to know."

"Like, perhaps, where I came from? Where I vanished to? Like, perchance, that you are a foul green-scummed risslaca, Glycas?"

He gaped. For an instant, his composure deserted him. With a jerky strut he bore down on me, the long sword pointed at my breast. He took my filthily-bearded chin in his hand and twisted my head up into the lantern light. Again he drew that hissing breath between his teeth. His fist gripping my chin shook.

"Drak, Kov of Delphond!"

"And now, perhaps, you will free me from these undignified chains, let me have a bath and scented oils, and then provide me with an explanation and an apology—"

"Silence!" he roared. He stood back and still he did not lower the long sword. He would not risk his neck in the same position as the guard commander's. "Enough. That you are Stylor, the wanted slave traitor, is enough for me. What else you have done to my sister, is between us, not of Magdag."

"I have done nothing to the Princess Susheeng," I said, before he hit me. "That is her trouble." Then he hit me.

I was to be used in the rituals to insure the return of the green sun, Genodras, and the rebirth of Grodno.

A medley of emotions tortured me. If I say that in some odd and hurtful way I was glad that this was to happen, I do not believe you will understand. Since this, my third period on Kregen, I had not been myself. Always, I had felt the unseen compulsion of the Star Lords — possibly, I thought then, of the Savanti also — forcing me into actions and deeds that were not truly of my nature. The suffocating sense of that shadowy doom I knew was reserved for me had inhibited me. Strange and mysterious powers had torn me from my own Earth, and I had responded eagerly, gladly. But the doom-laden feelings I could not shake off had soured all my thoughts and actions. Clearly, here in the great Hall na Priags of Magdag, I had been abandoned by the Star Lords, their plans for me betrayed, my usefulness at an end.

I felt, suddenly, free, lightened, ready to be once again plain Dray Prescot, of Earth, and to face that menacing doom with all the callous courage I could summon up.

Captives of the highest rank were used in the ritual games of Magdag to propitiate, entreat, and insure the return of Genodras. We were bundled into iron-barred cages overlooking the great Hall na Priags so that we might see what awaited us and shudder at our fate. I stood gripping the bars, staring out on that fantastic scene as the lamplight and torchlight flickered and flared on the massive walls with their festoons of paintings and carvings, their murals exalting the power of Magdag, their sculptures of the beast-gods, the overwhelming decorative detail.

What I saw astonished me.

Around the cleared area where we would be tortured to death in manners weird and horrible to the mind of a sane man the rows of Magdaggian overlords waited. They waited for the entrance of the high overlord of this Hall na Priags, who was Glycas, in ceremonial procession. A sigh went up as the smoke swirled and lifted and the priests and the sacred guards walked sedately into that vast chamber. Glycas, as square, as hard, as corrupt as ever marched with the sacred golden covering held above his head by four nobles. I looked about. I was astonished.

Every single person present wore red.

Clad all in red, they waited or walked in a rhythmic swing toward the dais, all in red, and at their sides swung long swords, broken in half, their jagged edges protruding past the ripped-away ends of split scabbards.

All in red.

Here, in the heart of Magdag, stronghold of Grodno the Green!

Here, then, was part of the secret, part of the reason why only overlords and nobles were allowed to witness these rituals to insure the return of the green sun. We sacrifices, of course, were not expected to live. And I guessed at a part of that secret.

The green sun Genodras had been swallowed by the red sun Zim. What more natural, therefore, since there was now only a red sun in the sky of Kregen, that the worshipers of Grodno should seek to placate Zair, the deity of the red sun Zim! What, indeed! But, how shameful a fact to own in the world. How they must hate what they now did, clad in the hated red, parading to the glory not of Grodno, but of Zair. Begging, pleading, entreating, not Grodno, for the return of Genodras — but Zair!

"The blasphemers!" A naked man with the marks of the whip on his back clawed at the bars, cursing. The others with me in the sacrificial cages shouted and yelled, but the men of Magdag were accustomed to that. They ignored us.

In that moment had I any pity in my heart for the men of Magdag surely, then, I would have felt a pang, condemned as they were by the laws of astronomy to lose their godhead at each eclipse.

But very quickly they were taking the sacrifices out, poking them with sharp swords, forcing them into the center of the cleared area where the torturers waited. What was done was fiendish, diabolical; and it was all done in the name of religious superstition.

The stink of incense, which has always sickened me, the noise of shouting, the resonant chanting rising ever and anon, the shrieks of the victims, the harsh feel of the iron bars in my fists, all melded into a hideous series of concussions in my brain. Around the hall were sited huge banners, of red cloth, embroidered with the devices and blazons of Sanurkazz, and of other southern cities, Zamu, Tremzo, Zond, and of citadels like Felteraz, and of individuals like Zazz, and Zenkiren — and Dray, Lord of Strombor! — and of organizations and orders like The Red Brethren of Lizz, and the Krozairs of Zy.

Then I noticed the diabolical cunning in the thinking. As each victim fell to his death one of the red banners was removed, torn into pieces and cast upon the sacrificial fire. Here was an example of the twisted logic available to the fanatical mind in pursuit of a single desired object. And yet each ritual test was designed so that there was a chance, a slim one, perhaps one in a thousand, for the victim to escape and come through safely. If he did so the banner he had saved from the fire was relegated, but he was returned immediately to the cages to await a further trial. This was leem and woflo with a vengeance!

I had a hope I might come through safely.

My test was devilish and simple.

Over a gangway beneath which a series of razor-sharp knives moved jerkily, I had to run carrying a squirming half-grown leem. The leem is furry, feline, vicious, with eight legs, and sinuous like a ferret, with a wedge-shaped head equipped with fangs that can strike through lenk. When full-grown it is of a size with an Earthly leopard. This one was about the size of a spaniel; at once it sought to sink its fangs into me. I gripped it about the neck and started ruthlessly to choke it to death even as long swords prodded me over the gangway. I ran. Men and women of Magdag, laughing, swayed the gangway about so that I staggered and almost lost my footing to plunge bodily onto those circling scythe-like knives. But I gripped the leem which struggled and flailed its eight legs. It could not shriek, for I gripped it. Oh, how I gripped it! And I ran. When I reached the far side men with swords met me and I flung the leem full at them. They cut it down instantly, and sword points prodded my breast, forced me back to the cage.

But I saw the deviced banner of Pur Zenkiren moved away from the sacrificial fire, and I exulted.

I would await my next ordeal.

Feasting, singing, and ritual dancing went on all the time the sacrifices underwent their ordeals, and died. Slowly but remorselessly the victims and the brave red banners lessened in number.

The hideous burs passed.

Then, as though in a daze, I saw, sitting at her brother's side, laughing and drinking wine from a crystal goblet from Loh, the Princess Susheeng. Barbaric and gorgeous, she looked, clad all in red, the blood coloring her face, her eyes brilliant with kohl and her mouth a scarlet pout of sensual desire.

She had seen me run. She had seen me, naked, the sweat pouring down my chest, my muscles bunching with frenzied energy, as I gripped the leem and ran above that pit of death.

When I looked again, after the agonized scream of a poor devil who had failed to draw his head back in time so that the buzz-saw-like wheel of knives had decapitated him, Susheeng was gone.

The sacrificial cages opened by small and well-guarded barred gates onto the great hall. To the rear lay the entrances through which we had been escorted. Beyond them lay the complex of this megalithic structure, one with possibly a score of halls like this, where even now other rituals were being played out in death.

Within the structures, used only during these times, lay kitchens, bedrooms, dressing rooms, and all the facilities the overlords would need. The rear door opened and more sacrifices were thrust in at the points of swords. An overlord in mail gripped my arm. He jerked me back from the bars.

"This way, rast. And quietly."

I followed him. We left the cage and, with six other guards, walked along the stone corridor. I understood then that someone who knew me had sent these men. Seven guards, overlords all, had been considered essential. Along the corridors guards and sacrifices moved, with personal slaves, pampered pets of the palace household, scurrying about their business. They would never be allowed into the great halls at this time.

The leem I had carried had managed to rake one of his clawed pads down my chest. The blood oozed.

The seven guards were overlords of the second class. Their drooping moustaches were extravagantly long. They carried their swords naked in their hands. They had been told about me.

We entered a high, narrow room, hung with brilliant tapestries depicting the hunt of Galliphron when he discovered the succulence of a vosk rasher grilled over an open fire. The guards went out; they backed away from me and the last I saw of them was the tips of their swords.

The other door opened and the Princess Susheeng entered.

She looked pale, the spots of color burning in her cheeks. Her manner was frightened, wild, inflamed, jerky.

"Drak — Drak! I saw you—" She bit her lip, staring at me. I regarded her calmly. She held out a gray slave breechclout and a tunic embroidered with the black and green device of the overseer of the balass. Beneath her arm she carried the balass stick. She was still clad all in red, and her bosom heaved uncontrollably. Her eyes were large and hypnotic upon me.

"Why, Susheeng?" I asked.

"I could not see you die thus! I do not know — do not ask me. I cannot explain. Hurry, you calsany!"

I put on the gray slave clothes. I took the balass. I did not strike her with it.

"You must hide until Genodras returns—"

"It would be better, Susheeng, if I left now, would it not?"

"Ah, Drak! Cannot you stay, even now! Even after I have risked—"

"I thank you, Princess, for what you have done." I looked at her. She was exceedingly beautiful, in her lush overblown way. "I think you have forgiven me for what happened in the Palace of the Emerald Eye."

"No!" She flamed at me. "I have offered you everything! Yet you ridiculed me. Oh, how I rejoiced when those two cramphs betrayed you to my brother! How I thought I would glee in your death, in agony! But — but—"

"Who?"

She shrugged those full shoulders, pouting. "It does not matter. Two cramphs of workers. They have been condemned now—"

"Who!"

My face must have worked its usual havoc. She shrank back. "Two overseers of the balass — Pugnarses, I believe, and Genal—"

"No!" I said. I felt the hurt, the agony, there, that I had never felt when a sword bit, when a leem's claws struck.

She saw that. Triumph spurred her on. "They betrayed you! Pugnarses, because the fool thought to wear the mail and sword of an overlord! And the other, because Pugnarses talked him into it, made him out of jealousy of a girl—"

"Holly!" I said.

"Yes," she said, the venom biting. "A disgusting girl — cramph, Holly, who even now awaits my brother's pleasure."

"And the two — Pugnarses and Genal?" Again she moved those rounded shoulders, indifferent to their fates. She had always taken what she wanted; she still believed she could take me if she tried hard enough. "They are to be sacrifices. It is just. They presumed."

"Just! Is that Magdaggian justice?"

"What do you, a Kov of Vallia, know of Magdaggian justice?"

I gripped her shoulder.

"I would like to find those two—"

"To kill them? To take your revenge?" She let me grasp her and swayed into me, clasping me in her arms. "Ah, no, Drak. No! Let them go. Escape. I have it all

237

arranged. When Genodras returns and the world is green once again — then we can ride!"

"Where to? Sanurkazz?"

She shook her head against my chest. "No. I have wide estates. No one will question the Princess Susheeng. I will create a new identity for you, my Drak. We can return to Magdag. I have wealth enough for us both, and to spare—"

I had had, for the moment, enough of new identities.

She had been clever in not attempting to find a hauberk of width enough to encompass those shoulders of mine, and an overseer of the balass was nicely balanced to move about the megalithic complex without question within the hierarchical structure. I moved to the door. My face was set.

"Where are you — Drak! No! Please — NO!"

"I thank you for your help, Susheeng. I do not blame you for what you are. That is not of your manufacture." I opened the door. "If you wish to call the guards, that is your privilege."

She ran to me, caught the gray slave tunic. Outside, a guard detail passed with a sacrifice screaming between them.

"Drak! I will come with you!"

We went out together. She preceded me, as was proper, and she led me through the maze of corridors, avoiding the halls from which floated the horrid sounds of the rituals. There was nothing I could do for those men of Zair now, here in a hive of mailed Magdaggian might. But my blood boiled and my heart thumped the quicker, and I had to hold myself very stiff and straight as we passed those men of Magdag.

Genal and Pugnarses were chained together in a cell, awaiting their call to the sacrificial games.

They looked miserable and woebegone and defeated. I was glad to notice they did not look frightened. They had had time to think, chained naked in a Magdag dungeon.

They saw me over the shoulder of the guard. Their eyes popped and they would have spoken out and so betrayed me once again had I not struck the guard on his chin, above the opened ventail. I took his keys and his sword.

I stood looking at them, as Susheeng hovered uncertainly at the door, peering with frightened eyes into the corridor. I shook the keys before them.

"Stylor—" Genal swallowed. He looked sick. "If you are going to kill us, do it now. I deserve it, for I betrayed you."

Pugnarses, in turn, swallowed. He stared at the sword as a man stares at a snake. "Strike hard, Stylor."

"You pair of fools!" I said. I spoke fiercely, hotly, angrily, feeling all the hurt in me. "You betrayed me because of Holly. Did you not see the pile of corpses — of our own men? The group leaders dead, the glorious revolution finished?"

"We—" croaked Genal.

"I persuaded Genal," said Pugnarses. "I wanted to be an overlord! I thought they would believe two of us more than one alone. I must take the blame, Stylor—"

"And see what the men of Magdag do in return, how they repay your treach-

ery!" My face, I could see, made them believe all was over for them. "I can understand either of you doing anything for love of a girl, and I suppose you thought
she must choose one of you! Betraying a rival is a small thing to a man so obsessed with a girl. But you betrayed everyone and everything we worked and
struggled for. You betrayed more than me, Stylor!"

I lifted the sword. Both of them stared at me, unflinching.

I reached across with the keys, threw down the sword, and snapped open the
locks.

"Now," I said. "Old vosk heads. We fight!"

But first — there was Holly.

I handed the sword to Susheeng. She hesitated. A party of guards moved past
a cross corridor. I motioned to them. "A shout, Princess, and how do you explain
this?"

She flung herself around, taking the sword, and almost, I believe, the impulse
to cut us down mastered her. Then she led us on. The swing of her hips as she
walked ahead of us made a fascinating sight

"Wait here," she said outside her brother's palatial apartments within the
megalith. "I will bring the girl."

When she had gone, Pugnarses said: "Can we trust her?"

Genal said: "We have to. She, and Stylor, are our only hope."

"And when we get back to the warrens," I said, "what is to become of her then?"

Genal looked at me, and away. He felt his disgrace keenly. Pugnarses, unchar-
acteristically, said: "At another time, Stylor, I would have counseled: 'Kill her!'
But I do not think you will do that." He eyed me. "Do you love her?"

"No."

"But she loves you."

"She believes so. She will get over it."

"And — Holly?"

"Holly," I said, "is a sweet child. But my love lies far away from here, in another
land, and I remain here only because it is a stricture laid on me. As soon as I have
finished my work, then — then, believe me, I shall leave Magdag and all its evil
ways far behind me!"

I spoke with a passion that forced them to believe. Holly, following Susheeng
meekly, came out then, and she saw me and the color flooded her cheeks.

I merely said: "Hurry, Princess."

There was no time, as I saw it, for a traumatic and emotional outbreak. I
wanted to get back to the warrens. We all knew what would happen as soon as
Genodras reappeared in the sky above Kregen and the overlords of Magdag were
freed from their superstitious imprisonment in the megalithic complexes.

Susheeng, it was clear, still believed she could persuade me to accede to her plan.
To her it would appear the only sensible plan, indeed, the only and inevitable one.

Why would a man, a Kov of Delphond, choose to return to a stinking rasts'
nest of workers and slaves?

We hurried through the corridors. Truth to tell, I was beginning to think we
would break clear away without trouble.

"This way," panted Susheeng. "Up this narrow staircase lies a bridge and then a descent to the outside. I dare not venture out while Genodras is gone from the sky. We can wait."

I did not say anything to that. I would not wait.

At the top of that steep flight of stairs, walled with enameled tiles depicting fantastic birds, animals, and beasts, two mailed guards were descending. Torch-light struck back from their mail. Between them they marched a captive, a fresh sacrifice for the ritual games. He was haggard, bearded, filthy. But I recognized him. I moved aside to let them pass.

But Rophren, that certain Rophren who had been first lieutenant aboard Pur Zenkiren's *Lilac Bird* and had failed in the rashoon, recognized me too.

A shout lifted from the foot of the stairs. More torches spattered lurid orange light upon the brilliant tiles.

"Hai! Princess! Princess Susheeng — that man is Stylor! They are escaped slaves! They are dangerous!"

I took the first guard's sword away and chopped him over the back of the neck. He pitched forward and tumbled all the way to the bottom. Pugnarses and Genal dealt with the second guard, who joined the first in a tumbled heap at the feet of his comrades. They started up.

"Run!" screamed Susheeng.

We now had three long swords.

Rophren reached out a hand.

His haggard face looked uplifted, lightened. He squared his shoulders with a gesture at once instinctive and defiant.

"Lahal, Pur Dray," he said. His voice sounded thick, drugged. "Give me a sword. I would be pleased to exchange hand blows with these Zair-benighted rasts of Magdag. You go on and take the women with you."

He knew I could not do that. But he meant it. I looked at him.

"Lahal, Rophren," I said.

"I am of the Red Brethren of Lizz," he said proudly, with a lift of his head. "I wished to be a Krozair of Zy, but the rashoon stopped all my hopes there. Give me the sword. I will die here, and none will pass until I am dead."

"I believe you, Rophren. I will stay with you."

I reached for the long sword Susheeng held. She was looking at me with a wild light in her eyes and she shrank back. "What—?"

Rophren took the sword. He hefted it. The mailed overlords of Magdag were hurrying up the stairs toward us. "It is good to feel a sword in my fist again," he said. "I have been captive too long." He laughed then, and swung the blade. "Stay, as you will, Pur Dray, my Lord of Strombor, you who are a Krozair of Zy. It will be a great fight. Stay and you, a Krozair, may see how a Red Brother of Lizz can die!"

Susheeng was staring at me with all of horror and hell in her eyes. "A Krozair," she whispered. "You — the Lord of Strombor!"

Eighteen

My Vosk-Helmets greet the overlords of Magdag

Truth to tell, all during this imprisonment in the colossal structures of Magdag where I was a sacrificial victim in the ritual games to insure the return of Geno-dras, I had been half hoping against all reason that the workers and slaves of the warrens would continue our plans, would mount the attack despite the cata-strophic loss of their leaders. If ever there was a need for them to put in an appearance, it was now.

Even while the Princess Susheeng shrank back from me, her face a white mask of fury and despair, a seething agony of acrimony I could well understand impel-ling her to turn from me at last and finally, the mailed men ran up the flight of stairs.

"A Krozair!" she said. Her fists struck again and again at my chest. "A pest-rid-den rast of a Sanurkazz pirate! The vilest Sanurkazzian Krozair of them all, Pur Dray Prezcot, the Lord of Strombor!" She was laughing and shrieking now, mad and wild with the frenzy that tore her. Holly came up and took her shoulders and wrenched her away. Holly's face was as blanched and set as those of Pugnarses and Genal. To them it was inconceivable that an escaped galley slave hiding in the warrens might be a Krozair. Krozairs, they knew, fought to the death.

"They come," grunted Rophren. He had wanted to be a Krozair of Zy, and his crisis of nerves during the rashoon had blasted his hopes. But the Red Brethren of Lizz were a renowned order. He had redeemed himself; he would die well. I do not subscribe to the view that a single act of courage can wash out all a man's crimes, as is so often said; but Rophren, for me, had committed no crime save that of being unfit to be a sailor.

We stood, Rophren, Pugnarses, and I, with our long swords eager to smite down on the coifs of the advancing overlords. We fought. There were only ten of them and in accounting for five of them I felt I had betrayed my comrades, for Pugnarses was wrestling his sword out of the cranium of one while Genal strug-gled hand-to-hand with another who sought to cut down Pugnarses from the side — and Rophren was down, on his knees, bending over with his life's blood bubbling through his fingers.

But there were ten dead overlords littering the stair.

We stepped back from the carnage. Pugnarses, with a curse, kicked the bodies down the steps. I knelt by Rophren. He tried to smile. "Say Lahal and Remberee for me to Pur Zenkiren," he whispered, and so died.

Pugnarses and Genal were collecting the swords.

"Why burden yourself with them?" I asked. Susheeng was vomiting all over those brilliant tiles. I knew it was not because she had seen men die.

"We can give them to the slaves!" snapped Pugnarses. "They will fight—"

241

"As you have just done, Pugnarses? With your blade wedged in your opponent's head? The skill, Pugnarses, the skill."

He swore vilely, bitterly, but he kept the swords.

I approached the Princess Susheeng. She looked up. Her cheeks were stained with tears, vomit slicked on her ripe lips.

"Will you stay here, Princess? You will be safe, for none know now how we escaped."

I felt sorry for her. She had suffered exceedingly; and now she had discovered that the man for whom she conceived she bore a lifelong love had turned, at a single disastrous stroke, into a hereditary enemy. Truly, I think she had suffered enough.

"And are you truly Pur Dray, Krozair, the Lord of Strombor?"

"I am." Did I speak boastfully? I do not think so. Did I speak pridefully? Ah, there, I think I did.

"How can I love a man of Zair?" she wailed.

"You do not love me, Susheeng—"

"Have I not proved it?" she flashed back at me.

I could not answer that. There was no answer.

Holly made a small movement, and I turned, and she stood there, clad in the gray slave breechclout, with a sword in her little fist. "We had best be going, Stylor."

"Yes," I said. I turned back. "Susheeng — try not to think ill of me. You do not understand the compulsions that drive me. I am not as other men. I do not love you — but I think you have touched a chord in me."

She stood up. In that moment, with the tears and the vomit smearing her face, her hair unbound and disarrayed, she looked as close to a human being as I had ever seen her. I thought, then, that if she had the luck to fall in love with the right man she would turn out well. But that is something not of that pressing moment when we stood on the stairs with their florid tiles, in the megalith of Magdag.

"I cannot go with you into the warrens, Drak," she said.

"No. I did not expect you to. Try to think well of me, Susheeng, for red and green will not always be in conflict." I bent and kissed her. She did not move or respond. I suspect that she was trying to hate me, then, and failing. Her emotions had been drained from her, her will power exhausted. "Go down to your friends, Susheeng. As long as we live, we will not forget this moment."

She started to walk down the steps. She moved like a mechanical doll of Loh struts, jerkily, almost tottering at each step. She halted. She looked up. "You will all be killed when Genodras returns to the sky." The words seemed hardly to mean anything to her. "Remberee, Kov Drak."

"Remberee, Princess Susheeng."

She walked away from us, her hated red dress draggling on the flight of stairs, under torches, between those brilliant tiles of winged birds and horned beasts.

We descended the opposite flight and passed out into the brilliance of a day on Kregen when only Zim, the red sun, shone in the sky.

With our news, and with what they suspected, and the wailing over the pile of corpses of their group leaders, the warrens were in uproar.

"The overlords will ride in and destroy us all!" shouted Bolan. His bald head gleamed orange in the light.

We had avoided the half-human guards on our way in. But I knew they would happily fulfill their contracts with the men of Magdag and charge into warrens to discipline us. We faced the kind of decision I think must face any man, any group of men, if he or they wish eventually to taste their rightful portion of life.

Because the orbit of Kregen is slanted steeply to the plane of the ecliptic the green sun during this eclipse appeared to descend at a sharp angle on the red; it would appear at the opposite side at the same angle. I looked about. Were there green tints returning to the orange colors of Kregen?

Soon men and women were running and screaming through the alleys and maze of courts.

"Genodras is returning! Woe! Woe!"

By reason of the place where the green sun was appearing from the red I knew what the men of Zair would say was happening. How that information, that I was a Krozair, had shattered Susheeng! Genal and Pugnarses had little conception; I was still Stylor to them. And I was still their military commander. I ordered the Prophet to be found.

He came up, his beard as defiant as ever. Holly, Pugnarses, Genal, and Bolan gathered at the head of slaves and workers from all over the warrens. I climbed onto the roof of our hovel to harangue them. What I said was a long series of clichés about liberty, freedom, what we had planned, vengeance for our dead. I roused them. I pointed out that from our barricaded warrens we stood a chance of defeating the mailed men.

In the uproar and the driven dust, a furry form glided to the front, leaped up beside me. Sheemiff, the girl Fristle, screamed for attention. When some quiet returned, she shouted:

"We must fight, or we must die. If we die without fighting, what better off are we if we die having tried and struggled to win? This man Stylor, he is a great Jikai — follow him! Fight!"

"My comrades!" I shouted. "We will fight. And we can win by using the weapons we have made and trained ourselves to use. We will fight — and we will win!"

After that there followed all the bustle and hectic activity attending the preparations for a siege as we dragged our clumsy barricades across the mouths of alleys, set our rope and spike traps, brought out the pikes and the shields, the crossbows and the sheaves of bolts. Finally, like a field of daffodils opening all together in the yellow sun of my old Earth, we donned our yellow-painted vosk-helmets. Then, accoutered, ready to fight and die, we took our posts.

Other leaders were appointed to take command of the groups. We four — Bolan, Pugnarses, Genal, and I — would each take a point of the compass, north, south, east, and west, and hold it. We swore to hold until death. We gripped hands, and went to our posts.

I looked up into the sky and saw a white dove circling up there. I swallowed down a knot in my throat. The Savanti, then, had not forgotten me. It had been a long time.

The mailed men, the overlords of Magdag, rode out to crush the slave revolt. With them marched their half-human, half-beast mercenaries: Fristles, Ochs, Rapas, Chuliks, all bent on our destruction.

I placed Holly in command of the sextets of steel-bowed crossbowmen. The shields were raised, carried by lads whose task it was to shield our men from the shafts of the foe. The pike phalanxes waited, ready to thrust out on my command. I intended to leave the Prophet to handle a great deal of my post, that facing away from the city, for I wished to be everywhere the attack was most hotly pressed. Pugnarses had insisted on taking the post facing the city of Magdag. He licked his lips. Though he wore a long sword scabbarded to his hip, he carried a halberd.

We had all snatched time for a little sleep, but a sailor's life had inured me to working through long periods of sleeplessness. The last of the youngsters, boys and girls both, returned from scattering the caltrops in the spaces before the alley openings into the warrens. Various ugly chevaux-de-frise had likewise been fixed across openings. Horses would not face them and I did not think the sectrixes would, either. I would not have dreamed of lifting a zorca against them, and I would have thought twice of the ability of a vove to surmount them. Behind our crude but, I hoped, effective barricades, our weapons in our hands, our eyes bright, and our breaths hard and short, we awaited the onslaught from the mailed men, the overlords of Magdag.

A little wind lifted the dust. Birds were singing with incongruously cheerful notes into the early air, and a gyp — a brown and white spotted gyp, I recall, very like a Dalmatian — lolloped yelping and alone between the caltrops.

The overlords, confident in their muscle, might, and habitual authority in riding down at will the workers and slaves, attacked firmly and in strength and directly. They knew we had made weapons for ourselves, for Genal, not without the agony of remorse burning him, told me he had shown them an example of a halberd and a glaive. Getting a pike and a crossbow out of the warrens and into the palace had not been possible, for obvious reasons. I sensed that Genal, if not Pugnarses, had regretted his weak decision to betray us for love of a girl at a very early stage. Pugnarses — and I believe he could not rid himself of the sight of Rophren dying on the stairs — remained sullen and hating and determined to prove himself what he truly was: a worker, never an overlord.

That first furious onslaught when the overlords tried to charge into the warrens in their usual fashion foundered on the cruel iron spikes of the caltrops and the chevaux-de-frise.

The mailed cavalry drew off, surprised but undaunted, and the half-human mercenaries ran forward to remove the obstructions covered by a brisk barrage of arrows. Looking down from our barricade I could see the quick movements of the Ochs and the Rapas. Chuliks, of course, would be reserved for more positive and noble kinds of fighting. Pugnarses stood next to me. He looked haggard, lean, and wolfish. He said: "Shall we shoot them down?"

An arrow sailed past our heads, to carom from the upraised shield of a young armor-bearer. I looked at him and, instinctively, he straightened up from his flinch and his jaw set stubbornly.

"No. I want to reserve the bows for the overlords."

"Hah!" said Pugnarses. He looked extraordinarily mean.

When a lane had been cleared through the caltrops the mailed might charged again. They came straight for us in a great thundering roll of mail and upraised swords. I lifted my own long sword, the one I had retrieved from the straw of my bed, the long sword that was the gift of Mayfwy. I slashed it down.

At once the shooters of the crossbows discharged their bolts. With a smooth and practiced flow of action the shooters handed the discharged bow to the hander, took a freshly-loaded bow, and let fly with that. Behind the shooter his loaders and spanners worked like maniacs to maintain the rate of discharge I demanded. Bolts whickered through the hot air. Mailed men reared back in their saddles. Quarrels struck through their mail, pierced their mounts, lanced into their faces. A shrill screaming arose. The mailed charge lashed in confusion, like a sea running all crisscross on a rocky coast.

And all the time the crossbows twanged and clanged and scattered their death upon the overlords of Magdag.

The overlords had never experienced this before. They reeled back. Their sectrixes galloped away. Dismounted men ran after their comrades and my marksmen shot them down without mercy, for we expected none.

Six times they charged.

Six times we cut them to pieces.

Because there was nowhere near enough mail to equip all my men, I disdained it. Also, I felt a savage affection for people and places and things long past. So I wore a scarlet breechclout strapped around with the leather belt from which swung the long sword. I fancied old Great Aunt Shusha would have smiled could she see me in that moment on the barricades of the warrens. And Maspero, too — for this was a pale replica of the Savanti hunting leathers I had grown to know so well. On my head I wore a yellow-painted vosk skull, like my men, for there were vosk skulls to spare.

On the seventh charge, just as it was falling back in confusion, an uproar began over on the flank of the warrens fronting the river. Here Genal commanded. And here the overlords while keeping us in play with their own mailed cavalry had sent in the Chuliks. Those savage and prideful warriors with their yellow skins and their uprearing tusks had fought through the arrow storm and were now at handstrokes all along the barricades linking the alley mouths. I had known, given the extent of the warrens, that complete defense at every point would be well-nigh impossible, but the Chuliks had stormed through more rapidly than I liked.

With a shout of good cheer to Pugnarses I hurried off toward the river flank.

The Chuliks met me in a plaza, scattering before them a spray of running slaves who dropped their weapons the better to run.

Everything happened very fast, as is the way during moments of crisis. I shouted to Holly as her crossbows fanned out.

"Fast and accurately, Holly!"

She nodded. Her breast heaved beneath the gray tunic with its mailed coat beneath — a hauberk I had insisted she wear — and the yellow and black badges flashed bravely. She rattled out her orders; the sextets formed, like a series of wedges, and then they went into action. I watched, filled with suspense, for this was a severe trial for my bowmen.

"May Zair shine on you now!" said I. "Shoot straight!"

Over the open plaza the Chuliks, strong and agile, should have reached the slave and worker bowmen with ease. But, for a reason those in command could not at first understand, the Chuliks were falling, lying in heaps and droves across the dust and the bloodied mud. Those that did pass through the arrow storm were met by the halberdiers and the swordsmen of the support groups, protecting the bows. We shot and shot. The Chuliks hesitated; they turned — Holly shouted: "Up, all! *Loose!*"

And every sextet let fly with six bolts.

The Chuliks were never a force in the battle after that.

It raged, that battle; slowly we were forced in, past one barricade after another as the mailed overlords dismounted from their sectrixes and went at it as infantry, with flashing swords. We held them off. The issue hung for some time in the balance.

But the morale of our men, our slaves and workers, grew and increased even as they were being pressed back. For they saw the death toll they were taking. They saw how our armor-bearers, our lads carrying shields, could protect us from the arrow storm until the moment when the arme blanche men stepped out to throw back yet another attack. It went on for a long time, for the overlords could not understand, they could not conceive, that their habitual authority could no longer be imposed. They were used to riding bravely into the warrens and harrying anything they saw. Now, what they saw wore a yellow vosk-helmet and shot a crossbow, or speared with a deadly pike point. They could not understand; but as their losses mounted and they saw their friends writhing in the dust with their mail pierced or shattered, the blood spouting, as they heard the frenzied shrieks of their brothers or cousins in the throes of death, they had to believe they could not subjugate the slaves and the workers.

And still the sleeting hail of the crossbow-shot bolts and quarrels burst about them. There were very many slaves in the warrens of Magdag, and many workers. We had manufactured a great many bolts for the crossbows — a very great many.

The body of longbowmen from Loh performed stoutly, and I used them as snipers and sharpshooters. I did not know how many surprised Magdaggian overlords pitched from their saddles with a cloth yard shaft in them — surprised in the few moments left before they died.

All over the city-end of the warrens slaves and workers were pushing back the overlords and their hired mercenary beast-men.

I sensed the victory within our grasp.

We had fought our way back toward the original line where the conflict had begun. I ordered my pikes to form phalanx ready for what I hoped would be the final charge. Holly prepared to march in the intervals to give cover. I was covered in a thick paste of sweat and mud and blood. It was not my blood; I looked past the torn-down barricade, out onto the open area from which the overlords had begun their attack and where now a mass of overlords on foot and mercenary beast-men milled. They were saddling up, out there, taking their sectrixes from their slave grooms. Was this their final charge, as we marched out?

I smiled, then, at the thought of mailed men charging my pike phalanx covered by my steel crossbows.

That, as a sight and a terrible retribution, would repay me much.

A single figure rode out toward us. Clad all in white, a long white trailing robe, the Princess Susheeng rode her sectrix out to parley with me, Dray Prescot.

"What can I say, Kov Drak?"

She could not bring herself, I could see, to use any other name for me. She was pale, her moist red lips now thinned, almost bloodless, shrunken. Her eyes glared out on me from deep bruised wells. Her hands fidgeted with her reins.

"There is nothing to say, Princess Susheeng. You and your brother, all the overlords of Magdag, you merely reap what you have sown."

"Do you hate me so much?"

"I—" I began. Then I hesitated. I had hated this woman. I still believed I hated all the men of green. I was young, then, and hatred was easy, Zair forgive me.

"You are a Krozair," she said, with some difficulty. "A Lord, a man of Zair. You could arrange a truce with Sanurkazz — you yourself said the red and the green would one day cease to fight." She leaned over toward me from the high saddle. "Why should not today be that day, Dray Prezcot, Kov Drak?"

"You still do not see. It is not between red and green. It is between the overlords and their slaves."

A harsh discordant shriek shattered the waiting silence as the two armies faced each other. I looked up, shading my eyes. Up there, wheeling in lazy hunting circles, a great scarlet and golden raptor swung on wide cruel pinions.

"Slaves!" Susheeng made a dismissive gesture. "Slaves are slaves. They are necessary. There will always be slaves." She looked down on me, and a spark of her old fire returned. "And, ma faril, you look ridiculous, standing there with an old vosk skull on your head!" She had not forgotten and she was paying me back.

"The old vosk skulls will win this fight, Susheeng."

"I appeal to you, Drak! Think what it is you do! Please — you owe me something, after all — Zair does not hold your true allegiance, you are not of the inner sea, the Eye of the World. Make peace between the red and the green, and we will settle the problem of the slaves—"

Now, in that shining sky as the twin suns of Kregen slanted, close together but separate now, toward the horizon, the scarlet and golden hunting bird was circling with a more deadly intent. A white dove was matching its moves, dive for dive, volplane for volplane. They circled and maneuvered like two fighter planes of a later age. Once again I sensed my own helplessness as the phantom forces of the Savanti and the Star Lords clashed in this world so far from the planet of my birth.

Susheeng saw my face. She moved irritably and I saw that she wore mail beneath that white robe. She twiddled her riding crop and the reins. She said: "I have appealed to you, Drak. Now hear the message I have brought from my brother, Glycas. If you do not all return to your warrens and lay down your arms you will all be destroyed—"

I moved back a pace.

"There is nothing left between us to be said, Princess. Tell Glycas my message is the same as I called him in the dungeon of the great Hall na Priags. He will understand."

A handful of overlords, impatient, were riding out toward us. They carried bows. The bows were bent and strung in their hands. Pugnarses began to walk out to me, tall and ugly with his mop of hair and his sprouting eyebrows. Susheeng lifted her crop.

An arrow arched from the overlords. It struck Pugnarses in the throat. He fell sideways, retching, clawing the arrow that had killed him.

"There!" I shouted, impassioned, savage with anger. "There is your answer to your foul brother!"

She brought the crop down hard on my face, but I turned my head down and the blow glanced harmlessly off the vosk-helmet.

When I looked up she was spurring back to her own kind.

I had to run, zigzagging and dodging, through a pelting rain of arrows, but I stopped to carry Pugnarses back to his friends. Holly bent over him, weeping.

"Prepare to move!" I yelled at my men — my men who were workers of the warrens, and slaves from the gangs, and girls like Holly, and youngsters with their shields. The phalanx stiffened. Holly looked up from Pugnarses' dead body. Genal was at her side. He lifted her up. "Yes!" I shouted at them. "Yes! We fight now in the last battle. We will utterly destroy the evil of the overlords of Magdag." I lifted the long sword. "*Forward!*"

Beneath the measured tramp of the phalanx of slaves the ground shook.

The phalanx advanced. The pikes were all held in their correct alignment, angled forward and upward. The yellow of the vosk skulls glowed in the streaming opaline light. The steel bows of the crossbowmen winked back brilliant reflections. All — everyone in my little army — all moved forward.

With us now were the thousands of other workers and slaves, men and women with snatched up weapons or implements to use as weapons in their hands. The dust rose chokingly. Trumpets shrilled and called. I strode on, wishing I had Mayfwy's mail coat about me now, but moving on, moving on...

I knew, as nearly as a man may know anything, that now we had these arrogant overlords. Against the new weapons of the phalanx and the pike, supported by the crossbows, they would be swept away. Exultantly I strode on. Shouts and rallying cries echoed. Arrows and bolts began to crisscross in the air.

"Krozair! Krozair!" I yelled, swinging the long sword and pressing on, the pikes all about me. Holly's sextets were lavishing loving care in their shooting. "Jikai! Jikai!"

We would win. Nothing could stop that.

In all that uproar, all that bedlam, with the pikes seeming to lean forward in their eagerness to get at these hated mailed overlords of Magdag, I looked up. I looked up. The scarlet and golden hunting bird circled up there — alone. The dove had gone.

"Against Magdag!" I yelled and my sword caught that falling streaming light and blazed like a flaming brand.

The light was changing. Blue tints crept in around the edges of my vision — and I knew what was happening. Arrows fell about me; the pikes were surging forward, stabbing; the halberdiers were hacking and cutting; Holly's bolts were swathing through the mailed ranks and the Prophet and Bolan and Genal were urging the men on. Even as we smashed solidly into that surging sea of armored men and moved on over them, so the blueness limned everything about me. I felt light. I felt myself being drawn upward.

"No!" I shouted. I lifted the long sword. "No! Not now! Not now — I will not return to Earth! Star Lords! If you can hear me — Savanti — let me stay on this world! I will not return to Earth!"

I thought of my Delia of Delphond, my Delia of the Blue Mountains. I would not be thrust through the interstellar void away from her again! I could not.

I struggled. I do not know how or why or what happened, but as the blueness grew and strengthened I fought back at it. In some way I had failed the Star Lords. Something I was doing was contrary to what they wanted to accomplish. I had vaunted that I would serve them in my own way — and this was my reward.

"Let me stay on Kregen!" I roared it up at that indifferent sky where the suns of Scorpio cast down their mingled light. Now I was scarcely conscious of the fight raging around me. Men were dying, heads and limbs were being lopped, bolts were piercing through mail, blood was being spilled on a prodigious scale.

I staggered. I was encompassed and floating in blueness. I gripped my long sword with the clutch of death. I felt myself falling, all lifting and exultation gone, falling and falling...

"I will not go back to Earth!"

Everything was blue now, roaring and twisting in my head, in my eyes and ears, tumbling me head over heels into a blue nothingness.

"I will stay on Kregen beneath the suns of Scorpio! *I will!*"

I, Dray Prescot of Earth, screamed it out. "I will stay on Kregen! *I will stay on Kregen!*"

Warrior of Scorpio

A brief note on the tapes from Africa

Although this is the third volume chronicling the strange and fascinating story of Dray Prescot, the editing has been so arranged that each book can be read as a separate and individual volume.

After publication of the first two volumes[vii] of the adventures of that remarkable man, Dray Prescot, on the planet Kregen beneath the Suns of Scorpio some four hundred light-years away, I was completely unsure of the reception they would be accorded. So far Prescot's story has been given to us in the form of cassettes he cut on Dan Fraser's tape recorder in that epidemic-stricken village in a famine area of West Africa. Having been afforded the privilege of editing the Tapes from Africa, I have kept the promise Fraser made to Dray Prescot, and I have already written of the profound impression that calm sure voice makes upon me, and of how I feel uplifted as that voice quickens as the fire of memory burns brighter in remembered images of passion and action and headlong adventure.

The response has been surprisingly profuse and laudatory and there has been no opportunity for me to make adequate reply. We feel, in truth, that it is to Dray Prescot himself that we must look for that reply. The value of this account of life on Kregen is incalculable and the absence of certain of the cassettes containing portions of the story is a tragic loss. To my urgent inquiries, my friend Geoffrey Dean, to whom Dan Fraser had entrusted the Tapes from Africa and from whom I had received the cassettes in Washington, replied with sad and shocking news.

Dray Prescot had unexpectedly appeared in the famine area in West Africa and had been assisted by and then in turn had assisted the young field worker Dan Fraser. Now, Geoffrey told me, Dan Fraser was dead. He had died, mockingly, cruelly, wastefully, unnecessarily, in a stupid automobile accident.

With the death of Dan Fraser we lose the only direct link we had with Prescot. For Fraser was the only one of us ever to have seen Prescot in the flesh. Dan described him as being a man a little above middling height, with straight brown hair, and brown eyes that hold a light of incisive intelligence and a strange dominating quality that goes with the abrasive honesty of the man. His shoulders made Dan's eyes pop. And now Dan Fraser is dead and the whereabouts of the missing cassettes may never be known.

We must, it is clear, be thankful for what we do have. Of the transcribed material I have deleted as little as is necessary, and have edited lightly; but a few items remain to be mentioned. The first is the pronunciation of the word Kregen. Prescot rolls this out as though an acute accent rides the first "e" — Kraygen — with a hard "g." Despite his long sojourn on Kregen he often refers to things as an Earthman would — for instance he will say "sunshine" when, as Kregen orbits the binary Antares, he means "suns-shine." "Sunshine," however, trips more easily from the tongue.

Clearly, since Dray Prescot cut these tapes in the 1970's, he must be possessed of much more information now about Kregen than he was at the times of which he speaks. The whole planet could have changed in character and the most powerful of impressions remains that if it has done so then Prescot himself will have had a large hand in that change. But those long-ago days were as new to Prescot then as they are to us now, and without artifice he recalls those stirring times as he felt and experienced them. But, nevertheless, there are two levels of story unfolding and we must be mindful of that as we read. I have sought the advice of a distinguished author of long experience whose help has been invaluable, and, good friend that he is, whose sage counsel will one day receive the acknowledgment that is its due. We agree that in speaking of his life, some scenes and impressions have remained more vividly with Dray Prescot; it is as though when he speaks into the microphone he is living through these episodes again.

Dray Prescot, born in 1775, presents an enigmatic picture of himself. Through his immersion in the pool of baptism of the River Zelph he is assured of a thousand years of life, as is his beloved, Delia of the Blue Mountains, for whose sake he was first hurled back to Earth by the Savanti. I feel it is clear he has thought long and carefully just what a millennium of life will mean and has come to adjust to and accept that fate. Returned to Kregen by the Star Lords — of whom he has given us no information — as a kind of interstellar troubleshooter, he rapidly rose to the position of Zorcander among his Clansmen of Felschraung in Segesthes, and then became the Lord of Strombor of the enclave city of Zenicce. At that point the Star Lords, apparently having no further use for him, returned him once more to Earth.

Some time elapsed before he was recalled to Kregen beneath Antares to find himself on the continent of Turismond, thousands of miles away from Segesthes, and up to his neck in problems. He witnessed the horrors perpetrated by the overlords of Magdag, escaped their slavery, became a corsair captain of a swifter — a Kregen galley — on the inner sea, the Eye of the World. We here lose portions of his story through the lamented absence of those missing cassettes, but we do know he was accepted into the mystic and military order of chivalry, the Krozairs of Zy, becoming Pur Dray. Returned to Magdag he organized the slaves and led a revolt which in the full tide of success was placed in jeopardy by the intervention of the Star Lords.

At the head of his slave phalanx he was surrounded by the lambent blue radiance that, together with the occasional appearance of a gigantic scorpion, accompanies a transition. In this case he was threatened with another ignominious return to Earth. However, once before he had managed by the exertion of a willpower we can only marvel at to negate the immediate effects and to remain on Kregen. So, now, he exerted all his willpower to remain on Kregen.

This volume, *Warrior of Scorpio,* takes up his adventures from that point and in the process almost exhausts the cassettes in our possession, leaving only a very few to see publication.

Unless Dray Prescot is able in some way to reveal some of his story, and this of course assumes he can in some way be afforded the opportunity of seeing the volumes already in print, this incredible saga of brilliant action and high adventure, of chilling cruelty and superlative courage, will come to an end.

Geoffrey Dean called me on the transatlantic phone to tell me of the tragic death of Dan Fraser.

"I am firmly convinced Dray Prescot is determined to have his story told," Geoffrey said over the line. "If it is humanly possibly — or superhumanly, given the intervention of the Star Lords — I believe, Alan, he will find a way of continuing to reach us and of carrying on with his story."

Even if the story does end here — and somehow I believe Geoffrey is right in his assessment and I await the confirmation that will come with a fresh communication from Dray Prescot — still I am convinced that on Kregen four hundred light-years away Dray Prescot, Pur Dray, Lord of Strombor, Kov of Delphond, Krozair of Zy, will continue his own living story.

Alan Burt Akers

One

Pawn of the Star Lords

"I will stay on Kregen!"

In my nostrils stank the odors of blood and sweat, oiled leather, dust, and my ears rang with the sounds of combat as swords clashed and clanged and pikes pierced mail and crossbow bolts punched into armored men. I could smell and hear, but I could see only an all-encompassing blueness lambent about me, and my gripping fist closed on emptiness where I should be grasping the hilt of my long sword.

"I will not go back to Earth!"

Everything was blue now, roaring and twisting in my head, in my eyes and ears, tumbling me head over heels into a blue nothingness.

"I will stay on Kregen beneath the suns of Scorpio! I will!"

I, Dray Prescot of Earth, screamed it out in my agony and despair. "I will stay on Kregen!"

A wind riffled my hair and I knew that old vosk-skull helmet with its panache of yellow paint had vanished with my long sword.

I was lying flat on my back. The noise of combat flowed away, dwindling. The screams of dying men and wounded sectrixes, the grunt and harshly indrawn breaths of men convulsed with the passions of battle, the clangor and scrape of weapons, all died. And the blue brilliance of light about me wavered and I sensed the inward struggle as obscure forms moved and merged past the edges of my vision. Against my back pressed hard earth — but was it the dirt of Kregen or of Earth?

That last battle against the overlords of Magdag had been violent and emotional and transforming, but any taint of battle-lust or battle-fever in me had been banished at a stroke by the unexpected intervention of the Star Lords. I have, I confess, sometimes been overwhelmed by the lust of battle, not often, and have little time for those who prate of that red curtain that falls before their eyes and to whose existence they point as an excuse for actions of the most barbarous and savage kind. Oh, yes, the scarlet curtain before the eyes exists, but it is capable of manipulation by those whose humanity has not been destroyed.

You who listen to these tapes spinning through their little cassettes will know how often I have succumbed, to my shame, to that red-roaring tide of exultant conflict.

So it was that as I sat up on that hard-packed ground the blood-lust of battle had cleared from my mind. But the fever of instant action still gripped my body. As I sat up, then, expecting I knew not what, a vast odiferous mass of squelchy straw laid me flat down on my back again.

Dung and straw smothered me. Spitting out a mouthful of vile-tasting straw I sat up, blinking, trying to see, vaguely making out a barn door black in the light as the blueness faded, and — smack down again I went as another heaping fork-ful of straw-laced manure slapped me across the face. I spat. I blinked. I cursed. With a roar of fury generated as much by indignation and a sense of the ludi-crous as much by anger I leaped to my feet.

This time I could dodge the flying forkful of dungy straw.

Thoroughly annoyed, I started for the barn door. As I expected, I was com-pletely naked. The Star Lords had snatched me from Magdag; where they had deposited me I did not know — but I had urgent problems before finding out, problems to do with people who threw dungy straw into my face.

A voice shouted something I didn't recognize, but even in the midst of intend-ing to deal with dung-hurlers I took comfort from the conviction that the language was not of Earth. It had that ring peculiar to the languages of Kregen, and I felt a surge of thanksgiving.

A man stepped out of the barn door.

My vision cleared and I saw this man bathed in the mingled streaming light of the twin suns of Antares. Then, without doubt, I knew the Star Lords had not snatched me from Kregen altogether and hurled me contemptuously back to Earth. Contemptuously, for I knew that in some way I had failed them, that I had not accomplished what they had brought me to Kregen and sent me to Magdag to do.

Staring at this man who stared back at me I was conscious only of a great and all-engulfing thankfulness. I was still on the same world as my Delia! I was not sundered from the only woman for me in two worlds by four hundred light-years of empty space. Somewhere in Vallia on this planet of Kregen my Delia of the Blue Mountains, my Delia of Delphond, lived and breathed and laughed and, I hoped and prayed, did not despair of me.

This man carried a pitchfork to which wisps of greasy straw still clung. He stood tall and lean, with the most infernal mocking smile taking in my naked-ness and the dungy straw clinging to my skin and broomsticking my hair — and then he saw my face. He lost his smile and the pitchfork came up in quick auto-matic response. He possessed a mane of intensely black hair. His eyes twinkled brightly blue upon me. There was about him an air of recklessness and of action-before-thought-of-consequences, and I judged he had not been slave for very long.

My thought of Delia had halted me — in the glory of knowing I was still tread-ing the same ground as my princess — so that this man was spared time enough to speak.

"Llahal!" he said, in the universal nonfamiliar greeting of Kregen. Had we been friends he would have said: "Lahal." He went on without waiting for my re-ply or for the making of pappattu. "You look a sight, dom!" And then he laughed. It was a light laugh, all mockery of myself gone from it and filled only with a de-light in the circumstances. Any man who cannot laugh at himself is truly dead. But, as I think you will know, I, Dray Prescot, do not, for others and out loud, laugh easily.

I started for him again with the intention of wrapping the pitchfork around his neck and then deciding what to do with the tines.

He skipped aside, still laughing.

His laughter changed to puzzlement.

"You must be one of the new slaves, dom. I am Seg Segutorio. If you've been sent to help me you'd better get started before we're both in trouble and tasting ol' snake."

The tines of the pitchfork looked exceedingly sharp. This man, this slave, handled the implement as a warrior handles a spear. Now he had recovered from the first shock of seeing that expression on my face that I have heard many men call the look of the devil; he balanced easily with the farmyard weapon covering me, confident in his own prowess. About to disabuse him of that idea, I checked.

We stood in a farmyard, with low buildings surrounding this stable area, with the rustic odors of dung and straw, urine and dust, heavy on the air. Over all the glorious rays of the twin suns of Scorpio streamed down in an opaline mingling of colors. Only moments before I had been leading the slave phalanx of my old vosk-skulls into headlong conflict with the mailed overlords of Magdag. Now, once more, I heard the shouts of men in furious strife and the screams of wounded, the shrilling of sectrixes, and the clamorous clangor of sword on sword.

A dog ran whining across the farmyard, his tail tucked down in between his legs.

Following him, a bedraggled band of slaves ran and fell and picked themselves up to stagger on. They were a mixed bunch of humans and half-humans, all wearing the gray slave breechclout, and their screams and crying panic made my hand reach out for a weapon. On Kregen a man without a ready weapon to hand is a man with a foot in the grave.

Flames shot up beyond the stable buildings and I guessed the great house itself would be burning. A rout of bloodied men-at-arms stumbled after the slaves, their mail coats ripped, their helmets dented and awry, some lost altogether. There were men and Rapas and Chuliks among the mercenary men-at-arms. Some had flung away their weapons in order to run faster.

"A raid!" Seg Segutorio hitched up the pitchfork. I didn't like the look on his face. "Those Froyvil-forgotten rasts of sorzarts!"

Now I could see them pelting around the stable buildings, squat on scaled legs, bedecked with gaudy strings of clanking bronze and copper ornaments, befeathered, cockscombed of helmeted head, fierce and predatory and shrilling war cries that struck absolute horror into the fleeing people of the peaceful farm. They wielded cut-down long swords and throwing spears not unlike narrow assegais, and they presented a sight calculated to overawe peasant opposition in the twinkling of the first blade. The few mercenary guards maintained by the farm had been powerless to halt this raid.

Although I had heard of these sorzarts, I had not previously encountered them. They inhabited a cluster of islands toward the northeastern end of the inner sea and were the subject of endless speculation among the other peoples of the Eye of the World as to who would instigate the great crusade against them and who would follow the Banners and when; but while the bitter enmity between the green north and the red south persisted the sorzarts were left unmolested. Their faces were vaguely lizard-like in their wide cheeks and virtual absence of forehead, but their eyes were quite unreptile-like, being dull and deeply set.

Everything, as is usual in moments of crisis, happened at breakneck speed and by the time Seg had leveled his pitchfork and broken into a run the sorzarts had mostly vanished beyond the opposite stable building. A woman clutching a child to her bosom ran into view, saw the last three sorzarts, swerved in her run, saw Seg Segutorio, and screamed at him. Her bared legs beneath the lavender gown covered the ground rapidly, but it was clear to us that the sorzarts would cut her off and catch her before she could reach us.

"Help me!" Even in her terror and despair the words cracked with the snap of habitual command. "Seg! Help me!"

"The mistress." Seg bounded forward afresh. "She bought me ten days ago and I have no love for her — but — but she is a woman."

That was an irrational thought in a culture possessed of many types of beast-humans and human-beasts encountered daily in ordinary social intercourse.

Now I knew why the Star Lords had condescended to keep me here on Kregen and why they had not flung me through the interstellar gulfs back to the Earth of my birth. They had found another task for my hands. As usual, they had dumped me down naked and defenseless in the midst of a situation of extreme peril. I knew that away in Magdag my slaves, wearing their old yellow-painted vosk-skulls and wielding the weapons I had created and taught them to use, were fighting with savage intent against the might of the overlords and, most probably now I had gone, losing. But I had been snatched from them and in return for not being banished to Earth had been presented with this crisis to resolve.

I scooped up a heaping double-armful of odiferous manure-fouled straw and sprinted after Seg. I passed him with ease and then I was beyond the woman and her child and facing the three sorzarts. They looked mean and ferocious and they held their weapons with the skill of long experience.

The nearest flicked his cut-down long sword at me and I angled my run so that he obscured the view of the second, who lifted his assegai in frustration, balked of his cast. I checked, lifted on my toes, and hurled my dung-straw full in the face of the first sorzart. He ducked lithely enough and avoided the straw. But his movement slowed him and then I was up to him. His back broke with a soggy snap and I had his sword and snatched it aloft to parry the assegai cast. The shaft rang against the blade. I lunged forward. The sword felt good in my fist. Longer than the short sword as used by my Clansmen, this brand balanced oddly; but it served its purpose and as I withdrew the blade befouled with the sorzart's blood there was time to meet the challenge of the third. He hesitated.

"Hai!" I said.

He eyed me warily from those deep-set eyes. Abruptly, like a striking lizard, with a bunching of muscles and a jangling of bronze and copper disks, he hurled his assegai. I brushed it aside. Seg saved me the final thrust, for, as I waited for the sorzart to draw his sword, the pitchfork flew past my ear and buried its two center tines deeply into the scaly neck.

"Why did you hesitate?" demanded Seg, panting. "You know these sorzarts are the most treacherous of beasts."

I wiped the blade on the sorzart's brown apron.

"I have killed a man before he has drawn to defend himself," I told Seg. "And, sink me, no doubt will do so again, Zair forgive me, if it is necessary. In this case it was not."

He looked at me oddly. Reckless and wild, as I was to find him, his ideas of warfare were also extremely practical.

The unpleasant sounds of raiding half-men reached us from beyond the stable block and the wind drew coils of greasy smoke from the burning house about our faces. The woman caught her breath. I had looked at her once, and then gone about my business. There has been more than enough in my life of seeing screaming women clutching their infants to them — the tears soaking into their dresses, their faces distraught, running blindly from rapacious reavers of all kinds — for me ever to treat such scenes lightly. People prate of the values of human life, and of how nothing outside the context of human activity is of worth, and on Kregen, willy-nilly, the existence of half-human, half-beast peoples must figure into that context, and yet I wonder how often such academic postulators have been presented with situations in which their actions must match their words. Of course I was not insensitive to this woman's naked bloody feet, the tears on her cheeks, the infant mess around her child's mouth and nose, his inflamed eyes and his crying blubbering. But raiders of the stamp of the sorzarts know well the weakness of men unmanned by women's sufferings.

I said: "We must leave here. Now. Come."

Without bothering to await their reply I stripped a length of brown cloth from a dead sorzart — the cleanest length — and wrapped it around my waist, pulled the end through between my legs, and tucked it in to form a breechclout. I balanced all three of the cut-down long swords and selected the one I felt the best. The belt and scabbard were neatly stitched from the skins of the little green and brown lizards called Tikos and as Seg picked up a sword and an assegai I thrust the sword I had chosen into the scabbard, took the third up together with the three assegais remaining. I ignored the helmets. This took but little time and during it the woman stood first on one leg and then on the other, hoisting her child up on her hip and shushing it, and staring at me with an uncertainty I had no time to bother over just then. She would know well enough I was not one of her slaves.

We set off in a line directly away from the burning house.

I felt completely confident that this woman and her infant were the people I had been sent here by the Star Lords to succor. Just why I should be so sure I did not know. My natural instincts sometimes coalesce with a darker and rarer judgment. I had saved Gahan Gannius and Valima there on the edge of the Grand Canal when, for the third time, I had found myself on Kregen. They had given me no thanks but had taken themselves off. Now I assumed they must play some part in the complicated games with destiny played over the years by the Star Lords — with assistance and interference from the Savanti. That these thoughts were true and just how the world of Kregen was influenced by my own interference, you shall hear.

We spoke little. I was concerned to find a riding mount for the woman. The stables were empty — the men out on an expedition and leaving the estate vulnerable to just this kind of sudden raid — and the quicker we found a sectrix, one of the six-legged riding animals of the inner sea littoral, or a calsany, or even an ass, the better. When Seg asked my name I had no hesitation in choosing my own among the plethora of names I already possessed — a quantity of nomenclature I found, to be honest, more amusing than otherwise.

"I am Dray Prescot," I said. And then: "Of Strombor."

The name meant nothing to them.

It was unlikely that they would know of Strombor as a place, for until I had resurrected that enclave in Zenicce with the gift of Great Aunt Shusha — who was not *my* great aunt, I must remember — the name of Strombor had been obscured for a hundred and fifty years by the house Esztercari. But since they had not heard the name of Pur Dray, Lord of Strombor, Krozair of Zy, renowned corsair upon the Eye of the World, it surely indicated the cut-off nature of their life. I had convinced myself that I must still be within the sphere of occupation around the inner sea, as witness the sorzarts, and so I was not unduly alarmed. Had I been so minded I might have chuckled at the haughty reception such ignorance of their noble names and deeds would have received from some of the swifter captains and Krozairs and Brethren of my acquaintance.

"This is the Lady Pulvia na Upalion," said Seg Segutorio, and despite the situation and his clear detestation of his slave status, some respect was evident in his words.

I looked at the woman. Nothing about her impressed me so much as the way her head came erect and her eyes widened to meet my regard. She was in no sense beautiful, rather she was a sturdy, strong-limbed woman habitually in command, conscious of her position, and no doubt in normal times somewhat in despair over the hint of a moustache beginning to darken her upper lip. I reached out my hands.

"Give me the child."

Instinctively she clasped the infant closer to her breast where tears and mucus stained the lavender material. She wore a gold and ruby trinket upon a slender gold chain. I gestured impatiently to her naked feet. She looked into my face and I saw her eyes darken in shock. Then, silently, she let me take the boy from her. He was no great weight. In a little group we left the stables and at once were among the standing crops, tall green-stemmed bloin loaded with golden fruit in which we were hidden as though by a million tongueless cathedral bells.

From the rear, black and oily smoke rose and spread to cast dark shadows from the mingled light of the twin suns of Scorpio.

Any thoughts I may have had that my task for the Star Lords was thus easily accomplished were speedily dispelled. With the three spare assegais tucked under my left arm which cradled the child, the second sword naked in my right fist, I brought up the rear, with Seg in the van.

The sorzarts must have landed from their raiding ships — for they habitually disliked voyaging with only a single ship — and marched inland to fall on this estate of Upalion, which I had already seen enough to know was composed of broad acres and rich land, heavy with crops. Upalion, some distance from the sea, had considered itself secure, as the weak mercenary force of men-at-arms testified.

Now the sorzarts burst into the wealth of golden bloin fruits, seeking our blood.

"You go on, Seg," I said, and handed him the child, pushing past the woman unceremoniously. "I will hold them."

"The mistress can take the child," said Seg. His eagerness to stand to die with me was surprising.

"Sink me!" I exclaimed, not angrily but exasperatedly amused. I can find amusement in strange situations. "She can barely walk, let alone run with the child. You must get her away, Seg, for the sweet sake of Zim-Zair. Do not argue!"

"By the veiled Froyvil—" began Seg, his black mane of hair wild among the golden fruits.

I cut him off, with a rolling Makki-Grodno oath.

"Go on!"

I own, then, that a deal of that unpleasant rasp must have sharpened my tones, a dominating, domineering almost, way of talking I assumed in automatic response to opposition and that came from many years walking the quarterdecks of King's Ships, of handling my Clansmen as Zorcander and Vovedeer, of reaving as a Krozair captain of a Sanurkazz swifter. Seg took a look at my face. He took the child.

"There are ruins of the sunset folk about a dwabur south," he said. That was all.

I felt I could get to know this volatile yet practical man.

Seg and the Lady Pulvia vanished among the golden bells.

The swords I now held had once been regular long swords. Now they had been cut down and sharpened with wedge-shaped points into a blade-length of some twenty-four inches. For a tiny nostalgic moment I thought of those superlative Savanti swords with which we had so lightheartedly gone from Aphrasöe the Swinging City clad in our Savanti hunting leathers in bloodless pursuit of the graint. Maybe these sorzarts knew more of swordsmanship than I guessed, more, even, than the Krozairs of Zy, although in my pride that seemed so remotely possible as to be unthinkable. Well, I would soon find out.

Harsh cries rose into the air and the golden bells of the bloin hanging from stems curving in such subtle beauty from their straight green stalks waved and twisted over our back path as agile scaled bodies thrust their way through.

A fighting-man's life is stitched together with vivid scarlet incidents patching the gray drabness of days and my experience had taught me that on Kregen the scarlet outweighed the gray. I thought of my Delia of the Blue Mountains, and prayed she would not despair of me away in her awe-inspiring Vallia.

Then, with weapons in my hands, I turned to face the dangers that had ensured my continuance on Kregen beneath Antares. It would need many swords to force me to flee from all that kept me on Kregen under the suns of Scorpio.

Two

Seg Segutorio

This was what life on Kregen was all about, this continuous challenge that set the blood pulsing through my veins, that brought all my alertness alive, that made me aware of myself as a man. Only moments before I had been fighting in the dust and sweat of my slave phalanx against the overlords of Magdag and then, because I had in some way unfathomable to me failed the Star Lords, I had been thrown into this new situation. Well — I thrust the second sword carefully down through the lizard-skin belt and hefted an assegai — well, the Star Lords or Savanti or scaled-skin sorzarts, all would meet my defiance distributed with an impartiality that held fast to one ideal only — I would win my way back to my Delia of the Blue Mountains. At that time the simplicity of this concept could hold no irony for me whatsoever.

The golden fruits waved and parted and the first lizard-man stepped through. I waited.

He was followed by another and then a third. Still I waited. They had not seen me yet, concealed by the dark-green stems of the bloin, and I did not move. The first was very near now, so near I could see the way his scales grew smaller and smaller as they reached his neck and spread over his face in a kind of pseudo-skin in which his snout-nose and mouth protruded beneath those deep-set eyes. The mingled red and green light fell across the bronze and copper ornaments slung about him and sheened golden from the tall helmet with its arrogant bronze cock's comb. He held his assegai slanting over his shoulder in the ready-to-cast position.

I saved that one for my sword.

His three companions went down, shrilling, each with an assegai through him, sprawling kicking among the brittle hard stems of the golden bloin.

The first sorzart's cast assegai sprang for my chest. My sword flicked free from the belt and knocked aside the flung assegai with a vibrating twang in that swift wrist-roll we Krozairs of Zy so often practiced against arrows. Then I was on him. This time my scruples about killing a man or half-man before he had time to draw could be put aside, with whatever of morality remained in this situation. Other sorzarts were following fast; three or four assegais whickered past. I lunged, withdrew, leaped back to avoid the next clump of assegais.

So far I had made no mistakes. I had not spoken; the full-scented odors of the golden bloin bells and the smell of blood and dust among the brittle green stems seemed to render out sounds, so that the dusty crackling of the stems as sorzarts sought my life came as through a golden afternoon haze. I did not know how many there were, but I did not intend to be chopped by their swords or struck by their assegais. I had no time, given what the Star Lords had brought me here to accomplish and that which I meant to accomplish for myself, to stay. In an instant I vanished from the lizard-men's sight among the silent golden bells of the bloin.

It would be useless just to scamper after Seg Segutorio and the Lady Pulvia. He would be hampered by her and the child and the sorzarts would catch up with them with results the Star Lords would disapprove of. So it was that those bold raiders of the inner sea were set on and bedeviled in their pursuit through the golden bloin and then — with more difficulty for myself — through orchards of gnarly-trunked samphron trees, whose juicy fruits with their glossy purple skins would soon be picked to be crushed into fragrant oil.

The second sword broke off short during one fierce interchange, but I came away with a replacement and with two more assegais that were almost immediately targeted off to good effect.

The blood that smothered my right arm was not mine. The two swords, I found, formed an interesting combination, rather like an overbalanced pair, a too-short long sword or broadsword for the right hand and a too-long main-gauche. The sorzarts probably shortened captured long swords because of the half-men's somewhat short stature, but they were nonetheless swift and sturdy fighters for all that.

Swords, of course, are objects of worth and price and not easily come by in a culture without an extensive metallurgy, either of bronze or iron. The sorzarts' assegais — not the true assegai of Africa, I hasten to add, but an altogether slighter and narrower-bladed weapon — were their own natural weapon. Not all the lizard-men by any means possessed swords. Many of those swords I saw were easily identifiable as to previous ownership by their armory marks; weapons from Gantz and Zulfiria, from Sanurkazz and far Magdag.

The twin suns of Scorpio moved across the heavens and the streaming light settled more regretfully across the land. Soon darkness would fall with the temperate-zone twilight of not overlong duration. Somewhat to my astonishment the sorzarts kept up their pursuit. I no longer count the men or beast-men I have slain and so I do not know how many they lost in that long and agonized pursuit. Only when the twin suns at last sank beyond a distant ridge of mountains that ran down from the interior into the inner sea could I discern any reluctance on their part to continue.

Sharp trilling cries rose from one and then another. The last one I dispatched — without regret, for he had nicked me with his flung assegai and would have killed me without compunction had I allowed him to finish his sword-blow — fell headfirst into a little brook that meandered from the borders of the last orchard and trended away through open meadowland toward the sea. Purple shadows gathered and the water glimmered like cold steel. Thoughtfully, I wiped my blade on the sorzart's breechclout, picked up all his weapons, and walked on south. Soon the darkness was complete and I could gaze upward at the Kregen night sky and see those strange yet blessedly familiar constellations wheel above my head.

A comfort could be taken from the distant chips of light that fancifully formed animals and people and monsters, pinpricks of light that could form meaningful patterns only in a man's mind, his own rationality plucking form from an inchoate star-spattered infinity. I saw the stellar images, and I stumbled over a thorn bush and I cursed, and thereafter kept my eyes fixed on my path with only the occasional navigating glance aloft.

All the warmth of combat had passed from me. I did not shiver, for the night was mild, but inwardly I felt once again the essential futility of blind killing. How often — I remember musing as I trod southward to fulfill whatever of destiny the Star Lords would allow me — I had seen men who appeared actually to enjoy inflicting pain on others. These were the uniformed men of the bludgeon and thewhip, who recruited their own warped desires into the punishment of the unfortunate. Did I enjoy the sensation as I cut a man down? Did I thrill to the jolt as my sword pierced a man's guts? God forgive me if I did — but I did not then and do not now. Perhaps my punishment is that in a situation in which it is kill or be killed I choose the easier path and kill to save my life and the lives of my loved ones.

Thus musing in a somber frame of mind — for I missed my Delia of the Blue Mountains beyond the mortal capacity to endure, or so I thought — I came to a rearing mass of toppled stone, twisted columns, broken arches, and collapsed domes all shining pinkly in the first of Kregen's nightly procession of moons.

The little stream broadened here and washed the worn steps of a landing jetty. Shadows jungle-hostile hung between truncated columns. I caught strange glimpses of pagan sculpture, serpentine forms that twined upon the surfaces of the blocks, hints of a demonology older than any current civilization thriving on this continent of Turismond.

The men of the sunrise had built their cities along the shores of the inner sea. Today, the shores lie mostly barren and untended except where the vicinity of a strong castle or fortified town or city affords some protection from corsair raids. I had raided the north shore myself, that shore of the green-sun deity Grodno; I had heard horrific tales of similar raids upon the red southern shore, dedicated to the sun Zim's deity, Zair. And the sorzarts raided both north and south and the eastern shore of Proconia — where I must now be — with the impartiality of the true unbeliever. I touched the hilt of one of my swords — for I remembered with affection the impressive armory of Hap Loder and my Clansmen of Felschraung — and went on.

"Stand and declare yourself — or you are a dead man!"

The voice sounded hard and confident and reckless. It was the voice of Seg Segutorio. I could not see him.

Undoubtedly, then, he was a warrior of skill.

"Dray Prescot," I said, and did not stop.

Seg and the Lady Pulvia waited beside the stone lip of a wide and shallow basin, shell-shaped, into which an arm of the stream poured continually, pinkly silver in the moons' light. Above them a chipped and defaced statue of a woman whose marble wings hung splintered from narrow shoulders cast a peaked shadow.

"You are safe, Dray?"

"Safe, Seg."

We had fallen into names thus easily, then.

"Thank the veiled Froyvil for that, then!"

"And you — the Lady Pulvia?"

She lifted her head from above her child as I asked, and gave me a blank, un-seeing stare that told me that we would have to support her on whatever further voyage we must undertake. She bent her head and crooned softly to the child, who lay, his soft mouth stoppered by a plump thumb, fast asleep.

For a moment I could not recall when I had last slept. In all my bones that lax-ity of alert feeling told me that I was tired, deadly tired, but a sea officer of a King's Ship comes early to learn the knack of using his strength against long pe-riods of wakefulness. I could go on for a space yet, but I considered the situation, knowing that sleep now would set store of strength by for later emergencies.

A movement in the purple shadows beneath the statue's splintered wings brought my sword out instantly, but Seg laughed and said: "Easy, Dray, you wild leem! That is Caphlander. A stylor, one of my lady's servants."

The man stepped into the moonlight. Tall, he walked with a stoop, and his sparse hair glinted in that wash of pink light. He wore a white robe bordered with a checkered design of red and green — a sight I must admit bewildered me for a moment with all the fierce clash of red and green still echoing in my skull — and his face reminded me somewhat of the ugly bird-head of a Rapa. There were sig-nificant differences, however, and his humanity seemed to me more pronounced than the remnant left to a Rapa. He was a Relt. Numbers of these usually gentle people when made slave pined near to death; others found reasons for living in serving their masters as librarians, stylors, accountants. His bright bird-like eyes studied us from a face held to one side, so that I knew his sight was affected in one of those eyes.

"Llahal!" he said, and then waited, stooping, subservient.

Brusquely, Seg said: "And?"

Caphlander the Relt wilted. "All burned," he said. "All dead. Such sights—"

"There's no going back, then. The Lord of Upalion having gone on his expedi-tion will return to dust and ashes and corpses."

The impression I gained then, briefly and fleetingly, was that Seg was not overly dismayed at this catastrophe to his master, the man who owned him as slave. And — no wonder.

"Is there no safe place for this woman, Seg?"

He looked at her and sucked in his lower lip.

"The city — that is the only safe place. And we would never reach it on foot now. The sorzarts must be out in force."

"The day of our doom is here." Caphlander spoke with complete subjection and acceptance of his fate.

"I do not believe that my day of doom is to be brought by a bunch of lizard-faced scaled beast-men. There are other ways to cities than by walking," I told Caphlander and Seg.

"All the sectrixes were taken—"

I lifted my head and sniffed. On the night air, whose lush odors of nocturnal plant life told of many of those immense moon-drinking flowers twining among the ruins, the tangier smell I knew so well infiltrated like liquor at a funeral.

"The sea is not far. This city—"

"Happapat," said Seg.

"This Happapat — is it a port?"

"Yes."

"Then let's go."

We reached the coast. Seg carried the child and I carried his mother. She lay in my arms, a soft flaccid sexless bundle, a human being for whom my only concern had been dictated by the Star Lords — whoever they might be. We rested in a rock cave halfway up the cliff as the night passed.

With the gaining light, and refreshed by a few burs' sleep, we could plan again. I think, even then, Seg Segutorio had realized something other than mere concern over the safety of his mistress impelled me, for his people may be wild and reckless and filled with song, but they also possess that hard streak of practicality that has maintained their independence.

As the first sheening light of Zim spread in scarlet and golden radiance across the calm waters of the inner sea we looked out and down onto the ships of the sorzarts.

"Eleven of them." Seg spat. I did not waste good saliva. "They have to voyage in company, for they cannot face a Pattelonian swifter in fair fight."

On the curved beach the ships had been drawn up stern first. Ladders were lowered with the dawn and the anchor watch began their preparations to welcome back their comrades with loot and gold and prisoners. My hand tightened on the hilt of one of the swords. We could wait here until the sorzarts sailed away...

Call me a fool. Call me a windbag full of braggadocio. Call me prideful. I do not care. All I know is that while my Delia sought me from her island home of Vallia by rider and flier and I yearned above all things to hold her dear form in my arms once more, I could not thus tamely crouch hiding in a cave. On the hilt of the sword were marked letters in the Kregish script: G.G.M. That meant that a mercenary warrior employed by Gahan Gannius had died some time in the past and his sword had been taken as battle booty by the sorzarts. I wondered what had happened to Gahan Gannius, whom I had rescued on my last return to Kregen, and if his manners and those of the girl Valima had improved.

The plan must be nicely made and as nicely decided. Those eleven ships down there on the beach beyond the nearest crumbling wall of the Pattelonian fishing village were not swifters nor were they broad ships. They were dromvilers. They had chosen to land directly at the fishing village — which are rare enough on the inner sea's coastline, Zair knows — to secure safe berthings. The coast here fell sheer into the sea. The people of the village, sentinels against just such raids, had been outwitted on this occasion, for a huddle of their fishing boats, the familiar muldavy with her dipping lugsail of the inner sea, were still drawn up on the beach by the wall. No one, then, had escaped.

But those ships of the sorzarts... I had heard of them, of course, during my seasons as a Krozair raider on the Eye of the World. But I had never before penetrated this far east. The dromvilers were, to phrase it loosely, a compromise between a galley and a sailing ship, although they were not galleasses. They were more like those classical ships sometimes remarked on by ancient writers, or the oared merchantmen of the Middle Ages used considerably in the trade to the Holy Land, shipping pilgrims.

Broader than a swifter, narrower than a broad ship, they carried single banks of twenty oars each crewed probably by three or four oarsmen, and two masts. I felt reasonably certain that the masts could carry topsails, and a grudging respect grew in me for the sorzarts' sailing skills, for from topsails can emerge all the panoply of sails, skysails and stunsails and all.

A further sobering thought occurred to me. With that number of oarsmen — something between one hundred and twenty and one hundred and sixty, plus essential reserves — the sorzarts could not be using slaves as oarsmen. A large war swifter can carry a thousand slave oarsmen, and feed and water and clean them after a fashion, by extraordinarily careful management. But a merchantman exists to transport goods. There would be no room aboard the sorzarts' ships for slaves. The oarsmen, then, were free — that is, they were sorzarts capable of standing and fighting along with the soldiers of the crew. Maybe the sorzarts were not the savage barbarians the men of Grodno and Zair believed them.

"I am thirsty," said the Lady Pulvia, breaking the silence. "And my son is thirsty. Also, we are hungry."

I said: "So am I. I will bring you food and water as soon as it is possible."

"And when will that be?" said Caphlander. He held his hands together, the long thin fingers intertwined. The veins stood out with a greenish-blue tinge.

I ignored him.

Why should I destroy these sorzarts? A peculiar feeling toward them of respect had been growing in me. They were small men — half-men — yet they fought well. They had adopted topsails. They employed themselves as free men as oarsmen. But I saw the fallacy of this materialistic argument. The Vikings had been free men employed as oarsmen — yet I would have had no hesitation, given this situation, in utterly destroying every Viking longship I could. The child gave a whimpering cry, which swelled until against all his mother's shushings it broke into a torrent of sobs. The child was hungry and thirsty and he reacted as nature ordained he should.

Often I have been faced with a problem and reacted as I did because that was the way of my nature. That scorpion, that frog, they were impelled by forces stronger than themselves. Well, I have boasted that I can control my impulses, but I think that boast is on occasion an empty one. I stood up.

"Caphlander. You will remain here. Do what you can for the Lady Pulvia and her son. Seg, please come with me."

Without giving any of them a chance to reply or argue I went out of the rock cave and began to climb to the cliff top.

Three

I dive back into the Eye of the World

Seg Segutorio looked at the bow in his hand and his mobile lips drew down in a lopsided grimace. The bow spanned about twelve Earthly inches. He had made it with swift expertise from a branch of the thin willowy tuffa trees in whose shade we stood. The string he had as rapidly fashioned from plaited strips torn from the living bark. I looked down over the edge of the cliff, squinting a little against glare striking back off the sea from the twin suns of Antares.

Our preparations were complete. It only remained to kindle fire.

Any distaste as a sailorman I felt for the task I had set myself had to be quashed.

Seg let loose a great sigh and lifted the bow to me. He shook his head. "Had I my own great bow I'd guarantee to pick off those sorzart rasts so fast they'd be pincushions before the first one hit the deck."

He surprised me. You must realize, you who listen to my story as these tapes rustle through your little machine, that despite Seg's black hair I had taken him to be a Proconian, who are, as I have said, mostly fair-headed. The remarks about his people I have made refer, of course, to his own true people; but they are re-marks made from hindsight, a crime you must forgive a man who has lived as long as I have. "Great bow?" I said.

He laughed. "Surely, even you — who are a stranger of strangers — must have heard of the longbows of Loh?"

"You are of Loh?"

Again he laughed. "Yes — and no!" That ancient look of blood pride suffused his face, an arrogant, proud expression so familiar in those who trace their an-cestry back and back into the dawn of their culture. I can understand it; but in many ways I am glad I do not share it, for that kind of pride so often leads to the chinless wonders who have so blighted life on our own Earth. But, with Seg Segutorio, as you shall hear, pride in race and ancestry burned with a steadier and truer flame.

"I am an Erthyr, of Erthyrdrin..."

Of Erthyrdrin, that convulsed mass of mountains and valleys forming the long northern promontory of Loh, I had indeed heard. I had used longbowmen from Loh as a special sniper force in my slave army when we went against the over-lords of Magdag, and some of them had had red hair, and some had not, and all had been superlative archers; but none had come from Erthyrdrin, although they had spoken of the place with some awe, some respect, and not a little bile.

Although tempted to contest a little in words with Seg over the relative values of my Clansmen's horn and steel compound reflex bows, I desisted. The wind was just right. The trees selected and bent and staked. The grasses gathered.

Now only the flame remained to be kindled.

"Go down to the Lady Pulvia, Seg. Prepare them. You know the boat. If I am delayed — do not wait for me."

"But—"

"Go, now—"

He handed me the bow, his face glowering. "I see that at a more suitable opportunity, Dray Prescot, I shall have to teach you some respect for a warrior of Erthyrdrin."

"Willingly, my friend. I trust the good Zair will grant it—"

"Pagan gods!" he said, with a flash of cutting temper. "The mountaintops whereon the veiled Froyvil sends out his divine music from his golden and ivory harp would soon teach you the true values, my sad and unhappy friend."

"As to that," I said, taking the bow and squatting down to work, "I make no claims for Zair beyond those his followers make. And," I added, looking up suddenly, "they have been known to claim by the edge of the sword."

He made some kind of exasperated snort and hurried off down to the rock cave.

I shook my head over Seg Segutorio. From what I had heard of Erthyrdrin, that mountainous promontory of the continent of Loh thrusting up into the Cyphren Sea between eastern Turismond and Vallia, he was a good representative of his race. They were reputed reckless and wild, forever screeching crazy songs and thrumming on their harps; yet I knew of the strong streak of realism stabilizing their characters and lending always the calculated risk to the actions that other men called foolhardy.

So Seg was a longbowman. That could prove interesting.

The little bow whizzed rapidly back and forth twirling the drill of harder sturm-wood against its sturm-wood hole wherein chippings and dry grasses awaited the first ember. Gently and then with greater boldness I blew on the glow. You, who are so accustomed to flicking your finger for heat or light or a naked flame must remember that I had known flint and steel from childhood; perhaps I was a little quicker and defter at thus creating fire than a modern civilized man would be. It is of little consequence.

By the time I had a twisted torch well alight, the flames pale and writhing in the twin suns' rays, I figured that Seg must have reached the rock cave and gathered up our companions. He should be creeping cautiously down toward the beach now and, as I had judged him aright, taking every opportunity for cover the way provided. I walked across to the first bundle of grasses, wrapped and wadded around a flighting stone, where it lay poised on the forked-branch end of a sapling bent over and staked into the ground. Seg had sighted these rude catapults, and I had let him do that and had then merely checked them. He seemed to me to have done an excellent job. My ballistic knowledge had been gained at the breeches of twelve pounders and then all the way down to four pounders and up to thirty-two pounders, with one stint I looked back on with a grimace on the clumsy old forty-two pounders. In addition I had handled varters aboard swift-ers from Sanurkazz, and added to all this a natural eye for estimating distance and elevation and trajectory, and I knew myself, with all the necessary modesty required, to be a first-class shot. As I sliced through the first retaining fiber and released the first weighted bundle of flame I knew Seg Segutorio, also, to be a great marksman.

That first flaming missile arced into the suns-lit air, some smoke trailed from it, then it was a roaring mass of consuming flame arcing high and over and down onto the deck of a sorzart vessel.

I ran along the line of staked-down tuffa trees, their supple stems bent into graceful arches, and I seemed somehow to sense all their necessary springing ef-fort as they flung themselves erect once more. It seemed to me all of their essential nature was pent up in those supple stems. One after another the spout-ing missiles of destruction plunged down onto the decks of the sorzarts' dromvilers. A pure pang of relief pierced me that the lizard-men would have no slaves chained to their dromvilers' benches. Already flames were licking malevo-lently at masts and rigging, shooting from oar ports; already the most dreaded foe of the seaman was consuming the wooden vessels and I knew, not without another pang, that nothing could be done now until the dromvilers burned down to the waterline — and their sterns were drawn up on the beach...

This was a sight I need not stop to watch; this was a sight I did not care to stay to watch. It sickened me.

The necessity of the act alone could make me burn a ship. Halfway down to-ward the rock cave I halted and looked over the drop toward the beach. All eleven ships were blazing, although the one farthest away, which we had had to reach with a smaller incendiary missile, showed signs of resisting. Gangs of sor-zarts were running like crazy people with buckets of seawater; others manned the pumps and streams of water jetted. I doubted they would hold back the flames. Once fire gets a hold aboard a wooden ship with her paint and tar and canvas and wood dried internally, there is practically no hope of extinguishing it.

At the cave I paused again, just to make sure they had gone. They had. On again and so down out of sight of the beach and around the last corner over the bluff above the fisher-folk's jetty wall.

Down there three figures struggled toward the boat we had chosen. The Lady Pulvia fell and Seg thrust the child at Caphlander and snatched up his mistress, slung her over his shoulder as he must have slung the bags of feed oats on her farm. They would reach the boat safely — and then I saw the group of sorzarts running from the heat and the smoke of their burning fleet.

I looked down.

It was a long way — a hundred and fifty feet in Terrestrial measurement. The sea looked blue and calm and serene. Shadows flitted across that surface as smoke clouds wafted by. The twin suns shone in all their resplendent glory. And, away in distant Vallia, my Delia of the Blue Mountains waited for me...

You have probably read of experiments carried out to test from what distance a man can safely fall without a parachute. There are remarkable cases on record. Impact velocities of the order of a hundred feet per second have resulted in the survival of the person — in what state depending very much on the angle of impact or entry into the water. I knew nothing of that, then. All I knew was that I had to get down to the beach rather quickly. There were things to be done down there which if left undone would bring the wrath of the Star Lords down on my mortal head.

Without stopping further to cogitate I put my arms out and dived.

Even now I can remember the sensations.

Free-fall diving from aircraft is a modern sport.

I have practiced it and enjoyed it.

Then, when I dived off the cliff in Proconia above a Pattelonian fishing village, with the sorzarts running with naked swords, I just dived and let what fates held me in their hands take control.

Mind you, I did assume a diving position, and I entered the water straight. Confused images of that immense waterfall in the sacred River Aph billowed and echoed in my mind, and my whole body felt as though I had been compressed in some giant vise. Then I was cleaving through the water, down and down, seeing the daylight fade, feeling the growing resistance in the water, curving up, rising and rising until my head popped out and I could shake my hair and look back at the beach.

That first gulp of air tasted very sweet.

The Lady Pulvia, Caphlander, and the child were in the boat. Seg had just hurled an assegai and brought down the leader of the band of vengeful sorzarts. I started to swim.

When I scrambled out Seg accounted for four more and was crossing swords with the sixth.

I must admit I had been extraordinarily lucky since neither the Star Lords nor the Savanti had taken a hand to preserve a life they might consider of use to them. Certainly the risk had been entirely of entry. The almost vertical cliffs of this coast had told me the water would be steep-to right up to the rock, deep and commodious enough for me to avoid knocking my brains out on the bottom. The overhang of the bluff assisted also. I had merely to swim around the tiny spit of land to reach the beach and Seg and the others.

"Hai Jikai!" I yelled. I drew my sword and slogged into the lizard-men. Seg circled a sword, thrust, recovered, shouted: "What kept you?"

A joke, a reprimand, mere bravado — I do not know. I never asked. But I felt a warm glow of elation at the presence of this black-haired and reckless man from Erthyrdrin.

There was no time for nicety in that fight. We had to dispose of this band of sorzarts — there were about eight left — very rapidly before their comrades left off hurling ineffectual buckets of water over their burning ships and hastened to their assistance. No niceties — that meant hard, fierce, dirty fighting. Tricks I had learned boarding enemy ships of the line in the battle-smoke of Earth, tricks I had picked up with my Clansmen, even a few passes from those days as a bravo-fighter in Zenicce came in useful. All the miraculous-seeking swordplay given me by the disciplines of the Krozairs of Zy, of course, enabled me to stay ahead of my opponent, but some of the stunts I pulled would have turned a young college boy fencer of this Earth green.

Seg and I — we very quickly cleared the sorzarts away.

"The three boats on your side, Seg!" I yelled.

Without a word he did as I directed, and together we stove in the bottoms of the boats lying in this huddle. One boat, the largest, a fifty-footer, lay some distance off, toward where the bonfires of the dromvilers spouted flame and smoke.

I started for it, waving Seg back to the boat we had selected.

The Lady Pulvia na Upalion stood up in the bows of the boat. Very erect, she stood.

"Leave that boat!" she shouted. "They are coming! Look! Hurry back and push this boat into the sea! Hurry!"

A further group following the non-reappearance of those sent to investigate, no doubt, was indeed running from the burning ships along the beach toward us. Suns-light glinted on their bronze and copper ornaments, from their tall golden helmets, and winked back from their naked weapons.

I turned to the Lady Pulvia.

"Get out and help Seg and Caphlander push the boat out! Move yourself! Hurry!"

Then, before she could give vent to her outraged anger and surprise, I yelled at Seg: "Get the boat off, Seg! Make her help — and the Relt. I will swim out to you." Then I hared off toward the remaining boat and the swiftly advancing party of sorzarts. When they saw me they shrilled their horrid war cries — but mere yelling has not so far harmed me at that distance.

Reaching the fifty-footer I stove the bottom in with four quick blows — not without once more that pang of displeasure at myself for this destruction of property that gave livelihood to the poor fisher-folk — and glared out to sea to get the best line for my swim.

The boat had not moved. The Lady Pulvia still stood in the bows, gesticulating to the two — Seg and Caphlander — who were vainly attempting to thrust the boat's keel into the water.

I kept down the immediate icy welling of rage. That, if I so chose, would come later.

The boat felt thick and hard beneath my hands as I reached it. At any moment the sorzarts would be within assegai-casting range.

"All together!"

We heaved. The boat lurched, the keel screeched, it stuck — we all bent and thrust with desperate effort — and then the boat jerked and slid free into the water. I took Caphlander around the waist and fairly flung him up into the boat. Seg went in over the other side and I, after a last fierce thrust that sent the craft surging out into the tiny waves, leaped in after him.

At once I seized the oars Seg had readied and fell to. I rowed with a long swing and now all those horrific days of labor when I was an oar slave aboard the swifters of Magdag paid handsome dividends. The boat clove the water. Spray danced inboard. I bent and pulled, bent and pulled, and only incidentally was aware of

Seg snatching an assegai from where it had plunged into the transom and, standing and balancing awkwardly, flinging it back into the throat of a sorzart prancing in fury on the beach.

A few more assegais plunged in alongside and then they were hissing into the water astern of us.

I steadied the rhythm of my stroke and glared with a most uncharitable wrath upon my Lady Pulvia na Upalion.

She saw that look, and her chin came up; then a deep flush spread over her cheeks and she lowered her eyes. She breathed unsteadily.

"The next time I give an order," I told her, knowing that infernal rasp was back in my voice, "you will obey instantly, do you understand?"

She made no reply.

"Do you understand, Lady Pulvia?" I repeated.

Caphlander started to burble something about being respectful to the mistress, but Seg shut him up. At last she raised her eyes. She had evidently made up her mind to be cutting, authoritative, contemptuous. But she saw my face and her resolution and no doubt her set speech faltered. She opened her mouth.

"Obey — understand," I said, not ceasing from rowing.

"Yes."

"Very well."

I rowed then in a simple long rhythm that sent the little boat out across the suns-lit waters of the Eye of the World.

Four

Rashoons command our course

I took no pleasure — on the contrary I experience no little shame — in thus browbeating a woman rightfully concerned over her child and attempting to uphold her own dignity and not give way to the fears that must have been clamoring to turn her into a sobbing ball of defenseless weakness. But there can be, as I know to my cost, only one captain aboard ship.

And — she was a slave-holder, and a representative of that class of authority most distasteful to me after my experiences in far-off Zenicce, and more lately in Magdag.

We sailed the muldavy with her dipping lug rig safely to the town, the port and arsenal and fortress of Happapat, and delivered the Lady Pulvia na Upalion into the hands of relations who cooed over her and the child and whisked her off to their palace.

When their guards — fair-haired Proconians clad in the iron ring mail of warriors all around the coasts of the inner sea, and armed with long swords that were not cut down — marched Seg and me off to the local barracoon, I felt no surprise whatsoever.

274

This kind of attitude on the part of slave-holders seemed inseparable from their nature, as abhorrent to Seg as to myself.

We wasted no time in breaking out, whooping, cracking a few skulls in the process, and with a couple of wineskins and a vosk thigh tastefully cooked and browned, we helter-skeltered off to the harbor. The fishing muldavy we had stolen in order to rescue the Lady Pulvia and her child and Caphlander lay still tied up where we had left her. In her, I knew, there was a full breaker of water. We tossed our meager belongings in and cut the painter — a gesture of defiance, that — and rowed out. We had the lugsail up and were foaming off into the suns-set long before the guards had pulled their scattered wits about them.

"And so, Dray Prescot," said Seg Segutorio, "what now?"

I stared with a glad affection at this volatile man with the lean tanned face and those shrewd yet reckless eyes. He was a good sword-companion, and for a moment I remembered with a choked nostalgia all those other good companions I had known. I am essentially a lonely man, a loner, one who stands or falls on his own merits and I take ill to being beholden to anyone. This is a fault in me. I thought of Nath and Zolta, my two oar comrades, those two rascals who could not keep away from wine and women. And I remembered how Nath would lean back and quaff a full tankard, and wipe his forearm across his shining lips, and belch, and say: "Mother Zinzu the Blessed! I needed that!" and how Zolta would already have the prettiest girl in the inn perched laughing on his knee.

Sitting resting on the oars and looking at Seg Segutorio with an awakening awareness — I cannot dwell on that, as you will come to understand — I remembered Zorg of Felteraz, my other oar brother, and I thought of Prince Varden Wanek, and of Gloag, and of Hap Loder — and — and remember I was still young at the time as age is measured on Kregen — I wondered how it was that Seg Segutorio could sit on the opposite thwart and look back at me so cheerfully and say so matter-of-factly: "Well, Dray Prescot, and what now?"

These memories of my comrades affected me, and I admit to a tired, dejected, defeated feeling creeping over me then. You would be forgiven if, from all I have so far said, you jump to the conclusion that Kregen is essentially a man's world. Despite the Princess Natema Cydones, and the Princess Susheeng, and other highborn ladies of enormous power, including among their number the Lady Pulvia na Upalion whom we had just rescued and delivered safely to her kinfolk, you might well think that Kregen is dominated by the male principle where brawn and muscle and fighting ability count for everything.

You would, of course, be wrong.

Through this sudden gloom on my part for my old comrades I never for a single instant forgot my twin destiny on Kregen beneath the suns of Scorpio.

Whatever plans the Star Lords had mapped out for me as a troubleshooter, I held to my own purposes. First, I would find my beloved Delia of the Blue Mountains. And, when that had been accomplished, I would travel this world of Kregen to find my way back to Aphrasöe, the City of the Savanti, the Swinging City, for there I believed paradise awaited me. In all these simple and primitive emotions and ambitions I could still find joy that I did not seek vengeance.

We sailed out into the waters of the inner sea, and Seg appeared perfectly satisfied to allow me the conn and to run the muldavy. As he said, with a laugh: "We Erthyr are a mountain people. The sea is not a second home to us."

The night breathed gently about us. The sea ran with a calmness that cradled the little boat. The stars glittered above our heads. The wind blew a mere zephyr.

I looked at the stars. I knew them well. I had studied them night after night from the deck of my swifter as we sailed in unexpected nocturnal raids against the overlords of Magdag, or any of the green cities of the northern shore. I had often shocked my crew by this nighttime sailing; their ideas were those of daytime sailing only and a safe beach at night.

I steered to the west.

It was necessary that I return to Magdag as soon as possible. From thence, before the rebellion, I had sent the Vallian Vomanus back to his home island with a message for Delia. He would return — that I knew with fair certainty — and if he landed at Magdag now, his life would be snuffed out in an instant as a friend of the arch-criminal Pur Dray of Strombor, Krozair, arch-fiend and deadly foe to Magdag.

We steadied on our course west and the wind gusted up suddenly and heeled the muldavy so that water creamed in over the lee gunwale until I let her pay off a trifle. I frowned. The wind veered and strengthened. Now the stars were being blotted out in great clumps at a time as clouds gathered. A brilliant zigzag of fire split the heavens. The thunder, when it reached us, rolled and reverberated around our ears. Rain started to slice into the sea in an abrupt and deafening uproar. In moments we were soaked, our hair tangled about our ears. Seg started to bale. The wind blew directly from the west.

I knew.

This storm not only confirmed my fears that the Star Lords would not allow me to return to Magdag, it also strengthened my suspicion that after my summary ejection from the fight as my slave phalanx in their old yellow-painted vosk-helmets raged on to tear the mailed overlords of Magdag to pieces the battle had swung against us. Perhaps I had overstepped my authority when I had really and truly organized the slaves and workers of the warrens so that they could actually win the fight against the overlords? Perhaps the Star Lords did not want the overlords of Magdag crushed and banished? It could be their plans called for whatever I had done to slumber a while, to gather subterranean strength, to smolder until at some time in the Star Lords' plans for Kregen that spirit I had kindled with the help of the Prophet could burst out in renewed fury. I did not know.

What I did know was that I could not reach Magdag.

Very well, then. Gradually a kind of structure of devices for coping with the Star Lords — if this was truly their work and not the mortal but nonetheless superhuman work of the Savanti — was being wrought out in my mind. I had successfully appealed and been granted reprieve the last time, in that I had been permitted to stay on Kregen, in a dissimilar fashion to the way in which I had been reprieved at Akhram. The idea began to grow that provided I did not actively contest the dictates of the Star Lords — The Everoinye — I might go about my own business on Kregen beneath Antares.

Yes — very well, then. I put the steering oar up and we surged away on the starboard tack. I would go to Pattelonia. Vomanus would be there if I was lucky, and I could stop him from going on to Magdag. Then — then we would take over the Hostile Territories to Port Tavetus from whence we could sail direct for Vallia.

And then — Delia!

Immediately our bows swung to the eastward with the necessary touch of southerly in the heading for Pattelonia, the wind eased off and the rain ceased. Amid a last grumbling of thunder I heard the harsh croaking shriek as of a giant bird. I looked up. In the darkness I could not see the Gdoinye — but I knew without shadow of a doubt that the gorgeous scarlet and golden raptor of the Star Lords had swung over us in its wide hunting circles.

"In the name of the veiled Froyvil himself!" said Seg. He looked about. "What was that?"

"A seabird," I said, "caught in the gale. It seems, friend Seg, we must sail to Pattelonia — rather the chief city on the eastern coast of Proconia than any other, yes? — and we will reach it safely, never fear. You asked me what now — this is your answer. What do you say?"

"Pattelonia." Seg spat the name. "That may be the chief city, but the fighting-men disgust me."

"Oh?"

He swaggered up a wineskin and stoppered his mouth to the spout very expertly, as the boat surged along, considering he considered himself no sailor. When he had gulped and wiped his mouth and said, "By Blessed Mother Zinzu, that fires up the cockles of my heart!" — and what a pang of Nath there was in that for me! — he went on to say: "I hired out as mercenary to Pattelonia in one of their infernal wars, you know?"

I nodded. "I know."

His story was commonplace, ugly, and painful. Men of Loh could usually find employment as mercenaries without trouble, for their prowess as archers was renowned throughout the known lands of Kregen. Seg had entered the inner sea by the western end, through the Grand Canal past the Dam of Days. I reflected that he had seen that colossal construction; I had not. I forbore to mention that to him; it would arouse too many questions. His fighting career had been of the normal routine and monotonous kind associated with mercenary fighting; when the Pattelonians had been defeated by a combined force of a number of the Proconian cities assisted by Magdag, he had been captured and sold as slave.

"So Pattelonia fell," I said.

"Mayhap. I did hear that Sanurkazz was coming to our assistance, but I tripped into that damned thorn-hole and was scooped up by a diabolical overlord before it did me any good."

I made suitable sympathetic noises.

"There are friends in Pattelonia, Seg, although I have never been there. We will be returning to Vallia." This was a lie. I could never return to Vallia for I had never been there in the first place; but as I had told Kov Tharu of Vindelka, I thought of Vallia for all its frightening reputation as home simply because my Delia lived there.

"Vallia?" Seg drank more wine, his shape a dark expressive blot beneath the starlight. "I took passage aboard a ship of Pandahem. The Vallian was too dear. But I know Vallia — they maintain a great fortress depot on the northernmost tip of Erthyrdrin. Many times have my people gone down against them."

"You don't like Vallians?"

He laughed. "That was in the past. Since Walfarg broke apart like a rotten samphron the Vallians have been markedly more friendly toward us, and now we tolerate their fortress depot and it has grown into a sizable city, and we do business with them, for they are essentially a nation of traders."

Walfarg was a name I had heard here and there, a mighty empire of the past which had broken apart. It had originated in Walfarg itself, a country of Loh, and some of the stories of Loh hung about its faded glories. There are many countries in the continents and islands of Kregen; only Vallia, as far as I know, boasts that it is a single land mass under one government.

And that boast was to cost it dear, as you shall hear.

"So you are for Pattelonia, then?"

"A pity, Dray Prescot, your friends could not await you at a point nearer the Dam of Days. From Pattelonia we have — oh, I am not sure of the distance, five hundred dwaburs, is it? — to cover before we even reach the outer ocean. Then we must sail south past skeleton coasts to Donengil and thus swing around up the Zim-Stream and so to the Cyphren Sea — and there, before us, lies Erthyrdrin!"

For the moment I was content to let Seg believe this.

He said, with a sharpness to his voice, "You are not a Vallian?"

Vallians, I knew from the example of the glorious hair of my Delia, were often brown-haired, as I am. I had successfully passed as Kov Drak in Magdag, acting the part of a Vallian duke. But I did not wish to lie unnecessarily to Seg Segutorio.

"I am Dray Prescot of Strombor," I said.

"So you have told me. But — Strombor. Where might that be?"

Of course — what was now the enclave of Strombor would have been Esztercari for all Seg's life. A fierce joy welled up in me as I thought of my Clansmen riding across the Great Plains of Segesthes, of the way with good friends' help we had taken what was to become my enclave fortress of Strombor within the city of Zenicce.

"Strombor, Seg, is in Zenicce—"

"Ah! A Segesthan — well, even that I wonder about, for I call you a stranger of strangers, and I know what I know."

"What do you know, Seg?"

But he would not answer. That fey quality associated with mountain folk must have alerted his senses; but I was doubtful that he could guess I came from a planet distant from Kregen by four hundred light-years.

He swung away from that as the muldavy creamed through the night sea and the stars once more reappeared above. The twin second moons of Kregen, the two that revolve one about the other as they orbit the planet, sailed above the horizon and in their wash of pinkish light, strengthened by the presence of two more of Kregen's seven moons, I saw Seg watching me with an enclosed and contained look on his lean face. He brushed a hand through his black hair.

"Very well, Dray Prescot, of Strombor, I will go with you to Pattelonia." He chuckled. "For all that the army in which I served lost the fight, the Proconians still owe me my fair hire, and they shall pay me."

"Good, Seg," was all I considered necessary to say.

"And I refuse by all the shattered targes in Mount Hlabro to return to slavery."

We slept on and off during the night and when the twin suns rose to burn away a few patches of mist, there, broad on our larboard beam, lay one of the many islands that dot the inner sea. I steered to pass it with plenty of sea room, for islands are notorious as the lair of pirates and corsairs — I had used them enough times myself — when Seg noticed what I had seen and mentally filed as part of the habitual stock-taking of a sea officer the moment he reaches the deck.

He pointed aft where a low black and purple cloud like a massive bruise against the gleaming sky whirled onward.

"A rashoon!"

At the moment I was more concerned with the identity of the swifter shooting out from the lee of the island. She was large, that I could tell — and then as flags broke from her mast and flagpoles I saw their color. My lips compressed.

Every flag was green!

"A Magdag swifter," I said to Seg. "Hold on — we are going into some fancy evolutions now—"

And then the rashoon enveloped us and we fought the lug down until I could control the muldavy in the screeching wind. The seas piled and knotted about us. We went sweeping on, and the swifter was left floundering. Even then I noted the seamanlike way in which her skipper brought her around and scuttled back with all his double-banks of oars stamping the sea in neat parallel lines, back into the shelter of the island. We were sent weltering past and out to sea. When the rashoon had blown itself out and we could get back to an even keel and rehoist the lugsail and take stock, I found Seg with an expression on his face which, allied to the green tinge around his jaws, gave me an odd feeling of compassion and unholy glee.

I offered him a thick juicy slice from the vosk thigh.

He refused.

It pains me now, in recollection, to think how badly I treated Seg Segutorio then as we hauled up for Pattelonia across the Eye of the World.

We called in at various islands on the way to water and to acquire fresh provisions, mostly fruit and vegetables, for we avoided the habitations of men and half-men. Seg told me much of his home in Erthyrdrin — which I shall relate when it becomes necessary — but one fact he told me made me think on.

"Arrow heads?" he said one day as we burbled across the sea with the limpid sky above. "You won't find an Erthyr archer using steel in an arrow head. By Froyvil, Dray! Steel is hard to come by in my country."

"So what do you use, bronze?"

He laughed. "Not a chance. It's a pretty metal, is bronze, and I have an affection for it. But we use flint, Dray, good honest Erthyrin flint. Why, we kids could flint-knap as pretty a point as you could wish to see when we were three years old! And, mark you, flint will pierce solid lenk better than almost anything. Perhaps your steel is better, but not bronze, certainly not copper, or bone or horn, or even iron."

I stored that away in my mind, thinking of the sleeting rain of arrows my Clansmen could put down. But then, the city of Zenicce controlled what was in effect a vast metallurgical industry, with immense iron deposits nearby with woodlands to furnish charcoal. The same was true of both Magdag and Sanurkazz here on the inner sea.

In talking into this little cassette tape recorder in these heartrending surroundings of famine and despair I have sometimes found it difficult to give a coherent account of Kregen. The planet is real, it is a living, breathing, fully-functioning world of real living people, both men and women and beast-men and beast-women besides all the monsters you could desire. Things happen there as they do on Earth, because necessity impels men to invent and to go on developing these inventions. There could be no long crisp loaves of Kregan bread without cornfields opening to the twin suns, with back-breaking labor to plow and plant and hoe and harvest, with mills to grind and bakers to bake. No man who values life can take anything that life offers for granted — even the air he breathes must be tended and cared for, otherwise the pollution that so worries you here on Earth will poison the uncaring hosts.

So Seg and I talked as we sailed toward Pattelonia, the chief city of Proconia, and the city to which I had been posted as a swifter captain of the forces of Sanurkazz before I had taken off in that abortive journey to Vallia that had terminated back in Magdag, hereditary foe of Sanurkazz. Whoever ruled now in Pattelonia ruled by right of sword, whether red or green or Proconian. Navigation was simple; the suns and the stars kept me on course over seas I have never traversed before, and soon I calculated we must be approaching waters in which more traffic must be expected.

By this time Seg could take a trick at the steering oar and he it was who was conning the muldavy when another of those inconsiderate rashoons whirled down upon us in a whining torrent of wind and a lumping roaring sea.

At once I leaped to the dipping lug and rattled the yard down, leaving a mere peak to give us steerage way. White water began to sluice inboard and I took up the baler and started in on flinging it back from whence it had come. We steadied up and I could look back at Seg Segutorio. He clung onto the steering oar with a most ferocious expression on his face. He fought the waves with the same elemental force as he would expend in hunting among his beloved mountains of Erthyrdrin. He fought a new element with a courage and a high heart that warmed me.

Smiling and laughing do not come easily to me, except in some ludicrous or dangerous situations, as you know; but now I looked on Seg Segutorio and my lips widened in a mocking smile, an ironic grimace to which he responded with a savage wrench on the steering oar and a rolling string of blasphemies that burst about my head as the rashoon was bursting.

We rolled and rocked and I baled, and Seg hung onto his oar and kept our head up and steered us through. Again I look back in sorrow at the way I treated poor Seg Segutorio. He was a man to delight the heart.

When we came through it, Seg heaved in a tremendous breath, blew it out, glared at me, and then ignored me altogether. I did not laugh; now I am sorry I did not, for he expected it.

Following the wild moments of the tempest in the inner sea — the rashoons varied as to name and nature — we glided on over a sea that fell calm with only a long heaving swell.

The broad ship lay low in the water, wrecked by the rashoon, her masts gone by the board and her people running about her decks in panic. Then we saw the cause of that alarm.

Circling in toward the broad ship — a merchantman Seg told me by her devices as being from Pattelonia — the long narrow wicked shape of a swifter cleft the water in absolute and arrogant knowledge of her own power. As we watched, the swifter broke her colors. All her flags were green.

A swifter from Magdag! Attacking a broad ship from Pattelonia. From that I deduced that Sanurkazz had succeeded in retaking the city, and I felt a bound of delight.

Now if I have not made it clear that Seg Segutorio was reckless to the extreme, despite that streak of practicality, then I have not drawn the man aright. He stared at the green-bedecked swifter and his nostrils tightened up. He turned the steering oar so that our head bore on the two vessels.

"What, Seg, and you're going to attack a Magdaggian swifter on your own?"

He looked at me as if he had not heard.

"She's a big one, Seg. A hundred-and-fiftyswifter. I'd judge, by her lines, she's a seven-six-six."

The faint zephyr of wind bore us on.

"We don't even have a knife, let alone a sword, Seg."

Our prow rustled through the water.

Oh, how I regret baiting Seg Segutorio!

Perhaps, just perhaps, then, when I was young, I had not forgotten that forkful of dungy straw smacking me full in the face.

"They're from Magdag," Seg said. "They made me slave."

We bore on over the sea and now the sound of shrieks and screams reached us, the ugly sound of metal on metal. I was a Krozair of Zy, dedicated to combating the false green Grodno — no other course occurred to me.

Five

The fight aboard the swifter

"It's the oldest, hoariest trick there is, Seg," I said as we slid through the calm water toward the Pattelonian broad ship and the Magdag swifter. "But it's all we have to work with. It's worked in the past and no doubt it will work again, in the future. All we're concerned with now is that it works for us this time."

"How many men, Dray?" was all Seg Segutorio said.

"The swifter's a seven-six-six, one hundred and fifty. That means she has three banks of oars each side, twenty-five oars a bank. The upper deck oars are crewed by seven men each, the two lower banks by six men to an oar. That's about a thousand men or more, given spare oarsmen carried below."

"And all slave?"

"All slave."

"You seem to know about these things, Dray."

"I know."

"And the warriors?"

"That varies. Depends on the purpose for which the swifter has been put into commission. I'd guess, again, that there won't be less than a couple of hundred. If they're on a big one, there will be a lot more." I thought of my days as a slave aboard swifters from Magdag. "They crowd the men, Seg. They keep them chained to the oars and they feed them water and onions and slop and cheese and they douse them out with seawater twice a day and they fling them overboard when they're exhausted and all the strength has gone from them and they're lashed to death."

"We're approaching nicely," said Segutorio. He laughed. "All I regret is — I do not have my own longbow with me, my bow I made myself from the sacred Yerthyr tree that grew up on Kak Kakutorio's land. He near caught me, the day I cut my stave. I was twelve, then. I built that bow for use when I'd gained my full stature — and when I did she balanced out just right. Kak's tree was almost black, so dark and secret green it was. He near caught me—"

Seg checked himself. I saw the way his shoulders hunched. That streak of practical common sense had thrust hard at his reckless spirit and he could apprehend clearly just what we were getting into. He was driven by hatred for the green deity worshipers and by a habitual recklessness. I was impelled by my vows, my own dark memories — and because I was a Krozair of Zy.

Being privileged to be a member of the Order of Krozairs of Zy means a very great deal to me. That they are a small group of dedicated men tucked away in an inland sea on a planet four hundred light-years away, bound up with their fanatical adherence to a mythical red deity and in absolute opposition to an equally mythical green deity, has no bearing on their inner strengths, their gallantry,

282

their selflessness, their mysticism — which contains profundities beyond profundities — their remarkable disciplines of the sword, their essential courageous integrity. These are qualities found only in a debased coinage on the Earth you inhabit today, it sometimes seems.

Seg Segutorio hated slavery and slave-holders — as did I. Yet only when I had been the captain of a Sanurkazzian swifter and a Krozair had I, too, employed slaves. They had rowed for me in conditions little better than those of my own misery when I had pulled for Magdag. This surely must mark the power of the Order of Krozairs of Zy over me. When I had attempted to free my slaves and had adopted free oarsmen I and my crew had been so close to a horrific and murderous end as to cause nightmares.[viii]

So, thus thinking, I waited as the muldavy closed the final gap between us and the swifter's stern. Everyone aboard had their attention occupied by the dying moments of the struggle to take possession of the broad ship. I had thought she was sinking; no doubt the swifter captain considered he could plunder her and take her people prisoners before she sank. Now the high upflung curve of the stern rose from the water before us.

The swell slopped us up and down. I stood up in the bows. The swifter was large and her apostis, the rectangular rowing frame, extended well out from the smooth curves of her hull. Her oarsmen, arranged *alla scaloccio*, still held to their looms as the blades were all, every one, in perfect alignment. Every now and again the drum-deldar would give a signal double-beat of his bass and tenor drums and precisely together all the oars of either the larboard or starboard banks would dip and give a short jabbing thrust to keep the swifter lined up against the broad ship, beak extended and jutting over her beam.

I looked up the arrogantly upflung stern and put aside instinctive thoughts of equally arrogantly upflung tails of scorpions.

Among the elaborate scrollwork and what we would call gingerbread I found easy handholds. As my bare feet gripped and heaved me up so Seg followed. We were both unarmed. I wore simply the same strip of brown cloth taken from the sorzart, and Seg wore his gray slave breechclout. Carefully, now, I put a hand on the deck below the rail. One of the steering oars extended past my back. I lifted myself gently. I looked.

The steering-deldar lay on his oar, ready with curling movements to keep the head of the swifter against the broadship in time with his companion on the other side and the occasional thrusts from the oars. The drum-deldar would be sitting with his drumsticks poised, and the oar-master would be sitting in his little tabernacle below the break of the quarterdeck. An officer — very resplendent in green silk and gold lace — strode about looking pleased with himself. I cursed his black Magdaggian heart.

As carefully I lowered myself.

Seg was looking at me. His face was wrinkled up, his whole expression one of absolute distaste.

"They stink," he said.

"Yes."

Swifters are built on lines laid down by naval architects of varying talents. I recognized the lines of this example and I knew my way about her as slave or captain. We made an entry into the aft lower cabin — what would on an Earthly seventy-four be called the gun room — and found the space deserted of life. Beyond the doors opening onto the lower or thalamite bank of oars lay the manpower I needed. This galley was of the cataphract variety so that her upper thranite banks of rowers were protected by a fenced bulwark. At the time I was still undecided, as I was undecided between the long keel and the short keel theories, whether the open un-bulwarked style, the aphract with its free passage of air, was better than the cataphract which did at least offer some protection from arrows. However that might be, that extra protection afforded us an extra level of concealment as we went about our work.

First out of the double-folding doors I saw the nearest whip-deldar and before he could so much as turn I held him in a grip from which he slumped lifeless to the gangway.

The slaves stared up with lackluster eyes. Their heads were bushy mops, clear indication that the swifter had been at sea for some time, for the heads of oar slaves when they clear the mole at Magdag are shaved as smooth as a shot trimmed for a twenty-four pounder bowchaser.

Seg started for the other whip-deldar at a dead run.

Down here in the odors and the confinement the whip-deldars took turns at duty, or received thalamite duty as a punishment.

The fellow I had dropped carried a knife. It took me only a few moments to pick the lock of the great chain to which all the other chains were attached.

The nearest slave looked at me in a puzzled fashion. His back carried the marks of his trade. The one next to him also looked up, his jaw slack and mumbling over broken, decaying teeth behind thick slobbering lips. I experienced a moment of despair.

These slaves were completely broken. Would they rise, as they *must* rise, if we were to succeed?

There would be no question here of an immediate flinging off of the great chain, a gathering of their own chains into vengeful fists, and an immediate abandonment of the habits of slavery. They must see what could be done. But — the lower deck held the recalcitrants as a rule, the troublemakers, the extra-tough. Had I disastrously miscalculated?

Then from that twin channel of upturned faces, bearded, filthy, a man clambered up dragging his chains. He stared at me.

"Pur Dray!"

I did not recognize him. But he knew me. I sensed the change, then. I heard the word "Krozair!" and I hurriedly raised my hands.

"Be silent! Free yourselves now the great chain is loosed. Keep the oars at the level — you know. We will free our comrades above — and then — *silence!*"

Of course, they could not keep silent Once the traumatic bludgeon of release had shocked them, once they suddenly realized that they need not be slaves again, there was no holding them.

Whip-marked naked bodies began to spill out into the central gangway with its slits of sky above and the long rows of naked legs of the oarsmen of the upper two banks. A whip-deldar looked over his narrow split-deck and yelled. I hurled the knife as I had hurled the woman's weapon of my Clansmen, the terchick, and he toppled over spouting blood from his mouth. I put my foot on his body and drew the knife from his throat. I rather cared for that economical use of a weapon.

The slaves were clambering up the supporting timbers of the upper banks, hauling themselves up over the inboard ends of the oar looms where they rested in the level position within the patterned rowing-frames. They were screeching and yelling and waving their chains. I knew few of them would think to release their comrades; their minds were now shocked into one desire only — to kill the overlords of Magdag. Mind you — that was a desire I then considered eminently worthy — Zair forgive me.

Like some grundal of the rocks I went up hand over hand, the bloody knife between my teeth. That, I admit, is one time when I grin.

The twisted and pulped body of a whip-deldar crunched underfoot as I leaped for the locks of the zygites' great chain. The knife point probed, there was a click clearly audible above the uproar, and then the zygites, prepared by the astonishing appearance of their fellows from below, were roaring and raging with chains in their fists.

A few arrows fleeted down and a slave shrieked and toppled back with a shaft through him. The crew had reacted swiftly.

I had not expected otherwise.

Only the overwhelming manpower of the slaves could win the swifter for us.

It is difficult to conceive of the uproar and violence of those moments. In an exceedingly long and narrow space, a mere slot walled in by timbers and chains, naked hairy men howled and struggled to reach the light. Up we went and with us went Seg Segutorio, brandishing a whip with which he took the ankles from under a whip-deldar and so brought him screeching down into the merciless talons of the slaves.

On the upper deck with its central gangway and gratings to either side over the lower banks the slaves were raging like a sea breaking against cliffs. The task of reaching the locks of the thranites' great chain would be difficult. Already soldiers of Magdag in their iron-linked hauberks were running back from the bows. Arrows were flickering through the air. I took off in a long run toward the oar-master and his tabernacle. The drum-deldar let out a single long scream and went scuttling aft. Up there the officer I had seen drew his long sword.

I wanted that sword.

Still — the locks must come first. Then Seg was with me. His whip flicked the oar-master into a gibbering panic. I bent to the first lock and an arrow feathered into the deck at my side. The officer ran toward us, leaned over, shouting. His face, browned by wind and sun, looked in the last stages of apoplectic fury.

I clicked the lock, stood up, let fly the knife.

The officer gurgled, slumped, toppled down.

I caught the long sword as it spun through the air, taking its bone grip —
which I dislike — leanly into my fist. It would have been a fine catch at first slip.

"Forward!" shouted Seg. "The rasts are waiting for us!"

Indeed, the battle to take the broad ship was over. Now the swifters crew and
soldiers were turning about to face the frenzied slaves. We had begun with the
lowest bank so as to avoid detection. Now that all the slaves were free nothing
stopped us from hurling ourselves into the fight.

"Grab a sword first, Seg!" I yelled.

"Had I my bow—" he yelled back.

I sprinted forward along the gangway, hurdling various bodies, until I could
thrust through the back of the press. Hundreds of slaves were crowding forward,
waving their chains, humming them about their heads in deadly arcs. But many
were going down as the swifter archers shot with flat trajectories, rapidly and
professionally.

The struggle for me to reach the front ranks was severe; but in a few moments
I pushed aside the body of a slave who, swinging his chains, had been thrust
through the belly, by a long sword. I stepped out, the long sword held in the fighting grip of the Krozairs of Zy.

Blades crossed. An arrow brushed through my hair. I kept on the move. The
long sword was a fine weapon despite its bone grip and I felt it slog crushingly
into the rib cage of the first Magdaggian, biting through the mesh. He fell away.
There was another, whose face above the ventail I smashed in. More arrows were
fleeting past — then I realized some were going the other way. An overlord before me abruptly threw his hands in the air, dropping his sword. An arrow stood
out from his right eye.

Seg Segutorio had found himself a weapon he knew how to use and was in action.

Now the sheer mass of slaves told. Perhaps there were as many as three hundred men of Magdag aboard: overlords, overlords of the second class, soldiers,
and crew. Of them all the captain of the swifter seemed alone to be alive as I
reached the entrance ramp onto the lower beak. The scene was fantastic. The
whole upperworks of the swifter were crowded with the naked bodies of slaves,
all howling and screeching like — no, not like, they were — demented souls.

I knew what emotions they were experiencing.

The long extended beak of the swifter hung over the water-slopping deck of
the merchantman. She had had two masts, their stumps now jagged tangles
among the raffle of wreckage, so she was a fair-sized craft. Her forecastle — it
was that, proper, and not a fo'c'sle — had been badly battered by the swifter's varters. These were mounted somewhat higher in the bows of the galley than I
considered proper, and had been rigged to hurl stones, as was fit in the circumstances. The merchantman's sterncastle, an imposing edifice of two decks, was
cluttered by the raffle fallen from the mainmast. Bodies lay everywhere.

The swifter captain glared up at me. He was a big man, his mail bulging, his
long sword a weapon of exceptional size. Around him among the circle of slain
slaves lay sprawled other men in mail and half-mail, mercenary marines carried
by the merchantman.

"Hail!" he called up.

He waved his sword in a gesture that plainly said: "Come down here where I can chop you."

He knew that against all those enraged slaves he had no chance of survival.

He was of Magdag — yet he was a brave man. Even then, when I was young and bore a hatred for the green burning in my breast, I recognized a man's courage.

I leaped down to him.

With only a breechclout to cover my nakedness I fought at a disadvantage against his mail. But also, against his knowledge that he was doomed and his desperate determination to make a fight of it and die well, I could put my skill and my own determination, the red against the green.

Our blades crossed once, and I felt the strength in his arm.

The broad ship lurched beneath our feet as water gushed in.

"You will die, slave, and join your fellows here!"

I did not answer. Again the blades crossed and I swung on the disengage, but be was quick even on that cumbered deck and avoided my blow. He bore down on me, anxious to kill me and take as many as he could with him to the ice floes of Sicce.

A slave shouted from the deck, high and exultant.

"Jikai! Chop him, Pur Dray, my Lord of Strombor, Krozair!"

The swifter captain's blade faltered. He drew back. On his face grew such a look of fury and despair as sickened me to see.

"You—" he choked. "You are the Lord of Strombor — Krozair!"

Without bothering to reply — for I felt the broad ship's sluggish wallowing movements and knew she would go down any instant — I leaped forward. And now our blades clanged and rang with that ferocious screech of steel blade on steel blade. He was good and he was strong but I was in a hurry now and in a quick passage of murderous blows he fell.

Someone shouted: "The ship's going!"

And amid the tumultuous shouts of the freed slaves as they saw the hated Magdag overlord dead at their feet I leaped nimbly up onto the swifter's beak. A florid but sea-bitten man rushed forward, his slashed blue finery proclaiming him the captain of the merchantman.

Seg was there and with the help of slaves who seemed to carry some authority among their fellows a space was cleared. The merchant skipper grasped my left hand, babbling his thanks. His ship had gone, but his life was safe. Overside now the broad ship wallowed deeper, and thrashing around her and waiting for their grisly harvest the chanks with their twin stiff upright fins, the sharks of the inner sea, patrolled hungrily.

"May Ta'temsk shine upon you, my Lord of Strombor!" He let my hand go as I began to strip away the bloodied brown rag from my loins. "We fought as well as we could, but the rashoon dismasted us. My crew fought like demons, as you can see — even my passengers fought — ah, how they fought—"

"Passengers?" I had found a length of red cloth wound about the body of a dead man — evidently one of the passengers the merchant skipper was speaking of — and I wrapped it around my waist and drew the end up between my legs and tucked it in. The brave scarlet color cheered me. "Yes — a strange lot. The men fought like men possessed. Look, Pur Dray — there is one now, dying, and yet still he thinks he fights."

Hauled out of the way beneath a varter a man lay dying. What the skipper said was true, for he kept opening his arms wide and closing them again in the rapier and main-gauche drill known as the "flower" although his right hand was empty. He wore long black boots and a snug-waisted brown coat which flared wide over his hips and up to his shoulders. He wore no hat, but I could guess what sort of hat he would own. In his left hand he carried a bejeweled main-gauche with which he kept up his laborious flow of passages at arms.

I knelt by his side.

"You were with Vomanus?" I said. I spoke as gently as I might, but my words cracked harsh and impatiently for all that.

"Vallians," said the merchant skipper. "A strange lot."

"Sterncastle," gasped the dying man. Blood dribbled from his mouth. I looked up at the broadship's captain.

"Alas, my Lord of Strombor. The men of Vallia were insistent that every care should be taken of the passengers and so on my orders they were shut up in the Sterncastle, for safekeeping. But the fall of the mainmast, and the ferocity of the attack — we could not get them out. I fear they are doomed." I was puzzled. Granted that Vomanus had shipped aboard this vessel now sinking into a chank-infested sea, I couldn't understand my not seeing him. He would never be shut up in a safe place when there was a fight brewing. The Vallian was young, handsome, with a long brown moustache and neatly trimmed beard. He tried to speak, spat blood, tried again, managed to blurt out: "They must be saved!"

"There is no saving them now," said the captain, with a grim nod at the decks of his ship about to submerge beneath the water and the twin fins of the chanks circling nearer. "My old ship is taking them to their grave, may Ta'temsk smile on them."

The dying Vallian opened his eyes and there was reason in them. He had stopped his ghastly phantom swordplay. I took the dagger from him, gently, respectfully. Blood gushed from his mouth as he burst into an impassioned and mortal shout.

"You must save her! She is trapped, drowning, doomed — you must! The Princess Majestrix of Vallia! Princess—"

The blood choked him. I felt — I thought — I —

Delia! My Delia! *Delia!*

Six

Delia of Delphond and I swim together

I have no memory until I stood before the doors to the broad ship's aftercastle with its hideous tangle of wreckage blocking them off, tearing at them with my bare hands, the dagger naked in my clenched teeth.

It was all a long time ago and four hundred light-years distant, a drama played out on a distant sea beneath the lurid fires of the twin suns of Antares; and yet — and yet!

Water slopped about my thighs, pouring in an ever-thickening flood over the gunwales. I heaved timber aside, used the keen dagger edge to slash through water-soaked ropes. I reached the door and now I became aware of the yells and shouts from the swifter.

"It is too late!" "Come back!" "You will be drowned!" and — "My Lord — the chanks!"

I ignored the jabbering.

A stubborn balk impeded me and I put my shoulders to it — those shoulders that had been the despair of my ever-sewing mother — and heaved up until the blood seemed to compress all my brains and threatened to burst from my eyes and nostrils. My muscles rippled and bunched and I heaved — how I heaved!

With an abrupt screech the balk slid aside and I lurched forward into the doors. I used that lurch — there was no time to draw back — and smashed solidly into them. I heard metal snap. Water roiled around my waist now and I felt the ship wallowing and lurching like a drunk staggering from The Fleeced Ponsho in Sanurkazz.

I kicked the doors in and a frenzied woman was in my arms, all dark hair about my face like damp laundry, and softness against my naked chest, and a screaming mouth and fiercely clawing fingers.

A voice yelled in my ear.

"Pass her back!"

"Here, Seg."

I knew it was him, and there was no time for my gratitude. He was no seaman, he could probably swim with a dog-crawl; he was risking more than I here, on the deck of this sinking ship.

I plunged into the cabin.

The whole ship shuddered and the ominous roar of thousands of gallons of water suddenly victorious pouring into her told me she was gone. Water smashed me forward and I swirled around in the sudden green gloom.

With the dagger between my teeth again I held my breath.

And then—

Delia! My Delia of the Blue Mountains, my Delia of Delphond was once more in my arms and I held her dear form to me in that water-choked cabin of a sinking ship. I felt her waist as lissome and as lithe as I remembered, and I swung around and struck out for the door. Timber and cordage and canvas floated like octopuses with groping tendrils, seeking to ensnare us and drag us back. But we pushed through the door and the gloom decreased. Light struck down from above. I kicked with a savage exultant fierceness and we rose upward.

I could see the whole extent of the deck of the broad ship with only a few bubbles bursting from her shattered hatches and all the miserable aftermath of the battle. And, among those twisted shapes of corpses, hunting like ghouls, the long sinuous shapes of the chanks nosed in from all sides.

We broke surface.

The swifter's proembolion had nudged off the sinking merchantman. She moved now some distance away. Nearer to us swam the little muldavy in which Seg and I had escaped from Happapat. We had to reach that before the chanks reached us.

I looked down.

Too late…The chank was already here, was nosing up with that characteristic shark-like belly roll to expose all his corpse-white underbelly. I thrust Delia away from me, took the dagger into my right hand.

"Swim for the boat, Delia! *Swim!*"

The breath I drew in scorched my lungs. I dived. The chank saw me coming and half rolled. I went with him. I would not grasp his pseudo-scaled skin for those scales would lacerate my own human flesh like rasps.

As he rolled so I rolled with him and nicked aside so that his gape-jawed attack sliced water. As he went past I thrust the dagger in as hard and as fast as I could. Blood poured out to roil in a thick cloud-like mass in the water. He went on and slowly began to roll, his tail seesawing. A quick look around showed me no more ominous shapes immediately in my vicinity and I kicked hard after Delia.

The water was limpid clear, with the surface, the exotic silver sky, all rippled and chiaroscuro-shot with color.

I caught Delia around the waist and heaved her up into the muldavy.

I had to be sure.

I ducked down and, sure enough, another chank was circling in. He would razor off my legs before I could scramble into the boat. As I went under again I headed straight for him. He moved aside, those immense jaws gaping, then straightened and headed for me, trying to roll sideways at me. Chanks only need to roll over to seize their prey when it is above them on the surface. Otherwise they are quite capable of gulping a man down from any position.

I went with him, then scissored my legs in a frantic explosion of energy, scythed around his thrusting snout, and buried the dagger six times into his belly. Blood streamed out like a wake. He went on, turning slowly, and I glared up against the radiance. The curved wedge-shape of the muldavy's bottom showed like a balloon against that silver sky, water-rippled. I shot up stiff-legged, burst from the water, hooked an arm over the gunwale, and hauled. I could feel the expected snap of gigantic chank jaws and expected to pull a legless torso aboard.

When my feet hit the bottom boards the jolt came as a reassuring bolt. I was light-headed, for I would not have attempted to leave the water had I anticipated the chank could return to the attack before I could clear the surface.

The muldavy bounced.

The chank — or another — had returned and was trying to overset us.

I saw Delia standing up, lithe and lovely in a blue short skirt and tunic, hefting the water breaker up over her head. She tensed and then, *whoosh* — down went the water breaker over the side to bash the chank on the snout. With a flick of his tail he took himself off.

She stood there above me, gazing down, her water-soaked garments shining and clinging, and she smiled — she smiled!

"Dray!"

We were in each other's arms, then, and if the muldavy had rolled over spilling us into the chank-swarming sea I do not believe we would have noticed.

When we returned to a semblance of sanity a hail reached us and I saw the swifter turning and moving gently down on us, twenty or thirty oars clumsily splashing. Seg shouted again.

"You are all right?"

I waved and shouted something.

"Thank the veiled Froyvil for that, then!"

"Thelda!" Delia said suddenly, her sweet face changing expression to one of concerned alarm.

"If that is the buxom hell-cat who near scratched my eyes out back there in the cabin," I said, "friend Seg took her off me. Thank the Black Chunkrah," I added, lapsing into a blasphemy of my Clansmen.

"I am glad," Delia said. "For Thelda means well." And she laughed in that old thrilling spine-tingling way. How incomparable a woman is my Delia of the Blue Mountains!

The muldavy was hoisted aboard the swifter. Thelda rushed to Delia and gathered her in her arms, cooing and sighing and sobbing. Thelda's hair, already drying in the suns-light, was a darker, deeper brown than Delia's without those glorious auburn highlights. She tended to plumpness — I would not go so far as to say fatness — and she bubbled with eagerness. She was all over Delia. Her ripe red lips smiled easily. I saw Seg giving her his undivided attention, and sighed, for I foresaw only problems for him there. In that, as you will hear, I sadly underestimated the whole truth.

Somewhat on the stocky side was Thelda, but she was built magnificently, with thick ankles somewhat detracting from her attempts at languorous beauty when she remembered to forget her eagerness. I cannot be too cruel to Thelda, for Delia clearly suffered her with a good heart.

The first order was obtained. With so many men aboard unchained I had thoughts of mass rape; but the knowledge that I was Pur Dray, the Lord of Strombor, a famed and feared Krozair of Zy, corsair of the Eye of the World, had impressed the ex-slaves. Very willingly they agreed to return to their oar benches, this time as free men, and pull for Sanurkazz. I took hands with many of them, and was not surprised to feel that secret sign of the Krozair from many of them. Also there were men of The Red Brethren of Lizz, and others from the Krozairs of Zamu — famous fighting Orders of Chivalry dedicated to Zair. But none, as I had known even before I was one, as strict, as famous, as notorious where it mattered as the Krozairs of Zy.

One of the ex-slaves who had given me the secret sign, a man of superlative musculature, as must any man possess if he is to survive at the oar, a massive black beard and a head of that curly black Sanurkazzian hair, gripped my hand and said: "You do not recognize me, Pur Dray?"

I studied him closely. Seg was taking care of the girls as I sorted out the swifter. I shook my head, then halted that instinctive negative.

"By Zim-Zair! Pur Mazak! Pur Mazak, Lord of Frentozz!"

We clasped hands again.

"We shared a raid against Goforeng, you and I, Pur Dray. You with your *Zorg* and I with my *Heart of Zair*. You recall?"

"Can I forget! We took — what was it? — twelve broadships and dispatched three large swifters into the bargain! Great days, Pur Mazak."

"Aye, great days."

"Well. They will come again for you." I had made a decision. We must pull for Sanurkazz. Now I had Delia with me again we might spend a little time on the inner sea, for there were things still to be done there.

But as soon as we settled down on our course, south with a heading of west in it, that damnable gale got up, the sea rose, lightnings and thunders raged and roared. I shouted to the helm-deldars — men from the slave benches who had been rudder-deldars before their capture — to ease off and head east. As miraculously as it had arisen, the gale, which was not a rashoon, died away.

"Pattelonia," I said to Delia, and I saw her face light up.

Arrangements were speedily made.

Clearly, the Star Lords wanted me out of the inner sea. Well, that suited me well enough. I felt sincere regret that I would not again see — for how long I knew not — my two oar comrades and rascals, Nath and Zolta, or Pur Zenkiren, or dear Mayfwy — I had wanted muchly for Delia and Mayfwy to meet, for I could not express adequately the thanks I owed Mayfwy, widow of my oar comrade and friend Pur Zorg.

As for Delia, she had loyally agreed to accompany me to Sanurkazz, but there was no denying her joy that we were to go directly to Pattelonia and from thence to Vallia. There was no problem over who would command the swifter we had captured — her name was *Sword of Genodras* — and I clasped hands again with Pur Mazak and entrusted him with the ship.

"She is a fine vessel, even if the apostis is a trifle bulky for my taste," I said. "I would be inclined to pack a few more benches in along the upper deck — but that is of another time." Mazak looked at me with the calm firm gaze of a true brother in Zy, and I knew the prize was in good hands. I gave him instructions that should the king, Zo, allow, *Sword of Genodras* should be bought into the service under the aegis of Felteraz, for I owed Mayfwy much. "At any rate," I said.

"My shares go to the Lady Mayfwy of Felteraz. You will speak with my agent, Shallan, who is as honest a rogue as any agent can ever be. And now, Zair go with you, Pur Mazak."

"Remberee!" The shouts came across the water as the swifter gathered way. Delia, Thelda, Seg, and I watched from the muldavy which had been hoisted over the side and fully provisioned and watered. "Remberee!" and "Remberee!"

From the mass of booty and other materials in the aft cabins I had selected a number of fine Sanurkazzian long swords. Also I had fine silks from Pandahem, and leather of Sanurkazz, cloaks woven from the finest curly ponsho wool from Wloclef and, to prove how villainous a character I am, there was also a strong leather purse bulging with silver and golden oars of Magdag, as well as the varied currency of the southern shore. Seg had also helped himself, and in particular had taken a full score of the small bows. He grumbled about them, their puniness, with which I fully agreed. Nonetheless, I felt safer — if I may admit to such a feeling, for Delia was now in my safekeeping — with the archer from Erthyrdrin aboard.

As we hoisted the dipping lug and set sail for Pattelonia, I was able to hear Delia's story. Characteristically, she remained silent about the parts I could guess had given her the most problems.

Vomanus, whom I had sent with a reassuring message to Vallia, had told his princess and then had been sent off on some errand or other by Delia's father, the emperor. Instead of Vomanus returning with an airboat for me, he was traveling in the opposite direction, toward Segesthes, and nothing was done about me. I fully understood about that, for I knew a little of the fierce opposition aroused in Vallian political circles by the Princess Majestrix's decision to marry an unknown near-barbarian Clansman, for all he styled himself the Lord of Strombor. So — Delia had immediately set about flying herself. With a few trusted companions of her personal guard, and with her lady companion, Thelda, she took off. There had been no trouble at Pattelonia after the long flight across the fearsome mountain ranges collectively entitled The Stratemsk that walled off the inner sea from eastern Turismond. The broad ship had been sailing, and Delia had taken passage, intending to transfer subsequently and so find her way to Magdag. I shuddered to think what would have happened had she arrived at that wicked city and fallen into the hands of the Princess Susheeng, or those of her evil brother, Glycas; for I was growing more and more convinced as I pondered the matter that the Star Lords had ensured my old vosk-skulls would not overcome in their revolt.

A keen sorrow for her slain guards made Delia need the comfort I could give her in my rough way.

"But, Dray — you are safe! I sometimes feel what a monster I am when I consider that I really cannot regret anyone's death if it helps you — my poor lads died in vain, but you are alive!"

She was no monster. I knew without a trace of remorse that I would wade through seas of blood if necessary so that not one hair of my Delia's head should be harmed. Kregen is a world of violence and ugliness as well as a wonderful world of vivid life and beauty and love.

Condemn me as you will. I know where my loyalties lie.

Thelda made a great fuss of me. She fussed and fussed, until I felt stultified, and poor Seg, who was getting absolutely nowhere with the buxom girl, glowered and took himself off to the foresheets to fiddle with his little bows.

Delia laughed and joyed in my discomfort, whereat I longed to take her in my arms and show her just who it was I required attentions from. As it was, we made a somewhat strange little party sailing across the eastern end of the Eye of the World to the Proconian shore and the city of Pattelonia.

We reached the island city without incident and I felt a great leap of joy as I saw the multitudes of red flags floating above the ramparts and the towers and the long seawalls. So Sanurkazz still held the city — we sailed in feeling in very much of a holiday mood.

Seven

Thelda cuts hair and Seg cuts a bow-stave

Thelda it was who insisted on trimming my shaggy mop of hair, my long fierce moustache and my beard before we entered harbor. My hair was normally worn quite straight and almost to my shoulders. My moustache is of that kind that juts most arrogantly upward — sometimes I despair of its unruly nature — and my beard of that trimmed and pointed kind associated with cavaliers, lace, and rapiers. As a sea officer of wooden ships on Earth in the last days of the eighteenth century I had of course been clean-shaven; very often I reverted to shaving, but I had vowed never to return to wearing the queue.

The custom of growing a great long mass of hair so that it may be twisted up and worn as padding and protection beneath a helmet is a survival of primitive times in the evolution of ever-more sophisticated armor. I prefer a properly padded helmet — or basinet, sallet or, perhaps a favorite with me, a burgonet — and neatly trimmed hair.

All the time Thelda whickered the long dagger about my head and clumps of my brown hair tumbled onto the bottom boards, Seg sat glowering on a thwart. Fighting-men require haircuts as do other people. Merely to rely on a band around the head can be fatal in battle when a shrewd stroke can split the band to release a mop of thick uncut hair to shroud the face and obscure vision; you may wake up in some celestial barbershop in the sky with the blood still oozing from the wound your foeman's steel snickered in when you were brushing the hair from your eyes.

Delia caught my eye. She was lolling back with the steering oar tucked neatly into its notch and held in her small capable hands. She was laughing at me without moving a muscle of her gorgeous face! She was thoroughly enjoying my discomfiture as I sat shifting on the thwart, muttering and mumbling, wincing as the dagger sliced perilously close past my ear. I glared back at her and made a face whereat she burst into a peal of laughter that would have turned them all out of heaven to listen.

"It was sweet of Thelda to think of your hair, was it not, Dray Prescot?"

"Huh," I said, and then added, quickly: "Of course. Yes. Thank you, Thelda."

She lowered her eyes and a flush stained her cheeks.

I had to finish this somehow.

"And now it is Seg's turn—"

But Seg said: "I am happy as I am, shaggy as a thyrrix."

Delia chuckled with delight. She had seen me before when I myself was as disreputable as any mountain thyrrix, that grundal-nimble animal of the mountains of Seg's home, and I knew so long as I was all in one piece that was enough; she would take me as I was.

"For the man who wants to marry the Princess Majestrix," said Thelda, her habitual pushing eagerness evident, "you must take more pride in your appearance, Dray Prescot."

The mole drew closer as we approached and I could see the usual waterfront activity. The pharos here stood a good hundred feet less in height than the one at Sanurkazz. Nonetheless the smoke that curled from its summit by day and the light by night could be seen well out to sea. Whoever was in command here then, whether Proconian or Sanurkazzian, must feel confident. The overlords of Magdag must have been pushed back, they and their Proconian allies defeated, at least temporarily. Interference in an internecine war is never pleasant; and in the usual way Sanurkazz left Proconia strictly alone in the interminable feuds they waged; but once the green of Genodras had made its loathsome appearance the red of Zair must reply.

When we touched the jetty I was first out of the boat.

This was habitual; this was a mistake — I heard Thelda gasp and then I had turned and leaning down seized Delia under the armpits and swung her high into the air before setting her feet on the stones.

"There!" I said, to cover my lapse. "I may not look the part as the future consort to the Princess Majestrix of Vallia, but I do know how to help a lady from a boat."

Delia knew, of course, and she laughed back at me, and leaned close so that all her intoxicating scent wafted into my nostrils, dizzying me, and whispered close to my ear: "Poor Thelda — you mustn't mind her, dear heart — she means well."

We made the necessary calls on the port authorities, and were cleared for entry, for the peoples of the inner sea are more than somewhat lax over quarantine regulations. And the ideas of customs and excise which they employ are either barbaric — if you are on the paying end — or remarkably mild — if you are trying to build the seawalls of your city. We were rapidly able to walk up to the hostelry from which Delia, Thelda, and her young men had started off. Everywhere mixed up with the Pattelonian soldiery were the armed and armored men of Sanurkazz, fraternizing with them, laughing, arms draped over shoulders, engaging in friendly drinking bouts at the taverns, chasing wenches in the customary tactful way of the men from the southern shore. Evidently, a battle had recently been successfully fought and won.

A messenger arrived at the hostelry as I was downing a blackjack of Chremson wine — a vintage I had found as much to my taste as the superlative Zond wine so favored by Nath.

The messenger brought news that came as a staggering surprise and a most joyful reunion.

Four sectrixes had been provided, richly harnessed, and the messenger led us up through the terraced avenues of the city, wending past palace and villa, workshop and store, until we reached the lofty eminence of the governor's palace. Away on a neighboring hill, distinct in the limpid air, the palace of the Pattelonian ruler showed a multitude of Proconian flags. Where we stood the air seemed filled with the red banners of Zair.

From this height we could see around the curve of the island to the mainland side and there harsh black scars in the blocks of white houses showed where the city had burned. The struggle to take and retake Pattelonia had been severe, I could see easily enough. Also from here we could see the naval harbor with its placid waters disturbed by the passage of swifters, in and out. The long galleys lay ranked alongside the jetties and the columns of men carrying stores out to them wended like armies of warrior ants from the African jungles.

I recognized some of the swifters down there. But I could not wait now to count them and to check their condition and to remember. I heard a firm tread on the flagstones, and swung around, my hand outstretched in greeting.

"Lahal, Pur Dray!"

"Lahal, Pur Zenkiren!"

Our hands met and clasped in the firm grip of friendship and brotherhood in Zy.

He looked just the same, Zenkiren of Sanurkazz, tall and limber, with that bronzed fearless face, that fiercely up-brushed black moustache below his carved beak of a nose, that shining mass of curled black hair. On his white tunic above the apron the coruscating device of the hubless spoked wheel within the circle, embroidered in silks of blue and orange and yellow, blazed into my eyes. He smiled with warm affection upon me and I leaped in my heart to see him again, and although I did not smile the pressure of my hand told him of my joy in seeing him. He knew me — or that me who had fought as a Krozair and a swifter captain on the Eye of the World — did Pur Zenkiren, Krozair of Zy, admiral in the king's fleet, Grand Archbold elect of the Krozairs of Zy.

Introductions were made, and I noticed the courtly way in which Zenkiren treated my Delia. He did not miss our own heightened emotions, so that when I asked him of Mayfwy he replied she was well, that her son and daughter prospered, that she remained still a widow, not remarried, and that she missed seeing me. Nath and Zolta I heard, to my disappointment, had gone a-roving aboard a swifter into the western end of the inner sea. I would not achieve this joyful reunion with those two rogues here, then.

Seg, who I felt with an uncomfortable start of guilt, must have been feeling a little left out in all this handshaking and greetings, said: "Mayhap you will see them on your way through the Grand Canal and past the Dam of Days."

I looked at him, bemused for a moment. Then Delia nudged me and I managed to reply something and went on to tell Zenkiren of all that had happened to me since we had said "Remberee" in Sanurkazz. We went into the palace and were served wine and we helped ourselves to a heaping pile of palines from a silver dish. Time passed most pleasantly. I urged Zenkiren that now was the time to strike at Magdag. He agreed, and immediately sent off messages to the king, Zo, in Sanurkazz.

"My duty lies here, Dray, to help our Pattelonian allies against their foes and the devils from Magdag. I urge you, Pur Dray, now you have found your Delia of the Blue Mountains, to remain here. There is much to be done. We are pushing them back. Our army has gained success after success. Soon the call we all long for will go out, and all the men of Zair will rise and go up against the evil of Grodno."

"Greatly would I desire to do that, Zenkiren. But—"

The twin suns were slipping into the sea, far away across the western horizon. I persuaded Zenkiren to order a fleet liburna out. As we stood on the poop — she had no quarterdeck — and watched the single banks of oars, three men to an oar, pulling in that metronomic rhythm inseparable from the ideal of the swifter, I waited with apprehension.

That apprehension was for what I hoped would not occur.

But it did.

The wind roared, the sea got up, the thunders and the lightnings cracked and fizzled about us. We turned for the harbor and the gale dropped.

"I do not care to inquire too closely into these things," said Zenkiren, with a gravity habitual to him in weighty affairs. "No doubt Pur Zazz could fathom the meaning. But I take your point. You are fated to travel east — away over The Stratemsk, over the Hostile Territories. I wish you well, Brother, for the way is difficult, Zair knows."

"Pur Zazz has told me of many marvels and wonders in the Hostile Territories. I am happy to know the Grand Archbold still lives."

"Zair has him in his keeping, Dray. I pray he will live until my work here is accomplished."

I knew what he meant.

"When you are Grand Archbold, Zenkiren, and the call comes for all the Krozairs of Zy to answer — I will not fail."

He inclined his head in acknowledgment. But he was a sad man that I could not go with him on this last expedition against the forces of Magdag arrayed against us in the eastern end of the Eye of the World.

I believe that Delia took an opportunity to speak privately to Zenkiren, and can guess at some of the many questions she asked about my life on the inner sea, and that she asked about Mayfwy, too; I am glad that when we two spoke of these things together we could be absolutely frank with each other. Mayfwy, the widow of my friend Zorg of Felteraz, was a wonderful person and a glorious girl; but there can only ever be one woman in my life — my Delia, my Delia of Delphond!

Still and all, I gave Zenkiren the charge of making sure that my agent Shallan got the best price for the prize swifter *Sword of Genodras* and that all my shares should be paid to Mayfwy.

"After all, young Zorg will be growing up soon, and he must command the finest swifter that can be provided," I said. My old oar comrade Zorg — I would not let his widow or his son or daughter suffer if any way lay open to me to prevent it. I knew my two rascals, Nath and Zolta, felt exactly the same way.

During the short time we spent at Pattelonia, in a sense getting our wind for the next stage of our journey to Vallia, Seg kept much to himself. He was still trying his best to win some sign of recognition from Thelda, but she persisted in her fussing smothering of me, much to my annoyance and Delia's hidden and mocking amusement.

Seg came in one day bearing a monstrous stave of wood of so dark a green as to appear black. He flicked it about, speaking slightingly of it, but he was pleased.

"This is not true Yerthyr wood," he said. "The Yerthyr tree is deadly poisonous to the weak animals hereabouts, and the people do not like to grow it. In Erthyrdrin our nimble thyrrixes are able to digest the wood and bark and the leaves in their second stomach."

"So?"

"This stave will make a passable bow-stave after I have dealt with it." He ran his thumb along it, feeling. "But had I my own longbow — ah, then, Dray Prescot, you would see!"

A commotion broke out at the door, for we had by Zenkiren's kind invitation removed from the hostelry and quartered ourselves in commodious suites in the governor's palace. A Sanurkazzian guard — a young lad in a new hauberk and with a shiny new long sword, a parting present from his father — jumped back as a voluble, gesticulating, furiously angry Proconian popped in. Orange and green sunshine lay in slanting stripes on the patio outside the doors, and exotic blooms depended on vines from the white walls.

"Vandals! Pirates! Thieves!" the Proconian spluttered. He was plump, flabby, with ringed hands and a nose which wine had coarsened into a knob, and he wore no sword. His robes were twisted about him in the fury of his movements.

"I am sorry, Pur Dray," said the guard. "He insisted — and short of cutting him down there was no way of stopping him..."

"It is all right, Fazmarl," I said, turning away from Seg and his bow-stave. "Let the gentleman in."

The gentleman shook a fist under my nose, saw Seg and let out a screech. "There he is, the plunderer, the reaver, the barbarian! He holds my property, Pur Dray — and he has destroyed the finest tree in the women's quarters—"

"Oh-ho!" I said. I looked at Seg. He gripped the stave with the clutch of a man sliding over the side of an airboat.

"I did but cut the best stave suited to a bow."

The little man danced and spluttered and shook his fist.

"Only! And ripped it out of the heart — the very heart — of the tree that gives shade to my favorite wife—"

The Proconians believed in the quaint habit of marrying three wives. They were a punishment-loving race.

"Is the tree mortally wounded, sir?"

"Mortally! It has suffered a wound from which nothing can save it. My tree — my favorite wife's favorite tree!"

"Then, if nothing can be done to save the tree, I think it best to uproot it and plant another."

He gobbled over that, and wiped his forehead, and found a chair and collapsed into it. I nodded at Seg and that reckless man had sense enough to fill to brimming a silver-chased goblet with noble Chremson wine and hurry it across. The Proconian wiped his lips and gulped the wine, and gasped and palpitated, a hand to his heart, and gulped some more.

"Very good," he said, looking at the wine afresh. "Booty from Chremson, I take it?"

I inclined my head, but the word booty had inflamed him anew. "Plunderers, reavers — that is all you red-raiders from Sanurkazz are! You tear down my best tree, leave it in shattered fragments across my tessellated pavement so that my second wife barks her pretty shin and removes at least a palm of skin—"

"Come, sir," I said, putting the merest fraction of that rasp into my voice. "You have not yet favored me with your name. I do not know it was your tree. You could be fabricating the entire story to gain my sympathy — and my wine!"

He staggered upright with the assistance of the chair back. He tried to speak and his fat lips popped and blew and his cheeks turned purple and his eyes stood out. Then: "By the fair hair of the Primate Proc himself! I am Uppippoo of Lower Pattelonia! I am respected in this city, with wide lands on the mainland beyond Perithia, owner of ten broad ships, and with three of the most delectable wives a man could boast — and now they have kicked me out because their shaded garden has been ruined!"

Seg couldn't hold himself in and spilled wine trying to stop from bursting a gut laughing. I remained severe.

"Very well, Uppippoo of Lower Pattelonia. I would not wish a man to suffer, particularly from three wives. Rest assured, I shall make complete restitution." A thought occurred to me. "Can another tree be procured?"

A kind of frenzy possessed Uppippoo. "You imbecile! Those trees take a hundred years to grow!"

That was half a lifetime or so on Kregen.

"In that case, my friend here, who comes from Erthyrdrin, will be returning to his country shortly. I know he will immediately take steps to have a fresh tree prepared and shipped out to you. There, sir, what can be fairer than that?"

Uppippoo merely goggled at us.

"In the meantime, if you would accept a little common gold, which is nowhere as romantic as a tree, you could purchase a length of colorfully-striped awning, and thus protect your charming wives from the suns."

And I put down carefully onto a table a handful of gold scooped out of my waist-belt — for I had now, in the city, perforce to dress as a citizen with tunic, apron, and accouterments.

Uppippoo looked at the gold.

"An — awning?"

"Why — yes."

"An awning." He considered. "But a tree is alive, it looks beautiful, it soughs in the wind and its leaves create the most delightful patterns of shade and light upon my pavements — and the tesselae are renowned in Pattelonia, Pur Dray, renowned."

"Quite so. Take the gold. Buy an awning or buy a new tree of a different kind. But, Uppippoo, I would wish you to leave now. Do you understand me? The gold is fair payment, I think."

Uppippoo for the first time took care to look at me, instead of raging and roaring and blow-harding and glaring at Seg and the offending dismembered limb of his wife's tree. He saw my face. I was not conscious of any change in my countenance, but Uppippoo's snorts and ragings and breathy threats halted as though he had been gripped by the throat.

He backed a step. He bent his back, stealthily, reaching forward to take the gold from the table. He backed away. His protruding eyes were fixed on my face; his tongue kept licking his fat lips.

"Fazmarl!" I called. "The gentleman is leaving now."

The young guard showed the Proconian gentleman out.

He had not uttered a word since he'd had a fair sight of my ugly face.

Seg collapsed moaning onto a chair.

"As for you, Seg Segutorio, you should be ashamed of yourself. Cutting a stick from a tree — that's what kids do."

"Aye!" he roared joyously. "Just as I did when I cut my stave from Kak Kakutorio's tree! Hai — I could hurt myself laughing."

I must admit that I felt like allowing myself a laugh, also.

The incident of Seg's bow-stave and the shade tree of Uppippoo's wives convinced me that I had no need to worry so much about Seg Segutorio. He was still in form despite his conspicuous lack of success with Thelda.

Delia was anxious to leave, and now that I could not serve a useful part in the campaign I had nothing to tie me here. I told Seg, somewhat brutally, I fear, that he would have no time to put his new bow-stave into pickle. He chuckled with a grim sardonic humor that made me stare at him.

"You have a poor opinion of the bowmen of Erthyrdrin if you believe they are unable to fashion a bow-stave anywhere on this earth — aye, and pickle it, too. Put me thigh-deep in the mire of the Marshes of Malar with a stave and I'll fashion you a bow that can split the chunkrah's eye." He was as good as his word. He contrived a tall narrow tube of treated leather, well-stoppered, and into this with his precious stave he poured a concoction of his own — that stank to Zim itself — and shook it up and glared at me with a satisfied defiant stare on his face.

"By the time we are past the Dam of Days she'll be pickled—"

Even then I couldn't tell Seg just how we were traveling to Vallia, and there was no reason for this holding back. Delia knew exactly where the flier from Port Tavetus, on the eastern coast of Turismond beyond the Hostile Territories, had been hidden in the foothills which gloamed blue and orange and purple on the far mainland horizon. The people of Havilfar, where airboats are manufactured, did not care to have their products exposed on the inner sea. I gathered the air-boats gave trouble, too, as I had before experienced. Thelda cooed over me and ignored Seg and so we passed the last days before we took off. Again it was time to say "Remberee" to Pur Zenkiren.

Everything that should be done was done. Our belongings were carefully packed into satchels and leather sacks, for Delia with a strict flier's wisdom wanted no sharp-edged packing crates aboard, and were stowed aboard the calsanys that would take them down to the jetty. I detected a strange look of sadness on the face of young Fazmarl as I bid him good-bye. I clapped him on the back — a somewhat awesome experience for so young a would-be warrior of Sanurkazz from a swifter captain and a Krozair — and felt I must be getting old and walked down with Zenkiren and Delia to the jetty. Thelda had gone with the baggage — riding a calsany — to superintend, although we all knew she didn't care over-much for walking. Seg marched behind with his revolting leather pipe of bow-stave-pickling over his shoulder.

At the jetty we all climbed down into the boat and this time we were not using our old stolen muldavy which I had made arrangements to have, when possible, returned to its owners with a suitable sum in gold to compensate for those we had smashed. We were using the admiral's barge, no less, and twenty stalwart wights pulled lustily at the oars. As we cleared the mole and the barge's head swung toward the mainland, Seg looked back at me, sitting next to Delia. He was puzzled.

"I do not see our ship, Dray. And, why are we heading for the mainland?"

I realized he did not connect the storms that arose when we steered west with our very act of heading on that course, and I had not discussed that problem with him at all, as I had merely hinted at it with Zenkiren. The mysticism of the Krozairs of Zy armored Zenkiren against marvels of that kind. But now the time had surely come when I must be honest with Seg Segutorio and tell him of our means of travel. I told him.

He gaped for a moment at me as the barge pulled through the suns-lit water. Everyone was watching him.

"A flier," he said, at last, surprising me. "As to them, I have seen them and I welcome the opportunity to fly in one. But—"

"But, Seg?"

"The Stratemsk! The Hostile Territories! Man — do you know what you're doing? They're murder."

Delia said: "We are going home to Vallia, and you, Seg, to Erthyrdrin, if you wish. We would like you to be with us, but if you do not come we understand." She added, mischievously: "Anyway, that's the way Thelda and I got here..."

Eight

Through The Stratemsk

"Ossa they would pile upon Olympos; and upon Ossa, Pelion with its rustling forests, that the very heavens might be scaled."

This ambition of the Aloadai, Otos and Ephialtes, had always seemed to me a laudable goal, seeing that I myself had scrambled my way up through the hawsehole from the lower deck to the quarterdeck, and, since my startling arrival on Kregen beneath Antares, had fought my way to various arrogant-sounding posts and positions. But I had always thought of the tall twins' activities of ambition as rhetorical. The actual idea of mountains piled one atop another had always seemed to me figures of speech, devices of the imagination. I have seen the Himalaya — the other mountain ranges of the world are subsumed in the lofty and frightening grandeur of the Himalaya — and I had been suitably impressed and awed.

But The Stratemsk — Kabru piled on Nanda Devi upon Kangchenjunga upon Annapurna upon Nanga Parbat — with Chimborazo from the Andes thrown in as foothills — with K2 and Everest lofting beyond reason above — Yes, The Stratemsk, although not the loftiest or most extensive range of mountains on Kregen under the suns of Scorpio, are quite out of this world with the awe-inspiring terror and beauty of outraged nature flaunting her powers. The Stratemsk are big and wide and tall. They shatter reason. Snow mantles their upper slopes and pinnacles in an eternal and unbroken whiteness. The clouds hover around their feet. Savage and voracious animals haunt their lower ranges and gigantic birds and flying animals forever circle their valleys and passes with cruel talons and fangs seeking prey.

Above these mind-freezing precipices and crags and icy glaciers we flew, Delia, Seg, Thelda, and I, in our frail airboat through the cutting air.

We huddled close together warmly wrapped in flying silks and leathers, with immense furs wrapped about us.

The airboat was a mere shell of wood upon metal formers, shaped into the likeness of a petal and streamlined well enough with a windshield and leather thongs and wooden guard-rails. If it failed, as airboats notoriously failed, we were doomed. Below us lay certain death.

That death might come from cold and exposure. It might come from starvation or madness. It might come in the ravening jaws of some semimystical monster of the higher slopes where the tree line thinned and the screes stretched for miles before the snow line was reached in ice and penetrating cold.

Or — that death might come to us from the fangs and talons of any one of the many species of giant birds and animals who flew voraciously among the passes and valleys seeking what prey they might snatch. From their high aeries they could plummet down, their eyes sighted on a target so small at that distance only eyes su-perlatively endowed by nature could ever make out what manner of animal or beast it might be below them. We saw the ominous dots flying far off. I grasped my long sword hilt and determined that should anything or any monster attack us only my death would prevent me from protecting my Delia until none remained.

Coal-black impiters, corths, xi — the iridescent-scaled winged lizards of the humid jungle-valleys sunk in broad tracts within The Stratemsk — bisbis, zizils, the yellow eagles of Wyndhai, and many other monstrous flying beasts are to be found within the massive confines of The Stratemsk — or, to be practical about this matter, better not found.

For the first upward trending slopes before we rose high to seek the easiest of the passes opening out before us we flew over many crude encampments of the man-beasts who occupy the outer portions of The Stratemsk. There are many tribes, but they are referred to in general as crofermen, savage, untamed, cruel and suspicious, who delight in nothing so much as raiding down the outer slopes of The Stratemsk. It was their ponshos that the great winged beasts of the air would seize if given the chance. Life, indeed, was a hard and demanding exist-ence within The Stratemsk.

So that with the sheer size and immensity of the mountains and the crofermen incessantly raiding and the monstrous winged beasts, The Stratemsk had pro-vided a barrier between the Eye of the World and eastern Turismond that had endured for century after century.

And my Delia of the Blue Mountains had braved these terrors and these dan-gers in order once more to clasp me in her arms!

No wonder the sailors of the outer oceans would sail all the weary way around by the Cyphren Sea past Donengil and up the skeleton coasts to enter the inner sea via the Dam of Days. For besides the dangers of The Stratemsk there lay ahead of us the unknown perils of the Hostile Territories.

We had safely negotiated the first passes and left the peaks on either hand and Delia had the control levers thrust full to maximum when she touched my arm and pointed.

"Look, Dray—"

The gorgeous scarlet and golden accipiter with those deadly talons extended flew above our heads, turning in lazy hunting circles. I knew it. Messenger or ob-server of the Star Lords, the Gdoinye croaked a harsh challenging call — either that, a challenge, or a farewell — and swung away. I did not think that any corth or zizil or other flying monster would seek to attack that blazing raptor of the Star Lords.

We waited out the flying time, eating and drinking sparingly as the dwaburs unreeled below us. The air remained thin and cold, for Delia would not dip down into the shrouded valleys for warmth for the iridescent shapes of the xi cir-cled there, seeking their prey in the humid jungles beneath.

Gradually the high peaks passed away over our shoulders. Slowly the whole convulsed mass of The Stratemsk with its shining silver spears thrusting into dazzlement above dropped away behind us, but it would be days before those high peaks fell below the horizon. And slowly and gradually I came to thinking that we had successfully surmounted — or threaded our way through — the first great obstacle.

And then the impiters struck.

They swooped in a wide-winged onslaught from a distant ledge, swirling about us in a monstrous beating of wings. They tried to pluck us from the sky. Massive talons extended like the claws of some Earthly power excavator. Raucous croakings of their fanged mouths from which the forked tongues emerged in a constant licking were designed to frighten us into frozen immobility. The airboat rocked. The impiters were wild and savage, but I protected Delia of Delphond and my wildness and savagery met and mastered theirs.

My long sword whirled, thick with blood. And Seg's arrows flew as fast as he could draw back the string and loose. In truth, he dispatched far more than did I, although I was forced to tackle those posing the greater threat as they sought to impale us with their whip-barbed tails or rend us with their claws or snatch us up in their gape-jaws.

Massive they were, the impiters, giants of the air, and yet they cavorted in the empty levels with the speed and agility of an Earthly falcon. My sword arm bunched with muscle and I struck and struck and still they came. Now the airboat faltered, it dipped, dropped, fell away.

"She won't respond!" shouted Delia.

Thelda was screaming away and impeding me in my work as she sought to throw herself into my arms. I knocked her back into the bottom of the airboat and yelled at Delia.

"Grab her, Delia! She'll have her head taken off if she sticks it out here!"

Arrows spurted from Seg's bow. My sword lopped and slashed. The impiters continued to attack as the airboat sank lower. There was no chance of my seeing where we were falling; every straining effort had to be bent on to picking the next flying beast, sensing his line of attack, guessing whether he would strike with his jaws or flick himself over to lash with that deadly barbed tail. I saw a tail strike into the wood of the rail, splintering it. The barbs did not hold; some muscular mechanism seemed to fold them in the instant the impiter knew it had missed its stroke. I hacked the tail off.

How long that insane aerial battle went on I do not know. Now my chest was crisscrossed by red welts where the barbed tails had struck, and blood — my blood — slicked down my belly and thighs. But I battled on. I could stand up and brace myself against the movement of the airboat. My long sea training gave me at least that advantage. But Seg, too, stuck to his task, loosing arrows as though from some fabled machine-crossbow of the ancient men of the sunrise.

Trees abruptly swooshed past and a branch almost accomplished what the impiters had failed to do. I ducked and just managed to get the long sword's swing to intersect neatly with an impiter's jaw. He screeched and spun away and then — suddenly, miraculously, enormously — we were surrounded by a vindictively smothering swarm of tiny pink and yellow bodies. Tiny birds! Thousands of them.

Tiny pink and yellow birds with shrill cheeping cries were hurling themselves at the massive impiters, were darting in to sink their long sharp beaks into tender spots, where wings met body, at the juncture of tail, into the glaring, bloodshot eyes. The impiters went mad. I threw the long sword down — it had served me well but all my arms-training could not prevent me from doing what I had to do the quickest way I knew. I seized Delia and thrust her hard under a heaping pile of silks and leathers. I shouted.

"Seg! Cover yourself up — grab that idiot Thelda! Hurry!"

We cowered there, the four of us beneath silks and furs, as we let a myriad tiny birds harass and torture the mighty impiters into ignoble retreat. We could hear the sounds of that strife clear across the broad valley into which we had descended. The screechings and the shriekings persisted for some time and then gradually faded and I was able to poke a cautious head out from our cover to see the last of the flying monsters circling aloft with heavy wingbeats as the tiny dots of the little pink and yellow birds clustered thickly about.

Thelda was shaking all over and sobbing hysterically.

That was a normal reaction and I thought nothing of it. Seg tried to comfort her, but she wiped her eyes and turned a shoulder on him. Across that smooth skin lay a vivid weal.

"Well," said my Delia. "I shall always have a soft spot in my heart for those little birds. What were they, anyway?"

No one knew their name; none of us had ever heard of them. There is much to know of Kregen, and much that I tell you now I picked up later — but to spoil the effect of those thousands of little birds with their vindictive feud with the impiters is something I cannot do. We were shaken, bruised, cut — but alive.

After inspection, Delia pronounced the airboat as unusable.

Whether from a blow from the impiters or from an inherent failure we didn't know. What we did know was that from here on in we must walk if we wished to reach Port Tavetus.

All across the western skyline and extending out of sight to north and south stretched the colossal mass of The Stratemsk.

Before us lay a valley, and then open country with the glint of rivers and the clumping of trees amid the grasses.

"We walk," I said.

Thelda had recovered and we had drunk and eaten. Now she made a face. "I never did like walking. It's so unladylike."

Our preparations at the beginning were ambitious.

Thelda insisted on our bringing with us a mass of equipment she said was, "Absolutely vital."

I threw a handsome silver-mounted mirror into the grass.

"Sheer lumber, Thelda. If you want to preen — use a pool."

She started to argue and Delia started to try to persuade her, but I just said, "If you want to bring all that junk you must carry it yourself."

That settled that.

We took long swords, bows and arrows, daggers and knives. We took sleeping equipment. We took what food I thought we would need before we got into our stride and could hunt what would be necessary. We took water bottles, large canteens of Sanurkazz leather, which is the best tanned and treated of the inner sea although perhaps not as fine, in the manner of tooling, as that of Magdag — Zair rot them!

On Delia's suggestion we buried all the treasures — the gold and jewels, the luxury trappings. If ever we passed this way again we might retrieve them, and if some unknown warrior stalking this way found the marker he would be suddenly rich, and good luck to him. As for footwear, we took every item we had, for although I prefer to walk barefooted, the others were mindful of the discomforts of the way — Seg must be used to hunting barefoot over his mountains of Erthyrdrin, and Delia, I knew from the time we had escaped from the roof-garden of the Princess Natema and had spent a wonderful time on the Plains of Segesthes, could cope adequately without shoes. No, it was a way of saying we thought Thelda would not keep up with us without shoes.

Poor Thelda!

Poor Seg!

He perfectly resigned himself to carrying her, if needs be.

I must admit that I had not a care in the world. We had landed safely. We had arms and food, we were fit, and we had a continent to explore. Vallia would be there when we got there. I was in no hurry to reach that mysterious, potent, terrible island empire and face the emperor-father of the girl I wanted to marry. The future would take care of itself; only the here and now mattered — for was not Delia of the Blue Mountains, my Delia of Delphond, walking so lightly and freely at my side?

Nine

Into the Hostile Territories

Delia sang.

As we marched along Delia sang.

My chest itched.

As soon as Thelda had recovered herself and seen the weals crisscrossing my chest she had cooed and pursed up her fat lips and gone off to pick some brilliantly-mauve wild flowers which she bashed and mixed into a paste. Delia had wondered across and bent down and looked closely at the flowers and at Thelda's intensely absorbed face as she pounded and stirred, and had smiled slantingly at me, and gone off, humming.

Now Thelda had splattered the mauve paste all over my fiery chest, saying: "This will do you the world of good, Dray! It's an old Vallian remedy and wonderfully efficacious. Why, these little vilmy flowers will have your poor dear chest healed in no time!" The confounded paste was irritating and fretting me like a hive of bees fastened to my chest.

And Delia marched on at the head of our little caravan and sang.

She sang wonderfully. Gay, rollicking airs that sped our feet over the grass, sad little laments that made me, for one, think back on all the great times and powerful men I had known who were now no more, silly little catch-phrase songs in which we all joined — Thelda with a self-important air of consciousness of the effect she was creating, Seg with a most powerful and musical tenor that truly delighted me, and me with my own wild and savage bellowings that always made Thelda jump and Delia sing on superbly.

But that damn chest itched until I could stand it no more.

"May the Black Chunkrah take it!" I yelled. I ripped the whole sticky mauve plastery mass off and flung it into the grass and jumped on it "My chest's on fire!"

"Really, Dray!" sighed Thelda, sorely tried by my ingratitude. "You must persevere. You must give it time to work its healing magic."

"Healing magic nothing!" I shouted at her. "You try it! You stick it on your own imposing chest and see what it feels like!"

"Dray Prescot!"

"We-ell—"

The tinkling of a stream a short distance off by a line of salitas trees gave me the excuse not to exhibit further my sullen disgrace. I ran across and dived in and if all the monsters from the fabulous book called the *Legends of Spitz and His Enchanted Sword* that had been popular at the time I'd spent in Zenicce had started for me with gnashing jaws and talons I'd have scrubbed that confounded chest of mine clean first. Since Delia and I had taken that baptism by immersion in the sacred pool on the River Zelph in distant Aphrasöe — distant! No one knew where Aphrasöe, the City of the Savanti, was located! — we seemed to have picked up the valuable attribute of not only remaining healthy and with a promised life span of a thousand years but also of recovering with remarkable rapidity from wounds. We never seemed to get sick.

I rejoined them and I heard Delia, in a musing kind of voice, talking about a little blue flower she had picked.

"How pretty it is, Seg! See the petals, and the stamens, and the curious little silverish shape on each petal, like a heart—"

Thelda said "Oh!" and put a hand to her mouth.

"You are not well, Thelda?" inquired Seg, most anxiously.

"Oh! How silly — Oh, Dray, what you must think of me!"

"Now I've got rid of that debased paste from my chest I don't think anything," I said. I saw Delia's face, all glowing and glorious and I knew Something Was Up —

"Oh, Dray!" wailed Thelda. "What I picked was not vilmy at all! It didn't have the silver heart — I forgot! It was fallimy, that we use to scour cisterns clean — and I put it on your chest! Oh, Dray!"

I looked at her.

She put her hands over her face and started to sob, so I had to yell at her: "You silly girl — it doesn't matter! I'm not mortally wounded — oh, for the sweet sake of Zim-Zair, stop that infernal racket!"

"Say — say you — will forgive — me! I'm so — so stupid!"

"Now, now, Thelda!" said Delia, rather more sharply than I expected.

Seg tried to put his arm around the lady companion's shoulders, but somehow she eluded him and the next moment she was up against my abused chest and snuggling up to me, crying: "I am such a silly girl, dear Dray! What you must think of me — but—"

"Thelda!"

Delia hefted her pack and nodded at Seg.

"It's time we marched!"

I couldn't have agreed more. I managed to tuck Thelda somewhere around my left hip bone — she clung on — and started off after the other two.

Oh, how my Delia had joyed in all that! She was no white-skinned flaccid lump of lard who would lie back motionlessly. She was lithe and vibrant, a sprite, alive, full of mockery and yet absolutely dedicated and honest and fearless in our love. We had met and loved and we formed the perfect whole, meeting on all levels, profound and ethereal — no, there is no woman in two worlds like my Delia of the Blue Mountains.

The country closed in soon after that into a series of knobby rounded hills through which we followed the bank of the stream. Thick vegetation choked the hills but we found animal tracks beside the river and made good progress, always on the alert for the makers of these trails. Insects tended to be a nuisance, but Delia found a herb of pale and delicate green which, when she had crushed it and made a clear syrupy liquid seemed to my eyes a better proposition than poor Thelda's thick mauve paste. With this smeared over our faces and bodies the insects left us severely alone; I quite liked the scent of it.

Once more the country opened out and now we could see distant mountains — mere knobs on the ground compared with The Stratemsk; but nonetheless for that mountains through which we must find a way, walking. Numerous species of wild deer roamed the plains and I sighed for a fleet zorca between my knees. As it was Seg did some crafty stalking and with a single arrow provided us with our supper. We selected carefully-chosen campsites, for the horrific stories of the Hostile Territories, although so far nowhere borne out in what we had encountered, still rang in our minds. And so we proceeded across the land toward the far-off mountains. Twice we saw smoke rising from distant elevations in the plain, but these places we avoided.

Who — or what — lived here we did not know and had no desire to make their acquaintance.

An earnest of the wisdom of that decision came on a morning when the twin suns of Scorpio flamed into the sky and threw slanting sunshine gloriously through fluffed and meandering clouds above. We broke camp and strapped up and set off. The trail we were following dipped through a defile and so, naturally, we detoured that, clambering over scrubby hillsides and around thorn-ivy bushes. Ambushes are no places to take the girl one loves.

"Look—" said Seg in a low voice.

Ahead of us, in a crevice in the hillside that trended down to the defile below, something glittered. We approached with the silent tread of the hunter — Seg's learned in his mountains of Erthyrdrin and mine with my Clansmen in Seges-thes.

Two dead bodies lay there. They were not men. Neither, for that matter, were they members of any of the races of half-men of Kregen with which I was at that time acquainted, Fristle, Och, Rapa, Chulik, Sorzart, or other — and my com-panions had never met these people before. Of medium height, they possessed two legs and two arms. Their faces reminded me of the hunting dogs of some of the clans that roamed the Great Plains of Segesthes, but there was a considerable admixture of the leem there, too. I was struck by the vast forward-thrusting lower jaw and the dewlaps that hung down. Mind you, the bodies were decom-posing and the flies — they get everywhere — were busy. The girls moved back, out of range of the stink, but Seg and I were professionals and we knew what we had to find out.

Weapons first: Short thrusting swords like the short swords of my Clansmen. Long and slender lances with many-barbed tips. Tomahawk-like axes. Knives. Metal: From the mixture of steel and bronze, we judged these people to be in much the same area of development as the people of the inner sea where steel would be used if it could be come by, and bronze if not. Armor: Practically non-existent, consisting of leather arm-guards, a leather cap, and a leather breastplate with strips of some pretty hard substance stitched into it. Seg thought this was a bone or a horn of some kind. Clothes: Minimal, breechclouts as worn all over Kregen, with a padding vest beneath the breastplate. No shoes or sandals. Accouterments: The usual leather belts and pouches.

Then we both looked at what had killed these beast-men.

From the face of each one protruded a long arrow. An exceptionally long ar-row. Working carefully with his knife Seg got the arrows out. He gave a grunt and lifted the points for my inspection. They were not the steel piles I would have ex-pected.

"Flint," Seg said. His tanned face screwed up. "Seems I have relations around here."

He did a few quick flip-overs of his outstretched fingers, measuring the shaft, and then he whistled.

"They're from a master-bow." I knew that the esoteric of toxophily dominated much of Seg's life. Various grades of bow each had its name, every part, every ac-tion, every function, had its name and its ranking. The necessity of this was obvious. Seg, during our time together, had taught me much of the longbow, as I had swapped details with him of the compound bow of my Clansmen and the crossbow I had introduced to my old vosk-skulls. He had built himself a number of longbows, none, of course, from Yerthyr wood, and we had shot together in friendly rivalry. As was to be expected, at first he had outshot me by a margin. Then, as I got the hang of the longbow and mastered the transition from the compound reflex bow with which I was thoroughly familiar, as I have men-tioned, I gave him a run for his money. They say you must start to train a longbowman by beginning with his grandfather. Once the society exists, how-ever, and a man like myself with a lot of time to devote to the practice of arms is dropped into it, with the necessary requirements of an archer already existing, a great bowman may be made of him — as I had demonstrated on the Plains of Segesthes.

"You recognize the flight, Seg?"

He shook his head. "An expected master-set." He mentioned the technical jargon for the way the feathers were cut and set, the angle of the cock-feather, the twining and slotting. "Whoever loosed these knew his business."

"Whoever he was, he was ambushed and dealt with it."

"But good."

"These beast-men have no missile weapons. They must have flung them—"

"Much good it did them — nothing," said Seg Segutorio, "can stand against the longbow of Loh."

We marched on. All we took were the two arrows. The other weapons would merely weigh us down, although I regretted leaving them.

As we walked through this land, wary and always alert, we were able to talk. I believe you must have realized that having Delia with me had released my tensions, had loosened me up so that more than once I was astonished to find myself in the midst of a rib-straining laugh. A genuine laugh, at a joke, a witty remark, a funny situation. So we talked and joked and sang as we walked on toward the east coast of Turismond and Port Tavetus from whence we would ship to Vallia.

Thelda wore out the first pair of shoes and then the second. She persisted in her bright eager chattering and her pushing concern over me, but with Delia walking so lithely at my side I could put up with far worse than a boring woman. Seg and I grew closer together, too, as we joined in hunting for our sustenance. I remember those days as we walked steadily eastward away from The Stratemsk across the eastern plains of Turismond with a warm affectionate nostalgia. My search for Delia had been accomplished; we were together again. Vallia could wait, and as for Aphrasöe, to which Swinging City I fully intended to return some day, that was of the distant future. Everything was of the present. The journey itself was the adventure, the joy, the laughter, the zest.

Seg told me of Erthyrdrin, that country of his, that convulsed mass of mountains and valleys occupying the northern tip of Loh and peopled by a highly individualistic kind of person. The valleys resounded with song and the mountain peaks with the music of the harp. There were cliff-top strongholds everywhere, mere single towers of stone, some of them. Others had grown into battlemented fortresses of four or five towers linked by walls, and all were fiercely independent and devoted to protecting their crops and their flocks from neighboring raiders. Many of the young men hired out as mercenaries, for their longbows which had been developed over the centuries as hunting weapons proved mighty and invincible in battle. The Yerthyr trees were revered on the score of the quality of bow-staves they could produce; but it was considered a man's prerogative to cut his stave from the best tree he could find, wherever he could find it. The Yerthyr trees contained a deadly poison that killed any animal who ate of its leaves, and only, according to Seg, were the thyrrixes protected by virtue of their second stomach.

"We men of Erthyrdrin were the backbone of the armies of Walfarg. I doubt not but the bowman whose handiwork we witnessed came in the long ago from Erthyrdrin. Walfarg was a mighty country — it still is — but in its great days it ruled an empire over all Loh, and Pandahem to the east and south, and Kothmir and Lashenda, and over the eastern portions of Turismond. Only The Stratemsk halted the onward flow of the empire of Loh to the west."

"So all these so-called Hostile Territories were once a part of the empire of Loh?"

"Yes. I hold nothing in my heart for Loh as a country. They failed because they failed. Then the raiding barbarians from northern Turismond moved in, fiercer and ever more fierce. What are now the Hostile Territories became walled off to the east by barbarous tribes of men and half-men and nowadays only a scattering of cities and trading posts on the eastern seaboard remain open to the men of the outer ocean." He gestured about him. "As for what goes on in the Hostile Territories now — who knows?"

Seg Segutorio would sing of the old days of Loh as well as his own high-flavored culture. I do not care to render into English the words of his songs. They roared and rattled and boomed in my head — and I can sing them now — but they are of Kregen.

They echoed with deep rolling sounds — "oi" and "oom" and reverberating drumrolls and profound bassoon-like resonances, with the splatter of hard syllables like hail against taut canvas. One of his songs of which he was particularly fond reminded me instantly of "Lord Randolph My Son" and I believe the frontier and border cultures of both worlds hold much in common.

We saw occasional hunting parties roaming the wide plains but we invariably went to earth until they had passed. Strange beasts riding strange beasts — how those words recalled another time and another place to me! — were of no concern of ours now. Although I sensed a growing need in Delia for us to push on. She wanted to get back to Vallia.

"I cannot contract a legal marriage outside Vallia, Dray. It is all part of this silly business of my being the Princess Majestrix — you know."

"I can wait, my Delia — just."

"We must soon be there." She glanced at me quizzically as we threaded the aisles of a forest which appeared to bar our approach and around which we had been unable to trek. "If you have any—" and then she stopped, to start again: "If you feel somewhat—" And again halted.

"I know little of Vallia, Delia. All I know is that I wish our union to be one in which you will take pride. I know your father is the emperor and I have heard of the puissance of his island empire. Maybe—"

"Maybe nothing! You will be my husband and the Prince Majister! Have faith, Dray. It will not be so great an ordeal."

"As to that," I said, somewhat offhandedly and a little thoughtlessly, as I realized afterward, "We have to reach there yet."

"We will, dear heart! We will!"

Whenever we saw flying specks in the sky we took cover at once and instinctively, without stopping to think.

Through this forest we did not expect to find impiters or corths and so we trod along with a firmer tread. As night dropped with the refulgent sinking of the twin suns spearing in topaz fire through the intertwined branches we sought a resting place and soon enough ran across a series of old caves sunken into an earth bank. Gnarled tree roots thrust forth, naked and shining. The leaves around looked untrodden, the dirt trails unmarked. Seg nodded. We set about gathering wood and preparing camp.

I felt a slight twinge of concern lest Delia consider I was chary of visiting her notorious home and of meeting that powerful man, her father the emperor. Well, it was something I would have to do if I wished to claim Delia before the world, and having said that, that was sufficient. Nothing would stop me from doing just that — nothing...

Settling down for the night in our sleeping bags we had fashioned from the soft Sanurkazzian leather with plenty of luxurious silk for linings I lay back for a moment reflecting as I often do before sleep. I could well understand Delia's desire to return home. As for me, now, my home was on Kregen and with Delia. But, still and all, I had felt very much at home riding with my wild Clansmen, and I acknowledged the surge of barbaric pleasure that savage and free life could always invoke in me. Seg had mentioned the barbarians who had swarmed down out of north Turismond to ravage and destroy the remnants of the empire created by Walfarg. I wondered if they were more violent and more barbaric than I and my Clansmen could be...

As I was sinking into sleep I heard a tiny scraping sound from the rear of the cave.

Before the sluggish reactions of a city dweller of Earth would have prised his eyelids open in yawning query I was up out of the sleeping bag and with my naked long sword in my fist facing at a crouch whatever menace lurked there in the cave.

Seg said: "What?"

He stood beside me, a sword in his hand. Delia said: "Do not make a sound, Thelda," and I heard the squashy sound of a palm over fat red lips.

Again the noise reached us and then the whole back end of the cave fell outward. We had searched the place carefully before taking up our occupation; we had not expected this. Pink light from the moons of Kregen washed in with a reflective uncanny glow.

In that wash of pink radiance I could see the squat ovoid outline of something moving. I saw two squat legs bending to bring the bulk of the body into the cave, and I saw the array of tendril-like arms bunching from arched shoulders. The thing's head was hunched down and in the darkened silhouette was invisible to me. The thought occurred as such thoughts will that perhaps the thing had no head at all.

It kept emitting a wheezing hiss, rather more like a faulty deck pump than a snake but nerve-chilling for all that.

Seg shouted. "Hai!" and charged, his sword high.

He brought the sword down in a brutal butchering blow and a tendril uncurled and caught his forearm and snapped straight. The long sword poised immobile over the thing's bunched tendrils. Two more grasped Seg about the waist, lifted him, began to draw him forward into the pink-tinged shadows.

I did not yell but ran forward fleetly, my head bent to avoid the overhang, and sliced the two gripping tendrils away.

They fell to the floor and writhed away into cracks in the rocks like snakes.

The thing shrieked — whether of rage or pain I did not know — and Seg managed to get his sword-arm free.

"The point, Seg!"

As I yelled I ran in again and buried my own weapon up to the hilt into the thing's body. Everything had happened fast. I know now that these things are inimical to most living beings and the thing had been clearly bent on surprising us by its trick back-end to the cave. Quasi-intelligent, the morfangs, quick and treacherous and incredibly strong. As the beast lay on the ground we could all see in that streaming light from Kregen's moons the gaped mouth with its serrated rows of fangs, the tiny malicious eyes, the thin black lips, the slit nostrils where a nose should be. It hissed as it expired. We found out about these morfangs later on; what we did not know then was — they habitually hunted in groups.

From the dimmer radiance at the mouth of the cave where the overhang cast shade, figures moved with unhurried purpose. I leaped for the opening. A quick glance showed me six of the tendriled beasts. Thelda was heaving and moaning and Delia was holding her down. I had no time for Thelda now. My Delia was in mortal peril.

"Seg! Gather what we need. Grab the girls! Hurry!"

I checked the back exit to the cave where the surprise had come from. Quasi-intelligent, these things, but clever. We were supposed to run screaming from its sudden surprise appearance — run straight into the tendrils of its fellows waiting outside. The back, which opened into a small shaft filled with moons-light, was clear.

"Seg!" I said again, harsh and dominating. "Take the girls out the back way — hurry—"

He tried to argue and I beat him down with a snarl and a look.

Thelda was clutching herself and rocking and moaning. Seg hoisted her up beneath the armpits and half carried her. Delia took our gear and as she went out she cast a look back and stopped, ready to throw down the sleeping bags and the food and the medicines and jump to my assistance, a long jeweled dagger in her hand.

"For my sake, Delia! Go — Hide and then create a little noise — not much, enough to draw them off — you understand?"

"Yes, Dray — oh, my—"

I didn't give her time to finish but waved her off with a most ugly look. Then I turned to face the front opening of the cave.

Ten

Great beasts of the air

The noise from the cave had not been what these tendriled monsters expected. In a body they headed for the entrance to the cave.

Pink moonlight lay thickly on the leaves, on the spilled earth, limned the branches of the trees, weaved and twisted with purple shadows in the coiling and uncoiling tendrils.

I stood at the entrance. I could feel my feet thrusting at the earth, the dirt of Kregen four hundred light-years from the planet of my birth. I could feel my heart thumping with a regular anticipatory pulse, kept unpanicked by the disciplines so carefully and painfully learned from the Krozairs of Zy. I could feel the heft of the long sword in my fist, and the balance of it, and the beginning movements that would turn that bar of cold steel into a palely glimmering instrument of pallid destruction until the clean steel glitter fouled and slicked with blood.

As I stood there I must have presented a wild and terrible picture, with the defiance that would not be beaten down because the girl I loved was in peril, with my ugly face ricked into an expression I am sure would have prevented me from shaving had I seen it in a mirror, with my muscles limber and lithe and ready instantly to bunch and exert all the monstrous power of which — sometimes to my shame — they were capable.

These morfangs were quasi-intelligent, as I learned later; that they clearly were not fully-intelligent is obvious. Had they sense enough they would have run from me, shrieking.

But not unintelligent — as soon as they saw me they halted in their advance and their hissing increased. One bent, picked up a stone, and threw it. I struck it away with my sword as one makes an on-drive to mid-on. The ringing clang acted as a gong-like signal. The half dozen of them, hissing and screeching, leaped toward me and the lashing forest of tendrils writhed above my head seeking to trap me and draw me into the fanged crevices of their jaws.

And now I struck and struck again and the keen edge bit and sliced and any pity or sorrow I might have had for these voracious beasts burned away in the fire of action. Only the sword could have saved me. Their intent was quick and deadly and obvious. Those tendrils clustered in seeking, groping, twining bunches, with immense coiled power striving to drag me into the crag-like sharpnesses of their mouths. Unarmed, I know I would not have lasted five minutes.

As it was I was forced to hack and skip and jump and strike again as though I were some phantom woodsman fated to hack his way through an animate mobile forest. All the time they kept up their jangling-nerved hissing screeching; and, too, I became convinced that shrilling was of anger and fury and not of pain.

For the severed tendrils looped up with muscular strength and writhed like the furious contents of an overturned snake basket. And, too — instead of writhing off into the woods as the severed tendrils had wriggled into crevices in the cave, these serpent-like tendrils writhed toward me. They crept over the ground and began to drag themselves up my legs. I could feel their clammy coils lapping about me, constricting my muscles, and as I stepped back and chopped them free so each new severed portion began instantly to coil sinuously toward me over the leaves and the dirt.

Only one way waited for me if I wished to escape.

With full force I brought the long sword down onto the head of the nearest creature. That head split and gushed ichor and brain and the sword sliced on past the coat-hanger-like shoulders with their five-a-side ranks of lashing tentacles, drove cleaving on down into the ovoid body. The thing fell backward and I had to exert tremendous strength to jerk the sword free.

In that instant of hesitation tendrils lapped my neck.

Instantly my left hand whipped the main-gauche across and the razor-edged steel — razor-edged because when I shaved I found this weapon a useful implement on my stubble — sliced down the bunched coils. It left a thin scarlet line on my own neck, too.

This could not go on.

Now two of the beasts were down and then a third staggered away on one leg. I breathed in with long deep breaths, timing them to the swing of the sword. The main-gauche went into the eye of an attacker on my left — too deeply, for I was again hung up on the withdrawal and only barely managed to fend the sword blade above my head, shearing tendrils. More tentacles looped me from behind and I felt myself toppling backward off balance.

"Hai!" I yelled — a complete waste of breath and yet a psychological reminder. I twisted as I fell and thrust the sword up so that the beast in falling into me fell instead on the sword with its pommel thrust hard into the ground.

Dragging myself clear I shook my head. Two left, if the others were truly hors de combat, and a host of writhing wriggling tentacle-remnants like a pit of snakes from hell; long odds they were, yet.

Then I heard a shout — Seg's voice: "Hai!"

The remaining beasts hesitated. Quasi-intelligent they were, knowing when to stop fighting as well as when to go on with unintelligent viciousness to death. Had they been armed...

I shouted.

"Hai! Jikai!"

I leaped forward.

The sword blurred. Left, right, left, right. I struck now with the impassioned zeal of a man who knows he must finish it fast.

The two morfangs dropped and I dragged the smeared sword back. Now, with the death of the last two, all the free snake-like tendrils wriggled away into the moon-drenched forest. I guessed then, and was later proved right, that they would grow each into a new morfang beast-monster. Moments later I had rejoined my comrades, guided by their voices, able to reassure them. We began a night march at once to clear the confines of this accursed forest.

There had been only six. They had given me more trouble than twice their number of armed men. One of the reasons lay in those coat-hanger shoulders, each with five whipping tendrils. Even allowing a man two arms, which on Kregen is usual although by no means universal, the count was as though I had fought thirty men. I touched the hilt of the sword. I had lived then, by the sword. The balance of the thought lay leaden and ugly in my mind, and I did not speak as we marched through the pink-shot moonlight of the Kregen night.

After that we redoubled our vigilance and only through extraordinary good fortune were we able to avoid similar encounters. The tendril monsters roamed over a goodly-sized portion of the land here and we found ourselves traveling in constant apprehension. A considerable extent of badlands worked its way in from the south as we trended east, forcing us to carry on in a slanting angle to the east-northeast. Delia shook her head and remarked that she did not recall flying over this kind of country at all when she'd come in from Port Tavetus. Although the feeling was marginal, I had, with that sea officer's sense of navigational direction, felt we had veered to the north during our passage through The Stratemsk and the attack by the impiters had further driven us off course.

But I did not express my concern, thankful that we were still alive and still fit to travel. Thelda was hardening, and Delia positively glowed with the fresh air and exercise.

The climactic shadow of The Stratemsk lay to our rear now, the forests indicated that, and the badlands must be an effect of absence of soil or presence of minerals and poor soil and the millennia-long erosion. The mountains had been traversed and although we did not know their names we were conscious of their puniness in contrast to The Stratemsk; all the same, they were arduous on foot, and we near froze a couple of times. On the eastern side the whole country changed in character.

Now we were hard-pressed to avoid cultivated areas, to bypass towns and villages, to keep off the highroads that intersected at towns and posting stations and gave us clear indication that this land was populated.

We would scout with the minutest attention to every detail of the land that lay ahead. From whatever eminence we could climb we would plot our passage. Some of the towns we saw and avoided were nearer cities than towns. Many times we lay in hedgerows while cavalcades of armed men and trundling wagons rolled along paved roads. The roads were, indeed, objects of wonder. I was reminded of the old Inca or Roman roads, and I suspected that they were still in such good condition only through the skill of their builders, for the present inhabitants of this land looked hard and brutal and contemptuous of labor, lusting after silver and gold and the good things of life.

"They remind me of my own people in their hardness," said Seg. "These cities and towns must be constantly warring one with another."

"I agree," said Delia. "The roads link them, but between each city and its surrounding cultivation lies barrenness."

More than once we saw high-flying birds or winged beasts, and concealed ourselves, for we knew what to expect.

Now we began more fully to understand why all the continent lying between The Stratemsk and the eastern coast of Turismond had been dubbed the Hostile Territories. The true hostility came from men and not from nature or the animals of the wild.

I continued to feel concern over the northerly drift of our course; but in the nature of things with an infuriating obstinacy events conspired to force us more northerly still. I knew that Turismond extended in a bold out-thrust promontory into the Cyphren Sea and if we were traveling eastward we could march as much as five hundred unnecessary miles to the east with the sea away down to our south. But I was not prepared to risk an encounter with the inhabitants of these pinnacled cities, these battlemented fortresses, for I sensed from what we saw of them that they differed in kind from those peoples I had already met on Kregen.

More than once we bypassed cities inhabited by beast-men, half-men of races with which none of us was familiar, although given the strangeness of human nature I felt a comical sense of relief when the semi-humans of these cities turned out to be Ochs or Rapas, much though I distrusted the former and detested the latter — emotions which, I hasten to add, were germane to my continued existence at the time, whatever subsequent changes a long life and a great experience have brought.

None of us had the slightest hesitation in giving the widest of wide berths to the sprawling city filled with Chuliks upon which we almost stumbled as we came down out of a hill-cleft into a wide valley.

We crawled back up into the hills again and when I tried to lay off a course southerly we were halted by a river on the banks of which a string of guard-towers had been built. Perforce we struck northward once more.

The whole land was cut up into city-states. Antiquaries say there were ninety city-states of the ancient Minoan civilization in Crete. They must have been very small. Here the city-states sprawled over vast areas of land, or huddled around a natural fortress-holding on a hill within a valley. The state of savagery of the intervening areas can best be judged if I tell you that Seg and I had often to cope with sudden attacks from leem, those eight-legged demons, furred, feline, and vicious, whose fangs in their wedge-shaped heads can strike through lenk. And, too, we met graints, those wonderfully vital and obstinate animals I had met and battled outside Aphrasöe with the magical swords of the Savanti that did not kill but merely stunned. These, and other wild animals, were not in the usual way to be found anywhere close to settled human or half-human habitations.

'According to my calculations," Delia said to me as we rested in a fold of gentle, grass-clad hills, eating the rich flesh of a deer-like animal Seg had brought down and the girls had cooked, "I figure we have something like two hundred dwaburs between The Stratemsk and Port Tavetus."

"Yes."

"We must have covered that by now — we've been walking for ages—"

"Yes, Delia. But we are north of our course—"

"Oh, yes, I know you have been concerned..." She pondered. Then, briskly, she said, with that defiant tilt to her chin: "All right, then. The airboat carried us a good way, and we have marched a long way. We do not seem to be able to head south — so we must go on. I think we will find the next Vallian port city up the coast will be Ventrusa Thole. There are port cities of Pandahem, but I think we would be wise to avoid them."

Pandahem, I knew, was a great rival of Vallia's in the carrying trade and in business of the outer oceans. But there was a quiet animosity in Delia's tones that startled me.

"Do you hate them so much, then, my Delia?"

"Hate? No, not really. We both seek to enrich ourselves on the leavings of the empire of Loh. We both maintain settlements on the eastern coast of Turismond. We both try to extend our business contacts to the west—"

"And a fat lot of good that does!" broke in Thelda. She pushed up on an elbow. Thelda had lost weight on our journey and her figure had trimmed off into statuesque beauty that poor Seg found mightily disturbing. "By Vox!" she said, with some force. "I heartily wish all the devils from Pandahem a watery grave!"

"Quite still!" said Seg. His voice cracked. The green radiance of Genodras lay on his face and turned that lean tanned visage into a ghoul-skull newly-risen from the grave with the grave-mold crumbling upon it.

We all remained absolutely still.

Now I could hear the beat of many wings. From the sky that susurration floated down, ominous, breath-catching.

Shadows flitted across the grassy hills, twinned-shadows from the twin suns, at first in ones and twos, and then in clumpings until the whole sky darkened. We did not look up.

Delia still looked at me and I at her, and her face remained calm, her eyes bright and mocking on my face, and I yearned to take her in my arms. But we lay there rigid and unmoving.

And now I could hear a strange clinking from the sky, mixed with the massive gusting as enormous wings beat at the air.

The noise dwindled and the fleeting shadows drifted away again into twos and threes. Seg touched me on the arm, for he had been able to watch everything.

"Gone."

We looked and saw the host of flying beasts like a low cloud vanishing beyond the farther hills.

Seg's face remained grave and serious, despite Thelda's babblings of relief.

"What is it, Seg?" asked Delia.

"I have heard the tales — all men of Loh have heard the tales of our great empire that Walfarg forged on Turismond. The legends that creak with age and are hung with cobwebs. But—" He wiped a hand over his forehead and I saw the sweat slick there. "But I never thought to see them come to life!"

"What do you mean?"

"They were impiters. But — they carried men upon their backs!"

At once I remembered what Pur Zazz, the Grand Archbold of the Krozairs of

318

Zy, had spoken to me when we had said Remberee. "I would welcome news, Pur Dray, of your adventures and the sights you encounter. Men say that beyond the mountains, in the Hostile Territories, there are whole tribes who fly on the backs of great beasts of the air."

And so there were.

Of course, when one considers that men on this Earth have tamed horses and camels and donkeys and ride them as a mere fact of everyday life, and on Kregen men and half-men ride zorcas and voves and sectrixes and yulankas and many more wonderful animals, and given that the impiters and corths we had seen were large enough to support a man's weight in the air, the wonder would be if there were not men flying birds and beasts, the miracle would be if men did not form aerial cavalries.

And so it was that I felt no surprise at Seg Segutorio's words.

"They did not see us," I said, "thanks to Seg's sharp eyes. But, by Zim-Zair, had we four of those flying beasts we could manage this journey to Port Tavetus or Ventrusa Thole with less damage to our feet."

Delia looked at me sharply. Her surprise was understandable; she knew how much this leisurely progress meant to me and then she smiled as the realization that I really did want to go to Vallia pleased her. And yet, she still felt doubts of the outcome, that I knew. Her father's reputation was a frightening reality.

"Aye!" said Seg, leaping up. "And we'd soon unravel the knot of how to fly the beasties. They must be well-trained."

"Assuredly," I said, "otherwise the riders would either fall off or hang upside down between the beasts' legs."

So saying, we gathered our belongings and took up our weapons and continued our journey.

Below us, in the valley, an army marched.

At once we sank down below the crest. We looked out and down onto infantry and cavalry and artillery — different types of varters and catapults — and I heard Seg whistle softly between his teeth.

"Tell me, Seg."

"It is as though I am Loh-borne again," he said. His eyes stared with a fey hunger on the marching host. "It is as though I am looking through the illuminated scrolls of my people — for I tell you, Dray Prescot, that army marching there is an army from the past!"

I said nothing, respecting the mood that had overtaken him. He had told me of the pictures in the illuminated scrolls of his people. They were artifacts common in lands where literacy was not high or widespread, and conveyed stories by many thousands of pictures stretching along scrolls that might be, when rolled up, as thick around as a chunkrah thigh. Many men dedicated their lives and the contents of their paint-pots to producing these items, and many of them were objects of great beauty in their own right, irrespective of the story they told.

Now Seg drew in a shuddery breath. "An army from the past, an army of Loh, marching in all the glory of the empire of Walfarg!"

In my time on Earth and on Kregen I have seen many armies on the march, and there are ways to assess the qualities and the strengths as well as the weaknesses of hosts of marching men. These men below me marched with a swing, in step and in ranks, their spears all slanted at identical angles. Cavalry rode picket. Artillery — strange-looking varters to me, used to the ballistae of the inner sea — all arranged in a neat symmetry. I studied the way in which the army marched, and came to certain conclusions. But it was Delia, watching with us that army of something like ten thousand men, who pointed out the most important observation of all.

"I feel like swearing just like Thelda!" said Delia, crossly. "For — do you see? — they are marching in exactly the same direction as the way we wish to go!"

And — as I said with a nice round Makki-Grodno oath — they were.

There was nothing for it but to wait out their progress and then follow along with the utmost caution, for as Seg and I observed, their scouts were very good.

"Although," I said, with a trace of dubiousness, "they seem a little too good."

"How come?"

"Well — they scout ahead, checking every knoll and defile, and they're spread to the flanks. But it seems to me, somehow, done by rote, as though each man has a drill book in his hand." The English word was: mechanical. "For instance — if I was commanding that army I would want to know if four desperadoes were lurking on a neighboring hill — there might be more."

Thelda looked alarmed for an instant, and then she laughed, and tapped me on the bicep, and said, "Oh, Dray! You mean — us!"

Very gravely, I said, "Yes, Thelda."

As we trailed them Seg relaxed his first incredulous disquiet and told us that the uniforms worn by the soldiers were those of three hundred years or so ago, and I was quite prepared to believe him, for in the main the uniforms of Kregen are colorful, practical affairs that change slowly. Although life and culture on Kregen varies widely from place to place, in general culture is outward-looking and thrusting forward, new lands opening up, new kingdoms raised, new empires being formed. Many new peoples were lifting their fortunes on the debris of the empire of Loh, and here in the Hostile Territories we had stumbled across an army constituted as Loh would have organized it.

"For a moment," said Seg, and his laugh did not sound genuine to me, "I thought they were an army of ghosts!"

The truth was that in the collapse of the old empire and the inrush of barbarian hordes, fragments of culture from Loh, Lohvian attitudes and customs, had survived. Clearly, this army belonged to a city-state that had retained its Lohvian character. I confess, now, that at that moment the idea cheered me. With a civilized people we might find shelter in this crazy patchwork of Hostile Territories and rest and relax.

Why then, do you ask, did I not run down and introduce myself to the army commander?

My friend — whoever you are listening to this tape — if you think that, you have not listened well to my tale of Kregen.

Since the eclipse of the green sun Genodras by the red sun Zim — an event that had entailed direful consequences for me in distant Magdag — the green sun preceded the red in sunrise and sunset. When we camped that night in the amber rays of Zim falling slanting across the land we could see the campfires of the army like a miniature flame-filled reflection of the stars above us.

In the morning the army formed up in a welter of heel-clicking and rigidly correct lines; there was much drilling about, parading, and wheeling past fluttering colors before they at last set off. My suspicions of the army spread out below me grew — and shattering confirmation came when that ominous low cloud dashed into sight above a crest a dwabur away.

We watched, fascinated.

The fight was not our concern and we wanted nothing of it. We sheltered in the lee of a crest and watched. We had drunk refreshingly from an upland lake, a little tarn, and we had palines to munch, and we did not wish to become embroiled in what was going on between the Lohvian army and the boiling mass of wing-beating animals and ferocious men. The flying armada came on with cloud-driven swiftness and immediately began a long series of diving attacks on the men on the ground. These reacted with all the strict order of men obeying the rule book. And this was where I saw the weaknesses I had suspected revealed. Their dispositions for combating the aerial attack were excellent, but the manner in which they carried out their instructions left them shattered and confused.

The flying beasts were impiters, right enough, possibly the same group we had seen before, possibly another tribe. The men perched on their backs were too distant to discern properly, but I guessed they would possess some, at least, of the attributes of humanity along with their obvious bestiality.

"Look at them!" screamed Thelda, and Seg had to reach up a hand to drag her down, so carried away by excitement was she.

The flying beasts would swoop down and the men on their backs would loose arrows or fling javelins. Then they would zoom up again and reverse to swoop again. The Lohvians were shooting upward, and many flying beasts fell, but the army was split, segments were running wildly. The whole confused area before us became covered with hundreds of separate combats.

"No, no, no!" Seg was saying, over and over. His eyes betrayed his excitement. His hands kept gripping into fists and relaxing, gripping and relaxing. He held his longbow now, and I said, softly: "Seg?"

He looked at me with blank, drugged eyes. He breathed very quickly.

"They are of Loh!"

"You are of Erthyrdrin, Seg. But, if you will it..."

I started to bend my longbow and Delia said: *"No!"*

"No, Dray! This is madness! Suicide!"

"Oh, Dray!" wailed Thelda.

Only one woman in two worlds could hope to sway me in any decision I make, right or wrong.

I, Dray Prescot, hesitated...

And then a dark shadowed shape gusted above us and there were a dozen great winged beasts circling us and circling, too, the dazed little group of riders who had spurred their mounts at the hill in the hopes of riding beyond it to safety.

The riding beasts were nactrixes, cousins of the familiar sectrixes, with their six legs and their blunt heads; but they were deeper of chest and taller, with an altogether more hardy look about them. Their slatey-blue hides were covered with a more profuse coat of hair, which was trimmed and cropped.

The riders were officers, with sumptuous saddle gear and brocaded cloths, with as much finery about their mounts as about themselves. Some attempted to shoot their arrows aloft, but absolute concern over their own safety drove them on and the shafts flew wide of their marks.

Thelda screamed.

Seg cursed. He drew, let fly, and his shaft hurtled true to bury itself in the body of one of the aerial attackers.

Even as the screech rang out and the great body pitched from the sky my own shaft winged its way to its mark.

At once Seg and I were in action. All about us beat the massive pinions of the impiters, shining and heavy, feather-flurried in the wind of their smiting. We dodged and ducked and avoided the flung javelin and the loosed shaft. In return our own shafts plunged home in wing and belly, in breast and head. I saw three of the barbaric riders shriek and topple from their high saddles, to swing wildly from restraining straps as their mounts struggled to stay aloft.

"Your back, Dray!"

Delia's voice.

I swung about and ducked and saw the monstrous talons graze past my head. They swerved with the swaying of the impiter's body and closed about the head and shoulders of a man upon a nactrix and dragged him screaming upward. Seg loosed and a blast of air from a slashing wing deflected his shaft. I saw another swooping flying-monster, and the creature upon its back, vicious, with narrow-set eyes and square clamped mouth, whose hair floated freely aft of his blunt head in a waving mane, dyed all a brilliant indigo. I saw the maleficent glare in those close-set eyes and I dodged the flung javelin, seizing it as it spun past in the empty air, and reversing it and hurling it back so that its flint head smashed into the leem-skin pelt and copper and bronze ornaments on the man's chest. The impiter swerved away, but I saw its rider jerk and open that square mouth and cough a bright stream of his life's blood.

A nactrix trailing its intestines galloped madly past. Its rider fell sprawling at my feet, and I bent and lifted him as an arrow feathered into the grass beside us. His young, pale face sheened with sweat; one eye was closed and swelling purple-black and his fiery-red hair clotted into a great wound across his scalp.

"Take your sword and fight them off!" I said, twisting him upright.

His eyes widened and the horrified look of absolute panic on his face creased away into the semblance of sanity amid an insane world. He drew his sword — a toothpick compared with the great long swords worn by Seg and myself — and put himself into something of the stance of a fighting-man.

Thelda was still screaming.

I saw Seg loose three arrows so fast that all were in flight together before all three smote their targets, and three more of the indigo-haired aerial attackers shrieked and slumped in their flying straps.

My own bow sang and another square-mouthed man astride his impiter sagged back, and, writhing horribly, slid down and under his mount's neck so that its wings smashed remorselessly into his body as it sought to struggle upward.

Around us the sward was splashed with blood, nactrixes lay dead, with the bodies of their riders; but the young man whom I had forcibly pushed back from the pit of madness waved his sword, his red hair bright under the morning suns, and shouted brave, silly, vain words of defiance.

Seg gasped and loosed again and an impiter in its flight went straight on, with extended wings, straight on into the ground with the arrow imbedded through its eye into its brain.

I started across to deal with the rider, who leaped free very nimbly, and drew a long and thin sword. His leem pelt glowed with the dyes lavished upon it, his bronze buckles and buttons burnished to a blazing brilliance blinded me in the brilliant suns-shine. Still with my longbow in my left hand I drew my long sword with my right. He faced me most determinedly, aware that he had only to fight me off to be saved by his companions. Over his shoulder I saw one of his comrades shake the reins of his flying beast, drive in his leather-wrapped legs and feet, and wheel that monstrous bulk toward me, and I prepared myself to face two enemies at once.

"Hai!" yelled my man on the ground, and charged.

Meeting his blade with a solid shock, I caught that sliver of fine steel, looped it around, and thrust and with the thrust went on with my lunge, doubling up and jerking the brand free from his belly, doubling up and rolling over on the ground. I felt the beat of immense wings and felt the cold downrush of air. Almost, I made it; but a raking talon smashed searingly down my side, knocking the breath from my lungs and sending gouts of racking pain through me.

I could understand and deal with pain. I staggered up, gasping for air, still clutching my sword, and turned to see Delia being whisked aloft in the cruel clutching talons of an impiter.

I shouted — something, I know not what — as I saw my Delia being whipped up. The attackers were retreating now, unwilling to lose more men to these merciless foemen below. Then, from somewhere, a blow sledged down on my head and I pitched forward into the bloodied grass.

I rolled over sluggishly. Then I could not move. I lay there, seeing Seg topple as a last flung javelin bounced from his leg. I lay there and watched that accursed impiter as it sailed away bearing my Delia fast-clenched in its claws. The thing upon its back waved its spear and screeched in a high mocking crow of victory and revenge.

My Delia was gone, snatched away by as vile and merciless a being as any I had seen. Lost and gone, my Delia of Delphond, lost and gone…With the blackness that closed over me closed also complete and utter despair.

Eleven

Assassins in the corthdrome

The performance of *Sooten and Her Twelve Suitors* presented in the covered theater aroused intense enthusiasm from the audience, and although I quite admired this tragedy known almost over the entire Kregen world of culture, the action irritated me, the words seemed trite, the melodious phrases mere cant. The crack on my skull had healed with the customary rapidity of wounds inflicted on my carcass, a useful by-product of my immersion in the pool of baptism of the River Zelph that had given me the promise of a thousand years of life.

But of what use or goodness or value were a thousand years if my Delia of the Blue Mountains was not there to share them with me?

A kind of psychic numbness had overtaken me. Seg had been wounded, also, and was being nursed back to health and strength in this city of Hiclantung, which he appeared to regard in much the same way as a denizen of my own time living in a remote corner of Cornwall would regard a recreation of Chaucer's London. As for Thelda, I had to resort to lies and trickery to obtain some respite from her constant lamentations and protestations and tears. At this moment she was under the impression I was lying fast asleep in the apartments given over to our use in the villa of red brick and white stone situated on a southern declivity of the city just a comfortable ten murs' walk within the walls. Sooten, in her interminable trickeries of the clamoring suitors — something, I fear, of a Kregan Penelope — wearied me in my numb and dissociated mood. All savagery and wild anger had shriveled. Without Delia the whole universe meant nothing.

If you marvel that we, three friendless wanderers, had so fallen on our feet as to have a comfortable villa in the Loh style given over to our use, I can remember my feelings then. The young man I had snapped into a semblance of sanity had, as was clearly evident from his trappings and hauteur, a high post in the army of Hiclantung. Young Hwang — for such was his name with the very necessary additions of many sonorous titles and ranks and indications of estate-holdings — was the nephew of the Queen of the city, and although we had made her acquaintance in the most formal of ways she yet remained a stranger to us. Yet, it was she who in gratitude had given orders that we were to be well-treated.

Seg had wrinkled up his nose about this Queen, but he refused to comment when Thelda chided him.

There is no real coincidence in this train of events. Any fighting-man knows that on an open battlefield if he renders some distinguished service to a man dressed in brilliant uniform or otherwise marked for a man of distinction, then the gratitude of the powerful can be expected — *ceteris paribus* — and he may expect to benefit from that action. We had saved the Queen's nephew. So we were rewarded.

I would gladly have consigned all the Queen's nephews in the whole of Kregen to the Ice Floes of Sicce to have my Delia back.

A hand touched my arm.

"You are bored with the entertainment, Dray Prescot?"

"I know the piece well, Hwang, and admire the dexterity of construction — after all, I am told there are fragments of this play extant on clay tablets dating from five thousand years ago. But no; it's not the play. I am at fault."

Hwang, despite his somewhat foppish manner and his desperate loss of identity on a battlefield, was nonetheless for that a fine young man from whom something better than average might be made given the lad was conceded a chance. Now he laughed and said: "I can show you more full-blooded sport if you wish."

I had declined this sort of offer before in Zenicce, and so I said, simply: "I thank you; but no. I will walk a while."

Outside the covered theater the largest moon of Kregen — the maiden with the many smiles — sailed clear of clouds. The whole city lay floating in pink moonlight. Presently the two second moons would rise, eternally orbiting each other, the twins, to add their luster to the scene. As we walked along in this tide of radiance dark figures detached themselves from shadowy alcoves and fell in to our rear. Young Hwang's bodyguard, provided by the Queen, an insurance that her line would continue, and an infernal nuisance to a man like myself who wanted to be alone.

Every house and building in Hiclantung possessed a roof which stoppered the night air, every roof-garden had its sliding ceiling panels, and they were unfailingly closed each night. Over the roofs thin strong wires stretched, wires patiently drawn by hand and forged and hammered hour after hour. Metal spikes projected in serrated and ugly fans at every vantage point of cornice and ledge. All the architecture had been designed to offer no single vantage point unprotected. Tall and thin columnar towers rose everywhere, and at their summits they broadened like tulips into minor fortresses with pointed roofs — tulip-shaped, onion-shaped, domed and spired, but never flat. No canopies with gilt-spearheaded posts projected with their awnings, as were everywhere visible in the other cities I had visited. Nothing was provided that could offer a perch.

"The dancing girls at Shling-feraeo are exceptionally fine," said Hwang. I was well aware that he had not yet summed me up; he didn't yet know what to make of me. Had I cared what he thought or did not think of me I still would not have bothered to worry over his enlightenment.

"Thank you, Hwang. But dancing girls, no matter how fine, do not suit my mood this night."

Under that moon-glow Hwang's red hair gleamed a curious color, rich and thick and curled. He was a good-hearted young fellow, I thought, amazingly friendly given the circumstances of his upbringing. He would benefit from a season or two with Hap Loder and my Clansmen of Felschraung out on the Great Plains of Segesthes.

He it was who had filled in the background picture of this city, this anachronism, this civilized survivor in a wilderness of barbarity. When the great empire carved out by Walfarg had fallen through dissension at home in Loh, here, in eastern Turismond, the cities had drawn their own culture tightly about them and resisted to their best the invaders from the north, away past the northern outskirts of The Stratemsk. Some had fallen and were now mere shells, inhabited by leem and plains-wolves and risslaca. Others had survived as cities but were now the homes of barbarians, of beast-men and half-men. And yet — some, some had retained all their old Lohvian culture and civilization and went on their own paths as cities and city-states, islands of light amid a sea of darkness.

Of Loh, they now knew nothing.

Legends and fables, garbled histories, and the occasional venturesome traveler alone provided any link with their ancient homeland.

I could foresee that both Vallia and Pandahem, the new, lusty, sprawlingly-vigorous powers establishing themselves on the eastern coast, would not find this country easy, their penetration a mere matter of barter and sword.

Hwang, to do him justice, tried to jolly me out of this mood of black depression.

"If not dancing girls, then come with me to the nactrix stables. I have had to buy fresh mounts—" He stopped talking, and coughed. I knew well enough why he was forced to buy fresh nactrixes.

"I thank you, Hwang — but—"

He halted me with an upraised hand. His bodyguard froze behind us in the shadows.

Living was an everyday precious affair for the Lohvians of Hiclantung; they valued continued existence, always struggling against the seas of barbarism beating upon their ancient walls. These robes we wore now, old but finely woven and superbly maintained, were a part of that tradition. Loh had withdrawn and there was no way home for these people through the Hostile Territories occupied by beast and barbarian — even had they wished to leave their own homes and hearths. So I was not as hard on young Hwang as I might have been. No other thoughts had much place in my skull at that time except agonized fears and mocking, now they were gone, memories of Delia of Delphond.

"Then," said Hwang with youthful force, "we will go to see the corths that rascal Nath is trying to sell me."

I perked up at once; then reality supervened. Nath is a common name on Kregen — already in my life at this time there had been Nath the Thief from Zenicce, and my old oar comrade Nath of Sanurkazz, and I was to meet more.

This Nath was a fat but jolly man with a stub-nose and liquid eyes and a kind of loosely-rolled turban that slanted down over one ear in which a whole pagoda-like construct swung dwarfing any normal earring. His robes were new, embroidered in the Lohvian way with serpentine risslaca and orchids twining with the moon-blooms, and his slippers — to my intense disappointment — were mere plain squat-ended herring-boxes. He should have worn slippers flaunting extraordinarily long and up-curled points.

"Lahal, Dray Prescot," he said, when what passed for pappattu had been made

— I did not have to fight him or give him obi as was customary on other portions, equally civilized, of Kregen — and he rolled his girth around and resumed his seat on a pile of trappings, cushions, gear, and flying silks. Hwang was already inspecting the corths, all securely chained up by wing and leg to their perches, beneath the arched roof of the corthdrome.

"A couple are to my liking, Nath," he said, without any attempt at bargaining. They began to talk prices, and I wandered across to take a closer look at the representatives of the flying monsters who had menaced our flight through The Stratemsk.

The corth is a truer bird than the impiter, although not as large or fierce — I believe that only two other flying animals of Kregen better the impiter — and in general will carry no more than two passengers. These birds possessed the large round eyes, the sleek feathered heads, the deep chests and wide wings of faithful fliers, their legs short and sturdy and varying as to the amount of feather-covering in different species. Now they shifted from side to side and cocked their heads to stare at me first down one side of their beaks and then the other. In color they ranged through the spectrum, with patterns of variegated feathers lending a powerful beauty to their forms. Compared to the fanged and whip-tailed impiters with their coal-black plumage, the corths were indeed beautiful.

On a question from me, Nath laughed so that his array of chins and stomachs shook. "Oh dear me, no! We would not allow our beautiful corths to perch on a bar outside our windows! Why — the barbarians would simply dive on them and kill them and then they would have the perch on which to land freely provided for them. We make it difficult for fliers to land in Hiclantung."

"I had noticed."

The corthdrome had been built at the summit of a high building on one of the hills of the city, on the southern declivity of which our villa lay. I thought of Seg, slowly recovering, of Thelda, keeping as she thought a vigilant night-time watch over my sick bed. They were good comrades. When we quitted the place, to Nath the Corthman's wheezy: "Remberee, Dray Prescot!" and the chinkling of the fresh golden coin in his wallet, I was ready to turn in.

Hwang held me back. His face tautened. Looking down the long flight of stairs that led to the street, each section of twenty treads with a separate side wall looped for arrow-slits, I saw a body of armed men climbing the white stone that glimmered duskily pink and purple in the moons-light, for the twins were now wheeling across the sky after the maiden with many smiles.

Hwang suddenly laughed softly and I was aware of the rapid putting away of the longbows in the hands of his bodyguard.

The two parties met

"You are abroad late, Hwang."

"Yes, Majestrix." Hwang inclined. They inclined in Zenicce, and I had never liked the custom, so, as before, I merely bowed. Queen Lilah of Hiclantung looked upon me, there in the fuzzy pink moonlight.

"It seems I have pierced two impiters with a single shaft. I came to haggle for corths from that fat corthman Nath, and now I find the pleasure of meeting you,

Dray Prescot. I had planned a more formal meeting, for I fear I have not thanked you enough for saving the miserable skin of my foolish nephew."

Against that kind of polite nonsense, a plain sea officer and a fighting-man is usually out of his depth. I merely bowed again and said: "The pleasure is mine, I assure you."

How long the inanities would have gone I do not know. This Queen Lilah stood very tall, her dark eyes on a level with my own brown ones, and her red hair had been coiffed into a high pile resplendent with gems and strings of pearls. Her dark blue gown, thickly embroidered and stiff with bullion and gold and silver threads, gave no hint of her figure; but her face was very white, unlined, her eyes picked out with kohl and her mouth painted into a cupid's bow of allure. She gazed at me most intently as we spoke, and I gathered something of her power and her majesty, the immediate response she could always elicit, for that pallid face tinged with the pink radiance from the moons of Kregen and those darkly glittering eyes held a kind of hypnotic power, emphasized by the shadowing beneath her cheeks and the upslanted eyebrows, the widow's peak of red hair over her forehead.

A man with her, elegant in dark green robes — dark green! — and with a powerful bearded face and eloquent hands adorned with many rings on the carefully tended fingers, was speaking of the lack of news of the scouts sent out to track the destination of the flying tribe who had so sorely bested the Hiclantung army and carried off Delia.

"But in a day or two they will return," said this man, one Orpus, a councilor high in the Queen's confidence. "Then we will know what to do."

"I doubt not but they were employed by those rasts of Chersonang. Soon, now, our plans will be ready and then—" The Queen did not finish her words, and the inanities might have turned into some conversation more welcome to my ears, for Chersonang was a city-state of great power whose borders marched with those of Hiclantung and with whom, as was to be expected, there was constant friction, had it not been for the sudden and wholly unexpected slaughter caused by a shower of arrows that whistled down about our ears.

At the same instant a body of men in dark garments rushed upon us. The next second I was fighting for my life.

"Stand firm!" roared a Hikdar and went down screeching with a cloth-yard shaft in his breast. An arrow hissed by me and buried itself in the back of a bodyguard who had swung around to face the oncoming assassins. Hwang was yelling and tugging at the Queen's sleeve. I saw her face, pale and pinkly-illuminated in that streaming radiance, and she looked firm and powerful, and yet haggard and ill, all at the same time. And, too, I saw the harsh lines curving about that painted mouth and understood more of the burdens she carried and the absolute intolerance with which she carried out what she conceived of as her duty.

Then, to what must have appeared as the seal of our doom to those attacking us, a cloud of impiter-mounted men swooped from the sky and gusting in over the walled stairway fell upon us with all the impetuosity of a chunkrah charge.

If we were to come out of this alive not a moment could be lost. Hwang had still not budged the Queen, who stood, tall and straight in those heavy brocaded garments. Her bodyguard fell about her, and now it was clearly apparent that these night raiders had planned this assault to carry off the Queen.

"The Queen!" someone shouted.

"To the death!" screeched the defiant answers from the bodyguard.

Hwang's little sword flickered in and out very expertly. My own great long sword, suddenly clumsy in this civilized company, swept away three of the attackers, lopped heads and arms; but they pressed me back and soon Hwang and I were left isolated with the Queen at our backs, pressed against the stairway wall.

I felt cramped in, hemmed and penned. I had not used a rapier and main-gauche as a pair in a long time, the Jiktar and the Hikdar, and all the advantages of a long sword were being lost to me.

"We must break through and reach the corthdrome," I shouted at Hwang. If only Seg were here! I felled a man who lunged at me, skipping aside from his glittering point with accustomed unthinking skill. "You must force the Queen—"

'They will never take me alive."

Queen Lilah of Hiclantung held a dagger, jeweled and ornate, but needle-sharp for all that. I knew that dagger would plunge into her breast when the end came. Somehow, in my agony for my Delia I found a strange sense of outrage that another beautiful woman should die.

I leaped forward, whirling my sword in tremendous overhand circles, rather in the fashion of the Clansmen of Viktrik with the Danish ax, and cleared a space in which the ghastly slashed trunks and sliced heads of my opponents sank down bloodily. Moving now very rapidly, even for me, I scooped up Queen Lilah, hoisted her under my left arm, and with a great yell to Hwang to follow, bounded up the stairway.

Two, three, four of the dark-clad assassins I slew as I raced up the steps. I forced my breathing to fall into that old familiar regular rhythm. The only thing that would stop me now would be an arrow through the spine. Even then, such was my wrath, that I believe I would have reached the lofty doors of the corth-drome with a quiver-full of arrows feathering in my back.

Just as we reached those arched doorways a figure scuttled out and the doors began to close. In seconds they would slam in our faces. From below us on the wide stairway the beast yells lifted and the rapid patter of feet and the clink of steel eloquently told of what fate lay in store for us there.

I let rip with a furious, atavistic, enraged yell and bounded up the last flight, shoved my shoulder against those closing valves, and thrust vigorously.

A frightened squeak answered from within, and then we were through and Nath the Corthman and three or four of his stable slaves were pushing frantically at the doors again. Hwang pitched in to help them.

"Put me down, you great oaf!"

I had forgotten the Queen, bundled up under my arm. As I set her on her feet, she called out in her most imperial way: "The bar, you fools! Put the bar across! By Hlo-Hli — hurry!"

Nath the Corthman was dancing around and wringing his hands and sobbing.

"My beautiful corths! These barbarian beasts will take them all, or slay them, my flying wonders of the sky!"

"Cease your babbling, cramph, or I will nick your ears!"

Nath bobbed and bowed before the Queen as we struggled to close the doors, our feet slipping on the tessellated paving, our muscles bulging, our breaths clogging in our throats.

Flint-headed spears thrust through the slit opening between the two valves. Arrows flew through. We could hear the yelling outside, the whip-like crack of orders, and hear the bestial grunting of the assassins as they sought to thrust the doors wide and rush in upon us.

Behind us the corths, whose unease manifested itself in a great whistling chirruping, had now begun to emit their strange feathery-dusty odor. I glanced up. Long before we could unchain a corth and open the ceiling valves, which drew back in segments, the assassins would have completed their work.

As we surged against the doors Queen Lilah stood back from us, tall and regal, her embroidered robes falling in sheer lines to her feet, her face as waxy white as a votive candle, the dagger in her hand catching the light from torches in their wall brackets and splintering strange and disturbing colors over the scene.

"The defense wires had been removed from this stairway," she said. Her voice cracked as flat and hard as a falchion blade. "There were men waiting in hiding. Oh, Orpus, unhappy man! If you have survived it were better had you not!"

If the high councilor had been a party to the plot then he wouldn't hang around Hiclantung; if he had not been then he would be lying on the stairway weltering in his own blood.

The doors groaned as weights thrust unequally against them. Their bronze hinges squealed. Slowly, the stable slaves and Hwang and I were being thrust back. It was a mere matter of moments before the murderers broke in.

All my natural instincts urged me to fling wide the doors and with my sword in my fist to hurl myself upon these beast-men.

Such a course — which is deplorable in itself — often seems to me the most natural one in two worlds in circumstances like those when I fought the assassins in the corthdrome of Hiclantung. I can wait for an attacker to expose himself and then counter-strike. I can charge headlong and carry the fight to him. But now — such a course would mean the inevitable deaths of Hwang and Queen Lilah. I glanced back at the torchlit interior of the corthdrome.

Beyond the ranked perches where the corths whistled and shrilled and ruffled their feathers beneath the arched roof a narrow stair ran winding around the interior wall. At its summit a narrow door of lenk wood gave ingress to the windlass room, where were situated the necessary drums and levers and apparatus for opening the roof. I shouted at Hwang.

"Hwang! Do not argue! Take the Queen up there — at once!"

Before Hwang could reply she had stamped her foot and rejected the suggestion in an icy manner of high hauteur.

"If you do not go, Lilah," I said, "I shall put you under my arm again, and this time I shall beat you."

"You would not dare!" Her eyes flamed at me. "I am the Queen!"

"Aye— and you'll be a dead Queen, by Zim-Zair, if you don't do as I say! Now *go!*"

She looked at my face in the vivid light of the torches and I must have been wearing that old ugly look of demoniac power that transfigures my features into a devil's mask, for she shuddered and turned away.

"Go!"

With what I took to be either a curse or a sob she lifted the heavy brocaded hem of her robe and I saw her slippered feet twinkling as she ran across the floor between the perches and started on the lung-bursting climb.

"After her, Hwang!"

"But you!"

"If I am to die, then this is as well a way to go as any other." I shooed him away and the doors squealed as they opened further. To the stable slaves in their gray slave breechclouts I said: "When I give you leave — run! Hide! These evil men do not desire to kill you!"

"Aye, master," they wailed, thrusting with their lean naked arms, the sweat running down their lined faces.

I stripped off the gorgeous Lohvian robes with their rich and encumbering embroidery. Against a long sword the cloth mass I bundled around my left arm would be useless, but these flying men used long and thin swords — not rapiers — and I could perhaps deflect them enough to strike back. From a natural nostalgia I had selected a brilliant scarlet loincloth and I own I felt a thrill of the old pride in the color nerve me — vain young words and feelings, to my shame!

Also, I kicked off the elegant sandals provided by my Lohvian hosts in Hiclantung. The long swords we had picked up here and there on our travels had not been the great long sword of the Krozairs — but Zenkiren had graciously given me a real Krozair long sword when we had parted in Pattelonia. Its handle was a full four fists' width in length, perfectly balanced for single-handed work, deadly when counterpoised by the left fist beneath the pommel with all that leverage that could be exerted. It was, perhaps, when wielded by a practiced and expert two-handed swordsman even faster than a single-hander — I knew this, yet I needed some protection for my left arm initially, and I could wield the sword two-handed even with the embroidered cloth bundled about my left arm.

"Now — go!"

With frightened shrieks the stable slaves scampered away from the doors and vanished into the shadows.

I poised, ready, and I felt the night breeze upon my naked chest and thighs, the floor hard and firm beneath my feet, the grip of the Krozair sword in my fist.

Yes — my Delia, my Delia of the Blue Mountains — if I was to die then this was the way I would go.

The doors smashed back.

Like an indigo tide the assassins poured in and I met them headlong, with a bestial roar that stopped them in their tracks. I was among them, smiting, thrusting, before they were aware, and they recoiled as though from some inhuman monster of legend.

331

"Hai!" I roared, leaping and slashing. "Hai, Jikai!"

We were too close-packed for them to bring the mighty Lohvian longbows into action. I swung the sword in economical strokes now, aiming for targets, smiting them to the ground. Twice I was able to wrest the thin sword from the grip of a surprised man, and, leaping forward, grasp him about the throat with my left hand and, after throttling him, hurl him back among his fellows.

How long I might have gone on thus I do not know. Not forever, that is certain. But then I heard a high-pitched, cracking voice from the interior of the corth-drome.

"Dray!"

And I knew Hwang and the Queen had reached the door to the windlass room.

For an exit I surged into the nearest man, hoisted him over my head, flung him horizontally into the men jostling to get in through the doors over the bloodied bodies of their comrades. Swiftly, then, for I did not relish this part, I turned and ran. I, Dray Prescot, Lord of Strombor, turned and ran. But I ran with a set purpose. I reached the foot of the stairs before they had recovered and I went up in gigantic leaping strides that must surely have confused those men of Kregen who had never witnessed an Earthman's muscles exerting their full power against the fractionally weaker gravity of their planet. Halfway up I judged to be the moment of danger, and a yell from Hwang from above confirmed that.

I swung about, the Krozair sword lifted, and I beat away the arrows as we used to do in those strict and demanding disciplines on the island of Zy in the Eye of the World.

Up again, and a turn, and more arrows to be dodged or beaten away with sword or robes, and up yet again.

Now the indigo-haired men were at the foot of the stairs and were racing up, their swords slivers of steely glitter in the torchlight. They wanted the Queen; they would dare anything for that end.

At the top I struck sideways an arrow that would have found Hwang, and then we were through the small lenk door.

I slammed it and barred it. I breathed deeply and easily, aware of the sweat shining on my chest and thighs, runneling down between the ridged muscles. Blood dripped thickly from my sword and gobbets and gouts of it matted the hair on my chest.

"You—" stammered Queen Lilah of Hiclantung.

A new and stronger roaring began outside the barred door and the first few blows upon its stout lenk wood were the only ones. We could hear, distantly, the shouting of men and the clash of steel.

"The guards!" exclaimed Hwang. His face radiated a fresh and sudden confidence. "We are saved!"

I grunted.

I put my hand to the bar.

Queen Lilah stood, and I could see the heaving tumult of her bosom thrusting now against the concealing stiff brocade. "Dray—" she began, then, again: "Dray Prescot?"

I looked at her, eyes on a level with eyes.

"You have witnessed what few have ever seen," I told her, unaware then of the irony of it. "You have seen Dray Prescot run from his foes. Now I go back to settle with them."

Of course — that evil and fascinating blood fever was upon me then.

I lifted the bar.

She put a small white hand on my arm.

"No, Dray Prescot. There is no need. The guards will deal with those rasts of assassins. But — I would not wish you wounded now, perhaps killed."

"You would have me skulk behind a locked door?"

She shook her head angrily, her dark eyes filled with a reflected torchlight that made of them a dazzlement and a glory.

"I would have you live, Dray Prescot — and do not forget, I am the Queen! My word is law! You would do well not to cross me, Dray Prescot — stranger!"

"I agree — and I would do even better to obey my own wishes!"

And I lifted the bar and opened the door and ran down the stairs.

Twelve

The Queen of Pain

"Oh, Dray Prescot!" said Thelda. "I just don't know what I'm going to do with you!"

We stood in the sunny morning room of the villa and Thelda regarded me with her head on one side, her ripe red lips pursed up and her hands on her hips. She wore a scarlet — because she thought that would please me — breechclout and a simple silvery-tissue blouse that was as near as made no difference to being transparent. Her dark brown hair had been meticulously coiffed by one of the house slaves we had been obligated to accept — we had no powers to free them, as Seg and I would have instantly done — and the lush coils sparkled with gems and pearls. Her fingernails and toe-nails had been lacquered a pleasant scarlet. Her face received such care and attention as it had surely never known since leaving Vallia. She did look alluring and lovely and voluptuous, no question of it, now that her fat had been worked off and the natural firm and Junoesque lines of her figure could be seen. She stood with her legs braced, her hands on her hips, and she regarded me as a risslaca regards a rabbit.

"You, Dray Prescot, recovering from a terrible wound, go slallyfanting about the city at the dead of night — getting into fights — rescuing the Queen — oh, Dray — look out for her! She is a deep and devious one. I know, for Seg has told me of the notorious Queens of Loh—"

"I know," I said. "I have heard. They call her the Queen of Pain. But only when she cannot overhear them."

"They were terrible — the Queens of Loh! The things they did turned my stomach over when Seg merely hinted at them. And this one is right in the line. I wouldn't like to inquire into just how many husbands — husbands! That's a laugh! — how many poor silly believing men she's toyed with and discarded and had tortured to death..."

"Thelda! It's you who are slallyfanting, not me."

"But surely you can see why I am so worried about you, Dray!"

"No. And, anyway, since the Walfarg empire crumpled Loh has left only some of its culture behind here — why, the women don't wear veils, as they do in their mysterious walled gardens of Loh."

"You have been to Loh, Dray?"

"No. But I have heard of it—"

She was standing straight and firm, but now she seemed to melt and flow, the tenseness leaving her thighs and calves, her shoulders, and she bent and flowed and moved against me so that she pressed into my chest. I was wearing a plain white loincloth, having come straight from the bath, with my hair still wet, and I could feel the warmth of her through the silver tissue. Quite evidently she expected me to put my arms about her as she put hers about me, tilting her head to gaze up at me, her lips half parted, moist and clinging in that way that can madden almost any man of sensibility. I kept my arms away from her.

"Oh, you fond, silly, silly man! Don't you know why I worry so over you, so that my heart seems to burst right out of my bosom?" She unclasped one hand, and grasped my fingers. "Feel my heart, Dray, and you will know how passionately it beats—"

I had had enough of this. I simply didn't let my arm bend in, and I said, gently: "I think Seg is up and about. His wound mends well—"

She flounced away, her lips plainly wanting to rick into a snarl and yet forced by a will I was coming to recognize to curve into a fetching pout.

"It is no good thinking of Delia, Dray—"

"What?"

She wouldn't be checked now.

"Why — didn't you see? I thought you knew—"

I was at her side and I gripped her by the shoulders, crumpling the silver tissue, dragging her half upward so that she staggered up onto her toes. I glared down on her upturned face where now that silly pouting look vanished to be replaced by a sudden startlement.

"Knew what, Thelda?"

She gasped as my fingers dug into her shoulders.

"Dray — you're hurting—"

I let her down, but I still held her hard.

"Tell me!"

"Delia — the Princess Majestrix — the impiter dropped her, Dray — I thought you knew! It dropped her into a pond — you know, one of the little tarns that you find all over the uplands — and I screamed — why did you think I was screaming, Dray, for myself?" She wriggled and licked her lips. "I knew Delia was dead, and I was screaming in fear for you, Dray!"

334

I let her drop so that she went down in a flurry of silver tissue with the brave scarlet breechclout sprawling in an ungainly back-slide, and turned away, and Seg said: "I did not see Delia fall from the impiter! By the veiled Froyvil — she cannot be dead! It would not be allowed!"

He came into the room with most of his old reckless air still about him; his limp had almost gone. He was better, he was the old Seg again, with the reckless laugh and the damn-you-to-hell manner.

"No," I said, my voice a croak. "No — it would be unthinkable — it could not be allowed. My Delia, she is not dead—" I swung to Thelda, who raised herself on her arms, the silver tissue bulging and crumpling with the force of her breathing. "What tarn was it, Thelda? I will go to this pond and see for myself!"

Nothing would stop me.

When Hwang pointed out the dangers, that travel between cities anywhere in this land was beset with peril, that the winged host might still be in the vicinity, that wild beasts would rend me, I brushed all that tomfoolery aside. I donned my scarlet breechclout, buckled on my long sword, and I found a blanket roll, and some odd items of food. I took my new longbow in my hand, slung the quiver over my shoulders, mounted a borrowed nactrix, and I was off.

As I had expected Seg soon spurred up to ride at my side.

By the time we had ridden back over that ground and found the site of the battle — massacre, really — where the bones lay white and bleaching under the suns of Scorpio, Hwang and a regiment of his own cavalry were hard on our heels. I had heard from the Queen's nephew something of the reasons for that disastrous battle in the valley; that the men cherished their traditions and fought in disciplined bodies held together by rules sacrosanct with age. That the treacherous councilor Forpacheng — and not Orpus whom the Queen had suspected and who had miraculously escaped the ambush on the stairway — had led the troops into the valley, and had then let them be cut to pieces. That the discipline had broken under Forpacheng's malicious and contradictory orders. Now, Hwang had said, a new army was being forged from the remnants and new recruits, and they would not repeat the mistakes of the past.

The pool lay black and ominous beneath the suns.

I dived. I dived and swam beneath the water until my lungs burned and all the suns of the universe flamed before my eyes; I did not find my Delia.

Memories of that time blur. I remember men talking to me and urging me not to continue; and of myself taking deep agonizing breaths and cleaving the dark water of the tarn and swimming, swimming, swimming, and always that nightmarish expectancy that my groping hands would close on the obscenely bloated, water-logged, half eaten body of my Delia of Delphond.

Exhaustion had no place in my scheme of things. I would search every single square inch of the bottom of the pool, and every cubic inch of its water; and if I did not find my Delia, then I would begin all over again. I did not want to find her there, God knows; but I did not want to leave the task unfinished and be haunted for the rest of my days.

Perhaps, in the end, I was only saved from insanity by the arrival of Orpus and more soldiers. They seemed to my dulled senses smart enough, Zair knows. With them rode a man whose hair was dyed a deep indigo.

I reared up and from somewhere my long sword was in my fist and I started for this man with the indigo hair and I heard Seg shout and his hand gripped my arm.

"No, no, Dray! He is of Hiclantung — his hair is dyed because he has been scouting—"

"A spy," I said stupidly.

"Yes, yes — and listen! He believes he has found where Delia is held captive!"

When I had somewhat recovered my senses and the news had been expounded, my next step was obvious.

The name I now focused on with an intensity of purpose at once hateful and vengeful and obsessional was — Umgar Stro.

The spy, one Naghan, a common name on Kregen, had been clever; clearly he was a courageous and resourceful man. Charged with the task of discovering who had instigated the nighttime attack upon the Queen he had begun by making inquiries in Chersonang, the rival city-state of Hiclantung, only to discover that the whole political situation had changed. A new force had entered this area of the Hostile Territories. From far to the northwest a fresh barbarian horde had swung southward as they had done when the empire of Walfarg in Loh had fallen. From the windy heights past The Stratemsk they had flown astride their impiters and corths and zizils, intent on carving a new land for themselves. They had taken over a country inhabited by Rapas, killing the vulturine people by the thousand, installing themselves as overlords. And here their leader, this Umgar Stro, had suborned and paid the traitor Forpacheng. But now — Umgar Stro had announced his intentions of dominating the entire section of nations centering on his new capital of Plicla, that had once been Rapa, and then of taking over the whole of the Hostile Territories, and the eastern seaboard with its scattering of settlements of nations of the outer ocean, and, so he had said, boldly, he would also march across The Stratemsk and attack whatever lay beyond.

Of course, the inner sea, the Eye of the World, was unknown to these people except in the vaguest of myth and legend.

"And Delia is held in a tower in Plicla. May the veiled Froyvil guard her and keep her from harm!"

"You are sure?" I asked Naghan as Seg's anxious words died.

"I cannot be certain that the girl captured is the princess you seek," said Naghan, omitting all forms of ceremonial or obsequious address. "I never saw her." He was short and strong, with a faded look around his eyes. He had built his face up into a blunt profile with oiled clays, but no one would think him one of Umgar Stro's half-men in any kind of decent light. He had taken his life in his hands to bring me this information, and I was grateful to him. "I can give you all the information of the tower you require; externally, that is. Once inside—" He spread his hands.

Umgar Stro.

The whole area between The Stratemsk and the eastern seaboard had been turned into a place containing a very large number of petty kingdoms. The so-called Hostile Territories were places where a series of nations each followed its own destiny. There were tracts where the original inhabitants remained, there were barbarian nomads, there were cities of half-men and beast-men, there were nations of half-civilized barbarians, there were the cities which had managed to retain much of their Lohvian heritage. The whole was a great quilt of conflicting cultures.

Umgar Stro.

With the legacies left by Walfarg — the long well-constructed and surfaced roads, a common currency, the use of arms, a common law that the barbarians naturally disrupted, a religion based on worship of the female principle in life and the interesting ramifications following on that — all these elements of existence held in common had in an ironic way helped rather than hindered the dissolution and conquest of the land by factions. A raiding army could move rapidly down the roads, but they would be exposed to attack at known places by the flying hosts.

Umgar Stro.

"Once I am inside Umgar Stro's tower," I told Naghan, the spy, "I shall be satisfied."

He looked at my face, and turned away, and fidgeted with his sword.

"What is the name of this barbarian nation that flies its impiters against Hiclantung?"

"They come from Ullardrin, somewhere north of The Stratemsk and they are called the Ullars."

"We'll need to fly, Dray," said Seg.

"Yes," I said. "I hear the men of Hiclantung do not really relish flying — the corths are few and far between in the city." This was true. Corth-flying was in the nature of a sport for the nobles and the high councilors; the ordinary people and the soldiers hated all flying beasts, and one could well understand why. Their ancestors had waged ceaseless war against the aerial barbarians, and it still went on today. They had developed effective tricks and weapons they could deploy against impiters and corths and only through Forpacheng's treachery were they deprived of them on the day of the army massacre.

We hurried back to the city.

Thelda with tears and protestations tried to stop me from going. She had seen Delia fall into the tarn and if I went to this dreadful Umgar Stro's high tower I would surely be killed.

There was much to be learned about riding a corth and I put her aside and shouted for Seg. Hwang had insisted on putting his two best birds at our disposal, and we went along to fat Nath the Corthman to find out all we could.

Everyone treated us as though we were mad, and everyone was careful to make full, polite, and emotional Remberee of us before they let us go.

I told Seg I did not want him to accompany me.

He laughed.

"I'll grant I've never seen a swordsman like you, Dray — no, and never likely

337

to! But I know that however good you may be with the longbow, you cannot best me; and bows will be needed, you will see. Consequently, I shall come with you." He stared at me and I warmed to the look on his lean, tanned face, the light of understanding and resolution in his blue eyes, the wild mane of black hair. "And," he said, offhandedly, "I, too, value your Delia Majestrix."

I couldn't speak for a moment, and grasped his hand. I was not fool enough to say what I had been about to say, namely, that I had thought he would welcome the opportunity to stay with Thelda. She had been worrying me, and I wished she would turn to Seg, although I wouldn't have wished her on my comrade for the world — either one — had he not devoutly wished that disaster for himself.

In the confused tangling of politics going on all around me as Queen Lilah sought for strength and allies against the menace of the Ullars, I was conscious only of one objective: I had to reach Umgar Stro's high tower and bring my Delia safely back to me.

I called her "my Delia" and she called me "my Dray" but neither one of us regarded it as selfish possession in thus speaking; rather we recognized we were but halves of a complete whole.

To add to our normal weapons and accouterments we took warm flying furs and silks, extra quivers of arrows, and a couple of heavy flint-headed spears. I packed a complete set of warm clothing for Delia. I had no doubts, now.

That evening I went up to the palace — imposing but, because of the absolute necessity not to allow any perching place for birds or animals, somehow spiritless and without that fantasy of architecture so beloved by the builders of Kregen — to pay my respects to the Queen.

Lilah received me in a small withdrawing room in which the lamps picked out the sumptuous furnishings, the furs and rugs, the weapons on the walls, the leather upholstery and all the crystal wink and glitter, the golden glows and the silver sheen of absolute luxury. The Queen of Pain, men called her, behind their hands. I had heard dark stories about her wayward manner with men; how she used them and tossed them aside. I had met, as I then thought, women of her stamp before. Those fabulous Queens of Loh, notorious, sadistic, cruel, had a devoted disciple in this tall woman with the widow's peak of dark red hair, the upslanting eyebrows, the shaded cheekbones, and the small firm mouth. She welcomed me kindly and we drank purple wine of Hiclantung, and munched palines. She wore a jeweled mesh of clothes so that her white skin gleamed through the interstices. Lovely and desirable she looked; and yet, hard and remote, a true queen with destinies and cares above the mere carnal satisfactions of the flesh. I had the thought that my Delia, however greater an empire she might one day rule, would never take on that hard, polished, ruthless look of despotism.

"You have saved my life, Dray Prescot, and now you rush off to risk that life, precious to me, in the wayward service of another woman."

"Not any woman, Lilah."

"And am I not any woman! I am the Queen — I have told you; my word is law. You flouted my wishes, there in the windlass room of the corthdrome. Many men have died for less."

"Mayhap they have. I do not intend to die for that."

She drew in a breath and the gems about her body winked and flashed in the lamplight. Gracefully she stretched out a white arm and lifted her goblet. The wine stained her lips for an instant, turning them purple and cruel.

"I need a man like you, Dray Prescot. I can give you any thing you desire — as you have seen. Now that the Ullars are forcing themselves on us, I need a fighting-man to lead my regiments. They are well-disciplined, but they do not fight well. The barbarians scorn us."

"Men will fight if they believe in what they fight for."

"I believe in Hiclantung! And I believe in myself!"

I nodded.

"Sit upon my throne alongside me, Dray! I implore you — and there could be a great sweetness between us — more than you can imagine." She was breathing faster now, and her mouth opened with the passions she felt. I — what did I think, then, when every fiber of my being shrieked to be off and away in search of my Delia of the Blue Mountains?

"You honor me, Lilah. Indeed, you are beautiful."

Before I could go on she had thrown herself upon me, her arms were about my neck, and I could feel the gems upon her person pressing into my flesh beneath the white robe I wore. Her mouth, all hot and moist, sought mine. I recoiled.

"Dray!" she moaned. "If I were a true queen I would have had you quartered for what you did! So bold, so reckless, so impious — you defied me, the Queen of Hiclantung. And yet you live and I am prostrate at your feet, imploring you—"

"Please, Lilah!" I managed to disengage, and she slumped to the floor on the gorgeous rugs and stared up lustfully at me. She was breathing in great gasps now, her body convulsed with her own passions. "Please, you are the Queen and a great one. You have wonderful deeds to accomplish for your city, and I will help you — that I swear—"

"You—?"

"I must go to Umgar Stro's tower, Lilah. If I may not do that then I will not do anything else."

She jumped up, her eyes murderous upon me, and I knew that in an instant I might be struck down on that carpet before her, my head rolling and spouting blood over her pretty jeweled naked feet.

She opened her mouth and a palace slave — a pretty girl with the gray slave breechclout edged in gold lace, and a pair of enormous dark eyes that fairly danced in a goggling kind of amazement at the scene within — put her curly head in at the door and started to say: "The Lady Thelda of Vallia—" when she was pushed aside and Thelda marched in.

The tableau held. It held, I confess, until despite all my lack of laughter I wanted to roar my mirth at these two.

For these two were standing up very straight and erect, bosoms jutting, chins up, hands held quiveringly at their sides, their eyes darting and flashing like rapiers crossing, so charged with emotion were these two ladies — and over a hulking great brute of a man with an ugly face and shoulders wide enough to have encompassed the pair of them — a man, moreover, who wanted nothing so much as to be rid of the pair of them and wing into the night to seek his true love.

So much for the tantrums of beauty!

They did not fight, or spit, or scratch — and, indeed, it would have been an overmatched contest — but the danger signals that flashed between them crackled with eloquent if silent rivalries.

Queen Lilah seemed perfectly to accept Thelda's arrival. I suppose she could, if she wished, have tossed us both into some dank dungeon and had us tortured to death, licking her lips over us the while.

As it was, Lilah simply said with devastating regality: "Does this — woman — mean anything to you, Dray?"

The question differed entirely from that question of like meaning put to me by the Princess Natema on her garden rooftop in the Opal Palace of the Esztercari hold in Zenicce. Then I had lied to save my Delia's life. I did not need to lie now to save Thelda's. And yet — she did mean something to me, although not what either she longed for or Lilah suspected.

"I have the highest respect for the Lady Thelda," I said, with crude formality. The image of the night sky and a rushing wind and the tower of Umgar Stro reared into my mind's eye. I could not wait longer. "I hold her in the same deep and cherished affection as I hold your esteemed and regal person, Lilah. No more — and no less."

"Oh — Dray!" The wail could have come from either woman.

"I must go."

I laid my hand on my sword hilt. An almost instinctive gesture, it brought a flush to Lilah's pallid countenance. Such boorish behavior, clearly, was unknown in her civilized palace. Thelda started across and took my arm. She glared haughtily upon the Queen.

"I am responsible for the safe-keeping of my Lord of Strombor," she said. "Now that his betrothed, the Princess Majestrix of Vallia, is dead."

I would not let her say any more. I turned my wrist and took her hand in my own and crushed it, and smiled at Lilah, the Queen, and said firmly but without rancor: "I am eternally in your debt, Lilah, for your goodness to me and my friends. Now I must go to seek out this Umgar Stro and, if necessary, kill him. I believe I am doing you a good favor, Lilah, in doing that, so do not hurt Thelda here or hinder me. I am a good friend — I would not wish you to understand the depth of my enmity."

This was all good fustian staff, but it had its effect.

As though coming to a decision, the Queen nodded, and the stiffness went out of her poise. Her figure was good, if a trifle on the thin side, but this merely added to the regality of her presence. She put a hand to her breast, over her heart, and pressed it in. Distinctly, I saw a gigantic diamond, scintillant and brilliant in the lamplight, cut into her flesh.

Her gasp forced its way past psychic, mental levels of pain completely unknown to her body.

"Very well, Dray Prescot. Wreak your vengeance on Umgar Stro. I shall not forget. I shall be here when you return. Then we will talk more; for what I have spoken to you I sincerely mean."

"I am sure you do."

"As for you, my Lady Thelda, I would advise a more circumspect tongue. Do you understand?"

Before Thelda, whose blood was up, could answer, I dug my fingers into her hand, so that she winced. Then I dragged her off.

Lilah, tall and resplendent in the jeweled lamplight, called after me: "I wish you well, Dray Prescot. Remberee!"

"Remberee, Lilah!" I called back.

As we got outside, Thelda jerked free and spat out: "The female cramph! I could scratch her eyes out!"

Then, and with some bewilderment, I admit, I chuckled.

Thirteen

I go swinging at the tower of Umgar Stro

That image of a dark night and a rushing wind I had experienced in the scented withdrawing room of Lilah's palace had come true.

Seg and I had taken off before the twins — the two second moons of Kregen eternally orbiting each other — had appeared above the horizon and with the maiden of many smiles sinking over the western rim of the world. By her dying light we saw the sleeping city beneath us, all its watchtowers spiring into the sky where restless men kept their long vigils, and only the faint lamp-glow falling from their arrow slits to tell of life within.

We passed over the manufacturing quarters where in the enclosed atrium-style houses the work-people lay asleep, and all the long alleyways between the houses lay silent and deserted beneath the stars. Down there the forge fires softly sloughed away into grayness and cold, the hammers stilled, the bellows silent from their slave-driven wheezing. Bronze and copper and iron for implements and weapons of war, silver and gold and nathium for trinkets and objects of art, all lay quietly in their racks awaiting the morrow's labors, for the Queen maintained her industry at a thriving rate against the tide of barbarism.

Farther off lay the tanners' quarters, and the potters' and the glaziers'; great cities do not exist as mere palaces and villas, streets and temples, without visible means of support. As soon as Genodras flooded down in the morning the gates would open and the country folk, ever-fearful of barbarian raids, would trundle in their carts, pulled by asses or calsanys, or trudge stolidly with great burdens swinging over their shoulders at either end of long supple poles of tuffa wood, all seeking to find the best and most advantageous places within the covered markets to display their produce. The city slept; save for its guardians in their spires and along its walls. On the morrow it would awake to a new day and fresh life, and would thank its pagan female goddesses that it still survived.

I wondered, not without real concern for Seg, if we two would still live to welcome that morrow.

The corths Hwang had provided, not without a deal of cutting sarcasm directed against Nath the Corthman, were docile but sturdy beasts. Their wings beat steadily and we rose and fell in the night air in a strong and soothing rhythm. They were well-trained, as any flying mount for a man must be, and we felt confident that they would do all that we required of them. We rode two and I had attached the long leading rein of the third to my flying saddle. Warmly clad in furs and silks, we lay in a semi-prone position just abaft the birds' heads. We had to be clear of the arc the powerful wings cut in the air. A bird shaped, say, like a falcon or a hawk would be difficult if not impossible to ride; a saddle bird must needs possess a neck of some strength and length if its rider's legs are not to smash catastrophically against its wings.

The sensation of flying thus, of hurtling through the level air, exhilarated me. This was very different from aerial navigation aboard a flier from Havilfar. I began to wonder if we would have stood a better chance of negotiating The Stratemsk astride an aerial monster like the corth, or the impiter which was so much bigger, fiercer, and more powerful.

We winged on our way following the faint glimmer of the road beneath that ran almost straight from Hiclantung. We had been given our instructions — briefed, you would say — and we had no fears of failing to find Plicla, the city of the Rapas that was now the city of Umgar Stro.

Plicla was situated amid a mass of broken hills and dales, good flying country with its updrafts, and yet dangerous with its sudden precipices and vortices of air. The city had been founded by Rapas who had drifted into the area as slaves or mercenaries in the long ago, employed by Loh no less than her foes, and who now had banded together to found their own Rapa nation. Umgar Stro and his Ullars had altered all that.

We saw the high towers, the craggy cliffs supporting the massive walls, with their tops raking for the sky. A suspicious, smelly, unpleasant race, the Rapas, so I thought then, when I was young and new to Kregen and had only unpleasant experience of them to judge them by. Their bird-like faces, their fierce agile ability, made them valued as guards and mercenaries, no less than slaves. I wondered what they would be like as mere citizens of their own city-state.

Natural caution among mercenary-employing nations impelled them to hire mercenaries from many different races. Chuliks, Rapas, Ochs, Fristles — of those I had already met on Kregen — and all the other strange half-men and beast-men I was to encounter, also, when employed by a single government would rest secure in the knowledge that each individual detachment of mercenaries would scarcely ever allow itself to be cozened into a rebellion in association with any other detachment. Mutual suspicion would keep the hired soldiers apart. And no single detachment would of itself be powerful enough to topple the hiring government, when all the others would leap in to combat the first hint of insurrection. In general, then, mercenaries on Kregen can be trusted to earn their hire.

But — there were always the exceptions. And I, Dray Prescot from Earth, took a perverse delight in finding those exceptions and turning them to the general good.

Now Umgar Stro and his Ullars from far Ullardrin with their indigo-dyed hair ruled in Rapa Plicla.

Naghan the spy had given us exact directions.

We could not, of course, converse at the distance apart the wingspread of the corths forced us to fly, and into the teeth of the blustering wind; but at my pointing spear Seg nodded, and we did as we had been taught with the simple reins of the birds and began to glide down.

The tower seemed to grow in size and girth as we floated down to it.

Away to the north we could make out the stone-piled enclosures surrounding the Yerthyr trees to keep out the animals of the city. Seg had reported to me on the quality of the trees of Hiclantung. Wherever we went in our travels it was noticeable how Seg's expert appraising eye dealt with the forestry details. Hiclantung's Yerthyr trees, according to Seg, were excellent and the bows with which we had been furnished brought a smile of delight to Seg's lips.

This first rapid approach was to be a reconnaissance. Our corths, which would never be mistaken for impiter or yuelshi, could no more make a landing on the tower or its battlemented curtain walls on either hand as could one of the Ullars' mounts land on a roof in Hiclantung. The same rules of elementary tactics applied. My corth — a fine fellow with the boldly delineated eye and pigment streaks running from it that distinguish the Earthly cormorant — wheeled with easy power, swooping past the tower and so away again with a giant rustling of wings off into the concealing darkness. A couple of Kregen's lesser moons were in process of hurtling across the nighted sky, but until the twins rose we had the comforting concealment of semidarkness.

I suppose it is a natural part of nature's progress that more than one species should exist simultaneously — many hundreds insure the survival of at least some — and it would have been extraordinary if Kregen had developed through the years only one kind of flying animal or bird. Think of the enormous multitude of birds on Earth, and given the much greater size of the Kregish fliers, partially due, I imagine, to the slightly lessened gravity, it would be unthinkable for only one kind of giant flying animal to exist on Kregen beneath Antares.

The twins would soon roll above the eastern horizon and flood their pinkish light down over the jagged hills and the gaunt towers of Plicla. Seg knew exactly what he had to do, the doing of which as I had ordered being the only reason I had accepted his insistent offer to come along. I knew he would have come, anyway; I just didn't want to get him killed unnecessarily.

I made a sign to him in the wind-rushing darkness and I saw his wild head nod against the starlight.

Swerving my corth back toward the tower of Umgar Stro I began my final preparations. No normal landing was possible. So the abnormal became necessary.

All my old sailor skills surged up afresh as I knotted the leather thongs. The Hiclantung leather was good, even though I considered it not so fine as that of Sanurkazz. The corth's reins were extended in length. From the flying saddle I unwound the already-prepared thongs and dropped them to swing madly in the rushing wind of our flight. At their ends the trapeze and the loops did not look particularly inviting. I took a breath and then unfastened the flying straps and bands that held me to the saddle and slid over the side. My feet kicked wildly for an instant, then I had control and was able to lower myself down until I sat astride the trapeze, my hands in the loops above me and gripping the ends of the long extended reins that ran over crude blocks on the saddle bow.

An overwhelming nostalgic sweep of memory carried me back to my days in Aphrasöe, the city of the Savanti, and to the swingers. How I had joyed then in swinging in wild free hurtling flight from plant to plant! Now I was swinging again — although this time I clung beneath the hooked talons of a giant flying bird and swung not from pleasure but to save the life of the girl I loved.

The cold struck at me shrewdly, but I took no notice.

Umgar Stro's tower seemed to me to swing and sway before my eyes. I fought to make my reeling senses understand that the tower remained still, that it was me, Dray Prescot, swinging so sickeningly. Long practice over the years in straddling out along the topgallant yardarms saved me, then, and I could estimate distance and force my senses to compose themselves.

Seg's corth billowed in from the side, the fingerlike wing-tip feathers altering angles and curvatures as with superb aerial control the great bird matched velocities with my own corth and the led bird. Seg would have to grab the reins of my mount — somehow — and keep it ready for our departure.

The roof of the tower spiked up toward me.

I pulled on the reins gingerly, and the world tilted; then the tower became perpendicular and I could see the fans of cruel iron spikes, the trip wires, the slanting lines of tiling that gave no secure perch anywhere.

I inched forward on the trapeze as the wind bellowed past my head, whipping my hair back, lacerating my eyes and cheeks.

Closer — closer — would the corth never haul up?

At the last moment to the savage jerking of the reins the bird abruptly fluttered his wide vulture-like wingspread. His body reared up into the air exposing his underside, his legs and claws stabbed forward and down. The trapeze hit the tiles with an almighty thump and I pitched off and rolled.

As I rolled and slithered to the sheer drop to the cliffs beneath, the corth, without alighting, fluttered hugely and was airborne. The led corth followed and the two birds wheeled away. I had no time to hope that Seg would catch them.

The lip of the slanted roof was coming up at me with frightening speed. If I went over that there would be nothing anymore — no Delia, no Vallia, no Aphrasöe...

My hand smashed numbingly into an iron fan spike. My fingers curled and gripped without conscious volition. I hung there, spread-eagled on the roof, blatted at by the wind, seeing only the faint star-shot shadows all about me.

After a moment I had breath enough to draw myself up into a posture less exposed. The trapdoor through which inspection parties must come to check the roof defenses opened after I gave it a taste of my long sword. I dropped down, bent-legged, my sword in my fist. Only dust, cobwebs, litter...

From the attic I found the ladder leading below and descended wondering, for the first time, at the silence of this place.

So far the information given me by Naghan, the spy, had proved correct. But he had not penetrated here. From now on I entered unknown dangers. For me, Dray Prescot, that is not an unusual hazard.

It seemed to me that the stone wall and floors of the chamber within the tower still reeked faintly of the distinctive Rapa odor. I padded on, guided from one dim pool of illumination in the palpable darkness to the next where torches guttered low. Desperately I sought to convince myself that my mission had not already proved in vain. But the atmosphere here smelled of abandonment — and then I tensed.

Voices, ahead of me, talking lazily, in half grumbling, half resigned accents brought all my senses alert as I crept stealthily upon the two Ullar guards.

"By the violet offal of the snow-blind feister-feelt! I swear my throat is more parched than the ripe-rotten south lands themselves! Nath! Fetch me a pannikin of that Chremson."

The voices were those of Ullars, fierce, resonant, the voices of men accustomed to shouting across the windy gulfs as their impiters crossed the sky. But — Nath!

"Aye," answered he who was named Nath. "And I'll drink you swallow for swallow, Bargo, and see you carried out heels first."

I crept closer in the gloom. The guardroom had been situated within a circular enclosure jutting out from the main bulk of the tower, and from this aerie the guards could obtain an unimpeded view. My sword did not tremble in my hand. The sound of wine gurgling from a leather wine-bottle reassured me.

"When they left us on guard they did us a mortal mischief, my cloth-headed dom." More drinking sounds. "I've not missed a sack since we left Ullardrin—"

"No more have I, Bargo, no more have I."

A gulping and then a resonant belch. Now I was up to the corner, ready to swoop in through the half open door of lenk. I could just catch a glimpse of them, or one of them, with his indigo-dyed hair flowing from that blunt head, that square mouth pursed to the upended blackjack. The handle of a pannikin showed, moving up and down, up and down, as the other Ullar drank. They were so nearly men, so much more like men than the Rapas they had chased from this tower. They wore leather studded with bronze and copper, and as I moved in, slowly and more slowly to bring them both into view, I could see how much alike they were, fierce, belligerent, habitual conquerors and masters of the sky. Each had a bundle of leather thongs cunningly draped and knotted about his waist, and, although I knew little of the ins and outs of their mystique then, I knew enough to know this was the clerketer, the meticulously maintained harness with which they fastened themselves to their impiters and on which their lives would depend in the air.

"More wine, Nath, by the ice needles of Ullarkor, more wine!"

I had feathered shafts into men like these and seen them screech and swing out to dangle from that restraining harness, the clerketer.

Each of these — Nath and Bargo — carried himself with a swagger, that was clear enough. On a bench near them lay the leem pelts with which they kept warm in flight. Their long narrow swords were tucked up, thrusting, important, intended to scare and impress by their very angles of attack when seen against the chunky body, the blunt head and those close-set narrow eyes, that luxuriant mane of indigo hair.

I judged the time was ripe.

I entered the room very fast, and struck Nath upon that mane of indigo hair with the hilt of my sword, so that he dropped to the stone and blood burst from his nostrils and mouth. To the one called Bargo I showed the sword point, pushed against the leather over his heart. I leaned on the blade and it punctured leather and skin. Bargo's square harsh mouth clamped down. He glared at me, and there was death in my face, and he read it there, and he scowled back in savage defiance.

"Where is the prisoner, Bargo?" I spoke roughly, yet in a normal voice. I believe that frightened him more.

He gave me back look for look; then he lowered indigo-stained eyelids over his eyes and said: "Below—"

The wild leap of my heart must be quelled, instantly...

There were no other occupants of the guardroom. Leaning against the wall behind the opened door stood two of the bamboo-hafted, gladius-bladed, and single-edge bitted toonons, the personal weapon of the Ullars, favored by them over all others when in the air. Each bamboo haft was twelve feet in length; with a two-handed grip on that, well-spaced, an Ullar could wield a wide swath of destruction about him in the air. The idea of carrying a short sword aloft was incongruous and ludicrous; what the Ullars had done was to mount the short sword upon this extended haft, reinforce it with a single ax-edge, narrow and deeply curved, and thus bring swordplay into a semblance of possibility aboard the back of a bird, albeit they had in reality constructed a kind of halberd.

Bargo's narrow and deeply-set eyes were focused upon my sword as its point thrust against the leathers over his chest. He wore a brave gold-laced sash about his waist. His legs, clad in the bound leather and cloth that gave him protection when in flight, were quivering. I knew that a moment's relaxation of watchfulness with him would be enough; he would be upon me like a plains leem.

"Lead, Bargo." Again I spoke almost normally.

The only precaution I took with him as I shifted the sword so that he could precede me from the guardroom was to relieve him of his sword. The blade was exceptionally long and thin. It was steel, flexible, keen, suited to the kind of blows a man must deliver if he fights from impiter back. I threw it down into a corner. I fancied my Krozair long sword would overmatch these impiter blades. Bargo's torch sputtered redly.

As we walked steadily down the winding stairs noises hitherto unheard became audible at the lower level. The distant sound of laughter, shouting, music from the single-bagpipes and the wilder, melancholy strains wrenched from the triple-bagpipes; I could even hear, I fancied now and then, the chink of bottles and the rattle of the dice cups, the tinkle of money. We went down the stairs in perfect silence. Bargo understood that his life meant nothing to me.

So confident was I of success that I could worry about Seg now, and hope he could keep clear of the impiter patrols the Ullars would have flying about Plicla.

The stones were old with that distinctive Rapa odor upon them still. We entered a corridor where dust lay thickly, marked by a central trail of darker footprints. At each cell door the dust lay undisturbed, at each one — save one!

To this Bargo unhesitatingly led.

"Open it, Bargo."

This he did, in silence, with the keys from his belt; great clumsy wooden keys they were, each a good nine inches in length, cunningly cut from lenk. The door opened, creaking. I looked inside, my emotions held tightly under, and—

An old man rose from his filthy bed of straw, gazing up with weak eyes, blinking, his near-lipless wrinkled mouth working, trying to distinguish us in the torchlit gloom.

"I have told you, and told you," he said in a voice that quavered as much from age as fear. "I cannot do it — you must believe me, Umgar Stro — there are some things forbidden and some things impossible for the Wizards of Loh."

I took Bargo by the front of his leather tunic and I lifted his feet from the floor. My sword point nestled into his throat. He was very near death, then, and he knew it.

"Where is she, you fool? The prisoner, the girl — tell me, quickly!"

He gargled. He managed to spit out words. "This is the prisoner! By the snow-blind feister-feelt, I swear it!"

"There is another, rast! A girl — the fairest girl you have ever seen. Where?

He shook his head weakly, and his blunt snout wrinkled with his fear. His indigo hair hung lankly down his shoulders.

"There is no other!"

I threw him down and my sword struck like a risslaca; but in the instant of striking I turned the blade so that the flat took him across the head and he pitched forward and lay still without uttering a sound.

"You are not of the Ullars, Jikai." The old man stood more firmly now, clutching his rags about him. His eyes in the random light from the fallen torch caught reflections and glowed like spilled wine drops in the wrinkled map of his face. His nose was long and narrow, his lips nonexistent, and the hair that wisped about his temples was still as red as any man of Loh's. It looked blue-black in that half light, but I knew it was red.

"Have you seen another prisoner, old man, a girl, a girl so wondrous—"

He shook that head and I wondered why it did not creak as the cell door had creaked.

"There is only me, Lu-si-Yuong. Have you means to escape from this accursed tower, Jikai?"

"Yes. But I do not go without the girl for whom I came."

"Then you will spend eternity here."

In all the clamor of thoughts echoing in my skull I think I knew, then, that Delia was not here.

"You have been here long, old man?"

"I am Lu-si-Yuong, and you address me as San."[ix]

I nodded. The title of San was ancient and revered, bearing a meaning akin to master, dominie, sage. Clearly, this representative of the Wizards of Loh not only considered himself an important personage, but was indeed truly so. I do not mind using a title when it is earned.

"Tell me, San, please. Have you any knowledge of the girl captured by Umgar Stro and brought to this tower?"

"I, alone, of the prisoners was spared. The Ullars know of the powers of the Wizards of Loh and they thought to avail themselves of my services. All the other prisoners were slain."

I stood there, I, Dray Prescot, and heard this old sage's thin voice whispering words that meant the end of everything of importance to me in two worlds.

I wanted to leap forward and choke a denial from his narrow mouth, to grip his corded throat in my two hands and wrench words I must hear from him. I think he saw my distress, for he said, again: "I cannot help you in this, Jikai. But I can help in — other — ways if you will rescue me—"

For a moment I could not answer him, could not respond. My Delia — surely, she could not have been so wantonly killed? It did not make sense — who could callously snuff out so much beauty?

San Young was whispering again, bending stiffly to pick up Bargo's spluttering torch. "They revel tonight, below. There are many of them, fierce, bold barbarians of the skies. To fight your way through them, Jikai, is a superhuman task—"

"We go up," I said, and I was short with him. All my instincts clashed there, in that cobwebby tower cell of Umgar Stro, torturing me with indecision, with doubt, with a mad and futile rage. She must be here! She must! But everything pointed to the opposite being true. This Wizard — why should he lie? Except, to cozen me into rescuing him!

I faced him. He had recovered his composure now, had drawn himself up so that the torchlight flowed over his gaunt features, over those wine-dark eyes, that long supercilious nose, that near-lipless mouth. He looked at me, clutching his rags, and he was well aware of the horror and superstitious awe in which common folk held the Wizards of Loh.

Indeed, there was power about him in an aura no one could overlook. Many and many a time have the Wizards of Loh performed deeds any normal man would dub impossible, and what their secrets may be are still a mystery to me. They demand and obtain instant obedience from the common folk — of whom, Zair be praised, there are many sturdy souls — and for the lordly of the land they reserve a kind of watching, cynical and amused tolerance, an armed truce of checks and balances of interest. Umgar Stro, for instance, could torture this old man to obtain his services, and his men might murmur but, being barbarians, they would not react in the same way that a man of Walfarg might.

Once having obtained his services, Umgar Stro would have to kill him; for, judging by all the stories I had heard, if he did not then a retribution as horrible as it was inevitable would overtake him as surely as Zim and Genodras rose with each new day.

So it was that this Wizard of Loh, this Lu-si-Yuong, thought he could now safely dictate what was to occur.

He stared at me and I saw the torchlight flicker over his grimed yet pallid face. He took a step backward.

"Listen to me, San. If you speak true, if there is no girl prisoner here, then swear it be so by all you hold sacred of Loh. For, Lu-si-Yuong, if you lie to me then you will die — as surely as anything you know of in your world!"

His tongue rasped those wrinkled sandpaper edges of his mouth.

"It is true. I swear to you by Hlo-Hli herself and by the seven arcades, I am the only prisoner here."

We stood facing each other for what seemed a long time.

I was scarcely aware when I lowered the sword point from his shrunken breast.

"Very well." I could not break out, not now; I could not allow myself to despair and to abandon myself to my grief. Not now, not when faithful Seg orbited outside awaiting me, in mortal danger. "Come, old man. Pray to all your pagan gods you have spoken the truth — and yet, and yet I wish you lied!"

We left the cell and walked on the footprinted way between the dust and so up the spiral stairs, past the guardroom and up to the attic. For me, Dray Prescot, this was a skulking, an undignified way, of tackling my foes.

Thelda had told me Delia had dropped into a tarn and been drowned. San Yuong told me she was not here. Did they both lie?

I told Lu-si-Yuong to wait and went back to the guardroom and took up the two toonons. The bamboo was not a true bamboo but came from the Marshes of Buranaccl. I wondered what Seg would make of the weapon. My mind was beginning to function again.

Seg was mightily joyed to see us. He brought the corths in with supple skill and I bundled up onto the trapeze with the fragile form of the Wizard tucked under my arm. We swung away into the Kregan night and the glow from the twins rolled across the eastern horizon laying pink icing across the towers, battlements, and roofs of Rapa Plicla.

The strong vulturine-shaped wings of the corths beat up and down, up and down, and we rode the sky levels away from the fortress of Umgar Stro until we could alight in a clearing among tuffa trees and so rearrange ourselves for our flight back to Hiclantung.

Seg was very quiet.

He did say, savagely: "I would have welcomed an opposition back there. We need a fight, Dray."

"Aye," I said. And let it lie there.

I did not believe my Delia was dead. Not after all we had been through. Only when I held Umgar Stro's throat in my fists and choked the truth from him would I believe. And, even then, even then, I would go on hoping...

Fourteen

"It is my Dray! My Dray Prescot you covet!"

One of the strange and, if the truth be told, weird, aspects of the Wizards of Loh was revealed in that grove of tuffa trees as we rested our corths and rearranged our flight program. Lu-si-Yuong, without a word of explanation to Seg or myself, squatted himself down on the ground in the pinkish light from the twin moons, composed himself and, lifting his veined hands to his eyes, threw his head back and so remained still and silent and unmoving.

Seg whispered: "I think, Dray, he is in lupu."

"Oh?" I really hardly cared.

"Yes. They say the Wizards of Loh can see into the future—"

"A simple story for simple minds. The credulous will believe any mumbo jumbo and it puts a copper into the hands of clever tricksters."

Seg glanced obliquely at me, his mouth open. He shut his mouth, and looked back at Yuong, and did not say what he so clearly thought. I had a mind to speak more kindly toward him, for he was of Loh, but I forbore. Delia! I remembered my anguish when among the tents and the wagons and chunkrah herds of the Clansmen of Felschraung I had heard my Delia was dead, and I recalled my determination to remain alive and fighting strong so that if, as I truly believed, she was not dead, I would be able to render her what aid I could. Now, as the Wizard of Loh went through his mumbo jumbo I made the same solemn vow.

Quietly, I said to Seg: "I came away from the tower tonight, Seg, for there were reasons why I should do so. I cannot believe that Delia is truly dead. I shall go on until I find Umgar Stro, wherever he may be. I think he was lucky not to be home tonight, and yet more unfortunate, too."

"How is that, dom?" asked Seg in a neutral voice.

"I would have killed him tonight, stone dead. But if it takes me long to find him then there will be that amount more time in which to store resentment, and to think of ways of making him talk and — pay!"

Seg turned his eyes away from my face.

Lu-si-Yuong began to tremble. His thin shoulders shook and over all his scrawny body beneath the rags he shuddered and then he began slowly to draw his palms from before his eyes. His eyeballs were rolled up, displaying the whites like a bird-befouled marble statue's, and his breathing had practically ceased.

"Lupu," I said. "Is that it?"

"Aye, Dray, that is being in lupu. He is having visions. Who can tell where his mind is wandering now—"

"Get a grip on yourself, Seg!"

All the fey characteristics of his race predominated in Seg Segutorio now, all

350

the dark and hidden lore in his native hills of Erthyrdrin pulsed and answered the weirdness of this old man, this San, this Wizard of Loh.

As the streaming pink moons-light fell upon that gaunt upturned face and turned those blind eyes into cracked yellow pits I looked about the grove of tuffa trees and at the three corths uneasily picking and pecking their feathers, and I, Dray Prescot of Earth, wondered at the faces of Kregen I had not yet seen.

A gargling cry wailed from Yuong. His trembling ceased. Unsteadily, waveringly, he tottered to his feet. He opened his arms wide, the fingers rigid and outspread. Like some blasphemous cross he gyrated, like a cyclone-torn scarecrow, like a whirling dervish in the last stages of exhaustion. Then, as abruptly as he had begun, he sank down, resumed his contemplative position, and so lowered his hands flat to the ground and opened his eyes and looked on us.

"And have you looked into the future, old man?" I said.

"Dray!" Seg's outraged cry affected me not at all.

San Yuong looked at me. I think, even then, he did not know how to size me up or to read me in the context of those people with whom he was accustomed to deal. I do know now, and admit it with only the slightest diffidence, that I must have been in a state of shock still, and hardly recking of what I did or said. In any event Yuong decided to treat me with caution. For this I was later duly grateful; at the time I merely remarked to myself that I must be wearing that old devil's mask of a face again — and joying in it, Zair help me, joying in my pain.

"The future does not concern me at this moment, my friend. I shall thank you properly for rescuing me at a suitable time. What I have been discovering is how I will be received by Queen Lilah—"

"She does not blame you for the defeat of her army in the massacre," I said. "At least, she did not mention you in that context — or at all."

"She would not."

"What have you discovered, San?" asked Seg.

"The Queen will need my guidance and advice in what is to come. But she was cold — distant and cold. There is a woman, another woman, they have fought bitterly—"

"Thelda!" exclaimed Seg. He stared at me in dismay.

I was intrigued. Could this old man in some way have seen what was even now happening in Hiclantung? Impossible! But, remember, then I was young and new to the ways of Kregen and especially to the wiles of the Wizards of Loh.

"The Queen has imprisoned this woman, this Thelda, and she weeps for her lost lover." Yuong canted his head so that his supercilious nose aimed itself over my right shoulder. "Perchance she dreams of you, Jikai?"

"If she does," I said, "she does so without my permission."

"Since when has a maid required permission to long for a man?"

I didn't want to continue this, not with Seg looking and listening, so I went across to my corth and inspected its harness.

"Let us go," I said. "If Queen Lilah has flung Thelda into prison we must get her out again. We owe her that much, at least."

Seg vaulted into his saddle. His fist gripped into his rein knot — and his other hand made sure his great longbow was in position, handy as to bending and loosing, the feather of his arrows protruding from their quiver past his right ear.

I could see the irony in this situation; more than irony, deadly mockery of all I held dear. Here I was setting out to rescue my Delia from the clutches of a malevolent monster and instead was hurrying back to our friends to rescue a tiresome woman.

How all the Clansmen would have roared their appreciation of the joke — until I silenced them with my upraised sword!

We soared aloft with those initial convulsive rippling movements of the corths' wide wings driving us low across the clearing until we had picked up enough speed to rise and bank out past the trees. I scanned three hundred and sixty degrees as I would have done the moment I stepped onto the quarterdeck of *Roscommon* back on Earth — only now I had to sweep again below as well as above the level of our flight height. It was almost with regret that I saw no pursuing impiters, no vengeful corths, no varter-towing yuelshi.

Had I been of the stuff from which the romantic heroes of Kregan legends are constructed — all manliness and pride and stoicism and lofty indifference to personal pain — I would not have felt then as I did, all the agony and the remorse clawing and tearing my spirit. I knew only that I must go on — somehow.

We alighted on the outskirts of Hiclantung.

"If Thelda truly has been imprisoned by Lilah," I said, "then it would be foolish simply to fly back when day dawns."

"Yes," said Seg.

I knew how he felt. His constant cheerfulness with me both heartened and saddened me, for Seg had tried most desperately to interest Thelda in himself and had as desperately failed.

The corths snuffled around, ruffling their feathers, giving clear indication they wished to rest. I looked at Yuong.

"Tell me, San. Can you reach out with your mind and find the woman I seek?"

"Speak more plainly, Jikai. Do you mean Thelda, whom you would rescue from the Queen, or do you mean the woman you love?"

I started violently.

Fool! Why had I not thought of this myself — and before!

I gripped his thin shoulder. He did not wince but stared up at me placidly. I began to speak, but he shook his head.

"Is this woman you love as beautiful as you say?"

"Yes."

"Incredibly lovely?"

"Yes."

He moved my hand away. I let him. "I cannot find her for you, for I have no means of location, as I had with Thelda, who was with the Queen." He started back at my movement. Pink moonshine runneled along his jaws. "But, if she is as beautiful as you say, I believe she still lives. Umgar Stro values beautiful objects."

"Delia of the Blue Mountains is not an object!"

"With Umgar Stro all women are objects."

I turned away from him. Old as he was, cocksure as he was, weird as he was, if I had not turned away I believe I would have struck him down.

"By the veiled Froyvil, Dray! Let us get on!"

San Lu-si-Yuong went through his pantomime again. I call it a pantomime, for that is how I thought then when I was under tremendous strain, tensed up, desperate and weary and vengeful. Yuong did, however, play fair by us.

"She is with the Queen even now, in the Paline Bower—"

"I know it!" said Seg.

"I shall humor you," went on Yuong, "and go into lupu in the morning when the gates are open and we may enter the city."

Seg started violently.

I said: "You do not think Seg and I are men to wait tamely out here for them to open the gates for us, do you?"

He nodded that stringy lipless head with the wine-dark eyes somber and yet full of a spritely malice. "What else will you do, Jikai?"

Seg laughed.

I do not laugh easily, as I have said; I simply stood up and went across to my corth — the one with the trapeze and the thongs — and readied him for flight. Seg followed me.

When the corth was ready I turned to Yuong.

"You had best fly with us — there are leems hereabouts—"

He shook his head.

"Nay, Jikai. If you lend me one of those thick anachronistic flint-headed spears, I will fare well enough."

"As you wish. The spears were unnecessary, after all. They were a failure, like my plans."

"Dray!" said Seg. "All is not yet lost."

"Come!" I said, and I was abrupt with Seg. So we left the Wizard of Loh, San Lu-si-Yuong, there with a flint-headed spear to await the dawnrise of the twin suns of Scorpio and the opening of the gates to Hiclantung.

We rode the same corth for the short journey and by taking turns we both dropped off the swinging trapeze onto the trip-wired and fan-spiked roof of the Queen's palace and let the corth go where he willed. I fancied that sharp eyes peering out in the pink light of the twins would have spotted us from one of the many watchtowers rising in the city. That did not concern me as yet. We padded down stairs carpentered from sturm-wood and opened lenken doors with our swords. We did not kill the guards we encountered, for these were, after all, our hosts.

No incongruity of repetition struck me as we crept silently down past the guards, for this time I carried no high palpitations of hope and fear for my Delia; now we were merely attempting to do the right thing by a comrade — and then I remembered the way Seg felt about the callous and shallow Thelda, and I sighed, and wondered just what I did wish for this baffling comrade of mine.

Truth to tell, I felt a queasy sense of responsibility for Yuong; how could his frailty stand up against the awesome ferocity of a wild leem, flint-headed spear or no?

A young Hiclantung guardsman very smart in the ornate robes of a Queen's spearman with the gold and silver buttons and buckles in place of workmanlike bronze or bone was very pleased to assist us when Seg placed his dagger at the lad's throat. We were led past a doorway into an area of dust and cobwebs. It was a long narrow passage and every now and then thin slits let lamplight fall across the floor, so I knew it to be one of those seemingly essential items to certain palaces — the place of observation hidden behind the walls of the chambers. I have used these observation galleries many times, and no doubt will do so in the future. For some reason the minds of many rulers on the world of Kregen are obsessed with this desire for secrecy and for hidden observers ready to leap out in surprise and deal with the slightest hint of treachery or assassination. I have used these galleries many times — but not for the purpose for which they were built.

Seg tapped the lad lightly on the head when he indicated we had reached the correct loophole and I caught him in my arms and eased him silently to the dusty floor. Then Seg below and I above looked through the slit.

This was a small chamber within the Paline Bower which nestled securely beneath a wing of the palace. The first thing I noticed — before either of the women — was the chased silver dish containing a pile of palines, luscious, full-bodied, juicy, invigorating, and I licked my lips thirstily.

Seg whispered: "The Queen has a dagger in her hand!" The mellow light from the samphron oil lamps shining through wafer-thin scraped-bone shades splintered back in hard-edged reflections from the jewels in the dagger hilt. A star winked and dazzled from the dagger's point. That point hovered over Thelda's breast.

I felt for the edges of the crack that would reveal the doorway. Seg was breathing loudly, almost gasping.

That secret chamber was furnished in casual unostentatious luxury, with ling furs upon the low couches, silks and satins scattered here and there in a riot of colors between the tumbled cushions.

"You forget that I am the Queen!"

"And you forget that I am a Lady of Vallia!"

"Vallia! I spit on your Vallia!"

"What is this miserable dung-heap called Hiclantung? My country is a great nation, united under an all-powerful emperor! The power of Vallia is like a leem compared to the puny rast-city of Hiclantung!"

"By Hlo-Hli! You will pay for this insolence!" I sighed. The girls were at it again. But poor Seg was taking it all in with a very visible distress.

Lilah wore a long scarlet gown, very tight as to the bodice, slit up the sides to reveal her long legs. Her hair and bosom and arms were smothered with gems. Much of that satanic look about her that came from the widow's peak and her upslanting eyebrows and the shadows beneath her cheekbones was absent now as she argued and wrangled with Thelda. Thelda — poor Thelda — another man than Dray Prescot might have chuckled at her now, knowing what I knew about these two. Thelda was clad in a short and raggedy brown shift that left her thick thighs naked, that hung lopsidedly on her shoulders, sagging, and her wrists were bound behind her back with golden cords. Yet she lifted her head defiantly, and I had to admire her, despite all the ludicrous scenes that had passed between us.

"I know why you're so much of a female cramph!" spat Thelda now, her face flushed, her eyes bright, her breast heaving like the seas of the Eye of the World after a rashoon has passed. "It's my Dray! My Dray Prescot you covet!"

"Your Dray!"

"Yes! You know nothing of what we mean to each other. I love him and, now the Princess Majestrix is gone, he will love me! I know—"

"You know nothing, rast! What can you offer him? I am the Queen, a Queen in all her glory, Queen of a great city and a great nation—"

"Surrounded by enemies waiting to tear your heart out!"

"They may wish to — but they will never succeed. I can offer Dray Prescot everything — you—"

Thelda threw back her dark brown hair and opened those plump lips and laughed. "You!" she spluttered. "A skinny rast-bag like you! Dray Prescot needs a woman, a real woman!"

Lilah's hand trembled and the dagger shot sparks of fire into the corners of the room. "You great fat lump of lard! Dray needs a woman of fire and passion who can meet him, breast to breast, spirit for spirit!"

Seg put his hand on the secret panel. I suffered for my comrade during those minutes.

A sharp rap on the door opposite brought Lilah around, catlike, the dagger upraised. The knock also halted Seg's pushing hand. The door opened and a little slave wench with golden bands upon her gray slave kirtle skipped in, bending and genuflecting, showing in Councilor Orpus. His powerful bearded face was filled with extreme animation and the many rings on his fingers flashed in the lamplight. He swept his embroidered robes to one side as he inclined deeply. When he straightened up, he said: "Forgive this intrusion, oh Queen! But — great news! We think we have discovered the location of Umgar Stro."

"What do you mean — you think?" Lilah replaced the dagger in its sheath at her waist. She advanced on Orpus like a leem. She was all queen now, all regality, lofty and cold and demanding, merciless to failure.

"The scouts report—"

"Wait." Lilah beckoned. "Guards! Take this miserable creature to the cells; let her rot there until my pleasure is known. Come, Orpus. We must go to the council chamber — summon the scouts, my generals, and my councilors. We must plan — now!"

As Orpus stood aside to let the Queen sweep past him, her long scarlet gown trailing, her naked legs strong and thrusting before, her guards inclined, their helmets low. They moved into the chamber, and their Deldar prodded Thelda with his spear point. That spear point was steel, as befitted a spearman of the Queen's guard.

"Up, little one. We have need of playthings such as you in the cells!"

They closed upon Thelda and dragged her away and as she went she screamed most piteously.

Seg put his hand to the secret panel, but it was my foot that kicked it open.

Together, Seg and I, we burst into the empty chamber. Our swords were in our fists. Shoulder to shoulder we started for the door.

Fifteen

Seg, Thelda, and I stand before Queen Lilah

On the way across to the door I used my left hand to scoop up a great mass of the palines. Juice dribbled through my fingers.

"Here, Seg. Munch on these—"

"No time, Dray! Don't you realize what they're going to do to Thelda?"

I pushed the palines at him.

"Take them, Seg! You need them!"

I stared at him, eye to eye. With a savage curse he pushed past me, scooped up a mass of the palines and stuffed them into his mouth. Then, and only then, I ran for the door.

The guards had just reached the first turn in the corridor. We ran swiftly and silently down toward that corner. I checked at the bend beside an alabaster statue of a risslaca seizing a leem, and the leem in its turn seizing the risslaca, and peered around. Seg hopped with impatience. The guards were moving Thelda along briskly. A few other slaves and functionaries moved along the corridor, which here broadened with a supporting aisle of thick-bodied columns down its center. I had visited the palace enough times to have a vague and general idea of its layout; but unlike most of the palaces I had encountered on Kregen this one, because it had been built in the midst of a city closed up around it within its encircling walls, had not sprawled out in an ever-growing maze of passages and courts and halls.

We marched smartly out and cut along the corridor.

Slaves looked at us, but slaves are slaves, and they took only enough notice of us, two warriors, to keep out of our way. I hate and detest slavery; here was one facet of slavery clearly apparent. The guards hustled Thelda around another bend. When we reached the corner where a vast pot of Pandahem ware — and how old it was I wouldn't care to guess — brought up a few memories, I saw before me a double-corridor I recognized from its decoration. Down that corridor lay the council chamber where Lilah, the Queen, was now meeting the scouts who had brought information of the whereabouts of Umgar Stro.

Without hesitation I started off down the corridor.

"Dray! They went this way..."

I turned. Seg was looking at me, and I could not read the expression on his tanned face. A stray shaft of torchlight caught in his blue eyes and gleamed back lambently.

"Umgar Stro—" I said.

"The guards have taken Thelda down here, into the dungeons!"

At once I came to myself. This was Seg Segutorio, the man who had unhesitatingly followed me to the tower of Umgar Stro in Plicla to rescue Delia. Now I must go with him to rescue Thelda. Of course. How could I have thought otherwise? I would fight my way to Umgar Stro — never fear. So I thought as I ran after Seg down the corridor branching at right angles, through the bronze-bound lenken door at its end, and down bare stone steps into the dungeons of the Queen of Pain.

It was not as easy as I have made it sound. Every cell of my body screamed in agony that I must go to seek my Delia, my Delia of the Blue Mountains. I did not think then, I could not, of what might be happening to her. But the agony I suffered would only increase if I allowed poor Thelda and Seg to be destroyed. I knew my Delia would understand that and approve; and I also knew I used her acquiescence as a mere excuse.

The guards had been joined by men in the traditional uniform of their trade. They wore black aprons and black masks and their brawny arms were bare. Thelda's pitiful brown rag had been stripped from her and she huddled against a stone wall where iron rings fixed into the stone gaped open for her. Two sets along they supported a skeleton clothed in decayed scraps of flesh and skin.

One of the men gripped Thelda and lifted her arm toward the iron ring. Beneath the mask his fleshy face showed a vastly unpleasant sniggering enjoyment.

Seg had sheathed his sword.

Before I could run in with my brand naked in my fist Seg's first arrow punched meatily into the broad black-leather-clad back. The torturer screamed like a de-gutted vosk and toppled away. Then I was in among the guards. I laid about me with the flat of my sword, for in all the desperate anger blazing in me I still retained sense enough to try to mitigate the Queen's rage. One torturer she might overlook; more would cause untold problems for Seg and myself.

"Don't kill them, Seg!" I yelled, as I felled the Deldar and swung back and laid my blade flat into his companion's guts, bringing the hilt down on his head as he doubled.

Seg gasped and swore and stowed that great longbow away and thwacked his long sword down onto the guards. So sudden, so vicious, so fierce was our onslaught that the guards wilted and fell in swathes. Only two managed to bring their steel-tipped spears up and these we slashed through with our brands and then knocked their wielders out, a neat one-two flicker of movement,

"I'll make a swordsman of you yet, Seg!" I said. The brisk action had stirred my sluggish blood.

But Seg Segutorio was cradling Thelda in his arms, holding her naked body to him, crooning unintelligible words over her.

"Oh, Dray!" shrieked Thelda. "I knew you would come! I knew you would save me!"

"Thank Seg," I said with a harshness of tone I had no need to simulate.

"But — Dray—" She struggled free of Seg. She stood there, her arms out-

357

spread, her bosom panting, her color very high and flushed. "That Lilah — that Queen — female cramph! I hate her! But you, Dray — you have saved me!"

I did not look at Seg.

He said, in a hard clipped voice: "We must get out of here. Now. Before these sleeping beauties awake."

"Put your dress on, Thelda," I said. "You and Seg must get away at once." I stripped a long, lavishly embroidered cloth from the Deldar, rolling him over and over so that his nose squashed on the filth of the stone floor. "Put this on, too, as a cape. You can make the outside safely; you know the way—"

"Dray! Aren't you coming?"

I did not laugh. "I have a matter to discuss with Lilah."

Thelda started back as though I had struck her.

"You — Dray — you — and the Queen! *No!*"

For all her words a change had come over Thelda, my lady of Vallia. Much of her bounce had gone. I remembered her screams as the guards had dragged her off. She thought then that she was doomed; dark fears of that memory would haunt her for the rest of her days, I expected. She looked more haggard, the plumpness of her sagging; her eyes looked dull.

"Not Lilah and me, Thelda, no — not like that. She has news of Umgar Stro, and I must have news, also."

"If you go to stand before the Queen," said Seg, "then I go with you to stand at your side."

"Seg—"

"And me?" shrieked Thelda. "I dare not go—"

"I do not think, Thelda, the Queen will harm you if Dray intercedes for us all."

Seg's words, so calm, so sure, so filled with all the dark wisdom of his hills of Erthyrdrin, rattled me. Loh was, indeed, a continent of mystery.

"I am frightened—" Thelda looked it, too.

I started to walk out of the chamber, back up the stone stairs. "The Queen will listen to me," I said. "Let us go."

We were not molested on our way to Queen Lilah's council chamber.

It is a strange fact to me now to recall that I have only the dimmest memories of her council chamber. Oh, it was wide and lofty and supported by the massive Hiclantung pillars with their garlands of risslaca and snake, and with pediments fashioned in the form of corths; there was color and torchlight and many people; but I recall only the tall scarlet form of Lilah, with her piled mass of gem-encrusted red hair with its wedge-shape over her forehead, of her deep dark eyes and the upslanting eyebrows, the shadows beneath her cheekbones and that scarlet-painted, small, firm, and yet sensuous mouth.

"So you have come back to me, Dray Prescot."

I remembered her, prostrate before me, groveling, imploring me to take a seat at her side on her throne, offering me everything. Her chin lifted as though she, too, understood my thoughts.

"If you have news of Umgar Stro, oh Queen, then tell me that I may take his throat between my hands and squeeze until he is as lifeless as a rag doll."

"Gently, gently, my Lord of Strombor! It is not sure. The scouts believe; we await confirmation."

"Tell me where and I will confirm—"

"Not so fast." Lilah looked at Thelda. Guards surrounded us, their steel spear-points glinting. Seg held his strung bow in his left hand, and idly held an arrow in his right hand. I knew he could bend the bow and send that shaft clear through the heart of this Queen of Pain long before he was cut down by her spearmen. "Not so fast. What is this — woman — doing with you?"

I stared at Lilah, challengingly, eye to eye. I forced my meaning upon her.

"She is innocent in all this, oh Queen. We found her in circumstances that would displease me mightily if I thought they were of your doing."

She returned my stare. Our eyes locked.

"I see."

"There is a man, a Wizard of Loh, a San, one called Lu-si-Yuong."

She gasped. "What of San Yuong?"

"Seg Segutorio and I rescued him from the tower in Plicla. He was the only prisoner. He will enter Hiclantung when the gates are open at dawn, although I venture he would find it a blessing if you sent guards to let him in now. There are leems."

"Yes." She gestured and a Hikdar moved off at once to carry out her unspoken orders. "The San is precious to me. I grieved at his loss in the massacre. And you have rescued him!"

"Seg Segutorio and I."

"Yes." She seemed somewhat at a loss. It was with a considerable reduction of her powers that she said: "It seems I am in your debt again, Dray Prescot."

"You know what I seek. Umgar Stro. Tell me—"

"As soon as the news of that evil person's whereabouts is brought to me you shall be told. But, my Lord of Strombor, I put a thought to you. We believe he is in Chersonang."

Chersonang was the adjoining country and city in hereditary rivalry with Hi-clantung. I could foresee problems.

Lilah leaned forward a little on her throne, her white hand beneath her white chin, brooding on me. "I shall send all my army up against Umgar Stro in Chersonang. I believe we can break both him and them, together. This will be your opportunity, Dray Prescot, to seek and find the woman you desire. I offer you the chance to command my army, with my generals, to go up against Umgar Stro at the head of a host. Come, what do you say?"

At my side Thelda gasped.

The guards pressed more closely about us now.

There was no need to discuss with myself my answer.

"I thank you, Lilah, for your offer. It is generous of you. But I cannot wait. I will leave for Chersonang at once — sleep will have to wait, instead."

"You fool!"

I turned to go and Seg's hand flashed up with the arrow between his fingers and a spear point tripped him so that he fell sprawling before the throne. My sword was half drawn when something — a spear butt, the flat of a sword — sledged down on my head and I tumbled down that long smooth slope of black oblivion.

Sixteen

The army of Hiclantung marches out

If you choose to think my actions at this time — and, indeed, for some time past — had been irrational, I could not argue the point with you.

Truly, I now feel that the belief my Delia was dead had deranged me. I know I had acted in ways completely outside my usual fashion, and, yet, too, in ways I have been told are typical of me, as witness that wild moment when I defied the Queen of Pain to rush out from the windlass room in the corthdrome upon the indigo-haired assassins of Umgar Stro. I must have been in a state of shock that allowed me to walk and talk and act and yet held me all the time in a kind of mental stasis.

The ancient Chinese, we are told, had perfected the art of torture by water, the expected drop of liquid crashing onto the victim's forehead like a weight crushing into his brain. A single small drop could not do that; it was the expectation and the mounting terror of the inevitable, alternated with the passive bouts of cringing waiting. First I had thought Delia dead, then I had heard she might be alive, then her death was once more certain, and now again she might be missing and, perhaps, better dead. The sheer vibrationary pressure, the nightmare nutcracker rhythm of it all, had made of me a different animal from the man who had flown over The Stratemsk.

Of only one thing could I be sure. Whether dead or alive, Delia would fiercely insist that I go on with life, that I persevere, that I never give in.

Seg and I recovered quietly in a comfortable room set deep within the palace. The room was as luxuriously furnished as anyone could wish, windowless, lit with samphron oil lamps, and set everywhere with the motionless and watchful figure of guards, spearmen of the Queen's own household in their embroidered robes and gleaming helmets, their steel-tipped spears. We were both naked. We had no weapons.

Seg said: "We could take the spears from these dummies, easily, you and I, Dray!"

I said: "We could. We could fight our way clear if we went together. But — what of Thelda?"

His look distressed me.

"Thelda," he said, and he bowed that mane of black hair to his brawny forearms.

So we pondered our chances of breaking free and taking the plump Lady of Vallia with us.

Wherever we were marched within the Queen's palace we were accompanied by an overwhelming escort, consisting of spearmen and bowmen. These latter, we knew, effectively prevented the sudden dash for freedom. And yet, even then, we knew we were not prisoners in any ordinary sense of that term. We became aware of a sense of heightened purpose within Hiclantung. Soldiers moved everywhere. Preparations were being made and Seg was moved to express a fierce dark satisfaction in the demeanor of the men.

"They have not forgotten what Umgar Stro did to them. Through the treachery of one man, that Forpacheng, their pride was humbled." Seg moved his hands meaningfully. "Well, now they are regrouping, remembering their traditions. They will not suffer the same fate again."

Hwang, the Queen's nephew, came to see us, distressed by what Lilah was forced to do to us — as he said, for our own good.

His young face wore the kind of look one associates with a child's awareness of some mischief, and the desire to brazen it out. He flung his embroidered robes away from his legs, kicking them petulantly, as he sat down. Seg hospitably poured wine — it was a purple beverage of excellent vintage, I recall, full-bodied yet not too sweet, from the western slopes of Mount Storr — and Hwang took the goblet as though prepared to sup and to forget what was on his mind.

"I have just come from the dancing girls at Shling-feraeo," he said. "They bored me."

"Umgar Stro," I said.

Hwang nodded. "Yes, Dray Prescot. You have it aright."

We began a technical discussion concerning the equipment and tactics of the army of Hiclantung, in which Seg pressed hard. I might have felt amusement, with another man, at another time without worries, at the way Seg so passionately concerned himself with the prospects of this lame remnant of the glorious empire of Walfarg. Much of Seg's home country, that mysterious land of mountains and valleys called Erthyrdrin, I came to know later; but nothing could quench the burning pride in Seg, a pride echoed in Hwang, that the ancient virtues of Loh should survive, and that he, as a man of Erthyrdrin, should participate to the full in their perpetuation. Perhaps I caught a glimpse, there in that silken scented prison room of the palace of Hiclantung, of the breaking of barriers of nationality that was so much to affect my life on Kregen.

Seg was a man of Erthyrdrin, and he had told me how his people were feared by the other peoples of Loh — there had been much wild free talk between us — and now, here he was, dourly determined to smash unknown enemies of the Lohvians.

For the enemies were unknown in the sense that the people of Chersonang were unknown to Seg and myself, and Umgar Stro clearly had not flexed all his military muscle and therefore was unknown to Hwang and the Lohvian army of Hiclantung.

Presently Hwang said to me, with a smile and a gesture of the hand holding the wine goblet: "You are a wise man, Dray Prescot, not to attempt escape. You are a man I think could escape if you willed it. But you have put both the Queen and myself into your debt; and we are conscious of that—"

"You are not in my debt."

"For myself, thinking of you as a friend, I am glad you go up against Umgar Stro with an army, and not alone."

"Huh," said Seg Segutorio.

Hwang inclined his head, squinting along the goblet.

"Assuredly, Seg. By alone I meant with you and without my army."

"You are in command?" I said.

"In a manner of speaking. Orpus holds joint-command. There are other generals. We believe you will join us, Dray Prescot, to give us the wisdom of your advice."

"Seg is perfectly accustomed to commanding men in combat."

Hwang looked with a strange kind of affection upon my comrade. "Yes. Seg is of Erthyrdrin, and we who remain of Walfarg know of them well. There was once a time… Well" — he drained the goblet — "no matter."

He stood up to go.

Then, looking down on us, for protocol was not respected by me so long as I remained a prisoner, Hwang said: "I have had a messenger from Naghan. You remember Naghan, the spy?"

"Yes."

"He will return very soon. His report — and it is cautious as befits a spy — says he will have news of Delia—"

Hwang's shoulder was gripped in my fist and my ugly face blazed down into his. "What?"

He wriggled. I took my hand away, drawing a breath, glowering.

"When Naghan reports I will bring him to speak with you."

"Do that, Hwang. Pray God, Zair, my life — his news is good!"

We had insisted we be allowed exercise and the guard commander would march us to a wide hall where Seg and I jumped and ran and thwacked at each other with quarter staffs until we both slumped sweating and aching and thoroughly worked out. I cannot say we were tired, for this make-believe action merely titillated the muscles of men accustomed to the real hardships of campaigns and battles.

At last Naghan the spy returned.

Queen Lilah, Orpus, and Hwang came to our luxurious prison room with Naghan. With them, also, a grim armored body of the Queen's spearmen indicated clearly she would stand no nonsense from Seg or myself. Also — surprisingly — Thelda walked in with them, dressed in her old brown short-skirted garment and with her hands bound behind her with golden cords. Her color was high. Her bosom jutted. Her head was held erect and arrogantly. She stared around contemptuously, saw Seg and myself, and all her composure crumbled so that, for just an instant, we saw the lonely frightened girl she really was. Then she caught herself, and resumed that haughty patrician air that remained to her the only bastion against insanity.

"Speak, Naghan," commanded Lilah.

The spy did not cringe. He looked at me curiously. His short body was clad in a simple robe with the minimum of embroidery, and his faded eyes sized me up in a way I knew few had done upon Kregen beneath Antares.

He opened his mouth, he started to speak, to say, "I now know for certain that the Princess Delia of Vallia is—" when Lilah stopped him with a single word.

She faced me. Since that dramatic meeting in her private room where we had drunk wine and she had lain at my feet with her garment of gems winking and flashing upon her white body, we had not encountered each other alone. I guessed she had been unsure of herself, unwilling to confront me again without the presence of her courtiers and her generals and her guards imposing an iron restraint upon her conduct.

"Let him speak, Lilah," I said.

"After we have spoken, Dray Prescot."

"Then be brief."

"I desire you to go with my army against Umgar Stro. You will lead them, inspire them. With you at their head they will attack to the victory."

"That is easy enough — it might suffice for vengeance. Is there more than vengeance to be found in Chersonang, Lilah?"

She frowned. Her red widow's peak of hair drew down, it seemed, with the movement of her face, so that she presented a brooding and devilish look. She wore a tunic of green — not the green of Magdag or the green of Esztercari, but green nonetheless — and a short skirt of green over leather-clad legs. Her embroidered robes were put away. Around her narrow waist a golden belt tightened her figure, emphasizing the fact she was a woman, and from it swung a jeweled sword. In her left hand she carried a switch. All the time we spoke and without conscious effort on my part a portion of my attention concentrated on that switch.

"I want you to give me your word, by the sacred name of Hlo-Hli, by whatever pagan goddesses rule you, that you will not leave my army until you have led it to victory."

"And what if the host of Umgar Stro prevails?"

"In that case, the issue will not matter to anyone."

"Nothing is certain in war."

Her whole attitude bespoke extreme uncertainty; she was bandying words with me, and she a queen.

"Give me your word—"

"I will do what I can for your army against Umgar Stro, because that happens to fit into my own desires, Lilah. Beyond that even your Hlo-Hli can do nothing. Now give Naghan leave to speak."

Her small mouth compressed and the switch lifted. But she turned to Naghan calmly enough and told him to report.

"The Princess Delia of Vallia is now known to me for certain as not the name of the female prisoner on whose track I spent a great deal of time—"

I stood there. I could not speak or move. I simply glared at this calm matter-of-fact man called Naghan the spy, and he saw my eyes and he swallowed, that grave courageous man, and went on: "As San Yuong has said, all the prisoners except himself were killed at Plicla. I have been in Chersonang. There is a female prisoner there, who may or may not be the Princess Delia of Vallia. I have discovered only that she is kept penned in a dungeon, miserably. I have had no opportunity to speak with her, but she has female servants and slaves. The talk is that Umgar Stro is too busy to win conquests at this time; when the battle has been won he will deign to try his mettle with her."

Queen Lilah sniffed. "From what I hear of Umgar Stro that fits his contemptible character. He likes his women pliable; drugged, eager for love. He will not waste time fighting a woman; he demands they yield to him with counterfeit joy."

"I know that type of sub-man," said Seg. He would not look at me.

Before anyone could stop her, Thelda burst out: "And is the man who forces a girl any the less of a sub-man, then?"

Orpus stroked his beard, which, as always, lent weight to what he was saying. "No. Passion in either case is unlawful and vile. But — I put it to you that no woman can be raped unless she desires it."

Thelda gasped, looking shocked, and Lilah smiled reflectively. I remembered the stories of her cast-off lovers, the abandoned detritus of the Queen of Pain.

I said: "When do we leave?"

"On the morrow." Orpus nodded, and he seemed pleased. "The plans are perfectly laid. You will ride at the apex of the host, Dray Prescot. The Queen's generals have planned everything with meticulous attention—"

Seg Segutorio, highly incensed, cut into Orpus' words.

"What of Delia?"

Naghan remained silent. Lilah moved her switch, but she, too, did not say anything.

"Delia may be the woman," Seg said. "We do not know—"

"We will ride at the head of the host, Seg, you and I," I said. "We will fight. If the army of Hiclantung can follow me, then it may. But I shall fight through to Umgar Stro, I think, or I will be cut down."

Orpus nodded briskly. "Excellent. Our plans call for a great charge that will reduce the cramphs of Chersonang to slime beneath our feet. They are but Harfnars—"

"Harfnars, yes," said Naghan in his quiet voice. "But they fight exceedingly well. And Umgar Stro with his Ullars has drilled and strengthened them. Halfmen they may be, but they will fight."

Orpus boomed a great basso laugh.

"There will be no treachery in our ranks, this time, when the Ullars fly down upon us. We have learned how to defend ourselves against impiters and corths. When the accursed Harfnars see their new allies retreating, bloodied and torn, they will not fight as they have done in the past."

Clearly the sense of historic conflict sounded in Orpus' words. For many years the hatred and rivalry between Hiclantung and Chersonang had festered. Now a new element in the Ullars had been added. There was sense in what Orpus said — sense, and a deadly danger these Lohvians would not see.

So we sallied forth on the morrow, a proud and eager company. Queen Lilah was with the host. Wearing her green tunic and with a glittering gilded breastplate, she led out for a space. With Seg and myself, mounted upon nactrixes, rode Hwang's regiment of cavalry. Heavy horsemen, with long lances and armor, and with a breathtaking panoply of embroidery and silken banners, they rode arrogantly, confident in their own prowess.

The infantry marched in their regimented formations. Varters rumbled in the intervals. There were also many strange contrivances mounted on carriages whose purpose I was to come to understand passing well in later years. At this time I saw them in action but the once, and was impressed.

Thelda rode with Seg and me. Lilah wanted to keep her under her eye. Seg and I wore half-armor, bronze breastplates and shoulder-pieces, beautifully made. There comes a time in a people when armor is so splendidly made that its very beauty cancels out much of its function. The empire of Walfarg had fallen to interior problems as much as by barbarian invasions, and a symptom of that ancient disease showed in the conspicuous artistry of the armor, its incredible standard of workmanship, its comfortable fit, its padding, its cunning fastenings — and in the ominous clefts between piece and piece, the gaps at neck and shoulder.

I did not care.

I felt a lightening of my spirits. I had been imprisoned in a silken bower unable to break free; and now I once more rode beneath the twin suns of Scorpio and advanced into Kregan warfare. I did not know if Delia lived. I would find out. Of that I was certain.

The whole glittering procession marched firmly toward Chersonang and following us tailed a massive baggage train. No comforts would be missed on a Lohvian campaign. We would, in any case, spend only a few days on the march before we crossed the border and approached Chersonang city.

"You do realize, Dray, that that she-leem only wants you to lead her army? She wants you to rush in first and break a way for the rest of her lackeys. You've had no say in the strategy, have you?"

"Yes, Thelda, and no, Thelda," I said. "I have more or less promised. You must understand why I agreed."

"But there's no need!" She bit her lip while Seg shot a quick glance at her as she rode between us. She wore a proper riding habit, and once more looked a great lady, her switch in her gloved hand.

"Oh?"

Her nactrix jostled closer to mine; she reached out her hand to me and her face showed a strange look, of compassion, baffled desire, remorse — self-doubt, even. Thelda had never been one to exhibit the slightest self-doubt; even the business of the vilmy and fallimy flowers had not fazed her for long.

About to pay attention to what was festering in her, I was caught by the long shrilling sounds of Hiclantung trumpets, those fabled silver trumpets of Loh. Intense activity boiled up.

"Look!"

Low over the horizon, skimming the ground and rising and falling over groves of trees, a myriad black shapes darted down on us. A swarm of midges they appeared at first; and in seconds the narrowing distance converted them into fanged and wide-winged impiters, metal-jangling, with fearsome Ullars perched on their backs waving their spears in ferocious glee at the onslaught.

Between the scattered clumps of trees the ground undulated gently in waves of rippling grasses, a motionless sea endlessly in motion. The Ullars flew their mounts directly down on us, disdaining any attempt to stalk us from the sun. Instantly the compact formations of the Hiclantung infantry shook out into fresh patterns and I saw the forest of upraised left arms, the longbows bent, the sunlight glinting from the jagged arrow barbs.

"They will not catch us again!" yelled Seg.

He lifted in his stirrups, dragging out his long sword, his whole body animate with a dreadful yearning.

The strange contrivances of Hiclantung now revealed their purposes. As the impiter host struck so rose the arrow storm to drive feathered shafts deep into breast and wing and belly. And, with that rustling arrow storm rose spiraling, tumbling, spreading, spinning nets, and chains, and bolas, and starred-blades. Great was the execution that day, as the army of Hiclantung repaid their score, as they showed the fliers of Umgar Stro how they treated any impetuous airborne assault.

A warrior flying a great bird, even a creature so fierce and powerful as an impiter, must necessarily be at a disadvantage against a warrior on his own two legs armed with a projectile weapon. It is difficult to shoot an accurate shaft from horseback — or zorcaback or sectrixback — and even more difficult from the wind-gyrating back of a corth or an impiter. It can be done by expert marksmen; and such marksmen were these indigo-haired half-men of Ullardrin. But the longbowmen of Hiclantung outshot them with ease. Aerial beast and man, one after another, more and more, fell helplessly from the sky.

I saw two impiters entangled in the same net, their wings striving to beat and break the strands, saw them twist and fall and smash terminally into the ground. All around us the flying host was falling. Occasionally men of Hiclantung staggered back with an arrow shafted into them, or a spear gouging its way down past the soft skin between neck and collarbone. But the winged attackers had met their match. Discipline, training, knowledge of weapons, and no taint of treachery brought the victory.

Watching those half-men up there as they wheeled aimlessly about above us, screeching their hatred and their defiance, shaking their weapons, trying to loose shafts down upon us, I was vividly reminded of the useless French cavalry charges I had witnessed on the field of Waterloo — and I began to build together ideas on how one should use this aerial cavalry, the proper function of airborne infantry.

In all the blaze of action I had not loosed a single shaft.

Despite his exultant energy, Seg, too, had not shot. We both sat our nactrixes with full quivers strapped to our backs.

Queen Lilah rode across, her peak of hair giving her narrow face that demon-haunted look, her mouth open and shouting. She indicated by her carriage, the brightness of her eyes, the abandon of her gestures, how great the victory was. Everywhere over those undulating hills the sprawled corpses of impiter and Ullar showed how sorely the half-men had paid, how bloody had been the vengeance of the men of Hiclantung.

"You see, Dray Prescot!" Lilah screamed across at us.

"I see, Lilah."

"Nothing can stand against us now!"

I pointed.

Over the crest of the hill appeared a long dark line. I could see the wink of suns-light on spear and sword, on bronze helmet and breastplate. Regiment after regiment, already deployed, broke into a jog-trot down the slope of the hill. And then, around the flanks broke a spray of cavalry, squadron on squadron of nactrixes. Their riders whooped in the saddle, lifting, their weapons glittering bright.

Lilah's face twisted into itself. Her switch came down with a thwack into her nactrix's flank. Before she bounded away she screamed at me: "There is your enemy, Dray Prescot! There are the Harfnar of Chersonang! Charge! Destroy them all!"

But, already, it was too late.

Whoever had organized this affair, be it Orpus or Hwang or Lilah herself, had miscalculated. After the formations adopted by the Hiclantung army which had so successfully defeated the flying troops of Umgar Stro, they were in no position to resist the punishing and sudden attack from the army of Chersonang. In an instant the leading echelons were upon us. Even as the men of Hiclantung broke and ran I was surrounded by viciously-striking half-men. Queen Lilah's army was converted in an instant into a running, shrieking, panic-stricken mob. And Seg, Thelda, and I were marooned in a savage and destructive sea of hostile blades.

Seventeen

Of downfall and of bondage

I fought

Oh yes, I fought. To have once more a tangible foeman before me, to feel the bite of his steel on my blade, to swing and feel that psychic shock as my brand bit back into his skull or body or limb, to feel the electric energy of it tingling up my arm, to do and feel all these things came to me with a great and dark joy. I confess it now; I joyed, then, in that battle as I seldom joy in mere fighting and killing. It seemed to me that every foeman who came up against me might be Umgar Stro, although common sense told me he would be directing the battle from some safe spot in the rear. I felt a personal animosity against every one of these Ullars and these Harfnars. For, between them, had they not taken my Delia of Delphond from me?

The Harfnars were a strange-looking people, and yet close to men as men are known on this Earth, and in nowise as weird or uncanny as the Rapas or Ochs or Fristles with whom I was familiar.

Hereditary foemen of Hiclantung, they were, whose animosity stretched back to the day when the Harfnars had taken over the city of Chersonang after the withdrawal of Walfarg's forces. They were strong, cunning, devilish, with flat noses as wide across their faces as their lips, with brilliant lemur-like eyes set above, which gave their countenances a curious boxlike construction, forcibly abetted by the squared-off chin and forehead. They were brightly clad in checkered garments of flowing silk and satin and humespack, trimmed with fur, with the dull gleam of bronze corselet and pauldrons shining through ominously.

So we fought, Seg and I, seeking to protect Thelda and reach a solid knot of Hiclantung cavalry isolated on the crest of one of the small hills. This was the remnant of Hwang's regiment.

Arrows darkened the air about us. The turf stank sodden with the tang of newly-spilled blood. The hooves of our nactrixes pounded out erratically as we jerked the reins, this way and that. Seg's longbow sang and sang again. Every shaft found its mark. He shot rearward, turning with supple ease in the saddle, shooting with contemptuous ease. Anyone who came within reach of my long sword died.

With Thelda crouched low in the saddle in the lead we thundered toward Hwang's remnant.

They opened ranks for us, then closed. Each man there knew he must die. I could see the knowledge stark on their faces, deep within their eyes, but they stood and they fought and they died.

We skidded to a halt and dismounted. Hwang greeted us with a grim and brooding humor whose genesis I recognized with a pang; his imperturbable mien outraged Thelda.

"The army ran away!" she said. She sank down to the ground, sobbing with fury.

Seg tried to comfort her and — to my joy and amazement — she welcomed his attention. I saw her put her hand in his. He did not look back at me, but I saw the way his back straightened and the way his head went to one side. They talked together as the battle outside eddied past. There would be plenty of time for Seg to loose the remainder of his shafts.

"Is all really lost, Dray?" asked Hwang.

"We are not dead yet."

"The Queen? Have you seen her? Is she safe?"

"I do not know."

I looked over the ranks of troopers who shot with precision and care, breaking up attack after attack. There was nothing wrong with the soldiers of Hiclantung; first treachery and then bungling had undone them. The army of Chersonang swirled into the pursuit, and the Hiclantung rout vanished over the hills. There was still time...

"If you break for it now, Hwang, a regiment like yours can break out, can carve a way through."

"Perhaps."

What had happened to Hwang had happened many times to many men in an abruptly lost battle.

"Do not joy in sacrifice," I said. "Rather, rage at death. This is no worthwhile sacrifice. If your regiment can be saved, then it is your duty to save them. It is not arguable."

"Perhaps."

"If you are to do it, it must be done before the Ullars rally and return. Isolated as you are and without your varters, you will not repel them as easily as—"

An arrow thunked into the turf at our feet.

The wounded had been collected in a huddle to one side of the nactrix lines. The uneasy beasts chomped and snorted, but they kept under good control. I did not know the full extent of the field supply situation, but I figured that the army, being a sophisticated part of a civilization descended from a great empire, would have ample regulations. The arrow supply would hold out yet; men were continually running from the supply carts with great sheaves up to the shooting lines. Hwang's officers kept a tight rein on their men. Order, efficiency, going by the book — all these undoubted benefits were amply demonstrated — but...

"You've got to break out, Hwang, before you are all cut to pieces!"

He started again to say, "Perhaps," when Seg approached followed by Thelda. She looked dreadful, the tearstains shining on her cheeks. Seg looked mean.

"You can't stay here," he began at once. "We'll all be chopped. Mount and ride! The longbows of Loh can ride through granite walls!"

Hwang looked from Seg to me, and back. He took a grip on himself, and I could fully sympathize with his position. As for myself, I was perfectly content with what I must do. Then Thelda took my arm as Seg and Hwang, arguing hotly, moved off to confer with Hwang's staff officers.

"Dray—"

I found a scrap of cloth and wiped her face.

"You'll get out all right, Thelda. Seg will see to that."

"Dear Seg—"

"He is the finest man you're likely to meet, in Vallia or elsewhere, Thelda."

"I know. And I've treated him so badly. But, Dray, I had to! Surely you see that? I had to!"

"I don't see it."

Above the bending ranks of bows and the nodding plumes of Hwang's men sudden onslaughts of the Harfnars boiled up to the lines and then the long lances thrust in drilled precision, the slender swords disemboweled, and the onrush turned once more into a retreat. But every mur that passed thinned the ranks of the soldiers of Hiclantung. Unless Hwang broke out soon the end was very near.

Thelda gulped, and her hands gripped and twisted together. She looked as though she had reached the last of her strength.

"But I had to! I was ordered to—"

"Ordered?"

"Yes, Dray. You know how the proposed marriage between yourself, a mere Lord of the Clansmen, and the Princess Majestrix is viewed in Vallia? Even the Presidio could not agree on a complete approval. Each member has his own rapier to sharpen."

I did not smile at her — we would say "ax to grind" — but I had already guessed what she would say. Indeed, only a credulous idiot like Dray Prescot would have missed the unmistakable signs before. "Go on, Thelda, my Lady of Vallia."

"Oh, Dray! Say you don't hate me, please!"

"I don't hate you, Thelda."

She regarded me with a wary misery through her tears.

"When Delia insisted on flying out herself I, as her hand-lady, also would go. The Ractor party gave me my instructions and they are very strong, Dray, terribly powerful!"

I nodded.

"They have their own candidates for the princess' hand. They are determined you shall never marry her—"

"So you were told to deflect my interest from Delia — to yourself."

Poor Thelda! How could she imagine that any woman in two worlds could prevent me from thinking of Delia for a single instant? Even Mayfwy, dear, loyal, wonderful Mayfwy, had not deflected me.

The battle could not go on for very much longer. The lines of wounded stretched now past the uneasy nactrixes. I fancied Hwang would not abandon his casualties and he would need every man in the ranks who could wield a sword. I reached down a hand to Thelda, to touch her shoulder and reassure her, but she gripped my hand and pressed it to her face and I could feel the tears, hot and sticky.

"I had my instructions, and I tried to follow them. And, in truth, Dray, I did fall in love with you. I believe any woman would. But Seg — he is—"

"For your own sake, Thelda, forget me. Care for Seg Segutorio. He will afford you all the love and shelter any woman could desire."

She lifted her eyes to me, and the tears brimmed there, silver and shining.

"But, Dray — I have been foolish, for I have been brought up to obey. The Ractors demand instant and total obedience in their schemes. But, Dray—"

She was trying to tell me something extra, a fact she had to force out. Seg shouted and I turned. He waved an arm. In all the uproar of shouting and screams, of the shrieks of wounded men and beasts, the incessant clang of steel on steel and steel on bronze, I just caught the tag end of his words.

"...now and not a moment to lose!"

Hwang's men were going through their drill with the precision of English Guards. Now the missiles were flint-tipped arrows. But they could strike through the bronze we wore, they could slice into the heart through the interstices in our armor, gaudy and beautiful as it was.

"We're leaving, Thelda. Up you come. And mind you stick close to Seg!"

She came up softly into my arms, limp and trembling.

"But, Dray — I must tell you! I must!"

I held her as the roaring battle smashed and boomed about us.

"Dray — Delia did not fall into the tarn. I did not see that. I said that to make you forget her—"

The roaring was in my head now. This story, this falsehood of Delia tumbling into the tarn had been the single dominant fear, bringing on all the rest; if she had not died then, she would still be alive now. I knew it. I felt it with every fiber of my being. No cynicism could deter me, now. Delia lived — I believed that. Delia lived!

The Lohvian soldiery of Hiclantung ran smartly to their nactrix lines, mounted. Detachments maintained a covering shower of arrows. With an excess of energy like the release of icy water in the spring thaws of the north, I flung Thelda up into her saddle. I straddled my own mount. Seg was with us.

Hwang shouted. The emptied supply cars were loaded with wounded. A wedge formed. I thrust my way to the apex — thinking ironically that this was the spot Queen Lilah had wished me to occupy, a spot in which my own foolhardy valor would spur on and encourage her army. Now I obeyed her wishes in order to save a paltry remnant of the Lohvians of Hiclantung.

Like some bursting summer storm cloud we broke away down the grassy slope. The nactrix hooves pounded. Arrows crisscrossed. Men and beasts shrieked and reared and fell away. We went bounding on, bouncing in our saddles, and yet maintaining that incredible accuracy of shooting that is the pride of the Lohvian.

Seg spurred up with me, his bow bending and releasing with a smooth inflexible rhythm. He controlled his mount with his knees, as did most of the men of Erthyrdrin, although some cavalrymen of Hiclantung tended to gather up their reins in the hands that grasped their longbows. I had followed the example of Seg, although my training stemmed from those far-off days riding with Hap Loder and my Clansmen across the Great Plains of Segesthes. Had I a phalanx of voves at my back now — we would smash like a roller of the gods across the Harfnars of Chersonang!

Seg turned his tanned flushed face toward me. Every thing about him was instinct with the passion of battle. I saw his face change; the expression of absolute horror and then of fanatical determination that crossed his features told me, without the need of personal verification, what had happened.

With a tremendous shout Seg swirled about. He thrust his great longbow away as he spurred cruelly back.

Back there Thelda's nactrix had taken an arrow in the belly.

She was sprawled across the grass to one side of the following wedge of cavalry. Arrows nicked the air. Arrows feathered into men and beasts. The carts rolled and bucked as they bounced after the cavalry wedge, their wounded occupants shrieking in time to the jouncing. Dust spurted. In all the crazed uproar I knew Seg could see only Thelda.

As he reached her a flying wing of Chersonang cavalry swept over them. I saw his long sword shining red; then he was down.

Somewhere in that melee of spurring beast-men and trampling nactrixes, of cutting steel and thrusting lances, lay Seg and Thelda.

I thought of Queen Lilah, and of my place at the apex of the wedge — but we were in retreat, we were not charging to victory. I brought the nactrix around with as much cruelty as Seg had shown, dug in my spurs, sent the half mad beast crashing back.

Harfnars with their flashing weapons reared before me.

Arrows cut the plumes from my helmet. Arrows clanged away flintily from the armor. One sank deeply into the neck of the nactrix. It went on and over in a somersault. I flew from its back, turning over, still grasping my long sword. I did not see Seg and Thelda again in that maelstrom of barbaric savagery.

Then, for a space, I did not see anything at all save a red-flaming blackness.

During this period of misted movement and dulled perception I was aware of a voice speaking in the common language of Kregen, so I knew it would be an indigo-haired Ullar talking to a Harfnar of Chersonang.

"Bring him. He will furnish sport for a while."

There followed movement and the sensation of flying and the thrashing sounds of great wings beating the air. The ache in my head diminished to proportions just short of bearable and I came back to my senses chained and bound and strapped up to a granite wall in a dark dungeon.

Dungeons are dungeons, as I have remarked before, and some are worse than others. This particular specimen contained all the unpleasant features a human-operated dungeon would have, plus a few the Harfnars had thought up out of their own culture of bestiality.

A groaning and moaning sound told me there were others of the men of Hiclantung with me, reserved for sport. There was no need to elaborate on what was in store for us. Cultures approximate, given the original dark impulse that began the gene trail.

By the time the first set of jailers flung open the lenken door and descended the greasy steps toward us I had freed my left wrist and partially broken away the links chaining my right. Under the impression that it was now or never I exerted all my force. My shoulders are not only wide, they are blessed with roping muscles that can surprise even me. The last link parted with a ringing ping.

In the fresh dazzlement of light I blinked and caught two of the Harfnar jailers about their throats and squeezed and flung them into their companions. All the time a low bestial growling rumbled and raged in the dungeon. The Harfnars hoisted themselves up, yelling, and their swords flicked out. They approached me warily. I was still securely fastened by my legs, so that between fending off the beast-men with swung chains I bent and tried feverishly to unfasten my legs, only having to straighten up and lash out again to make them keep their distance.

"Put down your chains, you Hiclantung cramph!"

"I'll slit your belly up to your throat, rast!"

At first I did not deign to answer them as they yelled at me and I worked on my bonds and swung the chains and all the time that sullen bestial roaring boomed and thundered in the dungeon.

"Keep them occupied!" shouted a Hiclantung cavalryman. The other captives were attempting to break their bonds, but they could not succeed. I still do not recall the exact strengths I exerted to snap those chains.

"Smash him over the head!" screeched the guard commander.

They danced in, one went down with his face ripped off, then they had entangled the chains, were bringing up spears to strike at me.

"Come on, rasts, and by the Black Chunkrah, come to your deaths!"

As I shouted the words, that bestial roaring stopped in the dungeon. Only then was the realization borne in on me that it was I, Dray Prescot, who had been roaring and thundering in so savage a fashion.

The shock sobered me.

In that instant the dungeon door was blocked off by the entry of a bulky half-man and the guards finally lost their patience with me and one thrust hard and in deadly earnest. His spear point darted for my breast.

I smashed it away and took him by the throat with my left hand, held him squirming and kicking in the air as I snap-reversed the spear and de-gutted the next guard. Then I hurled the one I held into their midst and swung the spear down again in low port.

"What are you waiting for, offal and dung feeders?"

They hesitated. They were splashed with the blood of their comrades. They could see the dead bodies sprawled on the dungeon floor, dreadfully mutilated. And all this from a man chained up by his legs!

The newcomer shouted, harshly, loudly, angrily, beside himself with fury.

"Dunderheaded dolts! By Hlo-Hli the Debased! I'll flog every man of you! Take him! *Take him now!*"

Goaded by twin fears, the Harfnars flung themselves upon me in a body. They entangled my left arm in flung ropes and dragged me down cruelly. I gasped and forced myself upright. A spear blade slogged down on my temple and I only half broke its force. But I slashed through the ropes — the flint-headed spear was sharper than any cheap steel — and reared back, blood obscuring my vision, my legs clamped as though trapped by a chank of the inner sea.

The man giving the orders moved closer. He peered at me in the light streaming down the dungeon steps. He put both hands on his hips and jutted his head forward, so that his indigo-stained beard shot forward like the ram of a swifter.

"You must be the one they call Dray Prescot, Lord of Strombor."

"And if I am, much good it will do you!" I shouted and hurled the spear full into his stomach. He gobbled and fell back, his hands clawing himself, seeking to stem the dark rush of blood welling past the neat flint-knapped semicircles of the blade.

His opened mouth sought to shriek, but only blood poured forth.

He fell.

And then I, Dray Prescot, laughed.

It did not last long after that.

The other captives were taken out one by one and when it was my turn I was tightly wrapped around in chains and ropes and carried up the dungeon steps. I saw clearly on the square boxlike faces of my captors a gloating kind of good humor. They knew what lay in store for me and they joyed in their dark fashion for the horrors I must endure. Indigo-haired Ullars met the cortege — an apt word, I remember thinking, wryly — at the entrance of arched brick where the brilliant hues of the suns of Scorpio flooded down in topaz and opal and incandescent light.

We entered an open area rather in the fashion of a theater or arena. The antiflier defense had been rolled away, and hung in nets at the sides, rather after the style of a Roman velarium not paid for by the gladiatorial promoter presently putting his show on and awaiting the next one, who had.

The amphitheater-like atmosphere continued in the storied series of seating terraces, all jam-packed with spectators. Dark blood lay seeping into the sand. Ullars moved about officiously. I looked for Umgar Stro. He must, I considered, be the chief man among the lolling group of dignitaries and nobles gawking down from an awning-draped box over the arena steps.

In the air and cutting through the familiar reeks of spilled blood and dust and sand and sweat a new and strangely disturbing odor laid a nasty taste in my mouth.

At the far end of the stretch of sand a monstrous erection of red brick reared. It was barred down the front. Beyond I caught the vaguest of glimpses of writhing motion, a flicker of evil eyes, the sway of tentacles.

And then — and then!

A wooden stake reared from the sand, surmounted by a triangle of logs, all bound together with thongs.

Naked she was.

All naked and white in the suns-light.

Thick and heavy ropes bound her to the triangle of logs, their rough bark harsh upon her soft skin. All white, her body glowed in the suns-light, bound by the constricting ropes that crossed over her spread-eagled legs, cutting into her thighs, her stomach, her arms, her throat.

Openly displayed, she hung there naked before the taunting gaze of the Ullars and the Harfnars, hung there by express order of Umgar Stro, baffled of a willing conquest, victim of his lusts for sadistic pleasure as much as the sweeter pleasure of voluptuous surrender. White and virginal and hanging, Delia, my Delia of Delphond, hung there awaiting the doom that writhed beyond the iron bars. And I stood stupidly before her, bound head and foot, helpless.

Eighteen

On my own two feet, then

Some little Ullar with his silly blue-dyed hair was prancing and yammering on the sand before me, but I could not pay much attention to him, even when he jabbed a spear into my stomach, because I was looking and looking at Delia. She hung there in her bonds, roped to that blasphemous triangle of rough-bark wood. Her head was raised in defiance, her chin high, and her glorious brown hair shone radiantly with those outrageous auburn tints beneath the suns of Scorpio.

She saw me.

She did not scream out.

We looked at each other, Delia and I, we looked, and between us passed the knowledge that if we were to die now, at least, we died together.

The Ullar was shouting and his flint-headed spear was becoming decidedly uncomfortable.

I managed to fall sideways against my chains and the Ullar on my right side, and as his arms automatically constricted about me to support me I lifted myself against him. Like a jackknife I doubled up in the chains and my feet shot out and crashed into the Ullar's face. He yowled and went over and I heard the answering roar from the massed spectators.

Yes, we were a spectacle, staked out for the enjoyment of the half-men peoples of Chersonang. Well-divided they were, I noticed; Ullars to my right and Harf-nars to my left. The ornately canopied box of Umgar Stro frowned over the assemblage. The Ullar picked himself up, clasping his nose from which the blood poured. He would have done for me with his spear then, but a shout arrested him and he swung away under orders from Umgar Stro.

All around the walls of the stadium perched giant impiters. Their coal-black plumage cut stark arabesques against the bright sky. The heat stifled down, intense and sweaty. I went on working with the chains, testing, seeking, straining.

Was that a link, thinner than the rest? Malleable? Subject to a straining twist? Surreptitiously I pulled and levered, feeling the thinner link distorting its shape.

We prisoners to be offered up as sacrifices had been fed some nauseating swill so as to keep our strength up to prevent us from fainting and so cheating the populace of their spectacle. If ever I had needed strength in my life, I needed it then.

Now the noise from the rows of seats began to settle into a rhythm and recognizable words beat out in a roar of sound.

"The Ullgishoa! The Ullgishoa!"

As if in response to some blasphemous call the thing in the iron-barred cage stirred and rippled its tentacles.

Whatever the thing was, the Ullars had evidently brought it with them from far Ullardrin. As I watched and worked on the chain everyone's attention centered on the cage and the thing within.

"The Ullgishoa!"

Half-men with their indigo hair streaming ran joyfully across the blood-soaked sand. Approaching the cage, they moved with a sureness of purpose that contrasted oddly with their sudden and completely unfeigned caution. Quickly the iron bars were flung back. Like a scatter of leaves before a gust of wind the Ullars scampered back to the side walls. The cage gaped open.

Movement. Slithering, sly, obscene movement. The Ullgishoa sprawled forward out of the cage, spilling over the iron lip onto the suns-warmed sand. I took a single look and then went at my chains with the crazed fury of a madman.

Huge, the thing was, squamous, slimy, its scales extending only over the upper portion of its hemispherical back, its lower portions a writhing mass of tentacles. But those tentacles! Each undulated and squirmed and writhed like a beckoning finger. Each began at the thing's body with a thickness of a man's calf, but as the tentacle thickness neared the tip it lessened until it was perhaps as large as a man's thumb, finished with a protruding lump that glistened scarlet and black, ichor dripping.

Inch by inch the Ullgishoa crept over the sand. Set in the center just below the squamous back a single eye stared lidlessly, yellow and red, focused unerringly upon the white, bound form of Delia. I knew what that thing would do once its tentacles were within reach of my Delia's body.

I struggled as the devils of Dante's Hell must struggle. If Hell exists, then it took this scene as its template.

I felt the link weakening. I felt it bending, slightly, and now the very technology of Kregen came to my assistance. I have mentioned how of necessity culture varied over the surface of Kregen, and as a corollary, technology and science varied also. It is manifestly unrealistic to imagine a world with every part at exactly the same level of advancement, unless that world be one under a central government, or a world of the far future wherein our Utopians love to direct their thoughts. So the long thin swords of the Ullars and the men of Hiclantung had to be forged from iron of a good quality. I knew because Hwang had often complained that the iron deposits around his city in nowise matched in quality the ores of ancient Loh; most of the swords had been handed down, from father to son, treasured heirlooms of a misty and grandiose past.

But for the iron of their commoner weapons and tools the men of the Hostile Territories had to employ local ores, and their weakness came now as a great blessing to me. I felt the link move, bending as I strained. All the time the people in the terraces howled and the stink of the Ullgishoa befouled my mouth, and I tried to think of iron technology and not of what those obscenely-seeking tentacles of the creeping monster would do to my Delia.

And, too, this lack of high-quality ore locally came as a surprising, but not unexpected, boon to me, as you shall hear.

The thing was almost upon Delia now.

She hung there, defiant, her head up, her face composed.

I risked a more obvious movement as I struggled. I braced my arms and stretched; those wide shoulders of mine gave me a leverage and my muscles jumped - and roped and bunched and — snap!

The link parted.

Now I must move with extraordinary swiftness.

The chains stripped from me with a clanking lost in the frenzied din of shouting from the thousands ranked on the terraces. Twin shadows from the suns of Scorpio paced me as I ran. Ullars must have attempted to stop me. I swung my bunched chains. I had become expert with swinging chains; I had had experience. I left a trail of blood and brains and shattered skulls strewing the sand.

376

The scarlet haze enveloping my sight concentrated vision only onto the Ull-gishoa and Delia.

Its tentacles were looping and coiling and reaching out for Delia. Each bloated head of scarlet and black dripped a foul ichor. They thrust and withdrew, thrust and withdrew, in congested anticipation. I ran.

Delia watched me.

As I reached the Ullgishoa her eyes widened.

"Jikai, Dray Prescot!"

I swung the chains. I swung the chains high and I put all my strength into that vicious and barbaric blow. Gone were the polite trappings of civilization. Gone the veneers of gentle conduct. Now I was a simple barbarian, filled with hate and loathing for this thing that sought so obscenely to destroy the woman I loved.

All that primordial savagery nerving me added cunning as well as bestial strength to my arms. The chains sliced cuttingly down upon that single lidless eye where mucus ran in a continuous dust-cleansing stream. The eye pulped and exploded into a scattered mass of scarlet and yellow. The stench sickened me — and yet nothing could sicken me now — not when Delia of the Blue Mountains watched as I fought for her life!

The Ullgishoa was not finished.

It emitted a high whickering shrill and its tentacles lashed back to envelop me. I skipped agilely aside and an arrow slashed past me. Again I moved, constantly maneuvering myself as more arrows sliced the bright air. Many of those shafts feathered into the bulk of the Ullgishoa — and I laughed!

I took the thick coarse ropes that bound Delia into my fists and I pulled and the rope snapped in a fray of threads.

She fell forward into my arms, her body against my chest, my face enveloped in her hair.

There was time for neither greeting nor the taking of a breath now.

The whole amphitheater was in turmoil. Ullars and Harfnars gesticulated and screamed, arrows scythed toward us, warriors ran fleetly over the sand, their swords and spears bright in the streaming mingled light of the suns of Antares.

"Umgar Stro!" I looked up at the ornate box.

I put Delia aside and met the first of the Ullars. I broke his neck, took his sword, slashed the face from the next, disemboweled the third. Delia had snatched a sword and fallen into place at my left side. I felt a terrible pang of fear for her safety there, but she urged me on: "Jikai!"

We ran in a jinking zigzag path. The sword broke and I took another from the first Ullar foolish enough to cross my path.

A flint-headed arrow scored a bloody line across my back. Another nicked a chunk of skin from my calf. I ran on. Delia's hair streamed behind her head as she paced me. Straight toward that awning-draped box we ran, and the bedlam in-creased and surged into a continuous shattering wash of sound.

Umgar Stro stood up and gripped the gilded rail before his royal box. Large he was, bulkier than me, with his indigo-dyed hair contorted into a fantastic pranc-ing shape above his head. His blunt features and those narrow close-set eyes brooded on his warriors as they sought to stop my advance. He wore a fancy gilded armor, risslaca and leem designs hammered onto the breastplate. His thick neck rose above, ridged with corded muscle and congested veins.

"Stop him, you fools!" he roared. "Cut him down!"

But I had seen what I wanted.

Strapped to Umgar Stro's side hung a great long sword that made the long thin swords of these people mere toothpicks in comparison. That sword was a Krozair long sword. It was the weapon given me by Pur Zenkiren in Pattelonia, before we set off to fly The Stratemsk and the Hostile Territories. I could well understand how a man like Umgar Stro would value such a brand.

An arrow hissed into the sand before my feet and I jumped and jinked and the following volley split air.

Delia paced me, running very quick, her circulation coming back and yet not impeding her movements. I knew what she was suffering and if it were possible my heart hardened even more against Umgar Stro and his Ullars and these Harfnars of Chersonang.

Only this man had prevented us from continuing our journey. He it was who had caused Seg and Thelda to go down before his allied cavalry. He owed me much, this half-man, this beast, this Umgar Stro. I ran toward him and I did not shout and he saw me coming. He drew that great brand that was my own and he threw himself into a posture of defense, cursing those about him.

Arrogant and conceited, puffed with pride like many Earthly Politicians, was Umgar Stro, but he did not lack courage.

His massive frame dangled and clanged with golden ornaments, barbaric dyed leem pelts flaunting weird colors. He towered there, glowering in the light from the Suns of Scorpio, his indigo-dyed hair waving with the violence of his movements, his arms bulging with muscle.

"If these cramphs of mine will not kill you, then, by the violet offal of the snow-blind feister-feelt, I will send you to hell myself!"

He vaulted the gilt rail and landed very nimbly, swinging at once into that trained posture of defense. He was a swordsman. I made no attempt to cross swords with him. I was only too well aware of the quality of the Krozair long sword he brandished; as to the blade I had snatched up, it was as like to break at the first blow for all I knew.

A sudden and tense silence descended. All eyes fixed on the drama being enacted before the royal box. Into that silence came the screech and hacksaw rasp of the impiters from their perches around the amphitheater. There was one, a giant of the air, fluffing its feathers immediately over the awning.

There was no time for fancy swordsmanship, for feint and riposte, for lunge and parry. There was space for swordplay — of the brutal cut and thrust variety I knew so well and that had brought me thus far alive — space but no time. Umgar Stro's coarse and bloated features broke into a crude guffaw as he brandished that splendid sword before my eyes.

"Die, little man! Die and spit your guts on the ice needles of Ullarkor!"

Beyond him as he stood so confidently his companions in the royal box guffawed in lackey-like approval. There were scented and painted women, females of the Harfnars and the Ullars, jeweled courtiers and soldiers, impiter-masters, sword-masters. And there was one man, with the red hair of Loh, who sat unsmiling and tense, clad all in dark blue and unhappy. This, I guessed, must be Forpacheng. I marked him, too, for through his machinations my Delia had been snatched when he plotted the downfall of the Lohvian army of Hiclantung.

My great Krozair long sword slashed down — aimed at my head!

I dodged easily enough but I did not reply. Delia stood a little to one side, her toothpick sword lifted, her breast heaving; but her face showed the same strong resolution I had come to know so well through all adversity.

Umgar Stro shouted, and stamped his foot, and thrust. I risked the clang of blades as I parried and dodged — and the sword I wielded snapped clean at the hilt.

The gush of laughter from Umgar Stro was like an oil well breaking surface in the desert, dark and spouting and greasy.

"Dray!" shrieked Delia, then — and she lifted her weapon to fling it to me hilt first.

"Hold, my Delia!" I shouted. I jinked left, then right, took a spring and before Umgar Stro could orient himself I had vaulted clean over him. I landed and twisted like a leem. My left hand raked across and took his right arm biceps in my fingers. My right hand went around his neck and jerked his head back. I squeezed.

He tried to gargle something.

I exerted pressure with the fingers of my left hand and his right hand slowly opened so that the Krozair long sword fell to the sand. He sagged and then thrust with desperate strength. I hauled back. Without remorse, without pity and, now his time had come, without hatred, I pulled back until, loud and sharp, his backbone snapped.

I cast him from me.

I bent to retrieve my long sword and the arrows sang past me and, in that instant, the suns-light was choked off as a wide-winged shape plummeted from the walls.

Umgar Stro's own impiter! Come to avenge his death!

He was a monster, coal-black, wide of wing and ferocious of talon, with gape-jaws distended so that the rows of serrated teeth gleamed dull gold. His tail lashed wickedly at me so that I had to leap back. I shouted.

"Delia! This is our mount — be ready, my heart—"

"I am with you, always, dear heart!"

I intended to stand no nonsense from this savage beast. I leaped. I took the reins close up to the fanged jaw and I wrenched. I brought the flat of the sword around and laid it shrewdly alongside that narrow and vicious head.

"Let that teach you who is to be master here!"

I drew the impiter's head down, twistingly, dragged that beast low, hit him again, forced him to bend. Delia mounted with a supreme confidence that brought the breath clogging into my throat. As she wrapped the flying thongs about herself and adjusted the clerketer for me, I vaulted up and dragged the reins upward. The impiter's head rose. He was in a vile temper. An arrow whistled off the black sheen of his feathers and he rasped a hacksaw whine and struck three massive blows with his wings. He ran forward and then, with a massive fluttering and a great roaring of down-driven air, he was aloft. I had to strike but three more arrows away before we were well airborne and sailing above the anti-flier defense and away into the bright air of Kregen.

Below us in the amphitheater we left an incredible scene of confusion as Ullars whistled for their impiters, as Harfnars ran uselessly, shooting upward, only to see their shafts fall short. Strongly we beat across the sky. Umgar Stro — who was now dead — had trained his mount well. Crazed and savage and bewildered it might be; the impiter understood well enough what the point of my sword thrust into his side meant. His wings beat metronomically. The wind blasted back through our hair. Naked, we shivered in the slipstream. But up and up we flew, faster and faster, winging away from Chersonang and all the barbarity festering there.

For some time I fancied I could detect the foul taint from the deliquescing corpse of the Ullgishoa.

From the city of Chersonang behind us rose the black swarm of impiter-mounted warriors. Like a column of smoke they rose and leveled off and, wind-driven, soared after us. I jabbed the tip of my sword into the impiter and forced him to beat a faster stroke.

The twin suns of Scorpio cast their mingled light down upon us, and the land beneath spread out with its cultivated fields giving way to heath and wasteland cut through by the magnificent stone roads of the old empire. The host of impiters on our trail must have been visible for dwaburs in every direction. Our own beast flogged the air, driving us on, putting an increasing space between us and our pursuers. As befitted the power and glory, as well as the bulk, of Umgar Stro his impiter was a king among fliers. But the double burden would tell in the long flight, and eventually the flying nemesis would catch us.

If such a thing as Fate exists, it has sometimes come to my aid as well as dealing me many shrewd blows. Unaccustomed to such things, I confess it was Delia who first spotted the distant dot, and who cried out in joy — and then alarm as other reasons for the presence of an airboat here, over the Hostile Territories, occurred to her.

But there was nothing else for it. The distant flier changed course and bore through the upper levels straight toward us.

We strained our eyes. I made out a lean petal-shape, high as to stern, a much larger craft than the one in which we had flown The Stratemsk; larger, even, than those airboats of the Savanti in unknown Aphrasöe. Flags fluttered from the up-perworks. Delia screwed her eyes up. I felt her body close and warm against me, and my arms tightened in instinctive protection.

"I think, my darling, I think—" she said. And: "Yes! It is! She is from Vallia!"

"Thank Zair for his mercies," I said.

She must have spotted the massed fliers from a long distance off, for I knew the Vallians possessed telescopes. I knew without doubt why the Vallian airboat was here, why it turned at once, sensing the answer to her quest lay with that flying host of impiters. The airboat swung alongside. I hauled the impiter up and looked down.

The craft was compact and trim. I was reminded of the order and discipline of a King's ship or of those swifters I had commanded on the Eye of the World. The sights of varters of design strange to me then snouted upward at us. At the first sign of treachery or the first false move we would be blasted from the sky. A group of men on the high stern looked up, and I saw the familiar Vallian costume mingled with a smart dark blue uniform I took to be that of the air service of Vallia.

"Jump down, Princess!" shouted one of the men, a barrel-bodied individual in dark blue, with wide shoulder wings, and a flaring orange cloak. At his side swung a rapier, matched by the main-gauche on the other. He wore a curly-brimmed hat with a blazing device of gold on the front band, and an orange tuft of feathers. His face was seamed and wind-lined, the crow's-feet at the corners of his eyes testimony to his days in the air scanning distant horizons.

Carefully I edged the impiter lower so that the ratings below ducked against the beat of wings. Delia went over first and I followed to be caught instantly in strong hands. Umgar Stro's impiter, relieved, spun away into the bright sky.

"Princess Majestrix!" said the burly man, a Chuktar, an exalted rank in any man's army or navy or, as I encountered for the first time, air force.

"My Lord Farris!" said Delia. She was wrapped in a swathing orange cloak, and her face showed high and proud and yet mightily relieved. "You are most welcome."

The Lord Farris, the Chuktar in command of this airboat, the name of which was *Lorenztone,* bowed deeply. He did not incline, a depraved custom, and this pleased me. "And this—?" He gestured toward me in a way that was most polite.

Delia smiled. "This is Dray Prescot, Lord of Strombor, Kov of Delphond, and betrothed of the Princess Majestrix."

Farris bent his head in a stiff but exquisitely formal little bow. He turned back to Delia. "The Emperor, your father, learned that you had taken a flier and—" He hesitated and I could guess the scenes that had followed on that discovery. "There have been many airboats seeking you, Princess, and I am overjoyed that it was to me and *Lorenztone,* that the honor of finding you has been given."

"I am pleased, also, Farris. But—"

A lookout sang out from forward.

Everyone turned. The sky seemed filled with impiters.

Farris looked pleased. He smiled and rubbed his hands.

"Now these debased descendants of a decadent empire will see what a new nation can do!" His orders were given in a calm and matter-of-fact tone of voice that heartened me.

During that fight as the winged hordes of Umgar Stro fell on us I was mightily impressed by the way the air service men of Vallia handled themselves. Their swivel-mounted varters coughed a steady stream of projectiles. Impiters fell fluttering from the sky. Archers using smaller bows than those of Loh, it is true, took a toll. Any Ullar venturesome and lucky enough to gain a footing on the deck was instantly cut down. The Vallians, in this kind of aerial fighting, did not deign to disregard the effective uses of a boarding pike. With my long sword, which they looked at with a kind of amused awe, I joined in. The battle, in a sense, came to me as an anticlimax. Delia was safe, now, and before us lay the flight to Vallia and then the meeting with her father, that imperious, relentless, awe-inspiring man, the emperor of all Vallia.

At last the impiters and their Ullar warriors gave up.

We forged on across the landscape of the Hostile Territories as gradually the twin suns, Zim and Genodras, sank to the horizon. I took stock of this Vallian airboat, this *Lorenztone*. She was all of fifty feet long and her widest beam, which came some two-fifths of her length aft, was twenty feet. Her leanness of appearance came from the sheer of her bows and the sweep of her stern where the sterncastle raised. Varters lined the bulwarks much after the fashion of the broadside guns of the ships of Earth with which I was familiar. Somewhere below her deck in a safe place would be that mysterious mechanism — mysterious to me then — by which this bulk was upheld in thin air.

The designs on the many flags she bore surprised me with their functional formality; but some were so embroidered that leems and risslaca, graints and zhantils as well as chank and sectrix, figured in that fluttering panoply.

An obliging crewman found me a length of cloth. He handed it to me expecting me to wrap my nakedness in it. It was green. I merely wiped the bloodied blade of my long sword upon it, carefully, mindful of the way that young tearaway of a Vallian, Vomanus, had so carelessly wiped his ornate rapier, and handed it back. From a great pile of flying silks I selected a length of blazing scarlet. This, with as always a pang of memory, I wrapped around my waist, drew up between my legs, and tucked the end in. Delia came up with a broad leather belt, of a leather I did not then recognize, soft and pliable, with a massive silver buckle. With this I kept the breechclout in place.

"There will be no scabbard for your great sword, Dray; not until we can have one stitched up for you."

"No matter. It can hang at my side naked, with a fold of cloth to keep me from being cut—"

After the action the reaction — we were both just making noises. The airboat rushed on through the sky levels. Delia looked at me, her head a little to one side, her face grave.

"Seg? And — Thelda?"

I shook my head.

She gave a little gasp, immediately choked off, and lowered that mane of glorious brown hair, shining in the dying light, and put her dear head into my shoulder. So for a space we stood there on the deck of the airboat as the twin suns sank and the strange and yet familiar constellations crept into the night sky with three of the lesser moons of Kregen hurtling low over the horizon.

Presently we were called away for food and we sat to a fine aerial feast in the aft cabin. The Chuktar, the Lord Farris of Vomansoir, introduced his officers and other high dignitaries who had been assigned the craft searching for the emperor's daughter. I caught at some of the conversations, guessing at hidden meanings, trying to sort out the people who would not object to Delia marrying me from those who took a violent exception. I did not think I would meet any Vallian who would actively wish me to marry Delia — not even Vomanus, if I cared to dwell on it.

I noticed one young man, with a mane of blond hair and a frank and open face, with that high beaked nose of the Vallians — a characteristic in noses that I myself shared — and took particular notice of him after he had said, with a light laugh: "I have never seen so large a sword wielded so expertly, my Lord of Strombor. I venture to think that a regiment of cavalrymen well-versed in its use would rattle even the best infantry line."

His name was Tele Karkis, and he did not appear to be the lord of anywhere, which was refreshing. He was a Hikdar. If I paint him in flat and stereotyped colors, it is because that was how be appeared to be then, when I first met him. I leaned over the table to help myself to a handful of palines, and before I popped the first luscious morsel into my mouth, I said: "And on what steed would you mount these hypothetical cavalrymen of yours, Hikdar Karkis?"

He laughed, not easily, but without unease. "I have heard of the voves your Clansmen ride on the Great Plains of Segesthes, my Lord of Strombor."

I nodded. "I hope," I said with the politeness habitual to the cultured Vallian, "that you will have the opportunity one day to pay us a visit and be our guest."

Then *Lorenztone* shuddered and lurched and Chuktar Farris spilled his wine and reared away from the table.

"By Vox!" he said. "I'd like to teach those rasts of Havilfar how to build like honest men!"

A man with a face I had taken no notice of at first sight, and thereby should have been warned, let out a string of oaths that were mere fancy verbiage, and quite fit for the ears of a lady, even for a princess. He was one Naghan Vanki, the lord of domains on one of the outlying islands of Vallia. He wore, unlike the air service men and the soldiers and court dignitaries, a simple silver and black outfit in the Vallian style. There was more about him than his name to remind me of Naghan, the Hiclantung spy.

We all went on deck.

The airboat was sinking and nothing the crew could do would bring her up. In the event we camped for the night among thorn-ivy bushes by a stream and were not too uncomfortable. Delia and I were quartered well away from each other, as was proper. As we prepared for sleep we all talked in a low-key kind of grumbling way about the profiteers of Havilfar. The name of Pandahem also figured in the conversation, usually with a round Vox-like oath or two.

A fire was built and we sat around it for a last cup of warmed wine. Naghan Vanki kept on making casually sarcastic remarks about barbarians, and uncouth individuals, and praising the civilization of Vallia. Delia shifted uncomfortably as he spoke. I saw well enough he was digging at me, but I did not care. Was I not with my Delia of Delphond once again, on the way to Vallia, if temporarily halted until repairs could be effected, and was not the future rosy with prospect?

"The Emperor raised heaven and earth to seek you, Princess," said Farris, smiling now the mission was successful. "You mean a very great deal to him and to all the people of Vallia."

"I am grateful, Farris. I am also aware that I mean a very great deal to my Lord of Strombor, as he to me. Remember that."

"Still," said young Tele Karkis, unthinkingly, "it is going to be an ordeal, standing up to the Emperor." He spread his hands. "I would not relish crossing him—"

"Hikdar!" said Farris, and at his Chuktar's words young Karkis colored up and fell mute.

But the seed had no need to be sown; everyone there knew the ordeal I faced, and I guessed many of them secretly wondered if I had the nerve to go through with it.

Truly, all I had heard of Vallia warned me off the place.

The warmed wine we drank was a good vintage. I remember that. It came from the province of Gremivoh, so I was told, and was much favored in the air service. It held a sweet and yet bitter savor unfamiliar to me.

Delia leaned close just before we parted for sleep.

"You do not truly wish to go to Vallia, dearest?"

"Can you ask!" I took her hand in the firelight. "I shall go to Vallia and face your father, never fear."

"But—" she began. And then: "Yes, dear heart, I know you will."

Perhaps, I thought then, being back with her own people had shaken her belief in me; perhaps she had been shocked by my own uncouth ways into seeing me in a new light. I tried to shrug that feeling off, but it persisted.

I crawled into my blankets and silks and yawned. I felt sleepy — not surprisingly, perhaps, but — ah, if we could foretell the future, then—!

I awoke in the morning as the twin suns of Scorpio sent down daggers of fire through my eyes into my brain to find myself rolled into a hole beneath a thorn bush.

I staggered out, cursing the pricks, and looked about.

The airboat was gone.

Alone, I stood among the thorn-ivy bushes on that endless plain of the Hostile Territories, and as I stood I heard a screech from above and I looked up and there, floating in wide hunting circles above, the gorgeous golden and scarlet raptor of the Star Lords surveyed me with a bright and implacable eye.

I shook my fist at the Gdoinye.

A moment later the white dove of the Savanti flew into sight, but, this time, the birds ignored each other. They surveyed me for a few moments and then turned and flew away. Whatever my plight it did not interest either the Star Lords or the Savanti, then.

My position was perilous in the extreme. I had the mother and father of headaches, and a stomachache, to boot, and I realized — dolt that I was — that something in the food or the wine of the previous evening had poisoned me. Whether or not the intention had been to poison me to death I did not know. I stood up, feeling grim, and looked about.

Some way off a blazing spot of scarlet caught my eye.

The remains of the campfire and discarded rubbish showed where we had camped. The marks the airboat had made were still fresh; evidently the technicians among the crew had repaired the craft working overnight. I walked across to the scarlet patch.

It was a length of scarlet silk wrapped about my own long sword, a rapier and main-gauche, a bow and a quiver of arrows and, tucked in at the end, a water bottle and a satchel of provisions.

I was not fool enough to believe these had been left for my good.

Whoever had drugged me and had me dumped here had also taken the trouble to leave these items, typical of those a man would need if he must survive in a hostile territory, so as to color the impression that I had left voluntarily and surreptitiously. The plot had worked. The people aboard *Lorenztone* must believe I had run away because I was unable to face meeting their emperor.

And the people aboard included Delia — my Delia of Delphond!

Did she believe I had left her? Could she believe?

I did not think so — but... But so much pointed to a desire on my part to evade going home with her. However much I tried to tell myself my fears were groundless, that she would keep faith in me, the more I doubted. I was in low spirits. My guts hurt, my head throbbed like the freshly cut-out heart of a graint, my limbs trembled, and my vision blurred.

I snatched up the Krozair long sword.

This I believed in — I had been cruelly wronged. My beloved had been snatched from me, and I could not blame her if she believed the worst of me. I could imagine how the situation would look, and the pressures that would be brought to bear on her to renounce her love for me.

Well, the Star Lords clearly had had no hand in this. The Savanti, too, were not implicated. They had merely assured themselves that I still lived, ready, no doubt, to seize me and toss me once more into the turmoil of their plans when the occasion demanded. Until then, I had men for enemies, men of Vallia who sought to take my Delia from me. Well, then, I would go to Vallia, I would march all the way to the eastern seaboard of Turismond and take ship, and march all the way into the great palace of this dread emperor of Vallia, this father of Delia's, and confront them all to prove my love for Delia.

I picked up the gear and strapped it about myself. I took a great breath. I looked at the distant eastern horizon of hills.

Then, with my long sword in my fist, I took the first step onward.

Above me the suns of Scorpio blazed down and about me the land of Kregen opened out with the promise of danger and terror, of beauty and passion. I could not fail. Not with the vision of my Delia before me.

Steadily, I tramped on eastward to whatever destiny held in store.

Swordships of Scorpio

A note on the tapes from Rio De Janeiro

I had assumed, along with thousands of readers who I am sure shared the same genuine sorrow, that the saga of Prescot of Antares must come to an end with the final transcriptions of the tapes from Africa. The editing of the tapes that chronicle the incredible story of Dray Prescot on Kregen beneath the Suns of Scorpio, a task which by a fortunate chance had fallen to me, had been so arranged that each volume might be read as an individual story in its own right.

But this meant that there were but few pages left to see publication after the first three volumes.

After that — nothing. I had hoped that Dray Prescot might in some way have been able to see a volume of his saga and perhaps be moved to contact me. So far this hope has proved vain.

But the ways of the Star Lords, no less than the Savanti, are passing strange and beyond the comprehension of mere mortal men.

I had just written the words, "…and then I yelled," and pushed back in my chair in my old book-lined study, feeling as though I had screwed down the coffin-lid on the face of an old friend, all glory fled from two worlds, when the telephone rang and it was Geoffrey Dean, long-distance from Washington. The coincidence affected me profoundly for it had been Geoffrey, an old friend and now connected with the State Department, who had given me the tapes from Africa. He had received them from Dan Fraser, a young field worker, who had provided Dray Prescot with the cassette tape recorder in that epidemic-stricken village of West Africa where Prescot had saved the situation. Geoffrey was wildly excited.

His first words were: "I have more tapes from Dray Prescot, Alan!"

By the time we both had calmed down, I had arranged to fly out to see him at once. A mysterious box had that moment arrived, and he had opened it, all unknowing; but he began to suspect as he saw the packed cassettes, played the first one for a few seconds only — and then had phoned me. There was a letter he was having translated. The box had been all over the world, it appeared, but had been mailed from Rio de Janeiro. Geoffrey met me at the airport and I drove with him to his Washington hotel in an impatience I could barely control. As soon as we entered his room I saw them. The box had been left as he had opened it. The manila-wrapped cardboard box, carelessly slit open, rested on a chair, and paper and string hung down. From the box a whole heaping pile of tape cassettes lay tumbled — and I knew that they contained a great wonderful El Dorado of exotic adventures on Kregen beneath Antares, that fierce and beautiful, mystic and awe-inspiring planet four hundred light-years from our Earth.

Geoffrey was waving a letter in my face.

"Read this first, Alan!"

The letter in translation was curt to mystification.

Dear Mr. Fraser:
I have been asked by Mr. Dray Prescot to forward to you these cassettes. Mr.
Prescot was instrumental in foiling a skyjack attempt upon a jet liner in which I
was a passenger. The bandits were after ransom without political aims in their
act. We crashed in the jungle. None of the passengers would be alive today if Mr.
Prescot had not guided us all to safety and taken care of us along the way. We
would have done anything for him. All he required was the use of my tape
recorder - and a large number of cassettes. And a promise to send them to you.
With great pleasure this I now do. I regret I have been unable to listen to any of
them as my English is imperfect. Mr. Prescot has now left Rio de Janeiro. If you
see him please convey my deepest regard and warmest admiration.
(signed) Francisco Rodriguez.

"And a hotel address in Rio," I said.

Geoffrey sighed. "No trace of Rodriguez, I'm afraid."

I looked at the heaping pile of cassettes and my hands shook as I placed that marked *One* in the machine. The opening was garbled; but then a voice sounded out clearly. I knew that deep, powerful voice; I would know it anywhere. I cannot vouch for the truth of his story, but that calm sure voice inspires confidence — more, it demands belief.

The precious box had been sent by sea mail to Dan Fraser's address in Africa, had been shipped back to Washington by the agency and, because Dan had been tragically killed in an auto accident and had no relatives, had found its way to Geoffrey Dean, Dan's boss. Geoffrey had made inquiries about this skyjacking, but had discovered nothing at the various embassies he approached. "Whatever happened down there in South America we may never know. No one is talking."

But, beside this wonderful cache of undreamed-of treasure, I did not care. Now the world could once more share the adventures of Dray Prescot on Kregen under the Suns of Scorpio and revel in the barbaric color and headlong action of his life.

As described by Dan Fraser, Dray Prescot is above middle height, with straight brown hair and intelligent brown eyes that are level and oddly dominating, compelling. His shoulders made Dan's eyes pop. Dan sensed an abrasive honesty and a fearless courage about him. He moves, Dan said, like a great hunting cat, quiet and deadly.

Born in 1775, Dray Prescot had clawed his way up through the hawsehole to become a ship's officer; but thereafter had little success in this world. I believe it is clear that, even then, he perceived with an inner conviction that he was destined for some vast and unimaginable fate. When he was whirled away to Kregen he positively reveled in the perils set to test him, and through his immersion in the sacred pool of baptism in the River Zelph of Aphrasöe he is assured of a thousand years of life, as is his beloved, Delia of the Blue Mountains. Banished to Earth he was recalled by the Star Lords — of whom he tells us nothing — as a kind of interstellar troubleshooter, and he quickly rose to become Zorcander of his clansmen, and then Lord of Strombor, an enclave house of the city of Zenicce on the west coast of the continent of Segesthes. Hurled through the void once more he suffered the horrors of the overlords of Magdag and was instrumental in raising his army of slaves and workers in an attempt to overthrow them. In the midst of his final onslaught he was whisked to another part of Kregen's inner sea, and plunged once again into the Star Lords' schemes. He had become a member of the famous Krozairs of Zy, entitled to be called Pur Dray, dedicated to the red-sun deity Zair.

Determined to reach Vallia, and Delia, he set off toward the east. But Delia had set her emperor father's air service in motion to find him, and had come herself to the inner sea in search of her lost love. Delia and Dray Prescot flew through The Stratemsk, as Prescot describes them a truly horrific range of mountains walling off the inner sea from the land to the east, the Hostile Territories. With two companions, Seg and Thelda, they crash and go through adventure after adventure until, at last, with the death of the beast-man Umgar Stro at Prescot's hands and the rescue of Delia, they make a dash for it astride Umgar Stro's own impiter — a gigantic coal-black flying beast. Seg and Thelda, so Prescot relates with great sadness, had been ridden down by a host of half-men. A Vallian Air Service airboat picks them up; but there is treachery aboard this flier, *Lorenztone,* for Prescot awakes beneath a thorn-ivy bush. He has been drugged. He finds weapons and food tossed down to color the impression that he has fled because he is frightened to face Delia's father, the emperor. This is the work, he believes, of the Vallian Racter party, who do not wish the Princess Majestrix of Vallia to wed him, a man not of their choice.

At this point Dray Prescot picks himself up and says: "On my own two feet, then!"

At this point the present volume, *Swordships of Scorpio,* takes up the narrative. At the junction where the tapes from Africa end and the tapes from Rio begin, I have made a note. They do not run consecutively on; there is a gap. From study of the cassettes I am sure there are other gaps to come in the story we have. I repeat, we are superlatively lucky even to have what we do of the fascinating and pulse-stirring saga of Prescot of Antares.

Kregen under the Suns of Scorpio is a real world, savage and beautiful, marvelous and terrible. Dray Prescot is there now, I feel sure, carving out fresh adventures by the side of his Delia of Delphond, his Delia of the Blue Mountains.

Alan Burt Akers

One

I march toward Vallia

On my own two feet, then, I would march all the way across the Hostile Territories and take ship at whatever port I came across and sail to Vallia, and there I would march into the palace of the dread emperor of that proud empire and in sight of all claim from him my beloved, my Delia, my Delia of Delphond, my Delia of the Blue Mountains.

I would!

The deadly Krozair long sword felt good in my fist.

My head still ached from the effects of the poison and my insides felt as though an insane vintner of Zond were trying to stamp a premier vintage from my guts. But I went on. There was no stopping me now — or so I thought then, wrapped about in rage and frustration and the unhealthy desire to smash a few skulls...

The plain continued on in gentle undulations to the low hills ringing the horizon. Long pale green grasses blew in the wind sweeping past. Over all the scene that streaming mingled light of the twin suns of Antares scorched down. The water bottle was half-full. Evidently, whoever had poisoned me and thrown me into the hole beneath the thorn-ivy bush had tossed down the scarlet silk wrapped about weapons and food to fool those aboard the airboat. The food and water had not been meant to keep me alive; I had a shrewd idea that the poisoner thought me dead.

If I, Dray Prescot, with weapons at my disposal could not live off this land, then I did not deserve to survive.

As you will know I was no soft innocent from a big city who always walked on stone sidewalks, who took automobiles everywhere riding on concrete pavements, who pressed buttons for light and warmth, who ate pre-packaged food. Although I am a civilized man from Earth, I was then and have remained when circumstances require as much a savage barbarian as any of the primordial reavers ravaging out from the bleak northlands.

The first river I came to I swam across and the devil take what monsters might be lurking beneath the water.

Along the banks were mounds of bare earth. These I skirted respectfully.

Ahead the tall grasses gave way to a lower variety, and the ground lay bare and dusty in patches here and there. The long black and red-glinting column I did not wish to see advanced obliquely from my right. I had no hesitation whatsoever in turning in my eastward tramp and heading off to the northeast.

From a low hillock — a natural hillock — I could see the seemingly endless stream of ants. I give them their Earthly name, for the Kregen names for the varieties of ants would fill a book. These were shining black, active, prowling restlessly toward some destiny of their own. The twin suns sank slowly behind me and the land ahead filled with the flooding opaline radiance from Zim and Genodras.

The first screams ripped from the gathering shadows.

Now I knew where the stream of ants was headed.

Soldier ants, large fierce fellows, their mandibles perfectly capable of shearing through ordinary leather, kept watch on the flanks of the columns of workers. The soldier ants, I judged, were all of six nails in length. Six nails make a knuckle. A knuckle in Kregen mensuration is about four-point-two inches, say one hundred and eighty millimeters.

These were big fellows.

The screams continued.

I hurried on, parallel to the column, seeing the sinking suns-light glancing off armored bodies, glinting red from joint and mandible.

Ahead the column spread out. It seemed to me like some blasphemous ink-blot, spreading and pooling, ever-fed by new streams.

The man had been staked out.

His wrists and ankles were bound with rawhide to four thick stakes, their tops bruised and battered from the blows of hammers. He twisted and writhed; but the tide of black horrors swarmed over him, a living carpet eating him to the bone.

There was only one way to get him out of it.

My Krozair long sword had been in action against mighty foes before; now it would have to go up against tiny killers four inches long.

Four quick slashes released the thongs. I bent and hoisted the man, holding him in my left hand, swatting with the sword. Already the horrors were scuttling up my legs, over my back, along my arms. Agonizing pains stabbed my flesh. I danced and jumped and ran and shed crushed black bodies like a mincer.

The man was clearly dying. I had merely saved him from the kind of death the people — or things — had planned for him.

By the time I had got rid of the last ant, and had rubbed my skin and felt the slick blood greasy there, and had placed the man down gently against a grassy bank, I knew he had mere moments to live. Most of his lower abdomen and legs had been eaten away, his chest cavity was partially exposed, only his head — with the exception of the eyes — remained to appear as a reasonable facsimile of a man.

He was trying to speak, now, croaking sounds from his throat, gargling, his useless arms attempting to lift toward me.

"Rest easy, my friend," I said in the universal Kregish. "You will sleep soon, and have no more pain."

"So—," he said. "Sos—" He choked the words out. "Sosie!"

"Rest easy, dom." I uncorked my water bottle, filled it at the river, and poured water over his face and between his lips. His tongue licked greedily. Some of the blood washed away.

"Save my Sosie!"

"Yes."

He knew he was dying, I think, and his voice strengthened.

"I am Mangar na Arkasson. Sosie! She — the devils of Cherwangtung took her — they took her — they — the ants! The ants!"

I moistened his lips again. "Easy, dom, easy."

His black skin shone now with a sweat-sheen in the pink radiance from She of the Veils, the fourth moon of Kregen. He had been a proud and imposing man. His face, despite the contortions his agony wrought in his countenance, still showed hauteur and pride. His features were not the hawk like ones of Xoltemb, the caravan-master I had met on the plains of Segesthes, who came from the island of Xuntal. This man, this Mangar na Arkasson, had features more Negroid in their fashioning, hard and firm with a generous and mobile mouth.

"Swear!" Mangar na Arkasson whispered. "Swear you will save my Sosie from those devils of Cherwangtung. Swear!"

He was dying. He was a fellow human being.

I said, "I will do all I can to save your Sosie, Mangar na Arkasson. You have the word of Dray Prescot, Krozair, the Lord of Strombor."

"Good — good—"

His mind was wandering now and although I knew he did not have the slightest notion what a Krozair was, and had never heard of Strombor, yet I believe that he took with him into the grave the conviction — and I hope the comforting one — that I was a man who would do as I had sworn.

When he died, after a few mumbled and almost incoherent blasphemies and pleas, cries of strange gods, and, at my questioning, the statement that Cherwangtung stood at the confluence of two rivers, by a mountain, away to the northeast, I buried him. There was no way of judging what marker or memorial he would want, so I contented myself with manhandling a great stone over his grave. That would hold the plains lurfings at bay, for a time at least.

Few lurfings would attack a single man, even, unless there were a round dozen of them. Low-bellied, lean-flanked, gray-furred scavengers are lurfings, equipped with probing snout-like faces well-suited to the tasks nature has set them.

I stood up.

Four moons wheeled across the sky now, and their combined radiance lit up the night-land of Kregen, here on the eastern plains of Central Turismond. Far away to the east lay the coast. On the coast stood port cities, of Vallia, of Pandahem, of Murn-Chem, of a number of trading countries from overseas. I had to reach one, take ship, sail to Vallia...

But, first, I had given my word to a dying man.

I do not believe you, who listen to these tapes cut in this stricken famine-area of your own Earth, can condemn me for what I had sworn to do. I knew my Delia was safe. She was even now aboard the Vallian Air Service airboat Lorenztone securely on her way back to Vallia and her father the emperor. I need no longer suffer the cruel tortures for her safety I had recently gone through, when I believed her dead, then the captive of Umgar Stro whom I had slain, and so released her. No. With a clear conscience I could do what I had sworn.

My Delia, Delia of the Blue Mountains, would understand.

At that time I had, of course, had no experience of motive power for shipping other than the wind and the oar. The swifters of the inland sea with their massed banks of oars could sail independently of the wind — but I had gained the strong impression that I should judge the Vallian Air Service more from my own experience as a naval officer of a King's Ship of my own planet rather than from the wild times I had spent as a swifter oar slave and captain on the Eye of the World. I had in the nature of my profession heard of Claude Francois, Marquis de Jouffroy d'Abbans, who in 1783 had invented a paddle-boat and sailed her on the Seine at Paris, thus being, as far as I knew, the man to sail the world's first successful steam vessel. The first practical steamer had been built by the Scotsman, William Symington, whose Charlotte Dundas in 1801 proved herself by towing exercises. Robert Fulton, an American who would work for whoever paid him, had designed a paddle-steamer, Demologos, with the paddles between two hulls and armed with twenty-four thirty-two pounders. I wondered, then, as I strode across the pink-lit night-lands of eastern Turismond, just what this independence of the wind would mean in a vessel, in these sky ships built in far Havilfar.

All of which meant that I had no idea how long it would be before Delia reached her home in Vallia.

If the plans of the man who had poisoned me and dumped me under the thorn-ivy bush went as he envisaged, would Delia believe I had run off? Could she think I had quailed from meeting her formidable father, the emperor?

If she did so think — then I refused to contemplate that

If she did not think so she would very well do as she had done before and send a fleet of airboats scouring the world for me. That, I confess, was a comforting thought.

The men of Cherwangtung, having staked out Mangar na Arkasson for the soldier ants, had merely removed themselves from that immediate vicinity before they got up to their devil's tricks with Sosie na Arkasson.

She was not screaming and so the first sounds I heard were the stamp of naked feet on hard earth, the throbbing of drums, the chanting and leem-keening of the men of Cherwangtung as they danced around the central stake.

This was a scene I did not relish.

Bound to that stake the lissome form of Sosie gleamed in the torchlight, her black skin in startling contrast to the fish-belly white of the men who danced about her shaking axes and spears, their ankles festooned with bells and bones and feathers. They danced two forward, one back, stamp, stamp, slide, stamp, stamp, slide, and they shook their weapons and in the torchlight their faces showed corpse-white and lascivious and incredibly evil.

Sosie held her head up proudly. They had stripped her garments from her. Her hair, done in the fashion we know on this Earth as Afro, bristled. Dust and grass stems covered it, and there were long scratches on her thighs. I could not see her back, lashed to the stake; but I guessed that, too, was lacerated in like fashion as these men had dragged her here for sacrifice.

What the sacrifice was about, what they were going to do, what blasphemous gods they worshiped — of all that I knew nothing. It could be I was interfering in a ritual demanded by law and custom. Both Mangar and Sosie na Arkasson could have been criminals, meeting a just end.

But no civilized man binds a young naked girl to a post and dances around her in the torch glare, his every intention obvious. I felt sure that I was not committing a gross error as I took the bow contemptuously tossed down from *Lorenztone* into my hand. This was not a great longbow of Loh. I shut my mind to thoughts of Seg Segutorio, who was of Erthyrdrin, and who was a master bowman, and who was now — I had seen him fall beneath the nactrix hooves — dead and gone and best forgotten.

How could anyone forget Seg Segutorio?

I lifted the bow. I must put thoughts of Seg from my mind. There were twenty of them out there, and after perhaps the fourth or fifth shaft the rest would flee into the pink-lit shadows. They would not escape by running; but I would have to be quick.

If only Seg were at my side now!

Angrily — furious that thoughts of my comrade Seg, who was gone, smashed into my mind — I loosed the shafts as fast as I could snatch up the arrows, draw back the string, and let loose.

One, two, three, four — the four went down, coughing, with shafts feathered into them.

The chanting and drum-throbbing ceased.

One of the men yelled and I put a shaft through his mouth.

Others were shouting, and running, their naked white rumps gleaming in the pink moons-light.

I pinned three more and then they were gone, in every direction. From now on I would be the hunted, not they.

Speed...

Sosie regarded me as though I had appeared through the screen of a shadow play, in the round, flesh and blood, miraculously taking the place of a phantom.

"Sosie," I said. I spoke harshly. "I have come to take you away from these evil men. Mangar has sent me—" All the time I spoke I slashed her bonds free. As the ropes released, she buckled and fell. The agony of her returning circulation meant I must carry her. She was no Delia, who had been running fleetly at my side, wielding a sword, moments after I had cut her loose.

"Mangar, my father," she moaned. "I saw — I saw what they did! The ants! *The ants!*"

"Zair has him in his keeping now," I said.

Then, for a shocked instant, I wondered if these people of Arkasson worshiped Grodno, the false green-sun deity of the green sun Genodras. But Sosie gave no sign that she understood. I ran. Out from the torchlight and into the pink-shrouded darkness where that darkness was illusory, where the moons in Kregen's night sky cast down enough light so that one might read the small print of a directory, I ran — and then I stopped running. Sosie was bundled down by a small bush — not a thorn-ivy but, blessedly, a paline bush. Immediately she began to stuff the appetizing yellow palines into her mouth, drawing sustenance, refreshment, and surcease from them.

I scanned the horizon, lying down and looking up. One of the torturers showed against the skyline and he went down with an arrow in his guts.

His scream attracted two more, who ran, like fools, over to him, to be slain in their turn.

How many more were there? Another ten, I estimated, at least.

This crouching down was no way of fighting for me.

"Sosie." I spoke with an urgency that was not altogether feigned. I had to drive through to her mind. "Sosie! I am Dray Prescot. Your father made me swear to save you. Now, you lie hidden in this paline bush. Do not move. I will return for you."

She understood enough of that in her dazed condition for me to think it safe to leave her.

Then I went a-hunting men who tied girls to stakes, all black and naked, and tortured them.

They went down, one by one, until in the end five of them clumped together, brandishing their axes and spears, and charged me as I shafted one of their number who attempted to cast his spear into my belly.

Now was the moment I had hungered for, to my shame.

The bow went into the grass. The Krozair long sword ripped from my belt — that belt given me aboard the airboat by Delia — sliding against the fold of scarlet cloth on my thigh. I gripped the hilt in both fists, spreading them, the left against the pommel, the right hard up against the guard. That way the two-handed sword wielded by one cunning in its use could strike past and through the spears and axes of these white-skinned barbarians. They rushed against me, whooping, charged with anger, probably unable to comprehend just where I had come from or who I was — a man like themselves and no half-beast half-man of Kregen.

Like any man of Kregen who carries weapons they were skilled. But they could not match the swordsmanship of a Krozair. There is no boast in this; I merely state a fact.

By the time they had realized this, it was too late, and as I chopped the last of them — a wild and reckless stroke that took his head clean away from his shoulders — I was aware of the ostentatiousness of my behavior. They were men and not half-men; but they had been behaving like subhumans. That, I submit, is the only excuse I can offer for my savage conduct.

When I reached Sosie she was crying. Her slender body shook with her sobs. As tenderly as I could I lifted her.

"Where lies Arkasson, Sosie?"

"Over there."

She pointed due north.

I grunted. North in the compass bearing had bedeviled my progress through the Hostile Territories.

So, bearing a naked black girl in my arms, I set off to take her home.

Two

Of the black feathers & gemmed quiver of Sosie na Arkasson

"You cannot just go walking off across the Owlarh Waste, Dray Prescot!"

Sosie na Arkasson glared at me in a positive fury, her hands on her hips, her eyes bright; but her full lower lip quivered betrayingly.

"I have to, Sosie, and I must."

"But, Dray! There are leems, and stilangs, and graint, and even risslaca, besides those devils of Cherwangtung. You just can't go!"

I have never been a man who laughs easily — except in moments of stress or passion — and I could not force a laugh now. Had I done so, it is doubtful if it would have soothed Sosie's real fears. Arkasson had proved to be an interesting town, built against a sheer cliff of stone in which giant gems twinkled in the mingled light of Scorpio. The architecture ran to much convoluted tracery and scrollwork carved in stone, and massive drum towers capped with round pointed roofs built from the heavy slates from local quarries. There were open spaces in which greenery grew; but, still, echoing the inflexible rules of all towns and cities to the west within the Hostile Territories, no handy perching places had been overlooked. The defense against aerial attackers was not carried out with quite the same fanatical attention to every detail in Arkasson, and the walls cincturing the town were battlemented against ground troops as their first priority; but a force of aerial chivalry would stumble attempting to alight in Arkasson.

Mangar, who had died so cruelly, had been a leading man of the town; and although I met a number of the notables and was treated with universal kindness by them, I itched to press on to the east, to Vallia, and to Delia.

My pale skin, tanned by the Suns of Scorpio though it was, aroused intense interest in the black-skinned people of Arkasson. Sosie, indeed, had had to speak with rapidity and with lucidity to prevent a spear degutting me on that first arrival.

The people of Cherwangtung roamed the land all about during the nights, the land that hereabouts was called the Owlarh Waste, and retired to caves and hidey-holes during the day. From Arkasson they were regarded with loathing as beasts who made life difficult and dangerous. The farms ringing the town were all heavily defended by wall and moat; but the fiends from Cherwangtung would creep through by night and raid and burn and kill. Sosie's farm lay in ruins, blackened by the flames, her mother dead and now her father dead, also. The white-skinned savages had done that.

I still retain a vivid mental picture of that torture stake with the slim black form of Sosie bound naked to it, and the torchlight flickering wildly on the gyrating bodies of the white savages in their bells and feathers as they circled her screeching their menace, shaking their weapons, lusting for her blood.

"If you go, Dray Prescot — I shall never see you alive again."

"Oh, come now, Sosie! I can protect myself."

This was, in truth, a strange conversation.

When, at last, Sosie and her friends and the relatives with whom she was staying in Arkasson — until she had found a man and married and so ventured forth to rebuild her farm — understood that I fully intended to walk on toward the east, they insisted on loading me with presents. Any town must have food brought into it, and manufactures to sustain it, and Arkasson was no exception. The farms were the lifeblood of the town, and the white savages of Cherwangtung were attempting to bleed that lifeline dry.

Similar situations must exist all over the Hostile Territories; this one was none of my business. I had fulfilled my oath to Mangar na Arkasson; now I must be on my way.

From Sosie I accepted only food and drink, and a finely built Lohvian longbow. Memories of Seg ghosted up, to be firmly repressed. The longbow was all of six feet six inches in height, and the pull I judged to better a hundred pounds. It was a bow with which I would acquit myself well; had I not been trained by Seg Segutorio, the master bowman of Erthyrdrin?

Sosie smiled as she handed me the quiver fully stocked with shafts. There was in her eyes the look of a woman who bedecks a corpse for its final journey to the Ice Floes of Sicce. Out of politeness I examined the quiver, and noticed the exquisite bead-embroidery covering it, animals and flowers and border motifs, all stitched in brilliant colors. The beads glinted in the suns-light — and at that I frowned.

"These gems were gathered by myself from the cliffs, Dray. I have spent many years stitching this quiver. It—" She stopped, and her black face shone upon me and her everted lips trembled and she lowered her eyelids with their long curling black lashes. I thought, then, that I understood.

Her aunt confirmed my suspicions.

"A maiden of Arkasson, on marriage, is expected to hand to her bridegroom an embroidered quiver, and tunic, and shoes of buckskin, stitched with gems she has gathered from the cliffs with her own hand, and polished to perfection, and drilled without a flaw or chip. You are a strange man, Dray Prescot. But for the color of your skin you would be a worthy member of the noblest of Arkasson."

"And will no young man take her to wife if she cannot provide him with these trinkets?"

The aunt — one Slopa, with a lined face and graying hair, which meant she must be well over a hundred and fifty — looked affronted. "No."

"Sink me!" I burst out. "I can't take the quiver from Sosie! It's taken her years to make. If no gallant will have her without it, then she'll wait years and years more, gathering gems, polishing them, drilling them, stitching them to a new quiver. And what of her farm? Aunt Slopa — I can't take it!"

"You will hurt her cruelly if you do not."

"I know, by Zim-Zair, I know!"

Aunt Slopa pursed her full lips. "Sosie would not have done this just because you saved her life. There is more to this business than that."

"Can you bring me an undecorated quiver?"

"I can. But that—"

"Just bring it, please, Aunt Slopa."

When I had transferred all the shafts from the brilliant embroidered quiver into the plain one and had time to mark the perfection of the feather-setting — every feather was jet black — I took up the quiver that was the gift of Sosie na Arkasson and sought her out where she sat on a bench in a courtyard, the anti-flier wire stretching above her Afro hairstyle. She was reading a book — it was *The Quest of Kyr Nath,*[x] a rollicking tale of mythical adventure at least two thousand years old and known all over Kregen — and as I approached she put one slim black finger between the leaves to mark her place and looked up at me with a smile.

"Nath," I said. "I know a man called Nath, a dear comrade, and I intend to go drinking and carousing with him and Zolta again one of these fine days."

She looked at the quiver.

"I would like to live, Sosie, and yet you put me in mortal peril."

"I! Put you in peril, Dray Prescot! Why, how can you think it?"

"See how these marvelous gems and this incredibly lovely stitching gleam and wink and glitter in the light of Zim and Genodras!"

She reached out her free hand and stroked down the embroidery and the gem-stones. Her face showed satisfaction and pride, as was right and proper for a young girl who knows she has stitched well.

"Indeed, they do look fine. Over your back they will proclaim to the world that the quiver was made for you by a girl who—" She stopped. Again her soft everted lips trembled. She did not go on.

I said, in something of that foul and harshly-dominating tone I so much de-plore in myself, "The quiver is beautiful, Sosie. I am a rough adventurer, who must travel in wild and perilous lands. It could be the death of me. It would show the world where I was; it would show the world that I carried a fortune on my back. I would have no peace." She started to say something, quickly, hotly, but I shushed her and went on. "This should hang in the house of the man you marry, Sosie, the man you will love. For him, it will be a source of unceasing joy and pleasure. For me, it could bring death."

"But — Dray—" She was confused.

"You do see, Sosie. I appreciate—"

As I spoke, as I held out the scintillating quiver to her, she leaped to her feet with a choked cry. *Kyr Nath* went flying. Her arms went about me and she kissed me with a full fierce passion that held in it only an innocence and a sweetness.

That hot wet pressure on my lips shot through me with a spike of agony. Then Sosie released me and fled into the house.

I sighed. Bending, I retrieved the book.

Kyr Nath. Well. I read at random: "And in this wise did Kyr Nath astride his coal-black impiter smite the legions of Sicce, so that they recoiled from him in thunder and lightning, and Kyr Nath smote them from beyond the sunrise to the day of judgment, so that they fell to the ground and crawled into the caves beneath the Mountains of Pearl and Gold from whence issueth their fiery breath even to this day."

I put the book down. Sunrise. It said sunrise. I was still, as an Earthman, bothered over saying "suns-rise" instead of sunrise. Those ancient people of the Eye of the World who had lived and laughed along the coasts, who had built the Grand Canal and the Dam of Days, they were called the people of the sunrise or the people of the sunset. There were mysteries here that I had no way at all of unraveling.

Perhaps Maspero, in distant, unknown Aphrasöe, could have explained.

Also, and significantly, this copy of the book had Kyr Nath flying an impiter. Those coal-black flying animals with their huge wingspread were well known here, in the Hostile Territories, and I had alternately cursed and blessed them, as I had fought Ullars screeching wildly on their backs, and flown with my Delia astride Umgar Stro's great impiter away to find safety with the airboat *Lorenztone* from Vallia. In Sanurkazz the story would have had Kyr Nath riding a sectrix. Certainly, the story as I had first heard it, declaimed among the wagon circle of my Clansmen of Felschraung, had Kyr Nath riding a vove.

The culture of a whole planet is an intricately-woven tapestry — and, I can remember now, that I turned with that duly solemn thought to find Aunt Slopa regarding me mournfully.

"Sosie asks me to say to you that she quite understands."

Although I had faced many wild beasts, as you have heard, I felt the strongest disinclination to probe into the details of the scene that had preceded that announcement. What had been said between Slopa and Sosie was nothing to do with me. It was to do with me, really; but it could not be allowed to become of me.

The subject of conversation being turned, Aunt Slopa said in answer to my question: "When a man dies, his embroidered quiver and tunic and buckskins are laid up with him in the Glittering Caves."

"The Glittering Caves?"

She nodded to the overbearing cliff face dominating Arkasson. "The cliff is riddled with the caves. The gems within the rock glow and glitter."

Further comment from me did not seem required; but I did think that a fortune beyond calculation lay within that cliff, embedded in the rock and lying beside the dead bodies of generations of men in the Glittering Caves.

Before I left Sosie appeared. She had dried her tears and made herself look presentable, which, in reality, meant that she looked dazzlingly beautiful with her black skin gleaming and her Afro hairdo a puffed-up nimbus. She wore a simple dress of a dark orange color, heavily spattered with sewn gems, and her feet were clad in yellow slippers. I remember those yellow slippers.

I started to say, "You will forgive me, Sosie—"

She hushed me at once, for which I was grateful. I make it a rule never to apologize; sometimes — not often — that rule of life becomes tricky.

"So you are determined to travel the Owlarh Waste, Dray Prescot! I know, now, I cannot prevent that. I thank you for your kindness to me—"

"Now, Sosie, it is you who are kind!"

"But not kind enough."

That was spoken tartly enough. She was no weeping willow, was this Sosie na Arkasson.

"I wish you all the luck in the world, Sosie — all the luck in Kregen. May you find the man of your heart, and marry, and the farm prosper. May you be happy. Zair go with you."

As before, she did not question my use of the name Zair. They were tolerant, in Arkasson, of any man's religion, unlike the primitives of Cherwangtung.

"And with you, Dray Prescot"

Before me lay what Sosie called the Owlarh Waste. I took a few steps away from the frowning stone walls, out of their shadow and into the streaming light of the Suns of Scorpio, and I turned.

"Remberee, Sosie!"

She lifted her arm in farewell. "Remberee Dray Prescot. Remberee!"

With deliberate purpose I did not look back until the town of Arkasson had sunk into a blending gray against the lowering cliff upthrust beyond its walls.

During the midday break when I ate and drank sparingly was the time to take stock of myself.

Around my waist I wore the scarlet silk formed into a breechclout. Sosie had, without my knowledge, stitched up for me a scabbard and baldric from plain supple leather of lesten hide and the deadly Krozair long sword now snugged safely against my thigh. She had made some remarkably raucous comments on that sword which, to her eyes accustomed to the slender blades of the Hostile Territories, was so monstrous a brand. The broad belt Delia had given me aboard the airboat buckled up firmly about my waist, the silver buckle deliberately left tarnished, and kept the silken loincloth in place, for silk has this exasperating tendency to slip. The rapier hung at my left side. It did not hang parallel to the long sword but thrust out at a divergent angle. The main-gauche was scabbarded to my right side. You may smile at this plethora of weapons, and consider me a walking arsenal — remember Hap Loder! — but I was accustomed to be so accoutered and could manage athletic evolutions without the slightest inconvenience.

The quiver that had caused so much heart-searching I slung over my back, the black-feathered shafts protruding up past my right shoulder. This was for convenience in carrying. For rapid shooting the quiver would be carried slung low and angled forward on the left hip. The bow itself, all six feet six inches of it, I carried unstrung. In a waxed-leather pouch I had a dozen spare strings.

Also there were the food bag and the water bottle.

So, thus I found myself, Dray Prescot, walking on my bare feet toward the eastern coast of Turismond.

If I fail to mention the broad-bladed hunting knife sheathed onto the belt behind my right hip it is merely because a knife in that position has been my constant companion from the time I first stepped aboard a seventy-four.

In my long life I have handled many weapons and grown skilled in the use of weapons wholly strange to an Earthman. Armor in its right and proper place has also been of importance to me. Yet, however much I grow used to any one sword or rapier in particular, one special bow, I have never chained myself and my fortunes to just one single weapon. Many weapons have been presented to me, I have bought large numbers, and taken quantities from dead foemen; if I were to lose all this gaudy arsenal I would feel annoyance — an annoyance not, for instance, that I had lost this one particular Krozair long sword presented to me by Pur Zenkiren, but annoyance over the loss of any weapon in the midst of dangers.

The man who wishes to be an adventuring fighting-man had best not lock his fortune to one brand alone. Fate is all too often ready to snatch it from him, and seldom ready to offer it back — as I had snatched back my sword from Umgar Stro after I had snapped his backbone.

And with this goes the corollary that the true fighting-man can fight with whatever weapons come into his hands.

The twin suns of Antares passed across the sky, the smaller green Genodras now leading the giant red Zim, so that at the second sunset the land took on the tincture of rusted iron, a broad wash of orange and brown and crimson with the last few streaks and streamers of green pulsing through that ruby sky. Ahead the Owlarh Waste stretched in dust and thorn-ivy and prickly scrub. Finding safe anchorage for the night was not overly difficult and by the time Genodras reappeared ahead of me with its filaments of lacy green patterning the sky ahead and painting out the last stars I was well on my first leg of the day's journey.

There had been a noticeable lack of interference from the people of Cherwangtung and this could be explained in a number of ways, perhaps the best of these being Sosie's comment when I had left that the wild white men tended to lay up during the day and roam only at night. I was not naïve enough to believe they had spotted me and, remembering what I had done to their war party, were afraid to approach me. They might well have been; but that way lies arrogance, psychosis, self-delusion, and eventual destruction.

The land here in the Owlarh Waste was poor and getting worse as I tramped eastward. Arkasson was a town muchly cut off from the world, tending its own circle of farms and minding its own business. The problem facing me soon would be water. Dust kicked up at the unwary tread, behooving me to walk carefully. Leem prowled here, so Sosie had said, raiding into the farms if the fences were left unrepaired, at other times subsisting on the rabbit-like animals burrowing into the plain — animals on which I, too, must depend for food.

I had less concern that I might meet risslaca — of which there are innumerable varieties. The overlords of Magdag placed a bronze risslaca beneath the beaks of their swifters where the wales met. They more often than not took the fancy of using a mythical risslaca, a great lizard-dragon with fangs and forked tongue. Those that I had previously encountered during my runs ashore when I was fighting my way up as a swifter commander on the inner sea, the Eye of the World, had been impressive enough, saurian monsters, cold-blooded, fanged and clawed, armored with plate and scale, chilly of eye. Nath, Zolta, and I had fought our quota in defending Sanurkazz's southern boundaries. That all seemed a long time ago to me, now.[xi]

As you may well imagine, having encountered dinosaurs in the flesh on Kregen, I have, whenever the opportunity offered, studied the dinosaurs of our Earth. They form a subject for study that fascinates everyone, from the school child to the paleontologist. Just why this is so can be explained glibly — or with much psychological insight. I had the idea of trying to trace any comparisons, any parallels, between the long-gone saurian kings of the Earth and the very present flesh and blood risslaca of Kregen.

There were, of course, many points of similarity. Equally, risslaca existed — had chased me and been slain — that were unlike anything that we know stalked the Earth at the end of the mid Mesozoic Era, the Jurassic Period, all of one hundred and forty million years ago.

Many were quite dumb. Many emitted shrieks like bursting boilers. Many hunted by eye. Many hunted by scent.

It was a trio of the latter who picked me up toward the middle of the afternoon, when I had entered an area where the ground, although still poor, offered perfect conditions for fern growth. A river had wandered athwart my path and I had crossed it and carried on. The ferns grew in lush profusion. I felt the hunter's itch between my shoulder blades. The light from the twin suns burned down, orange and jade, shafts of sunlight striking down between the great ferns. The foliage curved over me. The unending stalks towered above. I walked very lightly, turning and twisting my head, and I had strung my bow with that practiced ease that Seg Segutorio exemplified best. I carried the longbow in my hand, an arrow nocked.

Walking thus lightly and alertly through the green and golden glory of the ferns with the jade and orange light falling all about me I came to a swampy area that I must bypass. Here and there the water gleamed like bronze. A wall moved before me. That wall rippled with scaled muscle. Blotches of color — amber, jade, jet — camouflaged the risslaca against the crowding ferns. I saw a narrow head greedily gulping ferns and the drooping leaves of the bristle-topped sickly trees that grew palm-like around the fringes of the water. A serpentine neck curled around. The head lifted from the ferns and cocked so that one eye could regard — *not* me! The eye looked coldly back down the twisted trail up which I had walked.

The three killers were there. They padded up on their three-toed feet — and I saw the first toe of each hind foot carried the long scythe-bladed claw, razor-sharp, that distinguished our Earthly deinonychus. The light from the twin suns of Antares fell luridly across their arrogantly gold and ebony-banded scales. Ten feet long, were the killers; seventy feet at least the camarasaurus-like herbivore.

And I stood between them.

The rudder-like tails of the deinonychus risslacas extended stiffly backward. Those long-curved scythe-claws caught the gleam of suns-light and glittered with deadly power.

With explosive, incredible ferocity, the three killers sprang.

Three

Into the Klackadrin

With reflexive action so fast the movement was completed before I saw the first risslaca's hind legs leave the ground the black feathers drew back to my ear, the last extra urge of muscle snapped out as the bow bent, my fingers released the arrow, and the shaft loosed.

So fast had I reacted, my aim exact, that thereby I was nearly killed.

For I had not expected the incredible jumping power of the reptile. It sailed up into the air, its tail rigidly extended backward, its body straightening into the upright position that would enable those slashing blades on its feet to slice me to the backbone. I have seen kangaroos in Australia, larger than these risslacas, leap fantastic distances. The dinosaurs were no sluggish, lethargic movers; they were agile, rapid, deadly — and these were killers.

The risslaca leaped above my point of aim. The arrow skewered past its belly and struck deeply into the junction of tail and body.

Sosie had given me a selection of arrows, so that I had the alternatives of the thin armor-piercing bodkin, the body punching pile, the broad meat-cleaving barb, or the utility arrowheaded point. Against what I had fancied would be after me for supper I had chosen the great barbed meat-slicing head. This slashed its way through the scale and flesh of the risslaca, gouging deeply. Chance had driven that arrow with deadly precision.

For deinonychus of the type on Kregen has the thick bunched tendons and muscles around the root of the tail so that the tail may be extended rigidly and thus give the animal the balance necessary for it to spring and use its lethal scythe-claw.

The arrow slashed all those staying tendons and muscles apart. The tail flopped. The risslaca, hissing, somersaulted, all balance and control gone.

In the same instant I darted into the shadows of the giant ferns.

The two following risslacas hurdled their screeching companion. They sprang again. High and viciously they curved into the air. I heard the shrieking snorting roar of the giant camarasaurus as they landed on its back, one high against the junction of neck and shoulders, the other lower down, so that its curved claws sank bloodily into the belly of the herbivore.

At that instant, simply by stepping forward and loosing twice, I could have slain both killers.

But I do not kill unnecessarily. I regret that sometimes in my long life I have been forced to kill. Certainly, I own to the weakness of being willing to slay first the man or beast attempting to slay me. It is a defect of character, no doubt. Here, though, nature was merely being followed. Since long before I had arrived so unexpectedly on Kregen and, without a doubt, long after I am gone, the risslacas hunt and kill as do all carnivores. It is in the nature of these fascinating creatures — just as it was in the nature of the scorpion to sting my father to death.

Judging by the noise and the thrashing among the giant curving ferns the killers were not having it all their own way.

Circumspectly, then, I left that scene that might have been wrenched from the scarlet pages of Earth's Jurassic and walked delicately on around the swamp.

Perhaps, by taking out one of the hunting party of carnivores, I had given the herbivore the better chance, at that.

You may be sure I walked long into the night, constantly alert, until I was well away from the swamps and ferns of the meandering river and once again treading the poor, dry and dusty ground. I camped that night without a fire and merely dozed. Three days and nights later and with the land still as unfriendly and with only a mouthful of water left in my canteen, I had to revert still further to our barbaric ancestors. My shaft drove skillfully, and slew me a darting rat-like creature — not a Kregen rast, although no doubt a species allied to those unpleasant creatures — and I drank its blood to slake my thirst.

I strode on, having recovered my arrow and cleaned it on the animal's gray and dusty fur, ever vigilant for predatory enemies. More to the point, I was also constantly on the lookout for food. So, I suppose, as is the way with men or the half-men of Kregen, I was the greater predator crossing that dismal and hostile wilderness.

Toward evening of the fifth day I ran across one of the broad high-banked roads left by the conquerors of the Empire of Walfarg who had driven through here from the eastern seaboard in the old days and taken their suzerainty of all the Hostile Territories.

The debate I carried out did not last long. Of a certainty I could travel far faster along the road with its squared slabs than across the arid plain. Those stones were still in remarkable condition, squared, their edges only slightly crumbled and the greenery that attempted to struggle through the interstices could subsist only on drifted soil, for the old engineers of Loh had built well. But on the road I would be marked.

So, keeping the road generally in sight, I traveled more safely if more slowly parallel to it, heading east.

On the eighth day I began to discern a jagged appearance to the eastern horizon. The skyline there did not bear the kind of outline I associated with a mountain range, and I hoped there was going to be nothing like The Stratemsk ahead of me. I did not relish that thought. We had flown through The Stratemsk, Delia and Seg and Thelda and I. That mountain chain lofted so high, extended so sprawlingly vast, that it defied all rational comprehension. It walled off with chilling finality the western end of the Hostile Territories from the eastern end of the lands on the eastern border of the inner sea. What happened there, in the Eye of the World, might have been happening back on my Earth for all that the people of the Hostile Territories knew. And, now, I began to entertain the deepest suspicions that another and equally hostile barrier existed between the Hostile Territories and the eastern seaboard of this continent of Turismond.

If it did, I would have to pass through, somehow, so as to reach the coast, take ship to Vallia, and reach my Delia of the Blue Mountains.

The terrain continued unpleasant, much cut up with dry gulches and razor-backed outcroppings of naked rock. Here — although I knew I must have trended well north of the parallel of latitude on which stood Pattelonia, the city of the eastern seaboard of the Eye of the World from which we had set out — the weather continued hot with the brazen Suns of Scorpio burning down. I had now to hunt my food and drink in earnest.

The jagged impression of the skyline before me continued when I was able to observe it from a higher-than-usual eminence, although the difficulty of the ground with its bare-bones, desiccated look meant I was more often than not confined between rocky walls. My back kept up an infernal itch and my head swiveled from side to side, constantly observing my back trail, like — if you will pardon the anachronistic image — the rear turret of a Lancaster. The only life that scraped a subsistence here larger than the insects and lizards and other burrowing animals seemed, from all that I observed, to be a kind of six-legged opossum and the wheeling birds, both of which fed on the life lower down the food-chain. You may easily understand how relieved I was that from day to day the birds that followed me were no larger in size than an Earthly vulture or kite. Why they were following me was obvious; but I had to reach my Delia of Delphond, and was in no mood to provide a meal for these scavengers of the air.

Harsh vegetation grew scrawnily along shadowed cracks in the uptilted rock faces. There were ants here, too, and I avoided their dwellings with great circumspection.

So it was that a quick and furtive movement beyond a boulder at the far end of a draw sent me at once to cover.

I waited.

Patience is not merely the virtue of the hunter — it is his life.

Presently a Chulik stepped out into the center of the draw.

I drew my breath in a gasp of amazement.

The Chuliks I had seen on Kregen before were full-fleshed men, with two arms and two legs, with a healthy, oily yellow skin. They habitually shaved their skulls with the exception of a long rope of hair that might grow to reach their waists. From the corners of their lips protruded two upward thrusting tusks a full three inches in length and, although they were human-seeming, they knew little of humanity. Normally they were highly prized as mercenaries and guards commanding higher prices than the Ochs or the Rapas, beast-men who performed similar functions. Some I had seen as slaves, not many.

This Chulik's hair grew matted and coarse and filthy. One of his tusks was broken jaggedly. He wore a scrap of black cloth about his middle, much covered with dust and dung and his yellow skin was likewise befouled. In one hand he carried a long pole fabricated from a number of spliced lengths cut from the twisted and scrawny bushes that were all that grew hereabouts, and the end of the pole carried a yoke-like fork. A basket woven of dry stems enclosed four of the little opossum creatures. The Chulik was busy about the task of catching a fifth, poking and prying down into a shallow hole beneath a boulder, moving with an alacrity pathetic in comparison with the lithe and vigorous movements of the Chuliks I had known.

I waited.

Moments later another figure joined the first.

Again I felt astonishment.

This was a Fristle, a half-man with a face as much like a cat's as anything else, furred, whiskered, slit-eyed, and fang-mouthed. Although I still had no love for Fristles — for Fristles had carried my Delia off to captivity in Zenicce so soon after I had been taken to Kregen for the second time — much of my dislike had been mitigated by the gallant actions of Sheemiff, the female Fristle, she who had called me her Jikai and had so proudly worn the yellow-painted vosk-skull helmet when my rabble army of slaves and workers revolted in Magdag.

This Fristle wore a black breechclout, was as filthy and downcast as the Chulik. He carried the curved scimitar that is the racial weapon of the Fristles, but its hangings and lockets were tarnished and broken.

What had brought these two representatives of proud and haughty races so low?

The impression grew in me strongly that I had nothing to fear from them.

The strangeness of that feeling must be apparent to you who have listened to my story so far.

I stepped out and lifted my hand.

"Llahal!" I called, using the double-L prefix, after the Welsh fashion, to the word of greeting, as was right when encountering strangers.

They looked up sluggishly.

After a time the Fristle said: "Llahal."

The Chulik said: "Why do you not work?"

"I am going to the coast."

For a moment they did not understand. Then the Fristle cackled. I know, now, that laughter for him and the others here occurred so infrequently that it might never have been invented; it came almost as seldom to them as it does to me.

"I have marched from the Hostile Territories, through the Owlarh Waste, and I have not come here to be laughed at — by a Fristle least of all."

In response the Fristle merely blinked. His hand did not even fall to his scimitar hilt.

The Chulik cowered back, but he did not lift the forked pole against me.

I rolled out a vile Makki-Grodno oath.

What had happened to these men? What power had so ferociously tamed them into pitiful wrecks of their former selves?

Also, the thought occurred to me, it is said there is hereditary enmity between Chulik and Fristle, except when they are engaged by the same employer.

Knowing that, I was profoundly impressed when the Fristle helped the Chulik hoist the cage containing the four opossum creatures onto his back. I caught a glimmering, then, that whatever horrific experiences these men had gone through had brought them closer together and by stripping away the artificialities of race and species had displayed them to each other in adversity as creatures together beneath Zair and Grodno.

"The grint has gone, now," said the Chulik. He spoke in the whine habitual to the slave. "Four will not be enough, but that is all the Phokaym will get."[xii]

At this name, this name of Phokaym, both Chulik and Fristle gave an involuntary shudder.

Before I could say another word they hunched around and slouched off, quickly vanishing into the tangle of boulders at the end of the draw.

I ran fleetingly enough after them; but when I entered the rock-strewn area I saw quickly that they had taken themselves off and lost me, traveling by secret paths and passages they would know well.

Pushing on through this country grew more difficult in the following few burs and so, at last, I chanced striding out along the old road of empire.

One vital fact was very clear. In this area lived some power of such strength that it could reduce arrogant beast-men to a cowering state lower than that of a whip-beaten slave. From the evidence of the Fristle's scimitar I judged that they were not slaves. All resistance had been knocked out of them, and warriors who had strode victoriously over a score of battlefields had been reduced to a state of abject degradation. All this was proved to be true — as I found to my cost, as you shall hear.

Occasionally I glimpsed over the twisted and fantastically jumbled landscape on either side of the road more of these subdued people, men and women, Ochs, Rapas, Fristles, and Chuliks, as well as Ullars and other half-beast, half-men I had not so far encountered closely enough to identify. They all scuttled at my approach, disappearing into crevices in the rock. None ventured onto the squared blocks of the road surface.

That night I camped uncomfortably in a rock crevice of my own close to the road and, apart from a few strips of dried meat hung on my belt, I went supperless to bed. I had the strongest conviction I should save as much food as possible for what the future held.

In the morning with that jade and ruby fire mingling and pulsing down I stood up and stretched and was at once alert and ready to face the terrors of the day. As I walked along that ancient road I saw that scummy water filled pools and hollows among the rocks, and that a weird and gnarled vegetation grew, all twisted and stunted, its roots curling like petrified serpents from the rocks into the fetid water. Indeed, the smells of indescribable foulness grew every yard I progressed. I began to feel a dizziness. I blinked and shook my head and pressed on. The road appeared to me to waver as does tar macadam at the brow of a hill in hot sunshine; a shimmering stream of interconnecting and vibrating images at once obscuring vision and lending it a fraudulent magnifying quality.

Now I walked all alone. No other living soul I could see stirred in that dismal expanse.

Ahead of me lay the east coast, and a ship, and Vallia — and Delia. No fainting fit would hold me back. I staggered as I marched. I hauled up, the sweat starting out all over my body as I stared directly ahead along that ancient road, there on the continent of Turismond on the planet of Kregen beneath the Suns of Scorpio — and saw a three-decker of a hundred and twelve guns lift her scarlet-lidded gun ports and saw the thirty-two pounders and the twenty-four pounders and the eighteen pounders run out, grinning at me, and belch in silent flame and smoke!

That smashing broadside would pulverize me in an instant. The familiar yellow smoke engulfed me and I could not prevent the old prayer rising to my lips — but even as I said, "For what we are about to receive," the three-decker vanished. In her place I saw a swifter of the inner sea, a lean deadly hundredswifter turning toward me so that her bronze rostrum aimed directly at the rib beneath my heart!

I yelled — and in that wavering mist and confusing smoke, the glint of the twin suns and the smothering feeling of madness rising in my mind I saw my friend Zorg — Zorg of Felteraz — smiling at me, his moustache curling. Zorg, dead, and gone and food for chanks in the inner sea!

His face was ripped away and next I saw Nath and Zolta, my oar comrades who with Zorg and I had labored at the oars as slaves. Nath and Zolta, chuckling, the one with a leather blackjack slopping wine, the other with a giggling wench on his knee.

I shouted.

I lurched forward — and now I saw Gloag, my good comrade from Zenicce who was not a full human being and yet who knew more of human kindness than — than Glycas, that cruel and cunning man of Magdag, and his sister, the beautiful and evil Princess Susheeng — and I saw Queen Lilah, the Queen of Pain of Hiclantung — and I saw Hap Loder and all of my clansmen in headlong cry astride their massive voves — I saw Prince Varden Wanek of the House of Eward. I saw many people, then, all replaying the roles they had played in my life.

I saw Seg Segutorio and Thelda — and I wept.

And then — then I saw my Delia, my Delia of Delphond, as she had walked with so lithe a swing down toward Great-Aunt Shusha and me. Delia I saw, wearing that flaunting scarlet breechclout and with the dazzlingly white ling furs I had given her aswing about her form, her long lissome legs very splendid in the suns-light.

Then I knew beyond a doubt that I dreamed.

I shook my head.

Knowledge of hallucinatory drugs is more widespread on this Earth than heretofore, and armed with modern knowledge I might have appreciated far more rapidly just what was happening to me. Opium and hashish were known to me, as was the more luscious and gentle if treacherous kaf used by the weak-willed on Kregen beneath Antares. Drug-taking for escape from life is generally the mark of a decadent or bored society — and on Kregen life was too vivid and headlong and demanding for those who sought life out for the taking of drugs to be more than a marginal nuisance. It has seemed to me that I have never had the time to investigate properly all this modern to-do over the drug habit and on Kregen I have always had far too much to do, even as slave, when my every thought has normally been set on escape.

So now I staggered and lurched along the old imperial road and the phantoms

410

from my mind took on form and substance and came to leer and gibber at me, to mock, or to smile and hold out their hands in friendly Lahal.

That first time I attempted to cross this barrier to the eastern coast — the barrier was called the Klackadrin, as you shall hear — I entered on the task as a young and innocent. Those scummy pools fed minerals to the scrawny plants, which breathed out their miasmic bedevilment, betraying the wits of men and beasts. The Klackadrin sealed the eastern flanks of the Hostile Territories as effectively as The Stratemsk sealed the western.

Delia's counterfeit image swung away and in her place pranced all the might of the cavalry aswirl about me at Waterloo. I brushed a hand across my eyes, and when I looked again I saw Umgar Stro, huge and ferocious, charging upon me with the ghostly replica of the sword I now carried!

Tendrils from the marshy pools set amid deep crevices of the rocks at the side of the road wriggled across the road at me. At first I thought them figments of my imagination, perhaps a reminder of those morfangs we had battled in that cave of the Hostile Territories. Then a thick and clutching tendril wrapped itself about my ankle. It hauled.

A single slash from my Krozair long sword severed the thing.

More of them crowded the road ahead, writhing, seeming obscenely beckoning arms, beseeching me to walk into their embrace. I would have to hack my way through.

A fresh sound obtruded. A hard, ringing clash of steel-like claws on the flagstones of the road.

I swung about.

I really believe, even now, that I thought I was bewitched still, seeing phantoms, seeing things that never were.

That belief, sluggish and obstinate, held me in a stasis that came from the foolish belief that of all these hallucinations none could harm me and that only from the beckoning and writhing tendrils had I any physical danger to fear.

What I saw impacted with the sense of physical nausea and yet, with all my experience of Kregen and its beast-men to give me a guide, I realized that these beast-men were not half-men half-beasts; these were half-beast half-monster. They were the Phokaym.

They rode cousins to those risslacas I had previously met, huge lumbering dinosaurs that yet moved with a quickness that would tax a sectrix to match. The Phokaym themselves, quite clearly, were racial descendants of risslacas. They were cold-blooded, as I discovered, with the wide-fanged mouth of the carnivorous risslaca, the small front legs that had adapted into manipulative arms and clawed hands, and the powerful hind legs and tail of the carnivorous dinosaur. They were perhaps twelve feet tall. They carried their tails curled up and around behind the ornate saddles. Each one was armed with spear and sword. They wore barbaric ornaments, and their scales were painted and lacquered into geometric patterns of cold reptilian beauty. Were they real?

Intelligent, armed, cold-blooded carnivorous dinosaurs riding spurred and bridled herbivorous dinosaurs? They were real.

Had they been more alien, more weird, more unearthly than their very forms suggested, I might have believed. There are so many unearthly life-forms on Kregen that one can understand the profusion of life and its multiplicity; had they been like those morfangs, or the wlachoffs — incredibly alien in appearance — or any other of the many unterrestrial creatures I have encountered on Kregen, I might have reacted sooner. As it was their very suggestion of Earthly dinosaurs riding Earthly dinosaurs, a conception staggering to me then, if not so much later, with its immediate impact of rejection and dissociation in that bath of hallucinogenic compounds, made me laggard and late.

Thick blood-red strands fell about me, tacky and binding, dragging my arm and long sword into my side, entangling my bow and quiver, wrapping me from shoulder to ankle. I fell.

The smash of the hard stone against my cheek awoke me.

But it was too late.

Enmeshed I was dragged along the hard stones of the road, back toward the west, back away from the coast, back into a slavery of the kind I had seen in those unfortunates skulking among the rocks and fetid pools.

Triumphantly shrilling, the Phokaym dragged me away.

Had they had eight limbs each, I would have believed in them, and my long sword would have drunk cold reptilian blood. Had they had eight legs, I would have believed.

Six legs, even...

Four

The Phokaym

An old crone of an Och came to me in the corner of a cave where the Phokaym had flung me, still tightly bound in the thick blood-red strands. She was old and her stringy bleached hair hung lankly down. She stood before me on her legs, holding the pannikin of foul water with her middle limbs, and brushed the scum from the surface of the water with one of her upper hands, while the other dipped the stone spoon and so dribbled water between my lips.

"They want you alive and healthy for the voryasen."

The spoon was merely a dumbbell-shaped piece of stone with one end hollowed out. Most of the water trickled down my chin and into my beard — which was longer and more ragged than I customarily allowed — but the drops I sucked in, despite my knowledge of their stinking condition, tasted like the best Zond wine.

The Och made no attempt to free me. She cringed at the slightest sound, shutting her eyes and hunching her head down into her neck. She spilled more water than I got, but at least I felt a little more myself. I asked her impatient questions, and when I mastered myself enough to soothe her, she was able to speak, albeit falteringly and with many frightened glances over her shoulder. Outside came the noise of people moving about, the rhythmical gong-like notes as stone struck against stone. The suns had set, but it was still hot.

"The Klackadrin." The old Och woman sighed. Her name, she said, was Ooloo. She had no clear memory of any life before this; yet she must have been brought here in some way, if she had not been born here. She did not remember. "The Klackadrin. It is evil, weird, ghosts and bad spirits dwell there. No one can cross it at all — only the roads, only the roads—"

How many of these poor devils had sought to escape via the roads, only to have the fearsome Phokaym astride their risslacas hunt them down and bind them with the blood-red cords and cast them to the voryasen?

"Devils," she said, muttering, and cast a terrified glance toward the cave mouth.

The Klackadrin, she told me, was not a great distance in an east-west direction, although its north-south axis, meandering and curving, stretched she did not know how far into North Turismond and ended, she thought, far down into the south, perhaps as far as the Cyphren Sea where the Zim Stream sweeps up from unknown oceans.

"Evil dreams, nightmares, madness, that is all the Klackadrin can offer. There are monsters there — monsters—" She shut her eyes. I had had no food and when I asked she brought me a piece of raw opossum which, as a warrior, I knew I must eat to keep up my strength, yet tasted hard and stringy and needed much chewing.

"One day, perhaps, the Phokaym will go away and leave us in peace," said Ooloo. It was pathetically transparent that she did not believe this would ever happen.

By continuous perseverance I discovered I could move my fingers a little within the constriction of the blood-red strands. I kept working away, pushing and pulling one muscle against the next in well-remembered drill, seeking to keep them flexible and the blood coursing through my body. If I was to escape I could not have the agony of blood returning to circulation slowing me down.

I was working on my upper arms when the Phokaym amid a loud noise of clashing weapons and scaled armor came for me.

"The voryasen!" whispered old Ooloo. As I was dragged out with a great shouting and much buffeting I heard her say, "Jikai, Jikai," and I thought she sobbed.

We warriors always felt a trifle contemptuous of Ochs with their little round shields when it came to combat; but I think I can trace my emergence of a better feeling for them from that encounter with old Ooloo there in the fetid caves of the Phokaym.

Clouds drifted across the sky and She of the Veils, the fourth moon, shone more fitfully even than usual, while the first moon, almost twice the size of our own moon, the Maiden with the Many Smiles, was already setting far across the Owlarh Waste.

The collection of food and the production of tools and utensils were the primary concerns of the crushed-down people, both men and half-men, under the despotic rule of the Phokaym.

Tonight was to be a spectacle night, an occasion when the risslaca Phokaym emphasized their absolute power. A man was to be tossed to the voryasen. Consequently, so I gathered, more torches than usual were lit, painfully gathered by the slaves from the waste, twisted and gnarled branches they had so painfully gathered set alight gleefully by the Phokaym to illuminate their celebrations.

I saw stone jugs passing from claw to claw as the Phokaym gathered. Their scales glittered in the torchlight. It was difficult to distinguish just what was armor and what was their own scaly hide. I was dragged toward the stone lip of a great pit. Above the pit an arrangement of wooden supports lashed together projected, like the boom of a crane. The Phokaym crowded toward this pit. I was hoisted upside down and my lashed ankles were fastened by a rope painstakingly woven from dry stems. Torchlight glared upon the scene, ruddy and orange, streaming light and driving weird shadows cavorting among the rocks and the stunted bushes.

Up I swung, twisting and turning, upside down, hanging from the rope. The boom moved and turned and I was carried out over the pit. I looked down.

A voryas is a form of risslaca one might imagine in nightmare, part crocodile, part tylosaurus, a giant fang-filled mouth, all jaw and muscle, and an agile scaly body and bludgeoning tail, that one would do well never to imagine, even in nightmare, let alone care to encounter.

Bound and helpless, with all my weapons about me and unable to use them, I swung upside down above a water-filled pit crawling with the saurian horrors.

They lifted from the surface of the water, hissing and spitting, their jaws wedges of fangs, their eyes red and wicked and glaring upon me with voracious intent.

The Phokaym had fun.

They kept paying out the rope and lowering me down toward the surface of the water so that the voryasen would leap up at me, giant scaled forms gleaming dully emerald and amber, surging upward to fall back, baffled, hissing their rage, as the rope was hastily hauled in.

Up and down I went, and the voryasen leaped and hissed, and the world turned scarlet from the thrum of blood in my head and my eyes threatened to start from their sockets, and my body grew numb.

By a stupendous effort I managed to jackknife my body and look upward. A Phokaym, his teeth glinting as carnivorously as any voryas in the pit below, held out a blazing torch. He was touching the fizzing and sputtering torch to the rope holding my bound body above the pit.

Furiously I struggled with the blood-red cords, but they would not yield.

If I could swing, I could reach the timber support of the boom from which I hung suspended. The smells, the shrieks, the whole cacophony of noises spurted up to rumble and roil in my head. I was helpless. Below me the carnivorous water-predators saw the flame of the torch and their hissing redoubled.

They knew what would happen when the torch burned through the rope. They knew!

I was sweating now; everything whirled about me. One crunch of those gigantic fanged jaws below and I would be cut into two bloody halves.

There could be no last-minute rescue. There was no one within a hundred dwaburs who could aid me now — no one anywhere on this wild and savage world of Kregen.

The pit yawned beneath my dangling head. Torchlight splintered back from the scales and the eyes of the voryasen below. Now their hissing bounced back in magnified echoes from the pit walls. I craned up again — the rope was burning!

I could see the frayed and blackened strands parting, one by one, curling out like spent matches.

The torchlight burned into my eyes.

The shrieking and yelling of the Phokaym deafened me.

I swung...

My mouth was wide open, but I was not yelling.

This might be the end of it all, of all the high dreams I had had, here on Kregen, of winning my princess and of taking her to my palace and estates in Zenicce, of once more riding with my loyal clansmen across the great plains of Segesthes...

I swung...

The world dizzied before my swimming eyes. Smoke and flame mingled and blinded me.

But I could see the fire of burning rope, see the strands parting, see the evil flickering flame gnawing through the only thing that supported me above the fangs and jaws of those merciless risslacas below...

I saw — I saw the last strand burn, the rope part and break and then I yelled—

At this point the tapes from Africa end.

The following narrative picks up the story later on in Prescot's life on Kregen. It begins in the middle of a sentence.

The end of the last cassette came with a noise — a sound — of such unimaginable ferocity as to chill me to the heart when I first heard it, and which I hesitate to play over again. After that the tape spins emptily through the heads. Whatever it was that made that frightful sound, I have grave doubts that even the African jungle harbors its creator.

The beginning of the fresh cassette is garbled and there is some confused noise as of laughter and — I guess — the popping of champagne corks. This, as I think you who have followed the saga of Prescot this far will agree, is well in keeping.

The writer who has been giving me invaluable assistance in editing these tapes, a distinguished author with an international reputation, when he heard this portion observed, with what I took to be wry admiration: "Dray Prescot has successfully pulled off one of the oldest classical clichés in the book."

"Of course," I told him. "That's Dray Prescot's style."

I do wonder, though, if we will ever be privileged to hear what failed to record at the beginning of this tape. Just how *did* Dray Prescot do it? Those of you who have followed his saga so far will have no doubts whatsoever that he *could* do it...

And, there is the yellow fang of the Phokaym Prescot gave to Pando to act as a clue...

Alan Burt Akers

…bringing me up out of the light doze into which I had fallen and this time louder and more urgent. I opened my eyes and cursed and stretched out a hand across the wide rumpled bed where the fused jade and ruby light from the twin suns threw a miniature landscape of mountain and valley. The light glinted back from the hilt of my rapier as I took it up into my fists. Again the scream knifed up the narrow black-wood stairs of *The Red Leem*. I cursed, and groaned, for my legs were still rubbery and my head throbbed as though an impiter smote me with his coal-black wings.

"What in the name of Makki-Grodno's diseased armpit is going on?" I yelled.

By the time the third scream ripped out I recognized Tilda's voice. I staggered a little, and gripped onto the bedpost. The wooden floor with its scattered rugs of bright Walfarg weave swayed under me like the deck of a frigate blockading Brest. I shook my head. I had my old scarlet breechclout wrapped around my middle and my rapier in my fist. Hastily I snatched up the main-gauche and started for the door.

The door burst open and young Pando appeared, his hair wild, his eyes reflecting more of the red light than the green, his whole body animated with anger and furious defiance. He shouted at me, his words tumbling over one another, a little dagger in his fist that shook with his passion.

"The Pandrite-forsaken devils!" He danced up and down. "They're insulting Mother — Dray! Come on! You've got to help!"

"I'm coming, Pando." I set straight for the door and bounced from the jamb. Pando grabbed my arm and steered me through the doorway. "You'd best not stick 'em with that toothpick, Pando," I said. "You'll only upset them."

"I'll degut 'em all!" he shrilled. He was only nine years old, as I had to remind myself, and he thought everything in life was black and white.

Then, as though commenting on my thoughts about him, he gave me a kick to help me on my way. I wobbled toward the black-wood stairs, twisted, my feet shot from under me on one of the Walfarg rugs, and down the stairs I went, bump, bump, bump, to the bottom. The bottom hit me hard.

Through the arched opening into the main room of the inn I could see the counter with its ranked amphorae, its trim rows of sparkling glass cups, the covers over the food, everything neat and tidy and waiting for evening when the men and women of Pa Mejab would crowd in for their evening's entertainment.

The chief source of their entertainment was now struggling in the grip of three men. They were ruffians, all right, intent on their prey. As I stood up, smarting, and stared blearily at them I fancied they were leem-hunters, men from the back hills away to the west and probably men who would venture almost to the Klackadrin itself. They wore clothes made from leem pelts, and broad leather harness, with swaggering rapiers and daggers and large riding boots and all seeming to me to be very powerful and blurry.

I blinked.

Tilda's blouse had ripped down over one shoulder and then the other, and the men laughed.

"Let go, you stinking cramphs!" Tilda was yelling. Her long mane of black hair floated freely from her head, swirling out, in truth, very much like the wings of an impiter. She got one arm free and slapped a leem-hunter across his leathery, whiskered cheeks, whereat he roared with laughter, and, catching that arm, bent it back and drew his face close to Tilda's.

"You won't dance for us, ma faril, when we ask all politely, so you'll dance to another tune now."

"Wait until we open our doors, rast!"

"Hold on!" shouted another of the men, too late, for Tilda's naked toes slammed into him. He doubled up, clutching himself, and rolled away, both laughing and retching.

Yes, they were ruffians, all right. In from the country and wanting their fun. Pando ran past me, straight up to them, and struck wildly with the dagger at the man gripping his mother.

"Pando!" I yelled, alarmed.

The man back-handed Pando off. He staggered back, cannoned into a table, went over spilling the vase of moon-flowers onto the floor. The man roared his good humor. About to bend again to Tilda he caught sight of me, in the doorway, the rapier and main-gauche in my fists.

He straightened up and threw Tilda into the arms of the third man, who grabbed her — most familiarly, I thought — whereat she squealed and tried both to kick and bite him.

"So what have we here, by the gross Armipand himself!"

He ripped his rapier from its sheath, and the dagger followed as quickly. The man Tilda had kicked hauled himself up, turning to face me, his features still twisted and the tears still in his eyes. For a moment the tableau held in the main room of *The Red Leem*. I was conscious of the stupidity of all this. My head rang as though a swifter's oars were beating my skull all the way along the hull of a two-hundred-and-tenswifter.

"You had best release the lady," I said with some difficulty.

They guffawed.

"A tavern wench a lady! Haw, haw!"

I shook my head in negation — and that was a mistake. All the bells of Beng-Kishi clanged resonantly inside my skull.

"She is not a tavern wench. She is Tilda, the famous entertainer, a dancer and actress. She is," I added with words more like myself, "not for scum of the likes of you."

"Ho! A ruffler!" The leader of the leem-hunters abruptly threw himself into the posture of the fighting-man. "A swagger with a rapier and dagger! Come on, little man, let us see you back your words with your sword point."

When I say my legs felt like rubber, it would be more correct to say I could hardly feel them at all, and my knees seemed like mashed banana. I took a step forward, and my rapier point described trembling circles.

The three men laughed hugely.

"Serve him as you served the landlord, Gorlan!"

Portly Nath, the landlord, lay huddled beyond an overturned table. All I could see of him were his legs and feet in their satin slippers, and his balding head, the face turned away from me, and a small trickle of blood. He was not dead, for he moaned; but he had been struck a shrewd blow.

"I am not a fat old innkeeper," I said.

"Then I will open your tripes and find out!" said this Gorlan, flickering his blade very swiftly before me.

He lunged.

My dagger seemed — of its own volition and without any conscious effort of my muscles — to do as it pleased. It sliced up, deflected the rapier blade in a screech of metal, and so drove Gorlan back, with a spring, his face abruptly blackening with thwarted anger.

"You miserable cramph!" he bellowed.

He drove in again, powerfully, overbearing me by sheer weight and ferocity. My twin blades beat him off. The metal slithered and clanged, sliding and twisting with many cunning tricks and turns. He scored a long slicing cut across my left arm and then my rapier point pressed into his throat and his dagger flew spinning across the inn. I did not hear it land.

"Oh, Gorlan," I said, rather thickly and with the world jumping and dancing with purple spots and streaks of white fire. "Oh pitiful little Gorlan!"

His face blanched. It was a very wonderful sight to see that swarthy visage drain of blood, the eyes glare in terror upon me, the lips go suddenly dry.

"Dray!" screeched Tilda.

I swiveled to my right, taking the rapier around ninety degrees and showing its point to the man Tilda had kicked and who was now rushing upon me with drawn sword. My left hand gripping the main-gauche swung around with my movement and my fist smashed sloggingly into Gorlan's jaw. He dropped like a sack.

The second man hauled up, his rapier engaging mine, and for a short space we circled. With an oath the man grasping Tilda flung her from him, drew his own weapons, and charged in upon me at the side of his companion. The difficulty of focusing nearly betrayed me; I did not want to kill these two, as I knew they would not wish to kill me. This was a tavern brawl over a woman — as far as they were concerned a tavern wench — and they knew the arm of the law of Pandahem stretched here to Pa Mejab. As for me, the same strictures obtained. That Tilda was in very truth a famous actress, here in this colonial port city of Pandahem only because she had married for love, and her soldier husband had been killed here, leaving her stranded with her nine-year-old son Pando, meant nothing to them, although it meant a great deal to me.

So I engaged, and parried, and feinted, and took their blades upon my dagger, and thrust in the attempt to disable them. And all the time the world pressed roaring and swirling in upon me, my sight dimmed. I felt my banana knees bucking, and their onslaughts grew stronger and stronger as I grew weaker.

By a desperate piece of sheer outrageous Spanish-style two-handed fencing that would have had my old master, the cunning Spaniard, Don Hurtado de Oquendo, foaming with outraged professionalism, I managed to disarm the second man and send him reeling back with blood spurting from a pierced bicep.

But the other fellow bored in and my sluggish legs wouldn't drag me around in time to meet his attack.

Then — like an avenging angel — Tilda rose up at his back and, two-handed, brought down a jug of purple wine upon his head.

He grunted and lurched forward and his rapier skewered the floorboards as he smashed on past, the blade vibrating backward and forward and the hilt seesawing like an upside down metronome.

As though hypnotized by that rhythmic motion I went to my knees, toppled slowly forward, and so came to rest beside the leem-hunter — and all of Kregen fell on me in blackness.

Five

A zhantil-skin tunic for Pando

Tilda would not tell anyone — not even me — any other name by which she might be known in Pandahem. Tilda was her professional name, her stage name, and by it she had become famous. What personal tragedy lay as the cause of her moldering, as I termed it, here in a distant colonial port city she also would not reveal. I gathered this had something to do with her husband, and of him all she would say was that he had married her against the wishes of his family. As a soldier he had been posted to Pa Mejab and, leading his squadron one day, had been slain.

She was fanatically proud and possessive of Pando, who was, as you have seen, an engaging imp of a rascal. She fretted continually over his safety and welfare, constantly chiding him for not wearing enough clothes, for not eating enough, for fighting the other children thronging the busy streets. But, in all this, she never lost sight with a clearheaded practicality that Pando was the son of a soldier, that she must look to him one day, and that he must develop as a man.

I confess that I grew to a better liking for both of them with each day that passed. My room at *The Red Leem* had always a vase of colorful flowers, and the sheets and sleeping furs were changed with hygienic regularity. Old Nath, the landlord, recovered of the knock on the head, consented to allowing me a reduced rent when I went on the guard duties by which, perforce, I earned my daily crust. He was only too well aware of the business Tilda brought into his inn. In the evening when she sang and danced, when she gave recitals of the great parts in Kregen drama, tragediennes and comediennes, performances so moving in both cases that they brought tears to the eyes of her audiences, rapt in silent admiration, Pando and I would sit companionably together and listen.

Pando, at nine years old, had the most fanatical admiration for his beautiful mother.

For, as I have said, Tilda was a beauty with her ivory skin and ebony hair, all swirling and glowing, with her firm figure that had no need of the theater's contrivances to drive men's blood singing through their veins. Her violet eyes and her voluptuous mouth could melt with passion, could become stern and regal, could blast all a man's hopes, could urge him to fire and ardor and unthinking gallantry — and all this on the tiny scrap of stage mounted at the far end of the main room of *The Red Leem!*

Pando is a familiar name for children of Pandahem, the great rival trading island to Vallia. It was only on the second day of my stint as a caravan guard that he was discovered hiding among the calsany drovers.

The overseer, a tough and chunky man with a cummerbund swathing the results of many a night at *The Red Leem,* and, probably, all the other inns and taverns of Pa Mejab, hauled Pando out by an ear and ran him up to me where I strode along on the left flank of the leading flight of calsanys.

"Dray!" roared the overseer, one Naghan the Paunch. "Dray Prescot! Look what has dropped with the nits from the hides of the calsanys!"

I sighed and stared at Pando with a greatly feigned air of complete despair.

"We have no room for passengers, Naghan. Therefore he must either be slain at once, or sent back alone — or—?" I cocked an eye at Naghan the Paunch.

He pondered deeply. "To slay him now would probably be best, for he would never reach Pa Mejab against the leems and the wlachoffs who would rend the flesh from his bones and devour him until not a morsel was left."

Pando, squirming against the brown hand that held his ear in so tight a grip, looked up, and the whites of his eyes showed.

"You wouldn't do that to me, Dray! What would Mother say?"

"Ah!" said Naghan the Paunch, enjoying himself. "Poor dear Tilda the Beautiful! Tilda of the Many Veils! How she will grieve for this limb of Sicce himself!"

"Dray!" yelped Pando.

I rubbed my beard. "On the other hand, Naghan, Pando did run with his dagger to protect Tilda the Beautiful when she was attacked by leem-hunters. If he could do that, might he not thus also attack the leems themselves?"

Naghan twisted the trapped ear. "Have you a dagger, boy?"

Pando was thoroughly aroused now. He tried to kick Naghan. "Had I a dagger, oh man of the Paunch, I would have stuck you with it long before this!"

"Oho!" quoth Naghan the Paunch, and laughed.

And I laughed, and so — I, Dray Prescot, laughing! — because we could not send Pando back across that dangerous land we had perforce to take him with us. He was a bright lad, full of wiles and mischievousness, and yet with an endearing streak of pleasant loyalty and quickness of wits, and a readiness to learn that I knew would stand him in good stead on Kregen, where a man must be a man if he wishes to survive.

His greatest vice was his inveterate untidiness. Nothing he touched could be found in the same condition, and even to enter his tiny cubicle-like room in *The Red Leem* was usually impossible for the chaos strewing every surface and the floor, unless one did as he did and took a flying leap onto the trundle bed.

The caravan, with its long lines of calsanys head-to-tail in their stubborn purposeful swaying movements and with the smaller numbers of plains asses separated from the calsanys, pressed on toward Pa Weinob in the northwest. Pa

Weinob was an outpost town, part of the spreading web of influence the men of Pandahem were spinning along the seaboard and hinterland of eastern Turismond. There was set a definite limit to their western expansion as the same limit was set for all the peoples seeking to extend westward here. The Klackadrin with its cold hallucinations and its Phokaym waited out there.

I have spoken a little at my chagrin at finding myself in a port city of Pandahem when I had wished to reach Port Tavetus, of, failing that, Ventrusa Thole, both colonial port cities of Vallia. The difficulty of finding a ship at all to take me to Vallia had been further compounded by this enforced arrival at a port locked in mortal combat with Vallia. Mention of Vallia here was — almost — as mad as mention of Sanurkazz in Magdag, or of Magdag in Sanurkazz. There was a faint gleam of light in that I detected less vicious acrimony between the men of Pandahem toward Vallia, more a kind of grudging respect and a direful determination to do them down, than the out-and-out obsessional hatred on the inner sea between the red and the green.

Tilda often wore a green gown; and I was used to that now.

Naghan the Paunch kept Pando very busy about the calsany lines, and the youngster learned very quickly not to be anywhere near them when they became frightened. Naghan himself rode a zorca — a fine powerful specimen of that graceful riding animal. It had been a long time since I had seen a zorca — a long, long time. In the lands fringing the Eye of the World men rode sectrixes, and in the Hostile Territories they rode the near cousin of the sectrix, the nactrix. I looked at that beautiful zorca and I felt my hands clench in envious longing, for I had to pad along on my bare feet.

This zorca, like all the breed very close-coupled and with four impossibly tall and spindly legs, possessed a particularly fine horn, twisted and proud, flaunting from the center of his forehead. I would march along and look at the zorca and think.

What little money I earned — heavy silver pieces of Pandahem coinage called dhems, and duller and often-chipped copper coins called obs, one eightieth of a dhem — I saved for my food and keep and lodging, and, most particularly, to buy myself a zorca. I had seen no voves. You must remember that this city and zonal region of Pa Mejab was civilized, or as civilized as any area of Kregen given its situation had any right to be, and I could not just knock over the first person I ran across and take his gear and weapons, mount and cash, as had been my lamentable habit in more savage times. I had to earn what I needed, as I must earn a passage to Vallia. Often I have laughed since to think that the great and puissant Dray Prescot, Krozair of Zy, Lord of Strombor, had been placed in this position; but there was no shame in it at all. Nothing had happened to me here to give me an opportunity, and a great deal of the blame for that must lie at the door of my terrible weakness that debilitated me as a result of my experiences. You will know that after my immersion in the pool of baptism in the River Zelph of far Aphrasöe I could look forward to a thousand years of life, and, equally, that I did not take to disease and mended quickly from wounds, so that my weak state gives some inkling of the ghastly passage of the Klackadrin.

Here I was once more in the sphere of influence of men and institutions that had surrounded me when I had first carved my way in Segesthes. Between this eastern coast of Turismond and the western coast of Segesthes lay the northern tip of Loh, that mountainous and mysterious land of Erthyrdrin, and Vallia, I was back among rapier and dagger men, among tall ships, among zorcas and voves — gone were swifters and sectrixes and the Krozairs of Zy.

Although — the Krozairs of Zy held now my undying loyalty.

Gone, too, were impiters and corths, although it was foolish to dream that those great flying beasts of the air might bear me across all the pitiless dwaburs to Vallia over the shining sea.

When I made inquiries to discover if the Pandaheem possessed airboats, those fliers manufactured in distant Havilfar and widely used by the Vallians, I was met by a curse and a shrug. Evidently, Havilfar did not sell their fliers to Pandahem. Equally evidently, the snub to trade was resented.

A light cheerful voice singing fragmentary snatches of the robust ditty "The Bowmen of Loh" brought me back to the present with a start. How that cunning and hilarious song brought back memories of Seg! Of how he and I, with my Delia and poor Thelda, had marched through the Hostile Territories singing!

Before I could yell, Obolya, an exceptionally tall and heavily-built man with a bristle of black hair all over his muscular body, cuffed Pando around the head.

"Sing somewhere else, you pestiferous brat! Little rast! Your screechings make my guts rumble!"

Obolya was a guard, a man whose profession as a mercenary had made of him a man embittered, callous, unfeeling. Whatever he once had been, growing as a young man at his mother's knee, seemed all to have been wiped away during his years of hard fighting and long tramping. He owned a preysany, a kind of superior calsany, used for riding by those whose estate in life did not extend to the purchase of a zorca. He considered himself invaluable to the caravan, and Naghan the Paunch treated him with some respect.

It was with Naghan himself that I had taken service, as I have related. Now Obolya was being tiresome again.

The word "one" has many definitions and names on Kregen, of which "ob" is — if you will pardon the pun — one. Obolya,[xiii] a common name in various forms, indicates that its recipient was the firstborn of the family's children. The Obolya who had just knocked Pando flying was tall, over a knuckle taller than I. Others of the guards on this left flank of the caravan with a few drovers crowded across to see the fun. Zair knew, walking caravan duty was monotonous enough so that any break in the routine was welcome. And Obolya was known of old; until every fresh guard knuckled down to him he would be ever seeking to force a confrontation which poor Naghan the Paunch, who valued Obolya's massive thews in defense, must condone.

Pando just managed to avoid the nearest calsany's instinctive response and scrambling up flew toward me.

"Just rest quietly, Pando," I said, "while I speak with this limb of Armipand."

Armipand was one of the devils in which many of the more credulous of the Pandaheem believed devoutly.

422

"Cramph!" roared Obolya. "You have a mouth wider than the Cyphren Sea! I must fill it — with my fist!"

"May Pandrite aid you now, Dray Prescot!" said Pando, overwhelmed by what had happened. He had known me long enough to know I would not shrug off an insult; but also he had seen me only as a weak and ill man, lucky to be employed by the overseer Naghan on the personal request of Tilda of the Many Veils. Pando sucked in his cheeks, and his eyes grew very round.

"Crawl back into the hairs of a calsany's belly where you belong," I said to Obolya.

He stuttered. The black bristles on his cheeks and chin quivered. He pointed at me, and threw back his head, and roared his contempt.

"You! Cramph-begotten rast! You who carry the leavings of a blacksmith's shop upon your back!"

This was a reference to the Krozair long sword. Now, in this culture of rapiers and daggers, I carried the long sword on my back, still in the sheath Sosie had made, beneath the quiver of which I have spoken. The weapon was in many respects anachronistic here. The guards carried short broad-bladed stabbing spears for butcher work until the rapiers came into action. This would be after the bows had taken the first toll, and it was as a bowman that I had been engaged by Naghan.

He would say to me, half surly, half jesting: "You carry your bow in your hand, strong, and with an arrow nocked, Dray Prescot, when you guard my caravan. That is what I pay you for."

The hope that by carrying the long sword over my back and thereby escaping its notice had not, in the case of Obolya, succeeded. Just how long he would go on hurling insults before he got down to action I did not know. I was almost back to my full strength, the fresh air and the suns-light and the daily marching had all combined in my recuperation. But, as always, hot though I am to resent authority, I attempted to avoid an unnecessary clash and a dangerous enmity. Pride and a hot temper are all very well for those who do not think; my trouble is that I think first — and then still go berserk, to my sorrow.

Obolya wore a bronze breastplate of a reasonably high standard of workmanship; but for more complete protection he had under it only a leather tunic. On his arms and legs were boiled-leather strappings, and he wore a boiled-leather cap reinforced with straps of iron. He was as well-enough armored as many men who work as mercenary guards for a living; his armor, of course, would have made my clansmen smile and evoked mirth from the mail-clad men of the inner sea. I wore only my scarlet breechclout. My sleeping gear, along with Pando's, was carried aboard one of the guard detachment's plains asses.

"You affront me, Obolya. But, as I do not wish to deprive you of your few remaining teeth, black and stinking though they be, I will refrain from fighting you now."

The crowd roared at this and Naghan the Paunch came running up, sweating, starting to yell and drive us back to our duties. But Obolya waved him down and Naghan, seeing how the wind blew, took himself off, sweating even more over the safety of the caravan he had contracted to protect. The crowd roared again as Obolya threw down his spear and crouched. He used a large and variegated collection of foul Makki-Grodno oaths. He advanced on me to, as he informed me with great relish, tear my head off and stuff it between my knees.

He wouldn't kill me, as he knew I would not kill him. This was a bull moose confrontation, to decide who was who in the hierarchy of the caravan guards.

I handed the longbow to Pando. "Hold it off the ground, Pando. The bow is more valuable than this kleesh."

A kleesh is violently unpleasant, repulsive, stinking — and the name was guaranteed to drive Obolya like a goad.

His infuriated roar was quite up to the standard of a leem caught in a pit.

He charged.

He sought to grapple me to his breastplate and, holding me there, bend me back until I cried quarter. I stepped to one side and drove my fist into his jaw — and Obolya was not there. His speed was surprising. He hit me higher on the chest than he'd intended, because I moved; and in that I was lucky, for a blow from those massive arms would have taken my breath.

"Dray!" yelled Pando, mightily excited.

I did not deign to rub my chest, where the dint spread a pain I ignored. This time I rushed — halted, with a twist — took the blow on my upraised forearm — smashed Obolya in the breadbasket — drove him to a knee — chopped down on the back of his neck — and so laid him on the grass, insensible.

Someone let out a screech. Someone else was swearing by the gross Armipand. Another was laughing.

In truth I had welcomed the exercise and now I regretted hitting Obolya hard enough to knock him out. A little more of fisticuffs would have suited me, then, for I was strangely slow in getting back to my usual form. The Phokaym and the Klackadrin had drained more from me than even I realized.

Pando bent and retrieved a yellow object from the grass. He held it out to me, holding it gingerly.

"This fell from your loincloth, Dray, when you fought."

I took it. It was a six-inch fang I had taken from the jaw of a Phokaym as a memento. About to stuff it back, I stopped. Pando was looking at it with undisguised curiosity.

"What is it, Dray? It looks like — like a risslaca fang."

If I told him what it truly was, he wouldn't believe. No one who did not know me, Dray Prescot, Lord of Strombor, would or could believe.

"It's a risslaca tooth, Pando. Here." I tossed it to him. "Keep it as a memento of the fight. Boys collect anything — your friends won't have anything to match that for a space, I'll wager."

Pando took it eagerly. But, turning it over in his hands, he said: "Young Enky has a risslaca fang almost as big. And Wil had a claw he said his father cut off a risslaca himself."

I was, as you may imagine, duly cut down to size.

Pando went babbling on about the fight. I took my bow and nocked an arrow —

for Naghan the Paunch only half jested — and resumed my station. Guards who had felt Obolya's fist were helping him up. I saw him shake his head, looking dazed, and he dragged his feet as they helped him along. All this time the caravan had not halted, and we were well into the outer cultivated areas surrounding Pa Weinob.

I said, "Don't let your mother hear you singing 'The Bowmen of Loh,' Pando. You're only nine."

At his reproachful glance, I went on, "As for me, it is a fine song, and you may sing it as you will. I do not think anyone else will tell you to stop."

"By the glorious Pandrite, they will not, Dray!"

A shouting at the head of the caravan followed by a series of shrieking roars heralded fresh trouble. I doubled up past the plodding calsanys, but by the time I reached the van the problem had been solved. The zhantil had been slashed to death by many thrusts from the broad-bladed spears of the advance guard. This zhantil was of moderate size, about the length of a leem, although his massive mane and forelegs lent much greater weight to his foreparts than has the weasel-shaped leem. He was magnificently banded in tiger-stripes of glowing umber and ruby, and his richly golden mane fell about him. His blood pumped out to foul all that rich and gaudy marking. I felt sorry for the beast, and I know many of the caravan felt as I did. Although, of necessity, we must defend ourselves from zhantils when they attacked us, we did not feel for them the loathing and determination to destroy with which we regarded leems.

Naghan the Paunch, puffing, rolled up and at once began berating the guards.

"Fools! Imbeciles! Look at the pelt! Aie, aie — that would have brought many dhems had you not slashed it to pieces!"

An archer guard, one Encar the Swarthy, cursed and said, "We slashed it, good Naghan, because it was trying to slash us!"

"Well," persisted Naghan, wiping his forehead and neck, "you might have slashed with a little more care not to spoil the pelt."

Pando and I looked at each other, and Pando broke first, and held his belly and roared. Some of the other guards and drovers, knowing Naghan the Paunch, chuckled at the jest.

I said, "Naghan — will you spare a portion of the pelt — a trifle — to give Pando here a fine new tunic? Remember, he is the son of Tilda the Beautiful."

Naghan put a foot into the stirrup of his zorca, who sniffed once at the zhantil, and finding it smelling dead, thereafter ignored it. He twisted around, his paunch straining that brilliant blue cummerbund.

"A tunic for Pando? Of zhantil skin? Ho — I think Tilda of the Many Veils would like that. Ay! She would part with a whole amphora of the best wine of Jholaix for such a zhantil tunic for her adored son!"

Jholaix, I knew, was the extreme northeastern country of Pandahem, which island is split up into a number of nations of the Pandaheem, and, further, I knew Jholaix wine to be scarce, dear, and extremely potent and pleasant to the tongue.

"You mercenary old rascal, Naghan the Paunch!" I said.

But he merely mounted his zorca, with an almighty belch, and winked down at me, whereat I nodded and said, "Done."

Between us, Pando and I took enough of the zhantil skin to make him a fine tunic, and, also, I cabbaged enough to make a belt for him, also. I would pay the cost of the amphora of Jholaix wine — and, thereby, put back the time when I could buy a passage out of Pa Mejab. But, looking at the rosy glory of Pando's young face, and the sparkle of sheer delight in his eyes, I knew my Delia of the Blue Mountains would forgive me.

Zair knows, she had much for which to forgive me...

Naghan's servant, a one-eyed shaven-headed Gon, remained with us to take the rest of the skin and the mane, all of which, by virtue of his office, were the property of Naghan. The caravan had gone perhaps a little farther on than was altogether advisable by the time we had finished, and I made Pando step out smartly. The bloody pelt, rolled, I slung over my left shoulder.

The shout for help, when it reached me, made me whirl about and fling the pelt down and draw my bow fully.

There was no need immediately for violence.

The man who crawled toward us from a clump of missal trees was smothered in blood, and the long ax he bore glistened with gore. He tried to stand up to run toward us, but collapsed and fell. He twitched once and then lay still.

"Dray!" yelled Pando.

"Pick up the pelt, Pando. Go back to the caravan — and hurry!" I shouted at the one-eyed Gon. "Run, too! Warn Naghan — the caravan is attacked!"

For, beyond the man collapsed in his own blood and that of his enemies, I could see the wolfish shapes of halflings riding preysanys coursing toward the caravan, their fleet forms half-hidden by the missals. The opaz glitter from the twin suns speared back blindingly from their brandished weapons. In scant seconds they would be upon the caravan.

I loosed at the nearest rider and then slung the bow, ran toward the fallen man, and hoisted him upon my back. He was incredibly tall and thin. As I lifted him his eyes opened and he gasped. His right hand did not relax its death-grip on the haft of his ax.

"Bandits!" He choked the word out, and I knew from the way he spoke he had summoned up all his strength of purpose to run and warn the caravan and had been struck down. "Bandits!"

"Quiet, dom," I said. "Rest easy."

Then I raced back toward the caravan where already I could hear the shrieks of men engaged in mortal combat, and the slither and clang of iron weapons.

Six

Concerning the taboos of Inch of Ng'groga

The guards around the center flight of calsanys were already in dire trouble. The caravan had come to a halt and the beasts were milling. Hastily dumping down that impossibly tall man with his ax beside Pando, and yelling to him to keep out of sight and trouble, I drew the longbow.

The time had almost passed when archery could help; but I was able to feather four of the bandits before a gang of them swung their preysanys and coursed in at me, waving their spears.

Getting the long sword out of Sosie's scabbard over my shoulder demanded a convulsion of effort, and I had to jump up and bend over in a most undignified fashion to do it. But, once the deadly Krozair brand was in my fists, I was ready to meet these throat-slitting bandits, and to earn the wages Naghan the Paunch paid me.

Since that long-gone day when I had met Hap Loder on the beach and we had made pappattu and then I had taken obi of him, I had learned much of sword fighting. Then I had been accounted a useful man with a cutlass, and had learned a great deal with those wonderful swords of the Savanti; but, all the same, when my clansmen armed with broadsword and short sword had gone up against the sophisticated rapier and dagger men of the city of Zenicce, I had worried about them. Now, I had all the skills and scientific knowledge, and the art and mystic practice, of the Krozairs of Zy to drive my nerves and impel my sword arm.

The rapier and the left-handed dagger are excellent weapons, as I have indicated, and they can between them take on much variegated weaponry. By this time the bandits and the guards were at it hammer-and-tongs, their broad-bladed spears flung down, and the rapiers and main-gauches, the Jiktars and the Hikdars, flaming and slicing, cutting and stabbing, in a welter of slivers of finely-honed steel.

I charged the bandits running at me with a great shout of: "Hai! Jikai!" and at once that terrible Krozair long sword was whirling a path of destruction through the bandits.

My own rapier and dagger bounced scabbarded at my side.

The long sword took the head off the first bandit — he was a man of uncertain origin (but of certain destination) — and sliced back to lop the rapier-wielding arm of the next one. They spurred their preysanys in to get at me, and this, I believe, led to their own destruction, for I could reach them with the long sword and they could not reach me. This fight roared and bloodied away. At least to me it appeared topsy-turvy, for the mounted men used weapons shorter than they should, given the fine length of their rapiers, and I had no long pole arm. In this fight I did not learn, truly, of the full problems of long sword against rapier and dagger. The fight taught me only that I had to get it over fast, for I caught a distorted glimpse of young Pando, with a snatched up dagger, trying to hamstring a bandit preysany. If anything happened to him...!

Already Tilda must be frantic with worry over where the little devil had got to — and if I returned and told her he had been with me, and had been killed... I couldn't face that.

So my long sword became a bloodied blur. The bandits fell before me. They were of many races of men and half-men: Fristles, Ochs, Rapas, Gons; alike they fell before my brand.

Obolya I saw, fighting like a demon, spitting his man, taking another's attack on his dagger, twirling with a laugh full of braggadocio, lunging into the belly. Naghan the Paunch I saw, also, striking about him with a broad-bladed spear that from his height on the zorca kept the bandits at bay.

I shortened the long sword and drove it carefully into the neck of an Och, sliding above his out-thrust shield. I body-swerved to avoid the thrust that his last involuntary movement impelled. I jumped over his falling body. Right-handedly I slashed away a Rapa who, wasting time screeching, tried to spit me. He went over with his beak sheared off.

I jumped over a preysany, my Earthly muscles back to full power and tone, chopping short and hard down onto the man who ducked far too late. I landed neatly enough, removed another Rapa beak, swung and slashed and so forged my gory way toward Pando.

He came up screeching, scooped under my left arm. I laid the flat of the sword across his rump, whereat he yelled like a trapped leem, and left a long blood smear there.

"Quiet, you imp of Sicce!"

Obolya was down.

A Rapa, his fiercely predatory bird face gobbling with blood lust, was in the act, seeming so deliberate, of thrusting his rapier down into Obolya's belly. Without pausing in my run I swung the long sword in a flat arc that intersected first with the Rapa's right arm, thus removing it and the rapier from Obolya's intestines, and then sheared on into the Rapa's side. He was wearing a bronze corselet. The Krozair blade smashed through in a screeching splintering of metal.

I wrenched the brand free, spun, caught a rapier and, with the supple wrist-twist that is easy enough with a rapier, damned difficult with a long sword, managed to thrust the blade into the bandit's throat. He vomited blood and went over.

Obolya was up. He glared at me.

"How many more are there, Obolya, in Zair's name?"

"Enough for me to repay you my life, Dray Prescot."

There was no time to wonder about that. The bandits pressed and we guards earned our money. When I had contrived to deposit Pando back among the plains asses — who were more restful and far less impossible than the calsanys, to whom everyone fighting gave a wide berth — and sorted out another group of bandits, I began to think we would best them.

They had waited for us here, on the outskirts of the cultivated areas, thinking that having traversed the dangerous lands we would relax our guard. As it was, with Naghan yelling us on, with Obolya fighting like a demon, and with my long sword that simply destroyed them, they had had enough.

The last we saw of them was the dust their preysanys kicked up as they ran.

Without pausing I ran across to a preysany from whose saddle a man hung with his foot entangled in the stirrup. I put my foot on his face and kicked him free. Then I swung up into the saddle.

Naghan yelled: "Don't pursue them, Dray. They won't be back."

I rode across to another preysany which stood nuzzling the bloody rags around the head and shoulders of the Gon, its late master. The head and the shoulders were separated by a space of bloody grass. I remembered that one. Grasping the reins, I pulled the animal away and, a little reluctantly, it followed.

I said to Naghan the Paunch: "I claim these two preysanys for Pando and me. Agreed?"

He huffed his paunch more comfortably in the saddle and nodded. "You may claim them, Dray Prescot, with pleasure. Under the terms of our contract they are mine, as you well know. You can work them out of your pay."

"Naghan the Paunch!" I yelled.

He was chuckling and wiping the blade of his spear and reveling in it. I did not chuckle; but I suddenly shouted: "Hai!" and the zorca started and leaped and Naghan went careering across the grass, wildly grasping anything to keep from falling off.

I heard a deep belly-rumble of laughter and turned and there was Obolya with his black-bristle face all crumpled with malicious mirth.

"You treat men hard, Dray Prescot."

No surprise showed on my face. This was only a petty border skirmish, a thing to be done and forgotten and not to be placed alongside the great battles and campaigns of my life; but a man can be killed as easily in a skirmish as a world-shaking battle.

"True, Obolya. To their deserts."

He eyed me a moment, and then went off about the business of a mercenary guard — stripping the dead of their valuables. In this I heartily agreed. Pickings are hard-come-by. But when I saw Pando engaged in the same occupation I started off at once to check him, outraged, wondering what Tilda would say if she could see her son — and then I stopped. This was life. This was what fighting and killing were all about. Let Pando learn the true facts, and then, perhaps, in later life he would not be so quick to provoke a quarrel or to seek to kill.

I went back to see about the tall and thin man I had rescued, with a parting shout to Pando: "Don't waste time on trifles, Pando. Pick the best."

On the way back I took three rings from bandit fingers. As it happened the rings came off easily enough, greased by blood. Had I had to hack the fingers off to get at the rings this I would have done. I needed cash to buy a passage to Vallia and my Delia.

The drivers were sorting out the calsanys now and soon the caravan got under way again.

The tall man, still smeared with blood, was loaded facedown onto one of the preysanys I had acquired and the loot obtained by Pando and myself bundled in our sleeping gear on the other. Pando was hopping wild with excitement still, running up and down and emitting shrill Red-Indian-like war whoops. I let him blow off steam. Any fancy modern notions that his mind had been affected by the horrific sights he had seen, of course, did not apply on Kregen, where the absence of such sights usually indicates abject slavery on one side. He was growing up into a world of great beauty and wonder, for Kregen is a planet at once gorgeous and barbaric and highly-colored; but at the same time he was also preparing himself to face the other side of Kregen, the terror and the horror and the continuous struggle for existence.

Young Zorg, the son of Zorg of Felteraz, Krozair of Zy, my friend and oar comrade now dead and eaten by chanks, and his sister Fwymay, were both preparing themselves to enter the adult world of Kregen, far away there in Felteraz on the shore of the inner sea. Their mother, Zorg's widow, Mayfwy and Tilda had little in common except a love for their children and the sense of loss for their husbands — but I thought of them both, then, as I strode along, thinking, as I always do, mostly of my Delia of the Blue Mountains, my Delia of Delphond.

When we camped that night the man I had rescued had so far recovered as to consent to being washed. I discovered that most of the blood splattering him was not his. He kept that great ax close by him. He had had a thwacking great thump on the head, that I judged had smashed beyond repair the helmet he had lost, and was still a little muzzy. After some wine — mediocre red stuff from a local Pa Mejab vintnery — and a morsel of bread from a long Kregan loaf, liberally smeared with yellow butter, he sat with his back wedged against a tree bole munching a handful of palines. They would soon clear his headache.

"I am Inch," he said. "From Ng'groga."

So far had I come from Magdag that all those "G's" did not worry me. Inch told us that Ng'groga was a nation situated on the southeastern part of the continent of Loh, facing the unknown southern sea. He was, himself, a somewhat amazing individual. He was, as I have said, incredibly tall, some seven feet of him from toe to the top of his head. That head was covered in long and silky yellow hair that hung to his waist and which he would bind up and coil when in action. He was thin, also, but I did not miss the bulge of muscle about that sinewy body. At the moment his only clothing was an old and tattered brown tunic, gathered in by a leather belt of lesten hide. Beside his great ax, which reminded me of the Danish pattern carried by the clansmen of Viktrik, with the addition of a daggered head after the fashion of my own clansmen of Felschraung and Longuelm, he bore at his waist a long knife. He had no sword.

"I shipped out as a mercenary, as so many youngsters do," he said. "The life suited me but ill. Then I was betrayed — that does not concern me now — and was sold as slave. So I escaped and joined the brigands. But, that life, also, was not for me."

"Then what happened?" demanded Pando. He was hunched up, eagerly listening to the story, which Inch embroidered far more than I have indicated.

"At last the bandits said they were going to attack the next caravan, slay all the men and — ah—" He cocked an eye at Pando, and went on after a cough. "Abduct all the girls. I had an argument with the chief of the bandits and left him, I fancy, with his ears wider apart than they had been."

As he spoke he moved his hand across the ax, and I could well imagine that mighty weapon splitting down through the skull of the bandit chief.

"And?"

"That was a foolish thing to do. My taboos had not warned me adequately, which was passing strange."

This was the first I had heard of Inch's taboos; but not the last, oh, certainly, not the last! As you shall hear.

"So I ran from them, and they pursued, and I killed many; but then Largan the Wily hurled a stone, and I fell, and they would have beaten my brains out but for my old helmet." He reached a long hand up to his head, and felt his yellow mane of hair. "I am sorry I lost that, by Ngrangi, yes!"

"Yes, yes!" said Pando. "And then?"

"Then, when I thought I was done for, and the caravan gone, I called out and this monstrous man here, Dray Prescot, came and took me up and shot Largan the Wily with that bow that, if I mistake not, is a true bow of Erthyrdrin."

"Yes," I said. I could not speak of Seg, not yet, to Inch.

For, from what Sosie had told me, I knew this Lohvian bow she had given me was a true bow of Erthyrdrin, made from true wood of the Yerthyr tree, long matured and sweetly seasoned. I thought even Seg Segutorio would be happy with this bow, although comparing it always unfavorably with his own stave he had cut himself from the private tree of Kak Kakutorio.

Gone — those days, gone and dead and best forgotten!

In Pa Weinob, a city of wooden, high-built houses and a wooden stockade with watchtowers, we waited for the goods to be collected for the caravan to take back to the coast in exchange for the manufactures we had brought here. During this period I had a local woman recommended to me cure and prepare Pando's zhantil skin. Another woman, a clever seamstress, sewed him a fine tunic and belt. When he donned the gear and turned to let us see, both Inch and I made all the necessary noises of surprise and gratification. In truth, Pando did cut a dashing figure, and he was as pleased as a woflo eating his way through a whole Loguetter cheese.

By the time the country produce had been baled and loaded and we set forth to return to Pa Mejab, Inch had been taken on as guard by Naghan the Paunch, and he and I and Pando had palled up in a way that surprised me, although Pando took it all in his stride.

One night when the Maiden with the Many Smiles shone down from a cloudless sky, Inch approached the fire where we were cooking a tasty vosk haunch purchased in the town. He crinkled up his nose at the delightful smell. Over his long fair hair he wore a huge mass of cloth, like a sloppily-wound turban. Not a scrap of his hair was visible.

Pando let out a yell.

"Hey! Inch! That's my sleeping cloth!"

Pando started to pull the bundle of cloth from Inch's head.

Inch went mad.

He jumped up, waving his arms, screaming words no one understood, words clearly of his local language of Ng'groga. A strand of hair fell loose. Inch shrieked as though his flesh was being wrung out by red-hot pincers. He jumped toward the fire — he jumped *into* the fire!

"Inch!"

"You have made me break a taboo!" he shrieked. He gyrated in the fire and his sandals smoldered and then burst into flames. He didn't seem to feel a thing. He gyrated around, scattering hot coals, and the guards yelled and scrambled away, beating at their clothes.

"When the Maiden with the Many Smiles is alone in the sky, she may not shine down upon a Ng'grogan's hair! It is taboo!"

I grabbed Pando and shouted to the other guards and we cleared off. We knew when to leave a fellow alone with his taboos.

After that when Inch went berserk, or solemnly took a cup of wine and threw it over his left shoulder, or dropped onto all fours and stuck his rump into the air and beat his head against the ground, we left him to it. It was a chancy business, living with Inch and his taboos.

Pa Mejab looked most welcome with its streets of wooden houses, some brick ones already shouldering out the earlier timber structures, and its cool groves of fruit trees, its harbor and vista of the sea. We were paid off by Naghan the Paunch, and precious little I had left after I had settled all my debts, what with the preysanys and the zhantil tunic, paid for by the amphora of wine from Jholaix.

"At least, Naghan, Inch and I can have a cupful of Jholaix with you tonight, eh?"

"Surely," he said, patting his paunch. "Naghan is the most generous of men."

"Ayee!" said Pando, most impudently.

We walked from the caravansary through the crowded streets to *The Red Leem*. If we walked with a trifle of a swagger — well, had we not crossed dangerous lands and fought wild beasts and wilder bandits, and brought the caravan safely home?

A shriek as of a Corybant broke upon our ears as we walked up to the tavern.

Tilda, trailing a green gown, her glorious black hair swirling about her like impiter's wings, flew down upon Pando. She caught him up, kicking and squirming, against her breast, and smothered him with kisses.

"Pando! My son, Pando!"

Then—

"Pando! You limb of Sicce! Where have you been?"

And with that, Tilda the Beautiful started laying into him with the flat of her hand, applied to the bottom of that brave new zhantil tunic, until Inch and I winced.

"He's been all right, Tilda," I said — like a fool. "He's been out with the caravan, with me—"

"With you! Dray Prescot! Out there — out there, wild beasts, bandits, drought, hunger, disease — out there — Dray Prescot, I'll — I'll—" She left off beating Pando long enough to scream: "Get out! Get out of *The Red Leem!* If you show your face in here again, you vile abductor, I'll scratch your eyes out!" She spared a hand to rip off a slipper and hurl it at me.

"Out! Out!"

Inch and I walked off, hurriedly and without dignity.

"Nice class of friend you have, Dray," was all Inch said.

Seven

How Tilda the Beautiful fared at *The Red Leem*

Tilda's anger against me did not last long when Pando managed to tell her what had happened. For his pains he was sent supperless to bed that night, as Inch and I quaffed best Jholaix in company with Naghan the Paunch and Obolya. Inch disappeared for a time and when he came back he winked at me and leaned over, whispering.

"Climbing the back wall was easy, Dray. That young devil is munching a vosk-pie now, and probably getting disgustingly drunk on a thimbleful of Jholaix."

"If Tilda catches him and he tells on you, Inch—"

Inch looked pleased with himself. "Sending boys to bed supperless is against my taboos," he said, and winked.

I perked up. Inch was turning into a comrade, rather than a companion. Now, if Seg were here — or Nath, or Zolta. Or, Gloag, or Varden, or Hap Loder…

I must not think of Seg, I thought then.

Inch was laughing and telling how a friend's taboos had given him a pair of horns, and Naghan and Obolya were laughing, too, and I could understand Naghan the Paunch, not Obolya.

If I was asked to describe the Pandaheem succinctly, I would show my interlocutor Naghan the Paunch. He was Pandaheem to the very last nail of him. Built for comfort, the Pandaheem, as were their ships.

Obolya, now, while he had changed since I had knocked that Rapa off him, was still as surly and vicious as ever to everyone. To me, he maintained a watchful respect, the result, I imagined, of our fight. He did not, to me, fit in with the men of Pandahem at all. I had discovered that the island of Pandahem, which lies to the east off the coast of Loh, due south of Vallia, was divided up into a number of separate nations, most of them governed by kings jealous of their own power and prestige, continually at loggerheads with their neighbors. They seldom united even against Vallia, whose single mighty empire operated from the secure base of an island under one government. This division weakened Pandahem. Pa Mejab, which lay well to the north of Ventrusa Thole and just tucked into the bay south of the great promontory projecting from Turismond into the Sunset Sea, was a colony city of the human nation of Pandahem called Tomboram.

Tomboram, as I learned, is a pleasant place in almost every respect, situated in the northern and eastern part of Pandahem, with Jholaix as a smaller country to the northeast. The Tomboramin are a happy folk, they had made me welcome, and although they would fight their neighbors, and Vallia, and the mysterious pirate ships that sailed up out of the southern oceans, they much preferred to sit in a tavern and drink, or watch and applaud a great dramatic performance. Industrious when working and idle when playing, the Tomboramin were people with whom I got on well.

And yet — I could not forget the bitterness with which Thelda, of Vallia, had spoken of the Pandaheem, of how she had sworn by Vox that they must all be destroyed one day.

My Delia was a Vallian — she was the Princess Delia, Princess Majestrix. These people among whom I sat and drank and sang were her bitter commercial rivals, and deadly foes upon the seas.

Even now a great deal of talk was in the air of the next expedition to probe southward to attack the Vallian colonial port city of Ventrusa Thole.

My distress you may imagine; my determination to reach Vallia, I assure you, was in no way impaired by all this newly-found good fellowship as we drank and roistered in *The Red Leem* and watched the incomparable actress, Tilda the Beautiful, perform so gracefully and movingly for us.

When Vallia was mentioned by the Tomboramin, it was with a curse and a bitter feeling of betrayal, a sense of dejection and doom. No, these good people of Pa Mejab did not care for Vallians. Listening to them, hearing tales of treachery and deceit, I absorbed some of that feeling. Vallia was overbearingly powerful, omnipotent, almost. Vallia scorned all other nations. Vallia made treaties and broke them, contemptuously, careless of good faith. Vallia was as perfidious as, I suppose, the England of my day was considered by France.

Albion Perfide was now Vallia Perfide — indeed!

These days I habitually left my long sword in my room and in deference to local custom wore only the rapier and dagger about the town.

Tilda, in conversation one day, mentioned that political difficulties were growing worse every day with the Pandahemic nation immediately to the west of Tomboram, a nation she called The Bloody Menaham. I took little notice, although I knew that Menaham had sited a colonial port at what appeared to be perilously few dwaburs to the north, being more concerned over my own problems and being a trifle irritated that the wrangles on one island of Kregen were preventing me from reaching another.

In this I should have been more careful; for The Bloody Menaham, no less than Tomboram, was to play a large part in my life before I found Delia again.

We discovered that it was taboo for Inch to eat the tiny and delicious fruit called squishes and Pando took a fiendish delight in bringing in great baskets of them from the orchards, for they were in season, and leaving heaping bowls of them everywhere in *The Red Leem*. Inch doted on squishes. This convinced me that his taboos differed radically from what is considered a taboo on Earth; there, had the squishes been taboo, he would never have eaten one in the first place. As it was, whenever we came upon Inch standing on his head, his face expressing the greatest anguish, we knew he had broken his taboo and gone munching squishes.

And Pando, the imp of Sicce, would laugh.

"I wonder, Dray," he said to me, very solemnly, with Inch on his head in a corner close by. "If I had to stand on my head every time I ate vosk-pie, would I go off vosk-pie?"

"Such gratitude!" said Inch, and succulent squish juice dribbled down into his eye.

"Stick to palines, Inch," I said. "There is nothing more sovereign."

He groaned, and shut his eye, thus winking at us when he had nothing in his head to warrant a merry wink — at all.

The time was fast approaching when the armada might be expected in from Pandahem and the caravans would be loading again and Naghan the Paunch would be hiring guards.

Due to the depredations of pirates — call them corsairs, rovers, buccaneers, privateers, as you will, to honest sailor-men of Kregen they were renders all — abroad on the outer oceans ships tended to sail whenever they could in great convoys called armadas. I heard Naghan shaking his chins and his paunch and saying, "The swordships make life hard for a merchant, may Armipand drag 'em down by the short and curlies. I sometimes make myself remember, when my caravan is attacked, that I am lucky not to be a ship's captain."

"Come now, Naghan!" I protested, out of my ignorance. "Surely the Sunset Sea and the Cyphren Sea do not harbor so very many swordships?"

"Enough and to spare, Pandrite rot 'em!"

Well, I had been to Segesthes and I was now in Turismond; but I had never traversed the seas that lay between.

When the bells began to ring and the people streamed out of their houses and ran in wild excitement down to the harbor you may be sure that Pando was well up with the leaders and I not far behind.

Everyone looked out over the sea, toward the southeast and a great cry went up when we saw that armada of sails.

The commotion and seething rushes, the fluttering scarves, the hats tossed into the air, the cheering, the ringing of bells, the frenzied scamperings of children and the mad gyrations of dogs through the crowds, the gusts of happy frothy laughter — all were prodigious.

With a somewhat more cynical eye, I, an old sailorman, looked at that distant white-glinting armada of sails, and the sea between, and felt the wind, and I remembered days hanging around in the Downs, and said to Pando, "I am thirsty, Pando, and am going back to *The Red Leem* for a drink."

"But the fleet, Dray! You'll miss the ships!"

"They will still be in the offing when I return, never fear." He wouldn't budge. "If you fall in," I told him, "apart from realizing that I told you so, swim to the steps and take your time. The seawall breaks the force of the waves."

After I had sunk a couple of glasses of the local red biddy — not for me the best

435

of Jholaix when I needed every ob — Inch joined me and we strolled back to the harbor. I was surprised. The first ship was already entering the stone-built entrance past the pharos, gulls swinging whitely about her three masts, her sails coming down, her crew gathering on her forecastle with ropes. A band was playing and the music lolloped into the air as this broad-beamed ship lolloped through the sea. I studied her lines critically.

The Pandaheem called these high-charged ships of the outer oceans argenters. They were rigged with square sails; had they been rigged with lateens they would have looked remarkably like caravels, with their high forecastles and their half decks, quarterdecks and sterncastles. As was to be expected they were decorated lavishly with much gilding and carving, fine gingerbread work that glittered in the opal glare.

They were broad in relation to their length, solid, heavily-built, comfortable ships — and, therefore, slow. They carried courses and topsails on their fore and mainmasts, and courses — a crossjack — on their mizzens, with a spritsail on the bowsprit. I gained the impression, watching the argenters glide solidly and squarely into port, of rolling argosies of sail, dependable, unimaginative, lofty as to hull, cautious as to sail area and plan.

As you know it has been my custom not to jump about in this narrative but, rather, to attempt to tell you of what happened to me on Kregen beneath Antares in as good a chronological order as I can contrive. Maybe that skyjacking has loosened up my time-sense. I will, therefore, quickly say that when I — at last, at long last! — saw the ships of Vallia I saw immediately how like galleons they were. And I mean a real galleon, the type of ship invented by the English: low, streamlined, fast, daringly sparred, superb sailers. Despite the plethora of names the Vallians use for their ships I have always thought of Vallian ships as galleons, and will so refer to them when the time in this narrative is ripe.

By contrast — and I thought of it then, as I stood with Pando and Inch and saw the Pandahemic argenters without knowledge of the Vallian galleons — these ships of this armada sailing into Pa Mejab were reminiscent of Portuguese and Spanish caravels and carracks. Maybe history does repeat itself, even though it takes place on different worlds separated by four hundred light-years of interstellar space.

To finish this anachronistic comment, the reason — or one of them — why I could never seem to catch a Vallian ship on the inner sea lay simply in the galleon's superb ability to drive on in wind that would have overset a swifter in a trice.

As well as varters — the ballistae as used by swifters of the inner sea — these ships carried catapults powered by many twisted strands of sinew and hair. Watching critically the evolutions of the ships as they lost way, brought their canvas in, dropped their hooks, and swung to, I was reasonably satisfied that they were seamanlike enough. They were not in a hurry. The reason they had gained the mouth of the harbor before I had expected was explained by their use of sweeps thrust through a few ports cut in their sides. People around me commented on this, giving as their judicious opinion that great news was carried aboard the ships, for using the sweeps meant hard work, and the Tomboramin only worked hard when a definite end lay in view.

The wind was free, was it not, dom? So why sweat at the oars?

If these men *were* in a hurry — I shuddered to think what their customary seamanship would be like.

With the taking in of the fore and main courses disappeared the huge and gorgeously painted devices of Tomboram. Tomboram proudly flaunted the pictured representation of a quombora, a mythical monster of devilish aspect, with much fangery and toothery and clawery, spitting flames and smoke, as her symbol. The fore and main topsails carried the painted devices of the individual ships and owners. Many bright blue flags fluttered.

A swarm of boats put off to the ships, and the first pair were being warped alongside the jetty to begin unloading. The show was over. My next and most immediate plan was somehow to arrange a passage on one of those ships when she returned to Pandahem. I would have to sign on before the mast. That procedure must — given the physical facts of sailing-ship travel in relatively primitive ships across many dwaburs of open ocean — entail prodigious suffering and discomfort which meant nothing, of course, beside my determination to seek out Delia.

In a directly straight line from Pa Mejab to the chief port of Tomboram the distance is approximately eight hundred dwaburs. Distances of this order might be covered by a ship without calling in for water and supplies; normally the armada would make port somewhere in northern Loh, along the coast of that great thrusting promontory of Erthyrdrin. As I understood it ships of many nations shared port facilities here, docile under the constraint of the sufferance of the Erthyr. From thence a journey due east or northeast would bring a ship to Vallia. For Pandahem the course would be southeast, either outside or inside the long chain of islands that parallel the northeastern coast of Loh.

Inch and Pando went back to *The Red Leem*, for there would be new customers to care for and probably, if old Nath was lucky, passengers to be accommodated, while I went to find Naghan the Paunch and explain that I would be unable to go with him on the next caravan. I knew he would shout and swear and call me an ingrate; but my purpose was set.

Naghan the Paunch did all these things. In addition he threw a wine bottle at me, for I found him soaking in the small room of *The Marsilus and Rokrell*. I ducked.

"Peace, good Naghan. Oh man of the Paunch, I have served you well and taken your silver dhems, let us then part in friendship."

He glared at me. Then he pulled up another glass and bottle, and poured, and lifted his glass to me, as I did to him. "You are the finest bowman I have ever engaged, Dray, you and that great Lohvian bow of yours. I have seen many bowmen, and some almost your equal." He drank and wiped the back of his hand across his lips. "But never, no never, have I seen anything like that damned great cleaver of yours!"

I drank to him, and said, "I shall not forget you, Naghan the Paunch. Care for young Pando, if you can, and Tilda the Beautiful, his mother."

"That I will always do. By the glory of Pandrite, I swear it!"

"Remberee, Naghan the Paunch."

"Remberee, Dray Prescot."

I went back to *The Red Leem*.

People were moving about the streets, all of them still excited over the arrival of the armada, and passengers were already coming ashore. I saw a cart trundle along, the two calsanys drawing it impatiently goaded by the imp in charge, the cart's master dragging them by their stubborn jaws. Bundles and bales and casks and kegs would be coming ashore, and Pa Mejab was coming alive again, fed through all those dwaburs of sea by the mother country. It was a gala day. Pa Mejab was not forgotten by the king and the nobles and the merchants and soldiers and all the people in their far-off homeland.

As you may well imagine, I had made all my usual inquiries, but no one had heard of Aphrasöe, the Swinging City.

About to put my foot on the fantamyrrh, the habitual unthinking act performed by every Kregan entering a house, I paused. Pando shot out of the doorway, wild-eyed, his hair tousled. He did not see me at once and just as his eyes fell on me a hand at the end of a long arm reached after him, clapped around his mouth and neck, jerked him back. He disappeared.

That long hand and arm did not, I thought, belong to Inch.

Young Pando was a handful, I knew that well enough, and an imp of mischief, and it could well be that he had so upset a new guest in the inn that chastisement had been considered necessary. Yet I hurried inside, anxious that no real harm should come to the lad, and, if the truth be told, growing indignant that someone else other than his mother should lay hands on the child.

The noise of people in the main room drowned out any sounds of beating that might be coming from the upper floor. Quite a crowd had gathered already as the news and gossip of far-off places were detailed, and the merry sound of clinking glasses and the throaty exclamations of amazement accompanied me, along with the heady smells of wine and cooking food, up that narrow blackwood stair.

As I reached the top I saw Tilda's door slam shut.

I stopped at once, making a face to myself. No man with a pennyweight of brains interferes between a widow and her son in moments like these. But then — a stir of unease ghosted over me. That had not been Tilda's slender and shapely ivory-skinned arm that had so roughly pulled Pando back, and I had not passed the owner of the offending arm on the stairs. Strange.

With a certain hesitation — an unfamiliar sensation for me — I moved quietly toward Tilda's door. I listened. I heard nothing except a hoarse breathing, close up against the polished wood. I kept my own breathing steady and quiet.

Then a man yelped in sudden pain — as though, for instance, a woman had driven her bare toes agonizingly into his middle — and a woman's voice rang out. Tilda's voice.

"Help! Help! Murder!"

Eight

Wedding plans for Delia, Princess Majestrix of Vallia

I smashed the door open with a single kick and leaped into the room.

These were no rapscallion leem-hunters out for a good time, unwilling to kill, ready for a bit of rough-and-tumble.

I knew this breed. These were killers. There were four of them. They were tall, lithe, poised men, all bronzed from the suns-light, muscular and predatory. Their rapiers and daggers were plain, workmanlike, efficient.

They wore dark clothing, plain tunics and well-oiled leathers, high black boots, and their broad-brimmed gray hats with the curling blue feathers cast shadows across their faces from which the gleam of their eyes in the suns-light through the windows struck leem-like.

One held Tilda around the waist and his dagger lifted above her ivory throat, poised to strike. Another stood holding his middle and retching — I did not smile — and the other two swung around to face me. Reasonable odds for the Lord of Strombor.

There was no time to consider. The dagger was about to plunge down into Tilda's throat, and all Pando's despairing yell as he struggled between the legs of the assassin would avail nothing. My rapier and dagger were in my hands. I threw the dagger. It flashed across the room like a streak of sunlight, buried itself in the neck above the squared tunic. The man gulped and dropped his own dagger. His knees buckled; but I could watch him no more for with a clang and a screech of steel the two assassins hurled themselves upon me.

Our blades met and parried and I had to dodge and skip for a few wild heartbeats as I avoided their attack, my left hand empty.

I spitted the first one in the guts, recovered, slashed savagely at the next and did not complete the stroke, leaping back so that he parried with his dagger against the empty air. I ran him through the heart, aiming delicately between the requisite rib members. As I withdrew, the meanness of these men showed itself in the last one's actions — for, knowing he faced a master swordsman and knowing he faced thereby his own death — he turned and dived headlong through the window taking the glass and the framing with him in a great splintering crashing.

One spring took me to the wreck of the window. I looked down.

The assassin was picking himself up, his face still with a greenish hue from Tilda's kick and blood on his face from the smashed glass.

Inch was walking up toward *The Red Leem*, whistling.

I shouted, "Inch! If it is not against your taboos, kindly take that fellow into custody. Don't treat him gently."

"Oho!" said Inch, and ran in and planted a tremendous kick upon the assassin's posterior as he attempted to stand up. I jumped out of the window, landed like a leem, grabbed the fellow by the tunic, and hit him savagely on the nose. Blood spurted. I did not knock him out.

"Talk, you rast! Or I'll spit your liver and roast it!"

He gabbled something, something about Marsilus, and gold, and then blood poured from his mouth and he collapsed.

Inch looked offended.

"I did not kick him hard enough for that, Dray. Nor would your blow upon the nose have hurt a fly — So why is he dead?"

I was annoyed.

"He must have smashed his guts up jumping through the window and falling awkwardly. By the disgusting nostrils of Makki-Grodno! The fellow is dead and that's an end to it."

We left him there to be collected by the mobiles of Pa Mejab, who were later fully satisfied with our explanation of four dead men, and went back to Tilda and Pando.

The assassin I had first run through was in the act of dying as we entered the room. There was nothing to be discovered. Pando collected four rapiers and four daggers, which I was pleased to sell later for good silver dhems, and Inch took the best of the leather boots which fitted him, for his feet were inordinately long and thin. I had a pair, also; as an addition to my wardrobe, just in case. Two of the broad-brimmed hats, also, with their curled blue feathers, might come in useful. The tunics would not fit either Inch or me — I was too wide in the shoulder and Inch too narrow — so we sold the rest of the gear.

"If they have any friends come asking for them," I said to Nath, the innkeeper, "then let us know, by Zim-Zair, and we will wring the truth from them."

But no one else bothered us thereafter on the score of the four assassins while we were in Pa Mejab.

"They swaggered in and demanded to know if the actress Tilda and her son Pando lodged here," said old Nath, mightily shaken up by the event. He kept a respectable house, as, indeed, he must, otherwise Tilda would not have lodged and performed there. These goings-on were not to his liking. They might be common in *The Silver Anchor* and *The Rampant Ponsho* along the waterfront, not here in this respectable street and *The Red Leem*.

Not one of the four dead men yielded any personal identification to prying fingers. Apart from money and the usual items to be found in the pockets and gear of any man they were devoid of information. Inch wondered if we might make a few discreet inquiries among the ships; but Tilda, rather alarmed, vetoed this idea at once.

Looking at her, I caught the impression that perhaps she knew more about this business than she was prepared to discuss with us. After all, Inch and I were strangers.

A considerable number of people had taken lodgings with old Nath and he had let all his rooms. The main room was crowded that evening. Tilda had insisted that she was perfectly all right and could go on. Old Nath, gallantly protesting that she should rest up after her ordeal, visibly showed his relief that she would give her performance, whose fame accounted for his vastly increased trade and profits. But I do not condemn him for that; he was good to me as well as others.

When Tilda made her final exit to rapturous applause that thundered to the rafters and set all the glass wine cups on the shelves ajingling, she came over to my table as was her custom. Old Nath did not mind me occupying a table just so long as I paid for what I consumed in the same way as an ordinary customer. Most often I did not bother, saving my scraped wealth, but this night was different. Just as we were preparing to listen to the beginning of Tilda's impassioned rendition of the execution scene from the music drama — not quite the same thing as an opera — known over most of Kregen as *The Fatal Love of Vela na Valka* — I had heard the light musical voice of a young woman say: "Oh, Pando — there is not a table left!"

A young couple stood in the doorway, looking disappointed. She was young, lissome in the normal way and with fine eyes; at the moment she was pregnant. Her husband was a soldier, a Hikdar, handsome in his Tomboramic uniform. Naturally, I offered them seats at my table, and Wil, who had been brought in to help, quickly brought glasses and wine — a yellow wine of Western Erthyrdrin — so that when Tilda joined us we had already been thrown into the quick and casual friendships of the frontier. Inch had discovered a taboo and now came across, brushing sawdust from his long fair hair, and sat down.

The young couple told us all the news. The Hikdar was a cavalryman and burning for adventure out here on the borders of the spreading empire of Pandahem. His name was Pando — the cause of my immediate reaction when they had entered — Pando na Memis. His wife's name was Leona.

"Memis," said Tilda, gracefully drinking the yellow wine. "I know it well, those tall red cliffs falling to the sea, the islands and their gulls — oh, millions of gulls! — and the wine there." She laughed. "It is far smoother on the tongue than this Erthyrdrin—"

Pando na Memis looked somewhat confused and beckoned quickly. I watched the byplay. Young Pando trotted up, he also having, for a change, been conscripted.

"Bring a better vintage than this, young one," said Pando na Memis. "It is not to the lady's liking."

Pando — the urchin of that distinguished name — made a face at me, whereat I lifted my fist, so that he scuttled off, laughing. Tilda looked gracious, oblivious of the exchange. Pando na Memis pushed the bottle of yellow wine away across the table — and a long lanky arm reached out from somewhere and Inch grasped the bottle by the neck. Leona na Memis had not missed a single nuance.

Much of the traffic and trade of Kregen is devoted to this kind of mutual exchange of commodities. It is an infuriating fact of human nature that the grass is always greener over the neighbor's fence; and that is why wine from Western Erthyrdrin reached Turismond, why in Zenicce we drank Pandahem wine when the good vintages of Zenicce were shipped to Vallia. As to Vallia, her wines were carried to the far corners of Kregen. Despite all that, I still preferred the fragrant tea brewed by my clansmen in far Segesthes.

441

Inch, I considered, would be happiest with a bottle of dopa, that fiendish stomach-rotting drink that I had seen at work in the warrens of Magdag.

Drunkenness is relative on Kregen. Few Kregans consider getting drunk the occupation of a fully rational man, and my two oar comrades, Nath and Zolta, although they might become as merry as nits in an eiderdown, seldom ever achieved that disgusting paralytic sick drunk common in certain so-called civilized countries of this Earth. Kregans love to roister; and that means enjoying themselves. Getting sick drunk and puking over everything is not, really, much idea of fun.

The conversation wended on, and we heard of Pando na Memis' plans for the future, of how he craved for action — at which Leona looked alarmed — and of how, soon, the Tomboramin would advance along the old Lohvian roads through the Klackadrin.

"After the old Empire of Walfarg fell," said Pando, "the land must have gone back. The Hostile Territories are still there, waiting for strong men to ride in and take over. One day, and soon, we of Tomboram will do just that, before the rasts of Vallia or Menaham or anyone else!"

I made the right noises, saying nothing.

Then the name Marsilus came up. A great noble of that name, old, crotchety, more than half-mad, had just died back in Tomboram and his estates, reputed valuable beyond price, had fallen into the hands of a nephew, who was also a nephew to the king. Pando na Memis whistled when Tilda, rather sharply, I thought, said: "Are the estates then so valuable?"

"Are they not! They rival the king's. Now that Murlock Marsilus, the nephew, has inherited, the king must be greatly pleased, for the kingdom may inherit also when the king dies. There was a son to old Marsilus. Unfortunately, he died."

Speaking very precisely, Tilda said, "Was the son disinherited, then?"

"By no means. But he is dead and — there was a story — he was banished in disgrace. Married out of turn, so the story goes. Everyone has heard it — you must have, surely?"

"Yes."

"I haven't," I said.

After I had given some explanation of myself, brief and almost totally untrue, Zair forgive me, Pando na Memis went on: "Murlock Marsilus is now Kov of Bormark, but the story goes that the old Kov, old Marsilus, screamed and shouted for his son on his deathbed. He relented of his punishment of the boy when he married. There was a grandson — but, of course, he stands no chance of the title and estates now that Murlock holds them under the king's agreement."

"The old man was stricken with the shrieking horrors," said Inch, wisely. "It is known. He wanted to go to the Ice Floes of Sicce with a clean mind and with clean hands. One can visualize the scene. Poor benighted of Ngrangi!"

I leaned forward. "The king," I said, "and this Marsilus, Kov of Bormark, who had died. They were brothers?"

"Yes," said Leona, smiling at me. "You must be from some wild and untamed part of the world!"

442

"I am," I told her. "Oh, yes, indeed, I am!"

The conversation changed course then; but I noticed Tilda was very quiet after that. The hated name of Vallia came up and with it tidbits of gossip and scandal. Of these I felt my heart lurch when Leona, speaking with a gentle malice quite natural in the circumstances, said: "The Princess Majestrix of Vallia! Such a proud hoity-toity madam! Her father, the emperor has ordered her to marry—"

"To marry!" I shouted — and they all leaned back from me, their faces shocked, expressive of bewilderment and disgust. They must have seen that devil's look on my face. I made myself calm down. My Delia! My Delia, Princess Majestrix of Vallia, ordered by the tyrant emperor, her father, to marry — to marry some blundering oaf of his choice. I had to hold onto my sanity and my temper then. I do not apologize, so I just said: "You were telling us of Delia, Princess Majestrix of Vallia, Leona. Please go on."

In a voice she struggled to keep from quavering, Leona went on speaking. And, as I listened, I felt a warm sweet relief flooding me, and I breathed easier.

For my Delia had defied her father!

She had flatly refused to marry the oaf picked out for her! She had stood up against his puissant majesty the emperor of Vallia, and told him flatly she would not marry. Not marry at all.

This made my heart lurch afresh.

My Delia vowing never to marry?

Did she — could she — believe that I had abandoned her, as that scheming villain had planned when I had been drugged and dumped under the thorn-ivy bush? Had that foul scheme worked?

I had to get to Vallia — and yet, was there any greater urgency now than there had been? At least I knew my Delia was safe and well. She refused to marry. The emperor was still hale and hearty and, so the scandal went, quite prepared to wait and let his only daughter rot in maidenhood until she decided to marry the man of her choice. He would not force her; he would let time and nature take their courses.

Once I had held Delia of the Blue Mountains in my arms and pressed her dear form close to my heart I had known that no other woman in two worlds could compare with her, no other woman could take her place. And I had known many women, blazingly beautiful women of arrogance and power, lovely women of lissome grace and refined artifice, women of passion and glory; and one had been to my Delia as a candle to the radiance of the red sun Zim. I had felt absolute confidence that Delia felt in exactly the same way about me, however little I deserved so marvelous a wonder. Delia was everything. No — she would not despair of me — she would not, she must not!

"You all right, dom?" said Inch.

"Assuredly, my long friend. Do I thus break a taboo?"

He chuckled and pushed the wine over to me and I drank and pushed the problem of Delia's father, the emperor of Vallia, away for a space. At that time I had not settled the question. It rankled. I had to walk away from it for a space.

Leona, having exhausted herself on the scandal of a princess majestrix disobeying her father the emperor, had harked back to the Kov of Bormark, and was saying how lovely it would be if all that money were her Pando's. Pando laughed. With what I considered to be deep wisdom, he said: "The money might be fun, Leona, my dearest; but what comes with it — ah, that is a different matter."

Tilda was still sitting silently and sipping her wine and I saw her face suddenly tauten. I swiveled. Young Pando, his naked legs flashing, his brave zhantil tunic laid aside for the humble job of waiter, his hair tousled, was fleeting between the tables. A big fellow in the blue of a sailorman reached out and cuffed Pando alongside the head.

"Bring me a flagon, you rast of an imp of Sicce! Hurry, you little devil!"

Pando picked up his tray and what glasses were not broken. Someone else — a newcomer off the ships — kicked him irritably as Pando bumped into his legs; but that was a reflex action.

Tilda put a hand to her breast. Her violet eyes were large with anguish. Her supple voluptuous mouth shone, half open, pained, vulnerable.

I stood up.

Old Nath waddled across. "Now, Dray, please…!"

The sailorman laughed coarsely among his mates. He was big and bluff, with the tattoos across his forehead and cheeks that some sailors believe indicate heightened sexual potency or, perhaps, will give them immunity to the demons and risslacas of the seas.

"You, Nath, have a stinking clientele in here, lately."

"Please, Dray—"

I went across to the sailor who was already roaring for the little rast of a waiter and picked him up by the scruff of his blue tunic. He started to thrash his legs about so I clouted him — once was enough — and carried him outside horizontally. It was done quickly and decently, and old Nath put his hands together and cast his eyes up to Zair and Grodno.

Outside I stood the big fellow up and said, "You hit a young boy, you kleesh. This may be wrong, it may be savage and barbaric, it may be against the divine dictates of Zair; but I do not like men like you who hit young boys."

So, somewhat sorrowfully, for I know I sinned, I struck him in the belly. I stood aside as he was noisily and smelly sick. Then I kicked him where Inch had kicked the assassin and told him to clear off. I went back into *The Red Leem* and I managed to force out some sort of smile for Tilda.

Old Nath had quickly whipped a round of drinks onto the sailor's table and his mates were drinking and ogling the local dancing girls Nath had hired especially for the night. Tilda never performed more than once an evening. These girls were fine strapping wenches who danced like chunkrahs. They made great play with gossamer veils, they were heavily made-up, and each one would roll a sailor this night, or she was no true daughter of Pa Mejab!

Pando na Memis said to me as I sat down: "That was the captain of an argenter, you know, Dray."

"I should hope so," I said. "Nath runs a respectable house."

Tilda said she was tired and we all stood up as she left the table. The night roared on and presently, mindful that I must see about a ship the next day, I, too, went to bed. Tilda stood by her door, beckoning to me. She had waited for me to retire. A lamp burned in her room. I had made plenty of noise coming up the stairs. Even then, I believe I knew what she was going to ask me.

I sat on the bed, but Tilda prowled restlessly. She wore a long gown of jade, a green glinting and glorious. How strange, how incongruous, that I, Pur Dray, Krozair of Zy, dedicated to the utter destruction of the Green of Grodno, could sit and watch and not be moved!

Her ivory skin gleamed against the silk. Her black hair swirled as she walked. She prowled like a caged leem, like one of those leem stalking in the leem pit below the palace of the Esztercari in far Zenicce when my Delia clung in the cage above their ferocious fangs and claws.

"You need not whisper, Dray. Pando is fast asleep and it will take the wrath of the invisible twins to wake him. I sent him up to bed after — I saw that." Her voluptuous lips tightened. "I saw that, and I made up my mind."

I said, "What kind of life can he have, out here, on the frontier, Tilda?"

She clenched and unclenched her hands. She padded up and down those carpets of Walfarg weave, up and down.

"Old Nath runs a respectable house, for Pa Mejab. Yet already you have seen what can happen, Tilda." I tried to make my face smile for her; but I gave that up, and said flatly and, I fear, brutally: "You must take him home and claim what is his right."

Her white hand flew to her throat. She halted, stricken, and gazed at me, those violet eyes enormous in her white face.

"What? You know — how can you know?"

"It is not difficult, Tilda. By Zim-Zair. His father must have been a man!"

"He was! Oh, yes, he was! Marker Marsilus! Who would have been Kov of Bormark this day, had he not died out here in this pestiferous hell-hole. And Pando is his son."

"You mean, Tilda, that your son Pando is really Pando Marsilus, Kov of Bormark. He is, rightfully and legally. Is this not so?"

She looked at me, still and alert, like a risslaca watching a bird. "He is, Dray Prescot. Rightfully and legally." She took a breath so that the green gown moved and slithered. What she said next rocked me back with surprise.

"I am going home to Tomboram and I am going to claim what is his right for Pando. Dray Prescot — will you come with me and help Pando and me? Will you be our champion?"

Nine

We sail southeast past Erthyrdrin

Ochs, Rapas, and Fristles do not make good seamen. Chuliks may be trained, given the methods to which I had been born and grown accustomed, the system of the late eighteenth century, consisting of the lash, the starters of the bosun's mates, a wall of marines — and the lash.

Rum, in its counterfeit of shipboard wine, also helped.

As a consequence the vast majority of the crew of *Dram Constant,* Captain Alkers, were men of recognizable Homo sapiens stock. The few halflings were, and on their own wishes, employed in noncritical functions aboard ship — waisters.

No captain in his right mind would enroll a Fristle. I saw one being aboard — he was not Homo sapiens — who interested me mightily. His body was square in the sense that the distance across his shoulders, waist, and hips was the same, and equaled the distance from his neck to his upper thigh. He had but two arms, and they were as long and thin as Inch's, while his legs, also long, were nearly as thick as Inch's, which is another way of saying he was spindly-legged in the extreme. His face bore a cheerful rubicund smile at all times, his ears stuck out, he had a snub nose, and he could run up the ratlines and around by the futtock shrouds into the top with the agility of a monkey. This man, one Tolly, was a member of the race of Hobolings, inhabiting a chain of islands that I have mentioned, that ran parallel to the northeastern coast of Loh from the tip of Erthyrdrin southeastward to the northwest corner of Pandahem opposite the land of Walfarg.

Dram Constant, as Captain Alkers was happy to tell me, was as fine and tight an argenter as it was possible to find plowing the Sunset Sea. He knew that this report of his ship had been the cause of our taking passage in her, our little party consisting of Tilda and Pando, and Inch and I as guards and champions to protect them and see they were not molested and reached their destination safely. I believe it is not necessary to dwell on the mental turmoil I went through after Tilda's offer. As the days passed and the dwaburs slipped past our keel, as we sailed in the armada toward Loh, I had again and again to rationalize out my decision. Delia of Delphond waited for me in Vallia; yet I was to travel to Pandahem. Not only was I sailing away from her, I was voyaging to a land in deadly rivalry with her own.

By taking an intense interest in every aspect of the argenter — an occupation easy to feign — I canceled out a great deal of my own misery and indecision. I thought Delia would understand, I prayed she would; and yet I doubted...

This argenter was about a hundred and thirty feet long — Captain Alkers told me she was a hundred feet on the keel — and almost fifty feet on the beam. She was thus little more than twice as long as she was broad. Captain Alkers also said she was eight hundred and fifty tons burdened; but this I tended to doubt. She was a fat, wallowy, comfortable ship, with good stowage place below. We quartered ourselves aft, within the three-decked aftercastle, and our cabins were of a roominess that at first amazed me, used to far more cramped quarters. One genuine improvement these sailors of the outer oceans had made in their ships over the swifters of the inner sea was in the use of a rudder and whipstaff in place of the twin steering oars.

With her three masts and her square sails, *Dram Constant* plunged gallantly onward, sheeting spray, and if she made a great deal of fuss about her passage she did make a passage over open and truly deep sea — if at a snail's rate of knots.

Pando loved to lie out along the bowsprit beneath the spritsail mast and watch the water smashing against the round cheeks of the bows, creaming and coiling away. *Dram Constant,* as it were, squashed her way through the sea.

Tilda was continuously on at Pando, and me, for the lad to come down where it was safe. After I showed him a few of the necessary tricks of the trade any sailorman must have, I felt a little more confident about him. But, all during that passage, he was a sore trial.

Probably in an attempt to get his mind off ships and to confine him to one spot, Tilda got me to teach him rapier and dagger work. In truth, he was of an age when this very necessary accomplishment would be vital for him to learn quickly.

A full-size Jiktar and Hikdar would have overweighted him, but we were fortunate in being able to borrow a practice pair belonging to one of the young gentlemen signed aboard *Dram Constant* to learn their trade. With these I had Pando puffing and lunging, riposting, parrying, drawing the main-gauche back in cunning feints, carrying out all the many evolutions of swordplay — the twin-thrust, the heart-thrust, the thigh stop, the flower, the neck riposte — until he was dripping with sweat and limp as a moonflower on a moonless night. Tilda would sometimes watch, and when the boy flagged, would say tartly: "Get on, Pando, get on! This is man's work now! Stick him!"

She did not, and for this I was mightily thankful, use that expression: "Jikai!"

Tilda and Pando proved excellent sailors.

Poor Inch lost a great deal of his dinner and his dignity over the side.

Memories ghosted up — to be instantly quelled.

For me to be back on the sea again was an invigorating experience, and I snuffed the sea breeze like an old hunter let out to the chase once more. The sky gleamed and glowed above us, a few clouds streamed in the wind, the breeze bore us on, all our flags and banners snapped and whistled in that breeze, our canvas strained, billowing with all the painted panoply gorgeous upon it. We plunged and reared in the sea and in our wake we left a broad swathing wash of creamy foam. Yes, for a time they were good days. I knew that I would reach my Delia; first I had to deliver Tilda and Pando — that imp of Sicce who was now Kov of Bormark — safely to Tomboram.

Tilda had not told Pando, yet, just who he was. That would come later. A wise decision, I felt.

We made landfall in due time at Northern Erthyrdrin, and took on fresh provisions and water and landed a man who had fallen and smashed up his pelvis. We shared berthing facilities with ships from other Pandahemic nations; but the peace was kept. I looked up at the gnarled mountains that thrust right up to the coast. Up there, in those mountains and valleys, lay Seg Segutorio's home. I could walk there. I knew the way, for he had told me often. But I was committed. I vowed that one day I would go there, for I could walk directly to where he had cut his bow-stave, where he had held the pass, right to his home and greet the people as though I had known them for years. But my honor and integrity — such as they are and have value — had been enlisted in support of Tilda and the young Kov. Yes, one day, I would walk the hills and valleys of Seg's home.

We were talking of the enforced amity of the different countries of Pandahem here, and I heard more stories of the horrors that did occur from time to time. There were massacres, and mutual extermination excursions, and tales of bitter fighting even when the Vallians laughed and stepped in to steal the prize. I came to recognize the different devices and characteristics that divided and marked one nation from another on Pandahem. In all this talk of division and what amounted to internecine warfare I began to wonder if the Star Lords had set another task to my hands.

As we sailed out in our armada and set our bows toward the southeast I leaned on the larboard rail and looked back over the larboard quarter. Out there, across the shining sea, lay Vallia...

As I stood there dreaming I heard a harsh and savage cry. I looked up. Up there, slanting against the mingled rays of the twin suns, a giant bird circled, a gorgeous scarlet-feathered raptor, with golden feathers about its neck, and wickedly clawed black talons. I knew that bird, circling in wide hunting circles. The Gdoinye, sent by the Star Lords. As I watched I saw the white dove fly smoothly above me, circle once, and then rise and wing away. The white dove of the Savanti!

I felt a tremendous sense of elation, of relief, of lightness. I had not been forgotten. The Star Lords, who had brought me to Kregen, and the Savanti, who also had brought me here and then thrust me out of their paradise of Aphrasöe, both were watching over me. They would not take a hand to halt the cruel thrusting spear or sword. They wanted me for their own inscrutable purposes. I wondered, again, if there was work for them to my hand in Pandahem.

"What weird bird was that, Dray?" demanded Pando. His mischievous face was all screwed up against the sun glare, and quite serious.

"A bird, Pando. An omen." I could not tell him the Gdoinye came from the Everoinye, the Star Lords. "It means that everything is going to be wonderful in Tomboram."

"Of course, I am excited at going there, and the sea, and the ships, and learning swordplay — but, Dray, tell me. Why is Mother going home?" His eyes searched my face. "Home to me is Pa Mejab. She knows that."

"When you get to Tomboram, Pando, there will be many wonderful and exciting things to do. You will be a man. I know you will do your best to look out for your mother. She is a woman alone."

"She said to me once, would I mind if she married again."

"What did you say?"

"I said I would not mind if she married you, Dray."

I pushed myself off the rail and swayed gently with the roll of the ship.

"That cannot be, Pando." I spoke seriously, man to man. "Your mother is a most wonderful woman. You must cherish her. Yes, she will marry again, I feel sure, I hope — but I cannot marry her—"

But he was staring at me with such a black look that I felt sick. "You don't like her!"

"Of course I do." I looked around the wide deck, which was largely deserted on the larboard side, most folk being over on the starboard watching the last of the land. I bent toward him. "Can you keep a secret?"

"Of course I can." He was most ungracious, his lips in a pout.

"I am engaged to a girl — a wonderful girl — and I—"

"Is she a princess?" Scornfully.

I eyed him. He had been hurt. But I did not intend to lie. Clearly, not even a princess was better than his mother — and how right and proper that attitude was, to be sure! — but if my betrothed was a princess that, so Pando must be reasoning, might go some way to explaining my boorish behavior. But I would never, quite, be the same to him again.

He was growing up.

"Do you know what a Kov is, Pando?"

"Of course — anyone does. He has lots of money and rides a zorca and is covered in jewels — and he has a flag — and—"

"All right." A Kov, a similar rank to our Earthly duke, is what Delia had more or less confirmed me as, after my masquerade as Drak, Kov of Delphond, in order to avoid being killed by the overlords of Magdag. The title had been given me and she had confirmed it; I was not foolish enough to believe her father would do the same. As for the Lord of Strombor — as for all the other lords of the enclaves of the city of Zenicce — we were a cut above a Kov!

"As far as I am concerned, Pando, your mother is a Kovneva."

He screwed his face up to me. He was jigging up and down now, as all small boys do, being compounded of spring wire and rubber. "A Kovneva? So I'm a Kov, then?"

I tried to laugh. I did laugh, after a fashion.

"And I am the captain of a swordship!"

He laughed, then, and we were friends again; but it had been a near squeak. I sensed that Pando, young as he was, perhaps because of the insights of that youth, felt in me a secret that I could not utter, something vast and portentous that might move mountains. That it was in truth merely the love of an ordinary mortal man for his princess might have seemed far too commonplace for him.

Because of the action we had seen together, and my rescue of his mother, and the swordplay I was teaching him, Pando had come in his boyish way to hero-worship me. I had tried to choke this off, being not so much embarrassed as aware of the dangers; but had had little success. Now I felt I had succeeded, violently, and at a stroke.

The days passed and we bore on southeastward, the weather remained fine with a moderate breeze generally from a few points north of east, so we were continually on the larboard tack. Two alternatives now lay before the admiral of the armada.

He might choose to swing to the east and so outside the long chain of islands stretching down to Pandahem. This choice would offer attack opportunities to privateers from Vallia, scouring across the Sunset Sea. Or, he could run down between the islands and the mainland of Loh, which was here the homeland of Walfarg, progenitor of a once-mighty empire. This choice would lay him open to attacks from all the swordships which lay in wait in their festering pirate nests among the islands.

If he took the latter course, however, he would have to swing due east when he reached the last of the islands and run clear across the northern coast of Pandahem and the countries having their seaboards there before he could reach Tomboram in the east. Also, to figure into the calculations, there was over twice as much sea room outside as inside the island chain. To me, a fighting sailor, sea room is vital.

The admiral hoisted his flags and Captain Alkers, not without a fitting comment on the importance of the occasion, put his telescope to his eye. He nodded his head with satisfaction. He lowered the glass and turned to the helmsman.

"Make it east!"

So we were to run clear of the islands, and then turn southeast for Tomboram directly — and to the Ice Floes of Sicce with the rasts of Vallia!

Every sixth day Captain Alkers conducted a short religious ceremony on the open quarterdeck. Most of the passengers attended and all the crew, both human and halfling. Tolly, I noticed, was particularly devout. In the inner sea the green of Grodno and the red of Zair hate and detest each other. In Zenicce they used to say: "The sky colors are ever in mortal combat." The people of Pandahem and Vallia had progressed some way along the path of a more live religion, for they held the view that the red and the green, Zim and Genodras, were a pair. They both shone down upon the one world, the twin suns mingling their light into an opal glory. They regarded their deity as an invisible pair, the invisible twins with which Tilda so often threatened Pando, and upon whom she called in time of trouble. The name often given to this twinned deity of invisible godhead was Opaz: a name conjoined from the light streaming and mingled from the Suns of Scorpio.

Despite my vows to the Krozairs of Zy, and my own half thoughtless swearing by Zair, I was happy to join the others in their worship, feeling no true blasphemy to my own God, feeling, rather, that these people were nearer to Him than many and many another I had known.

So we beat on east and then turned southeast and aimed for a quick run to Tomboram. The easting had cost us time, for we had had to make to windward by a long series of boards. But that weary tacking was paying off now. The spume flew, and the last of the gulls left us, and we were alone on the shining sea.

The lookouts were alert, and a most careful watch was kept at all times toward the east and northeast, from which we might expect the lean galleons of Vallia to pounce upon us.

As the days winged by and the weather remained fine we began to congratulate ourselves. Not a single speck of sail showed on the horizon rim. The galleons of Vallia had missed us, or were not at sea. The reason we discovered, to our disaster, when black clouds began to build up all along the eastern horizon. The twin suns shone down with a light I found uncomfortable. This was rashoon weather. When the blow came I discovered the difference between a rashoon of the inner sea and a hurricane of the outer oceans.

I have lived through many a hurricane and tempest, many a typhoon — on two worlds — but that was a bad one. We were driven helplessly toward the west. Our masts went by the board. We lost crewmen swept overboard. The blackness, the wind, the rain, and the violence of the waves battered at our physical bodies and smashed with a more awful punishment against our psyches. We suffered. We went careering past islands, seeing the fanged rocks spouting ghostly white, to see that spray ripped and splattered away in an instant. Onward we surged, a wreck, our seams opening, our timbers splintered, lost, it seemed, in the turmoil of the seas.

When the storm at last blew itself out and we poor souls, numbed and drenched, could crawl on deck and discover to our surprise that Zim and Genodras still smiled down upon us from a clear sky, the dreaded cry went up.

"Swordships! *Swordships!*"

The deck was in a frightful mess, cumbered with wreckage, raffles of cordage, splintered timbers, everything that had not been washed overboard. We rushed to the rail. There they came, long lean shapes spurring through the sea. With deadly intent they closed in on us. Helplessly, we wallowed in the sea as those sea-leem ringed us.

"*Swordships! Swordships!*"

Ten

Swordships

"Swordships!"

I eyed the lean low-lying leem-shapes surging through smothers of foam all about us. Slender, cranky, spray-drenched craft, they clearly had put out from some pirates' lair hidden on a nearby island. They were closing in for the kill. Soon our decks would run red with blood.

"Oh, Dray!" said Tilda, grasping my arm in a convulsive grip. Snuggled against her side and held by her other arm, Pando — who was a Kov although he did not know it — stared with all his boyish excitement and venom out to sea and those slender hungry shapes.

A hail from forward distracted my attention from the swordships for a moment.

Then I saw the cause. Tangled together in a raffle of mutual destruction two other argenters from our shattered armada wallowed toward the shore. I saw the scheme of the swordships now. They would wait until *Dram Constant* had run athwart those other two dismal wrecks and then they would have us all, three fat ponshos, in the killing circle.

On the drifting wrecks the frantic forms of men ran and scuttled, and I caught the gleam of weapons across the water.

Very well.

We would fight.

Captain Alkers, pale but determined, gave his orders and his men were issued with axes and spears, boarding pikes and bows. Bows! Yes — to begin with, a little artillery might soften up the opposition. I disengaged my arm, very gently, from Tilda.

"You did Inch and me the great honor of asking us to be your champions, Tilda the Beautiful. Now, we will see about honoring our side of the bargain."

"But, Dray!" she wailed. "There are so many of them."

About to make the habitual response, I checked, as Inch, with a gusty laugh, said it for me.

"All the more of them to kill, Tilda of the Many Veils!"

I cocked an eye at the suns as I went aft to the staterooms to collect my Lohvian longbow that was built of true Yerthyr wood. How old that bow might be I did not know; but it was of great, price, and I thanked Sosie once again as I brought it forth. I buckled my Krozair long sword at my waist, along with the rapier. There would be need of those later.

Ax in hand, Inch waited my return.

"It will be dark in three burs or so," I said. A Kregan bur, being some forty Earth minutes long, meant we had two hours before we stood a chance of escape in the darkness. Like any Kregan, I carried a kind of almanac of the motions of the seven moons in my head, and I knew we had a bur or so of true darkness, lit only fitfully by a small and hurtling lesser moon, before the twins, the two second moons of Kregen, eternally orbiting each other as they orbit the planet, would rise to cast down their pinkish light. Would they rise before we could escape? Would we all be dead before the last orange glow of Zim faded from the western sky?

Soon after the twins would rise She of the Veils. Then the darkness would be dispelled completely. We had to hold out against the swordships. We must!

The corsairs opened away before us and a single bank of oars flashed, dripping, rising and falling, from each lean flank as the swordships heaved and rolled in the running sea after the gale. Two-masters, the swordships, with a low profile extending into a familiar beak and rostrum forward, a compact forecastle, a sweeping length of deck packed with men and half-men half-beasts, and a single-decked castle aft from which blazed and fluttered many gaudy flags and banners. The swordships carried varters mounted forward and on the broadside. All our varter and catapult artillery had been smashed and swept away in the hurricane.

We were not entirely defenseless. I watched a swordship surging up alongside, as a ponsho-trag herding a straying ponsho, worrying, attempts to push the recalcitrant animal back among the others, and I saw the way the water broke over her deck. I saw the spume shooting up, and the way the oars flailed and lost their rhythm, and the quick falling-off of the head to the wind to ease the swordship's motion. Waterlogged, *Dram Constant* rolled sluggishly onward, steady as a half submerged rock.

Lifting the bow and doing all the instinctive complicated mathematics of wind and relative velocities instantly in my head, without conscious thought, I loosed. The shaft struck the helmsman. He threw both arms up and pitched forward.

A great yell went up from *Dram Constant.*

The next instant the swordship abaft the one I had so suddenly and summarily deprived of her steersman loosed her starboard bow varter. The chunk of rock, as large as a fine amphora, flew over our wreckage-cumbered decks and splashed into the sea well forward of our starboard beam.

Again the crew of *Dram Constant* cheered.

But there were bowmen of Loh aboard the swifters, also, and a dozen multicolored arrows sprouted from the timbers of the argenter, and a crewman staggered back, cursing wildly, a long shaft embedded in his shoulder, the dark blood running down.

Wasting arrows has been a pastime in which I have never been interested. I shot only when absolutely sure of hitting a target; and I made of those targets the chief men of the swordships, for one oarsman more or less will not halt a galleass in full course.

The island richly clothed in a choked and brilliant vegetation toward which we drifted was appreciably closer now. The swordships closed in. There were seven of them, and they worked as one, obviously under the orders of a single commander. I call them galleasses because, in truth, lean and low in the water though they were, they were built with a far greater freeboard than the swifters of the Eye of the World. They would have need of that freeboard on the outer oceans. To add to the correctness of my description they carried varters in the broadside position, shooting over the single bank of oars.

When an arrow feathered itself into the planking hard by Pando, and Tilda screamed, I told Inch to take them both into the aft staterooms. I wanted Inch out of this long-range stuff, just as much as Tilda and her son, for his ax would be invaluable at close-quarters; now he was merely a target.

The swordships kept on with their attack. I fancied they were as unhandy in the sea as is any compromise between the out-and-out galley form and the complete sailing vessel. They looked dangerous ships — dangerous to those who sailed them.

The very aftermath of the storm, the long deep-swell waves, were aiding us by preventing the typical galley tactic of ram and board.

Soon, however, we must tangle up with those other two hopeless wrecks and strike the shore. When that happened the swordships' crews would beach and board us. We had little chance, for the pirate ships carried large crews.

The long-range artillery duel went on as we drifted closer to the island and I grew more and more miserly in my husbanding of shafts. The swifters in which I had commanded varters had soon, under my brand of discipline, acquired accuracy and speed in rate of loosing. A King's Ship with the ever-present memory of Nelson to jog heart and mind and sinew is the best training ground for rapid shooting, even if accuracy is a subject scarcely mentioned, to my annoyance. But these swordship varter-men were plainly inept. Only twice they hit us. One chunk of rock smashed clear through the aftercabin and destroyed the crockery the storm had left unsmashed there. The other mashed three crewmen into a red puddle. That was all.

There is callousness and callousness. Do not think I did not grieve for those three men, still practically strangers; but I had seen all this before, and Tilda, Pando, and Inch were on my mind.

"Not long now, Dray Prescot," said Captain Alkers. He held his rapier in his hand, and he fiddled with the gay golden tassel dangling from the hilt. "We will give them a fight, though, before they take us."

I had seen on the nearest swordship a man strutting importantly on the low forecastle, shouting at the varter-men, and before I answered Captain Alkers I spitted the swordship varterist through the chest. He fell over the side and was much beaten by the oars, which pleased me. Then I answered the captain.

"We can hold them off long enough to get the women and children off and into the island, can we not?"

There is callousness and callousness, as I have said. That varterist did not merit overmuch regret, I warrant.

In this, as you will hear, I perhaps did the man an injustice.

On that particular swordship, a larger vessel with three masts, a bowman had been having a go at me with some consistency. His arrows had sung past my ears, three had buried themselves in the timbers of *Dram Constant's* rail shaving close, and one had slain a Rapa waister who had been set to collecting incoming arrows. Captain Alkers cursed.

"I didn't mean the fool Rapa to collect an arrow in himself, Opaz take him!"

These arrows, of which I took only the automatic notice of a fighting-man engaged in an archery duel — which meant that I examined them with minute care — were feathered all with lush and lovely royal blue flights. Although I had never seen that gorgeous lambent shot-silk blue before, I knew exactly what they were and from which bird they had been taken. Seg had told me. They were the flights from the king korf, the largest bird of Erthyrdrin. The king korf was large; but it was nowhere near the size of the corth of the Hostile Territories; it was not a saddle bird. From this I knew I was up against a master bowman of Erthyrdrin on that swordship. It was extraordinarily difficult to pick him out on the deck clustered with men shooting. On the forepart of the aftercastle that extended into a quasi-quarterdeck stood a figure in brilliant and, the fleeting thought occurred to me, dashingly discordant clothing. A pendulous figure, with a mass of plumes waving above its helmet, the shine and wink of gems all about it, in a profusion; yet I caught the impression of uncaring scruffiness there. Twice I had shot at this figure, which appeared to me to be the captain of the swordship, and twice a mere chance had deflected the shafts.

Captain Alkers came back, cursing.

"We will strike the shore in a jumble of wreckage with the other two argenters. One is poor Captain Loki's *Tombor Adventurer.* The other is too far gone for me to be really sure just who she is—"

At that moment a blue-flighted arrow sprouted from the deck between us. I jerked it free, ran my fingers along the shaft to feel the sweet trueness of it, saw the head was a plain arrow-barb, nocked it, drew, loosed, and lost that flaunting blue in the mass of men crowding the deck of the swordship.

Now we were within close range of the shore the movements of the ships became more discernible. The sword-ships were swooping up and down in the sea. We surged on, sluggishly, and in a moment the shattered stump of our bowsprit tangled with the tattered bravado of the sterncastle of *Tombor Adventurer* and together, with the other argenter now a mere waterlogged mass disintegrating visibly, the three ships grounded. We swung broadside amid a great rending of wood. Outside of us now the swordships nosed in. Our keel grated on sand, we heeled, heaved as a wave caught us, and smashed down solidly onto the sand. *Dram Constant* had made her last landfall.

Some confusion ensued. I put it like that to let you understand that some of us wanted to stand and fight and some wanted to run into the shrouding vegetation of the island. Inch appeared with his great ax cocked over a shoulder, carrying our most precious possessions bundled into a canvas dunnage bag in the other hand. Tilda kept fast hold of young Pando, who was brandishing a dagger.

Captain Alkers formed his crew. The swordship carrying the blue-flight archer with whom I had been having that duel bumped our seaward side, going up and down like an elevator through the giant plants of Aphrasöe. I glanced back. People were pouring off the three ships and racing up the beach. A number of the swordships had landed farther along and pirates were running from them, waving weapons.

"Inch!" I put all the old deviltry and arrogance and unpleasant authority into my voice. "Take Tilda and Pando and get into those trees. Hurry! I will join you later."

"But — Dray—"

"Don't argue, man! *Move!*"

He looked at my face. He nodded, once, and his own lean face went tight and intense. He and Tilda and Pando hared off.

We met the first pirate rush in a smothering welter of blades that left many a sea-bandit screeching and toppling into the water in the gap between the two hulls. The sword-ship was going up and down confusingly. Men tried to leap aboard, and missed, and so were crushed. Others reached the decks and were cut down. I had been handed a fresh sheaf of arrows by a Fristle deputed to the task, and with these, standing back a little, I shot out those men who climbed the rigging in their passionate attempts to board. Arrows splintered the deck about me and one sliced my thigh; I did not think I could last much longer.

A quick glance showed me the beach deserted, and the pirates from the grounded swordships now preparing to attack us from the landward side. Men on the other two argenters were yelling and fighting and dying. Pirates forced their way onto the foredeck of *Dram Constant*. Captain Alkers was yelling his men on, clutching his left arm from which the blood splattered.

"Get into them, you calsanys! Fight! Fight!"

I slung the bow and ripped out my long sword. I leaped for the deck where the pirates were now shoving and pushing aft, shouting in triumph. I leaped — and I, too, shouted.

"Hai! Jikai!"

The Krozair brand gleamed brilliantly silver in the air; then it reeked a crimson gleam more dreadful as I lifted it for the next blow. With the argenter's crew I pressed forward. The pirates fought well, employing a miscellany of weapons; but we concentrated our strength and, just for the moment, were too many for the few who had boarded. We cleared the deck. But now, from the two shoreward ships came fresh sounds of conflict. In moments we would be attacked on two sides.

Captain Alkers' arm was bandaged; blood soaked through already. He glared about, panting, the rapier in his fist dripping blood.

"They want our valuables and our goods. They will overpower us for sure. We have done all we can, as honest sailors."

One of his mates, blood seeping from a slash across his forehead, shouted: "By Pandrite the Glorious! We have done that, Captain!"

"Abandon ship!"

Of that call so horrific to a sailor, Captain Alkers made a benediction and a curse, all in one. I knew he was right I suppose, left to my own devices and being in the middle of a little fight, I might have stayed and tackled the swordship renders for the sheer hell of it. It is not in my nature to run from a fight. But I had the responsibility of Tilda and Pando — as well as Inch — and so I, Dray Prescot also went with the crew as we jumped across the other argenters which were already deserted, leaped to the sand, and after a brisk rearguard action gained the shelter of the trees.

Tolly, the squat little Hoboling who knew these islands, took the lead and we hurried into the interior. We met up with the passengers and I was reunited with my three traveling companions. Tolly led us to a safe resting place and then went back to reconnoiter the coast. Inch, with a somewhat sour comment to me about staying with our charges, went with him. When Tolly and Inch returned they reported the argenters about stripped and the swordships preparing to leave.

After that, feeling empty and let-down, we trailed off to a fishing village Tolly knew, where we were welcomed by the headman, who looked remarkably like an older version of Tolly, and where we were able to obtain food and drink and a roof for the night. That bur or so of darkness had passed and now the moons of Kregen shone refulgently in the sky. Tilda and Pando fell asleep at once. I stayed up with Inch talking with Tolly and Captain Alkers and some of his mates with the headman, one Tandy. Tandy expressed a deep hatred and contempt for the swordships.

"They ruin trade," he said. "And our fishing. We are simple people and we live simply. But we are never likely to make contact with the outer world while the swordships by their depredations prevent commercial contact."

We argued and talked into the night and then I slept. But I made it a point to give Tandy a fine jeweled dagger I had picked up — I had severed it and the fist grasping it from its previous owner's arm — and tried to smile at him. I felt that he and his people would be valuable, situated as they were on an island in the midst of this strategic but isolated sea battleground. They'd be down to the stranded ships first light tearing them to pieces. The sea brought them harvests.

We made the necessary arrangements to secure a passage to the nearest port fortress of Tomboram, situated on an island a little to the southward. They existed in an attempt to suppress the swordships, an attempt, I fear, largely futile. They ran their own little fleet of swordships which flew hither and yon chasing the pirates — a thankless life.

From there we shipped aboard *Pride of Pomdermam,* Captain Galna, and made an easy passage direct to Tomboram's chief port and capital, Pomdermam, and so I sailed into the next period of my life in Pandahem. Vallia lay to the north. I would reach there, one day, soon. That, I vowed.

Eleven

"You ingrate, Dray Prescot!"

Pando had a toothache.

His face looked like one of those lusciously overripe gregarians grown in the lush gardens of Felteraz, a species of fruit of which both Nath and Zolta had been fond and so had converted me to their taste. A toothache in my own time on my own world was a serious, painful, and dreary business. On Kregen, of course, Pando saw a dentist who neatly twirled a couple of needles into his ankle and then yanked with professional skill. As first teeth, these should have given Pando no trouble in coming out and, normally, none did; this one had gone bad on him. The acupuncture gave him a completely painless time of the dentistry, and we came out and ate huge helpings of palines at the first restaurant we ran across.

But all this domestic business had blurred the edges of just why I was in Pandahem at all.

I told Tilda. I explained reasonably that she had asked Inch and me to escort her to her home; this we had done, and therefore it was time for me to be pushing on. Inch, when sounded out by me, had made the same reply he had made back in Pa Mejab.

"I'm a rover of the world, Dray, a wanderer. As a mercenary guard I can earn an honest crust I'd as lief stay with you as not."

"I am heading for Vallia."

He whistled. "Vallia! May Ngrangi aid you! From Pandahem they'd as soon send you to the Ice Floes of Sicce as to Vallia."

"I know. Please don't mention our eventual destination. We have to push on. We'll find a ship, somewhere, never you fear."

Now, when I told Tilda as we squashed down ripe palines and Pando explored his cavity with a pink tongue, Tilda exploded.

"You ingrate, Dray Prescot!" Her fine ivory skin flushed with blood and her violet eyes clouded. She put a hand to her bosom, over the orange robe, and grasped the golden locket there. "You were to be our champion, Pando's and mine. And now, just when it is all to do, you are deserting us! Is this friendship?"

I sighed.

Tilda had made not the slightest sign of any advance toward me and I was comfortable in her company. Poor Thelda, now, had been all gushing, pushing and eagerness and help, and had thereby been a confounded nuisance.

Sosie, of course, had had her own secrets, and I felt a twinge of bafflement when I thought of her sweet black face and her great eyes and Afro hair. She had presented her own brand of problem. I got along with Tilda perfectly.

"What do you mean, Tilda? It is all to do? Surely, you are in your homeland—"

"Do you think this great untidy port of Pomdermam is my home?"

"Bormark?"

"Of course. Bormark lies on the extreme western border of Tomboram, and the lands run border with those of The Bloody Menaham. We have to reach Bormark, Dray, before Pando can claim his rightful inheritance."

I looked at Inch. He rubbed his ear and popped a paline into his mouth, and chewed, and refused to meet my eye — a mean and despicable act in a comrade.

"Is there no one here who can help?" I shot a shaft at a venture. "The king in his capital—"

"Him!" Scorn flashed from those lovely violet eyes. "King Nemo? He would as soon lock up Pando and me deep in a dark dungeon and throw the key away. I am sure he hates us, for being the relatives of his brother, Marsilus."

"All right, then. Anyone else?"

She picked up a paline and began to roll it on her palm. "I was an actress, Dray. Oh, I came from a famous theatrical family, we played all the best houses, and my way seemed set to follow in my family's footsteps. Then Marker came to the theater one night — and—" She looked at Pando, who was gazing at her, his mouth and eyes wide and the rich paline juice dribbling down his chin.

"Wipe your face, Pando! You look like an urchin!"

All the old adjustments had to be made by me. I was an urchin, a powder monkey who had climbed up through the hawsehole and trod the quarterdeck, bedecked with gold lace and a pair of shoes, cracked and with steel buckles, true. But urchins, to me, are comrades the two worlds over.

Tilda watched as Pando wiped. Then she said: "There is the Pallan Nicomeyn. He is old and wise. He was always fond of Marker — he tried to mitigate Marker's father's wrath; but uselessly."

A Pallan was the Pandahem equivalent of a minister of state, a name used, I discovered, also in Vallia.

"The Pallan Nicomeyn, then," I said. "Let us go and see him."

It was not as easy as all that to contrive a meeting, for we traveled under assumed names. But, eventually, we were shown into a small and windowless antechamber of the palace where guards — humans — stood at the folding doors. Presently the Pallan Nicomeyn entered. He was old, for his hair was gray and his face lined, destructions of time that do not overtake a Kregan until he is well past his hundred and fiftieth year. Whether or not he was wise remained to be seen.

As soon as he saw Tilda he turned and made a quick motion to the guards. Obediently they closed the folding doors and we were alone with him in private.

He wore a long gown of blue, girdled by a golden chain set with rubies, and he wore on his gray hair a flat velvet cap of a bright blue adorned with the blue tail feathers of the king korf. He carried a book which, I noticed, locked with a hasp and a golden padlock.

He advanced toward Tilda, his arms open to her.

"My dear! I never thought to see you again! You do not know the pleasure these old eyes of mine gain by once more gazing upon your beauty!"

They kissed and I thought this Pallan, this councillor or minister of state, showed some true feeling for Tilda.

"And is this—" He turned to Pando.

"This is my son, Pando."

"So," said Nicomeyn. "You are the young Kov—"

I said, loudly, so that they all jumped: "Pando is a fine boy. He doesn't know much, though."

"Dray!" said Pando, and he tried to kick me. I moved my foot and he kicked the chair, and I smiled. "Sit quietly, you young imp, and listen while your elders talk."

He used the Kregish expression for grups, which I ignored.

"So he does not know, eh?" said Nicomeyn. He nodded. He wasn't too slow to catch on. "Perhaps that is wise."

Pando, defying me, said: "Will I see the king?"

"All in good time, dear, all in good time," said Tilda. She faced Nicomeyn. "You know the truth. Will you help us?"

He pursed his lips so that the lines indented deeply around his mouth. He put a long white finger to those lips, and shut his eyes, and thought. Just as I was about to become angry, annoyed that he should thus insult Tilda the Beautiful, he spoke his own salvation.

"There is no need to ask *if* I will help, Tilda. The question is — *what* to do best?"

"Oh, Nicomeyn!" said Tilda. "Dear Nicomeyn."

"Old Marsilus was a drinking comrade of my youth. It is dangerous to compare a king to his brother. I will not say more."

I stood up. "Well, that's settled, then, and pleased I am, too. Now Inch and I can get on. Kregen is a large place." I began to make a polite farewell to Tilda, with Pando staring at me as though I had grown another head, when Nicomeyn cut in.

459

"Please do not prattle, young man. I do not know who you are, but I assume the Kovneva Tilda employs you as a bodyguard. Your brute strength and your sword will be needed now, as it has never been needed before. So sit down and listen."

Then — with a great swoosh of air, I laughed. The situation tickled me. Inch looked most offended and Pando glowered at me, pursing his lips and fidgeting up and down on the seat; but I had my laugh out.

Tilda stared at me and her plucked dark eyebrows rose.

Most men, speaking like that to me, would have woken up in the far corner minus a few teeth. But the Pallan Nicomeyn was deep in conversation with Tilda, and patently anxious to help, so that I was completely disarmed. He did not know me, that is true, and so he escaped the deserts of his rash talk; besides, he was old and he wanted to help Tilda and Pando.

A plan was concocted but of it all the most important lay in the few words Nicomeyn spoke to me. "I have labored long for this realm of Tomboram, and I know the family of Marsilus can play a great part in our future. My loyalties go a long way into the past. I would wish to see Pando where he belongs." I made no comment, frivolous or otherwise, on that pious hope. "If the usurper Murlock Marsilus can be deposed, and a fait accompli is presented to the king, then the law is clear. The rightful title lies—" He glanced at Pando, and finished: "The title lies where the law obliges it to lie, and cannot be challenged. But, the usurper must be deposed first. While he holds — possession counts for a great deal."

"And he's a bad lot?"

Nicomeyn made a face.

"I see. So we must first get rid of him and then it is plain sailing?"

"Yes." Nicomeyn looked at me. I was dressed in a sober blue tunic with leather shoulder straps rather like winged epaulettes, and my weaponry was belted about me as was my custom. Under the tunic I wore my scarlet breechclout, but that was invisible. I held the broad-brimmed gray hat with its curled blue feather on my knee. As though sizing me up in a different light from that with which he had first conned me, Nicomeyn said: "He is cunning, like a rast. He is strong, like a leem. He is stubborn, like a calsany. He will not be an easy person to dislodge."

Pando perked up, speaking his clear childish treble. "I don't know what it is you say, Uncle Nicomeyn. But if anyone can do anything, that one is Dray Prescot. I know."

I clumped my ex-assassin's boots on the floor and stood up. The part that Murlock would play was already clear; for he had sent the assassins after Tilda and Pando to make absolutely sure of his inheritance, that was patent. "We had better be about our work, then."

All the way out from the palace and into the suns-shine of Kregen I was hating myself. For I had once more engaged to do something that prevented me from rushing to my Delia, and claiming her before the world.

On the street with the busy pedestrians, and the zorca riders, and the calsany carts, and all the hurry and bustle of a great port that was also a capital city, Pando piped up, "Why did Uncle Nicomeyn call you a Kovneva, mother?"

Immediately I took his arm and bent and whispered: "Did I not tell you, oh boy of little faith?"

He looked up at me and giggled and then tried to kick me whereat I spun him around and Inch yanked him back onto the pavement and a passing zorca bucked and its rider cursed. I looked up at him, and his curses stopped in midstream, and he swallowed and smiled — rather a sickly smile — and dug in his spurs and cantered off.

"You'll have to tell him soon, Tilda," I said as Inch and Pando went ahead. "If we are to rouse support for you, he is bound to hear—"

She nodded. "You are right, of course, Dray. We have much to thank you for—"

"You have," I said. "But say nothing of that until the job is finished. Then—" and I chanced it, and took a breath, and said stubbornly: "And then, Tilda the Beautiful, I must be on my way to Vallia."

She halted. "Vallia!"

"So you can see why we are like two nits in a ponsho fleece. We both have a zhantil to saddle." Which is the Kregan way of saying we both had our own secret and dangerous purposes.

"But, Dray! Vallia! What can possess you to go to that dung-heap of a disgusting rast-nest?"

When a woman as beautiful and respectable and intelligent as Tilda of the Many Veils spoke like that about the country that was the home of my beloved — what could I say?

"I have good reasons, Tilda. I believe I can expect of you some trust, to believe you do not think me an imbecile."

If she was about to make some unthinking remarks about me being a spy, she thought better of it. To take care, I hoped, of that eventuality, and already regretting that I had opened my big mouth, I said: "I have come to like and admire your Tomboramin, Tilda, I get along with your people. I shall be sorry, I think, to leave for Vallia, for there I shall do much mischief."

And, by Zair! That was true!

Inch, ahead of us, took Pando's arm, as I took Tilda's, to thread safely through the maze of traffic thronging the street as we crossed to make our way down to the discreet tavern in which we were lodging. *The Admiral Mauplius* was situated in the cooler end of a square, overlooking the sea and gathering most of the sea breeze. The temperature was somewhat higher here in North Pandahem than I had found it anywhere else I had so far traveled on Kregen. I have remarked that Zenicce and the cities of the inner sea are situated close to the same parallel of latitude, and Vallia, also, lies with much of her island bulk on those parallels. It is a strange fact that the temperate zones extend over far greater an extent north-south than they do on Earth. From the most southerly tip of the most southerly promontory of South Pandahem, the equator is not so many dwaburs farther south. From South Pandahem directly southwestward lies the coast of Chem. The equator runs through the enormous, dripping rain-forests of Chem in Central Loh. While I mention North and South Pandahem, it is worth saying that they are separated by a range of mountains running generally southeast to northwest in a dogleg. The mountains extend on into the sea to form the long chain of islands that terminate off Erthyrdrin in Northern Loh. But the mountains do not stop, for there, in Seg's homeland, they rear and convulse into that misty land of song and then, abruptly, collapse into a few islands across in the Cyphren Sea around which the Zim Stream swirls in its northward progress.

The problem we faced now was to hoist this usurper Murlock Marsilus out of his title and possessions, knowing that the king and the law would not help us until we had performed the deed, and knowing, also, that Murlock had all the aces on his side. He had the estates; ergo he had the money and the people tied up.

"We must do a little crafty detaching, Inch."

"With Ngrangi's help, that will be a pleasure."

Inch, as you know, came from Ng'groga, which is right down in the southeast of Loh, well south of the equator. I wondered if he'd want to go home after this. If he did, he'd try to talk me into going with him.

"Murlock," I said, firmly and with some bite. "We hit the top from the beginning."

So strikingly beautiful a woman as Tilda was surely going to raise men's eyebrows, inter alia, and she had taken to wearing a loose semitransparent blue veil, after the fashion of the women of Loh. When I asked Inch about Loh, and its mysterious walled gardens, and its veils, he chuckled and said: "I come from Ng'groga. There we are somewhat different folk."

"The truth is, Inch, everyone all over the world is somewhat different."

From the capital Pomdermam we took a coaster, a vile little ship smelling abominably of fish, to the westward. We touched at various charming little ports along the great incurved sweep of the north coast which forms the extensive Bay of Panderk, voyaging steadily westward. On the third day we saw a swordship foaming toward us on a parallel course, the waves breaking clean over her long low hull as she wallowed and lunged in the sea, her oars bending with the strain, white spume skyrocketing high, all her blue banners and flags taut in the wind that bore us so comfortably on.

One of the crew spat overside. "A King's swordship," he said.

"The good Pandrite rot him," said another crewman, looking up from where he slapped dough to make the long Kregan loaves he would bake on the hot stove later during the morning. "My brother was sent to the swordships — for nothing. I'd like to—"

"Aye, Lart!" interrupted the first, scowling. "And your mouth is like to get you sent to join your brother in the galleys!"

I took note of this little interchange. Evidently, this King Nemo was not loved by all his subjects.

With the bread we ate cold vosk and taylyne soup. In the warmer weather here the cold soup was delicious, a thing I would normally never credit. Taylynes are pea-sized, scarlet and orange in their redness, and in conjunction with succulent vosk, superb.

"In Vallia," Tilda told me when we chanced on that awkward subject, "they drink their vosk and taylyne soup so hot it scalds their lips and mouths. Barbarous, they are, in Vallia."

She sighed. "Poor Meldi loved vosk and taylyne soup." Meldi was the bodyguard with whom she had fled from Tomboram, and from what I heard of him he had been a gentle giant, caring for Tilda and Pando, until sickness had carried him off just before my arrival in Pa Mejab.

On the fifth day we saw what at first I took to be a school of fish with tall almost-transparent dorsal fins. A cry went up and the crew rushed to the rail. Then, between the foam and the splashing I made out that this was all one huge and serpentine monster of the deep, with an oval body along the top of which grew that long fence-like fin. His head was impossibly out of proportion to his body, being immense, and equipped with a dredger of a fang-filled mouth.

"A sea-barynth," said Lart, whose brother rowed in a King's swordship. "Now if we could catch it we'd feast right royally this night."

However, the coaster's skipper was no intrepid huntsman, and we left the sea-barynth far astern wriggling and curving in the water. It had two large paddle fins beneath its head. I was told that the barynth, of a similar size and ugly ferocity, one was likely to meet in the swamps of Pandahem as elsewhere, was equipped with four clasping claw-armed legs beneath its head.

I do not believe I have mentioned that the general word in use in Kregish for sea is "splash." The oddity of this perfectly sound onomatopoeic word in English ears, I think, is sufficient justification for the hint of a smile I summoned when I heard it, and why I use the word sea in its stead. There is another aspect of translation worth mention here. The word in Kregish for "water" in the sense of a drink of water is one that could never be uttered in any respectable company where English is spoken. To hear a wounded man calling for water, on Kregen, is to experience heights of the surreal.

In the shambles of the gun deck of a seventy-four which has just received a broadside from enemy thirty-twos, of course, one would hear through the smoke and confusion both words in just about equal proportion.

On the day before we picked up the pharos for what would be our penultimate port of call Tilda discovered nits in Pando's hair and nearly went mad, ordering up huge copper kettles of boiling water, and formidable bars of Kregen soap which is designed to scour little boys' eyes and the backs of their ears and necks. When Pando had been nearly scalped, she pronounced him fit to enter decent company once again. I thought of those running-alive ponsho skins of the Magdag swifters. Conditions of life are all relative.

From this last port of call before we reached Port Marsilus, the entrepôt for Bormark, we sailed in a little convoy of eight ships, accompanied by a vessel paid for and maintained by Bormark and her neighboring dukedom to the east for just this purpose of escort against raiders from The Bloody Menaham which lay far too close for comfort to the west beyond the promontory and islands that terminated the Bay of Panderk. The vessel was an argenter, if of a slightly leaner build than those that plowed the outer oceans, equipped with varters and catapults and with a sizable crew. I studied her, and felt something could be made of her and her like.

From Port Marsilus, with Tilda still heavily veiled and under our assumed names, we hired two onkers for Tilda and Pando and two zorcas for Inch and myself. We rode to Tilda's home, a farm nestled among groves of samphron and muschafs, where her parents, having overcome their surprise, made us welcome. With a strict injunction to them to remain fast and not to stir abroad, and so be caught, Inch and I rode for the palace of Murlock Marsilus, the usurping Kov of Bormark.

Twelve

Murlock Marsilus and King Nemo inspect my dagger

This Murlock seemed to me to be no atavistic sport of the family of Marsilus — despite all I had heard of Marker Murlock, and all I had observed of his son Pando — for the old Kov had been relentless in his rage and malignance against not only Tilda, the girl his son had married in defiance of his wishes, but against her family also so that they had given up the stage and gone farming with distant relatives in that pleasant valley. Now, we left the valley and our zorcas' hooves rat-tatted with a more purposeful sound on the paved road.

"Pando will turn out all right, Dray," said Inch. He reflected, and added, "If he lives."

"The story of the old Kov's recantation on his deathbed and the known desire of his to have Pando recognized as his heir," I said. "They are slender weapons, it seems to me; but they are all we have."

"If what the Pallan Nicomeyn says is true — I expect it is — those weapons will be enough."

"Once we have Murlock."

"Ah!"

The palace of the Marsilus family stood on the highest eminence of a block of red cliffs that fell into the sea with a stark sheer of cliff reminiscent of those cliffs of the Eye of the World where I had dived in order to go to the assistance of Seg and the others in our flight from the sorzarts. Verdant glowing vegetation clothed the heights. The castle and palace, as richly red as the cliffs, reared above. Many flags floated there, and armed guards strode everywhere. We heard, in the inn where we stayed for a dram of Tomboram wine, that the news was that the king was visiting Tomboram and was even now on his way, traveling with a great company, coming on the pleasant coast-road, journeying in state and great comfort, surveying the domains.

"There is no time to waste," I told Inch. "Once the king gets his lodging and board in the palace—"

"By Ngrangi! We must strike quickly, Dray!"

So it was that that night we two, Inch, a gangling giant with his ax, and I, Dray Prescot, Lord of Strombor, with all my weapons about me, climbed that frowning red cliff in the light of the Maiden with the Many Smiles. We were gentle with the guards, for Pando, we hoped, would assume the overlordship of this pile and we did not wish to store up resentment against him. As it was, we left a trail of unconscious bodies until we penetrated clear through to Murlock's bed chamber, where Inch uprooted the nubile wench sharing his bed and I showed him the point of my dagger.

"You are coming with us, Murlock," I said, and at sight of my ugly face he flinched back. He was a fat man, but strong, and his jaws shook when I twiddled the dagger closer. "You may dress or not, as you please, but you had best make haste."

Shaking with the fear that must be torturing him with wonder how we two desperadoes had invaded his palace — for he could not know that Tilda had told us of the best secret ways in that she had learned from Marker — Murlock threw on his clothes and we three went out of his bedchamber leaving the wench neatly packaged in costly silks of Pandahem itself.

We carried him down the cliff on our backs, passing him from hand to hand like a carpet. He was near paralytic with fear; but he knew, for I had made it very plain, that a single cry would sink my dagger in his throat.

We loaded him aboard the spare mount, lashed wrist and ankles, and then we spurred in the streaming pink moonlight of Kregen along the metal-shining road. Tilda could hardly believe we had done what we had done. I shushed her up. Murlock had been blindfolded so he would not know where Tilda had hidden, and for this her people were grateful. We spurred hard toward the east, going through rich agricultural land, avoiding the farms, heading up toward the coast so that at last, with the coming of the twin suns, we were well on our way.

We rode for three days, keeping up a good pace, eating provisions we had brought and not venturing near another living soul. On the morning of that day we rode boldly into the camp of the king. His people, servants, grooms, courtiers, guards, were just rising and yawning and thinking about the day ahead.

I selected the biggest tent of all, with its blue flags, and jumped down before the guard. He was a man, in half-armor, clad in a blue tunic, and for weapon he carried as fancy a long-hafted spear as I had seen on Kregen. In addition he had, of course, his rapier and main-gauche.

"Keep away, rast," he growled, and the spear blade snapped down level with my stomach.

"Send a message to the king, insolent one, that the Lord of Strombor wishes to speak with him on a matter of treason."

The spear did not waver.

'Take yourself off, benighted of Armipand—" There would have been more, doubtless of a foulmouthed kind, but I stepped inside the spear, knocking it away, put a fist into his jaw, didn't bother to catch him, and pushed through the drapes into the tent.

In the anteroom with its bright silken walls other guards started up, and their Hikdar strode forward, puffy as to jaw, bloodshot as to eye.

"Hikdar!" I said, and my rasp sounded like a mill full of buzz saws. "I am the Lord of Strombor. Rouse the king. I have news for him."

The Hikdar hesitated and I did not miss the lifting of weapons of his men. At that moment a short and exceedingly fat man wearing the robes and insignia of a Pallan stepped out.

"What is going on?" he demanded, with some acerbity. "The king is dressing and orders that whoever is creating this disturbance shall be brought before him."

The Hikdar lost all his color.

"It was not me, Pallan Omallin, not me! This man — he claims to be the Lord of somewhere or other—"

I pushed past them both, tripping the Hikdar, shoved into the main body of the tent.

As I went I shouted back: "Bring 'em in, Inch! Come straight through. Take no notice of this rabble."

The scene in the king's tent was much as I had expected. Evidences of luxury lay everywhere. Rich carpets, brocaded coverings, cushions, arras to double-wall the tent, weapons glittering from the tent-poles, all I saw and ignored. On a sumptuously upholstered divan sat a corpulent man with a puffy face pulling on a pair of enormous black boots. Their spurs would cause agony to a zorca. His black bar moustache lifted as he stared at me. His eyes held a pale fanatical look. He licked his purple lips a great deal. I did not take to him, as you may wonder, for I am overly tolerant to other people until I read them through correctly.

This was the man, this King Nemo, in whose power I had placed myself and my friends. I knew of his bias toward Murlock; yet would he flout the law? There were witnesses, for the Pallan Omallin had scuttled in, gasping, after me, and the guards and their Hikdar also.

"You are the man creating the noise," the king said, speaking with a nasal rasp that irritated. "You will be taken to the cliff-top, flogged, and then thrown into the sea." He motioned to the guard Hikdar. "Take him away."

"You are mistaken, King," I said. I eyed him. "I am the Lord of Strombor. You know of the last wishes of your brother, the Kov of Bormark, concerning his grandson?"

The king reared up, puffing, scandalized, starting to shout. But Inch had walked in, and with his height ducking to get in through the tent opening. He carried Murlock over his shoulder. Tilda followed, holding Pando's hand.

"You are mad!" shouted the king. "You will all die!"

"We are not mad, King, and I think you will listen — else it will be you who will die."

And with that I caught his fat greasy neck in my left hand and showed him my dagger in my right.

He gobbled.

I thought his eyes would fall out and roll like marbles on the carpets.

"I come in friendship, King. I would not harm you, but you must listen to me. You know what your brother, Marsilus, desired. The usurper Murlock is here, a dead man if he fails me. Also here is the Kov of Bormark."

Murlock emitted a shrieking groan at this and Inch threw him down on the carpet. He groveled there, and I had it in my heart to feel sorry for him.

"Mercy! Mercy!" Murlock yelled. "They are madmen!"

"Not so." With the king threatened by my dagger no one was foolish enough to make a move against me. I thought that these men here were most unlike that Lart aboard the coaster, who would probably have driven his dagger home had he been in my position, and damn the consequences.

"What do you want?" squeaked the king. "I can see the Kov of Bormark — Murlock—"

"Here is the Kov of Bormark," I said. Tilda pushed Pando forward. He stood there, clad in his zhantil-skin tunic, gripping the hilt of his dagger, and he looked wild enough; but, withal, there was about him in the cut of his jaw some strength that showed through. I know that the king recognized in Pando's young face the true lineaments of the Marsilus family.

"By the laws of Tomboram," I said, in a loud voice, "Pando, the grandson of Marsilus, is the Kov of Bormark. Banish the usurper, or he dies now, beneath my sword."

Inch had unslung his great ax and was swinging it up and down, whistling softly through closed teeth.

Murlock groaned and squealed and managed to croak out: "Do not kill me! Yes, I did it!" He knew what to say, for I had made sure of my facts first. "I did send men to slay Tilda and Pando!"

The king was in a cleft stick, in one sense, for he knew nothing of Pando, who was a young lad completely out of his reckoning. He had had Murlock under his thumb. I released the king's neck and stood back. The guards tensed, but they did not jump forward. By my actions I hoped to convince them it was all over. Tilda lifted her veil and smiled on the king.

Perhaps, when all is said and done, that smile did the business.

The king gave his judgment, there and then. It was for Pando. Murlock was given twenty burs to get out of Tomboram. He slunk out of the tent. I knew there would be trouble from him in the future; but there was little to do about that right at that moment, save kill him. And murder in cold blood is not one of my hobbies.

Now was the time for me to be properly apologetic for manhandling King Nemo. I managed this with a straight face, and when breakfast was brought and we sat down to a good meal, and Pando demonstrated that he knew exactly what being a Kov entailed — at which I winced a little — and Tilda got along with the king, as I thought then, I did really believe we had pulled it off. The king set himself to statesmanship at once.

"I was visiting Murlock because The Bloody Menaham, may Mandate rot 'em, are planning to invade my realm. They march alongside your borders, Kov Pando. I shall need many men and much money from you to defend the frontiers."

With the simplicity of youth and with all the fiery ardor of which he was capable, Pando cried out: "You shall have all the men I can raise, and all the money in the treasury, King Nemo! We will teach The Bloody Menaham a lesson. We will march against them! We shall fight them, and kill them, and burn their farms! It will be a great victory!" He swung to me, animated and excited and hardly a little lad of ten years old any longer. "Is this not so, Dray Prescot, Lord of Strombor?"

About to try to calm him down, for Tilda had somehow succumbed to emotion, and was sitting, drinking Kregan tea and sniffling from time to time, I was brusquely interrupted by the king. He was in a jovial mood. I saw through the reason for that. He had been looking forward to an interview with Murlock that would be painful to both of them, for however much Murlock may have been under the king's thumb, any Kov is cautious when asked for men and money. And now the new Kov, a mere boy, was giving away all he had by the handful.

I saw that King Nemo felt he had done a good morning's business. He spoke to me, later on, in much the same terms, except that he left out all advantage for himself that had occurred during my handling of him.

"You fight well, Kyr Dray nal Strombor. Right well. I have room for you in my guard. I need a man who is loyal to his employers."

Without hesitation — and in that I made a foolish mistake — I said: "That cannot be, King. I have a mission in life, and having discharged my obligations to Tilda, the Kovneva, and to Pando, the Kov of Bormark, I must be on my way."

King Nemo frowned.

For all my detestation of authority and sheer hatred of it when it is unfairly imposed and in tyranny and oppression destroys good simple people, much of my life on Kregen has been spent among representatives of those very people who wield the authority. I am as happy among a lower deck gang of sailors as among a palace full of Kyrs, finding good qualities in both. I was still very young and green then, as you will know from my previous narrative spoken into the tape recorder in the epidemic-stricken village of West Africa. How I was to face Delia's father, the emperor, I had not yet decided. I simply could not stalk in and treat him as I had treated this flabby and shifty King Nemo. So I floundered on, then, in my ignorance, and only when the next morning, instead of awaking to the tent where I had been quartered, I awoke with chains galling my wrists and ankles, lying facedown in the bottom of a boat where bilge water sluiced over the floorboards, was the understanding forced in on me that I had sadly underestimated this King Nemo.

I was naked except for the gray slave breechclout.

I knew where I was destined.

The banquet the night before in Pando's honor had seen some agent of the king's slip a potion into my drink. He had not had me killed, despite the fact I had laid hands on him, and I guessed that, maybe, after my stint in the swordships, he would attempt to win me over again. If I give myself too much credit in thus thinking, there were good solid reasons for it.

In addition, he would be well aware that the punishment of a quick death would not satisfy him. The lingering agony of the slave benches would please him much more. Or so I tried to reason as we rowed out and were bundled aboard a swordship lying in the roads. I have told you of my life aboard a swifter as a galley slave. The differences now were there and noticeable, but the end result was much the same.

I raged and cursed and broke a few heads and swung my chains and was soundly beaten and came back for more, crippling a whip-deldar, and was flogged again and, at last, came to my senses. The previous experiences of being an oar-slave should have trained me far more rapidly into the required state of dumb and instinctively willing obedience. There would come an end to the torture of this life, hauling at the loom of the oar. There would have to be. I could look forward to a life of a thousand years, and here one of the drawbacks of that state made itself horribly clear — a thousand years of life as an oar-slave aboard a swordship of Kregen!

No!

That I would not tolerate.

The swordship on which I found myself was *Nemo Zhantil Faril Opaz*. This mouthful was itself an abbreviation, a kind of heraldic shorthand for a much longer name which meant, in effect: "King Nemo as courageous as a zhantil and beloved of Opaz." For a laugh, and I sorely needed something to lighten my spirits in those dark days, I translated this out into English as: "King Nemo the lion-hearted, beloved of God." And so cursed and struck the loom of my oar, and almost despaired of ever seeing my Delia again.

We rowed eight to an oar, usually, five pulling and three pushing. The swordship, usually known as *Nemo,* and by we slaves with a spit and curse also, had commissioned for service up among the islands chasing pirate swordships. She was a moderately large vessel, although I did not then ascertain her measurements, not being in a position to do so; but she rowed in her single bank of oars arranged *alla scaloccio* thirty oars a side. There were marked differences between this swordship and the swifters of the inner sea, differences dictated by the altered circumstances of sea and weather and distances.

Whereas a swifter needed little freeboard, a swordship must be built with freeboard sufficient to cope with the deeper swell-waves and the greater violence of the outer oceans. Only one bank of oars was employed. The old-fashioned zenzile method of rowing was still found among the swordships, but it was rapidly disappearing. Because of this the oars were that much heavier and longer and were not angled so sharply into the water. Up front she possessed the curved bronze ram or rostrum that is still regarded by many sailors as the principal weapon of the oared galley, despite the problems of entrapping and swamping entailed in the rammed galley's apostis. The proembolion, the second projecting wedge designed to thrust the rammed ship off the rostrum, was as well-developed among the swordships as among the swifters. Above that the beak extended forward, and here, too, a difference was found. The swifter beaks were movable, being lifted or slung down into position for boarding, rather after the fashion of a sophisticated and modernized Roman corvus. The swordship beaks were permanent structures and built so that they extended forward short of the point of the waterline ram, and they were extended aft into the foot of the low forecastle.

All in all, as I sweated at my oar with seven oarsmen around me, I fancied the swordships were as good a bargain a navy might get from the always unsatisfactory attempt to oar a sailing vessel, or sail a galley.

Their underwater lines were nowhere as fine as a swifter's and they were deeper in draft, which made them sea cows to row. But they were still long, lean, low, and they were cranky and dangerous and wet and hideously uncomfortable.

Every time I hauled the oar I cursed King Nemo. To liken him to a zhantil was a ludicrous slander on a noble beast; if anything, Nemo was a leem — or a cramph.

This swordship *Nemo* boasted three masts, unlike most of the pirate galleys I had previously encountered, and the captain seemed to me to be as unhandy a sailor as any I had shipped with and always preferred to use his oars. This made life hard. We sailed north and west up along the island chain, calling in at various of the port fortresses Tomboram maintained there. We did not sight a single pirate swordship.

We saw three scraps of sail on a bright day of fine visibility; but we sheered away and later the buzz went around the slave deck that the swordships had been from The Bloody Menaham. They would have been a relief to me. Mind you, I was well aware of the horror and the shambles of the rowing benches during a fight, but my mood was black and vicious and by this time I was ready to tear the throat out of a leem with my bare hands.

Nemo Zhantil Faril Opaz got her comeuppance at last in a way that was so ridiculous that every time I thought about it afterward I cursed in delighted wonder.

We had touched in at an island that Valka, a captured Vallian and a man who appealed to me and to whom I had been closest drawn of all those oar comrades, said was deserted. A party was about to go ashore for water when, peering through the oar-port I saw a sight that created, at once, a great shout of surprise and admiration and lust all over the swordship.

Onto the beach dashed a horde of half-naked girls.

They danced down to the water's edge and they held out their hands to the swordship in supplication. Many and various were the oaths that floated fruitily into the hot air.

"By Likshu the Treacherous!" said a yellow Chulik farther along on our oar. "Were I not held by these chains!"

We mocked him. "Were any of us not held by these chains, oh mighty Chulik!"

"Mother Zinzu the Blessed!" rang a clear call from somewhere farther along the rowing deck, at which I felt all that old pang of remembrance. Many and varied, the oaths, fruity and blasphemous and calling on gods and demons and heroes from a score or more of different cultures. But we were slaves, naked and chained, filthy and mop-beaded, bristling with hair and vermin. That rout of beautiful naked girls was not for us.

The captain and the crew brought not water from the island but rich wine in great round-bellied amphorae. The girls, clad in their strings of flowers and feathers, laughed and came out to the swordship as the twin suns sank in an opaz glory. We slaves crouched on our rowing benches and glowered and fed on crusts, an onion each, and a strip of old cheese like lenk. The Maiden with the Many Smiles rose before the suns had gone. A weird clashing of colors poured over the swordship. We slaves could imagine what was happening in the after-castle and the forecastle now; we could hear the peals of silvery laughter and the great gusts of sailor mirth.

And then, gradually, the sounds quieted down. We heard a shrill scream, and then another, fainter. Silence dropped on the swordship. We did not even hear the watch calling the turning of the sandglass.

Valka said to me, "Something is amiss." He roused the Gon who was nearest the gangway, an unpopular position as he was nearest the lash of the whip-deldar. "Hey, dom. What's afoot?"

The Gon's great bristling, malodorous thatch of bone-white hair lifted. Gons habitually shave their heads skull bare. If that is because they feel shame over a mop of white hair, one must sympathize with their own foolish beliefs. As it was, this Gon experienced deep shame over his unshaven head.

"Let be, Valka. I want to sleep, and dream of those women."

"Look aft, you hairy nit! Is the watch by the lamp?"

The Gon stretched. "The lamp is not lit."

"By Vox!" Valka galvanized himself into instant action. "This is the one night..." He began to tear at his chains, desperately, until his nails tore and the blood poured forth.

So far I had found no implement with which to file through the iron chains, as we had done in *Grace of Grodno* when Zorg, Nath, Zolta, and I planned escape. Yet Valka was right. This one night *was* our chance! But, through the most simple and elementary precautions of the crew, nothing convenient for a slave to rub through his chains lay handily about the deck. We might all have lost our reason, then, tearing at our fetters and trying to keep silent besides. Already the unlit lamp proved the routine of the swordship had been altered, and when we were not hosed down for the night we knew beyond doubt that the crew was otherwise engaged — and in our lascivious dreams how wrong we were!

For — in the lambent pink floods of moonlight a girl stepped up onto the central gangway. Every head turned to look — but there were no cries of admiration or lust or, even, of wonder.

In absolute silence that slip of a girl walked all the way along the central gangway, from aft forward, half-naked, her limbs gleaming pink in the moonglow, swinging her burden lightly from one little fist. She held that burden by its hair. Sightless eyes glared out upon the rowing benches.

From the severed neck from which still strips of gristle and flesh dangled dropped the dark blood. Drop by drop as she walked the blood fell upon the gangway.

No chance guided her choice of head thus to parade.

Every oar-slave recognized that hated face.

The uncanny contrast between that lithe slip of a girl, all gleaming beautiful and pink in the streaming moonlight, and that hideous severed head, dropping its blood as she walked so gracefully along, with a swing of her hips, laughing, affected every single one of us profoundly.

Not a man so much as moved. No one spoke. Every eye fixed on her and her burden, glaring like the jungle denizens stare upon their prey.

Drop by drop the blood fell upon the planks of the gangway.

Every oar-slave recognized that hated face. In a deep and scarcely comprehending silence we watched the girl carry the head along, laughing, swinging her hideous burden.

We knew that dead face.

It was the face of the chief whip-deldar.

Thirteen

Viridia the Render

We were given the usual alternatives.

Given them, I do not believe a single oar-slave took the choice that would see his carcass hurled over the side and feathered with arrows in sport.

What others considered as an omen I took, also, I confess, as some kind of pointer to the future, for all the seven moons of Kregen floated in the night sky above as Viridia spoke to us.

"Never disdain the power of women," said Viridia. "For my fighting-girls have laid the whole crew of this King's Swordship low, and have taken her, and now she is ours."

I could not see Viridia very clearly, for the stump end of a varter interposed its ratchets and its winding windlasses and loosing mechanism between, so that I caught only fragmentary glimpses of her as she moved about, gesticulating. Seeing her like that, however, meant that I immediately recognized that gaudy, pendulous, barbaric figure as the one I had seen strutting the quarterdeck of the swordship when *Dram Constant* had been destroyed, and when I had indulged in that pleasurable contest with the blue-feathering bowman of Erthyrdrin.

Her girls had successfully seduced the swordship's crew, poured them drugged wine, and seen them off to the Ice Floes of Sicce. To me, the masterstroke of psychology had been to parade the severed head of the man whom we slaves would recognize immediately as the instrument of our daily torture. Now we were members of the pirate band of Viridia. I hesitate, even now, and remembering her as I do, to call her a lady pirate. Viridia was no lady. She was a woman, wild, free, gross, sudden, a woman who always — or, nearly always, as you will hear — kept herself in complete control. She knew what she wanted, she knew how to go about getting it, and she did what was necessary; and if the blood reeked along the blades of her people, both women and men, halflings and beast-men, then that was the price she was prepared to have them pay.

Her control was normally such that when she indulged in her killing frenzies and heads rolled one who knew her could almost judge to the mur when she would snap out of it.

The pirates who infested these islands where through the geography of the region there would of necessity be heavy maritime traffic did not employ slaves to tug their oars. Through this area passed the commercial traffic from Pandahem and Loh, north and south, east and west. Many armadas tried to avoid the area as the admiral of the armada in which Captain Alkers' *Dram Constant* had sailed had attempted, and many ships simply avoided the islands altogether, as Tandy, the Hoboling, had so bitterly informed us; but, despite all that, the needs and demands of cities and peoples meant that ships must sail these seas. Viridia was only one of a great host of pirate chiefs. And, she was not the only woman pirate chief.

Everyone has heard of the famous women pirates of our own Earth. Lady Killigrew, Anne Bonney, and Mary Read all made the headlines of their day. Anne Bonney, who deserted her husband for John Rackam, the notorious pirate Calico Jack, was powerful enough as a lady pirate to make Calico Jack take second place in the fighting and boarding and arguments that are inseparable from a pirate's life. Mary Read, already a girl who had led an adventurous life in that she had fought as a soldier in Flanders by the side of her husband, was captured by Calico Jack. The joke was — at least by Kregen standards — that when the pirates were taken they were all drunk with the exception of the two women, who alone attempted to fight off the British warship. A ray of light does exist to alleviate the story in that both women, although sentenced to death, were not hanged and did escape Execution Dock.

"We carry no passengers," Viridia informed us. At her back stood four immense fellows, all rolling muscle and corded thews, bull-necked, their heads jutting forward so that the two stumpy but formidable horns they carried on their foreheads could jab in with ferocious power at an opponent's eyes. They had two arms and legs, massive and bulky, it is true, and their bodies were recognizable human torsos and stomachs, plated with muscle. They wore the gaudy clothes of the pirate trade. They also carried short swords of a heavier pattern than the merely cut-down rapiers often found among the pirates.

Rapiers and daggers also swung from their belts.

These were Womoxes. As I have mentioned previously, there are many and various peoples inhabiting Kregen beneath Antares, and I give some idea of any individual people, either halfling or human, when they come onto the stage of my narrative. By this time in my sojourn on Kregen I had seen many strange and marvelous peoples of whom I have given no idea here simply because I did not personally come into contact with a representative of them. When I did — then I describe them, as I believe to the benefit of your understanding. I had not previously encountered the Womoxes. They came from one of the islands off the coast of Vallia. They are a people at once fierce, independent, not overly original — their native art is markedly copyist of another people on an adjoining island — and much given among the males to head-butting contests to decide who shall do what or who shall mate with which maidens. In all this they never, at least to me, suggested very much of the bovine.

Perhaps I could mention here that I believe that the many differing races and peoples of Kregen are not distributed over that marvelous globe by any laws of nature that are easily discernible as they are on our own Earth. I believe, further, that the races of Kregen have been arbitrarily placed in the locations of their origin. If this be the work of the Star Lords, as I have more than half a mind it is, then more remains to be learned of their dark and secret purposes than I, even now, fully comprehend. I do not think the Savanti had a hand in the locations of the populations of Kregen; but their task, as I know, is the amelioration of the lot of all peoples.

There have been many ups and downs in my life and in this present situation, because for the moment there was nothing else to do, I flung myself into the business of being a pirate aboard a swordship plundering along the Hoboling islands. We took Pandahem ships and ships of Loh. Sorry as I was for the people who suffered, I had worked out a theory that of the Pandahemic nations none could be construed as friendly to me except Tomboram, and of that country only, really, could I look for real friendship from Pando and Bormark. I was worried over that imp's handling of his people. I hoped Tilda and Inch would be able to hold in check his very natural desires to go for a fight and cut a fine figure and make a name for himself. War, as I have learned, is not a game.

The nations of Pandahem, always at loggerheads, were driven in part by economic rivalries, partly by the ambitions of their kings to become emperors of all Pandahem. They had the bitter example of Vallia to spur them on. Vallia might make a treaty of friendship with one nation of Pandahem, and another would ignore that and raid Vallian shipping, with the consequence that Vallia quickly lost patience with all Pandahem.

I had to make a stand against casual killing of captives.

"You are throwing money away!" I said to Viridia. I stood with my hands on my hips on the deck of a fine argenter of Walfarg we had just finished sacking. The frightened people left of her huddled by the break of the quarterdeck. I wore a loincloth of that brave scarlet I favor, and a rapier and dagger taken from a prize swung at my sides. Viridia came to the quarterdeck rail and leaned on it and looked down on me.

"Stand aside, Dray Prescot!"

So she knew my name. I thought that odd, among so many new recruits to the render's trade. A render is a pirate, and yet the name carries overtones associated closely with the swordships. She was looking down on me as I glared up. An odd expression crossed her face. She was a large woman, bulky, with muscles that could swing an ax with the best, and I had always thought of her as coarse, bloated, careless as to her dress and manners, oafish, almost. She looked different, now, as we glared at each other, eye to eye.

"Listen, Viridia. You intend to kill these wretched people and burn the argenter. How foolish!"

A murmur of surprise and shock went up from the gathered pirates. I motioned to them, calculatingly.

"By killing and burning you deprive your fellow renders of their fair share of the prize!"

She roared down, her dark hair flapping about her face, her blue eyes fairly blazing with wrath. "Have a care how you speak, Prescot! I am Viridia!"

"Aye! And you cheat your comrades!"

Viridia put out a hand to stay the automatic charging response of her chief Womox. He was a veritable giant, a good seven feet tall, and a formidable antagonist.

"Explain yourself, rast, before you die."

"If I am a rast, then what are you, Viridia the Render? Send the ship into port, sell her for good silver dhems, claim a ransom for these people in our power. They are cash and they stand upon cash! Can you not see that, Viridia the Render?"

Some of the men at my back set up a yell supporting me, seeing the cash in their hands already, and chief among them was Valka, my oar comrade from Vallia.

"Silence!" shouted Viridia. Once she had fought her way up to captaincy she had not experienced resistance to her slightest whim or order. The experience came as a novel one to her. She frowned. I could sympathize with her. The problems she had overcome were capable of being overcome, as she, no less than Anne Bonney and Mary Read, had demonstrated. Birth control is well-understood on Kregen where beliefs are taught that teach it is better to have two or three fine healthy children for whom parents can give what of food and clothing and shelter is necessary, than it is to have a whole squalling brood of poor, undernourished, half-naked infants for whom there is not sustenance enough. Ignorant and wrong-headed religious feeling receives short shrift in these matters on Kregen, where what can clearly be seen to be so is taken as a guide. Because there are two suns in the sky images tend toward a dualism. Because unthought-out parenthood, selfish and cruel, can result in a family of misery, compassion and sympathy tend toward families of sizes where the children may receive all that is their due.

Now, no virgin but capable of love, unhampered, totally in command of her swordships, Viridia glared down on me and her knuckles whitened into skulls as she gripped the quarterdeck rail. In a second she could order me to be run through and tossed overboard. I would fight, of course, but there would be little of joy in that fight.

I had the impression that Valka, and one or two others, would fight with me.

"Why do you resist my wishes, Dray Prescot?"

"Because I know I am right and you are wrong."

Her broad face, tanned and strong, flinched with a muscle tremor beneath those blue eyes. "I do not take kindly to—"

"Do you want the value of this argenter and the ransoms of these prisoners, or do you want a heap of corpses and a pile of ashes, Viridia the Render?"

Valka shouted, "Dray Prescot speaks good sense."

The tenseness of the moment showed in the ridges muscling on the faces of the men gathered about, the way the Chuliks kept polishing their tusks, the Ochs twined their four upper limbs together, the Fristles kept stroking their fur.

Viridia looked down on us and who of us could say how that mercurial brain of hers would decide to go — up or down in the scales of our judgment?

She was, as I have said, a large woman, and yet from the way she was standing and the drape of her gaudy and impossible clothes I caught the impression that she wore armor beneath that show, and the robes and clothes hung loosely outside, as though worn deliberately for effect. She half drew her rapier, and sheathed it — a motion that brought an instant reaction from her four Womoxes, a reaction as instantly stilled — and she put a hand to her mouth, which was large and generous, and pondered on the problems that I had brought into her ordered render life.

"And who would take the prisoners for their ransom? You, Prescot, you would? And would we ever see you again?"

"Aye!" shouted the men, swayed her way.

"Does honor, then, count for nothing, here along the Hoboling islands?"

A growl greeted this, and Viridia flushed darkly; but she knew as well as I that honor among renders was a matter of convenience. I went on, quickly, "Send someone you trust, if you do not trust me." Then, as though clinching the argument, I spread my arms wide. "I simply want all the cash that is due me and my comrades. That is all."

The upshot of it was that Viridia did not kill the prisoners but sent them in the argenter to Walfarg for ransom. We hung about off the coast, most uncomfortably, while her lieutenant transacted the business. But when he returned and the canvas bags were opened and rich fat gold coins spilled across the deck — Lohvian gold! — everyone roared their approval. Even Viridia the Render was pleased.

She called me into her ornate and stuffy aft cabin where zhantil pelts covered the settee, arms were stowed everywhere, bits and pieces of clothing lay scattered on the deck, and toiletries cluttered a side table beneath a port. She looked at me with an expression I tried to fathom, and could not.

I knew I trod a tightrope.

With her, her lieutenant glared up at me in open distaste.

He was a man called Strom Erclan, rough and yet with a remnant of faded culture and manners. For "Strom" is the Kregan title, I suppose, most nearly paralleled by "Count." He liked the men to give him his title when they addressed him. I had considered it a harmless fad; but now, as I looked at the pair of them, I realized that this hankering after a titled man as her second-in-command was all of a piece with Viridia. Powers of life and death she had over the crews of her swordships. She fancied herself as one of those fabled Queens of Pain of ancient Loh. I thought of Queen Lilah of Hiclantung, who had been a Queen of Pain, with no pretense, and I sighed for poor Viridia the Render.

"You're getting too big for your boots, Prescot," said Strom Erclan.

I glanced down. I was, of course, barefoot. Erclan snarled at me. He managed his snarl as well as a leem. "Insolent cramph!"

I said, "I understood you wished to see me, Viridia. Do you allow a kleesh like this to mock your authority in your own cabin?"

Before Viridia could answer Erclan's rapier hissed from the scabbard and he was around Viridia's table at me. I drew, parried, twisted, and halted my blade at his throat.

I glared into his eyes. Almost, almost but not quite, I lost control and thrust him through.

"Kleesh, I said, Strom. Do you die now?"

Viridia shouted: "Hold, you fool, Prescot. If you slay him you'll never leave this cabin alive."

Then I saw, through the aft bulkhead partition, the sudden movement and the shadow of a Womox grasping a bent bow, the arrow nocked and drawn back to the pile.

I whipped my blade away and struck Strom Erclan across the face, open-handed with my left, toppled him squalling into a corner where he put his face into a great bowl of some nauseous ointment Viridia used to iron out the wrinkles on her skin.

Viridia — she shocked me, then — Viridia laughed.

"Oh, Strom Erclan, you onker! Leave this wild man and me to talk a mur or two."

Although the words bubbled through with laughter and Viridia clearly had abruptly snapped into a playful mood, Erclan was less than happy. Ointment smearing his face, he took himself off, glowering. Viridia lifted her left hand and the shadow of the bowman eased the bow and moved back out of sight.

"Don't try to toy with me, Viridia," I said. I remembered some of the vainglorious boasting the corsairs of the inner sea employed when promising King Zo what they would do to Magdag. "I've eaten bigger fish than that fool for breakfast, and spat out the bones. If he's the best you can do, forget him. And that horned Womox of yours — I can get to him and spit him long before his addled brains add up what's going on."

She bit her lip. Had she been what she pretended to be she'd have snapped her fingers to her Womox bodyguard and made me prove my words. So I finished: "Anyway, Viridia, I'd as lief stick you through as a Womox."

She rallied. She refused. She said, "I think I shall have you killed, at the end, Dray Prescot."

"But, until then, you wanted to ask me something."

"Not ask!" she flashed. "I ordered you to report to me so that I could tell you I want you to take command of the varters. Valka tells me you have some skill with them."

I nodded. But I did not answer.

"Well, Dray Prescot?" She was surprised and not a little mortified. "Have you no word of thanks?"

"For what? For being given the thankless task of drumming varter drill into the blockheads of your crew?"

Her bosom rose and fell, but with the constriction I had noticed before, as though armor cased her. "Take care, man! Viridia the Render is known through all the islands! My swordships take and burn and sink — we are feared wherever argenters sail—"

"Aye! And by ramming and boarding. I've seen your catapult and varter work. You're hopeless. If I am to train your calsanys, then I demand absolute obedience. Any man who argues back will be knocked down instantly. Is that clear?"

About to reply she was interrupted by a Fristle messenger who put his head in at the door and squeaked rather than shouted his news, his whiskers quivering.

"*Venus* is alongside and she's sinking!"

I give the name Venus to the swordship. I could not give her real name without causing offense. She was the ship in which, in company with a crew of oldsters and weird beings without interest in what they carried, the host of maidens of Viridia's renders was carried. They were female pirates, true; but I had already seen how their talents were best exercised in the delicate business of extracting largesse from the shipping of the islands.

We all raced on deck and there was *Venus* already shipping water and the lithe agile forms of her girls leaping aboard Viridia's flagship. I believe I have not given the name of Viridia's personal swordship, the flagship of her little fleet of eight craft. Seven, now that poor old *Venus* was sinking.

I know why I have not given it, for it displeased me. She had called her pirate craft *Viridia Jikai*. It made sense, of course; but I had been trained into a different school of thought where Jikai was concerned.

When all the pandemonium had subsided and *Venus* had sunk and Viridia started her court of inquiry, I was left to seek out Valka. He looked at me with a most ferocious grin, the while sharpening a nasty-looking boarding-pike.

I said, "You got me into giving drill to these calsanys. Hauling and winding and loosing varters, Valka. Well?"

He laughed and went on sharpening. "Certainly, Dray. I heard about you when they dumped you aboard the old *Nemo*." He looked up, suddenly. "Anyway, it gets us out of the rowing benches, does it not, dom?"

Well, there was that to be said for it — indubitably.

Fourteen

The fight on the beach

During this period of my sojourn on Kregen many incidents occurred, but I feel that my purpose will best be served by pressing on. I am, I fondly believe, a man tolerant of other people until they prove themselves unworthy of trust; perhaps I am tolerant to a fault. But when a task has been put into my hands I am intolerant — decidedly and sometimes cruelly so — of every phase of the task until it is completed. I made those renders of the islands aboard the swordships sweat blood over the varters and the catapults. I have previously told you of my attitude to gunnery; discipline and absolute efficiency alone count. Eagerness and willingness to work are excellent; indeed I welcome them as bonuses; but a gang of calsanys, given my methods, will stand to their weapons whether varters or thirty-two pounders, and fight a ship.

And, as I know from experience, by the time I have finished with a crew, no matter how recalcitrant and unusable they were at the start, by the end they are as keen and eager and willing in all genuine fervor to excel, as the best volunteer crew afloat.

As it happened I was afforded not enough time to turn Viridia's pack of sea-leems into gunners — if you will pardon the expression. We met one of the strange ships which sail up out of the southern oceans from whence no man knew, and fought her, and only a storm coming on saved us all from sinking. We ran with the gale and by the time we could shake a little more canvas out, the southerner had gone. I will talk more of these strange and terrible ships later.

The days floated by, and Valka and I hammered at the varter crews. We transferred from swordship to swordship, and when I rotated back to one I had given some instruction, and found the calsanys had forgotten it all, there were many bruised lips and black eyes. I was not popular. And yet, despite that, Valka told me that the men respected me, for they could understand my purpose.

"They know the risks involved in ramming and boarding. If you can force an argenter to surrender without their having to risk their hides, that will please them."

Valka, indeed, was a tower of strength to me in those days.

It was mainly through his instigation that I picked up, one from here, another from there, a tight little crew of men and halflings who in addition to their expertise with varters and catapults showed — again according to Valka — respect and loyalty to me personally. I was aware of the dangers. I handled these men carefully. The idea, simple, of course, of welding them into a crew, of obtaining a ship and of sailing away, occurred to me without any deep cogitation.

The deep cogitation lay in where I would direct the course of the ship.

Tomboram?

Vallia?

My duty to Tilda and Pando seemed to me to have been discharged.

I could, in all honor, sail for Vallia.

Valka, as a Vallian, would be invaluable.

I am a loner. I walk singly. And yet, I am constantly aware of this strange — power, attribute, thing? — call it what you will, this uncanny phenomenon I possess of attracting the utmost loyalty and devotion from men. It is passing strange. I do not seek it. Sometimes I am embarrassed by it. I notice that men look to me for leadership. Only can it be explained, in part, by the fact that I will never let a fellow down if it is humanly possible. Perhaps some of that personality trait is responsible. I do not know. But, there it is.

In tandem with this charisma there goes, I believe, its opposite. But you who listen to this narrative will already be aware of where that leads to...

The dangers to which I alluded were simply that if Viridia or any of her lieutenants got wind of a knot of men devoted to me they would smell mutiny on the instant, and the steel would flicker red. So, in pursuance of plans, I must tread warily.

Despite all you may think of me as a hotheaded barbarian warrior who flings himself into action before thinking, this is not so. The first lieutenant of a seventy-four never stops thinking and planning, believe me.

This habit of thinking ahead and, in the night watches, of planning how to react to every foreseeable disaster must have been the root cause of my decision not to attempt to seize the ship. She was surrounded by six of her consorts. Even if I captured Viridia and threatened to kill her unless we were given free passage, I had the hunch that the captains of the other swordships, Viridia's lieutenants all, would still attack and let Viridia take her chances.

One fine morning we espied a sail on the eastern horizon and bore up in chase. The swordships did not sail well on any point; but, as Viridia observed, they sailed well enough for the renders' purposes, and they could row at top speed when it mattered, which an argenter could not do.

We gained on this chase with a rapidity which led me to believe her bottom must be fouler than most. The cut of her sails was strange to me. She bore away but ever and anon kept trying to edge to the west and so reach the islands. Valka came up beside me at the fore starboard varter platform and stared across the tumbling sea. The weather was fine and the smartish breeze cooled the air gratifyingly.

"What do you make of her, Valka?"

He looked surprised. I had given him very little of my history, as he had given me none of his; our friendship, fragile as it was, was based in its entirety on our mutual slavery at the oars and now our positions as varterists. That varterist I had shot from *Dram Constant* in his passing had, weirdly, left the way open for me now.

"You don't recognize her, Dray?"

Incautiously, I said: "Should I? She has two masts, rigged square, and a bowsprit, and she looks a trifle unhandy. Her stern looks high but narrow. I fancy I'd redistribute the stepping of her masts had I the need to sail her any distance."

"She is from Zenicce."

"Oh," I said, and could say no more.

Zenicce! That great enclave city of a million souls, threaded by canals and boulevards, where Delia and I had been slave, where Princess Natema lived, happily married now to Prince Varden! Where I had met Gloag, my comrade who, although not a man, was all the more human for that. Where I had slaved in the black marble quarries. And where now my own powerful enclave of Strombor no doubt wondered what had happened to their Lord. I hoped that Great-Aunt Shusha — who was not my great-aunt — ran Strombor in my stead, as was her right. Then I saw the colors of the banners. They flaunted there, purple and ocher, blazing in the streaming light of the twin Suns of Scorpio.

"Ponthieu," I said. "She is of the House of Ponthieu."

Well, Prince Pracek had led my Delia to the altar to wed her, although his plans had tumbled at that point Ponthieu was an enclave aligned with the foes of Strombor. So...

Valka said, "Now how can you tell that, Dray? You must have visited Zenicce, to know the colors of the houses—"

"Not so, Valka. Any sea-leem knows the colors of his victims."

"True. Still, it is passing strange. All the Zeniccean colors are alike to me."

So Valka had not heard of me all he might that night I had been dumped down into the slave benches of the old *Nemo*.

We took her without trouble. I must give her name, for it was, having regard to her speed, ludicrous on two counts. Her name was *Splash Zorca*.

She was clinker-built. Swifters and swordships and argenters were all carvel-built. This made me ponder.

That same day we made the island of Careless Repose where lay our renders' nest. We had made a good cruise and the men were in the mood for relaxation. Viridia wanted to negotiate with another pirate captain for a new swordship to replace the ill-fated *Venus*. From this island with its entrance hidden by a small and unsuspected vegetation-clothed islet and with its beach of white sand and its village of comfortable houses we would sally forth on our roving raids against the sea commerce of the area. So far, no King's Swordship had discovered the anchorage.

The pirates, like any good Kregan given half a chance, started in carousing.

I went for a stroll along the white sand of the beach by the light of She of the Veils, brooding to myself. As was my custom I wore my scarlet breechclout and my weapons slung about me. In the warm weather of these latitudes that was ample clothing, even at night. By the pinkish light of the moons — for a lesser moon hurtled past above — I walked on with bent head, pondering.

Strom Erclan almost caught me.

He leaped on me from a boulder beside the vegetation's edge and I saw the wicked flash of his dagger. I got his wrist in my fist and jerked him back; but he kicked me low down and sprang away, ripping out his rapier as he saw he would have to fight me for real.

I drew.

"You stinking cramph!" This Strom was reputed good with a rapier and main-gauche. I had seen him in action when we boarded and he showed no fear. I put myself in a position for fighting and waited, for I had no wish to kill him — then. "You mildewed rast! You lump of offal!" He went on shouting for a space, hoping, no doubt, to enrage me.

After a bit, I said, "Kleesh. Walk away quietly, or you are a dead man."

Whether his breeding goaded him into madness, then, whether he was simply mad clear through with jealousy, matters little. He threw himself on me, his blades whirling and thrusting in a positive flurry of action and a fury of venom. I parried, caught him, twisted; but he eluded that one, having been caught once before. A swordsman need only see a fighting trick once to know it again. If he doesn't, he is dead, of course.

Our blades crossed and slithered with that teeth-vibrating screech of metal. He leaped, I forced him back, I thrust, he took my blade on his dagger and held and thrust for me to take his blade on my dagger in turn. For a space the four slivers of steel slanted up in the pink moonglow, evil and slick and lethal, smooth and unbloodied.

Then, quick as a striking leem, he withdrew his dagger and thrust low. I swayed sideways, recovered and once more we fell into our fighting stances.

He was good. There was no doubt of that. I thought of Galna, whom I had fought in that corridor in what was now my own palace of Strombor; yes, it is all a long time ago, now; but I can still feel the jar of steel on steel and I can hear yet again the ring of blades as they met and crossed. Then he essayed a complicated passage, and I took him, and in the pink wash of moonlight from She of the Veils, Strom Erclan slumped with my rapier through his heart.

Fifteen

I give an opinion at Careless Repose

Raucous shouts and good-humored arguments broke the stillness of the night as the renders of the islands caroused in the wooden houses of the pirates' lair.

In the fringe of the vegetation back along the beach lay the skewered body of Strom Erclan. Very soon the creeping crawling denizens of those woods would convert his body to bones and then these, too, would rot away until all that remained to show a man had existed would be the memory other men might carry in their minds.

I knew no one would mourn Strom Erclan for very long.

In the wooden barn-like house where most of the higher ranks in Viridia's confidence were carousing, the atmosphere billowed thick with the fumes of wines culled from the freight holds of a hundred ships. Heaping platters of food loaded the heavily-timbered tables. Disheveled wenches darted in and out avoiding clutching hands in giggles or shrieks or abuse, each according to her nature. Food appeared on the tables in bounteous abundance, and disappeared down gullets with fascinating speed. The wine that was drunk! Men would suddenly screech and leap up and dance a wild jig, or leap head-over-heels across the floor, or two would fall into a deadly dagger fight that ended with one coughing his guts out bloodily across the floor, the other ready to face the render court of inquiry. Other half-men half-beasts drank and caroused in their own ways, and all were equal here, under the captains.

To this select company Viridia had bidden me, Dray Prescot.

As I approached where she sat at the head of a long table, quaffing her wine and roaring like any jack-booted man of the sea, I noticed Valka sitting at the lower end of the table, his nose in a blackjack. He looked up as I passed, and winked. Shades of Inch, I said to myself, and planted my feet down on a clear space among the litter of bones and discarded meats on the floor.

One blessing there was in all that pandemonium and guzzling and drinking and wenching, one evil we were spared; the only smoke in the room came wafting in from the glowing cook fires or rose from the succulent dishes covering the tables.

"Dray Prescot!" shouted Viridia, lolling back. Her blue eyes were not clouded with wine and I saw in their depths a deep and shrewd intelligence; yet her body lolled and her head jerked and she laughed shrilly, as though she were drunk. Near her a Chulik captain sat, a mass of gold lace and crimson silk, his tusks gleaming and — a fashion I had noticed before — tipped with gold. He was plying Viridia with wine. She laughed and drained the cup, and thrust it forward for replenishment.

In general Chuliks can be trained into seamen; of the halflings the Hobolings are unquestionably the finest top-men in the business, and I wouldn't give berth space to a Fristle, be wary of an Och, and detesting Rapas as I then did, would haul up the gangplank before letting one aboard my command. I knew that the Relts, those more gentle cousins of the Rapas, went to sea as supercargoes and clerks, but I doubted even them.

This Chulik captain, one Chekumte, was trying to sell a swordship to Viridia. His ploy was transparent to me, and, I saw, to Viridia also. I fancied she could drink him under the table.

"She is a fleet craft, and nimble, Viridia," Chekumte was saying. He spilled wine as he slanted his cup in eagerness to lean forward in friendly converse. "She rows a hundred and twenty oars and sails like a king korf!"

"A hundred and twenty oars," said Viridia, properly contemptuous. "Zenzile fashion!"

"And what of that? She has served me well; but I have captured a new swordship from Walfarg, and my force is balanced so that I no longer need her."

"And you seek to dispose of your old scows to me, Chekumte."

I stood there, listening, for listening brings information.

Viridia lifted her cup to me. The fingers she wrapped around the glass stem glittered with gemmed rings. Her tanned face was, minute by minute, growing more flushed. "Dray Prescot! You are not drinking."

"When I find out what you wanted, Viridia, I will find some wine."

She scowled as though I had insulted her, but heaved up and glared sullenly at me.

"Have you seen Strom Erclan? I want him to discuss this business. Chekumte is a wily rogue, for a Chulik."

Chekumte guffawed, polished his tusks, and quaffed wine.

I would not lie. "I saw him up the beach half a bur ago."

"Wenching again, I'll be bound." Viridia slumped back, that sullen expression on her face turning all her features lumpy. "I keep my render maidens locked away from the likes of him."

I did not say: "You will have no need of that anymore."

It would have been a nice line, but I wanted no more trouble. If I had to tear the hearts out of all those here, I would do so if that was the only way to return to my Delia. But only a fool buys trouble.

Instead, I said, casually, "A zenzile swordship would not fit in with your squadron, Viridia. And if she rows only a hundred and twenty oars she must be short, and if short then narrow to retain her speed, and if narrow then useless in a sea. I can't get your calsanys to shoot straight from the deck of your flagship as it is."

Chekumte surged up. His eyes were bloodshot. His thin lips ricked back from those gold-tipped tusks. Little of humanity is known to a Chulik. About the only thing I have heard in their favor is that they are loyal to whoever pays them.

Mind you — that is a valuable attribute in any mercenary.

Now this Chulik glowered down on me and spouted obscenities at me. He rounded on Viridia. "Do you allow Likshu-spawned offal like this to teach you your trade, Viridia the Render?"

Viridia was annoyed. She twiddled with the hilt of her rapier. As though transmitting her anger to her Womoxes who stood in partial shadow at her back, she herself stood up. For a moment we three stood, confronting one another, and gradually the uproar died as the roisterers realized the tension gripping us.

Chuliks make a habit of adopting the weapons and customs of the race employing them. Now Chekumte was a render captain in his own right and he had adopted the weaponry of his peers. He drew his rapier and, slowly, pushed it forward until the point touched my breast. He did not prick the skin.

"This thing must be taught a lesson, Viridia."

I looked at her. This was a test for her. I knew that. I wondered if she had realized that yet.

"For the sake of the cursed Armipand, Chekumte! Leave him alone!"

"Not until he grovels on his knees and begs my pardon."

So far I had not moved. Still I looked beneath lowering brows at Viridia. Her bosom beneath that armor heaved. She was clearly in distress — and I marveled.

"Leave it, Chekumte! I will buy the swordship. There! Will you shake hands on it?"

But the Chulik kept his rapier point pressed against my breast.

"Not until this cramph apologizes!"

I said, "This island is called the island of Careless Repose. I did not expect to find a quarrel here."

"There is not a quarrel, cramph! You, Prescot! Down on your knees! Lick my boots! Beg my pardon else I run you through."

"Now, Chekumte!" protested Viridia. She began to lose her temper and a spark of that wildness flared. "I have men here! Would you drench our safe haven in blood?"

"This is a point of honor, Chulik honor! By Likshu the Treacherous! I'll have his tripes!"

Still I glowered down on Viridia the Render — and still she would not meet my gaze.

A ruffianly towheaded pirate down the board laughed and yelled. He was of The Bloody Menaham or Menahem — either spelling conveys the meaning — and he had no love for anyone of Tomboram, from which country he believed me to originate. "Stick him now, Chekumte! What are you waiting for?" He waved his goblet and spilled wine over the brilliant blue and green cummerbund he wore, the blue and green of his national colors.

"Hold!" shouted Viridia. Her blue eyes blazed on me now with a violence of passion I knew would break out any moment and that would be followed by a battle royal and bloody corpses strewing the pleasant island of Careless Repose.

"There seems no holding the Chulik, Viridia," I said. With a quick and startlingly sudden movement I stepped back so that Chekumte was left with his rapier pressed against thin air. I lifted my voice and shouted. "Listen, renders of the islands! I will fight this rast of a Chulik in fair fight! It lies between him and me! In all honor is this not so?"

After a great deal of yelling and cursing and argument, the general opinion was that, indeed, the quarrel lay between Chekumte and myself. He leaped the table and advanced on me.

"You have held me up to ridicule, human! Now you will die!"

I drew and faced him.

As Strom Erclan had been, as long-dead Galna had been, he was a master swordsman. The moment our blades crossed I felt the power in his thick wrists, and knew that I must put out every ounce of effort. And yet — and yet I sometimes wonder if I exaggerate the qualities of swordsman opponents in order to aggrandize my own prowess. I do not know. I know that I have faced many master swordsmen and fencers of high renown, famous in their own lands, and have bested them, every one. Is this the beginning of paranoia? Yet each time I cross blades with an opponent I know that this time, at last, I may have met my match. I think it is this tingling zest of the unknown, this awareness that every combat may be my last, that gives me the nervous energy to go on. I have met swordsmen who through years of absolute victory have thought themselves invincible and so they fought in order to kill and gloat in their killing. This, to me, is the mark of the beast. I detest killing, as I have said many times. If I thought that I could never lose a fight — where would be the fun of fighting? If, Zair forgive me, fighting is ever fun.

Chekumte the Chulik was extraordinarily good, as I remember, as I believe. He would have disposed of Strom Erclan in a mere passage or two. Chekumte came from one of the many Chulik islands that stretch northeastward up the coast of southeastern Segesthes, with the island of Xuntal in the south of the chain. There they train their children in all the varied weapons they are likely to encounter when they reach adulthood and sally forth as mercenaries, for this is the chief occupation of Chuliks. Chekumte had been well-trained, and by a master I would like to meet. In addition, he had turned pirate, which was unusual for a Chulik, and had fought his way up to the captaincy of his own band of renders.

We fought in a great glittering of blades, thrusting and parrying, rapier against main-gauche, whirling about and sliding and slipping on the discarded bones and meats of the floor.

But, in the end, I had with as pretty a passage as I recall forced him against a table so that he bent backward to escape being transfixed. He catapulted out, his dagger low, his rapier high. He feinted a thrust with the dagger and then, as swiftly as a striking leem, slashed diagonally down with his rapier. Here was the Jiktar and the Hikdar working in sweet unison. I heard a shrill chopped-off scream. Then I had taken that swooping lethal blade on my main-gauche and in a screech of steel deflected it and the next instant my own rapier stood out a foot past Chekumte's backbone.

In almost the same motion I withdrew and Chekumte dropped his weapons. He looked down in wonderment and then placed both his hands over the blood-seeping hole in his chest. My blade had gone through cleanly, without fouling bone; but he was done for.

"You fight well," he said, before the bright blood frothed from his lungs and out of his mouth in a gory stream. "For a human."

Then he fell.

Without a pause I strode across the floor and stood before the towheaded man of The Bloody Menaham. I showed him the stained blade of my rapier.

"You were saying?"

He eyed me. His face was corpse-white. "I said nothing, Dray Prescot."

"That is good. Make it so."

Chekumte's render band would choose their own new captain and I wanted none of that. They were an unsavory bunch. After the room had been tidied up the carousing began again. Some had not stopped drinking throughout the whole argument and fight. Later on Viridia sent for me, one of her Womoxes padding gigantic in the misty pink moonlight from She of the Veils. I went and I went alertly, for presumably Chekumte had friends. Had he comrades willing to fight for him, I did not meet a single one.

Her room in the pirate village was furnished in much the same barbaric splendor, the same untidy womanly bric-a-brac as her cabin aboard her flagship. She looked different as the Womox ushered me in and then retired. Then I saw she had taken off that armor — and it was as I had suspected. She did indeed wear armor, a pliant mesh-steel shirt that came, I guessed, not from an armory of the inner sea but from the mysterious and progressive land of Havilfar.

Now she stood by the samphron oil lamp, her tanned face highlighted and wearing makeup that suited oddly. She wore a long white shift that reached her feet. Her dark hair had been combed — and that was a job for Kyr Nath, the Kregan Hercules, if ever there was one — and her blue eyes looked on me with a melting expression that at once alerted and alarmed me. I had seen that look in the eyes of women before, and I knew the trouble it brought. I braced myself.

She advanced and held out her hands.

"You fought right well, Dray. Chekumte was feared throughout the islands as a swordsman." Her voice was not steady.

"You might have told me, Viridia, before," I said. I spoke lightly. I tried to be casual; but Viridia the Render had her own dark and secret purposes which were transparent and unwelcome to me.

"Do you then so much dislike me, Dray?"

"Of course not! You are what you are—"

She bit her lip. Her mouth was very generous, soft and sensuous in a way quite different from the voluptuous mouth of Tilda. Now, with Tilda, I had had no trouble at all...

"That is not — gallant."

"Why not? You choose to walk around as a render, a pirate captain, and you dress for the part. I understand you must be tougher and stronger and more violent than your men. So—"

"So now I am changed, Dray!" Her blue eyes caught the mellow gleam from the samphron oil lamp. She was trembling. "I have combed my hair, and I have taken the baths of nine, and I am clean and fragrant — and—"

"You are very beautiful, Viridia," I said, for this was true, as incongruous as it sounds. Her body thrust with firm bold curves against the sheer white robe. The material of the shift, some fabricated silk from Pandahem, was very sheer, very smooth, almost transparent. Her bosom rose and fell and the silk ruffled with her movements.

"Then why do you scorn me? You must have seen with what favor I have treated you—"

I did not laugh, but I felt my harsh lips curving into a gruesome smile. "Training a bunch of calsanys with heads of lenk! Fighting the most noted swordsman of the islands! Oh, yes, Viridia the Render, you have treated me with favor!"

She blew up then.

She jumped for me and began beating me on the chest with her fists, shouting and sobbing, the dark hair swirling all into my eyes, pins and priceless gemmed hair ornaments flying in all directions. She even, like Pando, tried to kick me. I grabbed her wrists and brought her arms down and so inclining toward me, we stared face to face.

On her cheeks thick tears coursed. Her rich lips shook and quivered. "Dray Prescot! I hate you! I hate you!"

"I do not hate you, Viridia. But, I do not love you. That cannot be so."

All the passion and fire left her. She sagged against me so that our gripping hands were trapped between our bodies and I could feel all the firm softness of her. She moaned.

"Say that is not so, Dray! Please! I am Viridia the Render! My word is law! I can have you taken out and tied up and my men will loose at you for sport! Do not say you do not love me!"

"Nothing your men can do could make me change my mind by a single degree, Viridia. And you know it, by Zair! You know it as well as you know my affection for you! But love — that I cannot give you."

She drew back and I let her go. Her sheer robe tautened against her as she pulled her shoulders erect. That maddening dark hair swirled now about her face and with an impatient gesture and the flash of a gem-encrusted white wrist she pushed it back.

"You do not know what you are saying—"

"I know. I will faithfully support you, Viridia, in our render raids. I will be a loyal member of your pirate band. Beyond that, it is forbidden for me to go."

I saw the glitter in the lamplit blue eyes. I saw the way her body tensed, the deep breath she drew, the way her hands hooked into claws. I poised.

"Get out! Get out, Dray Prescot! Oh, you fool! You fool! Get out! *Get out!*"

And so, for the love of my Delia of Delphond, I left Viridia the Render shaking with passion among her pirate trophies.

Truth to tell, I felt remarkably sorry for the girl.

Sixteen

Of a wooden long sword and a cargo of Jholaix

The next morning a macabre scene was enacted on the beach fronting the village of wooden houses with the swordships riding over their reflections in the harbor. The weather was fine and hot, with the twin suns pouring down molten rays of ruby and jade. Everyone flocked down to the beach to witness the punishment of a dozen men who had been caught stealing a boat with the intention — as they freely confessed — of sailing to the nearest fortress port of the islands. This fortress port happened to be one belonging to the country of Lome, situated in a triangle at the extreme northwest of Pandahem. Lome was not overlarge as nations go, but her colors of blue and green horizontal stripes were to be found fluttering from swordships. Even in this matter of policing the Hoboling islands and their renders' nests, no unity of action was displayed by the fractious countries of Pandahem.

I will not go into details of the fate of these poor unfortunates. Whether they were paid spies, whether they had merely become sickened of the pirate trade, or if they had had an argument with their render chief, I never discovered. I turned away as soon as the executions began and took myself off to think. Clearly, any plan to escape to Vallia must be thought out with exquisite care, else I would end up like those poor devils on the beach.

In the event, when we put to sea again I took care to take myself aboard a swordship that was not Viridia's flagship. We dug in the oars, for everyone took a turn on the rowers' benches, and for all that I was now varterist in chief — the varter Hikdar — I pulled and tugged with the rest.

My idea that I could for a space escape Viridia's observation through my duties as varter Hikdar were soon dispelled. Her flagship cut water perilously close to our oars, and a stentor bellowed across, in much the same way as the stentors bellow a passage for the swifters passing Sanurkazz from the Sea of Marshes into the inner sea. *"Dray Prescot to co-ome abo-oard!"*

So, rather like a ponsho-trag with his tail between his legs, I was rowed across. Valka and the men whom I had trained, ostensibly as my varter cadre, were rowed across, also.

Viridia was not on deck when I stepped aboard. A fine tall man with the red hair of Loh greeted me. He had been a lieutenant and now wore a smothering extra layer of gold lace and so I gathered this man, Arkhebi, had been promoted into Strom Erclan's place.

Overside the swordship I had left gathered her boats in and then, all as one, her oars struck into the sea and with a heaving surge she took up station again. I did not feel in the mood to sweat at an oar any further this morning, and so I said: "If you'll muster a broadside crew, Arkhebi, I'll start in giving them a little training. I'll make 'em jump!"

Arkhebi smiled. He was, as I remember, a ruffianly fellow; but he loved a good fight.

'The captain ordered for you to come across, special, Dray. But she's said no more and she's closeted in her cabin." He clapped me on the shoulder. "You steer small, Dray Prescot!"

"Aye, Arkhebi, I'll do that. And congratulations on your rank." I nodded to where our six consorts plowed the sea. "You'll be in command yourself, soon."

"Aye, I will be!" he said with a brightness I found charming. Reavers and rovers all, those renders, but genial with it — some of them.

With the starboard broadside crew I was soon hard at work on the varters. I concentrated more on them, for with the ballista-type weapon one could obtain a flatter trajectory than with the catapults — they were of a formidably varying nature and kind with a plethora of technical names — and I sought to obtain the kind of accuracy and rate of fire I would tolerate on any ship I commanded. It may seem a strange and crankish thing to say, but I sometimes missed the deep-throated thunder of the broadsides of our Earthly guns.

Presently the breeze increased enough for the oars to be shipped and all the canvas to be set. Courses on fore and main, crossjack on the mizzen, topsails on the fore and main, and the spritsail ahead on its mast and yard on the bowsprit, we surged wet and uncomfortable through the sea. Swordships are a pestiferous kind of sea-animal. I would as much have them rowed as sailed providing I am not lugging an oar. As it was, she lay over and the spray lashed our faces and solid sheets of water were shipped green. But we flew along. This was what being a render of the islands was all about: discomfort and danger and, at the end, prizes and jewels, silks and wines...

Our first victim bore fluttering at her masthead the diagonal stripes of blue and green that denoted an argenter from The Bloody Menaham. We bore down on her. A few accurate shots from our bow varters knocked away some spars, we saw the flash and gleam of weapons along her decks, and we were about to bear down, our keen bronze rostrum foaming through the sea, when Viridia, who had not appeared when called, stepped on deck.

"Avast, you dogs!" she roared, all her old callous roughness fully in evidence. "Prescot, you great calsany! Get your pestiferous varters going! Earn your plunder! Knock over that fat ponsho for me and save the blood of my men!"

To all that I simply shouted, "Aye aye!" and bent to the nearest varter. It was fully wound, a chunk of rock in the slide as big as a vosk-skull.

I touched the trigger as the swordship rose to the swell. The rock flew true. A great shout went up as the mainmast of the argenter toppled, leaned, and in a weltering smother of canvas and cordage plunged overside into the wake.

After that it was simply a matter of boarding, of brandishing our weapons, and of cleaning up.

We took spices, and silks, great jars of Pandahem ware, chests of jewels, weapons and trinkets, and amphorae by the score. Rich wine of a dozen different vintages was carried aboard by the happily sweating crew and the frightened passengers who were now our prisoners.

"We can soon jury-rig her," I said to Viridia, without really taking too much notice of her, as we watched the busy scene of activity. "She will bring much Lohvian gold."

"Aye, Dray Prescot. And does gold please you? Is that all you seek?"

I faced her. "Whatever you think, Viridia, I will be loyal to you and your renders. Never fear."

"You had best be, Dray!"

We sighted no other sail for the next two days, and Viridia was contemplating a return to our island of Careless Repose. We were running under all our canvas and the sea was such that oars would have been impracticable. Despite my disdain for mere wealth I knew I had, personally, amassed a fair-sized sum in these piratical pursuits. I just had to find a ship to take me to Vallia. This life was seducing me.

"Sail ho!"

An excited rush to the rail and up the ratlines confirmed the sail, a triangle of white on the horizon. We took the wind with us as we bore down on her and soon the tall superstructures of a great argenter came into view. She was a fine tall vessel, her three masts clad with billowing canvas, her flags all standing stiff and taut in the breeze. We had the heels of her, if none of our rigging carried away. The hands began to discuss just what prospects of fortune she carried, and if she would strike under varter bombardment or if we would have to board in steel and blood.

Then I saw the flags standing so proudly from her mastheads.

All blue, they were, a bright proud blue. And, in the center of that blue field glared the yellow-orange head of a zhantil, ferocious, roaring, untamed.

I knew that flag.

"She's from Tomboram!" shouted Arkhebi. As a Lohvian from Walfarg he would know the Pandahemic colors as well as he knew his colors of Walfarg, the flaunting horizontal stripes of red and gold.

"Aye, Arkhebi," I said. "And not only from Tomboram."

For I knew, for Pando had told me, with many a boyish twitch of muscular excitement, that he was going to charge a brave zhantil on the blue field of his flag, a zhantil in memory, so he said, of the zhantil-hide tunic I had had made for him, the courageous zhantil, he had said, that reminded him of me.

"Booty, there, mates!" roared a squat-bodied Brokelsh, laughing, pointing, the black bristle hairs on his muscular body all slick with sweat.

I remembered *Dram Constant* and her blue flags, and how we had waited for the onslaught of the sea-leems, and of how Captain Alkers had fought this very swordship on which I now found myself. I could imagine the horror aboard that argenter from Bormark in Tomboram now.

My conscience is a slippery beast. Going a-roving had seemed perfectly respectable to me when I plundered, as I believed, the enemies of Vallia and of Bormark.

But, now, I was faced with the task of capturing and perhaps destroying a ship of a friend. There was no alternative, no choice, about my dilemma; the problem was how to carry the thing off without having my head parted from my shoulders by a Womox.

"Haul that sheet tight!" roared Arkhebi in high excitement. Hands rushed to the sheet and hauled. We were catching all the breeze there was and we were overhauling the argenter as a zorca strides past a vove.

Our four consorts — for one had been sent away with the captured argenter of Menaham — were left far in our wake. They had been dragging their heels all the way. Now it was between us and this proud argenter of Pando's. I saw his face in my mind's eye, I saw Tilda's — but I truly believe it was memory of Captain Alkers that spurred into action what little of conscience I possess.

I picked up a long and stout length of timber that fitted snugly into my two spaced fists. I held it in my left hand and walked across to the bulwark. A boarding ax glittered in the hand of a man who stared with a leem-grin over the shining sea toward his prey. I took the ax from him without a word, swung around, and brought the keen glittering edge down across the main course braces and, in a motion so fast the ax blurred into a silvery circle in the hot air, sliced down across the main yard halyards.

In a wild flurry and tangle of parting braces and lines the main course billowed up with a gigantic snap, and the main yard smashed down across the deck.

At once everything was confusion.

Viridia screamed orders, Arkhebi ran shouting and gesticulating. I walked quickly forward and repeated my actions on the foremast

"Dray! You madman! Stop that!"

Viridia came leaping across the deck toward me and her four Womoxes followed, shaking out their swords, their ugly faces blank with anticipation of bloodletting. I knew they did not like me, and they were ferocious and powerful in the extreme.

"We cannot take that argenter, Viridia, that is all. The damage aboard here can be cleared up in no time."

Men surged in confusion, and the ship rolled, falling off as her crossjack swung her around so that any moment she would be in irons. I didn't care. Just so that I gave Pando's ship time to make good her escape. Immediately she had seen our plight she had at once worn and gone haring off across our bows, heading for the shelter of the islands which were smudges low on the western horizon.

If I had hoped that Viridia harbored any sentiment for me that would halt her vengeful orders I was mistaken.

Valka and the other men of my little group I could see clustered a little to one side and, quite clearly, they were at a loss. They couldn't understand my actions.

"That ship was from a country friendly to me!" I roared. "No man ravages my friends. Remember that!"

"And no man stands between me and plunder!" shrieked Viridia. She was absolutely furious, her face as red as my breechclout. She jerked her hand at her bodyguard.

"Seize him — do not kill. I will talk to him when you have bound him in iron chains!"

I saw two redheaded men lower their longbows, and so I knew I had a chance. I threw down the ax.

"I will not kill, then, also!" I shouted.

Then the Womoxes charged.

They sought to beat me down, to wound, not to kill. They rushed in with so furious an onslaught that I was beaten back and half to my knees. I used the length of timber to push myself back onto my feet. Then, gripping it as I would my own Krozair long sword I jammed the splintery end into the guts of the nearest Womox. Before he was down, vomiting, I had swung my wooden long sword full at the head of the next. He ducked with the instinctive grace of the fighting-man, but the timber cracked against one of his horns and splintered it redly from his head. He screamed. I was already dodging and weaving away from the blades of his fellows, and with that scream ringing in their ears they were out to kill. Blood-lust dominated them completely.

They thrust now with every intention of spitting me.

I heard Viridia yelling. I ignored her. By rapid and eye-deceiving movements, by a constant flow of action and blows I held the two Womoxes off until I could lay that wooden long sword across the ribs of one and then, as he doubled, short-arm the splinters into his face.

He reeled back, spraying blood.

The second had recovered from the loss of a horn and bored in. The last lowered his head as he fought and sought to rip my eyes out with his horns. I skipped back, swung the timber, cracked his skull wide open. The first one, who had been winded, joined his comrade and they rushed me together. Here was the danger. I circled them, weaving the wooden long sword. I do not believe they had experienced a long sword in the grip of a man who knew how to use one before. I dazzled them with a series of passes, ignored their daggers, which took skin from my ribs and slashed my wooden brand down across the face of one of them. He reeled back and I back-struck at the last, smashed in his rib cage and then leaped forward and finished off the sole survivor.

The fight had been hot and brisk, but nothing was settled yet — or so I thought.

Viridia was standing with her hand to her lips, her body gross in the swathing robes and armor.

"Dray..." she whispered.

"I bear you no malice, Viridia. But your bodyguard no longer exist."

At that moment I heard Valka's voice, high, screeching.

"Dray! Behind you!"

I whirled. The Brokelsh, an ax high, was swinging at my defenseless back. I sprang aside and as he lunged on with all the vicious power of his swing, I smashed the timber down upon his own back. He went on into the deck. But my wooden long sword, sorely abused, snapped clean across.

"You men!" I roared, brandishing the splintered stump. "We are comrades.

There are plenty of fat ponshos sailing the seas. Another will be borne by the wind any time!"

Viridia stood as though turned to stone. Even then I did not fully comprehend the disaster to her personally. I stepped close to her side. I tried to speak gently, although, Zair knows, that was difficult enough with the reeking blood splashed upon me.

"Please, Viridia. Try to think. Only do as I ask in this, that you respect the flag of an ally, and all will be well."

"You do not understand, do you, Dray Prescot?"

Before I could answer, a hail reached us.

"Sail ho!"

The reaction was immediate and unthinking. Everyone rushed to the rail, so great is the greed for plunder in a render's breast.

She was a broad-beamed argenter from Jholaix, as we could tell from her blue flag with the bright red amphora in its center. At sight of her I was inspired. Jholaix was fair prey.

I sprang up into the ratlines. I threw away the splintered stump of that long sword that had served me so well, albeit the brand was wood, a mere length of lumber. I drew my rapier.

"See!" I roared. "See what the gods have brought! Did I not say so?" I pointed with the rapier. "And you all know, you sea-leems, what a ship of Jholaix carries!"

"Aye!" they yelled back. "Aye, Dray Prescot! Wine of Jholaix, the best in all the islands!"

With that we set to like maniacs to repair our rigging. The task was accomplished with much cursing and bellowing and by the time our main yard was up and the canvas sheeted home our consorts had drawn level. Together we bore down on the wine ship from Jholaix. She offered not the slightest resistance, and we took her without loss of life.

By the time the twin suns had set across the sea with the distant humps of the Hoboling islands rising against that sheeting crimson and emerald glory most of the hands were rolling merry with bellies full of Jholaix wine. The ship carried a fortune in fine wines.

I drank a little of the best, and was well pleased.

Viridia approached me as I stood by the taffrail. She carried no sword. Her armor hung over her arm, limp, a sheen of mesh-steel in the growing light of She of the Veils.

"So, Dray Prescot, you have taken command."

I was astonished. "Not so, Viridia the Render—"

"Do not mock me, Dray Prescot! You are captain now."

"Why should you suppose that? Because you chose to set your beasties on me and I was forced to dispose of them? I want nothing of command of a crew of cutthroats like this! They are yours, still."

"They follow you, now. You have proved yourself. You are a lucky captain, for you conjure the best wine of Jholaix from the sea, when we have not seen an argenter from there for many a long cruise."

"I am a man of peace, Viridia."

"So I notice." In that flood of moonlight the slight curl to her upper lip was pronounced, and distressing. I did not, then, and I admit this with some strangeness, relish Viridia the Render's contempt.

"Put your armor back on. I do not wish to take your crew or your ship from you. You will find other bodyguards."

She stared at me. "I told them not to kill you, and so they did not use their Womox swords. But then—"

"They tried to kill right enough, Viridia. You saw that."

"Yes."

So we stood for a space, and I do not know what she thought.

Looking back, it occurs to me that perhaps you are wondering, as I was so obsessed with the desire to sail to Vallia and claim my Delia, why I did not assume command of the pirates. Then I would have a ship and could command my men to sail to Vallia. It would not have been as simple as that, of course, for a swordship would have made heavy weather of the passage. I can only say that such a course did not occur to me as being a course with a grain of sense in it. Why this should be I do not know. During the night I heard a harsh and ominous croaking from the moonshot sky above; but when I looked up I could not see the Gdoinye with the scarlet and gold feathers I knew was circling up there in wide planing hunting circles.

So, in uneasy alliance, Viridia and I sailed back to the island of Careless Repose.

Seventeen

A zenzile swordship displeases Valka

My changed status aboard aroused considerable controversy and speculation among the hands until I told Valka to lay it on the line for them. Viridia the Render was still the captain, still in command. We had had a little disagreement over plundering the ship of a friend of mine. That had been amicably settled. Now I was going to knock varter-work into their thick skulls — and they had seen the way I had dealt with the four Womoxes with my only weapon a wooden long sword — and they heeded my words. Valka wanted me to take over. I regarded him with a curiosity I did not conceal as we ran into the harbor and the anchorage and the hook plummeted into the calm water.

"You say you are from Vallia, Valka. You have told me nothing of your history." Among the render crew we dropped into the longboat and brawny arms dipped the oars and we fairly flew over the still waters to the white beach. "I do not expect you to tell me anything of yourself, but I am curious, I admit. Of what use would it be to you if I took command?" He began to speak in his quick and volatile way, but I held up a hand. "Remember, Valka, it would mean the death of Viridia. That is certain."

"So, Dray Prescot! That is why you did not take the captaincy! For concern of Viridia the Render!"

If he chose to think that, let him. Maybe I should have disabused him, then and there; but I am not a one for giving confidences to any but those I know and trust.

We walked up to the village and were soon well into a bottle taken from the argenter of Jholaix. The stuff was smooth and mellow and, perhaps, it loosened Valka's tongue.

"You know Vallia, Dray? You have been to that beautiful and wicked land?"

I considered for a moment. Then I said, "No, never."

He sighed and drank deep. "It is a land where anything the heart desires may be found — but only for those in the privileged positions of power and wealth and authority."

"That is everywhere the same."

"True, true, Dray, my old dom." He looked up and his eyes misted. "In the north of Vallia are the mountains — the wonderful mountains of Vallia! From them flow mighty rivers, pouring in a refreshing flood down to the coasts on east and west and south. Ah! The south coast. Nowhere in all of Kregen is there a place like it."

He was waxing semipoetical on me now; but I listened with care.

Delia had told me something of her homeland and I had heard of these mountains before. They were not the Blue Mountains. Valka drank and wiped his lips. "The whole island is connected with a network of canals. Canals flow everywhere. As a consequence, the roads are usually abominable. The canal folk are my folk. We form a community—" Then he stopped, and hiccupped, and roared some obscene jest at a render who grabbed a serving wench, and missed, and fell into a waste bucket. Full-flavored accidents like that often amuse the Kregans.

Then he said with as much bitterness as I ever heard him speak: "I offended against a law. The Racter party are all powerful. They do as they please, them and their mercenaries. So I ran away to sea. And was captured. And ended up here."

"And would you return to Vallia, if you had the chance?"

He grimaced. It was not a pretty sight. "By Vox! I miss the canals. But if I return home, they will hang me, for sure."

"The Racter party will, or the government?"

"Government?" He spat. "The emperor wields awful powers. He is a devil. But he must walk small when the Racters frown."

The noise of carousing bellowed on about us as we talked. Soon Valka had drunk enough for him to join in with the songs the renders yodeled out. They sang songs I had never heard of until then: "The Worm-eaten Swordship Gull-i-mo." The part song, "The Wines of Jholaix," which they were sober enough to sing more or less correctly through, swordship crew and swordship crew taking parts. "The Maid with the Single Veil," which brought on a rash of giggles from the serving wenches. And they sang the old ones, too: "The Bowmen of Loh." They even had a shot at various musicked stanzas of "The Canticles of the Rose City," but by that time most were too far gone for exact rendering of the cadences of those old myths, three thousand years old if they were a day.

When I wandered off to the room I had been assigned Valka and the knot of men I knew now were faithful to me, for I had seen their reactions during the aftermath of the fight aboard the flagship, accompanied me. They would sleep next door. I went in and the samphron oil lamp was lit and there was Viridia, smokily lovely in a short orange shift which showed her legs and her knees — which were dimpled, I swear it! — reclining on the bed.

In her combed hair a blaze of jewels reflected the light and glittered magnificently. I heard Valka and the others laughing. Viridia pushed up on her arms.

"You were asking Valka of Vallia, Dray." She smiled and that sensuous mouth parted enticingly. "Come and sit by me and I will tell you of Vallia, also."

"You are a Vallian?" In truth, I had heard a story that she was, but had doubted it.

"I will tell you, Dray; but come, sit by me."

I did not relish a repetition of that scene I had endured with Queen Lilah. I discounted women like Natema and Susheeng in this equation; because Viridia fancied herself as a Queen of Pain, which Queen Lilah had in truth been. If I give the impression of Viridia as being less of a person than she was, then I do her a disfavor. She was a real person in her own right, vibrant, alluring now she had tidied herself up, and a genuine force to be reckoned with. I fancied she wanted to place herself under my protection, now that her Womoxes were gone. As I thought of them I gave an involuntary shiver, for they had been gruesome and powerful antagonists indeed.

Viridia started up.

"Dray! You have a fever?"

"It is nothing, Viridia the Render. Now, listen to me, and listen to me carefully. I shall not tell you again."

At this she sat up on the bed and meekly put her hands together, down between her knees. Her tanned face, warm under the mellow light, assumed an expression of subservience, the eyes downcast. If she was playacting, she did it well. There were no slaves among the renders, but I guessed from this display that Viridia had been slave in her time.

"I listen, master."

About to bite her head off, I stopped. Very well, if this was the way she wanted to play it, so be it.

"You are now defenseless, except for the strength and skill of your own arms, Viridia. I know you can fight and swing an ax, for I have seen you. But men lust after you."

"That is true, master. I desire to be your slave. You must chastise me if I am bad, punish me with the knotted cord. I have killed many men who attempted me. But for you I will do as Chekumte desired you to do for him, and kiss your feet."

I began to think she meant it.

I was naked to the breechclout; but I began to get hot under the collar.

"Listen, Viridia. I do not want your Makki-Grodno pirates! Keep them, and the swordships. If you want me to be your master and carry on in this foolish fashion I shall lift that short nightie of yours and spank you soundly—"

She looked up and her eyelids flew up.

"Oh, yes, please, master!"

With a furious roar I scooped her up, opened the door with my free hand and then found that I could not, as I fully intended, throw her out, for she had wound both her naked arms around my neck. The next instant she had kissed me, a full, wet, soft kiss that — I confess — was pleasurable, most. Then, automatically, images of my Delia floated into my mind in a torrent and I laughed. Yes, I laughed.

"It is no use, Viridia. I like you exceedingly well. But I do not love you. Now go to your room and Arkhebi and Valka and I will stand turn and turn about at your door. You will be safe."

"But, Dray, my master." She said this with a charming pout. "I do not want to be safe from you."

I marveled. From the fierce tough she-leem of the seas, she had metamorphosed into this teasing, sensual, alluring woman. Just how much of an act was it all? Would she, when I was suitably disarmed, slip a dagger between my ribs?

The last thing she said was: "If I am to remain in command, Dray Prescot, then I will set you in command of the swordship I have just bought."

This sounded more promising.

Once I had a crew under my orders and was free of the other swordships, without their seeking a lead from me, I might plan escape.

"So be it, Viridia the Render," I said, and carried her to her room and threw her inside. I slammed the door. Then I roused out Valka and Arkhebi and we stood guard turn and turn about all that night.

The next day I went down to the anchorage to inspect the newest addition to Viridia's squadron and my future command.

The moment I saw her I exclaimed: "A sea scow! Viridia, you cunning she-leem! She's a zenzile! Old, ancient, leaky — a veritable tub!"

The smile Viridia cast at me upward and the way her blue eyes caught mine through her eyelashes made me want to spank her in very truth. I put my hands on my hips and jutted my beard out to the swordship.

"Yes, Dray Prescot — you may think she is all of those things. But, if you wish to command a render ship in my squadron — that is the swordship for you."

Valka, at my side, guffawed, so I said without looking at him: "Laugh all you like, Valka. Just remember, you'll be commanding her varters." At which Valka stopped laughing.

It had been my custom in the Eye of the World to name any swifter I commanded *Zorg*. This in memory of my oar comrade. Other swifter captains had known this, and respected my wishes. But I would never dream of calling this swaybacked old zenzile swordship *Zorg*.

Without another word to Viridia I strode off toward the nearest of our beached boats and my men, after one look at my face, clambered in silently and bent to the oars. I did not look back at Viridia. I knew she was laughing at me. But, in truth, this old zenzile swordship was not all that bad and she was a weapon of the sea, long, lean, low, lethal.

The old-fashioned zenzile way of rowing incorporates what was a wonderful invention when it was first used — and just how long ago that was let the academic pundits argue — of slanting the benches diagonally so that their inboard seat is farther aft than their outboard. With three oarsmen on each bench and using oars of different lengths so that the blades formed those impeccable parallel lines in the water, the swordship presented from the beam an impression of a single bank of oars arranged in clumps of threes.

One man rowed one oar, three oarsmen to each slanted bench, and the centers could be anything from three feet six inches to four feet apart, depending on the whims of the naval architect who designed the ship. There were twenty benches a side and thus a hundred and twenty oarsmen in all. I began to think, as I mounted the side and put my foot on the fantamyrrh and so stepped aboard my new command, that Viridia had indeed bought the scow Chekumte had been trying to sell her.

If she had, she had done it to spite me.

Well, that was a game two could play.

Valka was making unpleasant comments on the sword-ship and with the group of men loyal to me strode about the central gangway and hurdled over the benches and prowled the apostis, looking over the side, for she was of the anafract variety.

"Don't be too hard on her, Valka. Galleys like this have fought in many great engagements — aye, and they will continue to do so, just so long as men believe in them."

"Give me a good long oar and half a dozen men on it, any time," said Valka, with a curse.

"This is a zorca of the seas," I said. "At least in theory. This zenzile arrangement is fine for smaller galleys; when you come to a swifter — a swordship — of large size is when you need the packed power that *scaloccio* rowing gives you."

I suppose the last time galleys had been constructed after this pattern on the Earth of my birth had been back in the sixteenth century, for the *alla scaloccio* system had been dated, I gathered, to 1530. The Venetians were great galley men of the Mediterranean. Zenzile rowing died out on this Earth; but I suppose these seafaring folk of Kregen clung to their own ideas with a stubbornness I could recognize.

The name of this wonder craft was *Strigicaw*. A strigicaw is a powerful fast-running carnivore with a hide striped as to the shoulders and foreparts and double-spotted as to belly and haunches, in a variety of brown and red camouflage colors, and although looking not unlike a leem has only six legs instead of that voracious beast's eight.

She was a hundred feet in length — any more would have been too much for her power-propulsion — and had just the two masts, a main and a fore, both rigged with courses and topsails. At least, she did boast a rudder and whipstaff. This is a clumsy system long superseded on the ships of Earth; no doubt soon the naval architects of Kregen will develop the wheel and cylinder steering gear. I strode about her, and, despite all, despite that she would need constant pumping, I began to get the feel of her, and to know she was my command.

After the sinking of *Venus* Viridia's render maidens had been shipped aboard another of her squadron, whose crew had been distributed among the remaining ships, so that we had been crowded. Now I would have to look to bargaining and cajoling and arguing in order to obtain the crew I wanted.

As we so stood surveying our new swordship a booming horn note rolled weirdly over the anchorage. All the busy noise of hammering and shouting, of singing and whistling, all human sounds ceased.

Again that booming note mourned across the water.

"The alarm!" shouted Spitz, a redheaded archer from Loh. I had marked him from the first, and sought to woo him for my little company, for in his quiver he carried arrows fletched with the brilliant blue of the king korf — and also arrows fletched with jetty black feathers — feathers I knew had been set by Sosie na Arkasson — and given to me, and loosed by me against Spitz, and so retrieved by him for further use. "King's swordships!"

We tumbled down into the boat and rowed ashore in a welter of foam. The swordship — or swordships — prowling around the island of Careless Repose might come from any nation; but we usually dubbed any swordship attempting to police the islands the King's swordship. Viridia met us on the beach. She looked excited, her tanned face flushed, her strong body in the mesh steel armor firm in the suns-light.

"Be ready to repel them if they venture past the concealing islet!" she rapped out to her lieutenants, captains of their own vessels, of whom I was now one. "I and my warrior maidens will seek to do their business for them." She laughed, throwing her head back in the light so that the dark hair swirled. "As we have done before!"

"Aye, Viridia!" the man yelled. "Hai, Jikai, Viridia the Render!"

There was no malice in me, no regret, for the use of that great word here. Viridia, in that moment, was a lady pirate indeed.

She took her girls off to the other side of the island and the swordship crews repaired aboard their craft and made ready to pull around the point if Viridia's plan did not work. As I had no crew, apart from my own small company of loyals, I took them, with weapons in our hands, across the island after Viridia.

She might welcome a little help, when it came to the time.

As it happened, she needed no help, least of all from mere men.

A repetition of what had happened to the old *Nemo* took place. This swordship, commissioned to hunt down the renders and sailing out of the chief port of The Bloody Menaham, was taken in exactly the same way and by exactly the same means.

I daresay it was the same half-naked sprite who ran along the central gangway carrying the dripping head of the chief whip-deldar.

The King's swordship was rowed around the point and past the concealing islet and so into the anchorage where the slaves were freed from their oars. They set up a wonderful hullabaloo. All, I knew, would take the alternative of joining the pirates.

I studied the new ship. She was a smart and efficient-looking vessel, with three sails and a spritsail on her bowsprit. Her bronze ram was fashioned into the like-ness of a mythical bird of prey, something like a falcon, although, of course, the hooked beak had been smoothed into a single shaft of cutting bronze. Anything like a hook, as of an accipiter's beak, for a ram is idiocy. One has to be able to backwater and shove off from a rammed vessel, with the aid of the proembolion, before the water rushes into the cleft in her hull and the apostis, the rowing frame, settles down over your ram and drags you under.

As for her spritsail, that was a sailor-like rigged job, nicely forward and yet well clear of her beak. I watched the ex-slaves being ferried ashore. Among those on the beach I saw a group forming around some object on the sand, and I heard loud guffaws, and hearty laughter, and many merry curses. I strolled down.

A man, a very tall man, was upside down on the sand, his legs rhythmically bicy-cling in the air. Some of the men were attempting to push him over. He did, at that, look a sight. I heard him yelling. "Clear off, onkers! I must abjure my taboos!"

A guffawing render — a towheaded man from one of the islands past Erthy-rdrin — pushed the tall upside-down man and he rolled spraying sand.

Instantly, he was upside down again, his long fair hair sand-clogged, his legs rotating.

The renders and ex-slaves roared.

"Taboos!" They yodeled, getting set for their next prank.

I sighed.

I strode over and unlimbered my sword.

I stood before Inch.

"If any man wishes to push this man over while he abjures his taboos, he must pass this rapier first."

After that, Inch could get on with it, and I could only wait until he had worked all the accumulated taboo-breaks out of his system before I could ask him all the news.

Eighteen

The yellow cross on the scarlet field

Strigicaw prowled the seas in search of plunder.

"I never believed, Dray Prescot, that any man could claw back from the Ice Floes of Sicce."

"Since I don't believe in investigating that shivery region for many years to come, Inch, your surprise is unwarranted."

"But, man! You just disappeared!"

"Evidently, what happened to me happened to you." I told him, briefly, how King Nemo had disposed of me and he sighed and said: "Much the same. I sup-pose I was getting too big for my boots. When you vanished, no man knew whither, Tilda insisted I stay on. I had to — you see that, don't you, Dray?"

"Of course. It was the honorable thing to do."

My swordship, making a most unpleasant business of beating into a devilish strong wind from the wrong quarter and with a sea that made the use of oars out of the question, pitched and rolled. Spray drenched us. My flags flew stiff as boards.

Being anafract, that is, without armor protection for the rowers, my artillery — for I may use that word of varters — must be concentrated forward. We were far more a galley than a galleass, like the other swordships. The others of Viridia's squadron were sailing far more weatherly than we and were pulling away across the tumbled sea. Again I looked up at my flags. Up there the yellow cross of my clansmen had been charged on the scarlet of Strombor. A brilliant yellow upright cross on a scarlet field. Yes, those were my colors. A momentary stab of an emotion I did not want to recognizethe render flag, a shaft of conscience, almost, that the pirate flag should wave in company with my own.

Inch had given me the news. He had tried to assist Tilda, and keep Pando under some sort of control; but the wild zhantil had taken his newly-won status as a Kov to heart, and had lavished money and armament on the king and, with a great levy, had gone to war. I ached that I had not been there to help him — and by helping him to draw him back from the folly of war.

"I spoke out, Dray, and the next thing I knew was chained on the rowing beaches of a swordship — and, mark me — a swordship of The Bloody Menaham."

"I had noticed. They sold you, it seems."

"The war was not going well when I — ah — left."

"If that idiot Pando gets himself killed — although," I spoke hopefully— "I expect he would be held for ransom."

"We didn't handle him the best way. The Kovnate went to his head a little."

"Agreed. And, Inch, that was my fault. I was a fool."

Inch had not broken any taboos as yet since boarding *Strigicaw*, and I had swiftly adjusted to remembering. Now he shook his head. "Not so, Dray. You could always control him, and in the best way, without a strap. I tried. But after you went he turned wild. There was no holding him."

"Tilda?"

He smiled. "She is a good mother, and a wonderful woman and a superb actress. But I think being a Kovneva was a trifle out of her experience. She tries to cope, but she has been drinking—"

"No!"

"I am afraid so."

"We'll have to go back, Inch, and sort them out."

"Yes. It seems to me that is a task laid on us, for our sins."

"For our sins, Zair be thanked."

And so — what of Vallia? What of Delia of Delphond?

The strongest doubts existed that this wallowing swordship *Strigicaw* would ever live through a passage across the open sea. She was a swift galley built for coastal waters, up among the islands. Now, through the sheets of spray, our consorts were a full dwabur upwind of us, and going hull down. Vallia would have to wait. Delia — I know I prayed she would understand and forgive me. But I was tortured by the thought that her resistance had been broken down, and she had given into that imperial majesty, her father, and married the oaf of his choice.

"By Ngrangi!" exclaimed Inch as the ship rolled and the wind tore at our canvas and water slopped green. "This tub will founder beneath us!"

"Spitz!" I yelled to the archer from Loh. "Before the flagship disappears! Hoist the white flag from the main yard!"

With a yell Spitz ran to obey.

That white flag from our yardarm, plus the simultaneous hauling down of the pirate flag from the main truck, would indicate to Viridia, if her officers could pick the signal out, that we had been forced to return to Careful Repose.

In the midst of giving the orders that would turn our head toward the easiest point of the compass for the ship, Valka sprang up through the canvas coverings we had spread over the rowing benches to keep the sea out and raced along the central gangway toward me. He glared up to the quarterdeck.

"Only just about in time, Captain, if you ask me! The seams are working something horrible. We're shipping water faster than the pumps can clear."

"Muster a baling party," I told Valka. "See they jump to it. I'm taking this ship home — never fear — unless something better comes along."

They all laughed at that, as though it were a jest.

The new course, off the wind and sea, eased the ship and I made a tour of inspection in the wildly leaping vessel, feeling her working in the sea, and realized just how close we had been. The inspection I had given her before we sailed had not been as thorough as I would have liked, and now I could see that Viridia had been cheated — although, no doubt, that troubled her not a whit. The new swordship she had just taken would be fitted and ready by the time she returned from this cruise. Much of the underwater planking was rotten, and I could push the point of my dagger into the wood with ease. I began to entertain a conviction that the bottom would drop out before we made port. And all through the rush of departure!

Thinking baleful thoughts I climbed up on deck again and ordered a tot of good red wine for every man.

When Spitz, having hauled down the white flag, began to rehoist the pirate flag I growled at him. "Belay that!"

Certain ideas were meeting and melding in my head. I knew I was sick of the pirate trade — and yet, its fascination and its rewards, given that we would plunder only enemies, could not be denied.

"Sail ho!"

I stood on my ridiculous quarterdeck as we pitched and rolled and struggled in that sea, with a scrap of canvas showing to keep us from being merely a waterlogged lump of drifting wreckage, and watched as, on almost a reciprocal bearing, so close to the wind was she, a magnificent ship foamed toward us. She passed like a queen of the seas. She took absolutely no notice of us at all. In reality, working as we were, boarding would have been an operation too costly, as I judged. As it was that beautiful ship beat past us, leaning over, all her canvas as taut and trim as a guardsman's tunic, her colors snapping out insolently.

I gazed on that ship and on those colors.

A galleon, jutting of beak, sheer of line and curve, bold in the sea, built low with forecastle and quarterdeck and a small poop, four-masted, raked, aglitter with bright gilding and flamboyant colors. She moved surely against that sea in which we floundered. A galleon. A race-built galleon.

And the flags! A yellow cross, a saltire, on a red field.

I glanced up at my own flag.

That yellow Saint Andrew's cross on a red ground — I knew it. I knew from whence that proud ship hailed. From Vallia!

The galleon from Vallia roared past and was gone and was soon hull down and then the last scrap of her canvas winked over the sea horizon to the east.

"Damn the Vallians!" said Spitz. He held his Lohvian longbow in his hand, a kind of nervous reflex. "They think they own the sea and all who sail on it! By Hlo-Hli! They think they've been anointed and given the scepter of all Kregen!"

We struggled on and, to our vast relief, the sea went down, the wind backed, and we were able to make better weather of it. The twin suns of Kregen were slipping down toward the western horizon, first Genodras and then Zim, and soon the nightly procession of moons would arch through the swarming stars.

Again came the hail that warms a render's heart.

"Sail ho!"

She was a swordship from Yumapan, the country south of Lome, on the other side of the massive mountains that divide the island into North and South Pandahem, Her colors of vertical bars of green and blue in keeping with Pandahemic tradition fluttered in the dying breeze. She had seen us and was closing fast, and even as I watched she sprouted her oars and the long looms held, as though ruled parallel, like wings on either beam, before the drum-deldar gave his first stroke and the oars dipped as one.

Valka yelled at me, pointing.

"No oars!" I shouted back.

Now Spitz and others of my officers were shouting. I leaped into the main shrouds and roared them to silence.

"They are big and powerful and can take us — and who among you wants to row for the Yumapanim? Eh? Any volunteers?"

There rose a few scattered, uncertain laughs.

Yumapan, being situated across the sea to the east from Walfarg, had been one of that robust nation's first conquests on her road to empire in the long ago. Now that Walfarg's empire had crumbled, the Yumapan remembered, and aped those old ways; and they had long memories. Men even said they preferred a queen on the throne in Yumapan, in remembrance of the old Queens of Pain of Loh.

"But, Dray!" shouted Valka. "No oars! How can we fight?"

"We let her ram us, of course, you hairy calsany! Let her stick her rostrum up our guts — poor old *Strigicaw* is done for, anyway! Then, my sea-leem — *then!*"

"Aye!" they roared it back at me. "Then, Dray Prescot — *then!*"

And so, rolling like a washtub in the sea, we awaited the bronze-rammed shock from the Yumapan swordship.

When it came, with a roaring rending of wood and the screeching of bronze against iron nails, the smash of white water and the solid reeling shock as we nearly overset, my men knew what was required of them and knew the plan. Before the swordship captain could back his oars and draw free we were up over our side. Grapnels flew. Men leaped down from our rigging.

With Spitz in masterly control of our bowmen we shot out their quarterdeck. I went in at the head of my sea-leems, handing up over the bronze ram, up past the proembolion which was fashioned in bronze in the likeness of a zhantil-mask, up to the side of the beak and so, with a heave and a squirm, over onto the beak gangwalk. I snatched out my sword and, roaring and shouting, led my men down onto the central gangway. We fought. Oh, yes, we fought. We knew that if we failed we would either die and be tossed overside or be chained naked at the rowing beaches.

This was a fight that had some meaning to it.

This was a fight we had to win.

I saw Inch with a great ax, almost the equal of his own mighty weapon he had lost back in Bormark, smiting and smiting. In expert hands the great Saxon ax of Danish pattern is a frightful weapon of destruction. It cleaved a red path through the Yumapanim. Many men leaped overboard, shrieking, rather than face the tall form of Inch with those incredibly long arms smashing that gory ax in swaths of destruction.

And, obeying my orders, selected hands of my crew were jumping down between the rowing beaches, kicking away the ponsho skins, smashing the padlocks and breaking the chains. How those oar-slaves rose to us! With snatched-up weapons parceled out by my men, the ex-slaves vomited into the battle. We began at the prow and we finished at the taffrail, and all between was mine!

Of course, looking back, how can I take a pride in all that destruction of life? How can I feel a glow of satisfaction that good sailormen had been slain and thrown overboard? But then, at the head of my sea-leem, my bloodstained rapier in my hand, I felt the full tide of gratification and lust of conquest. I had scarcely heeded that this was a part of the render's trade. Yumapan was a foe of Vallia, was a foe of Tomboram — and, as I knew, was a foe also to Zenicce and Strombor. It was all part of the struggle that, all unbeknown, I was waging on Kregen under the Suns of Scorpio.

Poor *Strigicaw* was almost gone.

Before the waves closed over her we took what was necessary and transferred our goods and chattels to my new command.

That brave flag of mine, the brilliant yellow cross on the scarlet field I personally bent and hoisted, high, high at the truck of the mainmast. And there it blew, proclaiming to all that this swordship was mine!

Pride, and possession, and power — disastrous, disastrous!

The released slaves would join us.

The name of the swordship had been a long and complicated farrago of high-flown pomp and circumstance, which boiled down to her and her captain being the best on the sea, and the queen of Yumapan being the greatest Queen of Pain who had ever lived. I gave orders for the whole name to be expunged, and this was done by a certain amount of high-spirited chisel work and a triple splash in the sea.

I gathered everyone aft and addressed them from the quarterdeck, which was wide and spacious for a galleass, and ornate with fittings that already I had my eye on as further consignments to the deep.

"This swordship is now named *Freedom*."

They cheered at that.

"We return to Careless Repose. There is work set to my hand, work that will bring rich loot, plunder beyond your wildest dreams, prizes — gold, silver, wine and women! Do you follow me, lads?"

"Aye!" They roared it out. "Aye, Captain Prescot. We will follow you to the Ice Floes of Sicce!"

I saw Inch looking sideways at me, and I did not wink; but I know he took the gist of what I meant.

Freedom was indeed a fine ship. She rowed forty oars a side, and there were nine men on each bench — according to the Kregen and not the Earthly way of reckoning. So that meant seven hundred and twenty men hauled and pushed the oars. Also, there were the sailors, and the marines — so that she had to be a large vessel. Quite unlike the swifters, with their dangerously low freeboards and their serpentine lines, she had some run to her underwater lines, and with her three masts and spritsail could hold a wind. Compared with a galleon, of course, she sailed like a barge. Even then, even then, that proud and haughty Vallian galleon could not match the qualities of a first-class frigate of my own day, let us not forget that!

Her freeboard seemed immense, and her varters and catapults mounted on the broadside had a superb arc of training and commanding height. I felt I could sail her to Vallia, if the need arose — *if the need arose!*

How far I had come! Tilda and Pando must be sorted out and when that task had been accomplished to my satisfaction, then, then I would turn the proud beak of this beauty northeastwards to Vallia!

Inch was let into all the plans I had formulated, with the exception that he knew only that I intended to sail to Vallia, and, being a footloose mercenary warrior, that suited him fine. Valka and Spitz and the other of my officers were told enough to keep them happy. They were well-primed to do their work. I knew that by the time we arrived at the island of Careless Repose I would have a whole swordship crew devoted to carrying out what I wanted done, demanding, pleading, desperate to sail on my business.

If I have a good ship's crew ready to my hand I sometimes fancy I might move mountains.

At the pirates' lair we talked and held out dazzling promises and suborned good men. The big breakthrough came when a swordship brought in an argenter from The Bloody Menaham. The renders had taken to copying Viridia and instead of butchering their prisoners and burning the ships, ransomed them instead. Now I heard that The Bloody Menaham were on the attack against Tomboram, had marched in to invade Bormark, had crossed that Kovnate and were advancing on the capital, Pomdermam.

"Let us hit these Bloody Menaham, where it hurts, at home!" I urged the sea-leems. By the time Viridia returned, with but a poor coaster to show for her efforts, and thoroughly out of sorts, she was, willy-nilly, swept up in the feral enthusiasm.

By careful sea passages we could reach south of the islands, coast along the north shore of Pandahem, come storming in on the rear of The Bloody Menaham, from a quarter where they least expected assault. There was a great deal of flashing blades and shouts of "Hai! Jikai!" but I kept busily preparing plans for every swordship captain, and as the news of a great venture whose final destination was a secret from all but the captains buzzed around the islands, swordship after swordship nosed in until the anchorage filled and they had to lie up in secondary harbors.

For some time, everyone said, the renders had been aching to go on a great Jikai. Now, all agreed, was the time.

If you think me blind to what I was doing, then, in all humility, I suppose I was. But I wanted to get to Vallia, and I could not leave until I had honored my promise to Tilda and Pando.

The great day came at last. We had filled every quiver. All the ammunition lockers were filled to overflowing. Wine, water, food, arms, everything was crammed into the sword-ships. In a great fluttering of flags and booming of stentor horns, we lifted our hooks and pulled for the sea and Pandahem.

Nineteen

The Scorpion returns

As we shipped our oars and from the yards the topmen let fall our canvas and we began to heel to the breeze, I saw above me and flying in those familiar wide planing circles the gorgeous scarlet and gold form of the Gdoinye, the raptor sent as observer and sentinel by the Star Lords. Although I did not see the Savanti dove, I was heartened by the sight of the Gdoinye, taking it as a good omen for my venture. In this, as you will hear, I was foolishly naive.

We made a fine passage south and east, swinging wide of the northwest tip of Pandahem where the land of Lome meets the sea, and cruising eastward to make the island of Panderk which lies off the western end of the enormous Bay of Panderk, immediately north of the border between The Bloody Menaham and Tomboram. Here we sent spies ashore.

The news they brought back infuriated me — and drove me to commit a folly that nearly destroyed the fleet of render swordships and would have totally undone me; but then I believed I was acting out some small part of the scheme the Star Lords planned for Kregen, and so I believed that I would not fail.

The spies reported that the Menaham army was slogging on toward the capital of Tomboram, Pomdermam, and thereby keeping in play King Nemo and all his forces. But, secretly, across the wide waters of the Bay of Panderk, a mighty armada of ships of all descriptions was sailing on, packed with men, to come upon Pomdermam from the sea and in a sudden and savagely unexpected onslaught rout the Tomboramin utterly.

This was bad enough. But, at least for Inch and me, there was far worse information. One of the spies, an agile pirate who hailed from Menaham and had been consigned to the galleys and subsequently followed the usual path to the island of Careless Repose, reported a choice tidbit of gossip. The Kov of Bormark — "a mere stripling!" — and his mother had been forced to flee and were hiding somewhere, Pandrite knew where.

I said one word: "Murlock!"

Inch nodded. "It would be like him, the obvious thing for him to do."

"But he must be mad! Blind! Cannot he see that Menaham will use him and then toss him aside? He'll never recover his estates and his title, by the Black Chunkrah!"

"Murlock Marsilus," said the spy, his blackened teeth exposed as he smiled knowingly. "That's the name. But he is not with the fleet for Pomdermam. He was seen — a girl I know told me, with many giggles — heading for Pomdermam itself, astride a zorca that he rowelled as though Armipand himself, may Opaz rot him, was after him."

Then, bringing the problem squarely before me, the Menaham pirate nodded over the bulwark to the northeastern horizon. Black thunderheads piled there. All about our island anchorage the water lay listless and still, glassy, unbreathing.

"By Diproo the Nimble-fingered!" said the pirate, and spat — by which I knew him to have been a member of the thieves' fraternity. "That fleet may just scrape through to Pomdermam, but no ship will follow for days!"

Everyone, it seemed all of a sudden, was looking at me. I could feel their eyes, like scarlet leeches, sucking at me.

An instant decision would be easy, perhaps fatally wrong. Just how far these pirates would follow my lead remained also a factor to be considered. I grunted something to Inch and Valka and went into my cabin. I automatically looked around for the scarlet-coated marine sentry at attention with his musket and bayonet — so far gone aboard ship was I in problems.

This was Kregen, four hundred light-years from the nearest Royal Marine and his musket and bayonet. I already knew the answer, in truth, this atypical and cowardly hesitation was merely my self-excuse for once again failing Delia. I loved Delia, and Delia loved me. We both knew each loved the other. Therefore there could be between us none of these adolescent lovers' tiffs of immature passion, those fits of jealousy and rage — no lovers' quarrels. So much of the literature of Earth no less than Kregen is consumed by these juvenile lovers' quarrels, and disbeliefs, and worries over faithfulness. I knew Delia would not despair of me and I knew she would not marry of her own free will; it was chicanery that I feared for her, the deep plots of her autocratic father. She would know my duty lay with Tilda and Pando for the moment and then — then to face her father. I would have to be ruthless with him. Have to be...

Love gently forces one to adjust mental horizons. If love is selfish, crying: "She is *mine!*" and one destroys lives and hopes for the sake of this spurious love, one cannot truly love. Love demands sacrifices, it makes giving easy. And, in turn, it means that receiving, also, is a part of love.

I went out onto the quarterdeck and everyone fell silent. All those eyes leeched on me as I stood, holding myself up, my left hand gripping my rapier hilt, and I know my beard jutted out in its swifter-ram arrogance, and my face wore its old ugly look of devilish power. But, that is me, alas.

"There is much loot aboard the armada of The Bloody Menaham. That loot will be ours. Afterward, we will smash The Bloody Menaham and take from them wealth enough to make us all rich for the rest of our lives."

I turned to Valka, who stood now in the position of my first lieutenant, Spitz taking the responsibility of varter Hikdar. "Make the signal to weigh. We sail at once."

For a long moment there was complete silence.

Had I failed? Would they disobey? Then Inch tossed his hat in the air. "The Bloody Menaham!" he roared. "We rend them utterly! Hai, Jikai! Hai, Dray Prescot!"

After that it was a matter of getting the hook up and of setting all our oarsmen at pulling and heaving. One by one the other swordships followed our lead, for they recognized a strong hand at the helm and had no other plan. As we gathered into our stride a longboat rowed alongside, her oars splashing frantically. A tossed rope hauled up a chest and on its second cast fished up Viridia. She bounded onto the deck, shook the dark hair out of her eyes, and declared roundly: "By Opaz, Dray Prescot! You won't get rid of me so easily!"

Nodding to that ominous blackness all across the horizon, I said so that only she could hear: "You may have joined me for your last voyage, Viridia the Render."

She laughed recklessly, tossing the hair out of her eyes. "And if I have I would sail on that last voyage to the Ice Floes of Sicce with no other man than you, Dray Prescot."

The black storm clouds whirled up into the zenith and the opaz light of the twin suns was blotted out in a hell of roaring wind and smashing seas and of a blackness like an impiter's wings enfolding us. We battened everything down and held on under storm canvas. Now the swordships must prove if they were sea boats or not. Some render captains turned back, out of cowardice, out of prudence, out of dire necessity of a sinking vessel beneath their feet. But *Freedom* held on across the wide Bay of Panderk, and with her sailed through those bitter seas a goodly proportion of the render armada.

If we failed to get through, then Pomdermam was completely lost, and with the capital the country, and with the country Bormark, and Tilda, and Pando. We fought the sea, for we must not lose.

Relieving tackles were rigged so that more men could throw their weight on the rudder. Lines were rigged across the decks. I stood lashed on my quarter-deck, spray-drenched, soaked, the wind whipping through my hair and beard and stinging into my eyes, conning the ship. We fought all the elements that the ocean could throw at us, and on the second day we emerged, sorely bruised and battered but intact, and sailed on into a subsiding sea and a dying wind.

And then — "Sail ho!"

Ahead of us and spreading across the horizon in a great cloud of canvas toiled the armada from Menaham. They straggled. They had caught the outskirts of the gale's violence. The twin suns were sliding down into the sea, staining the vast expanse of ocean in bruised rubies and jades. Signals flashed from swordship to swordship, so that my fleet held back, riding out the last of the swell-waves, re-pairing damage, giving the tired crews time to rest and recuperate. Signals among shipping on Kregen had not reached to the sophistication of the signal book as invented by Kempenfelt and Popham; but by flag and lamp I was able to get my message across.

The fallacy that ships may be drilled like soldiers still holds among landsmen, and although the Navy had achieved remarkable evolutionary prowess, navies still could not under the conditions of sail and oar take up long neat lines of up-ward of a thousand ships, in four ranks, with outriders and scouts, as though they drilled on Salisbury Plain. For one thing, the length of lines of galleys, marshaled abeam, makes for vast acres of sea coverage, and the distances are such that signals take a good long time to reach from the commander in chief to the outer horns of his lines. So I had simply adapted a Nelsonian piece of advice: "Sail or row toward your enemy whenever you see him. Any render captain who places his swordship into the guts of his opponent will not do wrong."

Perhaps, at another time, I will speak more fully of that battle in the Bay of Panderk off Pomdermam.

With the coming of the twin Suns of Scorpio the sea woke to long swaths of crimson and emerald. Birds flew low over the water, screaming. The sea lay heaving in glassy swells after the storm, and the wind died to a zephyr, so that it was all oar-work, and rowing, with the men standing and flinging themselves against the oars. Benches are provided aboard swifters and swordships where anything from four to ten men may labor at a single loom, and these benches are thickly covered with ponsho skins. There is nothing of the genteel sitting in your seat and resting your feet in slides and rowing as though you pulled an eight in some university boat race. The one-man-to-one-oar zenzile craft share some-thing of that finesse. Not so the swordships. Here men stand and grip the loom and thrust it down and then, lifting it high, hurl themselves bodily backward, crashing down with numbed buttocks onto those benches and those thought-fully provided ponsho skins. The benches exist to prevent them from smashing back to the deck, to support them for the next convulsive effort of jumping up and thrusting down. All the body is used in rowing a swordship or a swifter. Every ounce concentrated on dragging those massive blades through the water. So we thrashed on through the water. So we thrashed on through the glassy swells, the white water creaming from our bronze rams, bearing on in lethal pursuit of the armada of The Bloody Menaham.

The greatest problem would be that of individual renders taking an argenter and stopping for plunder.

The drum-deldar thumped out his booming and commanding beat, bongg, bongg, bongg. A single beat, as is used aboard a swordship as opposed to the double, bass and treble, employed in swifters. Quicker and quicker the beat rose as I urged the oarsmen on. We foamed through the sea. Ahead of us spread the blue and green diagonally striped flags of the Menaham, fluttering from a hundred staffs. I selected our target. The helm-deldars swung the whipstaff. Our ram curled back the white running water. I measured the distance...

"Prepare to ram!"

Spitz's varter men hauled back and braced themselves. A single shining instant of poising hush, a fragile bubble when everything coalesced and rushed together — and then we smashed into the stern of the argenter and the world revolved in a rending smashing and a bright chaos. On the instant I released my handholds and leaped. From our beak I crashed forward and in through the stern windows of the argenter, to be met by a flickering wall of rapiers and boarding-pikes. With my sea-leems at my back we went through the defense and roared out onto the quarterdeck. In a few murs we had taken the ship. We battened the crew below and left a small prize crew and then it was back to the benches and more of that straining, lung-bursting heaving at the oars with the whole body flung backward to drag the blades through the resisting water. We took another argenter, and then avoided the deadly thrust of a Menaham sword-ship, and raked her all along her side so that our cat head pulped her oars even as our own rowers shipped theirs.

For the rest of the day we were engaged in chasing Menaham shipping and taking or sinking everything that flew the diagonal blue and green flag.

By the time the Maiden with the Many Smiles floated into the night sky and Inch wound a great turban around his fair hair, we were masters of the sea.

"And this is the great victory you promised, Dray!" cried Viridia, flushed, dripping blood, her gaudy clothes ripped and slashed away to reveal the mesh link armor clothing her firm body.

"Only a part, Viridia, only a part. Now we must land in Pomdermam!"

When we had invested the treasures of *Freedom* after we had taken the swordship, I had found, safely wrapped in tissue in great lenken chests in the aft stateroom, a great quantity of armor. Remember that *Freedom* had been a Yumapanim vessel and the Yumapanim aped the ways of old Loh, so the armor was of that refined and decorated kind I had worn when fighting for Queen Lilah of Hiclantung. Now I stripped it off, chipped and dented and blood-smeared as it was, and let it drop to the deck. I hung my rapier on a hook on the bulkhead. I was tired, but no more tired than I have been a thousand times in my life. Viridia stared at me, her eyes unreadable.

"Tomorrow, Viridia the Render, or the day after, we land at Pomdermam. After that we drive The Bloody Menaham back to their own frontiers — or beyond — or kill them all. I do not care which."

She said, "Why do I do this for you, Dray? Why do the renders of the islands follow you in such desperate ventures?"

"Plunder."

"Aye. That — and more."

I knew the fragility of the links that bound the renders to my schemes. They were pirates. They would seek always easy victims. They must be cajoled into following me against the army of Menaham. But they would follow me. I was determined on that.

"Once the renders are let loose in The Bloody Menaham, Viridia, I believe they will find ample reward."

She cocked her head on one side. "And why shouldn't we rend the Tombo-ramin?"

"Because, if you do, yours would be the first head to adorn a spike over the walls of Pomdermam!"

Because the bountiful and marvelous paline grows everywhere it possibly can on Kregen, it follows there must be different varieties, generally distinguishable by slight variations in the yellow of the fruit. A Kregan could tell you where a paline had grown by the color, and I was already picking up the knack. There are two main sorts, divided into those that grow their fruit on the old growth and those that grow it on the new, and it is of the latter variety that one may pluck a paline branch and sling it over one's shoulder for the journey. It is a nice custom of seafarers to take a pot-plant paline with them, hoping their water will hold out, and there was a wondrous specimen aboard *Freedom*. Now Viridia plucked a paline and set it between her teeth, and crunched, and sucked juice.

"You wouldn't, would you, Dray?"

"Don't try me, girl."

With that she gave her reckless laugh and began to strip off her oiled steel mesh which was as befouled as my own armor. I sent her out into an adjoining cabin, for the sword-ship was marvelously well-off for accommodation in her after-parts, if the men slept wrapped in furs and silks between the rowing benches and on the central gangway. Watches were set with a naval efficiency I saw was strictly kept.

From the Island of Panderk in a straight line to Pomdermam is about a hundred dwaburs, and what with the gale and the battle I figured on our making landfall the day after next. Some of the render captains had taken their prizes and gone roaring it back to the islands; but I was gratified to note that many still followed me, and their sails made a brave show against the brilliant sea and sky.

The first sight of Pomdermam, as is so often the case with any port of Kregen, is always the pharos. At Pomdermam there are two, one maintained by the government, the other by the Todalpheme of Pomdermam. These Todalpheme, the mystic mathematicians and philosophers of the oceans of Kregen, calculate the tidal effects and issue almanacs to give warning of impending high tides. The Todalpheme of Pomdermam wore purple tassels. Since the Hostile Territories through which I had traveled had no seaboards, there had been no Todalpheme there for me to ask: "Do you know of the scarlet-roped Todalpheme? Do you know of Aphrasöe?" That had been one of my first questions when Tilda, Pando, Inch, and I had stayed here. A shake of head was sufficient answer — sufficient! Sufficient disappointment.

I directed the course of our armada into a little cove someway to the west of the city. Although Kregen possesses a larger landmass than does Earth, there are fewer people, which is pleasant from the point of view of breathing space. No one as far as we could ascertain observed our swordships as they plummeted their anchors into the smooth water of the cove and the captains and the crews rowed ashore. I held a meeting; it was more an order group. I specifically ruled out any form of council of war. I do not, in general, believe in those.

"You render captains of the islands! You have fought well. You have sailed through a storm that would sink a sea-barynth. You have some wealth. Now we go up against The Bloody Menaham, and the booty will be enormous." I glared around on them, speaking from my perch atop a boulder. "If any one of you from Menaham wishes to pull out, that I understand. He is free to go, he and all his crew."

No one moved.

"Very well. We take the Menaham in the flank. They will not expect us — they think an army is coming to aid them across the sea instead of you shaggy sea-leems!"

There rose a gust of laughter at this. By Kregan standards that was a jest of high carat value.

So we set off, marching for we had no mounts, heading for Pomdermam. We were a motley bunch. Men and half-men of many races marched in that straggly army. But one thing we shared in common. We were all warriors of the first rank.

In the event we did not take the army of The Bloody Menaham in the flank.

We struck them from the rear.

They were engaged in storming the city and tearing down the walls and setting fire to the houses. The Tomboramin had fought well and stubbornly, but they were overwhelmed and beaten back. We saw the smoke and flames as we charged in. Everywhere the diagonal blue and green waved the renders charged like sea devils. Rapiers thrust and slashed. Boarding-pikes skewered past up-raised arms. Our bowmen sleeted their feathered death into the ranks of our foemen. For the Tomboramin this last-minute rescue was unbelievable.

Through all those wild scenes of carnage I fought at the head of my men, my loyals about me, driving on wedgelike into the enemy ranks. Above our heads floated my flag, the brave yellow cross on the field of scarlet. Viridia fought at my side. Inch and his incredible ax were there, striking and smiting. Valka, with a rapier like a blur of steel, thrust with me, thrust for thrust. Spitz and his bowmen cleared the path. Onward we drove and soon — very soon, to the destruction of the Menaham — we had them on the run and they were fleeing and we were looking about for booty.

"Touch nothing of the Tomboramin," I had told my render captains. "Any man found looting will be hanged." I remembered Wellington and his ways. "When we strike Menaham they will yield all the plunder you can imagine, for their armies will have been destroyed. The whole country will be yours." In that, I remembered Napoleon.

A stubborn knot of fiercely resisting Menaham cavalry still clustered about the palace of King Nemo. Their zorcas were down and they fought afoot, and they fought savagely and well. With perilously few men left to me I led the final charge upon them, driving into them, with the yellow cross on scarlet biting into the ranks of diagonal blue and green.

"That flag of yours leads men on!" panted Viridia as we hacked and hewed together. The cavalry wore armor, and we were making heavy weather of it. But, as though, indeed, that flag did lure men on to victory, we poured over a shattered breach and ravened in among the Menaham. Now, we could thrust with care, aiming to drive our blades between the armor joints.

"Follow the flag!" screamed Viridia. She had flung down her rapier and now gripped the flagpole, the shaft all bloody in her fingers. The yellow and scarlet flamed above us. "It is superb! Superb! On! On! Jikai! Jikai!"

Following that magnificent girl with her flaring dark hair and her steel-mesh clad figure waving the flag aloft the men bellowed over the last of the Menaham cavalry. Now were left only those who had run into the palace, ready, like cornered cramphs, to fight and die.

"She is superb!" grunted Inch, flicking blood drops from his ax.

"Aye!" said Valka, waving his rapier. "And so is the flag!"

We raced up the marble stairs, hurdling the dead bodies, and so came into King Nemo's palace.

As I had known I would, I found Murlock Marsilus.

Viridia, gripping the flag in her bloodied left hand, her right now wielding a fresh snatched-up rapier, used her booted foot on a double folding door, kicking it open with a crash. Spitz feathered three shafts into the room and then Inch and I leaped in. Half a dozen Menaham gathered there, three with Spitz's blue-feathered shafts in them. The other three went down before Inch, Valka and me. Then I saw the tableau in the adjoining room, clearly visible through flung open drapes.

Murlock was there, gripping a rapier, about to drive it down into Pando's back as he clutched his mother about the waist.

Tilda faced Murlock bravely. She swung a wine bottle at his head, reeling, and with a savage laugh Murlock smashed it away. But the diversion had been enough. He heard our entrance and swung about — and I reversed my rapier, hefted it, balanced, and hurled it as I had hurled javelins with my clansmen on the great plains of Segesthes.

The rapier flew true.

Murlock screamed, and the scream was choked off as my rapier transfixed his neck. He stood for an instant, staring, his face as horrible a mask of hatred and disbelief as any I have seen. Then he fell.

Tilda and Pando, with wild and abandoned shrieks, flew across the room, through the drapes, and flung themselves into my arms, all bloody as they were.

"Dray! Dray!" they babbled, grasping me. "Dray Prescot! You have come back to us!"

Viridia, all blood-smeared, grasping that old flag of mine, stared at me. Her tanned face with the dark hair flowing contrasted with the classical ivory beauty of Tilda and her jetty mane of gorgeous hair. Pando was gripping me and sobbing convulsively.

"So," said Viridia. "This is what you tricked me and my renders into! A woman and her brat! It was all for this that you schemed and fought!"

"Not so, Viridia the Render. This is Pando, Kov of Bormark. And this is Tilda, his mother, the Kovneva. They are my friends, and if you are my friend and comrade, then they are your friends, also. Do not forget that. As for me, my destiny lies elsewhere."

"Do not say it, Dray!" sobbed Tilda, grasping me, as Viridia stared at me with her wide blue eyes all aglitter from the samphron oil lamps' gleam. "Say you will not go to Vallia."

"Vallia!" said Viridia. "What is this of Vallia, Dray Prescot, render?"

I felt the cold anger in me, the desire to turn and smash everything in sight. Not for this petty wrangling had I risked all and turned my back on Vallia and my Delia, my Delia of the Blue Mountains!

"Vallia is where I am going, Viridia. And neither you nor Tilda can stop me." I lifted Pando up. He wore his old zhantil-hide tunic and belt, and I marveled. Tilda's long blue gown was torn over one shoulder, and an ivory globe and collarbone showed, gleaming, alluring, even there, in those circumstances. "Pando. You will stop all this nonsense of going to war, and fighting for pleasure. You are a Kov. You must rule your people wisely and well, and you must listen to your mother and to Inch. Otherwise I shall strap your backside. As for you, Tilda. You must smash the bottles of Jholaix. Pando needs guidance. You must listen to Inch. He knows my views."

If that sounds pompous, tyrannical, banal, blame yourself, not me. I spoke truths. Truths were needed then; for I could hardly hold myself under control. Vallia! Delia! The need for her flamed in my blood, drugged me with desire. Too long had I betrayed her, and dillydallied with renders and Kovs and all the petty glory of sailing a swordship sea under my old flag.

"You — will not desert us, Dray?" Tilda tried to wipe away the tears staining her cheeks. Her eyes rested on me in a new glory, and I knew that if I stayed I would now have the same trouble with her as I had with Viridia.

As for that pirate wench, she stood with my old flag draping her shoulders, her rapier all bloody, glaring at me.

"And if you go to Vallia, Dray Prescot the Render, what is to prevent me from going, also?"

I sighed. I tried to speak calmly.

"There is nothing but heartbreak for you in Vallia, Viridia."

"And is she so much more beautiful, more desirable than me, Dray?"

"Or me?" demanded Tilda passionately.

There was no answer that a gentleman might make, and although I am no gentleman, although a Krozair of Zy, I could make no answer, either. But my silence told them both. The moment held, awkwardly.

Then Pando broke it. He struggled free, wiping blood from my armor caught tackily on his hands down that zhantil tunic.

"And would you beat me, Dray?"

Then I laughed.

"I would flog you, Pando, you imp of Sicce, if you did not behave like a true Kov and have a care for your people of Bormark! Aye, flog you until you sobbed for mercy!"

Before Pando could answer the chamber filled with the pirates who had followed me here. They crowded in, forming a great excited mass of milling men and glittering steel about me. Arkhebi, his red hair all tousled, shouted the words, words taken up by the others in a flashing of lifted rapiers.

"Hai, Jikai! Dray Prescot! Hai! Jikai! Jikai!"

Well, they were happy in the knowledge that immense plunder awaited them in Menaham. I listened to the uproar, and that slit between my lips widened a trifle, hurtfully.

That glorious mingled sunshine of Antares flooded in from the tall windows to lie across the rich trappings, the colors, the steel of blade and armor, the flushed excited faces, the blood. The samphron oil lamps blinked dim. Someone had thrown back the shutters from the windows and all the opaz glory of the Suns of Scorpio poured in.

I looked through the windows into that bright dazzlement and saw a giant raptor, its scarlet and golden feathers brilliant in the streaming mingled light of the twin suns.

And coldness touched my heart.

Jerkily, moving with the stiffness of rheumatic old-age, I pushed through the shouting exultant renders, entered a small side room. I was vaguely conscious of Viridia and Tilda following me, suddenly anxious, but if they spoke I did not hear what they said. Behind them, I guessed, Inch and Valka and Spitz would be treading on fast, and Pando would be working his way through to catch me.

I felt dizzy.

Then — how I recall that moment of horror, of despair! — across that empty room before me I saw the scuttling running form of a scorpion.

A scorpion!

I knew, then...

I was to be returned to Earth, banished from Kregen beneath Antares, hurled back contemptuously to the planet of my birth.

As that cursed blue radiance limned all my vision and the sensations of falling clawed at my limbs, my body, my brain, I cried out, high, desperately, frantically.

"Remember me, remember Dray Prescot!"

And when I tried to shout my defiance of the Star Lords, and of the Savanti, who were so callously flinging me back to Earth, and to scream that I would not return to Earth, that I would stay on Kregen, no sound issued from my rigid lips.

The blueness grew.

It took on the semblance of a gigantic blue-glowing scorpion.

I was falling.

In my mind, unuttered, tearing and bursting with passion, I screamed: "Delia! My Delia of Delphond! My Delia of the Blue Mountains! I will come back! I will come back! Delia, I will return!"

I would return.

Prince of Scorpio

One

I bid Happy Swinging to Alex Hunter

I, Dray Prescot, of Earth and of Kregen, once more trod the beautiful and brutal planet of my adoption, and in the engaging way of the Star Lords who had brought me here, was faced instantly with headlong action and deadly danger.

A bulky man in black leathers ran full tilt upon me, seeking to pin me to the ground with his rapier. The slender blade glistened redly in the mingled light from the twin suns of Scorpio. I do not argue when a man tries to kill me.

The guttural shouts and hoarse screams in my ears, the flickering impression of frenzied action all about me, and the black galvanic forms of men contorted in violent conflict running and stabbing and caught up in a confused melee washed around me; but the burly man with the bushy brown moustaches and the eyes of a killer lunged down fiercely upon me.

I rolled.

He cursed and dragged his blade free of the thin earth that dribbled over bare rock, swung himself forward for another essay at mounting me like a butterfly in a glass case.

Nothing else mattered in the world — either this world or the world of Earth distant four hundred light-years — beside that professional killer and his blade.

"You panval cramph!" he said as he advanced, with a little more wariness this time, a trifle of cunning evident in his clear wish to spit me as I rolled.

I shoved up on my hands, getting my feet under me, not rising on hands and knees. I was, as always when I landed on Kregen, stark naked. There were no handy weapons — a sword, a spear, a helmet — just me, Dray Prescot, naked as the day I was born.

A shrieking man ran past, his matted hair streaming, pursued by another of the killers in his black leather uniform. This screaming wretch, too, was naked, and so I reasoned that no one was surprised at my absence of clothes.

"Rast of a panval!" The killer lunged and I sprang, attempting to slip beneath the blade and so grasp him in my arms and break his back.

But he was quick. He eluded me, and a line of bright red wealed up along my thigh.

Now it was my turn to curse.

Normally I never bother to shout and curse when in action; it wastes breath and I do not need my morale boosted in this way.

"By the Black Chunkrah!" I yelled. "I'll take your Makki-Grodno infested tripes out and wrap them around your diseased neck!"

He was coming in again as I shouted and he looked at my face. He hadn't bothered to look before; all slaves look alike to their indifferent guards. Now he looked. He checked. He faltered in his attack in so obvious a way that I knew I was wearing that old ugly powerful look, the facial expression men say gives me the look of the devil, and I did not waste my chance.

I fended off with my left hand and sent his rapier skewering empty air skyward. I took his throat in my right hand and squeezed, then I brought my left fist down and around and under and hit him in the belly.

He would have shrieked, but no air could get past my constricting fingers.

He wriggled and flailed and tried to shorten his blade to stab me in the back, but I glared into his eyes with what I know is a wild and maniacal stare habitual to me when someone is trying to kill me, and I choked him and flung him down like a harvested sheaf of grain. I took his rapier. His left-hand dagger swung still at his waist; of what need had he of main-gauche against an unarmed slave?

With the weapons in my fists I sprang up, and at a half-crouch, ready for the next fool to show up, I surveyed the scene.

The bare rocks, with their thin scattering of dirt cover in which straggly beach-grasses and thorn-ivy struggled to grow here and there, led down to a shaly beach. Scattered along the beach an enormous mass of timbers, bales, bundles, ropes, and spars indicated a shipwreck. At first I thought the naked, screaming running men and women had been oar-slaves, but what was left of the vessel did not match my knowledge either of a swifter of the Eye of the World or a swordship of the Sunset Sea.

A fellow rolling with muscle, vociferous, authoritarian, yelled and waved his rapier. "Round 'em all up, you calsanys! Every last one of the Pandrite-benighted panvals."

Like the other guards he was clad in black leathers, and tall black boots. Like them he wore beneath the leather tunic a garment whose sleeves covered his arms with bands of red and black. He wore a helmet, narrow-brimmed at the sides and curled up at the fore and aft brim, after the fashion of a morion. His face was congested, bloated, full of annoyance that his command had broken down in what to him was clearly a most messy business.

I looked at the sea — to me, then, an unknown sea — and felt the deep longing for the fresh sweep of the breeze and the clean feel of a keel beneath me scudding through the waves. Then I advanced on this man, this leader of men who slaughtered unarmed men and women as they shrieked and begged for mercy.

The jagged boulders beneath my feet felt decidedly uncomfortable after my sojourn on Earth wearing decent shoes, but I have spent most of my life barefoot, and I took little notice. The Star Lords, this time, evidently had asked a very great deal of me. As always I had been dumped down on Kregen naked and defenseless, and as always a crisis situation was presented to me. This time I had been flung headfirst right slap into the middle of the action.

I jumped down off the rocks onto the beach and for a moment the big ruffian was hidden from me by contorting bodies. A girl screamed right at my feet and I looked down and to my left. She sprawled on the shaly beach, and I saw that the chains between the fetters on her ankles had tripped and brought her down. A black-clad guard was quite callously, quite intentionally, preparing to drive his rapier through her stomach.

I bent and with the main-gauche slewed a scatter of the shale into his face. He cursed and sprang back. He saw me. His main-gauche came out with the practiced ease of the fighting-man, and I knew I would have to take him first.

He tried to circle me. That was a waste of time — of my time, for his was going to finish here and now.

A second guard ran across with a four-foot-long javelin and hurled it at me. I swayed and the missile hissed past. The second drew both his blades. The girl lay, staring up with wide eyes; fear had drugged her emotions, so that she could no longer weep or cry out.

I wanted to get over this fight quickly. There were well over a hundred naked men and women in chains, and something like fifteen or twenty guards methodically butchering them. The two split up, to take me from left and right.

I have fought many times, and no doubt will fight many more times. These two were fair to middling examples of rapier men, which meant that, combined, they added up to a combination that could always take the better single man. I just had to be better than both.

They both succumbed, one after the other, to timed thrusts.

The shipwreck, the black shale beach, the susurrations of that unknown sea, the black rocks, and the evil thorn-ivy bushes coalesced into the backdrop for wild action and devilish murder. I dispatched two more guards. I could hear a roaring and a raging nearer the scattered timbers of the wreck and I ran toward the focus of the sounds, dropping another guard as I ran.

On the beach the big bull-roarer of a guard captain was down. He sat on the black shale looking stupidly at the stump of his left arm. The red and black sleeved arm lay on the ground at his side, still with the hand clutching his dagger.

Three other guards were backtracking rapidly. I looked at the man facing them, and I felt a painful and thrilling thump of blood from my heart tingle all through my body.

Oh, yes, I recognized who that young man must be!

Fair and open of face, with smooth blond hair, and eyes of an icy-blue, he fought with a grace and a delicacy that warmed my heart. Young, strong, confident, bold, he weaved a net of glittering steel before him, and, one, two, three, down went those guards, gouting blood.

He wore soft leathers cincturing his waist and drawn up between his legs, the whole held in position by a wide belt the buckle of which gleamed dully gold. On his left arm he wore a stout leather bracer. He wore soft leather gloves. On his feet he wore leather hunting boots. I had worn that gear once, myself, in the long ago...

And his sword...

Oh, yes, I felt all the strife and evil of two worlds flowing out and away from me and the beginnings of a new and altogether glorious promise. Here, before me, was my passport to paradise!

"Hai!" shouted this gallant young man, and he charged headlong for a group of guards who withdrew their reeking blades from the corpses of their victims and sprang up to face him.

Before me, half crouched on the beach, a naked man clasped a woman close, the black iron of their chains harsh against their skin. They were middle-aged, with faces lined with care, and yet for all that, the man could look up at the young man with eyes wide with wonder.

"Now in the name of the twins! Where did he come from?"

"Hush, Jeniu, hush!" His wife dragged him down into the black shale, burrowing for shelter.

I jumped over them, and because it seemed the right thing to do, as I leaped I shouted down to them.

"Remain quiet and you will be safe."

"Opaz the all-glorious preserve us!"

So far I had seen no beings other than humans among these guards and the slaves they were butchering to prevent their escape. There were no representatives of the half-men half-beasts of Kregen, those other races of intelligent beings who share the planet with human men and women.

The young man — I had the fleeting wonder if he might not also come from the planet Earth — had engaged nobly with the guards, and in pressing them back, was displaying fine swordsmanship. As I fought, indeed, as I do almost anything, I kept a weather eye open and alert. If a fighting-man sought to leap on me from the rear he more often than not found me suddenly facing him with a naked brand in my fist.

If you tread dangerous paths that is an essential to staying alive — on Earth as on Kregen.

So it was that I had to stop twice more to deal with inopportunely-pressing men in black leather, with their red and black sleeves, and their morionlike helmets. I observed a naked man, with a shaggy mop of brown hair and brown hair on his body so that he resembled a great brown bear, wrapping his chains about the neck of a guard and apparently on the point of severing head from body. This huge man, as thick in the chest as the barrels in which palines are shipped for sea use, roared his delight. I saw the suns-light glisten and gleam along the hairy muscles of his forearms as he leaned back. He saw me as I stepped outside a guard's lunge, dazzle him with what — I confess — was a flamboyant flourish of my dagger, and bring the rapier in for the terminal thrust; and Brown Bear yelled, hugely delighted. "Hai, Jikai!"

"Hai, Jikai!" I roared back. "We will finish them all very soon — and then I will strike off your irons."

"Not until I am done with using them. Never, by Vaosh, would I have believed I could love my chains so much! Ha!"

All over the beach and the soil-covered rocks just above, the bodies of slain men and women sprawled. But many more had reached some kind of sanctuary among the rocks, and among the dead lay many more guards than any of the escaping slaves had any right to expect. Brown Bear had accounted for his share, and I, mine — and this glorious youngster to whose aid I now sprang had fought right well and nobly.

Perhaps he was too noble; certainly, for all his skill and training he lacked experience. Twice I had dodged flung javelins. I saw it all. I shouted — uselessly, vainly, stupidly. There was nothing else I could do but shout and hurl my dagger; but long before the dagger found its mark in the javelin-thrower's throat, the cruel steel head of the flung spear smashed bloodily red out through the chest of the gallant young fighter.

It is not easy for me to speak of that moment. I can clearly remember that sharp steel javelin-head sprouting from the lad's chest. I can recall with exact clarity the way the twin streaming mingled light of Zim and Genodras cast sharp ugly shadows down over the muscles of his chest and the smooth tanned stomach, before he doubled up and fell sideways, drew his legs in, and began to cough up blood.

After that my next memory is of drawing my rapier from the leather-clad body of a guard, and looking around for more, and finding them all lying dead in the abandoned postures of complete destruction along the beach. Evidently, at the end, they had tried to flee from me.

I looked back up the beach.

A small clump of naked men and women had gathered, and more were creeping out from their hiding places among the rocks and boulders and thorn-ivy bushes.

The huge brown bear of a man stood a little way in front.

All stared at me.

None would approach.

I ignored them.

I went back to the dying youngster.

He lay still on his side, for the javelin prevented him lying in another posture. He was conscious and his eyes followed me as I approached. Those blue eyes were still bright and brilliant, but the face had drained of blood.

"Llahal, Jikai," he said painfully, dribbling blood. "You fight right merrily."

I did not reply with the rolling double-L of the nonfamiliar greeting of "Llahal" of Kregen; instead I said: "Lahal," which is used only to those one knows.

He looked surprised, but his weakness made him incurious and unable to ponder the matter overlong. I knelt by his side. There was nothing material I could do for him.

I looked at him, and I waited until I felt a light of intelligence in those eyes, struggling up past the engulfing waves of blackness seeking to drag him down forever.

I spoke.

"Happy Swinging," I said. My voice was not my own; it was hoarse, strange, harsh. "Happy Swinging."

He looked at me with the same shock his face had shown when the javelin pierced him through.

"Happy Swinging—"

"Tell me, dom. Where lies Aphrasöe, the Swinging City?"

He coughed and blood dribbled from his mouth, for he was almost gone.

"Aphrasöe!" He tried to move and could not. "I was there — there in Aphrasöe — only moments ago. I talked with Maspero and bid him Rembaree — and then I was here. And—"

"Maspero is my friend. He was my tutor. Where lies Aphrasöe?"

The cords in his throat moved and shuddered, and I saw he was trying to shake his head. His voice was faint.

"I do not know. The transition was made — cold and darkness — and then — here..."

I had to know where Aphrasöe, the Swinging City, was situated on the planet of Kregen. Next to my concern for my Delia, Delia of Delphond, Delia of the Blue Mountains, next to my love for her, I must know the whereabouts of Aphrasöe. For Aphrasöe was paradise.

He was trying to speak again.

"Tell Maspero — tell him — Alex Hunter tried — tried—"

"Rest easy, Alex Hunter. You have come a long way from Earth, but now you are with friends."

He looked up into my ugly face with its gargoyle-look strong upon it, and the bright blueness of his eyes faded and he sighed, very softly. His blood-smeared mouth smiled — he smiled, looking upon me, Dray Prescot — and then he died.

I stood up.

I turned to face the gathered naked people.

"Are any guards left alive?" I called. My voice rose harshly, bitter and cutting.

The big brown bear of a man shouted back. "They are all dead."

I nodded.

"As well for them they are. By dying they escape my wrath."

Then I turned and looked out to that unknown sea and I did not weep. For many memories had poured upon me and I could face no one until I had purged myself of weakness.

Two

Sweet and refreshing is canalwater of Vallia

The released prisoners wanted to build the cooking fires into conflagrations of joy, and I had to explain to them as gently as I could — and, Zair knows, I am a gentle enough man when the occasion calls for it — that as no one of them knew where we were, and I did not, the night would almost certainly contain hostile eyes. We must cook our supper carefully, and post watches, and be ready with the gathered-up weapons to defend our newly-won freedom.

They all seemed to think I had been in the prison ship with them. On her way to the Penal Islands, a gale had driven her off course. No one knew where we were — but they all knew from whence they had come.

Vallia!

I was on an island off the southeast coast of Vallia. Somewhere over that sea lay the island empire ruled by the despotic father of my beloved. Over there lay my target, Vallia, the island I had vowed to reach and storm, bare-handed if necessary, and claim my Delia before all the world.

524

Prosaic matters obtruded themselves now, however. The released prisoners were far too weak to march, and we had espied not a sign of life or a habitation of any sort. The prisoners could not march; I could not stay here.

The big brown bear of a man — Borg — said, when I queried him: "Prisoners, dom? Aye, we are prisoners, truly enough. Politicals."

At a guess, I said, "The Racter party?"

He glowered. "Aye! The racters, may Gurush of the Bottomless Marsh take them all."

I have spoken of the Racter party, those great lords, landowners, and wealthy tycoons who were bitterly opposed to the wedding between myself and Delia. These people were almost all of the Panval party, a more popular front, although containing many folk, I suspected, who had joined together in mere opposition to the ractors as through any common ideology.

Borg was a canalman. The canals of Vallia are one of the wonders of Kregen, spreading out over the entire island, fed by the awe-inspiring Mountains of the North, which have various names in their various districts. The canalfolk are a people apart and a way of life apart. Borg's name was Ven Borg nal Ogier. *Ven* is a title applicable only to canalmen, as *Vena* for the canalwomen. Ogier was his canal, the Ogier Cut, from which he took his patronymic. That the canal was upward of six hundred miles long, with many branches and loops, spreading across many counties of Vallia, meant nothing. Mere land area was of no account to a canalman; he marked out his lineage in the canal his parents traversed.

"I shall go and find help," I told Borg. "These people must be cared for."

He had taken a guard's leather tunic, but his arms and legs were bare. He carried the rapier and left-handed dagger as though he knew how to use them. He nodded in agreement.

"Good. Then, Koter Drak, I will come with you."

Koter is pure Vallian, equivalent to our Earthly "mister."

"No, Ven Borg. If you will, you would do best to look after these people. And without disrespect to you, I can travel faster alone."

He glowered at me, and fingered the plain steel hilt of the rapier, but he saw my face, and agreed.

"By Vaosh the all-glorious! You are a hard man."

"Sometimes I have need to be."

My feelings after Alex Hunter had died revealed another facet, but I would not discuss that. The thought occurred to me to wonder if the Star Lords had brought me here because they knew Alex Hunter would fail? But that would indicate a prophecy, a power to foretell what would happen. I put nothing past the Star Lords in those days, but the idea made me prickle a little up the backbone. Then the further thought came to me that the Savanti had sent Alex Hunter on a mission similar to those I would have been sent on had I passed all the stringent tests of Aphrasöe, instead of having the Savanti boot me out of paradise. I still bore them no ill will for that. They had their nature as I had mine. Whatever the truth of the business, I was here on Kregen and — given I could avoid too obvious a collision with either the Savanti or the Star Lords — here I intended to stay and reach Vallia and claim Delia as my bride.

And such was my mood, I was beginning to feel to hell with her father.

So far, the thought that I must in some measure demean him in her eyes had halted me, had checked my footsteps, had held me back from the headlong rush to Vallia and the arrogant barging into Vondium I knew I would have, one day, to make.

I gently unwrapped and unstrapped Alex Hunter's Savanti hunting leathers from him, before I buried him with solemnity and two prayers. Then I washed the leathers in a stream of clear water — how marvelously supple is the hunting leather of the city of Aphrasöe! — and donned them, pulling the end up through my legs and buckling up the wide belt. I hesitated before pulling on the boots, but I might need them if the going became rough. After my march across the Owlarh Waste and through the Klackadrin I felt my foot soles could march across hell without flinching.

And the sword.

The Savanti sword!

It was a beautiful specimen, with that subtle straight blade that in some alchemical way combines all the best features of a rapier's flexibility with a shortsword's harsh thrusting action, together with the slashing capabilities of a broadsword. I felt, then, handling that superlative weapon with its basket hilt, that even a Krozair longsword could not compare with the Savanti sword. I suppose, in mundane weapons, it most resembled an English basket-hilted sword of about 1610 with that cunning Savanti curve to the hilt to enable rapier work to be put in. The blade retained a brilliant sharpness of edge without continuous honing. I had no conception of how it could be done, then, and even today I am sure that no metallurgists of Earth could reproduce that exact mix of metals, that fantastic alloy. But then, as I knew to my cost, the Savanti, although mere mortal men, were capable of superhuman powers.

"Well, Koter Drak," said Borg, proffering a rapier and left-handed dagger. "You had best go prepared."

I slung the baldric of the Savanti scabbard over my right shoulder and let the sword dangle at my left hip. "I will take this sword, Ven Borg."

"It is a strange blade, and yet a useful one, as I judge."

I took the baldric off. I had grown accustomed to having my sword scabbards attached to my belt in such a way that all my upper body was free from strappery. I fabricated a sling, and the lockets would serve. Borg watched me, critically.

"On the canals we use the rapier and the dagger, the Jiktar and the Hikdar, but rarely, they being weapons not easily come by."

"You have used them before, Ven Borg."

He chuckled. The camp fire threw his mass of brown hair into deep tangled shadows across his face. He bit hugely into the thigh of a bosk — a rather less stupid and smaller relative of the vosk — from the provisions we had taken from the wreck. "Aye. I was accounted a fair swordsman, along the Ogier Cut, Koter Drak."

I was not absolutely sure how these people had my name as Drak. Drak is the name of a legendary figure, part-human, part-god, who figures largely in the three-thousand-year-old myth-cycle the *Canticles of the Rose City*. Culture is widespread on Kregen, and the old legends and stories travel the world, and are repeated over and over again. Also, Drak had been the name of the Emperor's father when he ascended the throne. I had a dim memory of saying, in response to a query, "I am Dra—" and then of a shout or a scream interrupting me. I believe it was the women called the Theladours; they had found a guard half alive, and had finished him off with their hands. Anyway, the beginning of *Dray* and the instant associations with *Drak* had named me. I did not care, then, what they called me, for I intended to leave them in the morning when the twin suns rose, and after finding help for them, see about taking myself across the stretch of sea to Vallia to the west.

Also, I did not fail to realize that the continent of Segesthes, and the enclave city of Zenicce, lay across the Sunset Sea to the east. In Zenicce stood my own proud enclave of Strombor. I was the Lord of Strombor. But Strombor and all my friends there would have to wait — as they had waited for years — until I had won my Delia finally.

From the shattered remnants of the wrecked prison ship we took what we could of food and wine and I saw that the survivors, about a hundred and twenty or so of them, men and women, would not suffer from starvation before help could reach them. For what Borg said, I judged that he would be very careful how they accepted help; for as political prisoners their fate would depend much on the tendencies of their rescuers.

The political situation in Vallia was complex and finely balanced, the racters and the panvals in their eternal struggling for power, the Emperor now strong, now weak, eternally seeking help from one side, now the other, always asserting his own power and demanding absolute obedience from the citizenry. To hell with all that! Vallia, Vondium, and Delia!

Much banging and ringing of iron finally fell quiet and the last of the fetters had been cut off. I found a snug hole down between two boulders, and with a scrap of cloth from the ship to serve as padding and cover, went to sleep. On the morrow, after a great dish of fried bosk rashers and a jar of some sweet rose wine — a vintage of western Vallia, so Jeniu told me — I was ready to leave.

They waved to me as I set off. They were a starveling crew, eating properly for the first time in many a day, their nakedness covered as best they could manage. I waved back, and I confess, to my shame, that I scarcely thought more of them except as people to whom I owed the duty of what help I could give. Beyond that — Delia!

"Remberee, Koter Drak!"

"Remberee," I shouted back, striding on. "Remberee!"

Many times I have marched through country completely new to me, alone or with companions. Memories ghosted up — but I would not think of them now. I studied the land critically. It looked bleak, bare, somehow tired and dispirited. Clumps of thorn-ivy grew along the way and, a dismal prospect on Kregen, no palines. No palines! Not a country for me, I decided, and thereby, as you will hear, made a stultifying mistake.

The Suns of Scorpio cast down their opaz beams and the weather, although warm, was in no wise stifling. If what the prisoners had told me was true — and their ideas of where we might be were almost as chancy as mine — we must be on a latitude sixty or seventy dwaburs north of the southern coast of Vallia. That, as far as I could judge, would be on a latitude about the same distance south of Zenicce.

I marched on and soon I walked through the remains of a village. The houses had been constructed of wood, and they had burned. There were bones among the ashes. The sad relics of an abandoned living-site passed to either side as I walked through what had once been a bustling main street. No birds waited to scavenge. This had happened some time ago, for the dusty vegetation was creeping back.

The prospect opened up beyond this dismal scene and hills closed in on my left, so that I walked for a space beside a stream. Here vegetation had taken a hold and I saw many varieties of the myriad growths that flourish so freely on Kregen. Here, too, I came across paline bushes and so could pick a handful and munch them as I traveled.

Far away on my right and ahead, obscured occasionally by cloud and by intervening rises, the tall blue outlines of mountains jagged against the sky. Snow glistened on their peaks, so they were of a size. The forests thickened, and I saw lenk and sturm, an occasional sporfert, and many trees of secondary growths that are common both to Earth and Kregen. Grass grew more lushly — and then I walked out upon a great clearing where the neat rows of samphron bushes lay all untended, where the crops had ripened and seeded and rotted, and where I saw a small village laid waste, burned, destroyed, abandoned.

I began to wonder if I would ever find succor for the prisoner survivors here in this desolate land.

The way I followed had seemed to me to mark itself out by its contours as a track and when this wended into a valley and ran side by side with a sheet of water, I felt certain I trod a dirt-packed way that once had been a highroad. Now grass and weeds thrust through, worts, ragbladders, creeping vines, and here and there the banks had slipped into the water. At the far end of the lake I came across a lock. Its wooden gates were closed, and I was downstream. It was such a lock as I was perfectly accustomed to back home on Earth. The navigators had made of the country a different place, and the genius that had put the lock to work, so that narrow boats and barges might rise and fall through mountains, had laid the foundations for the Industrial Revolution.

Dangling over the lock gates a yellowing skeleton brought me sharply back to Kregen.

Wedged in the skeleton's backbone was an arrow.

I studied it. Knowledge of one's opponent's weapons is a psychological knowledge of him, as I have said before.

This arrow had not been loosed from a Lohvian longbow. It was shorter; the point was, although of steel, merely an arrow-shaped barbed wedge. The feathers, bedraggled, were not, to my mind, set by a master-fletcher. They were red and black.

Red and black had been the colors of the prison guards' sleeves.

I left the arrow where it was, and saluting the skeleton's departed spirit — what some Kregans call the *ib* — I passed on.

That night I had to face a decision. I could not cross the stretch of water and reach Vallia to the west without a boat, and to find a boat I needed help. But I had also my duty to the prisoners, prisoners no more, although for how long they would retain their freedom I did not care to speculate. If I circled — then I faced facts. This land had been raided dry. Slavers had done this. Their handiwork is all too plain. I must press on, look for the lay of the land where it was likely to find habitation, and then see about a boat.

The next day I swung a little more to the west, leaving the canal. I found only scorched earth and moldering skeletons. I wended back to the east, crossed the canal, and pressed on through woodlands and open spaces where great fires had raged and the growth was only just beginning to sprout through. This was hard going.

On the third day I came across a fine metal road. Oh, it was no road of Imperial Loh of ancient times, but it was easy to walk on. I felt absolute certainty that there was no other person near me; long before I suspected I was approaching humanity I would be off the road and into the trees.

The road struck off due east.

This was taking me away from the coast, and I must perforce accept that annoyance, for I now saw that this land had been struck by raiders from the sea who had ravaged the coastal belt clean. I suspected these signs of destruction were more than two seasons old, and the still-dangling skeleton seemed to confirm that the inhabitants had not dared return. I was on an island, therefore I might find someone on the eastern coast or in the inland massif.

Drink was no problem, for the canalwater was surprisingly sweet. On reflection I assumed this to be the result of the absence of traffic. I saw a string of sunken narrow boats. Food was relatively easy to come by, a few carefully laid traps of plaited reed, a spirited rush, and a stupid bosk wriggled in the trap. Also, there were palines.

The impression I gained was that this had been a prosperous farming community of interconnected villages and towns, and the wild animals I might have expected — leems, graint, zhantils, and the like — had been banished long ago and had not found their way back. These bosk, now, must be the descendants of domesticated herds. Then, as though to prove me right, I came walking down into a valley where crops grew in neat rows, tended crops, with the sign of mankind strong and orderly upon them. There were, however, indications that the harvest was poor, and here and there the ground showed dry and dusty. Indeed, it had not rained since I had landed here.

The canal I had been following had curved away the previous day, but the road which had tracked the canal had seemed the more likely prospect. Feeling I had been proved right I trod on — warily! — and was most surprised to discover the road, wending with the course of the valley, swing away from that glimpse I had had of crops. I walked on for a bur or so, pondering, and then the explanation occurred to me. The road did indeed follow the natural line; those crops I had seen and the village they suggested must lie adjacent to them, had been sited away from the road, off the beaten track, hidden. They had been revealed by some local flaw in the tree cover.

At once I turned off the road and headed straight down into the valley bottom.

In the event, my clever supposition, although right, was rendered totally unnecessary. As I slithered and scraped through the trees down the slope I saw below me the same confounded thorn-ivy hedge that surrounds any boundary of cultivated land against the wild. The thorn-ivy was not of recent growth, for what was wild had once been tamed, but it gave me a few nasty jabs and stabs and scratches before I went through.

Cursing, I stood up, and there, coming down smoothly and decently from the road above, was a side road, all neat and clean and easy. And I'd gone headfirst through a thorn-ivy boma!

So much for my cleverness.

"Sink me!" I started off to let rip a whole string of the curses of two worlds and several colorful cultures — and then I stopped. I didn't laugh, for as you know I laugh seldom and then in situations that seem not to call for laughter as the correct critical response; but I could see the humorous side of that slide down the valleyside and the crash through the boma. I was still picking thorns out of my shoulders when I walked into the single main street of the village.

The houses were more like huts: bark-logged walls, large leaves of the papishin trailed over a ridge-pole for roofs, mere holes for doors, and of windows not a sign. A pen contained a dozen or so bosks, squealing and grunting. A few ponshos, languid in the warmth, their fleeces, although heavy in poor condition, were actually nibbling the grass growing up between the logs of the huts. There was a well. I walked straight to it. It had adobe walls and a fractured cover, but there was a rope and a bucket. I threw the bucket down, hauled it up, and drank deeply, then plunged my head in the icy water.

When I lifted my head and shook it like a ponsho-trag a quavering voice said: "Llahal, dom."

I turned slowly. I turned carefully. I still held the well bucket in both hands and I could hurl that and draw my sword with blinding speed, if I had to.

The old man confronting me did not look any kind of threat.

He was old, for his hair was white and his thin beard draggled whitely across his shrunken chest. He must be at least two hundred years old, I judged. He wore a simple garment of orange cloth around his middle, hanging to his knees, with a broad fold thrown up and over his left shoulder. For only a single instant could the foolish fancy that he was a Todalpheme attract me; but I knew he was not, for around his waist he did not have a colored tasseled rope; the robe fell loosely.

"Llahal, dom," I replied.

His weak eyes regarded me. "You are welcome to our poor village. We have little, but what we have is yours."

The words might have been rote — as I wondered then, they might be a trap — but I sensed in this man that what he said was true; he and his people were friendly to me. I saw a number of other people gathering and saw instantly that they were all old or babes-in-arms, held by their great-grandmothers. I knew these signs of old.

They were desperately poor. The strong young men and the beautiful young girls had either been taken up as slaves or had run off into the central massif. These people were abject. They had been shattered by a continuous succession of slave raids, and they had no fight left. They accepted their fate with a fatalism that, while I could not share its abnegations, I could understand.

The old man, Theirson, led me to his hut and I sat on the packed dirt floor, and they gave me a bowl of fruit, gleaming rounds of the fabulous fruit of Kregen. I picked up a squish. I thought of Inch and his taboos, and then I did not think over those memories again. I munched a mouthful of squishes as old Theirson talked.

"You had best not linger here, Koter Drak. You are most welcome and we would love your help in the fields, for the work is hard and we are old. But no young man is safe. The aragorn, for whom the Ice Floes of Sicce most certainly wait, ride through and take what they will and no man dare say them nay."

His wife, Thisi the Fair — she was old and stringy and her hair as white as his own — shivered. "Do not speak of the aragorn, Theirson, I beg you. If only the old days were here!"

I felt a peculiar sensation in my stomach, and I rubbed it. I felt hot and yet I felt cold. I drank a cup of water. I wanted all the information I could get; yet the hut walls were receding and closing, swaying, rippling like the bed of a mountain stream. My tongue seemed as thick as a chunkrah's tongue.

Theirson, Thisi the Fair, and others were looking at me with kind expressions, and talking, but their words boomed and echoed and hurt my ears. I fell full length, and lay there, unable to move. They were all looking down on me with worried, concerned expressions, and Thisi felt my forehead.

"It is the sickness," she whispered. "Koter Drak — you must fight for your life!"

And then I swung away like a surfer on the bottom of a board with only the deep black-green of nothingness beneath me.

Three

Thisi the Fair borrows my Savanti sword

Many visions passed before my inward eye as I lay stricken by the hallucination-fever of the sickness. I saw the smoke and heard the monstrous concussions of the broadsides as I sailed so slowly down on the Franco-Spanish line off Cape Trafalgar; I saw the swirling charge of the cavalry as we held the ridge of Mont Saint Jean; I fought with my clansmen, and swaggered as a bravo-fighter in Zen-icce; I battled swifters of Magdag, and swordships with Viridia the Render laughing; I saw many things and I felt many things.

Through it all I, Dray Prescot, Pur Dray, Krozair of Zy, the Lord of Strombor, sunk so low and helpless, did not for one moment imagine that these old folk had poisoned me. In a way that only hindsight can justify I knew I could trust them.

For three days I lay there caught in that damned soup of fevered visions and for all that time they stayed by me and cared for me. On the morning of the fourth day I opened my eyes and looked through the open door and saw the jade and orange light of the twin suns falling in mingled radiance across the street, and knew I was once more myself, once more in control, once more a man. But I was as weak as an infant.

They were surprised.

"The sickness takes a man or a woman and holds them fast bound for a whole sennight."

I did not tell them that I had bathed in the sacred pool of the River Zelph, in unknown Aphrasöe, and was thus assured of a thousand years of life and a natural constitution to throw off wounds and diseases rapidly. I thanked them. I had been a burden to them. I was still very weak, weaker by far than I had been after those horrific experiences crossing the Klackadrin, and for a space all I could do was sit in the suns-shine at the mouth of the hut and rest and recuperate.

I know, now, that my sickness was the result of drinking the canalwater.

Sweet, it was, to be sure, and ever after was to prove so. But, to a man or woman not of the canals, to anyone not of the canalfolk, it was deadly. After the week's fever-dreams, the victim very often died. That I had not was a tribute to the pool of baptism of the Savanti in Aphrasöe. Three days — half the six that usually constitute a Kregan week, for all that I render it into English as a sennight — was astonishing to them. I just sat in the sun and watched the dust devils on the street and struggled to grow strong.

They had taken my Savanti hunting leathers to have them cleaned and I wore a simple breechclout of the orange cloth. The color came from squeezed berries abounding in the forests. I looked up as Theirson came from the hut with a bowl of bosk and taylyne soup. Just as Tilda the Beautiful had said, here in Vallia they did drink their soup hot. I sipped it gently, grateful for the soothing sensations in my abused guts.

"My sword?"

"It is safely hidden. Should the aragorn ride in and find a weapon—" Theirson's wrinkled mouth pursed dolefully. "Rest and get well, Drak. Then you may take up the sword again."

This did not seem good advice to me. About to argue with the old man and if necessary become objectionable until they brought out my sword, I became aware of a hush fallen over the village. Down the street and riding toward me through the streaming jade and crimson light advanced the aragorn.

Theirson let a low moan escape his lips, then his face took on the look of one of those alabaster statues from Tomboram. Still holding the soup bowl he stood, bent over a little, in the doorway of his hut. I continued to sit.

This was close to eventide now, when the people trudged back from the fields after a full day's work. I had seen them go out and I had seen them return. They were forced to work hard and relentlessly, persevering with the monotonous labors as the twin suns poured down their beams on the backs of their necks and their heads, until the old folk could barely stand to walk back in the evening.

The results of their labors were stacked in the low barns at the end of the village, for harvests here, as is common in much of Kregen, occur when the fruits and the corns and the vegetables are ripe and not as a result of some unvarying round of seasons.

The great thanksgiving time of harvest is understood, however, on Kregen, and these old folk put by to that end. The aragorn rode in. I just sat there, stupefied, weak, watching them as they made their grand gestures, gave their orders, as the produce was brought forth and loaded on the backs of calsanys. I, Dray Prescot, Krozair of Zy, just sat.

Whatever of harvest thanksgiving lay in the hearts and minds of these men, it did not touch the people of the village.

I looked at these aragorn.

They rode zorcas. Well they would, being proud and mailed men in their might. These zorcas were fine beasts, with the tall and spindly legs and the single twisted horn that brought back the memories of riding with the wind across the Great Plains of Segesthes. The aragorn had the habit of using the tight rein, so that the twisted horns upreared in a way at once proud and flaunting to observe, and damned uncomfortable for the poor zorcas.

They were men. On Kregen, of course, one habitually identifies species as well as race. Their armor shone resplendently: plate on back and breast and thigh, with thick purple-dyed leather for arm and leg. They wore the typical Vallian hat, with its low crown and wide brim with the dashing upcurled feather, and with those two slots cut in the brim over the forehead. At their saddle bows swung morions. They did not carry lances, and their weapons were rapier and main-gauche, and a sheaf of javelins.

I wanted to get up and challenge them, but lethargy like a spider's web adhering to my arms and legs drew me down.

The aragorn took the produce, hit a couple of old men over the head with their riding crops, stared around arrogantly, and announced they were staying overnight. From their small string of calsanys they produced food and wine of kinds that the villagers had not seen since this blight had been laid on the land. They turfed Theirson and Thisi out of their hut and Vulima and Totor out of theirs, commandeering them. There were six aragorn, with six slaves for servants, and three dancing girls, with golden chains through their nostrils and exotic transparent pantaloons and silver-mesh mantles. There was about these aragorn the simple belief that they were the masters, that what they said was law and must be instantly obeyed. No idea of opposition occurred to them.

I realize I have not given you any description of their faces. I find I approach this with diffidence. Even then, as I sat in the dust, I could see in their faces what so many people have seen in mine. There was the same harsh intolerance, the same fierce and predatory demands of instant obedience, the same intemperate damn-you-to-hell arrogance, that old devil's look I know I assume. And yet I know many women have looked on me with a kindly eye, and I get along with children famously, and I venture to think that if any traces of that show in my face they were absent from the countenances of the aragorn.

"Get this dolt out of the way," said one, as he swung down from his zorca.

"He is sick, master, badly sick."

"Then I'll drive out his disease!" and with that the aragorn put his boot up. He intended to kick me in the face. I moved my head sideways, yet I felt that treacherous lassitude upon me and I was slow. The aragorn's boot took me in the shoulder and I toppled backward into the dust.

They laughed.

A couple of the villagers scuttled across to help me up and away. I say scuttled advisedly. The villagers bowed, and remained bowed, in the presence of the aragorn.

The absolute terror these men spread about them could be seen in little things. In the way people ran to hold their zorcas' heads, for instance. The constant trembling in their bodies, their hands shaking, their words disconnected. In the sudden rigidity with which they reacted to the words of the aragorn, so it seemed as though mere words could strike them to stone. The aragorn took whatever they wanted, and destroyed casually and without thinking in their search for hidden food. All valuables had long since vanished.

I thought of my sword, hidden I knew not where, and sweated it out.

That night I heard the shrill laughter, and the clashing of ankle-bells — I have never made up my mind if ankle-bells are the height of refined sexuality or the depths of depravity, or if they merely denote shocking bad taste — and although I could not see these men I could guess the games they were up to, the wine they were drinking, the food they were guzzling.

I still felt weak in the morning.

"Where is my sword, Theirson?"

"No, Drak. No!"

Thisi the Fair moaned. "You will surely be killed."

"My sword!"

But these old folk possessed courage and tenacity where their friends were concerned. They could do nothing about the aragorn, and so were beaten. But for me, they could save my life. Who am I to say they did not? I was aware then, and subsequently have been more than grateful, that I was privileged to be called their friend.

So I, Dray Prescot, had to watch with bowed head and a face over which I had drawn a corner of an orange cloth as the aragorn, leisurely, insolently, prepared for departure and then rode out. They rode their zorcas well. Easily and lithely in the saddle; tall, bold, strong men, absolute masters, absolutely in command; oh, yes, they bore the outward semblance of warriors. But I knew that the ordinary fighting-men of Kregen among whose number I had been proud to include myself, were as different from these men, these aragorn, as are the zhantils from the leems.

When they had gone I said to Theirson: "Do they often ride in and take everything you have?"

"Whenever they wish. We cannot stop them."

I noticed that the villagers seemed to be beyond the point at which mere ordinary curses could do anything for them in their mortal anguish against the aragorn. The aragorn were mercenaries, of course, working with the slave-masters. Now they were living in high fettle in various of the castles and fortresses of the island, going out on their raids, drinking and wenching, quarreling, quite happy to live here on the backs and the sweat of those they had not run off into slavery.

"They make sure we have enough on which to survive. That way we can work for them."

"How long is it to go on for?" said Thisi. Her veined hands trembled. "We must have offended the invisible twins in some way not vouchsafed to us."

"Not so," I said. "These are men, and therefore may be killed. I am a man of peace, but now give me my sword."

They tried to dissuade me. I was arguing with them, most vehemently, when I found myself sitting on the ground. I was weak, still — damned weak! I struggled up, and swayed, and blinked my eyes, and Thisi gave me a cup of water, and I knew I must wait until the marvelous powers of the waters of baptism cleared the poison from my system altogether.

On the sixth day everyone carried out the simple devotions that marked the religious observances of these people, much after the fashion of those I had witnessed in the argenter *Dram Constant,* where the invisible twins were honored and revered as the mystical twinned godhead of all things.

Then, even though the sixth day might reasonably be called a day of rest, the people trudged off to the fields. The work would never wait. I tried to go with them, and fell down, and had to crawl back alone, for they could not be allowed to waste their effort on me, a stubborn onker, when the fields and the incessant work demanded everything they could give. For strong young lads and girls, the agricultural work would have been easy — as it had been in the good old days.

Four days after that I was strong enough to insist on being given my sword and chopping wood. I noticed how I had to make a conscious physical effort to slash through branches that normally I would have cut through with a supple twist of wrist and forearm. But I persevered. The people had told me that the rescued prisoners on the beach were not likely to be interfered with; all that area had been slaved out and the aragorn or the slave-masters no longer went there.

The island, I learned, was called Valka. Valka had been the name taken by an oar-slave who had been a good companion with me in the swordships. The nearest way of explaining his use of the name — for he came from the main island of Vallia — is to suggest that a man from California might choose the name of Tex as an alias.

I donned my Savanti hunting leathers.

There seems little point in belaboring my feelings at this time. You will know something of the kind of man I am; inaction in times of peril is anathema to me.

I resent an insult, and if a man seeks to kill me I own to the moral weakness, thoroughly reprehensible, of attempting to kill him first.

I chopped a great deal of wood in the next few days, swinging my sword arm, using my left arm, also, working the sinews and muscles, feeling the jolting power of the sword blows. What Maspero, that gentle man who had been my tutor, would say, I did not know. He swung a sword, complaining of his own weakness, also. But the swords the Savanti use in their sport deliver a psychic blow that does not kill, does not even harm. This sword had lost that power, assuming it had ever possessed it, and Alex Hunter had been equipped as an ordinary fighting-man of Kregen — with this single exception of the sword.

On a bright morning when a little pink mist lifted from the treetops and birds sang with what I can only describe as a trilling note I told Theirson I must say Remberee.

"For one thing, good Theirson, I am eating far too much."

"You are always welcome to share what we have, Drak."

"And for that I thank you. But I ought to return to the beach and tell the people there what has happened."

"They would be advised—" And then Theirson paused, and looked helpless. Indeed, what to advise those escaped prisoners?

"I will think of something," I said.

He sighed. "If only the old Strom were here. He was a man! He ruled Valka with a rod of iron, and with justice and mercy. A girl could walk from one end of the island to the other without fear in those days."

"Why does the Emperor permit these things?"

His distress was obvious. "We do not know. Perhaps the Emperor does not know what goes on in Valka. We are the most cut off of all the Stromnates."

I didn't necessarily believe that, but I knew what he meant.

A Strom is the nearest equivalent to a count, and a Kov to a duke; the Strom of Valka had been early killed in opposing the slave-masters and their mercenaries. After that the island had become a mere slave-droving ground. Although, so Theirson told me, in the central massif were many, many young men and women who had escaped from their villages and towns. The chief city of Valka, Valkanium, lay fast held in the clutches of the slavers and the aragorn, the men of prey who feasted on the carcass of the island.

"They guard themselves well behind their iron gates and their tall black towers," said old Theirson.

Thisi the Fair came hobbling fast along the main street. She panted. Her white hair had fallen free of the wooden pins holding it — for all her silver pins from the Street of the Silversmiths in Vandayha had long since been stolen — and the sunshine glistened off the sweat along her forehead.

"You must give me your sword, Drak!"

"Willingly, Thisi," I answered in as uncharacteristic a speech as ever I could make. "But give me a good reason."

She halted before me, twisted her head to look up, and tried to push her hair into place. "Why, I would clean the hilt for you, and, too, I would show it to

Tlemi, who would recapture his youth." She cackled, and there was strain in her laugh. "He is too old to work, and he lies on his pallet dreaming of the past."

"The hilt is clean, Thisi." I drew the sword and held it out to her, hilt first. "But show it to Tlemi, with my blessing, and tell him once a warrior always a warrior."

"Aye," she cackled, grasping the hilt and holding it as awkwardly as one can imagine. "I know about warriors, Drak."

"I will pause a while before going into the fields, Drak, and drink a cup of water with you."

"That will give me great pleasure, Theirson."

So we sat in the early sunshine and drank our water and talked of the lack of rain and the crops and the old days in Valka. Truth to tell, I recall, I wanted to learn as much as I could of this island of Valka. This village had been raided often, and the pitiful attempt to hide it away from the main road and canal had been completely unsuccessful. That the roads here were reasonably good was a result of the old Strom's grandfather, who liked to race zorca chariots, a sport he could not practice on the canals.

Presently Thisi came back. "Tlemi had tears in his eyes," she said. "The old fool. Over a mere sword!" She looked a great deal calmer.

Thisi leaned over and whispered to her husband.

He started, and looked down the road, and then at me, and back at Thisi. He swallowed. "Here, Drak. Cover yourself with this old cloth—"

But I understood, and I cursed myself for a credulous simpleton.

They cared for me, these old folk, and they did not wish me killed. I had done nothing for them. I had brought merely sickness, and another mouth to feed. More altruistic love for a fellow man is difficult to find.

I stood up.

"I will go to Tlemi's hut and get my sword, now—"

"It is too late, Drak. Look!"

I looked.

Riding in their pride and their power, the aragorn astride their zorcas moved up the street. The old folk stumbled to their knees as the mercenaries passed. Absolute power they held, absolute control, a will never challenged.

And I, Dray Prescot, stood like a loon in the dust before them, empty-handed.

Four

A surprise for the aragorn

Theirson's hand gripped my ankle and jerked, and stunned by the folly of my own actions, I lost my balance and tumbled into the dust at his side. He whispered fiercely, in an agony of terror.

"Put your forehead into the dirt, Drak! For the sake of the glorious Opaz himself! Else you are a doomed man — *and we with you*."

Those last words, alone, could make me bend my stubbornly and stupidly proud neck. I bowed. I cringed. I, Dray Prescot, double-inclined to these cramphs of aragorn.

The zorca hooves twinkled past. Following them the calsanys lumbered along, tails flicking. Tethered to the last two calsanys by lengths of rope were two people, a man and a woman. I could see only their naked legs. They stumbled as they were jerked along. The woman fell. Now I could see her. She was young, with long brown hair and a thin but vigorous figure, clad only in a wraparound of the orange Valkan cloth. She was dragged by her bound wrists. An aragorn reined back and beat her with his crop until she rose up silently, and stumbled on, dragged by the calsany.

Theirson's hand gripped my arm.

Then the party had passed and the aragorn were yelling for the headman and Theirson was rising and shuffling forward, head bent.

"Bibi!" said Thisi. I looked at her. Tears coursed down her cheeks. "Bibi — my granddaughter."

Many secret societies exist on Kregen, as anywhere else, I suppose. Societies exist devoted to this end and that. On Valka, with the absolute dominance of the slavers and the mercenaries, and the disappearance of so many of the younger people into the central massif, a clandestine organization must grow up to resist. Given the normal strengths and fears of human beings — and of the halflings, too — this is natural and inevitable. Bibi, Thisi's granddaughter, must have come down with a message from the center. They — she and her companion — had been caught. Now the aragorn wanted to find out why she was visiting here.

I stood up warily, and looked up the street.

Theirson was talking to the aragorn. They looked to be the same six, evidently backtracking because of their captives. Other village people crouched abjectly by their huts. The six slaves stood by the calsanys, and the three dancing girls put their heads out of their preysany-palanquin covers and chattered like parakeets. The palanquins were gorgeously decorated with filigree work, and the poles by which they were slung were lavishly bound with silver wire. The preysanys — a kind of superior calsany — were likewise highly decorated and feathered.

I stood there and I looked down on Thisi.

My voice carried all that harsh, intolerant authority, and I know my face must have glared with that hateful devil's look.

"Run, Thisi, and bring my sword. Tell Tlemi I have need of it."

"But, Drak—"

"Run."

She ran.

In the days immediately after I had been captured and taken as a slave into the marble quarries of Zenicce, coming at a stroke from Zorcander of my clansmen to slave, I fought blindly and obstinately against restraint until beaten into submission. That happened only when I was unconscious. I still react in the same way now, on occasion; but I have tried to school myself. As I stood there looking upon these indifferently cruel and despotic aragorn I kept telling myself to wait.

I had to wait for Thisi and my sword. I did stand, and how I did it is a mystery, for I longed above all else to hurl myself forward and fling myself upon these sadistic overlords and tear them from their jeweled saddles.

I was spared the wait.

One aragorn glanced at me. He frowned. He lifted his crop and beckoned.

"Stupid cramph! If you cannot incline before your master I will teach you! You will scream for mercy — but we aragorn no longer know what mercy means."

At this his companions guffawed.

The orange cloth hurriedly thrown around me still hung from my shoulders, and it was evident that the mercenary had not yet appreciated I was not an oldster like the rest. I shuffled forward. I kept my head lowered.

When I reached the zorca I looked up.

I had put that simpleton's look on my face. Zair forgive me, but I take a pride in that look, for it makes me look an idiot of idiots, and gives me great and unholy — and very petty, I confess — feelings of gaiety and secret knowledge that I play a prank, that I disguise Dray Prescot.

"You stupid, Doty-rotten cramph! I'll teach you—"

I looked up at him. His arm was raised to bring the crop down across my face, possibly to blind me, certainly to mark me. His companions laughed.

"Kleesh," I said.

I prided myself, then, that I spoke so rationally. A kleesh is violently unpleasant, stinking, repulsive; and yet applied to me the name serves only to make me yawn. Applied to most men, I have noticed with sure unconcern, it is a guaranteed explosive firecracker.

His face contorted, he roared and brought the crop down in a violent slashing blow.

I moved in, took his foot from the stirrup, jerked it up, hauled it out — I didn't care if his leg parted from his hipbone — and tossed him swinging over my shoulder into the dust. I took a pace toward him and brought my foot down on his face. Then, without thinking about it, I ducked.

The flung javelin scraped over my back. It struck the ground with such force that it snapped. I disregarded it. I leaped sideways, turned, surveyed the five remaining mercenaries. One was already in action, gouging in his spurs cruelly, hurtling down on me, his drawn rapier pointed and low, aiming to spit me. I slid off the orange cloth, whirled it once and enveloped that rapier in the folds, and dived to the side.

The others were reacting now. Bibi and her companion, a personable young fellow with a thin face but merry eyes, huddled together, bound and helpless. I shot a look down the road. No sign of Thisi. The aragorn had seen I was unarmed, and they were taking no chances of my reaching their fellow lying in the road with a red pudding for a face. Mercenaries are ever conscious of the value of seizing a weapon from an adversary. They were roaring and yelling all the time, of course, threats and curses and detailings of what they would do to me and the rest of the village. I needed nothing extra to spur me on; had I done so the threats against my friends here would have been a spur and a brand.

Two came at me, with a third cursing and trying to rein his zorca around with them. I had to dodge and duck and weave. They were even taunting me now, cries such as some warriors use, mercenary tricks that, even if they did not realize it, meant they had admitted they were not faced by a helpless old man of the village.

The utter surprise they had, the sheer impossibility of an old man suddenly dragging one of their number from the saddle and breaking his neck, had now passed. But that uncanny business of a helpless victim abruptly turning on them, savagely, had for a mur unnerved them. Now they were upon me again, ready to drive and hunt me, to have sport, to flick and lash with their rapiers, not to kill but to torture.

Forced thus to skip this way and that I worked my way to the side. They reined their beasts around, the spindly legs of the zorcas perfect for this kind of wheeling curveting work. They performed caracoles very well, these aragorn. But I wormed free, turned, leaped, and, as I had done on that beach so long ago in Segesthes, I was upon the haunches of the nearest zorca and with an arm around the neck of its rider was dragging him back. I had to be quick. If I knew these people they'd care nothing for their comrade and would hurl a javelin to kill me, risking his life.

I snapped his backbone and then made a grab for his rapier. But he had twisted in his agony and I missed. I had to let myself go and slide off the zorca. The javelin hissed into the dead man's back.

On the ground I danced, as it seemed, between javelins.

Again I risked a glance down the street — and here came Thisi, hurrying and stumbling. She carried my sword.

The calsanys were uneasy and were milling, the two bound prisoners were being dragged across, and I saw they would stagger between me and Thisi. A zorca rider saw Thisi. He shrilled his anger and drew a javelin from the sheath strapped to his saddle. I saw Bibi open her mouth, but her scream was drowned by the roars from the aragorn. Her companion staggered across and fell against the javelin-man's zorca. The javelin missed. The calsanys barged against Bibi's friend and he fell. The zorcaman reined away, raving, drawing his rapier. Bibi pulled her man into the calsanys. I could leave them, but not for long. The stink of blood and dust stung my nostrils, rank and raw, but they have been familiar smells to me all my life.

I ran toward Thisi.

"Here, Drak! May Opaz have you in his keeping."

I forced myself to speak. "Thank you, Thisi."

I took the brand. The hilt had never felt so good in my fist before.

I turned.

There were four of them left, and they were completely incapable for a single moment of understanding defeat. They had cowed these people, enslaved all their young men; their slightest word was law, their littlest whim a command. Here was a man, all but naked, impudently attempting to challenge them. That two of their comrades were dead would mean only an excuse for an orgy of revenge. They had no conception that they would not slay me.

They wore armor and the man on the zorca whose back I had broken had not died of the javelin, for it had failed to penetrate his backplate. I balanced easily, the sword held low, and I laughed at these professional killers.

A shrill screaming that had been fracturing the air all the time gurgled away as I laughed. The three dancing girls, who had so short a time ago been laughing from their preysany-palanquins, had been shrieking and screaming; but when I laughed they stopped, and they remained silent thereafter.

Then, I confess it not without a knowledge of how foolish and inflated it makes me appear, I shook the Savanti sword at them, and I shouted: "Bite on a sword for a change, you cowardly kleeshes who murder old men."

Their rage was a wonderful and edifying sight.

They dug in their spurs and they charged.

I am a clansman, of the Clan of Felschraung, and I have faced the earthshaking charge of a whole hostile clan astride their voves. The zorca is not an animal a clansman uses in the massive barrier-smashing charge.

"Fools!" I said, and set to work.

I here proved, at least to my own satisfaction, that the Savanti sword was, and again, at least in my hand, a better weapon than the rapier. I had no main-gauche. The first man simply tried to spit me through as though I were a target at practice. I flicked his blade aside and as he passed I struck his thigh. The stirrup alone kept his leg from falling off.

The second man, seeing this, attempted to rear his mount back and slash me down the face. The zorca is a nimble animal — perhaps there is no more nimble animal on all Kregen, certainly there is none on this Earth — but I was quicker and slid the blow, reaching up and forward, and so passed my blade through his guts just beneath the corselet rim. I withdrew and flung myself sideways. The next man's blow would have clanged off my helmet comb had I been wearing one.

Mind you, unless you are a superb horseman or zorca-man it is deucedly difficult to fix a man who insists on dodging all around you and intends to unseat you or smash you or in some other unpleasant way do for you first. The third aragorn came out of his stirrups all flailing with my left hand gripping his left boot. He tried to cut down on me, but my blade deflected his blow, and as he struck the ground I sliced the sword down. The way I was feeling must surely be indicated by the fact that his head jumped clean off his shoulders and rolled under the middle preysany-palanquin, whereat its occupant swooned and fell out, a heap of jumbled silks, gold, and bells in the dust.

The fourth aragorn had no intention of quitting, I'll give him that; he was angry, so enraged that he roared in, screaming abuse, swirling his rapier, madly intent on finishing me off. I didn't want to kill this one. Him, I would like to question; but the fool ran himself onto my blade. It went through his throat. By Zair, but he was a fool!

Mind you, I must take a share of the blame. But, there they were, six dead aragorn littering the dusty street of the village.

Then it began to rain.

If the villagers wanted to take that as an omen, they might. Certainly, the raindrops felt cool and sweet. I walked over to the palanquins. The two petal faces regarded me in horror. They were not particularly pretty girls, but curved and complaisant, as I judged, able to wiggle their hips and rotate their bellies and jangle their bells. I spoke quite pleasantly.

"How do you wish to die? Would you like to be hanged, burned, beheaded? Perhaps you prefer drowning? I am in no hurry. Just make up your minds and then let me know." They cowered back, shattered, shrunken, unable to implore, seeing in my face only darkness and evil. I swung back. "Oh — there might be a way — but no. I am sure you will wish to die."

Then I strode off and left them. Bibi and her man were freed. His name was Tom — yes, the same as our Earthly Tom, although not deriving from Thomas — and although thin he was well-muscled and active and a very merry man altogether. He eyed my sword.

"Lahal, Koter Drak," he said, for Thisi had whispered the name by which they knew me. He shook his head. "I would not have believed it possible had I not seen it with my own eyes."

"Lahal, Koter Tom of Vulheim," I said, for that was where he came from, a port town up the coast that was now a mere pile of rubble and burned beams, razed, destroyed, and abandoned.

He looked about, lifted his arms, and let them drop.

Certainly, the situation called for considerable thought.

The dancing girl woke up from her swoon and when she was given the news by her two companions promptly swooned again. The six slaves stood docilely by the calsanys, soothing them. They would be a problem. There were four men and two women, hardy, short-statured folk with thick oily black hair and flattish noses, bought in a market far from Valka, I judged. That made me realize they were probably in a special relationship with the aragorn; slaves, yes, but privileged slaves, doing domestic work and quite unlike the whipped and beaten slaves for which Valka was scoured.

"We had best tie 'em up, Tom," I said. We had quickly dropped formalities. But the use of *Koter* is obligatory in Vallia unless you know a man well. We felt, Tom and I that we did know each other tolerably well. Time telescopes when you fight together — and his action in spoiling the aim of the javelin man, when he must have thought he would be instantly cut down, was as brave a stroke as any in any being's book.

"Will you really kill the girls?" Theirson wrinkled his nose up. He eyed me with a look that struck me as altogether too knowing.

They had heard him, for we were using Kregish.

"Certainly," I said. "The aragorn are evil, and these perfumed dancing girls are likewise evil." I heard them squeak, and sniffle, and realized they were crying now. That was one crisis over. "Of course," I said loudly, taking Theirson by the arm and walking him away. "If they understand just how evil the aragorn are, and are prepared to mend their ways, then perhaps—"

By that time I had lowered my voice and walked sufficiently far off for them not to overhear us.

"I doubt that I could kill them, Theirson. I am a man of peace. I seldom kill in cold blood."

"Seldom?"

"For my sins."

"You are a strange man, Drak. Harsh and hard and merciless. Yet there is mercy in you. I will see what we can do with those girls."

Tom had joined us. He had possessed himself of the leathers of an aragorn, a rapier, and a main-gauche.

"They'll have to be watched. But they will give us valuable information." I told Tom about the released prisoners on the beach.

"Panvals?" he said. "They can be useful to us, too."

The street was cleared, and the bodies stripped and buried. The slaves were placed in a hut, and an old man with a rapier stood guard over them. The largesse on the calsanys was distributed and the calsanys and preysanys themselves herded in with the village animals. We made the place spick and span again. And then we discussed what best to do.

I made my position clear. I would find a boat and go to Vallia. I saw Tom looking at Theirson. Tom would marry Bibi as soon as that could be contrived, and between them they could look forward to no life at all. Unless...

No one did any work in the fields that day. That night we ate well and drank wine for the first time in many a long day.

Then we commanded the dancing girls, who were half dead with fright and horrendous expectations, to dance for us. The ordinary dancing girl, such as one finds in taverns and dopa dens and even in higher establishments of pleasure, never appeals greatly to me, almost certainly on account of my experiences with my clansmen where the girls dance gaily and freely and with a fierce joy that finds its greatest expression of art — and where they'd stick you with a terchick if you called them dancing girls. Slavery and dancing are obscene bedfellows.

I had never touched the Triangular Trade, but I knew.

After that I called the three of them over and said: "Have you chosen?"

They fell on their knees, the tears streaming — and, of course, I could not let the cruel farce continue any longer. I told them, simply, that they must henceforth cut themselves off from the aragorn, and help the villagers. Later, when things had worked themselves out, they might be dancing girls again. It was not a satisfactory solution, but I was afire to find a boat and sail to Vallia.

Tom was doubtful I'd find a single boat along the west coast of Valka. When he understood that I had no objections to stealing a boat from the slavers or the mercenaries, and if necessary, bashing in a few skulls in the process, he said that, yes, there were boats; but the skull bashing would be hectic and heavy.

That suited me only in one way; but Valka, however pleasant an island it really was despite the depredations, could not hold me at all, and if skull bashing was necessary, then skull bash I would. Speed, now I had almost reached my goal, seemed to me the prime requisite. Tom accompanied me back to the beach. The prisoners were astonished to see me. Under the direction of their self-elected leaders, of which Borg was one, they had begun to sketch out a camp for themselves off the beach and on the banks of a little river where we tracked them. They were warned about the water in the canals, whereat Borg laughed hugely, a true canalman.

Tom and I departed, and after some difficulty, discovered a slaver camp where we stole a boat. The skull bashing did not, in the event, prove necessary. Tom waved goodbye. "Remberee, Drak!" and: "Remberee, Tom!"

I hoisted the dipping lug and the little boat curled out across the sea. I felt at last my peculiar destiny was running in ways I could understand when the black clouds gathered and a gale blew with incredible, immediate violence and the waves broke mountainously high; with a sick heart I recognized all the symptoms I had met before. This had happened on the inner sea. The Star Lords were forcing me back. I could not go on. The Star Lords were saying plainly: "You may not go to Vallia! Return to Valka, Dray Prescot, and perform there the work to your hands."

Five

The true history of *The Fetching of Drak na Valka*

I would not accept this dictate of the Star Lords.

What did I know of these mysterious and lofty beings then? Practically nothing of value, save their power. They had flung me back and forth between Earth and Kregen like a tennis ball. They could rouse the wind and the sea against me.

The boat grounded and waves sheeted over me, and I stood up and shook my fist at the sky and cursed the Star Lords, horribly and comprehensively. The wind slackened and the stars shone through the cloud wrack.

She of the Veils, the fourth moon of Kregen, drifted like a wan ghost, and against the pallid orb the shape of a giant hunting bird stretched like an accusing brand.

"The Gdoinye!" I yelled up, my head thrown back. "What do I care for you? It is Vallia and Vondium for me," and I finished with a fine rattling series of foul oaths.

The raptor up there, black in the starlight, catching an occasional gleam from She of the Veils, was the messenger and spy of the Star Lords. A giant bird with, I knew, a scarlet coat of feathers and golden feathers about its eyes and throat, it circled above me now in wide planing hunting circles. That raptor had watched over many of the crises of my life on Kregen. Now I picked up a stone from the beach and hurled it aloft. Oh, yes, believe me, I was mad clean through.

And then — then something happened that had never occurred to me before on Kregen and was never likely to occur on Earth.

The Gdoinye folded its wings and stooped. It dropped like a shot from a tower straight toward my head. I shouted aloud in my glee and hauled out my sword and threw it up, the blade a pinkish-silver brand in the night.

"I'll tickle your feathers for you, you kleesh of a bird! You won't spy for the Star Lords when I've spit you and roasted you and thrown you to the vosks!"

With a harsh cry the bird spread those gorgeous wings all black in the moonlight and swooped over my head. It circled insolently low above me, contemptuous, out of my reach. At my side swung a main-gauche Tom had insisted I take, and I could have drawn it and hurled it fairly into that scarlet-feathered breast. But I continued to shake my sword and rave at the Gdoinye. Looking back, I know I had forgotten I carried the dagger. My rage was terrible and ludicrous, pathetic.

Then — then the thing happened that stunned my brain.

"Dray Prescot!"

I fell silent, numb, gaping.

The bird — the bird spoke to me!

"Dray Prescot, you are a fool."

How could I argue that?

"Dray Prescot, we did not bring you to Valka. Had you a grain of common sense you would have understood. Was not the lad Hunter from the Savanti? Were you not brought to aid him?"

My sword felt as heavy as the chest of gold we dragged from Dorval the Render's tower.

"Vallia!" I shouted up. "I must go to Vondium!"

"Not so, Dray Prescot. You have been selected. Therefore you must."

"As I did in Magdag? When you dragged me away in the hour of victory?"

"If you presume, you will be put down."

"Presume! I served you as I thought fit! Star Lords! You are less than rasts that crawl upon a dunghill!"

"We are what we are. The Savanti try to be what they are not. They brought you here untimely." Then the bird emitted a shrieking squawk that might have been the laughter of the gods, or the gloating of demons. "Your Delia does not miss you, Prescot—"

I interrupted. "In that you lie!"

"Listen, fool. You remember that Delia saw you the very next day after her capture in the Esztercari enclave, yet you had wandered and adventured and swaggered like any ruffler for years?"

Now I understood, or thought I did, and a tide of pure relief flooded me through and through. I had spent years with my clansmen and had been back to Earth, and for Delia it had all been like a single day. I saw the Gdoinye rising higher and I shouted something after it, but it merely screeched an accipiter-like insult at me, and winged away, vanishing in the moon-drenched shadows.

But — I felt free! I felt released from a bar of constricting steel. I would make my way to Vondium in Vallia and claim my Delia — and only I would suffer the pangs of parting and separation. To me, then, these thoughts came as a great benediction, for I did not care how I suffered so long as not a single hair of the head of my Delia was harmed.

A flutter of white beneath She of the Veils made me turn my head and there flew the white dove of the Savanti. It flew around, and I thought its flight as agitated as ever I had seen it. The white dove spied for the Savanti. I shook my fist at it and shouted: "And what have you to say for yourself?" But the dove merely circled and then flew off, a white fluttering speck, pink-lit, inconclusive under the moons of Kregen.

So it was I think you will understand that I started up the beach with a grim purpose.

Now for Valka!

To explain the high purpose and the desperate resolves of the next six years I would do best to quote you the song made by Erithor of Valkanium; but he was of Valka and composed in the Vallian tongue, the Vallish, and even when translated into Kregish the majesty and power of the words are lost, the alliterations meaningless, the rhythm fractured. To translate further into English, however marvelous a tongue our English language truly is, would be to cripple the beauty and the magic and leave only dry facts. And, in glory and blood and effort and sacrifice, the facts were never dry. There are many kinds of singers in Kregen; call them what you will, bards, skalds, troubadours, minstrels, trouvères, tsloivoidees, and of them all, few were held in higher repute than Erithor of Valkanium.

How we sang in the high hall of the fortress of Esser Rarioch overlooking Valkanium!

This song Erithor made, the song that is still sung and will be sung for as long as there are singers on Kregen, is called *The Fetching of Drak na Valka*. There are wild savage passages full of the purple passions of battle, storm, and onslaught; and there are the longer wailing laments that surge rhythmically into heroic acceptance of the good men dead and gone, good men never forgotten. The song tells of Kylie and Kylon, the famous twins who held the bridge to Ussanore Ovoidach, and Nath of Vandayha, Jeniu and Vokor, Carli and Vomanus, and Yathmin ti Vulheim, whose broken body I clasped in my arms as she died, seeking to stroke the blonde hair from her face where her blood matted and clotted and the shining brown eyes dimmed and dulled.

I can never listen to *The Fetching of Drak na Valka* without a reaction that brands me as a human being, full of folly and sentiment and sadness, and, yes, pride too, nonetheless that pride is bruised and broken, the foolishness of a man who has known good friends and lost them.

The song tells how we roused the island of Valka. How the prisoners huddled shivering on the beach took up arms, and how we marched, and how the aragorn resisted us, and how we routed them, and grew stronger. How the young men and women came down from the central mountains, the Heart Heights of Valka, and took weapons from the slavers and the aragorn and all their mercenaries, for the aragorn brought against us Ochs and Rapas, Fristles and Chuliks. And the singing notes of the harps rise and the drums roar and once again I am transported back to the many battlefields and the stratagems and the night surprises when the seven moons of Kregen shone upon courage and selflessness and high endeavor.

The Fetching of Drak na Valka!

No man knows the profundity of feeling I experience, for my name is indissolubly linked with the island I love, the island of Valka, that was to become a home in which I might find perfect peace and security, happiness and love. But, then, as we first sang the seven hundred and seventy-seven verses of the song, I had only the faintest inkling of what Valka was to become to me in the days ahead.

The song tells of Tom of Vulheim, and Ven Borg nal Ogier, Theirson and Thisi the Fair, and their granddaughter Bibi, old Jeniu, the wise counselor, and his wife, Thuri, who in supporting him supported us all.

And only when Jeniu presented me with the fiat of the whole assembly of Valka, the pitiful remnant of men and women who had formed the assembly in the old Strom's day, led still by Tharu ti Valkanium, was the double meaning of the song's title born in on me.

For we had cleared the island of the aragorn. We had killed until the rivers ran red. We had driven them into the sea and watched as their armored forms toppled from the chalk cliff-tops. We had taken the slavers and sent them packing.

And when more slavers came, seeking to scourge the island again and sweep up more human victims for their vile trade, we had met them with a wall of steel and an invincible purpose. We had organized, for I had put all my own experience in these matters at the disposal of the Valkans, and our Jiktars and Hikdars, our Deldars, had led disciplined formations into action. Once again the island was a fair and clean place in which to live and bring up children. And the word spread and the slavers came no more for, as the song triumphantly proclaims, no longer was Valka a supine carcass rotten for plunder. The slavers, with their patents from the court of Vallia, turned aside from Valka and sought easier conquests.

And then — and then I understood what they all meant by the word "fetching."

For I had fetched the men and women out of the Heart Heights, and I had fetched them weapons, and organization and the understanding that they could triumph if they willed it. And then they fetched me.

Grim Tharu ti Valkanium, sword-girted, robed in the orange of the high assembly, strode the length of the high hall of the fortress of Esser Rarioch, and inclined to me — whereat, I remember, I was moved to anger, and bade him stand up like the man he was, and never cringe — and, with a smile, he said: "And for you, Drak, Strom na Valka, all men will bow. Aye! And joy in it, for it will show the world what we think of our Strom!"

I was astonished.

But they were serious. Everything had been arranged behind my back. I had known nothing. The song does not tell of these circuitous dealings, the messages, the sacks of golden talens dispatched, the complicated resorts to law, and the quoting of precedents. I was the Strom of Valka. The whole island was my fief. Everything upon it, whether living or dead, whether of man or nature, was mine, inalienably mine.

I tried to refuse, and saw the hurt in their eyes. I sat back in my seat and marveled.

This, I felt sure, was no outcome envisaged by the Star Lords or, given that I had completed what poor Alex Hunter had set out to do, the Savanti, either. But I have remarked before of this strange and frightening charisma I possess, unasked, unsought, that serves me sometimes so well and sometimes so ill. Now I could only stand before them all, and humbly take what they offered.

The rapiers leaped, glittering in the torchlight in that great hall.

"Hai, Jikai! Drak, Strom na Valka! Hai, Jikai!"

And so the seven hundred and seventy-eighth verse was added to the song.

The emblem of Valka is the reflex-compound bow, placed horizontally, half drawn and aimed upward. Vertically upon this is a trident, as though about to be shot from the bow. The Valkans are great fisherfolk. Also, up in the rolling hills and wild crags of the Heart Heights that form the broad central massif of the island, they are proficient bowmen, using not the great longbow of Loh and Erthyrdrin but the shorter, stiffer, compound bow of cunning double-reflex curves, such as is used by my clansmen.

We had driven our arrow storm into the aragorn, and they had shriveled before us. But, once on a time, Tharu ti Valkanium said to me: "We of Valka are great bowmen. Yet the Emperor keeps a personal bodyguard of the Bowmen of Loh. We are just a distant province, rich for plunder, ripe for slaves."

And I had said to him: "You are great bowmen, still, Tharu; but no longer is Valka a province ripe for plunder!"

The other favorite weapon of the Valkans is the glaive. I do not mean by glaive a sword, in the archaic meaning of the word, gladius, a sword; but in the meaning in general use of a pole-arm, of the fifteenth century or so. The Valkan glaive is formed of a long narrow head, somewhat more robust than a bayonet, mounted on a shaft about five feet long. From the head along the sides run strengthening pieces of steel that serve also to prevent a slashing sword blow slicing the shaft in two. With the glaive the warriors of Valka go up against rapier men with complete confidence.

So, in the fullness of time I, Dray Prescot, of Earth, became Drak, Strom na Valka.

If there was any regret that my own name had, by a chance, not featured so far in Valka, I had quickly gone along with the name of Drak, for I saw that this might serve me well as a disguise and an alias when I penetrated Vallia. For the name of Dray Prescot, the Lord of Strombor, would be that of a wanted man there.

Also, through this incident, I had discovered that titles — for what they are worth — were obtainable as much by merit and effort as by birth and heredity in Vallia. Once I had cleared Valka and established myself in fact as the chief of the island, and the whole people concurring, I became a Strom and no one would say me nay. I did discover that a great deal was owed to the panvals I had rescued; for they had joyed in arranging the contracts, bribes, and agreements in Vondium, and in obtaining the Emperor's great seal and signature — Earthly custom is paralleled in this on Kregen — on the letters patent. The illuminated patent itself was kept safely locked away in the fortress of Esser Rarioch.

Now a Strom, with all the responsibilities of rebuilding the island's economy and reinforcing her people's confidence, I plunged headlong into work. Do not think I forgot Delia. More than once I took a boat out toward Vallia, to the west, and invariably the storm clouds gathered and the lightning and thunder roared and crackled menacingly, and the waves sought to smash the boat to fragments.

Valka was a rich province, as I found, and by management I made her richer and more pleasant. Also, storing up credit for the future I had sworn must come, I so arranged matters that the high assembly could function with greater and greater freedom and authority. Tharu ti Valkanium often told me I was placing power into their hands, whereat I would say: "And do you believe I do not trust you, Tharu? And the elders? After all we have been through together?" And, again, I would say: "One day, Tharu, I must leave Valka, for a space, and go upon a mission that is dear to my heart. When that day comes, I want the island to continue to prosper, andyou to remember me, so that when I return — with my bride — the whole future will be bright and glorious."

"We will not forget, Strom Drak, we will never forget."

Already, the girls were preparing the elaborate dresses and jewelry and all things needful that the Stromni, my bride, would require. Erithor of Valkanium could not make a song about that triumphal return yet, but he would strum out a merry tune, and hum words beneath his breath. When the girls of the place begged him to continue he would laugh and say: "Not so, you handmaidens of frivolity! I but tune my strings against the day the Stromni comes!"

How could I tell them that this Stromni was a princess, was the Princess Majestrix of all Vallia?

One day, among a group of friends on the terrace of Esser Rarioch with all of Valkanium spread beneath us and the suns of Antares blinding back from spire and tower and gabled roof, and the wide sweep of the bay beyond where the sea sparkled its impossible Kregan blue, I began idly to hum and then sing a few snatches of *The Bowmen of Loh*. There were no ladies present, and we had been drinking the strong red wine of southern Valka, a vintage called Vela's Tears, after the maiden who features in the music drama *The Fatal Love of Vela na Valka*, a drama which you may imagine is highly popular on Valka itself.

Erithor drew his slender fingers across the strings of his harp with a harsh and jangling discord.

I looked up in surprise. They were all looking at me — Tom, Tharu, Theirson, Logu, and even Borg, who was a Vallian, stared also — and I looked at them in surprise.

Tharu said: "We do not sing that song in Valka, Strom."

I never apologize. It is a weakness. I said: "The song is mild and harmless, but if I have offended you, my friends—" And then I stopped. We had sung songs together a hundred times more bawdy, and they had not complained.

"The Emperor keeps a personal bodyguard of Bowmen of Loh. Therefore we do not sing that song."

I nodded. "I see. Rest assured, it shall remain among the great unsung epics."

At this they all laughed. On Kregen there are many classics that are honored more in the breach than the observance in their rendition, as on Earth. The tension of the moment was broken, but I was displeased. I like that song. It reminds me of Seg Segutorio, and that memory, then, was bittersweet and full of a masochism I relished as a punishment. I was young then, as you know, young and headstrong and foolhardy, although trying to control myself. I could take pride that I had not, back in Theirson's village, rushed with empty hands on the aragorn. I was learning, slowly. What was more disturbing was the evident antipathy these good people of Valka had for the Emperor's choice of a personal bodyguard. I welcomed their hatred of the Racter party, who, although never in the open, were the instigators of the slaving raids, for they gained much of their wealth thereby. I did not relish this hatred of my beloved's father.

For all that I would have to walk in and teach him how to behave to a son-in-law, a prospect full of unpleasantness.

This incident, I believe, finally made me make up my mind to act positively. I had been growing lethargic — oh, not in the amount of work I dispatched each day, but in the attitude I had adopted. I love Valka and I could see all the fantastic promise of the island even then. I had become wrapped up in the place. I saw it as the home to which I would bring Delia of the Blue Mountains in triumph as my bride.

Encar of the Fields came in then with a query about the new acreage of samphron trees we were clearing — from the gnarly-trunked samphron trees we pick glossy purple fruits which the watermills crush into fragrant oil — and after Encar waddled Erdgar, fat and out of breath, with a problem on the supply of shaped and seasoned knees for the new ships he was building down in Valkanium's dockyards.

"Erdgar," I said. "There is a journey I must make. I shall need your best-found ship. *Rose of Valka,* possibly? And fully-provisioned."

"*Rose of Valka,*" wheezed Erdgar the Shipwright. He took a glass of wine, sniffing it appreciatively. "Aye, she is fleet and well-found and might venture into the Southern Ocean, if needs be."

This was a neat way of asking me my destination. The breeze blew on that high terrace of Esser Rarioch and the scent of yellow mushk, clustered with bees in its shelter, smelled very sweet. My friends were relaxing after the day's toil; soon we would go down to the great hall to eat and drink and sing the old songs — and the new, aye, the new! — and life was exceedingly good.

"Zenicce," I told Erdgar. "I will go to Strombor."

This, as it seemed to me, was a cunning plan, for I might thus be able to detour the gales that prevented me from reaching Vallia. And I had a hunger to see Strombor again.

"Strombor! The devils of Esztercari drove out the good folk of Strombor! There was a story that they had in their turn been driven out. I pray the invisible twins it is so."

Tharu drained his glass. "Many of us were born of parents who escaped from Strombor."

My surprise was complete.

It made sense. Valka lies about a hundred and fifty dwaburs southwest of Zenicce. And the Stromboramin were likely to stick together in the urgency of their departure in the few ships available to them in those days of horror.

While Erdgar the Shipwright wheezed and fussed over *Rose of Valka* I took a journey into the Heart Heights in connection with the construction of a new dam. I found I welcomed these duties of economist, husbandman, canalmaster, and organizer of a province. My party of engineers, secretaries, and supply officers traveled into the interior in a narrow boat. Through lock after lock that had been recently repaired and put back into service we mounted the ladder of water. The weather remained wonderful, the crops were ripening, there was not a slave within sight, and my only regret was that my Delia of Delphond was not at my side to share all these delights with me.

One warm and pinkly-golden evening as the Maiden with the Many Smiles and She of the Veils floated together in the sky I walked for a space on the canal bank, sunk in thought.

The glorious pink and golden evening turned blue with a lambent refulgence of blueness I recognized with a savage surge of feeling. I looked up. Against the starshot sky with those two moons of Kregen floating so serenely I saw the luminescent blue outline of a gigantic scorpion.

This was the sign! This scorpion with arrogantly upflung tail was the sign that in some way either brought me or indicated I was to be brought to Kregen. I had seen this phantom sky scorpion on Earth. Now I was seeing it on Kregen!

The old familiar blueness enveloped me and I was falling and twisting with the blueness roaring in my head — and I did not struggle, I did not shout my defiance, I merely waited for what the destiny of the scorpion would bring me.

Six

The scorpion and the glacier

It is not my intention to speak freely or to go into details of my life here on this planet of my birth. Although I usually returned to some crisis or other and I spent some exhilarating years here, to put it mildly, my chief interest and absorbing passions were ever fixed on the planet of Kregen orbiting Antares in the constellation of Scorpio four hundred light-years away.

Often I would stand and gaze into the starry sky, hoping and praying that the lambent-blue form of the ghostly scorpion would once more summon me, naked and unarmed, and pitch me headlong into bloody and violent adventure. The man whose name I do not mention who held my growing fortune in trust for me served me faithfully and well, and his descendants after him. He was always pleased to see me and asked no questions I could not answer. He and his sons knew of this habit of mine of looking up at the stars, but they passed no comment. I know they understood I was not as ordinary mortals.

I found myself in Paris during the July days of 1830.

There was a time loop involved here; I had had the word from the Gdoinye as to that. I did not understand what was involved then; and even today, the mechanics of time distortion remain vague. I had spent more Terrestrial-span years on Kregen than there were between my first arrival there floating down the River Aph to Aphrasöe, the Swinging City, to meet the Savanti in 1805, and 1830.

Caught up in the excitements of the dismissal of Charles X and the installation of Louis Phillipe, I played a part. Only after the seventh of August, however, was I free and able to walk alone by the Seine. The blue lambency caught me up swiftly, and the scorpion drew me willingly across the parsecs, hurtling through the empty dark to resume my destiny upon Kregen under the Suns of Scorpio.

Even before I opened my eyes I knew I landed in a part of Kregen I had never visited before.

The cold cut in like scalping knives.

As usual, I was unarmed, naked, left entirely to my own resources.

I felt free, overjoyed, triumphant, profoundly thankful.

What, I wondered, was the emergency that had brought me back this time?

Whatever it might be I would deal with it as fast as I could and then, ascertaining just where I had been flung on this terrifying if beautiful world of Kregen, make my way to Vallia, march into Vondium, and confront the Emperor, demand from him his daughter in marriage. Yes, I had hesitated and hung back long enough. Only the gift of a thousand years of life had made what I had done possible. But my patience had run out. By Zim-Zair! No matter if the Emperor was belittled in the eyes of his daughter, and thereby I ran the risk of hurting her feelings — I had absolutely no fears that I would lose her love, as she knew she would never lose mine. I would take that risk and inflict that amount of pain on my beloved, believing sincerely that she would understand I moved not only for my own pleasure and greed and pride, but also for her sake as well.

I opened my eyes.

I shivered.

Snow lay everywhere in a thick, pale pink blanket through which the dark firs thrust like withered fingers of a buried army of crones.

A hundred yards off lay the crumpled shape of an airboat.

My task lay before me.

The wind cut into my naked hide and I knew that if I did not find clothes and food very quickly I could give up all hopes and ideas of finding my Delia again.

The airboat had landed badly and her petal shape had been grotesquely twisted. From the small aft cabin I dragged out four bodies. These men were Vallians. Under the heavy ponsho fleeces they wore the buff coats and the long black boots I knew so well. Selecting the body of the largest, I stripped him and donned his gear. The warmth of the ponsho skin struck in most gratefully and I shivered in reciprocal delight. Now I could attend to the two men still alive. Unconscious, they breathed stertorously; but an examination convinced me they were not seriously injured. These two men, then, were the reason I had been returned to Kregen.

The airboat had crashed through spiky fir trees to come to rest in a V-shaped valley between peaks. Up there the snow and ice glistened uglily. The thought occurred to me that we were stranded in The Stratemsk, a fate of almost certain disaster. The Stratemsk, although not the greatest range of mountains upon Kregen, are so vast, so tall, so hostile, that the imagination shrinks from their contemplation. Downslope a panorama spread out where the valley ended, and between craggy outcrops the snow could not smooth or render less sinister a glacier began, vanishing below cloud. That, then, was our way out.

A cry brought my attention back to the flier. One of the men had crawled to the shattered opening. His face glared out on me more white, more stark, than the snow and the dark fir trees.

"What happened? Where are we? Who are you?" The voice carried that habitual ring of authority, so that I knew I was in the presence of a man accustomed to command, a high dignitary, a man of power.

"You crashed. We are in the mountains. I am Dray Prescot."

He moved back as I approached, and before I reached the opening the second man crawled out. He was younger, handsome, his brown hair a fairer tint than the normal Vallian, although nowise of that outrageous chestnut glory of my Delia's hair.

"Dray Prescot?"

The older man pushed through quickly and the younger was, perforce, thrust aside. The elder wriggled as he crawled out onto the snow, and turning his head spoke in a low voice to the younger. He stood up, and swayed, and I was at his side, supporting him.

"You'd best rest easy, dom. You've had a tidy whack."

He drew himself up, although still clutching my arm for support. Blood had dried along the clean-shaven upper edge of his beard, frozen, glittering coldly.

"I am Naghan Furtway, Kov of Falinur, and this is my nephew, Jenbar. You address me as Kov, and my nephew as Tyr. Is that understood?"

I held him and I looked into his eyes. I knew those eyes of old, I had seen their like many times in the faces of men accustomed to absolute power. Corrupt, sadistic, merciless, yes; but the eyes of men accustomed to moving the strings of this world, as they manipulate those of Earth. The friendly name of dom — the nearest equivalent in English is mate, and in American, pal — had affronted him.

It was necessary to put our relationship on its proper footing instantly, and now I cursed that my stay on Earth had loosened my tongue. For these men were Vallians, and I had given them my real name. I should have remained Drak, Strom of Valka. So I simply said: "Very good, Kov. We must collect what things are necessary and travel as far downslope as is possible before nightfall."

He grunted. "Quite so." He turned to his nephew. "Jenbar — do you feel fit enough to walk?"

"I do not!" Jenbar spat out, with a curse.

Naghan Furtway, Kov of Falinur, merely looked at the young man, and then pushed past back into the shattered cabin. I had buried the naked body of the man I had stripped, and if Furtway bothered to notice he probably assumed the

553

disappearance had been caused by the unfortunate man being flung out as the flier crashed. He began taking ponsho skins from the dead bodies.

Jenbar studied me.

"Koter Prescot," he said, at last, and his voice betrayed his weakness. "I ask you to pardon my ill-temper. But I think you will understand it when you see our condition, and good men dead. I thank you for your assistance. I will try to walk bravely."

I warmed to him then, responding to his frankness. I, too, would have been in a filthy temper had my airboat crashed in these surroundings.

In truth, our surroundings were unpleasant in the extreme, and if we were caught out here by nightfall, desperately dangerous. The airboat might provide some shelter, and I fancied we might manage a fire with tree wood, but I preferred to make the effort to reach lower altitudes before dark.

"Oolie Opaz!" exclaimed Jenbar. "What a miserable business!"

His expression warned me that there might be more than a mere curse in his intentions; for I had once seen the long lines of chanting men and women, garishly clad and strung with blossoms, winding in and out of the streets of Pomdermam, the capital of the nation of Tomboram on the island of Pandahem. "Oolie Opaz! Oolie Opaz! Oolie Opaz!" they would chant, singing and swaying, hour after hour the same metronomic hypnotic words, swinging up and down the scale, changing key, on and on maddeningly. This hypnotic chanting held power. It sucked a man in, singing, until his eyeballs rolled up and he drifted away to a white and empty state of which philosophers and mystics talk.

I contented myself with a nod to the ponsho fleeces.

"Best to dress yourself warmly, Tyr Jenbar. The way will be long and hard." Then, because he was young and there was in him a steely inner strength I could perceive, I added: "I know you will march well, but I will be here to help you if necessary."

He looked downslope. His features hardened and a ridge jumped into life along his jaw, for he was clean-shaven. His face held a strong damn-you-to-hell look, and I guessed that ferocity was not for me, perhaps not even for the fates that had flung him here, but for the hostility of the way we must tread.

He chuckled. "It will be a task for Tyr Nath! But we will win through, Koter Prescot. We of Falinur always win through to our desires in the end!"

"So be it," I said, and busied myself in making what small preparations we could.

So we set off, the three of us, and, in truth, had I not been with them, hurled there across the gulf of four hundred light-years by the inscrutable purposes of the Star Lords, they would not have survived. I fancied the Star Lords had brought me to Kregen this time, for this business bore all the hallmarks of their handiwork, and not that of the Savanti.

We struggled through waist-high snow, which glittered with the frosting colors of jade and crimson as the twin suns struck through from a sky of purple and indigo. We reached the end of the valley, after many halts, and there stretching below us lay the beginning of the glacier, a tumbled confused mass, with the clouds drifting above it, obscuring the panorama beyond.

I am no man to love fir trees, for they look thin and harsh and dispiriting; I am a man who loves the wide-leaved expansive openhearted trees of the south. Fir trees are valuable for spars, and other artifacts, but here I welcomed their presence as clear proof we were below the tree line. As soon as possible we must reach below the snow-line.

"We will slide," I said.

They did not argue. They had become stupefied — puggled is the old word for it — and they meekly accepted my dictates. I spread the ponsho fleeces. We lay upon them, belted together, and I pushed off — and we went.

We went!

It was a mad helter-skelter of a ride, a wild swooping rush of icy-cold wind and the hiss of the ice and jouncing bouncing and the desperate booted thrusting to avoid debris and the moraines that built up as side glaciers joined the main stem. Four times I had to haul us painfully to a halt, against the scraped sides, so that we might not crash full tilt into the low pile of rocks. Then we had to slip and slide over the obstacles, find a fresh glide path, and so down once more on the skins and take off with a breathless swooshing. My face was numb. Ice smothered me and I had to brush the crisp glassy crystals from my eyelids. The cold continued to cut intensely, and our very progress intensified its freezing grip.

We had taken rapiers and daggers — for very few men, and they either fools or protected in other ways, travel Kregen unarmed — and with a dagger in each hand I was in some measure able to control and direct our descent. I thrust the daggers angling downward, and by varying the pressures from side to side could both slow and steer us. But it was exhausting work and I sweated a little, which is excruciatingly unpleasant in such cold temperatures.

We plunged boldly into the clouds.

"Have a care, Koter Prescot!" Furtway's words were weak. The cold was numbing him through to the marrow. If he was to survive we must get down — and get down fast.

The rate of descent was slowed by the daggers. We left a wide swathe of ice chips spilling across the glacier after us. If we hit a rock now...

The clouds thinned, thickened, whereat I thrust hard with the daggers, thinned again and then we were through them and almost on the lip of the glacier.

I lunged sideways, plunging both daggers over onto the right. We swirled in a great fanning of ice chips and for an instant I thought we would skate right off the ponsho fleeces.

"Hold on!" I yelled, and ice cracked and flaked from my mouth.

We held on. Just short of the lip of the glacier, where it calved and in a great crevasse and a white thunder fell a thousand feet, we skidded and slewed into the side. We hit the scored bank of ice and snow, tumbled out, and so lay exhausted.

"Up!" I said.

They moaned.

"Let me lie, rast," said Naghan Furtway, Kov of Falinur. "I am tired and would like to rest."

"If you rest here you will never rise again."

His eyes were closed and so he did not see my face as I leaned over him. I gripped him beneath the shoulders and stood him up, but his legs buckled and he slid down again. I turned to his nephew.

"Up," I said. "Now is when you must march like a man."

He groaned and sat up, and tumbled over sideways.

"Life is sweet and there is much to live for," he said, the gush of white mist spuming from his lips at each word. "Now I know that, but I cannot feel it. I am done for. Leave me, Koter Prescot. It is soft and comfortable and warm here."

"It's as cold as the Ice Floes of Sicce," I said, "which is where you'll find yourself if you do not brace up."

I stared at them. If they died I would have failed the Star Lords, and then I would be flung contemptuously back to Earth. I might rot there for years. I could not face that. These men must be saved, so that I might remain on Kregen and seek my lost love and demand her from her all-powerful father.

The task was extraordinarily difficult and painful, but I got Furtway up on my back, bundled with ponsho fleeces, and buckled him in place. I put my left arm around Jenbar and dragged him up, and so, carrying one and dragging the other, I set off.

There was no ice pick, so I could not probe for crevasses. If we fell, we fell. The cold was biting into my brain now; all I could do was put one foot down in front of the other, thankful for the tall Vallian boots. Socks are known on Kregen, but, like the men of the Foreign Legion, most Kregans have no truck with socks. I would have welcomed a good thick warm pair right now.

The memories I have of that nightmare descent grow vague and more vague. I was aware of the green sun Genodras sinking in an eerie smothering of emerald and jade, and then the world turned into blood as the red sun Zim held for a short space the sole domination of the sky. At this time the overlords of Magdag would gather in their colossal buildings and pray to Grodno, the green-sun deity, for protection and grace. Or so the peoples of the Eye of the World believed; I had witnessed the rites held during an eclipse of the green by the red, and I guessed the overlords did not act as the world suspected.

I was no warmer, but the trees were thickening and the snow — the eternal, damned snow — was petering out in drifts and crunching sheets through which I plunged to feel the hard rocklike ground beneath. The Maiden of the Many Smiles floated up into the night sky among the hosts of stars, and two of the smaller moons hurtled low overhead. In their pinkish light I trudged on. I had no conception of time or distance; all I knew was that I must go downhill. There had been a vague glimpse of a vast hilly plain when we quitted the clouds, cloud-bedappled. Now, as I lifted my head to look up and so out over the plain beneath, I saw that dark expanse beneath the moons spattered and dotted by myriads of specks of light.

Nearer, five hundred yards downslope, a light beamed up, warm and friendly and beckoning. I headed for it, fell against the wooden door, and went on hitting the door until it opened.

Seven

Naghan Furtway and I play Jikaida

"You are a strange man, Koter Prescot."

"Many men have said that, Kov Furtway. And it is true."

We sat around the plain wooden table in the neat cabin and drank the superlative Kregan tea and warmed ourselves by the fire that crackled and sparked in the hearth, while Bibi, the lady of the house, fussed around us, delighted and yet awed at entertaining a real live kov in her house.

"How were you in the mountains, then, Koter Prescot?" asked Jenbar.

"I was lost. Believe me, I was hoping you were going to rescue me."

They laughed at that.

Warmth, a good sleep, and now a piping hot meal of roast rolled-vosk-loin and a vegetable-pot, together with chunks torn from a long Kregan loaf and that Kregan tea I had sampled with my clansmen, had revived the three of us.

Bibi's husband, Genal, was out chopping more wood. They lived well up here in the mountains, with a great store of food put by in the shed protected from snow-leem and deep-frozen by the weather, and Genal could bring in enough ice to be packed and shipped down to the plain to keep him and Bibi in moderate affluence. Genal the Ice, they called him down there.

"More tea?" fussed Bibi. "It is still fresh, Kov Furtway."

He held out his cup and watched as Bibi filled it and he drank. He did not say thank you. In everyday life he never had to say thank you to anyone, except...

"We bring our ice from Drak's Seat," said Jenbar. "By Vox! I've seen enough to last me a lifetime. In Vondium ice is all the rage, but not for me, Oolie Opaz, not for me!"

Vondium!

I was in Vallia. I must be. Vallia… *Vallia!*

'Tell me, Tyr Jenbar. Just how far away is Vondium?'

He stretched and yawned and answered offhandedly: "Oh, I don't know. Three hundred dwaburs perhaps, a bit more probably, something like that."

"At least that, Jenbar," said Furtway. "We had crossed most of these accursed Mountains of the North from Evir before we crashed. May the Invisible Twins smite those cramphs of Havilfar!"

I nodded. "One would think they did themselves a grave disservice by selling airboats that fail so often."

Furtway grunted and reached for the palines that Bibi placed in a diced-wood bowl upon the table.

"They are arrogant in their power. Only they, as far as we know, possess the mines. One day, Opaz willing, one day..."

Jenbar laughed and took up the palines.

"My uncle has an old dream, Koter Prescot.[xiv] We of Vallia are proud and strong; we produce all we require and may buy what we will all over the known world. But we cannot make an airboat."

I nodded and the conversation drifted. The impatience to be gone sawed at my nerves. Vondium lay something like fifteen hundred miles due south. I had to get there — and I managed to retain wit enough to understand that through these two, Furtway and Jenbar, I might reach my objective faster than I could by traveling alone. They would provide transport.

Evir, across the mountains to the north, was the most northerly province on the island proper, although, as is common on Kregen, the coastal waters were peppered with small islands. One of those islands — and not so small, at that — was Valka. If I said I was a Strom to these men now, they would not believe. But the name Dray Prescot was likely going to prove a handicap.

The clothes I wore, the black boots on my feet, the rapier and two daggers, were all from the corpse in the airboat. In addition, I had taken his money, as also the money from the others, for old mercenary habits die hard. The Kov and his nephew had not recognized either the clothes or the weapons, for they were of the plain and workmanlike cut common to the middle classes of Vallia. I suppose one might call that great mass of self-interested, self-centered, and intensely self-loyal people the gentry of Vallia. With this garb I fancied I could fend for myself in somewhat better style than I had when I had at last crossed the Klackadrin and reached Pa Mejab on the eastern coast of Turismond.

In my view neither Furtway nor Jenbar were fit to travel yet, for we were still high in the mountains and the weather was bitterly cold. Since Genal the Ice had told us he would be taking an ice-load down the mountain in three days' time, it was easy enough to persuade them to wait that long. I did not want to wait, but I already knew what Kov Furtway proposed.

Roads are not as good as they might be in Vallia, and no one, as far as I then knew, had shown the interest in zorca chariot racing that had caused the old Strom of Valka to pave a number of his roads across the island. The roads are, however, perfectly capable of speeding zorca couriers along their tracks which would not accept wheeled or sledged traffic. Heavy traffic goes by canal in Vallia. Furtway intended to dispatch a zorca courier from the post town below in a fold of the foothills with a message — and a damned intemperate one it would be, too, I could guess — to his villa in Vondium to send a fresh airboat for him.

On that airboat I intended to enter Vondium.

All the great lords of the provinces of Vallia maintain splendid and sumptuous villas in the capital city, and use them whenever business or pleasure calls them to Vondium. When the lord is not in residence the villa is kept up, if on a reduced scale, for no chatelaine knows from one day to the next if the lord might arrive. And if all is not in apple-pie order and everything ready immediately for comfortable occupation — exit one chatelaine and enter a sufficiently energetic and zealous new one.

So we had three days to kill.

We sang songs and we told stories and we played Jikaida.

Kov Furtway was inordinately fond of Jikaida. This is the board game popular on Kregen involving an elongated form of chessboard — the actual number of squares may vary along with the numbers of men, and the different sizes are dignified by different degrees — which, together with chess, checkers, and Halma-like moves for the men, combine to form an engrossing game of mock war. Genal the Ice and Bibi had a board, for one is usually to be found in every house in Kregen, if sometimes a little rooting about in cupboards is necessary, and we settled down to a tournament. The men were blue and yellow.

"Blue," said Furtway, not giving me the opportunity to guess his closed fists. "You take the damned blue."

Jenbar chuckled, but the sound was such as I had heard Thelda utter — or my many friends of Pandahem. "Blue, the color of the Opaz-forsaken Pandaheem cramphs! My uncle, Kr. Prescot, never plays the blue."

"As you wish." I thought of that great battle in Magdag. "I, too, have a fondness for the yellow."

We played. Furtway was skilled, tough, ruthless, unscrupulous when he could thus win a point or a piece. I reacted at first with vigor, and gradually the yellow pushed back the blue along the board, and I was aligning my sights on his left-wing Chuktar, when I paused and considered. I came to the conclusion it might be judicious to let this man win. After all, a board game can be turned into profit and advantage, as I well knew; and there is to some men a superior form of winning in contriving their own defeat. So I fumbled a Deldar's move, and with a flashing smile and a triumphant gesture, Furtway removed my right-wing Chuktar.

"Your concentration lapsed, Kr. Prescot. Always, at Jikaida, as in life, you must bend your mind to the task in hand."

"Yes, Kov Furtway. You are right, but I am most anxious to reach Vondium."

They had, of course, asked me my business in the capital. I had fobbed them off with a casual story of a consignment of cortilindens coming into the port, and turned the conversation, managing to bring up the subject of the Emperor and his wayward daughter. Both men did not attempt to hide their feelings.

"The Emperor is the Emperor, and his will is law. But we sometimes have to take measures for his own good. The Princess Majestrix, now, is willfully disobedient in refusing to marry."

I saw Jenbar nodding in agreement.

"She is the most beautiful girl in all Vallia — in all the world, I truly believe — and she must marry some day. Happy the man who claims her hand."

"The man whom the Emperor wishes her to marry," I said, speaking with care, and yet seeming casual. "He is a good choice?"

"That fool!" cried Furtway. "Why, Vektor of Aduimbrev is totally unsuited, for all that he is wealthy and powerful and has the Emperor's ear."

"Vektor is a get onker!" Jenbar spoke with passion. I knew of the passion my Delia could arouse in the hearts of the men in her bodyguard and retinue; I had seen its results aboard the swifter *Sword of Genodras,* and I warmly applauded his defense of my beloved. If there was any degree of this kind of feeling abroad in the country, then perhaps my task in persuading her father the Emperor that I was the one Delia of the Blue Mountains should marry would not be as difficult as I had surmised. But I wanted to know more narrowly where these men stood in the greatest enterprise of my life.

"But the racters, they desire it, do they not?"

Jenbar snorted. Furtway cunningly captured a zorca patrol led by a Hikdar and, with the blue pieces in his hand, stared at me. "The racters run the country, no one can deny that. But in this they are wrong."

"Yes," said Jenbar. "But where do you stand in this argument, Kr. Prescot?"

I was merely a Koter, and therefore only a small step up from the great mass of the ordinary folk among whom I truly belong, as I sometimes think; the question, however, was not patronizing, as might be supposed, coming from the nephew of a Kov. Jenbar really wanted to know.

"As for me," I said, attempting to forestall an imminent attack on my exposed right wing, "I do not think the Princess Majestrix should marry Vektor of Aduimbrev."

"Ah!" quoth Furtway, and demolished a Jiktar and two Hikdars. "You have lost the game. Place the pieces for another. As for Vektor — when your business with the cortilindens is finished, call at my villa. You will be welcome. You are a man of resource. I can find work for your hands, aye, and your brain."

"Thank you, Kov Furtway. I shall look forward to that."

This might be very useful. A man as powerful as a Kov on my side would weigh heavily in the scales. I played considerably better the next game, taking both his wing Chuktars, but eventually letting him push a strong force through the center and so rout me. His passion for the game was unslaked, and I saw how much of his life was reflected in the pieces on the board. Vallia, as I understood it, while being preeminent on the outer oceans, maintained a minuscule army, mainly composed of honor guards and the like, and employed mercenaries whenever land warfare was involved. The interior police, however, and the aragorn, were prominent in the political affairs of the islands.

On the third day a shrill cry brought us to the door and we saw toiling up the slope toward us a shaggy old quoffa dragging a cart on its runners, its wheels removed and slung on the sides. The quoffa looks like a perambulating hearth-rug with bunchy shoulders and hindquarters — it has six legs, but the Earthly nomenclature trips from the tongue — and a dogged old head from which the steam blew in great snorts like one of Mr. Stevenson's new engines. The carter was a Relt, at which I was much surprised. But the Relts, those less formidable cousins of the bird-headed Rapas, are often found in employment in many countries. He shouted again and Bibi chuckled and bustled about, for this was her regular delivery of four weeks' supplies. Also, the Relt would take away a heaping load of ice on the downward run, and Genal would give him orders for the number of carts he required for the main delivery.

After a great meal and a single glass of an excellent vintage from Procul, a full and rich red wine, we bade Rembaree to Genal the Ice and Bibi. They were given a handful of broad gold talens, with the head of the Emperor on one side and the — smaller — head of Furtway on the reverse, charged with a checkerboard. I considered this carrying a passion for a game to a fault, that it should be the man's emblem and figure on his coinage, but it turned out that the checkerboard was the Falinur insignia. I had privily sorted through the coins I had taken from the dead men and found some with the Emperor on the obverse, and faces and designs I did not recognize on the reverse; these I handed to Genal and Bibi with my sincere thanks.

Then we clambered aboard the cart, warmly wrapped against the chill of the ice blocks, even though Genal had reduced this load on our account to make a space, and off we went.

The sliding descent on the runners was wild enough, but when the Relt replaced the wheels, and off we went again, I felt my opinion change, and knew the wheels were worse. At last the faithful quoffa could be put back into the shafts and we trundled decorously into the large village, almost a small town, nestling in the valley.

Clean through the center of the town ran a broad canal, bridged here and there, but unmistakably the artery of commerce and travel. There were many long narrow boats afloat. The ice went straight aboard one of them, together with ice from other ice-gatherers, and the boat pushed off at once.

"I'd have thought it would melt too soon, aboard a barge," I said.

The Relt rubbed his beak in the habit they have, and said in his squeaky voice: "This is ice for only a few dwaburs south. Ice for farther afield goes by airboat. Look."

We all looked and there was an airboat — drab, gray, battered — rising over the houses and heading south.

"That is for us," said Furtway in the voice of the Kov. We paid the Relt and walked across to the airport. Yes, we could book a passage south, it would cost us the same price as it cost the ice-shippers, and we would have to provide our own food, sleeping equipment, and an indemnity. In case of accident we must sign away the right of our heirs to claim against the ice-shipping Company of Friends. I was to learn a great deal more of these Companies of Friends which control so much of the trade and industry of Vallia. Both my companions made no bones about signing, so neither did I.

The airboat carried us — not particularly comfortably and in somewhat chilly conditions — a hundred dwaburs south, where we were set down in the bustling market town of Therminsax.

From this place Furtway was able to dispatch a zorca courier — one of the officers charged with maintaining the zorca communications over the island — on payment of a sizable sum and proof that he was who he said he was. This he did by means of his seal-ring. My own seal-ring as Strom of Valka, the ring sent from the Emperor via my panval friends, lay now with my Savanti leathers and my Savanti sword on the towpath back in Valka. Although — surely my friends would have found that little pile of possessions by now. They must have been sorely puzzled wondering where I had gone. Perhaps they thought I had taken that journey I had told them of. If they thought that, they were almost right, but why I should choose to go stark naked must have driven them to their wits' end to find explanations.

While we waited we put up at *The Swordship and Barynth*. I have often noticed how nautical names for pubs are common in inland parts. The inn was comfortable and obliging. Furtway claimed Jenbar to play Jikaida. I went for walks about the town, soaking up the atmosphere, relishing the clean red and white houses, the tidy gardens, the squares and shady colonnades, spending a long time leaning on the canal wall overlooking the towpath and watching the narrow boats as they glided by.

Many of them were hauled by whole gangs and tribes of people, sturdy, open-faced folk in practical outfits, men and women, of breechclouts and short-sleeved tunics, open at the throat. They hauled with a will, and once the narrow boat was under way she could be kept going and on course by just half a dozen girls or lads to pull, and the old skipper to steer. I saw no draft animals, not a single quoffa, and this did not surprise me. There were very few halflings hauling the narrow boats, although I did see a complete outfit of two narrow boats in tandem dragged along by a squealing bunch of Ochs. On the second day I saw a sight that brought me, with my fists clenched, staring painfully at the canal.

A narrow boat approached. She was not gaily painted as were all the others I had seen, decorated with fantastic scenes from myth and legend, from song and story, and with all the flowers of the field — this boat was all a dun gray and she was large and clumsy. But the thing that so disturbed me was her motive power. Along the canal towpath trudged a gang of people, all stark naked, all hairy and dirty, all heaving at the tow rope under the merciless whips of guards.

I stared, hatred welling.

The guards were big fellows, mostly humans, but a Rapa or a Fristle stalked here and there. They whipped their charges on. The narrow boat moved lumpily through the water, heavily laden. I just stood there. The guards were dressed uniformly in buff leather jerkins, wide across the shoulder, and with the tall black Vallian boots. The sleeves of their shirts were banded red and black. I had seen those uniform colors before.

I, myself, wore the buff jerkin, but my sleeves were buff also. I knew that these banded sleeves in their color coding were the signs worn by servitors of great lords or parties; but this red and black, these were the colors of the government, of the Emperor!

I, Dray Prescot, could not just stand there.

But I had to.

For I dared not do as I instinctively desired to do and rush upon these slave-herders and rout them and free their slaves; the trouble that action has caused in the past is beyond calculation.

A girl stumbled and fell and dragged the tow rope down in her despairing clutch. She brought down an old man and one or two others, so telling me how weak they all were. The guards whipped them. But the girl just lay there. Her brown hair drifted out across the muddy tow-path. I saw the rawhide cutting into her. Could I just stand there? This same scene must be reenacted many times every day. One more repetition would make no difference at all.

None.

The girl moaned and tried to shield herself with her spindly arms. She shrieked afresh as the lash bit into her.

No difference.

I had been learning cleverness. I had controlled myself back there in Theirson's village. I had not rushed upon the aragorn until I had a weapon.

I had a weapon now.

But — the trouble this would cause. The Emperor in faraway Vondium, the Kov Furtway here, all my plans, the love I bore my Delia of the Blue Mountains. One young girl being whipped to death was a common enough sight, Zair knew. What had it to do with me?

There was nothing I could do. Nothing.

I jumped the wall and ran down to the towpath. I spoke in a rational and quiet voice, calmly, reasonably.

"To hit her any more will do no good. She cannot rise."

The guard swung, the whip poised. Four of his fellows turned toward me as the chanks of the inner sea turn toward their prey.

"This is no business of yours, dom. Clear off!"

"But," I said, "if the girl cannot pull, why beat her?"

"She'll pull." The guard had fine strong white teeth. He smiled. "She'll pull. Now clear off. This is Emperor's business, as you well know. We are not answerable to you."

"I think, dom, you are, unless you release her."

"Release her? You're either a get onker or you're mad! The Emperor's slaves are sequestered property. Clear off, or you'll be in more trouble than you can handle."

The guard sounded no more truculent than any man interrupted in his work. He spoke as reasonably as I. He could not understand what I was talking about. I tried for the last time.

"Please" — I said *please!* — "do not hit her any more. If you cannot release her give her time to rest."

Another guard ran up, swearing horribly. He wore a red and black cockade in his broad-brimmed hat, above the feather. The narrow boat had gone on with her momentum and now the tow rope stretched back from the bitts on her bows.

"What's going on here? If you Doty-rotten cramphs can't keep your rasts of haulers in line I'll soon Jikaida your backs! I'll make you yell, by Vomer the Vile!"

"It's this one here, sir," said the guard who had been trying to explain to me.

I said, "This girl cannot pull any more. Flogging her will do no good—"

I was interrupted. The guard wore a rapier. He ripped it out. He flourished it in my face. He looked to be in a most apoplectic rage.

"This barge is on the Emperor's service — as you well know! Take yourself off before it is too late! Jump, rast!"

I knew little of the pecking order in Vallia; that it is complicated is true; I didn't worry about my lack of knowledge.

"It seems you insist I must make you show mercy," I said. I started to draw my rapier. I was already working out how not to kill them all, when I heard a man in the towing party yell. "By Vaosh! Behind you, Ven!"

I turned. I was slow. The blow struck behind my ear and I pitched forward, struggling to retain my balance. A black booted foot kicked out. I heard a coarse laugh. "Swim in the canal, cramph!" And then I smashed face-first into blackness.

Eight

On the canals of Vallia

On my back I floated with the mild drift of the current, for here near the inflow of river water, controlled and sluiced, the canal waters possessed a definite movement of their own. The sky above me towered enormously high, palely blue, with the intolerable glare of Antares blinding down and streaming variegated highlights from the tiny waves I made as I floated. I knew what I was doing there. I had been stupid, as usual, and slow, which for a man in my trade is unforgivable. I knew, however, why I had been slow. My aims had been confused; a desire to do what naturally occurred to me to do and my so-clever newfound rationality had played me false. I would far better have simply rushed in swinging as in the old days. Then, instead of me floating in the canal with a muzzy head there would be six bully-boy guards floating there, and with rapier-thrusts through their bellies, like as not.

In the future I wouldn't be slow, and I'd hit first — as I usually did.

Worry over Delia had fogged my mind. Here I was, actually on the same landmass as her, breathing air that might waft down for her to breathe and so waft back to me. An idiotic notion, but one that suited my idiotic mood.

Through the water toward me the smooth stem of a narrow boat bore on. I saw the gaily painted strakes and the fanciful representations of monsters and flowers, musical instruments, and spreading proudly to either side of the stem, the lavishly decorated picture of a Talu, one of those eight-armed mythical — as I still thought — dancers of the sloe eyes and the cupid's-bow mouths. I had seen such a Talu carved from the mastodon tusk in that perfumed corridor of a decadent palace, when a slave girl in the gray slave breechclout had dropped and smashed a jar of water. I had cannoned into the statue and toppled with it in my arms, the eight arms a wagonwheel of wanton display about me, the fingertips touching.

I confess I was still thinking about that mastodon-tusk carving as the rope hissed into the water and I was hauled aboard.

The majority of Vallians have been blessed with the kind of strong beaked nose I have myself, and the man who stared down on me now wiped a hand across his powerful nose, and grunted:

"Welcome aboard—"

He did not add the customary Koter, or even dom, or, given the circumstances, Ven. I saw the expression on his face and knew precisely what he was thinking. If you're not a canalman, he was saying, without speaking, then you're a dead man.

"Thank you for pulling me out. It's all right. The water won't harm me."

He perked up at that, and smiled.

"You'd best come below. Dry you off." As I nodded to thank him and bent to descend the short companionway ladder, he whistled. I had lost my hat.

"That's a crack you've had on the back of your head, Ven. Like to have killed a man."

"I've a tolerably thick skull. Too thick for some folk."

Someone yelled from up forward and my host halted to yell back. "He's of the canalfolk. He's had a knock, but he'll live."

In the small but beautifully appointed cabin with everything in its place I sat at the table and drank strong Kregan tea. Made with the canalwater, it tasted somehow as good as any tea I have ever had. "I am Yelker, skipper of the old *Dancing Talu.*" I knew, from my talk with Borg, that he would be Ven Yelker nal Vomansoir, for this was the Vomansoir Cut.

Thinking of Ven Borg made me remember my resolve.

"I am Drak ti Valkanium," I said. This was true.

"We're headed south so I can't offer to take you back to Therminsax. It is a pleasant town, and we always enjoy our stopovers there. But we are for Vomansoir."

My clothes were drying, so I sat there with a blanket about me as a girl bustled in, tut-tutted at the way my tunic had been clumsily hung up by Yelker, glanced a quick and intense look in my direction, gathered up my gear, and started up the ladder again. She paused and tossed her heavy brown hair back and stared over her shoulder. She wore an off-the-shoulder white blouse, attractively tailored beneath her bodice, and the movement emphasized her beauty, as she well knew it would. I could guess all too easily why she did not wear one of the tunics or jerkins common to the canalfolk.

"You men can't look after a thing. I'll hang these on the line."

When she had gone with a flash of long bronzed legs, Yelker sighed. "That's Zyna, my daughter. Her mother didn't spank her enough when she was young enough for it to be effective." Then he roared into the speaking tube that led forward, the brass mouthpiece dazzling. "Mother! That girl of yours is showing off again."

A muffled series of shrieks and squawks spattered from the brass mouthpiece. Yelker shoved the whistle back and sighed.

"I don't know what good canalfolk are coming to these days."

"Ven Yelker. Will you take me south with you?" I reached for the lesten-hide bag of money I had taken from the dead men, and realized it was in the pocket of my tunic. "I will be happy to pay you—"

He held up a hand. "Not so, Ven Drak. You are a canalman, and I am a canalman. If one cannot do the other a goodness without seeking reward, then the spirit of the canals is dead."

"Did you see how I came to be in the canal?"

"I did not. I would not ask, but I own I am curious."

I told him of the incident. He frowned and bashed a fist down onto the table.

"Pardon me for saying it, Ven Drak. But you are a fool!"

I sat.

"Don't you have Emperor's barges on Valka?"

"I have not seen one. We pull our own boats, there." I had expressed my astonishment to Borg over the non-use of draft animals, and he had simply scratched his head and said that men and women always pulled the boats. How otherwise would they get exercise and build their muscles? Animals, to haul narrow boats! He thought the conceit highly amusing.

"Well, you surprise me. We hate them. They are unfair competition. And the poor devils who are sent to the Emperor's canal barges — well, just steer clear of them, that's all. They have absolute priority and right of way on any cut. They force us out into the center and make us drop our tow as they pass. Oh, and they do pass!"

I had seen what I had seen. I could imagine the horror of the haulers, racing to drag their unwieldy barges past the elegant narrow boats of the canalfolk, driven on by the whip and the knout.

"I do not like it, Ven Yelker."

"Neither do I, Ven Drak. But neither you nor I can do ought about it. And here comes Mother." I stood up, clutching my blanket, as Sosie descended into the cabin, a plump, smiling, brown-eyed dynamo of a woman. I saw that she kept Yelker in order. I wondered where he hid his booze.

"You'll need feeding up, young man," she said, and the sharpness of her tones made me smile — me, Dray Prescot, made me smile — for I detected the warmth and humanity aboard this narrow boat *Dancing Talu*. Other members of the family were introduced. There were ten of them, not all blood relations but crew members indentured from other families and other boats. More often than not two or three families crewed a boat. The big thing was to keep moving. Once the initial inertia of the boat had been overcome and she was gliding with that stately smooth passage of a craft on inland waters, the whole gang could cease hauling and leave two or three to keep her moving. Naturally, I took my turns at hauling. We were all busy at locks. Then we would sweat and haul until our muscles cracked and *Dancing Talu* was under way once more. Then young Wil would go haring off to close the paddles down and shut the lock gates, and then come racing back along the towpath to take a wild flying leap onto the deck. If young Wil with his wild mop of hair and his agility had been unable to drink the canalwater he'd have been a dead rascal inside a day.

We were going south!

We were riding the Vomansoir Cut and going south toward Vondium. I knew a man, a Chuktar, the Lord Farris, who came from Vomansoir. I had met him once, briefly, aboard the Vallian Air Service airboat *Lorenztone*. I did not think I would make inquiries and look him up. He knew me as Dray Prescot, the Lord of Strombor, and the man who aspired to the hand of the Princess Majestrix.

I needed to be a lot closer to Delia than Vomansoir when I revealed my identity.

Vallia is riddled with canals. Traffic flow remained dense and constant. The local authorities of towns maintained the cuts, under the Emperor's personal fiat, and they had put into operation a system of traffic control at intersections. Every lock worked and was efficient, and did not lose too much water. The suns shone, the sky remained clear, I hauled at the tow ropes, operated the locks, fetched and carried, and all the time we rode on southward and I was drawing nearer and nearer to my Delia. I think I achieved a kind of tranquility. I had always underestimated canals, I now realized. Also, I observed the strong fellow-feeling of the canalfolk, and as I absorbed their language and its peculiarities, a task made easy by the potency of the genetically-coded language pill given me in Aphrasöe by Maspero, I reached the understanding that they considered themselves not only a people apart from ordinary Vallians, but a cut above the rest. I was not going to give them an argument on that.

The weather grew warmer as we progressed south, although with the much greater band-spread of temperate climate on Kregen the differences between Vondium, in the south, and Evir, in the north, are nothing like what one would expect on Earth. The Mountains of the North are cruelly cold, as I had discovered.

Winding lazily southward through the center of Vallia flows the Great River, the Mother of Waters, She of Fecundity, which empties into the Sunset Sea where Vondium is situated. Because of the lazy windings of the river, which bears many names along its length, canals sometimes use it when convenient; most often they have been cut by men with a disregard of the river's course. Once we crossed the Great River on a long-striding aqueduct, like twenty Pontcysylltes rolled into one.

Through the low-rolling hills to the south we traveled past tree-hung banks where the mirrored reflections gave a strange duplicating effect of aerial navigation, as though we floated in air. The water changed color occasionally as minerals washed down from the hills; generally it reflected the sky and the clouds, the overhang of trees, the grasses, wild flowers, and rushes of the banks. In a glass it sparkled silvery pure, clean, sweet, refreshing, and — if you were not of canalfolk — deadly.

Between towns the thread of water ran through open country, vast sweeps of moorland, or massy forests, through tangled byways and past the outskirts of magnificent lordly holdings. Sometimes there were no traffic arrangements at crossings, where cut met cut.

Yelker roused himself on an afternoon of lazy sunshine and drifting cloud, and consulting with Rafee, the bulky-shouldered man who acted as his second-in-command, shouted an order to 'vast heaving. He jumped lithely to the bank and with Rafee strode ahead to where the canal curved beyond a clump of missals, leaning over the placid water. Only one other boat was in sight, a red and green craft that had been gently following us for the last day or so.

"What is it?" I said to Zyna.

She tossed her brown hair back and said: "The Ogier Cut. It crosses here."

"Oh," I said, thinking of Borg.

The deep, quietly green-breathing heart of the country surrounded us. The green of the banks reflected in a double bar along the edges of the canal, the placid water pent between, dimpled occasionally by the plop of a fish, the high arch of the sky, the faint refreshing breeze, all added up to create images of perfect peace and quietude. I jumped to the bank.

"I will come with you, Drak."

"With pleasure, Zyna."

We walked up the bank together, the towpath, as is usual, wide enough for three people abreast. Just past the clump of missals there was a winding-hole where boats might turn. A little beyond that the canal widened again and I saw the Ogier Cut coming in from the east and west. At this watery crossroads stood Yelker and Rafee, and they were frowning at the long procession of boats on the Ogier, streaming past at right angles to the Vomansoir.

"This will take time, Yelker," Rafee was saying.

I had picked a spike of grass and I was chewing this as I walked up. Yelker turned at sound of our footsteps.

'Time, Drak," he said. "And time is money. They will never pause to let us through."

"I don't see why not." I walked up to the ridge of the bank and looked east. The boats continued pulling steadily toward us for as far as I could see until the canal curved, a distance I estimated as three-fifths of a dwabur. "There are a lot of them. This, as Rafee says, will take time."

"We must then go back to the boat and brew up and wait."

"Why? Surely they can hold up just long enough for us to slip through?"

"There are no canal wardens out here. It is every man for himself."

About to ask him — almost tauntingly — what of the vaunted comradeship of the canalfolk, I stopped. They had accepted me as a canalman who had, sorrowfully enough, become mixed up with ordinary Vallians. I must be of the canals, for I could drink the water. But I must not show too much ignorance.

"I will take a little stroll," I said. And then as Zyna perked up, smiling, I added swiftly: "Alone."

Dancing Talu carried hoffiburs from Therminsax and if they did not reach Vomansoir in good time they would go rotten. Any delay was to be avoided. We could be stuck here for the rest of the day. From Vomansoir the boat would take lissium ore back to Therminsax, a busy and lucrative trade.

As I walked slowly along I could just see a shining sheet of water dim and vast along the eastern horizon, and knew this to be one of the many great lakes that make the interior of Vallia so pleasant a place. The procession of boats on the Ogier Cut passed endlessly. The haulers walked carelessly enough across the wooden bridges built over the Vomansoir Cut. Other bridges, of a distinctively different pattern, crossed the Ogier north-south. I walked along the western bridge and stood leaning on the parapet, chewing my grass stem.

The scrape of a bare foot on the bridge made me turn.

Zyna walked up, boldly enough, although there was a little diffidence she hid admirably. She smiled at me. Over her shoulder I could see the red and green boat had pulled in astern of *Dancing Talu,* and her people and ours were clumped on the bank, talking and gesticulating.

"You should not send me away, Drak." She pouted at me, and the glance from her man-killing eyes would have done the business for any young buck of the canals.

"Nevertheless, Zyna, go back to your father and tell him to unmoor and begin hauling. The other boat also. They must be ready to shoot through the Ogier the moment a gap appears."

"But—?"

"Do as I say, young Zyna, or by Vaosh, I'll tan your bottom!"

"You wouldn't dare!" she flashed back. And then — she giggled. I thought of Viridia the Render, and I sighed, and surmised that my handling of girls is calculated to make them exceedingly wroth with me.

"I guarantee, young woman, that if you believe you would enjoy that, you are wrong. I have a hard and horrifically horny hand."

Whereat she giggled again. I pushed up from the bridge parapet and took out my grass stem and threw it on the gray barges of the Emperor with their arrogant right-of-planks and advanced toward her — and she ran off, shrieking with merriment.

It was precisely at crossing places like this that the gray barges of the Emperor with their arrogant right-of-way held an advantage. They would simply haul straight on. The stentor braced in the bows would lift his triply-spiraled brass trumpet, maneuvering it up and around, with his arm thrust through the spiral, the blaring trumpet mouth high and blasting forward, and peal the shrill commanding notes that would make all canalfolk hauling give way before the Emperor's barge.

Those long low gray barges flew the flag of Vallia, the vivid yellow saltire on the red ground.

As I stared back down the towpath I saw Zyna reach the knot of folk clustered where the stem and the stern of the two narrow boats nuzzled. Faces turned to look up at me and I waved. It had not occurred to me to consider that Yelker would not instantly do as I had said, and I felt a twinge of astonishment as he and Rafee and a few others together with men and women of the red and green boat started off along the towpath toward me. Truly, the habits of a Strom, a Zorcander, a lord, do not wash with canalfolk!

"What is all this about, Ven Drak? By Vaosh, if we move into the Ogier our tows will be cut swifter than the throats of a litter of leems!"

"Maybe not so, Yelker, maybe not."

"You have a plan?"

I hadn't thought of any plan. "No. No, I'm just going down there and ask the first haulers I come to, to hold up for us."

They gaped at me.

A man with a black spade beard, the skipper of *Pride of Vomansoir,* guffawed. "Ho! You'll find yourself in Gurush's Bottomless Marshes if you try that, Ven Drak!"

"Why?"

But, of course, the reason was obvious. No hauler is going to ease his boat back to a stop if he can avoid it; the effort of overcoming inertia to begin movement again is the toughest chore of the canalfolk, in and out of locks.

I said, "They will do as I request."

Yelker said, "I am a man of peace, Drak. You possess a rapier, and we do not see many of those on the cuts. But your rapier is aboard, and I will not let you get it."

He didn't know the risks he ran by telling me I could not do something, but I had no desire to use an edged and pointed weapon in this fracas. All I knew was that time was running out and I must press on to Vondium and Delia, and a line of narrow boats prevented me.

"Then, so am I. But, nevertheless, Yelker, get ready."

And I turned away from him and walked down the bridge and so on the Ogier Cut.

Nine

The headless zorcamen

Narrow boats keep to the left riding the Vallian cuts and so by walking down from the western bridge I could walk back eastward along the southern bank of the Ogier Cut. Past me went the stream of boats. Their haulers looked up and some smiled, others nodded, one or two called out a casual "Llahal, Ven," to which I replied in as casual a fashion.

Six young folk on a rope passed, four jolly laughing girls and two young lads who seemed mightily bashful as they saw me watching them. I let them go. All along the placid deep-green water approaching me the boats swam smoothly on. They differed in a subtle fashion from those riding the Vomansoir Cut, but they were narrow boats, gaily decorated, brilliantly painted, their high central ridgepoles draped with multicolored canvas concealing the loads beneath. Now walked steadily a man and wife, robust, fresh-faced, firmly-muscled. I nodded to them as I climbed up the wooden bridge, giving them all the room they needed as they dragged the tow rope across the bridge railing. The wood was smooth and so highly polished by the passage of countless ropes that it shone blindingly in the light from Zim and Genodras. It took, on busy bridges, a surprisingly short time for the wood to wear away and become unsafe and so have to be replaced by the wardens.

I descended the other side of the southern bridge over the Vomansoir Cut. I let two barges go past, hauled by four men apiece, agile as they flexed out the tow ropes as they ascended the bridge. I walked on. Now I had to believe that Yelker would do as I had said. His argument had been surprising; I had to remind myself I was simply an ordinary mortal here, no longer a Strom. Ahead of me the narrow boats stretched out of sight, a moving, gliding patchwork of color along the glinting waters of the canal.

There are in any society men who for whatever obscure reasons of psychology desire to shine, to be noticed, to do things with an air that will draw the attention of everyone exclusively to them. We all know people like that. I had never been like that, but had found that simply by doing what I felt I had been impelled to do I had gained many of the results of a greater striving. Sometimes a man, to show his strength and prowess, would haul a narrow boat alone. The average rate was around a third of a dwabur a bur and by traveling at night the boats could cover sixteen dwaburs in a day. I was looking at this one man who wished to show off.

He came striding on, head down, muscles bared to the air with his jerkin unlaced and open over his chest. He was a fine-looking man, with plenty of manly hair on that chest, and a well-proportioned head with fiercely jutting beard and arrogant moustaches. He carried the tow rope over his left shoulder so that he could lay his weight against it to control his boat. I judged that, indeed, she was his, for after the fashion of many of the canalfolk he wore adornments of gold and silver about him, golden earrings and golden bands around his arms, and these were of a fine quality.

The sound of the boat's passage in that rhythmical series of gurglings and plashings swelled as he drew nearer. I could see no one on the deck of his boat, which was a large specimen of canal craft, a good hundred and fifty feet long in Terrestrial measurements. A brute to handle in a congested way, as I well knew.

I approached.

"You look as though you could do with some help over the bridge, Ven."

He looked up, not having heard my approach.

"I do not think so, Ven."

"Oh, I am sure you do."

I fell in at his side and walked pace for pace. Ahead of us the bridges grew nearer, and the Vomansoir Cut.

"I am Kutven Ban nal Ogier, and by your clothes you are not a canalman, by Vaosh! I need no help. Or do you wish to drink canalwater?"

A Kutven was a high-ranking man among the Vens. The canalfolk had many degrees, of course, and among them there was the Lord High Kov, and the Lord High Strom, and so on down to the ordinary Kutvens and Vens. I made myself laugh.

"Oh, come now, Kutven Ban! Of course you need help to climb that bridge." I put a hand on the rope.

I was keenly aware of the ludicrous situation. Here was I ready to brawl with a fellow canalman over rights of way, and yet all my thoughts were centered on the Princess Majestrix of this land. Truly, I relished the irony. "Take your hand off that rope. By Gurush of the Bottomless Marsh! Do you hear me, leepitix?"

"I hear, Ven, and I am not amused. I do not like being called a leepitix." A leepitix is a twelve-legged reptilian wriggler about a foot long who infests the canals and has a nasty bite. They can be frightened off by splashing. "Clear off!"

He let go the rope with his left hand and struck out. I ducked, tripped him up, yanked the rope in hard. It came with the peculiar soggy resistance and welling movement typical of a boat in narrow waters.

"I'm only trying to help you, Ven!"

He yelled and tried to stand up, whereat I cast a bight of the rope about his ankles and so pitched him over again.

"Look out!" I yelled. I jumped up and down and waved my arms at the boat which now headed majestically into the bank. "Look out, Ven! You'll have her aground!"

He was shrieking and raving by this time. A head popped up over the hatchway coaming of his boat. Yells floated up. The stem grounded about a yard out, and the stern began to swing. The cut, here, just after the winding-hole farther back, narrowed so as to present the shortest distance for the canal architects to bridge. The boat's stern drifted across and grounded on the far bank. Now people were yelling and running from all directions, it seemed, and I heard a series of splashes as people dived in to swim to the bank as the quickest way ashore. I yelled at a crone with gray hair who ran shrieking with her frying pan held aloft.

"Kutven Ban tangled himself up in the rope. Quick! We must help."

Other voices joined in a chorus of disbelief. I was making a great play of unwrapping the rope from Ban. He tried to hit me and I put my foot on his head, purely by accident, and he gobbled into the muddy grass of the towpath.

"Help us!" I shouted.

The crone started to hit me with the frying pan.

I ducked and Ban struggled up, foaming, and I gave the end of the rope a kick and it slid into the water like an eel. A big fellow with a red jerkin and silver earrings ran up. Two or three boys joined in and a couple of girls danced about. Other people formed a ring.

Ban was purple.

"He tangled in the tow rope and fell over," I shouted. I spread my hands. "Look at the following boats."

The fellow in the red jerkin spun around as though I had kicked him in his breechclout.

"Oh, by the mighty Vaosh himself!" he moaned.

Men and women were tumbling out of the boats to get onto the bank, where the haulers were laying back and being dragged on squeaking heels along the path. The next boat homed in on the boat wedged diagonally across the cut and bumped in a great groaning of wood. The following boats began to pile up. I looked around. Now boats were filling the cut in a series of zigzags and presenting a scene of utter confusion.

I looked around with a certain satisfaction on my handiwork.

Then I looked the other way and saw *Dancing Talu* and *Pride of Vomansoir* gliding across the empty stretch, and the other boats on the Ogier Cut calmly receding into the distance.

Ban glared up, spitting mud, struggling to rise.

"You really should be more careful," I said.

I could not immediately run off and jump aboard Yelker's boat. There might be reprisals. So I started in on a fresh series of explanations for the benefit of fresh arrivals.

"Poor Kutven Ban!" and: "Ban shouldn't do it all himself."

I looked at Ban. He shook his broad shoulders and cocked his fists, spat mud, bristled, and started for me.

I said, "It is better that it was an accident, Ban. I do not think I wish to hurt you, but if it is necessary, I will."

He roared, threw back his head to glare in hatred at me — he looked in my face. He stopped. He hesitated. His right foot scraped the towpath. He lowered his fists.

"Maybe, at that, 'twas an accident."

"By Vaosh, Ban," I said. "You're a man after my own heart."

The clustered ring of people quite clearly were prepared to take their cue from the Kutven. He suddenly began roaring and raving to such effect that the ring burst asunder, and men and women, boys and girls, flew to their boats and a gang tailed onto the tow ropes of Kutven Ban's boat and began to drag her parallel to the banks once more. I shouted in a very genial way, "Remberee!" and walked off.

Dancing Talu pushed on southerly and I hauled with a will, but I was not so prideful or so foolish as to wish to show off and haul by myself, although capable of it, and I noticed that Zyna would very often be there with me, hauling with her slender firmly-rounded body thrusting into the rope. In the normal course of events life on the cuts is leisurely, but now, because the cargo of hoffiburs might go rotten on Yelker, he maintained a good pace and by nightfall we had left *Pride of Vomansoir* well behind. We pushed on, the leading hauler with a lantern balanced in a lantern-hat, an arrangement of cradles and slings strapped onto the head and around the chin, angled back so that the lantern swung horizontally, although the hauler's head inclined down with the strain of pulling.

It was the next night we saw the headless zorcamen.

Yelker ran up onto the forepeak of the boat and yelled, and Zyna let out a shriek of pure fear.

"Get back on board!" roared Yelker. "Let the rope go!"

Zyna clasped my arm. Her fingers shook.

"Drak! Drak! The headless zorcamen!"

I slipped the rope off my shoulders, got a grip on Zyna, and plunged bodily into the water. A few quick overarm thrusts with my free hand and I could heft her clinging body up with my other hand to the waiting grip of Yelker and Rafee. I followed them up. I stood on the narrow catwalk around the sheeted cargo space, dripping water, and stared narrowly into the blackness.

My eyes adjusted quickly — and then I saw them.

A long line of cowled and cloaked figures they were, as I thought, dark against the sky where four moons floated. Then a closer inspection revealed that, indeed, the cowls were merely hunched shoulders, the cloaks trailing, and that the zorcamen rode headless across the moors.

"Rubbish!" I said. "By Zim-Zair, a trick, a cheap trick."

"Of course, Drak. They are men like you or me, dressed up to look horrific. But many men still believe them to be supernatural apparitions."

I had had experience of headless horsemen, and the headless coachman, for in the land of my youth smuggling was a fine art.

"What purpose do they serve, then, Yelker? And why do we stop?"

"They are dangerous men. Those they do not frighten off, they kill."

"Are we to stop, then, because of buffoons like that?"

"It is wise. So long as they believe they terrorize the district, we are safe. If they detected resistance, disbelief carried to action, they would strike us mercilessly." He coughed, and added: "And there are Mother and Zyna, Sisi, and the girls to consider."

"Yes," I said. After a pause, when I had sufficiently controlled myself, I said: "Who are these kleeshes?"

"They ride the moors. Hereabouts is all the domain of Faygar, the Strom of Vorgan. He is a known racter. But he owns allegiance to the Kov of Vomansoir."

"So?"

"So the racters must show their strength in some way when all the usual ways are denied them."

There were twenty of them, riding head to tail, a long serpentine line of hunched shapes against the moons. They looked eerie and menacing, completely horrifying to an untutored mind.

"By Zair!" I said. "I have a mind to take my sword and teach them a lesson. And, come to that, I could use a zorca."

Yelker passed no comment on my vainglorious boasting. He said: "You would leave us, Drak?"

My thoughts were turned to Vondium and Delia of the Blue Mountains. I had no wish to appear ungrateful to Yelker or his family aboard *Dancing Talu*. But I could not but speak the truth.

"I would be in Vondium as fast as the fleetest airboat could take me, Yelker!"

He sighed. "We shall lose you at Vomansoir, then. I value your presence aboard mightily. We would have lost much time crossing the Ogier Cut. By Va-osh, I would not have believed it!"

Rafee let out a cackle.

The zorcamen rode on, and their leader trended over the dark horizon, and so they vanished, one by one. Racters they were, out to terrorize the people of the district, to extort, to maim, and to kill. Well, they meant nothing to me. I had let my chance go. To the Ice Floes of Sicce with them all!

After a space we resumed our hauling, but Zyna remained aboard the boat.

I had detected in my actions since this arrival on Kregen a change of attitude, a laxness, a half-heartedness, a kind of softness most displeasing to me. I could guess why this was. You who have listened to my story will know that I tend to think like a civilized man, and to consider all the angles of a problem, and then to act like a savage barbarian, and jump in with my sword in my fist. Much of that must come from my Earthly ancestry mingled with the years I spent among my clansmen, fighting my way up to be Zorcander and Vovedeer. And, too, I am not a twentieth-century man, despite my veneer of the ways of speech and the auto-mated culture of these times. I come from a lusty, brawling, robust age, when a belaying pin or a sailor's knife settled an argument. I am not your ordinary hero of polite fictions, such as are still to be found in the scented courtly poems of Loh or of Vallia itself.

But, equally, I am not your simpleminded if quick-witted barbarian, like my good friend Wulk of the northern hills.

I had become soft and vacillating and slow. And I knew why this was. Despite all my protestations that I would go to Vallia and there confront Delia's father, this dread Emperor, I had quailed from the task. I thought Delia understood my reasons, I fancied she saw that I had no wish to tear down the image she held of her father, all the love and affection built up through childhood and girlhood, all that warm close family kinship to be torn asunder, broken, destroyed, by a rough uncouth clansman not even from her own world!

As the twins circled through the night sky of Kregen, forever orbiting each other, I hauled the tow rope and I faced my problem. I had to go on. My feet had been set on this path by the Star Lords themselves. I must go to Vondium and stalk into the Emperor's palace and there, before the world, claim my Delia.

I must!

There must be no more shilly-shallying. I made up my mind, then, in the puny pride of my heart, vaingloriously boasting to myself and to the moons and the stars, that I would fulfill whatever of destiny had called me to this strange and terrifying planet.

I can look back now at myself as I was then so long ago, and smile. But I can truly say that no thought of the actual power and might and majesty of Delia's father the Emperor entered my mind. He was just a man. He could be made to do what I wanted him to do. It was on Delia, and on Delia's feelings, that all my thoughts centered. This I swear.

We saw no more headless zorcamen and two days of hard pulling with many locks to bite into the actual distance traversed of our eighty-lock-miles-a-day travel, we came down into Vomansoir.

I had expected just another town, perhaps a city, something like Therminsax. What I saw enchanted me. Vallia is full of strange and exotic places and out-of-the-way retreats. Vomansoir straddled the Great River and six canals joined here in a wide stretch of hectically busy waterways. We trudged in and got our berthing ticket and tied up at the hoffiburs wharf run by a Company of Friends with whom Yelker usually dealt.

Every canal ran in through a series of lock flights, for Vomansoir is situated in a great natural bowl. As we descended we could see the surrounding slopes terraced and cultivated so that not a square inch of space was wasted. Colors rioted everywhere. Trees and bushes and flowers all blended into an enormous patchwork quilt of dizzying splendor. The river, She of Fecundity, ran in and out of the bowl through colossal canyons. Along the banks were moored vessels of surprising size. Beyond them the quays hummed with throngs of people busy about the everyday tasks of living. Zorca chariots clattered and whirred here and there, quoffas dragged carts of humbler duties, men and women rode saddle zorcas, and I saw again the half-voves I had last seen in Zenicce. Vallia, however, has no voves in the natural state, although there are small herds here and there bred up by men.

Everything was magnificent. The women wore flowing free gowns of myriads of colors; the men in their Vallian gear were not content thus to be left in the shade and their wide-shouldered tunics and jerkins were also brilliantly colored. I saw many of the men working on the quays and at the warehouses, as in the factories and the streets that dealt in various items of merchandise, wore the shirts with the banded sleeves, and while many of these banded colors were gray and yellow, the colors of Vomansoir, there were many also of other colors, sometimes three colors banded together. The red and black of the guards were in evidence, and I saw, with a bunching of my jaw muscles, gangs of slave haulers at work. Also, I saw men with black and white sleeves.

"Racters," said Yelker, when I questioned him. "You are cut off in Valka, Drak, to be sure. By Vaosh, but they flaunt their superiority!"

I witnessed a clash between men of a racter employer and men wearing white and green banded arms over the priority of unloading a narrow boat. They fought with cudgels. They struck each other doughty blows. Yelker put his hand on my shoulder.

"Let them be, Drak, my friend. I am a man of peace, and you, I know, are a man of violence. But they go their ways—"

I was profoundly shocked.

"I, too, am a man of peace, Yelker! How can you call me a man of violence?" I considered. "I only tripped Kutven Ban!"

Rafee let rip with his coarse cackle at this. I could see their point. But I was annoyed. I am never violent — at least, not stupidly so, not unthinkingly, not when it will hurt people for whom I cherish affection. At least, so I hope.

I turned to collect my gear from the cabin I had used, up in the bows. "At least," I said over my shoulder, "I never hit an old man or an old woman for fun."

Then I stopped. "Well, Yelker — and you, too, you grinning onker, Rafee — if I am violent it would be because I saw someone doing just that! I'd be inclined to hit him and thus attempt to show him the error of his ways." Like, I thought with some remorse, I had shown that argenter captain in Pa Mejab the error of his ways for slapping young Pando.

I bid them all Remberee and took myself off. They were sorry to see me go. I hoped they'd get back through the Ogier Cut without bother this time, although the lissium ore did not share the same urgency as the hoffiburs.

Finding a posting station was not easy, for I had made up my mind to continue by zorca. I did not have the price of an airboat ticket, assuming I could find a Company of Friends operating an airline here. The oldster with the stubbly chin scratched that stubble, and spat in the straw, and sized me up. My beard had been trimmed neatly. But folk in Vomansoir were clean-shaven as a rule.

"You must be in a mighty hurry, dom."

"I am. The zorca will be safe, for I am accustomed to riding them. Here." I held out coins with the portrait of the man I wished to see. "What will it cost?"

Strange words, those, for Dray Prescot on Kregen!

In the event I hired a zorca and left a whacking deposit as a guarantee of my honesty. Vallia has a functioning banking system, as must any country which trades at such a high intensity, and I could collect the deposit when the zorca was either returned or unsaddled at the Vondium stables. I bought some food, and with a few silver coins left clanking rather dismally in the lesten-hide bag, I set off.

Vallian roads are foul. They are better now, but I speak of the time when I rode south through the sun-drenched land seeking an interview with my prospective father-in-law. The zorca made good time, considering, and I wended my way south through towns and cities, crossing the canals, watching the lazy progress of the narrow boats, spurring on harshly when I saw a gang of hauler slaves dragging an Emperor's barge, giving a quick sailor eye to the boats sailing on the Mother of Waters. I passed huge cornfields that took a day to traverse, immense dark forests, where twice I fought off footpads. This made me frown, for I had taken Vallia to be civilized. I would not allow myself to become fatigued. The zorca held up wonderfully well, and I fancy he recognized he had a zorcaman on his back.

The twin Suns of Scorpio chased in jade and crimson across the sky each day, the nightly procession of moons cast down their pinkish light, and I hurried on.

I reached Vondium.

I will say nothing of that altogether marvelous place now, and, truth to tell, at the time I scarcely heeded all its marvels. It was all too easy for me to hear the news. It was the subject of conversation in all the myriads of pleasant open-air restaurants along the quays beside the canals and waterways.

"The Emperor? Oh, that naughty daughter of his! He is not in Vondium. He has gone to Delphond to teach her a lesson!"

Ten

From Delphond to the Blue Mountains

Delphond is a delightful, charming, cozy land of small fields and secluded hamlets, of winding brooks and gentle undulations of ground clad in the brilliant green of Kregan grass speckled with the prodigious abundance of Kregan flowers. It is a warm land, a soft and safe country, a place for lazy retirement and idle amusements, happy and carefree and going the old ways of its people. Tucked away in a southern bend of the coastline of the main island of Vallia, it receives all the benefit of the Zim Stream, that warm current sweeping up through the Cyphren Sea from the unknown southwestern oceans. From Delphond comes the finest vintage claret in all Kregen, or so I believe. Also there are apples, pears, gregarians, and squishes, and the people there rear a kind of ponsho whose fleece, besides being as soft and silky as any in two worlds, provides chops and shoulders and legs of a succulence not to be believed until eaten, fresh, crisp, and savory, with liberal helpings of mint sauce and with the small round yellow mo-molams, a tuber that Zair put on Kregen in holy wedlock with roast ponsho.

Also in Delphond are fat cattle, very like our Earthly bulls and cows, and the cream they make there... it is of a triple consistency, rich and thick and fit for Opaz himself.

Such a meal I ate in a pleasant raftered alehouse, with the twin suns slanting in at the open window and the bees busy about the mauve and white loomin flowers in a pottery jar of Pandahem ware on the windowsill. The good-natured innkeeper's wife bustled, bringing me her best, and I ate well, for the journey had been swift and eating of secondary importance. My booted feet stuck out across the polished sturm-wood floor and in other circumstances I would have been content. I munched a handful of palines after the meal was finished, considering.

In my lesten-hide bag there now reposed but three copper obs... I had squandered all my slender resources on this last meal. The people of Delphond are jolly, given to laughter, happy, tucked away in their corner of Vallia, secure in the knowledge that they own fealty to Delia of Delphond as their suzerain, than whom there is no more fair or perfect a girl in all their world — and, as I know, in two worlds.

But I was not pleased.

The Emperor had indeed visited Delphond and been received with the pomp and ceremony fitting to his exalted majesty. He had come by water, as was fitting, in a long train of narrow boats, traveling with a full thousand of his personal bodyguard, the Bowmen of Loh, and with many retainers, servitors, and slaves. Delia, like myself, recognizes that in certain circumstances slaves can be economical, but that in many areas of the economy they are not; effective or otherwise, slaves are not for Delia of Delphond. There had been trouble when she had emancipated the whole of Delphond, as soon as the gift of the estate had been received from her grandmother, as there had been trouble of a different kind when she had emancipated the slaves of the Blue Mountains. Now the country was in apple-pie order. The colors worn banded on the shirt sleeves of Delia's retainers were lavender and laypom — the laypom is a fruit rather like a peach but of a pale subtle yellow color, delicate and exquisite — and her servitors moved with the springy step and open shoulders and frank faces of free men and women.

But this could not charm me now, for the Emperor had not found Delia in Delphond. She had gone, and so he had followed her, I was told, to the Blue Mountains.

The Emperor could simply wave a hand and the haulers would take up their ropes and away would glide his whole caravan. I must fend for myself. Well, I had done that often enough before, and was like to do it often enough again. So with a good meal of the products of Delphond inside me I stirred up my faithful zorca and set off westward for the Blue Mountains.

There was in the character of the folk of Delphond a gentleness and a happy laughter, too, that I knew would serve Delia well in times of peace. I had grave doubts that I could raise an army here that would fight. In that, as you will hear, I did the Delphondi an injustice. But then, in my black, dispirited mood, I canceled them from my evil calculations. Even so, I could understand that I had no right to bring war and bloodshed to this pleasant estate, that I would truly be the evil man I know myself to be if I forced these gentle folk to take up the sword, and carried fire and slaughter through their comfortable country.

Delia had told me that Delphond, willed to her by her grandmother, was a tiny estate. It took me two full days to reach the western border from the port city of Delphond. Truly, the ideas of size of the Kregan people, with the much greater land-mass of the planet, are of a different scale from those of Earth. Even their methods of travel have no significant influence on their conceptions of distance, for whereas the canal boats travel so leisurely, the fliers cover vast distances very rapidly.

Astride my zorca I bid Remberee to Delphond, which her people call Del-phond the Blessed, and rode on into Thadelm, the neighboring country, owing allegiance to Vad Selnix. That land shared much of Delphond's rural beauty on its southeastern borders, but gradually changed in character as I wended northwestward, until the land sprawled gray and featureless beneath the glare of the suns, a wild expanse of moorland and rolling downland. A Vad is one of the intermediate ranks between a Kov and a Strom. I rode on and passed a pleasant "Llahal" with the few people I saw. I was able to catch a few rabbits — very much like Terrestrial rabbits, a meat of which I am not over-fond — and the ever-present palines worked their usual magic.

If necessary, I would beg.

By this time you must realize that I didn't care what I did just so long as I reached my Delia of the Blue Mountains, my Delia of Delphond.

By this means and that, and, I am relieved to be able to say, without doing any-thing of which I was truly ashamed, I traversed the country in a northwesterly direction, passing through Stromnates and Kovnates and Vadvars, and through a number of wide estates, as big as states in themselves, owned by the Emperor. When the mountains began to loft on the horizon I knew I was approaching my goal. I had sold one of the daggers, but I kept the rapier and remaining main-gauche, for I felt I might have need of them above the usual need a man has for weapons on Kregen. I fell in with a caravan of calsanys, with preysany-litters, and with a guard of zorcamen. The servants wore shirts with sleeves banded in bold and black.

A zorcaman wearing a close-fitting helmet of iron, with a nasal and a high flaunting plume of gold and black feathers, hauled across my path. He had no lance. His quiver of javelins was unstrapped and he balanced one of the long casting shafts in his right hand as he eyed me.

I said, as civilly as I could: "Llahal."

"Llahal," he replied. Then: "Who are you and whence do you travel?"

I knew what to say.

"I am Drak ti Valkanium, and I go to High Zorcady in the Blue Mountains."

"Your business?"

He was a big fellow, and beyond him the rest of his company jogged along es-corting the caravan. There were fifty of them, a sizable little squadron, and judging from the bulging sacks and panniers of the calsanys, they were extremely careful with what they carried. They were not a mere merchant's caravan, like that of Naghan the Paunch on far Turismond — or even of Xoltemb, in Segesthes, as far in the opposite direction.

"Who are you?"

The lifted javelin quivered. "I am asking the questions, dom."

"By what right?"

His laugh was intended to be scornful, but I detected a note of uncertainty.

"You travel alone, Kr. Drak. I am Hikdar Stovang, and I travel on the business of the Kov of Aduimbrev. We are about to enter the Blue Mountains, and I want no secret enemy at my back."

"You are one of Vektor of Aduimbrev's men!" I relished this. "That is good. If you will, I would like to travel with you. I, too, have no wish for unseen enemies at my back through the Blue Mountains."

He spat. He had shown his authority, had sized me up as a simple Koter, a gentleman, and was prepared now to let me join his caravan. "The Blue Mountains," he said. "When the Kov marries the Princess Majestrix I hope to Opaz I am not stuck out here on duty. The place is a death trap."

I was fascinatedly interested, but my questions must be of such a kind, and in such an order, as not to arouse his suspicions. We turned our zorcas together and rode knee to knee. He sheathed the javelin. He was a soldier, doing a job, and not much caring for it.

The retainers of Vektor were heartily sick of the whole business. The quicker their master married the Princess Majestrix and had a brood of children to carry on the imperial line, the better. Then perhaps they could all return to their old ways and all this chasing about, first here, then there, seeking to make Delia of the Blue Mountains make up her mind, could finish. "I've saddle sores on my saddle sores, Kr. Drak!" declared Hikdar Stovang. "By Vox, I'm black and blue where I sit down."

I smothered my chuckle. I can always react like a normal man where my Delia is concerned. She had been leading them a dance. Impudently refusing to marry the man of her father's choice, then arrogantly refusing to marry at all, she had held them all off, going from one of her estates to another, staying with friends — I felt my senses quicken at that — she had kept them all at bay ever since her mysterious arrival back in Vallia.

"But all the nonsense is going to stop, now, Kr. Drak. We carry the wedding gifts. The Emperor is in High Zorcady. The Princess Majestrix is there, also. So is Kov Vektor." Hikdar Stovang sounded like a man well-pleased that a difficult and unpleasant job is finished. "Where the Emperor is, then that is where the wedding will take place. And right glad, to the glory of the Invisible Twins, am I that it will soon be over."

Aduimbrev lay to the north midlands, and Stovang couldn't wait to return home. The Vomansoir Cut had not gone through Vektor's Kovnate, and I guessed we had flown over it in the ice airboat. Now I set my face forward. Oh, yes, I relished the irony of thus riding in with the very wedding gifts of my rival, but that rival held all the aces.

A few canals have been cut through the Blue Mountains, and one, the Quanscott Cut, is carried through the longest tunnel in Vallia, driven through the heart of the Blue Mountains to the coastal strip on the west where stands Quanscott, the major port on that stretch of coast. But the Emperor would be riding up to High Zorcady astride a zorca, unless he chose to ride like old women, monks, or children, and saddle a preysany.

I knew that here, all around me in the rolling wild country leading up to the Blue Mountains, roamed thousands, possibly millions, of zorcas. This was zorca country. The frowning citadel and the town that had grown up on the granite crags around it in sight and sound of rushing waterfalls was aptly named High Zorcady. On most days clouds drift around the highest towers. From the ramparts on a clear day you can look out and see so vast an expanse of country that the very coil of the world seems to lie beneath your feet.

We had some way to go yet before we reached that high and inaccessible place, full of crags and water-thunder, drifting with clouds and the wide-winged crested-korf. That night we camped in a hollow by a stream and I was able to appease my hunger with hot vosk and taylyne soup. I noticed that double guards were set. Stovang was jumpy. He had been carrying this treasure of wedding gifts all around Vallia, it seemed, in futile chase of Delia, on the run from her father's marriage plans, but I knew that he was not apprehensive on account of the gifts.

The Blue Mountains, it seemed, were notorious.

According to Hikdar Stovang, bandits and robbers and assassins lived in every cave and crevice of the rocks.

I could see I was welcome as an extra sword. Fifty zorca riders had not been considered too many guards. Among the zorca riders in the service of Vektor and wearing his colors and insignia — a butterfly on gold and black — were halfling mercenaries, Rapas, Fristles, a couple of Chuliks. They appeared a reasonably disciplined and efficient bunch, but I slept with a hand on my rapier hilt, and with a lifetime's experience I slept ready to leap up in an instant. This knack of sleeping soundly and yet with the ability to react to the noise that threatens usually serves me well, for it has been learned in the harsh life of seafaring, or adventuring on Kregen; it is not a gift of cloistered universities.

Among the zorca riders were two Womoxes. Although outwardly as composed and drilled as their companions, they exhibited to me clear signs of a much greater degree of agitation. I had fought Viridia's Womoxes, and found them formidable opponents, their stumpy horns mounted on their foreheads able to jab at an enemy's eyes with terrifying power. Now they made no pretense at sleep. They stayed on guard all night, alert, their weapons drawn, waiting.

The next day as we jogged northwestward Hikdar Stovang, who had taken to me as a new companion able to enliven the journey with new stories, enlightened me, although without realizing he did so. The island of the Womoxes lay directly westward of Vallia, with the inevitable cluttering of smaller islands and islets between, and the port serving the Blue Mountains, Quanscott, lay on the same parallel of latitude as the chief easternmost port of Womox. Before Vallia had achieved hegemony and then consolidation of all the different peoples that now formed part of the empire, clearly there had been long and bitter racial enmity between the Womoxes and the people of the Blue Mountains. They were all of one nation now, under one emperor, but the old antipathies persisted here, at least.

We rode on. Vektor's men lived well, and they did not grudge me my share of food. We were made welcome at a couple of towns, where there was an influx of people foreign to these parts; then, as we penetrated higher and higher into the Blue Mountains and by following narrow tracks winding beside gorges where streams splashed and roared a thousand feet below, we knew we had left not only the plains and foothills behind but the attitudes of mind to be found there. We stayed a night at a small mountain village where the atmosphere of hostility could be cut with a terchick. We pushed on. Here local politics, local grudges, and local vendettas were carried to extremes.

"We're all one people under the Emperor, aren't we? complained Stovang. "If this is the family my master the Kov is marrying into, Opaz help him, by Vox!"

I was puzzled. The antagonism of the inhabitants of the Blue Mountains was a tangible onslaught on a man's feelings; we were interlopers, unwanted, detested. Clannish feelings ran high here. Were the Blue Mountain people, as Stovang insisted, just a rabble gang of thieves and cutthroats?

What a contrast to Delphond!

Very often now, during the day, as we progressed laboriously along a narrow ledge, or negotiated a track perched between heaven and hell, we heard a long ululating call, echoing and rebounding from crag to crag. The high notes pealed in the clean chill air. The mountains rang with the gong-notes.

"We're under observation, Opaz rot 'em," grunted Stovang. We edged our zorcas along with care, and the animals put their dainty hooves down with a precision that showed they fully understood the situation. Highly intelligent, are zorcas.

This difficult path wended higher and higher, traversing a rampart wall of mountains. The peaks soared to either hand, their lower slopes falling away into gorge and crevasse, and so down and along and out to the foothills. Trees of all the mountain varieties grew here, and flowers of fragile beauty, and we saw mountain ponshos leaping like impiters from crag to crag. The peaks carried mantles of ice and snow. The snow-line lay high above us still, and the weather held none of that frigid bite of the Mountains of the North where I had met and rescued Furtway and his nephew Jenbar. I was grateful for that.

Once we had penetrated the rampart barrier, which curved in a gigantic oval, we could descend the other side and so ride out onto the great central plateau within the Blue Mountains. But, as Stovang said with as much pleasure as he could derive from the situation, we were not traveling that far. High Zorcady had been built on its serried peaks where the pass reached its highest point. Cupped by mountains, shielded by clouds, walled by crags, High Zorcady frowned down from the mist.

It was at that point, as we paused in a narrow defile to glare up at High Zorcady, eerie, pointed, and leering above us, that the Blue Mountain Boys jumped us.

All was instant confusion. The mercenaries drew their rapiers, some hurled javelins, their zorcas wheeling and colliding. I saw stones hurtling to smash against close-fitting helmets or thump against gold and black chests. I saw men in shaggy ponsho skins leaping from the rocks to lay their cudgels against skulls. I saw the frantic pandemonium of the fight, then I was down, and a man lifted a rock high over his head, straddled above me, laughing.

Eleven

I meet the Blue Mountain Boys and the shorgortz

I reached up and took the rock away from his brown fingers and he had to let it go or his fingers would have snapped. I threw the rock away. I took his wrists in my left hand, his throat in my right, and I squeezed — a little, not much, just enough to let him know who was master here.

"I could kill you now, dom. But I will not. I am not one of Kov Vektor's men. You should have seen that from my clothes."

He glared at me, his eyes bulging out, a bright and brilliant blue. That was interesting; nearly all Vallians have bright brown eyes, and brown hair, and some of them have the luck to have that outrageous blend of chestnut that so glorifies the hair of Delia of the Blue Mountains.

I released my grip a little and he choked and coughed.

A quick glance around confirmed that all the zorcamen were down. I saw one Womox with a broken horn and blood oozing from a smashed skull. The other I could not see, nor did I ever again see that particular Womox. A Chulik was backed against a rock, his rapier slashing desperately at the cudgels of the ring of Blue Mountain Boys. I looked for Stovang, but could not pick him out. The defile looked a mess, with calsanys and preysanys milling, zorcas standing with drooping reins, the bodies of unconscious men sprawled everywhere.

"Listen, dom. You have a leader. Tell me his name — quick!"

No thought of treachery occurred to him; he told me what, in other circumstances, could not have been dragged from him by torture.

"Korf Aighos!"

I nodded, satisfied. The man was named for the powerful iridescent blue bird of the mountains, a nickname, as one might say "Eagle Jack." The man tried to work his throat, and gulped. And I was satisfied he was cowed — how little I knew of the Blue Mountain Boys, how proud of them I am!

"Get up, dom. Shout for Korf Aighos. I would like to have words with him."

The man rose, dragging his ponsho skin about him. He wore decent leathers beneath and his body was of the whipcord toughness required of a mountaineer. His face, brown and lined, glanced back at me with a return of his natural arrogance.

"Shout, dom," I said.

He shouted.

There was a stir in the Blue Mountain Boys, and a man strode toward me. At first glance I knew I could do business with this man. He walked with a swinging alert gait, half arrogant, half cautious, that marks a man ready for what the world may bring him. He carried a sword, short and heavy, more of a large knife than a shortsword, and its tip shone clean and unbloodied. He was not overlarge, but his chest was massive and his arms roped with muscle. His eyes, too, were blue.

"What is this—" he began.

I chopped his words off brutally.

"Aighos! If you look you will see I am not Vektor's man!"

"By Vox! You speak out of turn, cramph! You must be a rast of Vektor's, or else why are you here?"

A little rascally fellow with snaggly teeth and shaggy ponsho fleeces flapping about his narrow shanks trotted up. He carried a cudgel almost as long as himself. He had but one eye.

"Stick him, Korf Aighos!" he cackled, waving the bludgeon. "Stick him and take the treasure—"

"Still your tongue, Ob-eye!" Aighos glared. "I will say who is to be stuck and who not. As for the treasure, throw it into the river for all I care."

One or two of the ruffians, forming a watchful circle about me, started at this. Ob-eye yelped as though hurt.

"But the treasure! Stick him, I say!"

"I will stick you, by Vox, you ob-eyed rast! You know the orders of my Lady of Strombor! No killing!"

I really felt those solid mountains lurch under me. My Lady of Strombor! I, Dray Prescot, was the Lord of Strombor! There were only two ladies of Strombor in all Kregen — and one, Great-Aunt Shusha, was still there, as far as I knew, still in Strombor in Zenicce. So — so Aighos could only be speaking of *my* Lady of Strombor, my Delia!

No real recollection remains of how I covered the intervening space, but I was gripping Korf Aighos by the scruff of the neck, and twisting him up to me, and glaring down into his face. He glared back — and that dark, betraying shadow passed over his eyes.

"What is this of my Lady of Strombor! Speak, and quickly, or I'll snap your neck like a rotten pitcher!"

He struggled, and a hand was laid on my shoulder preparatory to my being whirled about and struck. I back-heeled and a man screeched. I lifted Aighos, beating away his fists, for he had dropped his long knife, and I swung him about and I shouted at these Blue Mountain Boys.

"Listen to me, you creeping mountain cramphs! I mean you no harm. I visit your country and am set upon! If this rast is your leader then let him speak, or by Zim-Zair, he's a dead man!"

I saw Korf Aighos' eyes flick toward me, and, suddenly, he went limp in my fist.

"I will speak. But first, tell me who you are — and, for the sake of Opaz himself, put me down!"

I set him on his feet.

"I am Drak ti Valkanium," I said — and then wondered if that had been the best thing to say. But habit had become ingrained.

He glanced at me, sidelong. He shook his head. "Now, by the Invisible Twins, I wonder!"

"Tell me of my Lady of Strombor!"

At this, as though abruptly recollecting himself and where he was, his face took on an expression of alarm immediately succeeded by grim determination.

He glanced around. He said, in a whisper, "If I tell you that, Tyr Drak, the Opaz-forsaken guards of Vektor will hear. Then we shall have to kill them all. My Lady of Strombor has expressly forbidden killing, although—" Here he spread his hands and glanced around, not, I fancy, with any too-guilty a feeling. He finished: "Sometimes the knife or the rock are the only solution."

A pragmatist, Korf Aighos. We withdrew into a cleft in the rocks, and he eyed me so narrowly that I tensed up ready to beat him in whatever scheme he was brewing. Instead, and again the rocks of the solid mountains lurched, he said: "You called yourself Drak ti Valkanium. I gave you the honorable title of Tyr because you are clearly so. But I think if I called you another name you would answer."

I looked at him. I know that old devil's look flashed evilly from my face, for he swallowed, and hurried on.

"Pur Dray, Dray Prescot, the Lord of Strombor, Zorcander of the Clan of Felschraung — I know I am not wrong!"

"Yes," I said, shattered.

"The Princess said you would come. Long and long has she waited. By stratagem after stratagem has she fended them off. Her father, the Emperor, may Opaz have him in his keeping, and that perfumed idiot Vektor — and there are others. Welcome and thrice welcome, my Lord of Strombor, to the Blue Mountains!"

"Well, sink me!" I exclaimed.

Korf Aighos rattled on, his face eager, his whole bearing animated and intense. "The Princess uses her name as the Lady of Strombor as a disguise. She trusts me." He spoke that proudly, and I could not condemn him for that. "This idea was hers. If there are no wedding presents, there can be no wedding. She it was, the dear daring Princess, who discovered the real treasure was coming in this caravan the hard and little-used way, and the great parade of servants and slaves and guards along the Quanscott Cut was the fake treasure!"

"That sounds like Delia's style."

"Every man of the Blue Mountains would die for her! And of them all, the Blue Mountain Boys are her most devoted and loyal subjects."

I had to rise to this occasion. Implicitly, in all Aighos said, there was the fact that if he agreed with Delia that she would not marry Vektor, then he must agree to her marrying me. I had to show some fire, some spirit, act a part as the great man.

"I would thank you, Korf Aighos, for your love and loyalty. I agree that we should not kill Vektor's guards. But, my friend, I do not think you should hurl the loot into the river."

"No?" He sounded doubtful, at which I took heart.

"Carefully spread out and spent, it would bring in much for the people of the Blue Mountains."

"Loot!"

Had I gone too far? Was he an honest man in the sense that he wouldn't accept loot when it came his way? Was this stealing in the accepted sense of the word? I was sailing near the wind, even by Kregan standards which are notoriously laxer than Earth's. Perhaps—

I said quickly, "But as we are all honest men, then the treasure must be gathered together and returned to Vektor when the Princess Majestrix and I are married."

"Amen to that, my lord." Then he screwed up his blue eyes, and said, with a chuckle: "And I will take counsel on the question of the treasure. We are great bandits in the Blue Mountains!"

They are great ruffians, the Blue Mountain Boys.

The missing Womox had leaped voluntarily to his death, rushing back down the track out of the defile and so over a precipice. The other, the one with the broken tusk, sat crouched in mortal terror of the Blue Mountain men. I had seen the Womoxes in action, aboard Viridia the Render's swordship; now I saw how a member of that savage and sullen race was terrified in his turn.

And yet — my Delia was the princess of this cutthroat bunch!

Aighos bustled about superintending the tying of the guards' wrists. They would be set stumbling up the track the remainder of the distance to High Zorcady in the mist. The calsanys loaded with the treasure were prodded away down the track. I looked up and saw a line of airboats appear over a nearby crag. They followed in line astern formation as neat as a rulered line on a score, sailing through the upper levels. They did not see us, down among the rocks, and so serenely flew on. I could guess why the treasure had not been brought in by flier; no one was going to trust an airboat with all this treasure among these hostile crags. The thought drew from me a gesture of respect for the men of the Vallian Air Service.

Hikdar Stovang stumbled up, blood on his face, his helmet gone, his bright gold and black butterfly insignia ripped and stained.

"Traitor!" he yelled at me as I stood with Aighos. "I trusted you, you Opaz-forsaken cramph! Drak ti Valkanium! I shall remember that!"

Ob-eye swung his cudgel and slanted his one eye at Aighos, but the korf of the mountains laughed and said: "Let the braggart go!"

His men respected Aighos, that was very plain, and even Ob-eye, inclined to rumbustiousness, stayed in line, and with them all accepted me as Drak, a friend of Aighos. The korf considered it best for the time being to conceal my identity from everyone, with the exception of himself. I saw, with an amusement tinged with a wry affection for this korf of the mountains, this bandit, that he relished this knowledge, this secret he shared with a princess and a lord.

From the zorcas Aighos selected the finest specimen, that ridden by Hikdar Stovang. I remounted my own animal. The other Blue Mountain Boys selected zorcas and preysanys, and in a straggly procession we wended down away from High Zorcady.

I looked back. High Zorcady! There was a ring about that, a fineness, a sense of high yearning. The grim rearing pile spearing up into the clouds, its towers ringed with mist, the crested-korfs wheeling past its battlemented walls, all made a reality out of a fantasy of imagination. I knew I was sorry not to have visited High Zorcady.

The plan was to get me in, or to get Delia out, and once we had met, to make further plans. I did not care which, just so long as I could hold my Delia in my arms again.

"Pur Dray," said Aighos, and then coughed and fiddled with his reins and berated the poor zorca between his knees. "Kr. Drak! We shall find hospitality at my cousin's village. You rode past it and never saw it, so well are the houses hidden."

He spoke the truth. The walls and buildings constructed of the rock against which they stood remained extraordinarily difficult to detect. We drank strong Kregan tea and ate a specialty of the mountains, ponsho rolled in hibisum flour and baked slowly — baked for three whole days — and then drenched in a taylyne sauce and simmered for another day. By the time the meat reaches your lips it melts like the sweetest honey. Superb! We also, being good Vallians, drank a great deal of wine of various vintages. The messenger had been sent, a lithe young girl of the mountains, striding with her skirts tucked up, springing boldly over frightening chasms, carrying laundry. The laundry would get her past the guards, and once inside she was known to friends, who would conduct her directly to Delia. Perforce, I waited.

We had been quartered in the largest house, a two-story structure whose roof of sharply-angled slates would have towered over the other buildings but for the cunning use of overhanging rock-shelves. Each slate had to be fixed in place with severity; where torrents could wash over the rocks and sweep everything away the roofs had to be steep. There could be none of the shallow roofs of the valleys where the slates could lie and slumber without fear of slipping off.

I sat in a carved black-wood chair that must have been all of two hundred years old, and talked with the men. I had a strange peace, a tranquility, a sense of time standing still. So near I was to Delia that all my recent frantic scurryings appeared ludicrous. I had merely to sit here, eat and drink and talk, and she would appear in the doorway, radiant, glorious, alive!

In the corner stood a two-handed sword, fully seven feet long, of that peculiar kind used on Earth around the sixteenth century. Contrary to popular belief, these enormously long swords of war were used in combat, and not merely for color guards of honor or as symbols, but the man to wield them must be a man indeed. This one had a leather-wrapped grip, wide quillons, and also a wrapping of velvet around the blade before the quillons. The cotton would have come from Donengil and the silk, probably, from Loh. To protect the hand when grasping this shortening-section a pair of semi-quillons had been neatly set into the metal. The thing looked clean, without rust, but a casual test with my thumb showed it to be blunt.

"The great sword of war of the Blue Mountains," said Korf Aighos. He half laughed, half sighed. "They are out of fashion now. There was a time when men raced through the ravines wielding the swords of war and none could stand against them."

These men had never seen a Krozair longsword. Beside this enormous brute a Krozair two-hander was a subtle instrument. I had the sudden craving to feel a real Krozair longsword in my fists again.

The feeling made me realize why Aighos had recognized me. He had heard me use a Krozair oath — "By Zim-Zair!" — and no doubt Delia herself had let the resounding words fall from her lips, also, from time to time. She was fully entitled to do so.

A fracas started in the narrow walk and we went out, laughing and joking, carrying blackjacks of wine, expecting to see sport. A man raced past, screaming, his hair streaming, his face sweating, the eyes like livid coals.

"The shorgortz! The shorgortz!"

A woman screamed and snatched up her child and ran inside, slamming her lenken door. Aighos dropped his blackjack and the rich dark wine spread across the stones.

"The shorgortz," I said. 'Tell me, Korf, what is that?"

'Truly you are not yet of the Blue Mountains, Kr. Drak!'

"Bring fire!" a man yelled.

"Shelter within doors and pray!"

"Fire!"

"If you light torches," I said, at once adjusting to the peril, "you will tell the guards where we are."

"Better the Emperor's aragorn, or the mercenaries, than the shorgortz!"

So it was that serious, then...

I couldn't have them running about with torches alarming the neighborhood and alerting the men brought back by Hikdar Stovang. And, far more importantly, if there was some monster out there in the mountains, my Delia was coming... I did not hesitate. I went back into the house, snatched up the great sword of war, brushed past its protesting owner, and strode out into the street. Men were milling. I shouted loudly, stilling them by my anger.

"Tell me, you Blue Mountain Boys! Where is this Zair-forsaken shorgortz?"

They babbled. A hundred paces along the track from the village. Along the track my Delia must walk.

I ran.

I thought of the Ullgishoa and Umgar Stro. Then I had fought only with my chains and had not until later grasped the great Krozair longsword Pur Zenkiren had given me in Pattelonia. Now I held what was little more than a bar of steel. Mind you, I had bested four Womoxes with a length of lumber aboard Viridia's swordship... It had seemed to me that a great bashing, cutting instrument of some length would be the best weapon here, better, at any rate, than an ordinary rapier.

I saw the shorgortz.

The thing was immense, nauseating, powerful, and altogether repulsive. I did not hesitate in my headlong dash but went on, at top speed, hurling myself forward, the huge sword of war held high and cocked over my right shoulder.

The shorgortz was a reptile. It was not a risslaca, those dinosaurs of Kregen; it had twelve legs, bent and crooked, so that it walked with the body slung between. Its body was squamous, the scales rimmed with a crimson iridescence, their centers green-black. Its four eyes kept up a rapid blinking. Its tendrils groped forward, writhing, seeking, snatching at anything that ran, to snatch and grip and force the prey into the convulsively chewing parallel jaws that stretched back to the rear of its hideous head. It was of the size of, for example, a double-decker bus, and it stank. It reeked with its own effluvia and the rotting stenches of its victims.

The sword of war slashed down.

The blade struck the thing cleanly over the head — and bounced!

The damn thing was as blunt as a lead razor.

I struck again and again and then had to skip back as a tendril writhed out toward me. My blows had no apparent effect on the shorgortz. No doubt it was merely fulfilling its destiny. No doubt it was acting as its nature impelled it. But I knew that my Delia would come walking lightly down this track and if this obscene thing was alive to meet her... I would not think of that.

This time I did what I should have done at first. I ran in, thrusting, to plunge the sword of war into the top right-hand eye. Thick ichor pulsed forth, gagging with the smell of vomit.

The thing lashed its tail with tremendous force from side to side, splitting and pulverizing the rocks< I leaped, thrust again, and now the lower right-hand eye burst.

I dodged back. A tendril lapped my body and I had to let go the sword of war with my left hand, draw my dagger and cut through. The keen steel bit. Maybe the sword of war had been a mistake? I needed a weapon that would bite!

The shrieks and hissings of the reptile screeched higher. I kept the dagger in my left hand, the curved steel guard shielding, and began a systematic slashing away of the groping tendrils. Twice the massive tail arched over at me and smashed brutishly along the ground where I stood the instant before I leaped aside. I stuck the dagger into it, but it did no good. Thrusting the dagger between my teeth, dribbling and drooling the foul-tasting blood smearing it, I took the sword of war into my fists again. This time I slashed and hacked and thrust, blotted out the lower left eye. But the thing kept jerking back, protecting its last remaining orb, and I kept thrusting and missing. And now it began to clutch out at me with its forelegs. Wickedly sharp talons raked past me. I felt my leather tunic rip and a white-hot pain scored my side.

I kept on. I had to. My body was smothered with the ichor. Steam rose in the light of the mingled rays of the twin suns. I leaped and struck — I slipped and a foreleg darted for me. Only the reflex of muscles long trained and hardened barred the sword up, a barrier of steel, to chop off the blow. I felt the vibrations hammer through my hands.

On my feet, I leaped, aiming for the remaining eye. The head twisted, reared, the fanged mouth opened — I hauled back.

In blind anger I hurled the two-handed sword down. I hauled out the rapier. I launched myself at the beast.

Two, three, four thrusts at the eye, and all parried or blocked. I brought the rapier down in a swooshing cut and the sharp steel scythed into scale. Again and again I cut, but I could see, clearly and with growing desperation, that the rapier lacked the bulk, for all that the rapier is a cutting weapon, to slice through the armored scale. The bulk inched ponderously forward on the ten legs to the rear. The shorgortz was hesitant to push on. It must recognize that it faced some being not prepared to submit to being snatched up and stuffed down the fanged mouth.

Those fangs opened and closed, chewing angrily.

The thing was no more angry than me.

I leaped again, tried for the eye, missed, slashed down furiously, and the rapier pinged and broke across.

I threw the hilt at the eye.

It caromed off the snout.

Beneath the thing's foreclaws lay the sword of war.

I took the dagger out of my mouth and plunged it deeply between two claws. The leg wrenched back, taking the dagger with it. I seized the great sword.

A mere lump of steel. Blunt as a boxer's chin. I took a breath. I could feel the foul gunk all over me. I poised.

Then I leaped.

The point of the sword of war penetrated the left upper eye. It burst in a showering of liquid. I slipped, fell, rolled, saw a flailing claw descending on me, and rolled on.

The talons hit the rock at my side, gouting up dust.

I leaped up and with a last and desperate thrust got the sword through the broken lower left eye. This time I did not pull it out. I leaned on it and thrust as hard as my muscles could push. I sweated and panted and thrust, my feet swinging off the ground as the beast reared. It was shrieking and I was yelling. It roared in its last agony, and I roared in my agony that it would not die before my Delia passed by.

I felt the foreleg brush past me, felt the talons rip my tunic back. I felt, again, that white-hot line of acid scorch down my back.

My fingers slipped from the greasy hilt.

I toppled back.

The rocks came up, hard; but they did not knock me out, and I was able to claw up, ready to fight the thing with my bare hands if necessary.

I recall little after that.

I did hear a man shout, dimly and far off, "Hai! Jikai!"

But that held no meaning.

The thing was down, was gushing blood everywhere. I staggered back, bruised, cut, exhausted, empty-handed. Men surrounded me. I heard the clang of weapons. I heard a yelling, wrapped in the fog of nonunderstanding.

Then, sharp and clear, like a lance-thrust, words shocked out at me.

"That's Drak ti Valkanium! Take the rast! The traitor will die, slowly. Take him and bind him with iron chains!"

Twelve

Chained before the Emperor of Vallia

They took me and bound me with iron chains, and our sorry coffle wended painfully down the mountain trails to the plains and so to the canal.

I knew what was in store. I suppose, given that all things come to all men in the fullness of time, I had always known I would become a slave hauler and haul an Emperor's barge. This was fitting. This was the circle of vaol-paol complete.

The difference was that I and my comrades captured by mercenaries in the employ of the Emperor were noted brigands, outlaws, who had robbed the caravan of the Kov Vektor. The wedding gifts were lost and could not be found. I had no idea where they were, and — with a heartfelt relief that had nothing to do with the fact that I would not suffer — I learned that we would not be put to the question. Torture is commonplace in some areas of Kregen; it had been outlawed centuries ago in Vallia. The Emperor's authority was autocratic, although some men did not obey him, but he could not flout the rules of civilized behavior in this. We were being taken to Vondium to answer for our crimes before a properly constituted court. I say being taken — we were in the chained gangs of haulers who walked all the way there on bleeding feet.

With the vanishment of the wedding gifts, the Princess Majestrix could only refuse the wedding itself. No one could fault her in that. Presents must be exchanged on both sides. It was a civilized custom. There was no dowry and nothing from the other side; there was no buying of a wife and nothing on the other side. There was an exchange.

We were treated abominably enough on that journey. We hauled the barges at a fast rate, fairly running under the lash and the knout. We slept on a barge reserved for the purpose, and it stank of stale sweat, urine, and fear. All day and all night we kept up that steady progress, passing narrow boat after narrow boat on the way. The stentor with his curled-spiral trumpet sounded the warning of our coming long and loud before us, and the tows went splash, splash, splash, into the cut, and the narrow boat skippers poled out to the center to leave a clear right of way.

We were not just ordinary slave haulers; we were going to a just trial and then an execution, or a lifetime as haulers. I felt that most of my hauling comrades would welcome the first.

I will not dwell on that time of hauling. My hair and beard, which had grown unattended during my travels across Vallia in search of Delia, grew luxuriantly, like bushes, untidy, knotted, filthy, covering my face. The lacerations from the shorgortz's talons suppurated, and I knew that if I had not taken that bath of baptism in the sacred pool of the River Zelph, I would have been a dead man. The whips of the slave-masters and guards wealed me so that I was truly jikaidered. Sores covered my feet. The disgusting rag that had once been a gray slave breechclout around my loins stank and crawled with vermin. I tried to wash it and was flogged for my pains. Fresh water was provided for those people who could not drink the canal-water, and dry biscuits, with a minced stew of vosk and ponsho leavings. Each day we had a handful of palines, and I believe these alone kept people alive and going, and, in many cases, controlled the degree of their insanity.

The branding with the Emperor's mark on our right shoulders we all under-went did not unduly worry me, for I knew that a brand would, on me, slowly thin and vanish as subcutaneous and cutaneous cells rebuilt themselves. The painful part came in that I had to be rebranded. The scar tissue on a normal human skin usually remained permanently; but I knew there were many skills on Kregen. I had seen how a brand might be removed in Zenicce. But I annoyed the slave-masters, and they kept an eye on me, and lashed their whips and their knouts with special viciousness in my direction.

I was, all in all, during that passage, down in spirit.

The talons of the shorgortz must have exuded a poison, or a toxic fluid in the effluvia in which I had been drenched had penetrated my skin like an acid, for the wounds refused to heal. The guards took a perverse delight in laying their whips accurately across the old cuts. I was jikaidered well and truly. Jikaida is played on a checkered board; my hide was crisscrossed with the checkers of the lash.

As I hauled and tugged at the harsh tow rope I did not think even the archan-gel Gabriel would recognize me. I was in far worse condition than ever I had been as an oar-slave in the swifters of Magdag. Zorg, my old oar-comrade, now dead, or Nath and Zolta, my two rascals, could never have seen in this hairy, stinking, lashed specimen the man Dray Prescot they had known.

Of the country through which we passed I was aware only of the towpath. We slaves, in a ragged bunch roughly three abreast, clawed onto our leashes, knotted and spliced to the main tow rope, and pulled, heads down. I saw the muddy track beneath my feet. Also, occasionally, and with a relief that broke the monotony, I saw lock gates and the smooth wooden beams that had to be opened and closed. I was never allowed what would have been the pleasant diversion of turning the paddle handles. That was reserved for the favored of the slaves, girls usually, whom the guards pampered.

Somewhere, in this despairing mass of humanity like a clogging mass of in-sects at the end of a jam-sticky knife, trudged Korf Aighos. I did not even know how many of us had been captured, although the how of it was easy enough. The laundry girl had been captured, and the noise of my battle with that confounded shorgortz had drawn the guards like a magnet.

I couldn't feel enmity for Hikdar Stovang. But although I had borne him no malice, he had believed the worst of me, and here I was, hauling for the Emperor.

We were riding the various canals on our way back southeastward to Vondium. I hardly cared. We must have ridden the Vindelka Cut, for Vindelka lies immediately to the northwest of Vondium. Often as I trod after my fellow haulers I walked a sea of muddy blood.

Some damned alchemy of that reptilian monster's foul acid-dripping ichor refused to let my body heal up. My mind was cloudy for much of that passage. Sores covered me. The daily lashings merely kept my body bloody. I still had strength, and could march; those of the ordinary haulers who fell were left to die, if they were dying, or had their throats cut if they feigned death after repeated floggings. Those of the haulers facing court hearings were flogged every now and then and given a ride, and flogged again, so that they preferred to haul rather than face the incessant extra floggings.

If you think I came to hate these slave-guards — you are right.

The red and black bands on their sleeves burned into my brain.

But I said I would not dwell on this unhappy period of my life. I would prefer to forget it, although I do not believe I ever will.

At last we came to the flight of locks leading to the inner network of waterways of Vondium. We locked through and finally came to a long low stone warehouse where more guards waited for us.

The regular haulers were taken away to their barracks. We criminals were rounded up, loaded with chains — whereat many a man screamed as the harsh iron bit into his open wounds — and dragged off.

All I could see was the stone beneath my feet. The guards were mere blurs of dark crimson in the corner of my eyes. I heard them whistling as they strode along — a tune I knew, surely — *The Bowmen of Loh*. That did not belong to any part of my life now; that came from a distant and dimly-remembered time when I was fit and well, with clean clothes on my back, a full belly, laughter and wine, kind faces about me... I trudged and stumbled on over the stones, done for.

Down dank stairways we went, into dark dungeons where the leepitix darted and scrabbled, where the rats gnawed dead men's bones, where the vermin clustered in the corners waiting for fresh meat. We were chained to the wall.

I slumped down. I did not think I could raise a little finger to bash a guard, as I would customarily have struck with my fists until either the guards were dead or I was out like a light. I tried to rest and sleep, but phantasms thronged my brain, and I moaned. Chains rattled and clanked dismally. We were not fed. Guards came for us, men wearing the red and black, and we were hauled out. We were starving, for we had not eaten for two days. There were ten of us, I saw, ten starved lean scarecrows, all hairy, filthy, and covered in sores. We were moaning as we were dragged along, our chains rattling on the stones.

Up we were dragged, half throttled in the chains. Up and up. We were in the Emperor's palace in Vondium. We were pulled out onto a wide and shining floor. Sunshine lanced down, emerald and crimson. There was a great throng of people, courtiers, guards, Air Servicemen, women gorgeous in fine clothes. All was a dazzlement to me. I could barely stand. I was weak, I tottered and fell, and a boot kicked me up. Korf Aighos fell and was dragged. I fell and was dragged. We left a bloody trail across that shining floor.

I looked up. All distorted, on its side, a throne soared, it seemed to the ceiling, that shattered the light into a myriad shards like diamonds. A figure sat on the throne, a blaze of gold and crimson. A second throne stood at the side, gorgeous, splendid, not of the world I inhabited.

I was aware of the hum of conversation, and stray words spouted up, like black ice breaking free of the pack. We were the assassins, the murderers, the bandits, who stole and raped and killed.

The guards moved back. A wedge of dark crimson gave a backdrop to the thrones. I saw the white blurs of many faces. Jewels winked into my brain like fire and ice. I was down, done for, finished.

A voice boomed close.

"Here, my lord Emperor, are the malefactors for your justice!"

No trial, then—

I tried to stand up. I, Dray Prescot, wouldn't show these scum anything other than defiance, contempt; I tried to stand up, my chains dragging me down. I staggered. I fell. The hard polished floor came up cruelly. I lay, drugged with fatigue. Hunger was no longer noticeable, except that I couldn't stand up and call these people and this Emperor a pack of kleeshes.

Of what use any further struggle? I had failed. I had failed to do what I had so vaingloriously boasted. I had said I would stride before the Emperor and demand from him the hand of his daughter Delia in marriage.

And here I was, before the Emperor, swathed in chains like a wild beast, bearing the scars of floggings, the red blood running from open sores, covered in vermin, filthy, with my hair stinking in my own nostrils, bathed in repulsiveness.

Oh, Dray Prescot, how are the mighty fallen!

I heard a cry and then a shout of horror.

I struggled to stand up and could not.

They would take me out now and cut off my head.

I heard a rustling, and then a great soughing sobbing from a thousand throats around the enormous throne room. I felt that rustling close. I felt a breath of wind and then I smelled a clean, sweet, fresh scent — I felt warm soft arms go around me, all white and rosy, naked, taking me up as I was, as I was in my filth and degradation, clasping me to her beast.

"Oh, my Dray! My Dray! I have found you at last!"

Thirteen

"The man who kills Dray Prescot I'll have burned alive!"

My Delia!

Some resource then, some last vestige of — not pride — love, some last remnant of love for my Delia forced me up onto my knees. She held me close and she was sobbing in a way that gave me a deep hatred for anyone or anything who

594

could make her thus break her heart — and knowing that person was me. I stood up. She would not let me go.

"Dray! Oh, Dray, I have been frantic! Dray!"

"Delia," I managed to say. The throne room whirled about my head. I staggered dizzily, and she held me, her dear body firm against me. "I love you, my Delia. I shall never stop loving you."

She kept sobbing my name, over and over, and hugging and clasping me to her. I could see very little. Hands drew us apart. Soft, anxious, gentle hands of court ladies, noblewomen, tugging my Delia away. And harsh, fierce, cruel hands of slave-masters and guards dragging me away, with a blow from a whip-handle across the face to speed my going.

Delia screamed.

I struggled.

I do not know where the strength came from.

I took the whip-handle between my teeth and I jerked. I brought my head back and snapped it forward and the lash whistled. I forced myself to see, forcing my eyes to open and to tell me what was going on.

A blow smashed against the back of my head and I staggered forward. I spun clumsily. I reached up against all that dead weight of iron, took the whip from my mouth, and brought the handle down across the fellow's face. He toppled back spouting blood, shrieking. I lashed the whip at the guards, and one was caught around the neck. I dragged him toward me, broke his neck, and threw him aside. I was ready to do this as often as was required.

I heard a shrill scream — and recognized Delia's voice, the voice of the Majestrix. The first time I had ever heard her use her voice like that: "Do not kill him! *The man who kills Dray Prescot I'll have burned alive!*"

"Daughter, daughter!" The testy voice — the Emperor!

I flung back my head.

"I am Dray Prescot! I claim your daughter Delia! *She is mine!* Before all the world, she is mine!"

The guards pounced then, and I smashed and slashed them back. I yelled again, shouting into that golden haze.

"She is mine — *and I am hers!* There is nothing you can do, Emperor, *nothing!*"

A guard coiled his lash across the blood-fouled shining floor and tripped me. I bent, dragged the lash in, and before he could let go I kneed him, and then brought my fists down on his neck. His head hung strangely before he pitched to the floor.

I knew Delia was struggling in the hands of the nobles, who would be outraged at her behavior. I caught another guard and dispatched him. I felt nothing. I was a shining figure molded from blood. The Emperor was cursing; I could tell his voice and would not forget it.

"Take him away! Guards! Take him away and execute him. Now! *Now!*"

"You will gain nothing by my death, Emperor! I will win; my Delia will win; you can only lose! *Fool!* Think of the daughter you love! Think of Delia!"

"*Take him away!*"

I do not know how many guards leaped on me. The whip was smashed from my grasp. It seemed a hundred hands gripped me. I was twisted over, picked up like a rolled carpet. My head lolled. But I could see the shining golden haze where stood the father of Delia, and I shouted, high and strong and with great venom: "You fool, Emperor! *You have lost!*"

The grim words followed me as I left that throne room.

"Take off his head — now!"

To relate what I have is to make me sweat and throb and relive once again all the passions, the desires, the despairs of my youth. How my love for Delia shone upon all — and how her love for me transcended everything! Had any two lovers in two worlds ever loved as we did? I do not know: all I know is the depth and passion and greatness of our love; and I tend to think not.

Out of the throne room hurried the knot of guards. I was surrounded by a wall of dark crimson, a wall moving and flowing with powerful legs clad in dark scarlet. These were not the slave-guards, nor yet the aragorn, nor yet the warders with their red and black sleeves.

Some red roaring feelings were surging back now. I was aware of the infernal aches of my body. Well, my head would soon leap from that abused body and I could rest. My Delia — oh, how I would miss my Delia!

I could look up at groined ceilings. Around corners we went, along corridors. How many carrying me? Six? I heard a curse, and then another. We had reached a small antechamber; in the ceiling an octagon of light cast down the colors of the Suns of Scorpio. A man beside me coughed. They dropped me. I fell to the floor and rolled. My head rang, but I got to my hands, and tried to get my feet under me.

A man shrieked: "What are you doing — *aaagh!*"

I forced my eyes to take in what they saw, and transfer that information to my brain. I saw five dead men, all clad in the dark crimson. I saw a sixth with a bloody rapier in one hand and a bloody main-gauche in the other. He advanced on me and I thought this was the end. And—

"By the Veiled Froyvil, Dray! They were good men, all, and I slew them!"

My brain reeled.

I knew that voice.

I knew — I knew!

But — it could not be.

It was impossible.

I was dead already and treading the path toward the Ice Floes of Sicce.

The impossible voice spoke again.

"By all the shattered targes in Mount Hlabro, Dray! Perk up, my old dom!"

I shook my head. My hands trembled. I could see them, there before me, on the floor, shaking and beating against the marble where a trickle of blood flowed from a corpse slain by a corpse.

I lifted my head. I looked up. I whispered.

"Seg?"

"In the name of all the windy heights of Erthyrdrin, Dray! Get up, dom, and let us get out of here before the Froyvil-forsaken cramphs come arunning."

"Seg."

"Well, who else—" Then that old familiar voice, that well-loved voice, altered. Seg — for it was he, it was Seg Segutorio — came to me, knelt, and put a hand under my chin, and lifted. He looked into my face, and I smiled.

"Dray! You're in a bad way!"

"No, Seg. No — for you are alive, and I have mourned you long and long. Oh — Seg!"

He picked me up then, hoisting me high to his chest, and he carried me out and away, through corridors that led from and to I knew not where in that great palace of the Emperor of Vallia. Presently he brought me to a small space where he lay me on a trundle bed; there he carried water, bathed me, and ministered to my wounds.

"Seg—" I reached a trembling hand up and grasped his forearm. "Thelda?"

He smiled and continued bathing my wounds. "She is a proud mother now, Dray. A fine boy." Then a look of furtiveness crossed his face, and I could guess, and I said feebly: "He has my blessing. I will bring the Yerthyr shoot—"

"You're the same Dray, my old dom! The same Dray Prescot!"

"But—" I said. I still could not believe. Out there in the Hostile Territories when the army of Queen Lilah of Hiclantung had been defeated by the Harfnars of Cherwangtung, Seg, Thelda, and I had raced with the remnants of Hwang's proud regiment, and I had seen what I had seen. "You went down, Seg. Thelda and you. The nactrixes boiled over you like chanks in a bloody sea."

"True. By the Veiled Froyvil, but they were a ferocious bunch! I slew them until I could slay no more, and their corpses heaped above us. They left us to chase you. I thought you dead, then, Dray."

"But—"

He smiled and tilted a glass cup to my lips. It held water of an iciness I usually find disagreeable, but now it tasted like the best Zond wine.

"I heard what happened with you and Delia. You did not think, after you were missing from *Lorenztone,* that she would calmly fly off and leave, did you?"

I looked at him.

"Little you know Delia of Delphond, Dray Prescot, if you think that! Chuktar Farris of Vomansoir was ordered — and I can imagine your Delia telling him! — to return and search for you. They did not find you. They found Thelda and me."

"Thank God for that," I said. I said "thank God"; I did not say "thank Zair", or Opaz, or the Invisible Twins, or Pandrite, or use any of the colorful expressions of Kregen.

"So we came back to Vallia and I do not like to think what Delia went through then. Thelda and I were married—"

"And you have a son called Dray."

He started to look uncomfortable, then the old fey wildness broke through, and he glared at me. "Of course! What better name in all the world is there? Tell me that, you stubborn old onker!"

"And how did you come to be here?"

"Why, I am a bowman, or had you forgotten? I am a private Koter in the personal bodyguard of the Emperor, the crimson Bowmen of Loh—"

I tried to sing a certain stanza of that song, and although my voice cracked and wheezed like a leaky set of bagpipes, Seg got the message. The stanza is a particularly mocking one. It is often omitted. Seg threw back his head and laughed.

"Now, by Vox! I can live again, Dray Prescot!"

After that a confusion set in, and I was aware of shadows moving, and then of a woman sobbing and crying and laughing and holding me in her arms, whereat I grunted and pretended to be much more soggy than I was. Poor Thelda! She meant so well, with her pushy ways, and her constant exhibited concern for everyone's welfare. But, as I was to discover, she had changed enormously from the plump sweaty earnest girl who had marched with us across the Hostile Territories and tried to suborn me away from Delia on the orders of the racters.

I did say, itching an old sore: "Where are the fallimy flowers for my poultice, Thelda?"

At this she burst into a torrent of tears, all wet and sticky. I heard Seg chuckle, and Thelda went away, crying. Seg bent over me. "You must rest now, Dray. A doctor is coming. Then we will get you out of the palace."

I opened my mouth to say what I so desperately longed to ask. Then I shut my mouth. I was well enough aware of the situation and what had happened. I dare not ask for Delia. I knew people were risking their lives on my behalf. Seg was a private Koter in the Emperor's bodyguard, a crimson Bowman of Loh, and thus had been able to dispose of the men carrying me out to execution. They had been his own comrades; he had slain them for me. I felt the shame of that, the fierce leap of pride, and the dark agony of remorse, but it was done, and, in truth, for my Delia's sake I would wade through oceans of blood, as I have said. I am not a nice man.

"Don't take chances, Seg. Clear up all traces. For your sake, and Thelda's — and little Dray's."

"Do not fret, Dray. Erthyr the Bow is with me now."

At this I felt more reassurance, for Seg seldom called on the name of that puissant and powerful spirit, the supreme being of Erthyrdrin; that he felt like that, and I knew it was a genuine emotion, proved he was satisfied.

Later I discovered more of the reasons for that satisfaction. But, even now, Delia will toss her head, grow very hoity-toity, and refuse to discuss just what was contrived. I know a body was found and substituted for me, and a convincing explanation put forward for the absence of five bowmen, four private Koters, and a Jiktar. At dead of night, with only two smaller moons hurtling low across the sky, I was conveyed out of the palace and secreted in a hidden room built into the attic of a lopsided house leaning crazily at the end of a maze of alleyways well away from the canals. The Presidio, the high council answerable only to the Emperor, confirmed his haughty actions in condemning me to instant execution. Korf Aighos and the other eight Blue Mountain Boys were put on trial. I asked about them, and Seg nodded, his face alive with all the old fey qualities, the strengths, the joyousness, the sheer love of life of his character. His black hair and blue eyes looked dearly familiar to me.

"They have been found guilty — as they were, Froyvil knows — but Delia knows your feelings, she's known you long enough to read you like an illuminated scroll of my childhood, and we have plans to rescue them."

And, in due course of time, they were rescued and secreted in another safe house in Vondium.

The doctor came. A dried-up little stick of a man with tallow-yellow hair and a wispy moustache, he was competent enough. His first action was to snap the locks and open his velvet-lined sturm-wood case of acupuncture needles. His name was Nath the Needle. Doctor Nath the Needle. Well, there are many Naths in Kregen.

"I don't know how you survived, my lord," he said, sniffing. He wore a somber dark-brown suit of clothes, a decrepit old cloak, and a hat in which the two slots over the eyes had worn into a gaping hole, like two gun-ports smashed into one by a thirty-two-pounder roundshot. "The infection from a shorgortz is generally reckoned to result in a terminal disease. But, there, medicine is improving every day in Vallia, and no doubt the Blue Mountain men have acquired an immunity unknown to us. I must look into it, indeed, I must." He babbled on like this, but he gave me some foul-tasting gunk, and, indeed, I began to mend very quickly.

Delia, of course, was kept under strict surveillance.

I had an idea.

She would seek to find a way to throw off her servitors and guards and visit me, but danger lay there, for all she was the Princess Majestrix. Seg told me that as far as he could tell the Emperor cherished a very real affection for his daughter, but that his ideas on the majesty and aura of an emperor kept interfering with that ideal. He was determined she should marry. She was his only child, and his doctors had told him he could have no more. I had never heard Delia mention her mother, and I assumed she was dead. Now, after Delia's displays of temper, as the court gossip went, she was to be held on a very tight rein until the Kov Vektor provided a fresh king's ransom in wedding presents.

I told Seg what I required. He looked at me, chuckled, then laughed, and finally he roared with good humor. Feeling fitter than I had in weeks, I was duly shaved, and new clean clothes were brought in for me to put on. I stared into a mirror of real glass that was the proud possession of Paline Panifer, the girl Seg had found to care for me and the room. Paline is a common name for a young girl on Kregen, like Cherry on Earth, and she was fresh-complexioned, dark-eyed, a little solemn and overawed in my presence, but she cooked a truly delightful squish pie and she could make Kregan tea properly. Also she did the laundry with an amazingly tiny amount of soap.

"A boat is due tomorrow, Dray," Seg told me. I stood up. I felt good.

'Tomorrow, then, Seg.'

He didn't bother to wish me luck. I believe he thought I didn't need it. Both of us thought the other returned from the Ice Floes of Sicce; and after that — who needed luck?

The next morning, early, I put on my new gear. The buff leather tunic fitted well, and the buff shirt was clean and starched. The hat was gray with a fine curly set of feathers in red and white, the colors that servitors of Valka wore on their sleeves. The tall black boots shone with Paline's ministrations. I buckled on the belt with the rapier and main-gauche Seg had brought. As always, I sheathed a knife back of my right hip. Swathed in a voluminous gray cloak I went with Paline from that maze of alleys and out toward the canals and quays. The tang of fresh air braced me up. The twin Suns of Scorpio flamed overhead. All the bustle and uproar of a great metropolis flowed about me. The lesten-hide bag given me by Seg, who had had it from the hand of Delia, hung heavily inside my shirt. I looked up and there rose the forest of masts. I felt my pulses quicken. The Star Lords had forbidden me to venture on the sea for a space, but they could not prevent my quick interest in all I saw and in the sealore I absorbed, it seemed, through my pores.

I have spoken of the great galleons of Vallia. Now I could see them. The ship from Valka lay warped alongside the quay, and men were busily engaged in discharging her. Her captain gaped at me as though I had risen from the dead. I recognized him — as he did me.

"Captain Korer!" I said, shaking his hand. "I trust you are well?"

"My lord Strom!" he gasped.

He told me all the news of Valka and I drank it up, every word, for I love my island of Valka. The land prospered. We remained at peace. Trade thrived. Babies were being born at a rate that ensured the depredations of the slavers would soon be obliterated. All my old friends still lived and were happy; and yet all mourned my departure. I sensed the truth in this. Captain Korer was, in the cant phrase, a bluff old sea dog. He would not dissimulate to me, his Strom — or so I fancied.

"Your crew? They are trustworthy?"

"Every man and boy, Strom!"

"Good. Then I took passage with you and am just arrived."

"I understand."

After that it was easy to arrange. With a small guard of marines from the ship, and presents bought with Delia's money — presents that would not betray their origin — carried by smartly-clad men wearing the red and white banded shirt-sleeves, we went up to the palace. Gold bought us a way in. Once again I found myself in that immense throne room, under the blaze of gold and jewels. But this time I walked with cracking heels on that shining floor, with a sword at my side, and with my own men carrying gifts for the Emperor.

"Drak, Strom of Valka!"

The Emperor received me kindly, his chamberlain, with fresh gold to jingle, having smoothed the way. The Emperor — how to describe him? He had sired the most beautiful girl in two worlds. He was strong and passionate, fiery-eyed, dominating, accustomed to command — aye, and cruel and ruthless, too, when he had to be. I knew.

"I have a gift for the Princess Majestrix, Majister."

He grunted. He thought I wanted favors from him over the rights of Valka. "You will get no favors from that young lady, Strom Drak."

I rubbed my clean-shaven and shining chin. I felt that Paline had dosed me too liberally with scents and perfumes.

"As to that, Majister, I must, at the very least, pay my respects to the Princess Majestrix. Of favors I ask none."

"That makes a refreshing change." He stood up, at which there followed a great swirl of activity of protocol and bowing and sorting out of places. "I'll come with you, for, by Vox, I've little enough to please me these days."

In the guard of honor marched private Koter Segutorio.

We went through brilliant corridors hung with tapestries of such beauty and value that I could not refrain from looking at them. Past precious objects from all the known world we walked, and came to a marble stair, and then a door studded with gold bosses in the forms of zhantil-heads. Everywhere everything was of absolute luxury and refinement. And I wanted to drag my Delia away from all this! How I presumed!

Thick soft carpets from Walfarg beneath our feet, silks from Loh, the scent of spices from Askinard, all the wealth of a world spread out, as we went into the apartments of the Princess Majestrix. Here water tinkled coolly from fountains; brilliant birds fluttered and cooed; the very air breathed a soft and fragrant welcome. I was enchanted. Music wafted soothingly from a silver screen beyond which musicians played. I put my left hand on my rapier hilt and I gripped hard.

The Emperor strode on and we followed, his guards, my men with presents, courtiers, and attendants, and me, the Strom of Valka.

Delia had been sitting playing the harp. I didn't know she could play the harp. Handmaidens bowed low before the Emperor. Everyone moved with smooth court ritual into their appointed places, forming a ring around the central figures of the Emperor and his daughter. She looked up from the pile of cushions, and handmaidens, all superbly dressed in sumptuous gowns, took the harp away. Here there was nothing of the naked pearl-strung slave girls of other palaces I had visited.

These magnificent chambers were merely the outer portion of her apartments, to which a visiting nobleman might fittingly be brought. Farther into the recesses of the palace would lie her private apartments. The thought of their beauty and evidences of sensibility dizzied me.

She said: "I am glad you visit me, Father. We do not talk often enough."

"You know the subject on which I wish to speak, daughter. But not now. We have a visitor who brings fine gifts, and also, as I judge a man, knowing something of his history, a man who is not seeking self-advancement." He glanced at me. "I am aware of what you have done in Valka, Strom Drak. The racters must look elsewhere for slaves now."

I could see he welcomed that.

"My daughter," he said, and the icy mask of polite formality descended on him, "this is Drak, Strom of Valka."

Delia looked up at me. I stood there, clean-shaven, dressed up in my fine new clothes, trying to make my lips form into something that might pass as a smile, looking down on her as if nothing in the world lay between us.

"The Princess Majestrix of Vallia."

I performed a full incline. It was the perfectly proper thing to do, if somewhat florid, but I wanted to carry off the part. "Your most humble and devoted servant, my Princess," I said.

"You are most welcome, Strom," said Delia, Princess Majestrix.

Fourteen

Of presents and whispers

When I had been thrown down before her, with iron chains dragging on me, all bloody and foul and filthy, hairy and horrible, my Delia had recognized me instantly and flown to my side.

Now I stood before her, clean and shining and fresh, and she greeted me merely with, "You are most welcome, Strom," in the cold and distant words of formal politeness.

Had she not recognized me? What a comment on the experiences through which we had gone together!

The ritual of greetings and introductions over — I had noticed how the universal formal "Llahal" was used here — we could lapse into more relaxed conversation. Light wine and miscils, which are those tiny fragile cakes that melt on the tongue, were brought, and the presents were looked at. In truth, they had looked fine enough when bought, and although mightily lessened by these gorgeous surroundings, they were still presentable. I had tried for quality and not quantity.

I stood politely talking to Delia and the Emperor, and we exchanged pleasantries. He was interested in Valka, and I was able to assure him that all went well there, and that he himself had personally the loyalty of every man of Valka.

This seemed to me a sensible attitude.

How true it was remained to be seen.

I thought to copper-bottom my bet.

"These are, of course, only small items I could bring myself. I have surprises from Valka that should please Your Majesty mightily."

He made himself looked pleased. He had a lot of the strengths of Delia about him, her same clear brown eyes, but his hair, still abundant, contained none of those glorious chestnut tints. They must come from her mother. His face was furrowed with lines I could recognize, scars of experience put there by ruling a vast island empire. Then I realized why he was taking this interest in me, an obscure strom from a province many dwaburs away. He needed friends. He was desperately in need of allies against the racters, and the panvals, who were against the racters rather than for the Emperor, and a mysterious third party one heard whispers of.

He was a tragically lonely figure.

He had also ordered my head cut off.

It was worthwhile not forgetting that.

I said, "Has there been any news of Tharu of Vindelka?"

"How strange you ask that, Strom Drak! Vomanus of Vindelka has searched long and in vain — the world is strange and marvelous beyond the confines of Vallia — and he has been much in our thoughts lately." And here the Emperor glanced at Delia.

She said, "Vomanus is the heir and he searches for Tharu with a devotion I find commendable."

Point taken.

We talked on in general terms, and then Delia said, with a cool effrontery that amused me, "I had heard the Strom of Valka was a hairy man, very violent, who raped a tower of the maidens dedicated to the Maiden of the Many Smiles." She shot a look directly at me. "You do not look like that, Strom."

"That is not my idea of recreation." I had heard the calumny, put about by the racters. "The truth is that a certain Foke the Ob-handed did that foul deed. It happened on a tiny islet on the eastern coast of Valka. I was in the Heart Heights at the time. Foke has not been caught. When he is I shall string him as high as the topmost stone of that tower of the maidens."

The Emperor nodded, clucking his tongue.

"And very proper, too." He looked about, his eyes gleaming white, a sudden and revealing gesture from an Emperor. "He belongs to the racters, does he not?"

"He does, Majister."

"The racters." He did not say any more. Poor devil — here was I, Dray Prescot, feeling sorry for this dread Emperor!

Delia said, "We had no warning of your coming to Vondium, Strom Drak."

"I had business here, Princess."

"Did you know Drak was the name of my grandfather when he ascended the throne?"

I inclined my head. "I have always taken great pride in that, Princess. I feel that our destinies are linked."

If she could play this game, then so could I!

"Really!" She tinkled her laughter, so gay, so forced, so artificial. "I heard once — a story, a silly trifle — of a man called the Kov of Delphond. His name, so men said, was Drak." She laughed again, gesturing negligently with her arm. How I longed to take that rounded glowing arm and haul her to me and plant an enormous kiss on those luscious lips! "Delphond is a sweet place, very dear to me. If that man had been caught, assuming him to have existed, I would have asked you, Drak, Strom of Valka, to hoist him up to the topmost stone of the tower along with Foke the Ob-handed."

The Emperor threw his daughter a puzzled glance. He reached out his hand to the empty air and immediately a handmaid placed a goblet in his fingers. He had no fear of poison, I judged, and recollected that poison is used so rarely on Vallia that when it is, it is marked and noted and remembered.

He moved away, talking to the Chuktar of his guard. The courtiers moved with him, always at their respectful distance, and only Delia's handmaids were left with us. I had no idea how proper was my conduct in not moving with the Emperor.

"I ought to go, Princess, with the Emperor your father."

"That is all right, Strom, in private. Our protocol is not overpowering. Come, sit with me."

I looked at the Emperor in the instant that he turned to look back at me, his head half bent. He nodded. I bowed deeply. Then I turned around and sat down next to the Princess Majestrix. She waved her hand and the handmaidens seemed to become insubstantial wraiths.

She laughed aloud delightfully — and quite artificially to me, who had heard her laughing as we strode along through the Hostile Territories on our bare feet — and said: "Indeed, Strom, Valka sounds a most outlandish place. Tell me of it."

Then, leaning forward a little, she said in a voice that snickered in like a rapier between the ribs: "You great onker-headed idiot, Dray Prescot! What happens if the real Strom of Valka walks in?"

I couldn't stop myself.

I lay back on the silken cushions with their gold and silver embroidery and I laughed. I laughed fit to bust a gut.

The Emperor swung around. All conversation ceased. I was the focus of all eyes, staring at me, uncertain — scared!

I stood up and controlled myself.

I inclined to the Emperor.

"The Princess Majestrix is a worthy daughter to a great father," I said. I meant at least half of that. "She has the gift of arousing the best in any man, Your Majesty. I did not mean to offend anyone here."

He nodded, looking a little — puzzled, I thought. He turned away and went on with his conversation with the Chuktar, and I flopped back next to Delia.

"You glorious girl," I said, changing what I had been about to say to a cliché no one could take amiss. "I am the true strom."

"You mean — no, Dray, my darling! You can't be!"

And then I remembered what the Gdoinye, speaking to me for the very first time on Kregen, had said. There was a time loop here. I knew that Delia would have heard gossip and news of this ferocious Strom of Valka, and of how he had cleared out the slavers and aragorn from his island, and received his patent of nobility — and all this would have been happening before she parted with me in the Hostile Territories. I had been on Kregen in two different places at the same time!

No wonder the Star Lords sometimes barred me off from travel!

My explanation was fragmentary and in a low voice. To have to sit here on silken cushions next to my Delia, so close to my own sweet Delia of the Blue Mountains, and be unable so much as to touch her! I knew that a single contact with her would result in my being run outside and at the best having my head parted from my body — and more likely having my body torn apart by red-hot irons. The Princess Majestrix was sacrosanct.

As she should be, of course.

The situation was idiotic, ludicrous, and fraught with terrible danger.

Both of us wanted to gasp out our love for each other, to clasp each other in our arms, to tell all our news, and gaze deeply into the other's eyes in absolute joy and wonder; yet we must sit here, so prim and precise, under the watchful eyes of the guards and the courtiers. I knew there were many eyes of spies there, people working for the racters, for the panvals, men and women working for all the different parties and lords each of whom wanted his own advantage from the Emperor. Drak, Strom of Valka, was a marked man henceforth.

That wouldn't worry me.

I started to tell her that she must run away with me, at once, back to Valka and then, probably, to Strombor.

"Yes! Oh, yes, Dray, my darling!"

No hesitation, no regrets for leaving the sumptuousness all about her, no thoughts of her life here in Vallia as the Princess Majestrix. If the Strom of Valka kidnapped her, then his head would be forfeit and never more would she be able to return to her home. Strombor, then… But — no slightest hesitation. She agreed willingly, joyfully, eagerly. Oh, yes, there is no woman in two worlds like Delia of the Blue Mountains!

Everything within the palace of Vondium was — and still is — conducted with order and dignity. I felt the sense of impressiveness, even then, when my every thought was of abducting the Princess out of that palace.

We spent what really amounted to only a few murs together before that audience was over and I had to take my leave of the Princess Majestrix and return with the Emperor to the throne room. He had taken a shine to me. Later we took a meal together in a private apartment with a number of the high men of the realm. These men were strangers to me then, but how well I know them now! Some as good and loyal friends, others as bitter and deadly enemies. As they stride onto the stage of my story I will introduce them to you. But, as always, following my plan, I will speak only of people and places and things as they impacted on me at the time, when I met them, even though I knew of them before that.

The first of these to whom you should be introduced called on me the very next day at my new lodgings. He was Nath Larghos, the Trylon of the Black Mountains. A Trylon is a rank intermediate between a Vad and a Strom. The Black Mountains extend northward of the Blue Mountains and, although neither so lofty nor extensive, are composed of a black basaltic rock rich in minerals. Eastward the Trylonate runs into farming and agricultural products.

Trylon Larghos came unannounced into the sunny upper chamber of *The Rose of Valka* where I sat at breakfast. The comfortable inn and posting house was run by Young Bargom, the son of Old Bargom, who had fled from Valka in the bad days. Naturally, he had changed the name of the inn to remind them of happier times back in Valka, their homeland.

"Strom Drak?" said Trylon Larghos, coming forward into the patch of mingled sunlight by the windows. I did not rise. I was in the act of placing rich yellow butter upon a chunk torn from a crisp Kregan loaf, and that is an important operation. I did look up. I saw Larghos then, and I can see him in my mind's eye now. A big man running to fat, but with the muscles still supple and bulging on his arms and across his shoulders. He wore a Vallian tunic of leather, but instead of the decent buff, the leather had been dyed in a pattern of black and white. His sword hilt glittered with gems. His face, bearded and bewhiskered, contained a pair of close-set shrewd eyes, and his mouth was a rat-trap if ever I saw one. A man of whom to be wary. I summed him up instantly; dangerous, like a leem.

Before I could answer he went on: "You astonish me, my dear Strom, that you are not occupying your villa here in Vondium."

"The place has been deserted for many seasons."

"So? I am sorry to hear it. I was pleased to make your acquaintance yesterday, with the Emperor. He seemed to find you genial company."

The Emperor had been laughing a lot more, I recalled, when I took my leave. I did not offer Larghos a seat, but he sat down anyway. Maybe he thought that being a Trylon gave him the edge over a Strom.

There had certainly been no desire in my actions or stories to charm the Emperor — quite the reverse — but from the Trylon's expression he was clearly accusing me of toadying to the Emperor. I wanted to correct that impression.

"Many men have done so. And many others have not."

"I trust, by Opaz, that we shall get along together, Strom."

Whatever he was after, he would get from me only what I chose to give. However, there seemed no point in antagonizing him just yet, despite that I didn't like the look of him.

"Have you breakfasted, Trylon? Would you care to join me?"

He waved the suggestion away with a very white and plump beringed hand. I fancied, though, he could use a rapier.

"Thank you. I have. We are up early in Vondium."

"Do you then not often visit the Black Mountains?"

If that was a nasty remark he didn't react. "When I have to. The black rocks offend me. My life is here, in the capital, where politics are!"

We talked for a space until I had breakfasted and then he joined me in a cup of Kregan tea. He worked his way around to the purpose of his visit. He was a racter. The white and black would have told me that. I was an unknown. Oh, yes, he had heard of the panvals and what had happened in Valka, but that was in the past. Now we must face the new realities. The Emperor must have an heir who is not a willful girl; the racter candidate must be the one.

"And who is that, Trylon Larghos?"

He studied me a moment. I had sidestepped his more direct questions, but I had appeared to satisfy him that if the racters could offer me more than the panvals, then I was their man.

"Kov Vektor of Aduimbrev is the Emperor's choice," he said. He spoke with care.

He wore leathers dyed black and white. He was a racter and flaunted that. The racters were a party, composed of many people from all walks of life — except, I thought with bitterness, those who walked the canal towpaths. They were a power in the Presidio. They had the strength to banish panvals on trumped-up charges, but there were still many panvals who wore the green and white colors. A man might choose to flaunt his color allegiance, as Larghos did. Or, as Pallan

Eling, the minister responsible for the canals, did, wear merely a small black and white ribbon tucked into a buttonhole. I guessed Larghos' servitors would wear sleeves banded black and white, and the colors of the Black Mountain — appropriately enough black and purple — would appear elsewhere on their jerkins.

The older a lineage the less colors in the insignia, in general. Some men, like Tobi ti Chelmsturm, with five colors to their name very often preferred the dignity of using merely two colors for their men, and these would be colors of their party. Humans and halflings, we share the same failings.

I said, "I do not support Vektor in this."

"Good. He is a weakling, a sop. You can smell him coming a dwabur downwind, like a woman's hairdresser."

"You have a candidate for the Princess Majestrix? Who is that, Trylon?"

He made up his mind. When he spoke the name I felt the blood rise and sing in my head.

"Vomanus of Vindelka."

Fifteen

Ill news of Vomanus of Vindelka

I felt outraged, betrayed, soiled.

I spoke before I thought.

"I understood that Vomanus was — ineligible to marry the Princess!"

He stared at me narrowly, and lowered his cup. "Now where would you have heard that?"

Collecting my thoughts, I said, stumbling and bluffing my way through: "I am not certain — it seems it was a drunken evening, somewhere, men talking and boasting. But, clearly, it cannot be true."

He leaned back, sizing me up afresh, but he neither confirmed nor denied what I had suggested.

Back there in hated Magdag where I had intrigued and fought for my slaves and workers I had last seen Vomanus. I had sent him with a message to Delia. He had always treated me as a comrade, and although he was a young man whom I delighted to call "my lad," there had been a mystery about him. He had said, once: "Just take it from me, Drak, my friend, Kovs are Kovs and Kovs to me." No, he could never voluntarily seek Delia's hand in marriage, not when he knew the passion that flames between the Princess and me. Then — he must consider me dead! Yes, that could be the only explanation.

And then, of course, I felt the guilt and the remorse — emotions I always try to quell out of perversity — when I remembered how finely he had always supported me. And all the time he had loved Delia himself!

Trylon Larghos said, "Young Vomanus was willed the estates and lands of Vindelka. The Emperor approves. As to what happened to Tharu, out there in the wilds of the inner sea, who knows? Who cares?" He was too sophisticated a man to say, as many would, of the inner sea: "wherever that is." He knew well enough where it was, although he'd never travel that great distance all his life. "Tharu was an Emperor's man. He was a great power behind the throne. Now he is gone, Vomanus is one of us."

I felt the sadness and the sorrow, but if young Vomanus really loved Delia, then he would use whatever levers came to his hand. He would move heaven and hell, in Kregan terms, to win her. I could not blame him. What would he say when he learned I was still alive!

I decided to test that. Speaking casually enough, my cup at a jaunty angle, I said: "What of this hairy madman I have heard of — this wild clansman—"

"Dray Prescot, the Lord of Strombor?" Larghos laughed, and his laugh was most evil. "Whether the Princess loved him or not does not matter. Prescot is dead. And the devil can go to the Ice Floes of Sicce with my boot in his rear. He has caused far too much trouble. But now the time is ripe for the racters, for Vomanus, for me — and for you, too, Strom Drak!"

Just then Young Bargom trundled in with fresh tea. He said in his blunt Valkan way: "There is a Koter below, asking for you, my lord Strom. He does not give a name." Bargom glanced at Larghos. "He wears green and white, my lord Strom."

"A rast of a panval!" exclaimed Larghos. He had half drawn his rapier before he recollected himself. "If I can force an argument on him as I leave I'll do so, and spit his guts! Aye, by Vox! And laugh as I do it!"

He took his leave, promising to speak with me again, and he was well pleased with his morning's work. When he had gone Young Bargom shook his head and leaned out of the window.

"Hai! A racter is on his way out! I don't want trouble in my inn — hey, you there!"

He turned back to face me. "Your pardon, my lord Strom, but Trylon Larghos is a noted duelist. He says he'll spit this onker's guts, he'll spit them, mark my words, my lord Strom."

Suddenly it was borne in on me — what the blue blazing hell was I doing fiddling about with politics in Vondium? I had agreed to abduct my Delia, we would fly together to Valka, to Strombor — we would finish with Vallia and begin a new life, together.

Whoever the panval was, he took the threat seriously, for he did not show up. Bargom busied himself clearing away the breakfast things. He liked to talk.

"They say the headless zorcamen have been seen, my lord Strom. They were riding within sight of Vondium last night." He shivered. "They mean ill, mark my words, my lord Strom."

"You believe in them, Bargom?"

He straightened up, the tray balanced easily on one hand. "Of course, my lord Strom! They are evil, supernatural! They set fire to buildings, they abduct people — and a two-headed chunkrah was born only last week. Mark my words, my lord Strom, evil days are coming to Vondium!"

Ghosts and black towers and bats and apparitions, all these things, then, were believed in by Bargom. How many others in Vondium believed? If they were racters dressed up, why were they doing these things here, where the racters were all-powerful? Again I thought of this mysterious third party, but Bargom, who had heard whispers of them in his pot room, knew nothing solid about them.

They were called the third party, not because there were only three parties, but somehow people realized that they must rank as a force at least equal with the failing panvals, and possibly with the racters. The other parties — generally owning allegiance to territory as well as belief — were too small to be counted.

Just to the northeast of Vondium rises the strange height known as Drak's Seat. The two main peaks, when viewed from the center of Vondium, look uncannily like a great throne, lowering over the city. Drak's Seat. Snow and ice are found there — as Jenbar had told me — which last longer in good condition than a man might believe, when packed in the Kregan way in sawdust of sturm-wood. I detest ice in drinks, for together with worry it is a prime source of ulcers. And no truly civilized man relishes having the taste of a fine vintage destroyed by great chunks of frozen water floating in his glass.

Young Bargom chattered on telling me the gossip of Vondium. His life was here, now; with a wife from the city, and children, and his father's bones buried in the Opaz-sacred cemetery a dwabur beyond the eastern gate, he had nothing to draw him back to Valka. His talk told me much, and I saw how useful he could be to me. *TheRose of Valka* was situated on the eastern bank of the Great Northern Cut, a respectable house to which Koters could bring their ladies in complete confidence of a pleasant evening. He loved to chatter, and this talk sparked up confidences from his guests, particularly when their bellies were filled with selections from Young Bargom's cellars.

Of the third party he could tell me only that men whispered behind their hands that dual allegiances were involved. The great nobles were all playing for themselves. The Emperor sought for allies and friends. Evil days were coming to Vondium. The headless zorcamen were one symbol of that, a presentiment and a sign of terror.

Why should Nath Larghos, a Trylon with power that placed him extremely high in the councils of the racters, seek out a lowly Strom and attempt to win him over?

My own plans must come first. There was much to do. An airboat, it seemed to me, was the obvious choice; indeed, the only choice. Once I had abducted Delia we would have no peace until we reached Strombor in Zenicce.

Even then the Emperor might fit out a mighty expedition and dispatch his powerful fleet with thousands of mercenaries to bring his daughter back. I did not fancy myself in the part of Paris, and Delia could occasion the launch of many more than a thousand ships, aye, and fliers, too, for I knew without question she was far more beautiful and passionate and willful than Helen could ever have been. But I would not bring upon Strombor the fate of Troy; the Emperor and his Vallians would never be the Greeks in this tragedy. If necessary Delia and I would fly to Sanurkazz and go to Felteraz, where I knew how welcome we would be. Mayfwy would welcome us. That was certain. If the Emperor followed us there through all the long and perilous dangers, then where would we go?

I jumped up and overset the teapot.

"Goddamnit to hell!" I said. I would make a start, and go with my Delia to the ends of this strange world of Kregen, and let the fates play with their silken strands as they would.

Young Bargom came in somewhat rapidly, to investigate the overset teapot I thought. But in his hand he held a heavy knife, not quite a shortsword, something like a cleaver — a weapon he could with perfect truth say he had picked up from his kitchen — and his face held a down-drawn, savage look that surprised me. He saw me standing there, composed, he saw the teapot, and he didn't know where to put the knife.

"The teapot thought itself a flier, Bargom," I said. Then, "What troubled you?"

He blurted it out: "I thought some Vox-spawned rast had crept in here, my lord Strom, to do you a mischief."

The incident passed. But it added up. Bargom said there were many expatriate Valkans living in Vondium. They were anxiously desirous of paying their respects to their Strom. They had heard what had been done on Valka and many of their friends had left to return home. Many of those still remaining intended to return. Meanwhile, here in the city was their Strom, the man who had cleansed their home and made of it a place worthy to be lived in again, a place of which to be proud.

With a callous cynicism and a calculating appraisal of the advantages I could wring, I saw these people. They came in, in ones or twos, sometimes a family, and they brought little gifts, tokens of their esteem. All went on about how Valka was no longer merely a slave-province, of which there were more than two or three, and the letters they had had telling them of the great things being done there. Some of the women even kissed my hand. I began to feel the greatest cheat and impostor in all of Kregen. I have said I love the island of Valka. This is true. I believe in that upper room of the inn *The Rose of Valka*, I came to feel completely the same about the people.

One young lad there was, tall, strong, upright, with the glowing features of hero-worship about him I found most distasteful, whose name was Vangar ti Valkanium, told me he was a Deldar in the Vallian Air Service. He had come in mufti, the buff tunic and the wide-brimmed hat with the red and white colors in feathers and in a great cockade over his left shoulder. I told Vangar ti Valkanium something of my admiration for the Air Service people, and we talked very pleasantly. When he left I knew that I would feel a pang at abandoning my island of Valka.

But I would abandon any and everything in two worlds for the sake of my Delia of Delphond, my Delia of the Blue Mountains.

Sitting at the black-wood table in the window I felt a softly caressing touch stroke feather-light across the nape of my neck. It was there and gone in an instant. I took no notice. In the window on its own special pedestal stood a flick-flick. The plant has many names on Kregen, and as an example of the closeness of the Vallish to the Kregish, the fly-catcher is fleck-fleck in the Vallish and flick-flick in the Kregish. Its six-foot-long tendrils uncoil like steel springs, their honey-dew stickiness certain death for flies. The flowers are cone-shaped trumpets of a pale and subtle peach color, and they gobble flies like a starving elephant stuffing down buns. Most homes like to have a flick-flick, usually near the kitchen. Flies, as I have said, get everywhere.

The break made me stand up and stretch and look out of the window. Across the patio, with its tables and chairs and Young Bargom's clientele drinking happily, the canal ran along between meticulously upkept banks. And a great straggly gang of haulers passed, their gray slave breech-clouts filthy, the whip marks jikaidering their backs, bloody and filthy, hauling a huge gray barge with a cargo that brought the gunwales down to within a knuckle of the water.

I frowned.

Delia detested slavery as much as I did.

I had thought I had been brought to Kregen to help stamp out slavery. My own plans called for the fulfillment of my own selfish ends. To hell with the Star Lords and the Savanti! Delia was all I cared about.

Many times, as you have heard, I had been deflected from my intentions. Now, again, I was prevented from putting our plans into operation that day, as I had wished, by the distraught arrival of Kta. Angia.[xv] A plump, homey, beeswax kind of woman, she sobbed out her story. Her son was a proud and headstrong youth, but they were in debt, for he was a cabinet-maker and had had words with his employer and could not find fresh work. He would not ask friends of the Valkans here in Vondium for help. And now he had been dragged off to the bagnios. She was desperate. Could I help?

The story is quickly told. Quickly — in that I went with her to the bagnios and found her son, Anko the Chisel, and paid off his debt, and in the process being arrogant and insulting to the guards with their red and black sleeves. But not so quickly — in my discovery of the bagnios themselves. I have seen many slave barracks, and barracoons and bagnios, and those of Vallia were no worse than many. Here criminals, debtors, hostages, prisoners, those who had forfeited their liberty in any way, were kept for dispersal among the slave farms, or the haulers, or the mines, or in any of the many places that slaves were employed. We took Anko the Chisel out of that place and his mother, Kta. Angia, fell on her knees before me, whereat I felt all the nausea of myself rising, and I bid her get up and take her son home, and start again in the search for work.

The point I had had thrust upon me I did not want to face, would not face, refused even to countenance.

Delia. That thought alone was all that mattered.

Sixteen

A certain Bowman of Loh comments on the Archers of Valka

That evening everyone crowded in and *The Rose of Valka* rocked with the roistering songs of Kregen. And, chief among these, sung for all its seven hundred and seventy-eight stanzas, was *The Fetching of Drak na Valka*.

Among the Valkan revelers, dressed like them in the flaunting red and white, sat Seg Segutorio. I had told him, swiftly, not to start singing *The Bowmen of Loh*.

"I'll fight any man who denies me!" he had started to roar out and I had hustled him away up the black-wood stair to my upper chamber.

"By Zim-Zair, you onker-headed bowman!" I exclaimed. He calmed down and then, with that strong streak of practicality that runs intertwined with the feyness of the men of the mountains and valleys of Erthyrdrin, he nodded, understanding. "Although, Dray, you know that there is no better bow than the longbow. All these made-up sinew and bone and horn bows, curved like a pregnant duck; they are as toys beside the longbow."

"True, true. But — watch it!"

"All is ready. By the Veiled Froyvil, but Delia is a true princess! She has made the arrangements for the airboat. Thelda and I and little Dray are ready. We can—"

I felt shock.

"You — you wish to come, too, Seg?"

He looked at me as though I had slapped him around the face.

"Of course." His bright blue eyes glittered on me in the soft radiance of the samphron oil lamp. "You want me to, don't you, my old dom?"

I managed to say, "I couldn't get along without you," and turned away so that he should not see my face.

The noise from below was reaching fantastic proportions and we went down and took up the wine — it was the best of Jholaix, precious and rare and saved for super-special occasions — and joined in the singing. Vangar ti Valkanium sang. Anko the Chisel sang. Everyone sang. We sang of Valka. A lithe and lissome girl, very beautiful, with a heart-shaped face and a figure to stir men to immediate action, recited some of the more sublime passages from *The Fatal Love of Vela na Valka* and we all joined in the choruses. Then, for the third time, we roared out all the seven hundred and seventy-eight stanzas of the song commemorating my fetching of Valka out of the shadows and of the Valkans fetching me to be their Strom.

It takes a long time to sing seven hundred or so stanzas and when, at last, we threw the shutters back it was high noon outside in Vondium. Deldar Vangar had a mad scramble to get back to report for duty. He spoke of a visit the Emperor was paying to Vindelka, northwest of the city. No one took much notice, the fumes of wine coiling in our brains. Seg had left early, saying that as a private

Koter he had duties to perform he dare not let lapse now, so close to the time for our departure. He had mentioned Vindelka, too.

We had, in the Kregan idiom, a zhantil to saddle, and we all had our secret parts to perform.

To clear my head, after I had shaved that harsh chin of mine, I took a stroll along the quays and watched all the busy loading and unloading of the great galleons of Vallia. Produce from all over the known world flowed into Vondium, and the products of Vallia flowed out. Gulls wheeled overhead, shrieking. The twin suns shone gloriously. The air held that bracing tang of the sea. But — the Star Lords had expressly forbidden me to sail the seas of Kregen for a space. How I longed, then, to take my Delia up onto the deck of a great galleon and sail with her over the rim of the world!

When I returned to *The Rose of Valka* a sedan chair such as are commonly seen all over the city stood at the door. The two men who bore it were slaves, although decently clad in dark brown shifts, with a lotus-flower emblazoned on breast and back. With them were four soldiers and a Hikdar, wide of shoulder and lean of waist, their raffish hats sporting feathers of yellow and green, with a double red stripe slashed athwart their brightness. I went in, and Young Bargom presented a lady whose face was covered with a deep violet veil. My first glance convinced me this could not be Delia in disguise, and the leap of my heart stilled.

Bargom withdrew and the lady lifted her veil. She was young, pretty, but with a pallid squarish face in which the brown eyes held none of the luster and sparkle to which I was accustomed.

"I am Pela, my lord Strom, handmaid to the Kovneva Katrin. I am bid to tell you that the Kovneva must see you immediately."

"Yes? Do you know why, Pela?"

"No, my lord Strom. Only that it is urgent, very urgent."

"I do not know the Kovneva Katrin. Tell me of her."

"But, my lord Strom!" Her eyes opened wide and for all their dullness they expressed astonishment. "She is a great and powerful lady. Since the Kov died she has refused to marry. Now she is a devoted attendant upon the Princess Majestrix."

So that was it, I said to myself. I yelled for Bargom and between us we made me look presentable, with a buff jerkinlike tunic with wide winged shoulders which left the white silk shirt sleeves visible. I buckled on the rapier and main-gauche and took up the hat with the red and white feathers. Down the black-wood stairs I went, following Pela, who got into the sedan chair very quickly. The bearers lifted their poles, the Hikdar gave me a sketchy salute, rapped out his orders, and we started for the palace.

The effects of a rollicking night coupled with the fresh air left me feeling alert and breezy, although with the edges of fatigue beginning to creep along my bones. We climbed up through the crowded streets and along wide boulevards where the quoffa carts trundled and the zorca chariots whickered their tall wheels. There were fewer airboats than usual wheeling over the city today. The birds sensed this, and they swooped and gyrated against the twin suns.

Around to the western face of the palace we went beneath the frowning walls where the mercenary guards paced. In through a square opening, faced with marble and gold, and so up again along courtyards and colonnades, and into the rear of the apartments reserved for the Princess. In a small square room, with a lamp burning in the center which cast weird gleams upon the friezes of mythical beasts and birds, the sedan chair was placed down and Pela alighted. The Hikdar saluted and marched his men out.

Pela said, "Wait here, my lord Strom."

As soon as she had gone I loosened my rapier in its scabbard and looked about. There were but two doors, and Pela had left through the opposite one. When its sturm-wood panels bearing plaques of beaten silver opened and a woman walked in, attended only by Pela, I relaxed a little.

"Strom Drak, of Valka?"

"Yes."

"I am the Kovneva Katrin Rashumin of Rahartdrin and you address me as my lady Kovneva."

I said, "I haven't come here to play games. What do you want of me?"

She flinched back. My words were tantamount to my striking her across the face. I heard Pela gasp. If there was trouble for my Delia there was no time for protocol and fine manners. I took a step forward, fears for Delia uppermost in my mind. I stuck my face at this haughty Kovneva.

"Well?"

She put her hands to her breast. She wore a long silvery gown that fell to the marble floor, and was held over her shoulders by a mass of jewels. Her dark hair was coiffed and curled and smothered with a net of glittering gems. As for her face — it was hard in outline, of undoubted beauty, with fine dark eyes and a mouth rather too thin for my taste. She reminded me, as a candle reminds one of a samphron oil lamp, of Queen Lilah, that proud and sensuous Queen of Paul.

She managed to speak. "I will have you flogged! I will have you torn asunder! To speak to me, the Kovneva, this way! You are a fool, a rast, a cramph, a—"

I took her left wrist into my hand and lifted it before our faces. I glared down into her eyes. Her face altered in contour, changing, going slack, the soggy droop she would never admit appearing beneath her chin. I knew my face wore that old corrosive look of pure domination and harsh authority that, in other circumstances, I have so despaired of. Here it broke this woman's resistance down in a way that, however unpleasant it might have been, was desperately essential.

"The Emperor," she whispered. "He has gone to Vindelka. The Princess Majestrix flies with him. I am—" She swallowed. "I am bid by the Princess on behalf of the Emperor to command you to join them."

I let her wrist go and she rubbed it with her other hand, staring at me the while with a look that should have blasted me on the spot. I nodded.

"Very well, Kovneva. Let us go, in the name of Opaz!"

Pela's eyes were as round as palines.

"And," I said in that harsh and hateful voice, "you will receive from me all the deference that is your due. Next time don't shilly-shally when there are messages from the Emperor."

"I shall remember this—"

"That is good. Make sure you remember well."

From this unedifying scene of my bullying a silly woman I took no pleasure, particularly after I had, as I considered, been groveling before the Emperor. But all my fears for Delia had leaped into my mind, and almost I had said "messages from the Princess." Only a last-minute flash of common sense had made me change that to "Emperor."

Of course, all the plans were changed. Delia must have managed to remind her father of the Strom of Valka, and arranged for my presence at Vindelka. That she had chosen this woman, this Kovneva Katrin, to bring the message must surely mean she held her in some esteem, even if she didn't trust Katrin Rashumin. Rahartdrin — that is, the land of Rahart — is a large island off the southwestern tip of Vallia, south of the straits between Womox and the Blue Mountains. All these places I was hearing about now have since come to mean a great deal to me, and to become very familiar, as you shall hear. I was slowly learning my way around Vallia, the land of my Princess.

Rahartdrin is about five times as extensive as Valka. She was a Kovneva and I was a Strom. No wonder she balked at my cavalier treatment of her!

Muffled in cloaks, we went out swiftly and boarded the waiting airboat, and I wondered just what rapier to grind Katrin Rashumin had in all this. She was more than a mere messenger. How much of the Emperor's trust did she have? And, far more importantly, how loyal was she to Delia?

The airboat was of the usual pattern, petal-shaped, about fifty feet long, with a sumptuously appointed cabin taking up the aft third of the length. Atop this was a sun-deck. I noticed that while the usual flag of Vallia — the yellow saltire on the red ground — flew from the stern, Katrin's own flag — the lotus in yellow and green picked out in red — flew from a staff in the prow. Evidently, this was her own personal airboat.

The luxury of the cabin confirmed this, for it was furnished in a sybaritic and yet realistic way very much of a piece with her character. I threw my cloak onto a chaise longue and looked about for a drink. The airboat bore on through the levels toward Vindelka. The crew wore the yellow and green striped sleeves, with twin slashes of red through the yellow, and they looked competent enough. Although, no one could feel absolutely secure aboard an airboat; I recalled what Naghan Furtway, Kov of Falinur, had had to say about the rasts of Havilfar. Pela brought wine then, a good vintage, and I settled down to what I considered would be the monotony of the aerial voyage.

As soon as the wine was served, Katrin drove Pela out in an abrupt and yet not unkind way, to go and sit in the suns-shine on the forward deck, and then locked the door. I did not think I was going to try to escape from an airboat a thousand feet in the air.

"You know how the racters have forced the Presidio to tax Valka more heavily than is just?" she began without preamble.

"I know, Kovneva."

"This is why you are in Vondium?"

"Yes." It was as good an excuse as any. I felt the Emperor had sized me up — whether I liked the man or detested him I still didn't know — and he had not mentioned the tax situation. I thought then that if it had been my daughter claiming the horrible object that had been Dray Prescot in his chains and filth, I might have reacted as he had done.

"And you are not prepared to do anything about it?"

"Just what had you in mind?"

The very word tax is obscene, of course, to those who pay. To those who collect for causes their honor tells them are just, the word means different things. But then, any taxman believes his cause is just. My people of Valka paid heavy taxes, unjustly heavy, as I had discovered since reaching Vondium. My selfish desires about Delia had driven the matter from my head. Now this woman was obviously seeking allies against the racters.

"Valka is a rich island. Richer, I venture to suggest, than Rahartdrin."

She flared up at this. But then she nodded, and bit her lip.

"Since my husband, the Kov, died, things have gone to wrack and ruin."

"You need a man, Katrin."

Of course, I shouldn't have said that.

And, indeed, it wasn't necessarily true. I make no claims for the superiority of men in managing estates, and I know my Delia could manage Delphond like a dream. The Blue Mountains tended to be left in the capable hands of her elders in High Zorcady. But this Katrin Rashumin, Kovneva of Rahartdrin, took my words and read into them what my ugly face and foul manners had kindled in her, and thus confirmed that belief in her mind. She did, in sober truth, need a man.

She drank more wine. Then she unclasped her silvery robe and let it fall to the floor. She moved toward me, and threw her round arms about my neck. "Drak, Drak — you would be a Kov!" as though that must clinch the argument.

As gently as I could I detached her fingers from me. Her silvery robe lay strewn about the deck. Her jeweled hair had fallen into a great loose mass, and a fortune rolled about on the priceless carpets of Walfarg weave.

"I am a man, Katrin; not Strom or Kov or Prince have any meaning for me." I did not say that being a Krozair of Zy held meaning. She would not have understood. "You must find a man more complaisant to your desires."

She rested a while then, drinking wine, the slanting mingled rays of Zim and Genodras playing over her body. She would resume the fight shortly, I knew. No wonder she had locked the door. But I was learning all the time. I would be a Kov if I married her. I had become a Strom in all legality because I had won the position, and none could say me nay. How these nobles of Vallia had schemed and bribed and fought their way to power! And how they must be ever ready to fend off the plunderers forever following them! What a man could make of himself, what he could hold, that he was, in Vallia.

Of course, like any system of its kind, once you were in power, in the saddle, wielding the whip, you tended to build up reserves to keep you in power.

"No," I said. "No, Katrin. I will be your friend, if you wish that, and perhaps take a lash and an accounting book into the island of Rahart. More than that I cannot be."

"I have never met a man like you! In a few short burs I knew. Time has no meaning in affairs of the heart. The moment you spoke to me, so rudely, so intemperately, I knew you were the man! I felt myself turn to jelly—"

I didn't laugh, but it deserved it. Poor soul! But for her, it was all deadly serious.

"I will strike a bargain with you, Katrin. I will be your good friend. I will ride into Rahartdrin and see what is going wrong. And you, in your turn, wipe your face, put on your robe, and tidy your hair — and then help and support me with the Emperor."

If she rebelled at that, put on her icy hauteur and allowed her hatred to spew forth — well and good. I just wanted to know where we stood. But she was prepared to accept that heavy-handed patronizing attitude — for all that I meant sincerely what I said, it was still insufferably obnoxious — and she did as she was bid, and once more turned from a passionate sobbing submissive woman into a regal and distant Kovneva.

A call came down the tube. The border of Vindelka had long been passed and now we were heading in for a landing at Delka Ob. This was the capital of Vindelka, where Tharu and now Vomanus lorded it over fat realms. At Delka Dwa, right over on the northwestern border, lay a frontier town against the poor lands stretching away up there, lands over which I had trudged hauling the Emperor's barge.

There were few lakes in that area, the ground was thin and sorry, and the wind scoured the landscape into wild and fantastic shapes. Only a few leem-hunters and madmen looking for gold and jewels found much in these badlands over which to feel satisfaction. The River of Shining Spears which ran from the Blue Mountains into the Great River skirted south of these badlands. They were called the Ocher Limits.

Beyond them and sharing them as a common frontier, seldom visited, lay the Kovnate of Falinur.

Katrin and I went out on deck as the airboat slanted down for a landing. Away across to the west where the twin suns sank in a jumbled blaze of emerald and orange the sky was a mass of glorious color. Fierce black twisted, violent spirals of cloud coiled up, with the beams of the suns striking through and the glow extending far across the horizon.

"We made our landing just in time, my lady Kovneva," said the airboat captain. He looked ill at ease.

Katrin didn't bother to reply. We all stood there, watching that violence and glory in the sky to the west.

Delka Ob was a pleasant enough place, situated at the crossing of two canals, with much greenery, shade trees, and the soothing sounds of water tinkling from fountains and waterfalls created in the gardens of the houses. There was the usual labor section; but here, too, the houses looked neat and clean and the people moved with that alertness and firmness of tread I always welcome, for it means the taint of slavery is not embedded in their bones.

Without question, the Kovneva ordered her palanquin out from the flier's hold and gave instructions to be taken directly to the palace. This was the palace of Vomanus of Vindelka. Now it hosted the Emperor and the Princess Majestrix. Pela was carried in her sedan chair; I walked with the guards.

The suns were declining now, the air growing cooler. Our way from the landing field took us across one of the many bridges over a canal and here I heard the familiar hateful trilling of an Emperor's stentor, and looking over the bridge parapet down onto the towpath I saw the sorry procession of dun gray barges. The haulers were being flogged into a shambling run, for the guards were impatient. I guessed these barges were carrying supplies, furniture, clothes, all the habitual magnificences of the Emperor, to the palace of Delka Ob, and had been dispatched some time ago, when this visit had been arranged, timed to reach the city for the Emperor's arrival. This was so.

They had been held up — a canal had burst its banks and the work of reconstruction had chopped all the leeway out of the schedule. The chamberlain in charge of those barges was no doubt trembling in his boots. I saw the savage way the whips rose and fell, the way the knouts smashed down on the heads and backs of the haulers. The red and black arms rose and fell remorselessly. A girl collapsed and was immediately cut out from her leash and pushed aside. She would be dealt with later.

"Hurry, Strom Drak!" called Katrin, putting her head out between the curtains of her palanquin. "Just a moment, Kovneva," I said. I turned to go. I had seen enough. I turned to go and saw at the head of the struggling knot of figures of the next barge in line a tall man leaning into the rope and hauling and hauling. I stopped turning to go. I swung back, very sharply.

I knew that I grew perilously close to callousness over the Emperor's slaves. A single man, Strom or not, could not affect that issue at a blow; abolition would take time and immense effort over many years. But, that being so, I must do what appeared to me the right thing to do. Nepotism, if correctly used, can be a worthwhile tool, as witness Nelson and Collingwood, among others. So, feeling shame that I could do nothing for those other poor struggling devils, I ran quickly down off the bridge and onto the towpath.

A guard brought his lash down again and again onto the thin naked back of the tall man, striking with a passion of ferocity unwholesome to witness.

"Get on, you stinking cramph! Get on, you kleesh."

The next act of mine was all over before I had fairly realized it had begun. I struck the guard full on the jaw. He dropped, senseless. Other guards had seen. They came running, up. I looked at the tall man. Seven feet tall, he was, extraordinarily thin of arm and leg, but with a bunching of muscles there that showed the lean sinewy strength of him. From his head a long silky mass of yellow hair fell to his waist. Now that hair was filthy and befouled. And he'd been uncovered when the Maiden of the Many Smiles floated alone in the sky!

"What in the name of Opaz do you think you're doing, rast?"

The guards hesitated for a moment, as I did not draw but faced them. I glared at them and I know they saw the hatred in my face.

"If you do not instantly release this man, your barges will foul and choke the cut. The Emperor will not like that."

"Who in the name of Opaz are you to—" I drew the rapier. I drew slowly. "I am Drak, the Strom of Valka." All the time the haulers had been blindly hauling on, and I had backed to pace them. "I can kill you all, and will do so with pleasure. Release that man. I am seeing the Emperor now; I have been summoned to talk with him." They stared at me, their faces lumps in that eerie streaming light.

I jumped back and with a single blow sliced through the tow rope. The leading man, that incredibly tall and thin man with the silky mane of yellow hair, lurched forward. Relieved of the horrendous weight of the barge he hauled forward at nothing and collapsed into the bloody froth of the towpath.

A guard — he was a Deldar — yelled his anger and charged full on me, his rapier held correctly for an instant thrust.

I met him, twisted, and sank my blade in his belly. I withdrew. "If any more of you want the same, come on!"

The thin man rolled over. He lay on his back, looking up, and I saw his face go through a whole spectrum of expressions, from dumb animal wonder to a glorious sunrise of hope.

"I am Drak, Strom of Valka!" I shouted.

Katrin's voice lifted from the bridge. "What is going on, Strom Drak? The Emperor is waiting to speak with you!"

The guards checked at this. They looked at their comrade, coughing his guts out. They looked at my rapier. They looked — and longest — at my face.

"I will pay the necessary fees, indemnities, but this man is manumitted as of this moment," I said. I turned and looked down. "I am Drak," I said again, hammering it home. "I shall find you a long-hafted ax, for I think that will please you. Now, by Ngrangi the all-powerful, get up and let us go to the Emperor."

"With all my heart!" said Inch.

"And don't think of working off your taboos until I can find you a suitable place in which to do so."

"I don't believe, Dray — Drak. But I must. Now all praise to Ngrangi!" Inch of Ng'groga leaped up, his long arms and legs pinwheels against the sunset's glow. He looked wonderful in that moment. Inch — old Inch, of Ng'groga, my good comrade in many a fight, many a carouse.

Seventeen

Inch flies to High Zorcady

The Emperor and Delia, with their courtiers, nobles, retainers, and guards, had not stayed at Delka Ob but had flown immediately to Delka Dwa. I fumed at this news in a way I believe you will understand. Prepared instantly to take to the air again I was met by the captain of Katrin's airboat. His air of uneasiness persisted.

This, I quickly discovered, was caused by the sunset and the storm out there to the west.

Even as we spoke, myself intemperately, the captain apologetically and half dead with fright, and Katrin soothingly, the outriders of the wind swooped howling over the rooftops of the city. The palace shook under the hammer-blows of the elements. Much damage was caused in the city that night; it was clear we could not fly in this weather. The rain sluiced down and the gutters ran red. The town lay smothered in the ocher and brick-red dust swept up from the Ocher Limits and blown hurtling across the land, leaving a trail of blood.

I cursed.

"The storm will blow itself out in a day, two at most," Katrin said. "No zorca will get you there quicker if you start now — and travel in this is well-nigh impossible. My flier will span the distance rapidly as soon as the storm drops."

With that, perforce, I had to be content.

How the fates and the elements conspired to cheat me of what I most desired in two worlds!

In an inner chamber I set about putting Inch back together again. With all the solemnity which the occasion required he set about purging himself of all his broken taboos. The process took time. He stood on his head for burs at a time. He sat on his haunches and howled like a ponsho-trag. A fire was laid and he solemnly jumped in and out of it. He performed some amazing acts which left me either stupefied with wonder or helpless with laughter — me, Dray Prescot. By the time he had finished the night had passed, I had slept, and Inch could be kitted out and tell me all his news.

My first words were: "What of Tilda and Pando?"

Inch sat and ate crisp fluffy Kregan bread and honey, and wondered aloud if he should take another dish of lig eggs. The lig egg comes in various shapes and sizes, of which the one with the points at each end and the fat round body between is perhaps the most popular. A few of those and a layer of grilled vosk rashers provided a breakfast fit for an emperor.

"Pando needs your horny hand on his rear," said Inch. "Tilda is more beautiful than ever, a true Kovneva. Tomboram thrives, but Pando will have to take over as king before he grows much older. He needs responsibility to hold him down. He's like a nit in a ponsho skin."

I nodded. These were problems I had not forgotten. "And you?"

He made a face and drank wine, a whole glass, down in one swallow.

"That Ngrangi-forsaken canalwater! All the haulers who were not canalfolk were scared to death of it."

"So they should be. What of yourself?"

"The argenter was taken by a swordship. The swordship was taken by a Vallian. I was simply packed off along with the rest of the prisoners; they laughed at my suggestion of a ransom."

"The Vallians would. They are an exceedingly proud and rich people. They covet slaves, for they do not have the numbers that other countries possess."

"However that may be, I hauled barges for this rast of an Emperor."

"To whose presence we go as soon as the storm drops."

Inch, of course, was staggered to find me here. He wanted to know how I had left the inner room of the palace of King Nemo in Pomdermam. I could not tell him that in that triumphant moment of victory, with the renders shouting "Jikai! Dray Prescot! Jikai," I had seen the scorpion scuttle, and had looked up and seen that greater scorpion blue and dazzling, and so had been hurled back across four hundred light-years to the planet of my birth. So I made up a story that explained it, and he, knowing of my desire to go to Vallia, understood what he chose to understand. He was loyal, was Inch of Ng'groga, a good comrade.

A couple of Katrin's seamstresses ran up a buff Vallian tunic for Inch, extraordinarily long as to body and sleeves, and although they did it rapidly the stitching was of far finer quality than my own. Katrin, like a true Kovneva, employed only the best, and took them with her on her travels. A pair of tall black boots and a rakish hat with the two slots and a mass of red and white feathers made Inch look something like a Valkan. He found an ax, long-hafted and keen-bitted. Fit, clothed, fed, Inch was ready to march and fight at my side as we had before.

I own I felt him a great comfort to me.

Seg Segutorio had gone with the Bowmen of Loh with the Emperor. I knew he and Inch would get along together — by Zair! They would! Or I would know the reason why!

The wind blew savagely from the west for all of three days, and at times must have gusted up to a hundred miles an hour. There were many slates and tiles strewing the flags of the city. I prowled, restless as a caged leem. Katrin wanted to talk about the problems of her Kovnate of Rahartdrin, but I was in no mood for that, and kept out of her way. Most of the time I spent drinking and talking with Inch.

On the morning of the fourth day Katrin's captain reported the weather fit for us to fly. The wind had veered and dropped and the clouds were piling back into the sky from which the twin suns put in a watery appearance. We went to the airboat, climbed aboard, and took flight for Delka Dwa. I was not in a happy mood. For some reason I did not wish to fathom I felt cut off, isolated, marooned from events.

I had made up my mind what I was going to do, and the elements were merely holding me back. They could not change my mind.

I would fly to Delka Dwa, take Delia and whoever she wanted to accompany her aboard this airboat. Seg would join us. I would place my hands on this calsany of a captain's throat and he would fly Katrin's airboat to Vondium. We would pick up Thelda and little Dray, and then we would take flight for Strombor.

Yes. That was the plan. Simple, direct, and brutal.

The plan did not work out like that. You must remember that Kregen is not Earth. Oh, yes, most of its geography, customs, and people are like some of those of the Earth; but much there is strange and awe-inspiring and as different from Earth as an Eskimo is different from an Amazonian Indian.

We slanted down to a landing where green fields of cabbage ended, their rows wide-spread beneath the suns. On the other side of the landing field rose the craggy pile of Delka Dwa, a dun-colored mass of stone, roofed with pointed witches hats, moated, a triple-gate opened ready to receive us. I had the impression the gates would be slammed shut the instant we were inside over the drawbridge. Across the town hung shadows of high clouds. Beyond lay a rising stretch of land, mostly of a yellow dust-rock in which the glimpses of gray-green vegetation served only to emphasize the barrenness of that land, the emptiness of it, as it rose and became drier and gradually turned into the true Ocher Limits.

All was in turmoil.

The blood was still being scrubbed from the cobbles and the flagstones, scraped from the walls, washed from the costly tapestries and carpets.

The bodies had been collected and lay in rows beneath the walls, hurriedly wrapped in makeshift shrouds fashioned from sheeting.

Delka Dwa had been attacked four days ago, just before the great storm. Savage men and beast-men wearing colors of green and purple, their badge a hangman's noose, had ravaged the place searching for the Emperor.

I forced myself to hold on to my sanity.

Pallan Eling, with a bloody bandage around his head, lay in a long chair, and his scrawny frame shook. I asked him the questions torturing me.

"I do not know where the Princess is, Strom," he said. His voice quavered. I thought he shook no more than did I. "Now we know the colors and the badge of the third party! By Vox, I hope their bones rot and slime on the Ice Floes of Sicce."

In the corridors bowmen lay mingled with mercenaries, all wounded, all the Emperor's men who had fought. They had been overwhelmed.

A Hikdar told me, a Hikdar with a broken left arm strapped across his chest and acupuncture needles in him, dulling the pain. At his side lay his great longbow.

"Pallan Eling should go back to caring for the canals," the Hikdar said. "And leave fighting to warriors."

"Yes," I said, in a voice I did not recognize. "What happened?"

I was aware of Inch busily taking in what had happened and talking to the survivors. The Hikdar's head lolled.

"I was told to wait here. As soon as we arrived from Delka Ob the Emperor must have heard news, for he took to the air again at once. Half his force he took with him. We who stayed here received the attack designed to kill him. That is sure."

The real fear took me then and gripped my guts with a pain that made me cry out and rush upon the shrunken form of the Pallan Eling, the man responsible for canals. His face looked like an old potato left out in the sun for a week. He whimpered when I gripped him.

"You must tell me, Pallan Eling. Where is the Princess Majestrix?"

He cried out, and gazed on the scene about him as though reliving the scenes of horror. Then he closed his eyes and a shudder racked through his body. "Gone." He moaned, barely audible, and his old lips fluttered. "They came wearing the white and black, and said they were my friends, and asked for the Emperor — and I told them! I told them!"

"What did you tell them, old man?"

"Vomanus of Vindelka, it was; he knew. He warned the Emperor! They fled to The Dragon's Bones. There, Vomanus said, they would be safe." Eling abruptly sat up, gripped what was left of his hair, and tore at it like a madman. "And I told them where Vomanus had gone!"

I tried to calm myself, to think clearly, and, Zair knows, that was nigh impossible with the blood roaring in my head.

"And the Princess? Where is she?"

"She took an airboat with the others — with the Emperor—"

"*Inch!*" I bellowed.

He came running, swinging his ax.

"We go to The Dragon's Bones."

"Aye, Drak. Where may that be, then?"

I stared at him like a loon. I had no idea.

A Chulik sat with his back against a wall. One eye had been gouged out and the tusk on that side broken off. His chest was broken and a girl was trying clumsily to ease his pain. He stared up at me with that stoic calmness the Chuliks boast against pain. "The Dragon's Bones," he said, in a whisper. He wore sleeves of white and ocher, so he was of Vindelka.

I bent down. "By Likshu the Treacherous! Tell me where lies The Dragon's Bones, Chulik."

"Into the Ocher Limits — northwest — twenty, twenty-five dwaburs, more. There are bones there, millions of bones."

A Chuktar whose once-brilliant uniform was now mere rags, bloody and ripped, leaned up on an arm and coughed out: "There is no hope for the Emperor now. The third party has suborned good men. We stayed loyal to the Emperor, and this is our thanks. There is no one in the whole of Vallia who will fight for him now."

"No, no!" shrieked the Pallan Eling, and then he looked around furtively. "But it is true. I should have joined Trylon Larghos! I was asked — I was asked! All have turned against the Emperor!" He rocked to and fro in his agony. "Why did I not do so? My loyalty has destroyed me!"

Well, the whole sorry story was out in the open now.

And yet Vomanus had warned the Emperor, and they had fled. Yet Vomanus was Trylon Larghos' candidate for Delia's hand! There was treachery and double-treachery here.

The confounded roaring and shrieking persisted in my head. I couldn't think straight. Trylon Larghos. Building his third party, double-dealing the racters — I felt a jolt of surprise. If Vomanus had found out about that, and realized his hopes for Delia as the candidate of the racters meant nothing, he would have turned against the men of the white and black. He had warned the Emperor, but his motives may simply have been pure self-interest. But — Vomanus? I had to get to The Dragon's Bones and confront him — and Trylon Larghos.

I snatched up the bowman's great longbow, and half a dozen filled quivers. They told the story. The third party had come in the guise of racters, as friends, and then had struck with steel; the crimson Bowmen of Loh had gone down with their bows unstrung, the arrows still snugged in their quivers.

I took Katrin's airboat captain's neck between my fingers.

"You will take us instantly to The Dragon's Bones."

He cringed. He had no time to argue, to say a word. He was run outside, and I shouted at the men standing limply by the drawbridge in the gatehouse in such a way that the drawbridge smoked down, and bounced, spouting dust. Inch and I ran across with the flier captain propelled before us. Katrin's despairing cry followed.

"Strom Drak! You would not leave me?"

"Where I must go there is no place for you, Katrin! I will try to send your airboat back for you." I gave the captain a buffet to make him run faster. "You might get it back if you're lucky."

The captain yelped at this. I kicked him aboard his craft and he fell onto the deck. Rearing up, he saw my face and so gave his orders in a scared husky croak to his crew. We took to the air.

"Captain," I said. "I do not know your name. But you will obey me in all things. Is that understood?"

"Yes, my lord Strom. I am Hikdar Arkhebi. I will do as you order."

"Get us to The Dragon's Bones as though your life depended on it — for, believe you me, it does."

He took himself off to oversee his steersman, down in the engine compartment where were situated the two silver boxes which, with my limited knowledge then, I understood to control height, speed, and direction of the flier.

Inch said, "The raiders got in treacherously by wearing white and black. The Bowmen were very bitter about that."

"I just hope Seg is all right."

"From what you tell me of Seg, I think he can take care of himself."

Delia.

If she had been harmed — I did not relish that swift flight across the Ocher Limits to The Dragon's Bones. I couldn't remain still. I paced up and down the sundeck, flicking my rapier this way and that, aching, shivering, shrunken. Black thoughts flitted like evil bats through my brain.

The barren wastes, rugged and harsh, fled past beneath. The hot wind scorched into my face and stung my eyes. I could not descend into that sumptuous cabin where the Kovneva Katrin had besought me. I stayed on the sun-deck and Inch kept everyone away, and, up there, alone, I suffered through that blistering journey.

Inch had never met Delia. I know, now, that he came to a full understanding of what she meant to me.

Away ahead I saw the yellow-umber landscape with its dry gulches and its powdery screes lifting to a serrated ridge, saw-toothed, jagged. Across this we flew, and I was very conscious how this evil land fitted my mood. Beyond, in a depression, lay a fumarole. We flew over it and then another. This whole area looked much as the surface of Earth's moon looks, with volcano detritus and lava scattered everywhere, crater colliding and blending with crater. The glare of the twin suns beat back dazzlingly.

There was no need for Inch to stand upon any rung of the ladder to lift his head to the sundeck level. He shouted back: "Strom Drak! We approach The Dragon's Bones."

"Come up here, Inch."

He shambled up onto the sundeck and stood, braced against the slipstream, regarding me.

"They said, back there in Delka Dwa, that there was no one in all Vallia who would fight for the Emperor."

"Aye," said Inch, who had been a barge hauler.

"That may be true. I do not know and, truth to tell, do not much care. But there are men willing to fight for the Princess Majestrix."

Inch looked at me. "Now I know," he said. "I can feel a little sorrow for Tilda the Beautiful — and, by Ngrangi, for Viridia the Render, also."

"You," I said to Inch, and I spoke as reasonably as I could, and Inch, because he was my comrade, understood and remained patient and calm under the bitter lash of my voice. "Inch, go to the Blue Mountains. Go to High Zorcady. Ask for Korf Aighos, for I think he will have returned by now, recovered. If he has not, there will be other men willing to fight — aye, and die — for their Princess. Gather what men you can, in fliers, and bring them back here."

"But," said Inch, "this Hikdar Arkhebi — you remember our Arkhebi who took Strom Erclan's place? — he can take a message." Inch's eyebrows drew down. "I would rather fight at your side."

"And dearly would I have you there, Inch, you long warrior, but" — and here I rolled out a foul Makki-Grodno oath — "I don't trust him. Only you will carry the words to make them believe. Only Korf Aighos knows I am Dray Prescot, Krozair of Zy."

Even Inch did not fully comprehend what that meant. No one could, who had not sailed the inner sea, the Eye of the World.

Inch grumbled a great deal and swung his ax about and looked every inch of his seven feet a disgruntled man, but in the end I persuaded him. I had to. The Delphondi for all their loyalty were useless — as I then thought — and only the Blue Mountain Boys and all the other bandits, reavers, and moss troopers of the Blue Mountains could offer help.

I placed the point of my rapier against Hikdar Arkhebi's throat. It was a cheap gesture, theatrical, but I had summed up the man.

"You will fly directly to High Zorcady, Hikdar Arkhebi. Maybe, if you succeed, you will take the first step on the ladder leading to Jiktar. If you fail, you won't be a Deldar — you'll be a corpse, swinging rotting in a gibbet!"

"Yes, my lord Strom!" he gasped out, his lips ashen.

"And Inch, here, who is to be addressed as Tyr Inch, has my permission — no! by the Black Chunkrah! my orders — to degut you the instant you try to betray me. Is that clear?"

He gobbled it out. "Yes, my lord Strom!"

They landed me short of my target, which appeared to be a crater filled with bones, and Arkhebi took the airboat in a wide circle around The Dragon's Bones, and so on over the horizon to the west.

I stepped out smartly, for I was anxious to get where I was going. I wanted to speak with Trylon Nath Larghos of the Black Mountains. If he died, that would be his misfortune. I was approaching where my Delia was in deadly danger, and nothing could be allowed to stand in the way of her safety.

Eighteen

With Trylon Larghos at The Dragon's Bones

"So you did receive the message I left at *The Rose of Valka*," said Nath Larghos. "But why are you afoot? What took you so long?"

He eyed me strangely. I had myself under control. The Emperor, Delia, and their men were shut up in the mass of ruins at the center of the crater. Various roads led in and out scraped in the rock and dust, with the enormous bones dragged aside. They were risslaca bones, mainly, although there were some from mammals of a later time, all fossilized, a veritable treasure for paleontologists. I forced myself to act normally. Just for the moment, Delia's danger lay in abeyance.

"That Opaz-rotten storm," I grunted. "The airboat failed. One day, by Vox, we must teach those cramphs of Havilfar a lesson."

"Agreed, Strom Drak." He led me off to a cluster of tents. "Come, sit and drink wine and refresh yourself. You need a shave, if you will pardon the liberty of my mentioning it."

"Mayhap," I said, "I will grow a beard, Trylon."

The Circadian rhythms of my Earth ancestry adapted well to the longer day-and-night cycle of Kregen, and I had quickly adjusted — and, if the truth be told — with some relish, to the idea that a day demanded not four square meals but at the least six and preferably seven or eight.

We sat and drank wine — a fine vintage of Procul, rich and fortifying — and I knew that before I did what I screamed and hungered to do and rushed into the ruins to clasp Delia in my arms, I must find out everything I could of these third party members and their plans.

They had infiltrated all the other parties, the racters in particular, and built up a powerful and secret force. The headless zorcamen were their messengers, able to travel through the country where eyes would have followed the movements of any man wearing whatever colors. They had built up a network, and I heard news that struck me with a powerful horror. Trylon Larghos — of the Black Mountains! — had set his own followers in motion against the men of the Blue Mountains.

"Those bandits who forever raid us would have tried to protect the Princess, their liege lord; as it is, they are out of the reckoning."

I sat there, drinking stupid wine, and I trembled. And I had sent Inch there — I had sent him to his death!

Larghos went on to tell me how he had so arranged matters that one Kovnate, or any other great estate, had been set to put out of the issue the one most convenient. Neighbor had been set against neighbor. He rolled out the names with a kind of lip-licking glee. "Delphond, of course, means nothing in these affairs."

"No," I said, trying to speak normally. "They are a peaceful, luxury-loving lot down there."

"So, Strom Drak. I am glad you have brought Valka in on the right side. I had bargained for that; I think I would not have enjoyed settling the Qua'voils against you."

I stared at him, trying to mask my hatred. He would have loved doing that. The Qua'voils occupy the southeastern lobe of the large island to the west of Valka, and they are halflings, sharing the attributes of — as the best way of so describing them — porcupines with those of men. They were — and here the old bitter jest turned sour in my mind — a thorn in the flesh of Valka.

The large island to the west of Valka is called Canthirda. In the past it has been the scene of many bloody battles as Vallia, the main island, separated from Canthirda by a wide channel, sought to bring a single government over the whole archipelago. Many races had settled there and many species. The Qua'voils were always causing trouble. To the north of them the Emperor had settled in new lands a dependency of Relts, those more gentle cousins of the Rapas. The Valkas got on well with them, and it was to their land that Tom of Vulheim had advised me to go when I had sought to escape from Valka and reach Vallia, only to be halted by the express commands of the Star Lords in lightning and thunder. Now Larghos was speaking of fresh foulness.

"Those stupid bird-brained Relts! Now, Strom Drak, you must send orders to your warriors to join with the Qua'voils and march against the Relts. We will take over all of Canthirda and run it as it is meant to be run." He chuckled. "A Relt can haul a barge as well as anyone else, I fancy."

I managed to get out: "They remained loyal to the Emperor, Trylon?"

"More fool them. So did the Pallan Eling. I fancy he wishes he had joined us. The leader has already appointed another man as Pallan of Canals."

Not knowing what Larghos had put in the letter, save that it must have summoned me to join the revolt, I could not inquire after this leader. I had thought Trylon Larghos that man. He was looking pleased, so I ventured to congratulate him on being appointed the Pallan of Canals.

"You are right Strom Drak...The Pallans who will run the Presidio under the leader are all chosen. I feel that you will soon rise to office, should you wish to do so."

"That day may come, Trylon Larghos."

The attack on the tumbled mass of ruins was not being prosecuted with much zeal. I heard that a couple of hundred or so Bowmen of Loh, with other mercenaries, were shut up with the Emperor. They had bloodily repulsed the first impulsive attack. Now Larghos was waiting for the arrival of the leader with reinforcements. I talked more, seeming affable — and wanting to drive my dagger into this man's guts — and I learned.

He commented on the longbow, and I said I found it useful, although I would not care to shoot against a crimson Bowman. I knew that Seg Segutorio, the best bowman that Erthyrdrin — and therefore Loh — had produced, had shot against me, and although he had won, it had been by a whisker.

I had to learn the plans.

Drinking wine made Larghos boastful. "What are these talked-of Lohvian bowmen? Merely archers. They caught us in the open, unprepared, but the next time — why, the leader is bringing with him five hundred Undurkers. The crimson Bowmen have idled away their time, living in luxury provided by the Emperor, living on money extorted from us! The Undurkers can outshoot the Lohvians, by Vomer the Vile!"

I did not believe that, and I had experience to go on; but, certainly, the compound bows of the Undurkers were powerful and their reputation ferocious. I felt more and more fidgety, sitting here, drinking and talking; but for the moment Delia was safe and I was doing more valuable work here than blindly rushing into the ruins.

I walked about the third party's camp, after a while, and Larghos gave me a great green and purple favor to wear in my hat. I saw the men they had, the mercenaries, men who would remain loyal while they were paid and their duty unfinished. Tents had been set up. There was no siege equipment of any kind that I could see. The leader might bring some, went the word. The suns would soon decline in the west. I felt I had learned all that was useful. The next big attack would go in through an archway of bones, through the gigantic skeletons of monstrous dinosaurs dead a million years or more. I looked out from the jump-off point and marked the way to go.

I had asked Larghos about Vomanus, his candidate.

"Vomanus! If I see him I shall slay him. He must have guessed he was being used merely as a front. Once the Emperor was out of his palace we had him at our mercy. Vomanus agreed to invite him to Vindelka. He trusted Vomanus, for the sake of Tharu, when he would not have trusted one of us. Vomanus warned the Emperor, but they fled here. That old fool Pallan Eling told us. He was glad to tell us."

He looked sharply at me. I nodded.

"So," he went on. "As soon as the Emperor is dead, the leader will take over. His candidate will wed the Princess. Then we can all count the loot."

I fiddled with the crimson Bowman's shooting glove I had taken from him. I use a bracer and a shooting glove when they are available; like any Bowman of Loh I can shoot without them if I have to. It is a knack.

All across to the east stretched the badlands of the Ocher Limits. Oh, they were nowise as strange and fearful as the Owlarh Waste over which I had tramped leaving the Hostile Territories. And they did not compare with the Klackadrin, that frightful place of hallucinations and the risslaca riding risslaca, the Phokaym. The Klackadrin is a great rift in the planet's crust, gaseous, poisonous, fatal. The Ocher Limits were merely badlands. But that meant I wouldn't walk out without plentiful supplies and much water.

A shout went up and we turned our backs on the twin suns as they oblated in weird runnelings of jade and crimson, and stared up to see a fleet of fliers swinging in over the Ocher Limits. Bright pinpricks of light against the swathing darkness dropping down, they circled once. Then with a neat precision that, once again, made me give that mental nod of admiration for flier pilots, they settled onto the ocher sands.

Five hundred archers from the islands of Undurkor!

With them were many other mercenaries, men willing to fight for pay. Well, I had been a mercenary in my time, aye, and was to be again, as you will hear. Fristles, Ochs, Rapas, Brokelsh, Womoxes, and men, they crowded from the fliers, laughing and exchanging rough jokes with comrades from bygone campaigns they recognized in the crowd waiting to greet them. Among them the yellow skins and shaven heads of the Chuliks stood out, grim and menacing and altogether malefic.

I went with Trylon Larghos. I stood in the last of the mingled opaz light falling about the animated scene to greet this leader who would kill the Emperor and take his place, who would marry his own candidate to the Princess Majestrix.

With the feeling that it was my duty to count heads and to appraise potential in fighting, I studied the new arrivals.

Of the halflings I knew — and some were there I do not mention, for I had not run across them in such a way as to merit detailed descriptions yet to you in these tapes — I was sure enough that I knew their capabilities.

The Undurkers I knew, for they came from a string of islands situated in that enormous bay pent between the giant peninsula of South Segesthes and the smaller boot-shaped promontory to the west that separates Zenicce from Port Paros. We saw them often in Zenicce, and they had even made the attempt at a few settlements in Segesthes itself. But they seldom ventured onto the Great Plains. I rather fancied my wild clansmen would be a trifle too tough for them there.

Their conversation was loud and confident, brash, I thought. They carried their bows already strung and in fancifully decorated bow-sheaths slung under their left arms on straps, making a saltire shape with their arrow quivers. The bows themselves were very much like those of my clansmen, curved, compound, reflex, fabricated from horn, bone, and wood, with brilliant silver fittings. Lovers of ostentation to an extreme degree, are the Undurkers. Their faces always remind me of the snooty, supercilious, offended faces of borzois. Except for their eyes, which are mounted higher up for the essential binocular vision required, they do look like borzois — and that higher mounting for the eyes adds, if anything, to their expression of continual superiority.

They formed their camp a little apart from the rest of the brawling throng, where already, I guessed, some old scores were being paid off. A mercenary makes enemies as he goes through life. A young Strom with Larghos' party laughed nervously, and fingered his rapier hilt. An older Vad, with a beard far too long for current fashions, boomed a laugh and clapped the young Strom on the back, and bade him bear up and face the future, when the Emperor was dead, and men could plunge their hands to the elbows in rich red gold.

These Undurkers wore coiled artificial headdresses of hair plaited and colored from which rose their squarish helmets. Their clothes, of good Lohvian silks and Segesthan hides, were studded with bits of metal and base gems; their Jiktars would wear real gems. Their feet were hidden in heavy boots, and I knew why; the hands of the Undurkers are hands that would not look amiss hanging on the wrists of a man, but in their paws they betray their canine origin. They are, as the Gons are ashamed of their manes of white hair, ashamed of their hind-paws, and always wear heavy concealing boots. That was their business. I wanted a glimpse of the leader — and then nothing would stop me from heading through the piles of bones to the ruins in the center and all that waited there.

Food, drink, and fuel had been brought in and the camp fires blazed into the night sky, obliterating the last lingering ruby drops scattered across the western horizon as Zim sank in the wake of Genodras. I saw Berran the Vadvar of Rifuji, a lean dyspeptic man with a nervous tic about his left eye, laughing and jesting, and marked him, for his Jiktars were leading his men against Vomansoir to keep them out of play. Over most of Vallia that might have any hand in this business the third party had cast the web of their intrigues so that here, in isolation, the Emperor might be murdered and the new leader proclaimed. This was more than a palace revolution; this work would drench the empire in blood and over-turn old dynasties, set men's thoughts and actions into new paths that might last a thousand years.

Around the campfires I took a heaping handful of roast vosk. I was not too proud to eat with these men, for all that I might be slaying them before the Maiden of the Many Smiles had crossed the heavens. I shoved the six quivers of arrows away on the strap holding them together; I kept my eye on them.

"Hai, Strom Drak!" said Larghos, very merry, quaffing his wine, his eyes beads of glitter in the firelight. He swaggered over with a bunch of men of whom I knew some, and whom I knew I would make myself acquainted better later on. "The leader is busy, there is much to do, but he will see you when he can spare the time."

I swallowed vosk and nodded.

The thought came to me then that it might be accounted a great deed — as true Jikai — if when we met I plunged my rapier through the body of this leader.

Even today, I cannot say if I would have done that deed or not.

The leader stood by a great fire, half turned from me, talking to a group of the nobles of the third party caught up in his schemes. With them stood the Chuktar of the Undurkers. At the leader's side stood a younger man, laughing and full of merriment. This was the third party's candidate for the hand of the Princess Majestrix, through whose marriage the leader would seek to legitimize his claim to the throne. Larghos led me forward.

"Here is Berran, Vadvar of Rifuji," said Larghos. "And here also is Drak, Strom of Valka."

We went forward into the firelight.

The leader turned, a goblet of wine in his hand.

I saw him.

It was Naghan Furtway, Kov of Falinur.

At his side, laughing and jesting, stood his nephew, Jenbar.

I froze, for a stupid moment held in a stasis of self-contempt. These were the two I had rescued from the Mountains of the North at the instance of the Star Lords. I had saved their lives so that they might destroy mine and the girl's I loved.

Jenbar stopped laughing.

"Who?" he said. He peered closer.

"Berran, Vadvar—" began Larghos.

"No. The other."

"Drak, Strom of Valka."

"No, by Vox!" said Jenbar. His laughter returned, bright and evil in the firelight. His uncle looked at me. Kov Furtway stared at me — and I knew his thoughts, as those of his nephew's, went back with mine to those icy slopes and snowy mountains. They had known and had planned all this, then, and how they must have mocked their secret knowledge of me, then!

Furtway said, "We were surprised and disappointed when you disappeared from Therminsax. We would have taken you to Vondium, as you wished."

"Aye, by Vox!" said Jenbar, chuckling. "And the Emperor would have been mightily pleased to receive you."

"As, indeed, he did receive you." Furtway's smile altered in character. "Although how in the name of the Invisible Twins you escaped him I do not know."

"What?" said Trylon Larghos. "What are you saying, Kov?"

"Why, Nath Largos, do you not know who this man is, the man you call Drak, Strom of Valka?"

Larghos saw the evil undercurrents running here, and he stammered, and was silent. His fear of this leader, who was Kov Furtway of Falinur, was very great.

I poised. *Flight!* I, Dray Prescot, the Lord of Strombar, Krozair of Zy, must run from my foemen! Well, I had done that before, not often, and would do so again; now I must live to reach my Delia, stand by her side, and defy the might of Vallia arrayed against us.

"Chuktar Uncar," said Furtway. "Feather me this fool with arrows! Pull him down as the trags pull down a leem!"

The Undurker unshipped his bow. Larghos was babbling. Jenbar was laughing.

"That man, you fools," shouted Furtway, "is Dray Prescot! That wild clansman, the Lord of Strombor! Slay him!"

I swung about and ran from the firelight and into the avenue of dinosaur bones. And as I ran the whispering rain of arrows whistled about me and clanged from those millennia-old bones in a sleeting shower of death.

Nineteen

"...fit to be called Prince Majister of Vallia."

The very tangle and interlacing tapestry of bones over and under which I leaped and dived saved me. One arrow only nicked me, a slicing shear through the leather over my left shoulder; a scratch, nothing. I dodged and ducked as best I could. These ancient bones, fossilized over the millennia and then cast adrift once again on the desiccated surface of the secret crater where these great beasts had trekked to die, surrounded me and in a weird and ghoulish way afforded me protection.

The arrows sleeted about the iron-hard bones. I heard their chiming, like the bells of the damned, and I ran and leaped. One chance alone was left me now. A roaring bellow of rage pursued me. Kov Furtway had let loose his mercenaries, and the Undurkers, their proud supercilious noses high, were after me.

I remember as I ran, hurdling risslaca vertebrae and all the scattered skeletons of giants of the past, that I had a most uncharitable thought about these halflings from Undurkor. Their long noses meant they could not turn their heads when loosing, otherwise the strings would have given them bloody stripes down those snouts. They used a short compound bow, and they must draw it as far as they might, to the chest, the lip, the nose. It is from the long throw of the great longbow that all its awful power is obtained, that long energy-storing thrust that gives range and penetration, when the shorter flatter staccato of the small bow slaps out jerkily.

Mind you — if an Undurker arrow skewered me now it would be just as painful as a cloth-yard shaft.

The moons of Kregen floated past above and the shadows shifted strangely among that fossilized forest of bones. The hard clatter of booted feet pursued me. I ran. I dodged. There was no time for that old Krozair trick I so joyed in employing, of turning about and swatting the arrows away with my sword, something after the style of a flick-flick gobbling up flies on the wing.

"I'll marmelize you!" a voice screeched at my back.

I ignored that kind of drivel.

I kept my bowstave horizontal so as not to foul the arching rib cages. Had my bow been strung — for like any frugal bowman I kept the stave unstrung when possible — I'd have risked a turn and a shot. But I kept on. Inky shadows barring the path succeeded by patches of pink moonlight passed, and I raced on. The avenue twisted and turned where bones too large and heavy to lift from the way imposed a turning. These serpentine windings saved me. I roared out into a cleared area. In a great circle the bones enclosed this area like a fence of fossils. In the center rose the tumbled pile of ruins. I made out three corners of a tower, shafting up like a rotten tooth. Masses of rock lay strewn haphazardly. A few lights glimmered. I had to cross this open space somehow.

Head down I started off at a tremendous pace, my Earthly muscles gaining full effect from Kregen's gravity, knowing I had at best but a few murs before the first of my pursuers appeared at the mouth of the tunnel-like avenue through the bones.

As I went I shouted. I used up breath to bellow a warning of my approach.

"Friend!" I roared. "I'm Strom Drak! Let me in!"

A long arrow skeeted past my head. I let out a blistering Makki-Grodno oath and lifted my voice, as on this Earth I had hailed the foretop in a gale, and told them what I thought of a Vox-spawned Opaz-forgotten cramph of a bowman who tried to spit a comrade.

With all the hullabaloo I very nearly miscalculated and left my first dodging weaving too late. I slanted my run and then zigzagged back, and six arrows clumped against the rock, to carom ahead. Three of them snapped across, whereat I took note and would have smiled, were I given to that kind of facial contortion in interesting moments like this.

"Undurkers!" I screeched. "Feather a few rasts for me!"

I was almost there, now, in the shadow cast by one moon. Over my head rustled the near-silent covey of long arrows. I dodged again and then dived into the sprawled mass of ruins with the shrieks of skewered halflings in my ears.

I rolled over and jumped up. "By Vox! That sounds better for a fighting-man to hear!"

Seg said, "You took a chance, dom. I only just managed to knock Hakli's bow up in time."

"I knew you must have done so, Seg. Since when does a Bowman of Loh miss a running target coming straight for him!"

The dark crimson shape at Seg's side chuckled. "Aye, Seg Segutorio. This Drak of whom you spoke is indeed a man."

In the moonshot darkness a line of bowmen sank down into their places in the shelter of rocks and tumbled slabs of masonry. Hakli, his fire-red hair a weird color under the moons, chuckled again, and took up his station. "The cramphs have crept back among the bones, where they belong."

"They'll be out again, Hakli," I said. "They have archers of Undurkor with them now."

"Children with toddlers' bows, by Hlo-Hli! Flint fodder!"

I turned to Seg. "The Princess Majestrix, Seg. Where is she?"

Seg looked at me. I saw the lines on his face in the streaming pink moonshine. "Delia? She is not with us."

Once again that frightful sensation of the solid ground beneath my feet turning and plummeting sickeningly seized me. I gripped Seg's arm. We moved away, into the shadows.

"What do you mean, she is not with you? She left in an airboat when these kleeshes attacked Delta Dwa. She must be here!"

"No, Dray. She did not come with us. I was aboard the flier in which the Emperor fled. She did not land here."

There had been confusion when the Emperor, warned by Vomanus, had fled for safety to these ruins in The Dragon's Bones. Vomanus liked to come here to study the old remains; it was a hobby. There had been worse confusion when the courtiers, retainers, and guards had landed here, a chaos made worse by the great storm that had swept up the airboats like idle leaves upon a river and swept them into shattered destruction against the massive array of bones. Seg could have been mistaken.

"We're short on food and water, Dray. There have been a few attacks, not many, and we held them off without trouble. But the men may not fight if they are not fed."

"They have Undurkers with them out there now, Seg. If the crimson Bowmen of Loh do not fight, the Emperor is a dead man." I looked into the ruins. "I will seek him out now. Delia *must* be here. If she is not — he may know where she is."

Seg, looking at my face in the shadows, coughed, and said: "Remember, my old sea-leem. He is the Emperor. He is surrounded still by his men."

"I know, Seg. But I have come here to find Delia—" I told him, then, that I had sent Inch to what might be his death.

Seg said, "From what you tell me of Inch, Dray, he will fight his way out of anything."

I warmed at that. Seg's tour of sentry duty being finished he accompanied me as I went to find the Emperor. On all sides among the ruins the mercenaries were camped, and they appeared to be a sullen, dispirited lot. I could imagine the frightful problems they were revolving in their minds. A mercenary fights for pay and will remain loyal, but if you do not pay him, if you do not feed him and give him wine...

"Welcome, Strom Drak!" The Emperor held out his hand and we gripped in the Vallian way. He looked exhausted, with the betraying dark smudges beneath his eyes, his cheeks sunken. But there remained about him the same indomitable iron determination that kept his place as Emperor; this man would never give in until they shoveled earth down onto him. Perhaps that was where we differed, for I would not give in until I had clawed my way up and thrown down those hurling the dirt on me. "You are right welcome, Strom Drak. It is good to find loyal men still in Vallia."

The silly old fool! He thought I had fought my way here to rescue him, or to help him in his defense! Idiot! Onker! Calsany!

"Where is the Princess Majestrix, Majister?"

"I do not know." He made a flat, dismissive gesture. "At least, she is not trapped here with us. But, soon, my loyal subjects will arrive, as you have, Strom Drak, and will destroy utterly those treacherous rasts led by the Trylon Larghos, may Vox tear his guts out with white-hot pincers."

"But, Majister," I said. "The Princess Delia — she must—" I swallowed. I shook and couldn't stop myself. The Emperor looked coldly at me, for no stranger, no man not of the family, unless given permission, may call the Princess Majestrix anything other than that. Her name, like her person, is sacred. "She was in an air-boat — the storm — those mad leem out there..."

Pallan Rodway, the minister in charge of the Treasury, took my arm and tried to wheel me away from the Emperor. I would not be maneuvered. I glared at them, at this Emperor and the few loyal nobles and Pallans remaining to him as we stood in that shattered tower surrounded by ruins.

"Where is she!" I yelled it; it was a demand. "The Princess Majestrix!"

The Emperor returned my glare with all the apoplectic fury of complete authority. I saw that malignant glitter in his eyes and I know my eyes returned the same ugly, evil, hateful, utterly damn-you-to-hell look. What might have happened then I do not know — and didn't care, by Zim-Zair, then! — but the moment was broken by two almost simultaneous events.

A voice spoke, a voice I knew: "Well met, Drak! Come and drink wine with me, for there is much to tell."

I said, "Your words to me, Vomanus, were: 'I will do as you ask.' Do you remember?"

He came forward into the torchlight. "I remember." He looked just the same, handsome, careless, above the petty run of party politics, and yet...

And then a Chulik mercenary let out a tremendous bellow.

"The cramphs! They attack! The Undurkers! They come!"

I unslung the great Lohvian longbow and with the smooth practiced forward jerk, strung it. I looked at Seg and at Vomanus. Here one was a mere private Koter in the Emperor's bodyguard, the other a lord of a province; to me they were comrades both. We went to the perimeter of the ruins and we vied one bowman with another, in our picking off of the supercilious Undurkers as they strove to outshoot us. Nothing on Kregen, as I understood it then, outshoots the Lohvian longbow. The warriors of Kov Furtway, attacking, were feathered into heaps and piles as they sought to rush from the ruins under the cover of their own arrow shower. Oh, we took casualties. But we held that attack and hurled it back; at only one point did it come to handblows, and then our Chuliks with their chilling ferocity smashed the first wave, and the second recoiled and ran.

The metal-adorned backs of the mercenaries vanished into the fossilized forest of bones. Our wounded were cared for. The fourth moon, She of the Veils, cast down her pinkish light and picked out in a roseate glow the glimmer of weapons, the gleam from an eye-socket, the black sheen of blood, and the harsh rock and dust, the ring of bones, the ruins, the desolation.

Vomanus cornered me where a dead Rapa still clutched his sword, his bird-beak embedded in the dust, the Undurker arrow protruding through his neck.

"Dray! I never thought to see you alive again!"

We talked. Much of our conversation dealt with what I have already related to you. I found my surmise was true. He had allowed himself to become the candidate so as to discover the secret intentions of the Emperor's enemies. His warning had been almost too late. "And now we are done for, anyway, I think, Dray. We have had bonny times, but they are over."

From the corner of my eye I was aware of the dark crimson shape, hovering. I said, "Vomanus, tell me true — you have no desires to marry Delia? You continue to support me?"

"Of course! Need you ask? I have spoken with Delia, and no woman loved a man as she loves you." He chuckled, an incongruous sound in those surroundings. "Although why so ugly a looking devil as you should manage it when all the chivalry of Vallia have been spurned — Vox take it! But you are the man, Dray Prescot!"

I heard Seg gasp.

"Come here, Seg!"

These two, Vomanus of Vindelka and Seg Segutorio, stared at each other, and I recognized the amusement in me at their instinctive sizing up, their flash of temperament. I told them both a little of the fuller story, and finished: "So we three are dedicated to the service of Delia of Delphond. Very good. Very fine. But where, by the Black Chunkrah, is she?"

All that was certain was — she was not trapped with her father in the tumbled ruins at the center of The Dragon's Bones.

Naturally, I immediately took stock of the situation with the single obsessive desire to get out. I could make a run for it, and once inside the tangle of bones, no man or beast-man would catch me. Covering that open space would be the tricky part, for I would be shot at by Undurkers in front and by Lohvian Bowmen from the rear. Of the two I gave the Lohvians the best bet on feathering me.

"Sink me!" I burst out, and the other two looked at me strangely. I knew I must appear a black-hearted devil to them, a harsh, intolerant — and intolerable — man who demanded instant obedience. But other thoughts occurred to me. This man we defended was Delia's father. That he was the Emperor meant nothing in my book. But if I left now, and Furtway succeeded in murdering Delia's father in cold blood — what would she think? What would she think of *me*? I would be the man who had run away and left her father to die a miserable death.

Hell's bells and buckets of blood!

I was in a cleft stick and it was damned uncomfortable.

Furtway flung his men in again, and this time they surged up to our parapet of stones. We had a few brisk moments when the swords rang and slithered, and men screeched with steel skewering their bellies. Then the third party mercenaries broke and we spitted them all the way back to the bone ramparts.

Seg said, "I'm down to a dozen shafts."

"Here, take these quivers." I handed them out, sharing among the crimson Bowmen. They had lost all their Jiktars, their Chuktar was Opaz knew where, only three Deldars remained, and one badly wounded and dying Hikdar. Of the intermediate ranks, as you know, a man is called simply by the last and identifying portion of his full rank. Various organizations place varying numbers of degrees in each rank. The highest ranking of the three Deldars was a So-Deldar — that is, the third degree of Deldar — and he had seven more to go before he became a Hikdar. They were good men. But, as is my custom, I had been active in the fighting, shouting intemperate and callous orders in my brutal and domineering way, and they had listened to me, instinctively understanding that, for all my sins and ugly face, I was a leader, and they obeyed.

The Emperor came up and said abruptly, "Strom Drak. I have noticed how you fight, and I am pleased. Of the other matter we will talk by and by—"

I interrupted him. If you cannot imagine the full depth of my agony for Delia, the feelings of screaming madness possessing me, I can understand that. It has been given only to few men to grasp what I suffered then, and I would not wish that pain on anyone. So it was I interrupted the Emperor, and walked away, saying over my shoulder: "I will fight for you, Majister — aye, and slay those rasts for you! — but afterward we will talk, you and I."

Pallan Rodway, a Vadvar, the High Kov of Erstveheim, two Stroms, and all the other nobles gasped their outrage. I was aware of Vomanus talking hurriedly with the Emperor; but another attack came in then and we were busily occupied in hurling the mercenaries back. But our numbers were thinning. I heard a Rapa grumbling that he had a throat drier than the Ocher Limits themselves. I gripped him by his clumsy throat, glared madly into his birdlike eyes, and I screamed at him that he'd be a dead Rapa before he drank again if he didn't get back into the fight.

The Emperor watched all this. I was sane enough to realize that he was cunning enough to use men when it suited him; he had seen me fighting and wouldn't arrest me — or make the attempt, Zair rot him! — while I was useful to him. That's how he had remained Emperor so long. I caught a whiff of perfume, a sweet, gagging stench, completely out of place in those surroundings. Across the clearing raced foemen to attack us. I looked quickly down and there, wedged into a crevice between rocks, crouched a man. He was sumptuously dressed, with a great deal of lace, silk, and golden ornaments. He wore a rapier. He smelled like a barber's shop. I caught him by the collar and hauled him out.

"Get up and fight, you cramph!"

"No! No — I am no fighting-man!"

Once a Kregan reaches maturity he appears to age very little until the last years of his life, perhaps a few white hairs when he is a hundred and fifty or so; but I fancied this man was considerably older than my comrades. I kicked him.

"You fight, dom! You fight for your Emperor!"

An Undurker arrow whistled between us and clanged against the rock. He screeched. His face was covered in sweat. It sheened under She of the Veils like pink icing.

"Fight, cramph!"

He staggered up then, his face contorted into a look compounded of fear and hatred, pride and anger. For a second I thought he would take his place in the line of men and halflings now furiously battling with the waves of attackers as they sought to smash past the pitiful barrier of rocks. Then he crumpled and twisted away. In the wash of light I saw the colors, made meaningless by the pink moons' light, but the emblem was unmistakable. It was a great butterfly so I knew those colors were gold and black.

"I do not want to die!" he moaned now, all the hatred and anger gone, and the pride slipping until only fear was left.

"We've all got to die some time, you calsany! Better in a great fight than rotten with disease in a bed! Draw your sword! Fight!"

Some of the last vestiges of habitual unthinking pride clung to him and he looked up at me, a white face, delicate, weak, foolish. "Do you not know who I am, kleesh! I am Vektor, Kov of Aduimbrev! I do not take orders from a mere Strom."

I looked at him, and the Emperor moved his hand. Pallan Rodway and the High Kov of Erstveheim, two old men and therefore not required in the fighting line, lifted Vektor by the armpits and took him away. I glared sullenly at the Emperor.

"That is Vektor of Aduimbrev! That is the thing you wish to marry your daughter!"

And then I laughed. I roared out a great coarse insulting gutter-bred laugh.

"You thought to rule him when he was married, keep him from getting in your hair! I despise you, Emperor Majister! You sought to soil your daughter by marrying her to a thing like that to serve your own dark and evil ways." And then, because a wash of Chuliks poured in over the wall, such as it was, I pushed him aside. "Get yourself under cover or you will be killed."

An Undurker arrow arched in over the ruins and dropped full for the Emperor's chest. My rapier nicked out, cleanly as we Krozairs of Zy know how, and chopped the arrow away.

"Go on, you old fool Majister!" I roared. "I've a battle to fight and you're getting under my feet!"

The Emperor stared at me with eyes in which an agony had been born. Vomanus ran up. His sword dripped blood.

"They're through on the other side!"

"Thank the Emperor for that and the onker Vektor. They detained me when I should have been fighting. Get everyone back to the central tower, Vomanus. *Move!*"

He ran off and then the smash of Chuliks reached me and I had to skip and jump, slash and thrust, very busily for a space. I left the Chuliks stretched upon the dusty rocks and ran back. I could see the heads of the Bowmen of Loh in the ruined tower, but they were not loosing their deadly shafts.

We had expended all our arrows.

The smaller arrows of the Undurkers were not of great use, but some of the Bowmen, who boasted they could loose a leg of ponsho and hit the chunkrah's eye, let fly and brought down their men. Inside the tower I paused to take stock.

We had lost a lot of men. We were down to twenty-four Bowmen, and sixteen halfling mercenaries. Out there, Furtway, although he had lost large numbers, must still have three or four hundred to hurl against us. And without arrows we were in parlous state.

"Rocks!" I roared. "We will throw rocks down on them and break their skulls!"

"Aye!" shouted Seg Segutorio. "They haven't a chance!"

The men reacted to that. Now they had faced the reality of the situation they knew they must fight on. One reality was, of course, that they had seen me thrust a Fristle through the body when he had attempted to run out toward our foemen, his hands empty and high over his head. That had not been murder. That had been execution of a traitor. I hated it, but it was done in the heat of battle, when the blood sang, when that dreadful and despised red curtain of which I have spoken drops before the eyes, and a man who is a man must struggle to reach past it. The other reality was less starkly brutal; much more of the mores of Kregen. They would earn their pay, these hireling soldiers. They had no complaints now about food and drink, for they sensed they might not live long enough to want.

The Emperor approached me again. "Strom Drak, I would like to speak with you—"

"Not now, Majister. I'm busy. If you've a problem, see Vomanus, or Seg Segutorio."

I spun away and roared vilely at two Chuliks who, in their eagerness to procure rocks for skull-crushing, were prizing loose a stone that would have brought down the upper corner ruins. As we sorted out that, I looked over the jagged masonry wall and saw quite clearly the quick energetic figures of Furtway's men advancing. So Zim and Genodras had risen. So it was daylight.

"All the better for us to see them!" I roared. "They'll be sorry they messed with us!"

We met the enemy as they advanced with a shower of rocks. Men fell, to join the piles of other bodies feathered with the long Lohvian arrows. But they pressed on. I looked for Furtway, Jenbar, and Larghos.

Some new dynamic had been injected into the attack. They came on with a firm tread, ignoring their casualties, and so burst into the foot of the tower. I had ordered everyone aloft on the single rickety platform remaining. From this we hurled down rocks. Arrows sought us. Every now and then a Bowman or a halfling would clutch himself, looking stupidly at the arrow in him, and then pitch forward to crash to the stones beneath. Around then I realized — and despaired as far as ever I allow myself to despair — that the men with me believed all was lost. They did not think we would live through this.

The Emperor with his nobles had been perched right at the top in the highest of the three angled corners remaining. I prowled the canted platform below, urging my men to conserve their rocks and to hurl only when a foeman attempted too boldly to climb. I had brought us into an impasse. This was not my way of fighting. I couldn't get at those rasts down there.

There were few enough of us left now for a breakout to be a possibility. It was our only chance to save the Emperor and his men. I had to make that attempt to save him now. For my Delia's sake.

I went up and told him.

He looked at me, and a look on his face I could not fathom made me return it with as ugly a glare as any I have bestowed on an unfortunate in my life.

"We stand a good chance now, Majister, and we will leave no one behind except the wounded who cannot run. And," I added bitterly, "they are mostly below, poor devils, well on their way to the Ice Floes of Sicce."

The Emperor said, "You are a wild and strange man, Drak. I thought this even when I heard of your exploits on Valka, when I signed your patent of nobility." He pulled and pushed a ring on his middle left finger. "Well, Strom Drak. If you save me alive from here, I will do more than make you a Strom, or a Vad, or a Kov. You will be fit to be called Prince Majister of Vallia."

"You'll have to tie up your garments," I said. "And take a good grip on my tunic, and belt. If you let go I can't save you. I shall need both hands for climbing."

"Did you hear what I said?"

"Yes. No time now. Titles mean nothing to me. Your life, Majister, means only something you wouldn't understand."

Vomanus came over and reported a stir below. I looked down.

Trylon Larghos was there, full of life and good cheer, beaming up, confident of victory.

"Let me speak to the Emperor!"

I hurled a rock at him and, stupidly, missed, for he jumped aside. The rock splintered and a chip struck him in the eye, and screeching and spouting blood over his hands as he clasped his face, he collapsed. I went up again.

"Now is the time, Majister." He was ready. Vomanus and Seg assisted the other old men. We went to the back of the tower and squeezed through the lower windows. Opposite us the forest of petrified bones glittered in the mingled opaz light. We began that climb down the walls. The Emperor hung on my back a dead weight. I watched a Fristle let go and scream his way to the ground, landing in a red puddle, and I cursed the fool for betraying what we were doing.

We slid, slipped, and scraped our way down. In the song that has been made of the fight at The Dragon's Bones, the tempo becomes mocking here, talking of the loss of skin, the sweat in our eyes, the ripped fingernails, and the blood-streaks down the ruined walls. But that is the Kregan way. They often mock where their emotions run deep.

We reached the floor of the clearing and at once we started for the bones opposite.

I thought we would make it.

"Go on, Majister! I will take the rear — just in case."

They ran on, a clump of old men, halflings, and Bowmen. I found Seg at my side, and Vomanus at the other. All our weapons were caked with blood. I spoke viciously.

"Go on, you two! Stick with the Emperor."

Vomanus said, "You have been giving us orders very freely, Dray. Now, I think, we will disobey you."

Seg said, "You go with the Emperor, Dray, if you like."

Comrades.

We would do it. We were almost there.

A great swirling flood of mercenaries burst around the shattered corner of the tower and raced across the dust toward us. Many races and species were there, all thirsting for our blood. I could hear their shrill shrieks of triumph.

"Run, Majister!" I roared. "Run, by Vox, run for the sake of your daughter."

He half turned to look back, and I waved my rapier at him and yelled: "I didn't come here to rescue you! But you're rescued now! Get in among the bones and you're safe! *Run!*"

Then we three, Seg, Vomanus, and I, turned to face the death running so swiftly upon us.

Twenty

Delia

A great song has been made of the fight at The Dragon's Bones, but I will not give you its title. It runs to a mere seventy-eight stanzas, but every one is turned and polished like a gemstone, and when I hear it the blood thumps and thrills through my veins. Perhaps, at least to me, there is no finer passage than that which follows. But I, speaking in English, can only tell you in my plain sailor-man's prose what happened. You must dream of the wonder-images, the defeat and triumph, the despair and hope, the smell of blood and sweat, the slick taste of dust, the feel of a rapier hilt hard in the fingers, the main-gauche gripped in the left fist; hear the devilish shrieks and yells of the wounded and maimed, the screams of the dying. You must blend all this into a mighty uproar in the brain.

We fought.

Vomanus was a fine rapier man, as I knew. Seg Segutorio was the finest archer in two worlds. Yet we wouldnot have lasted more than a few murs, but for the wonder.

How to tell you of that moment?

We heard yells, surprised shouts, and the press upon us slackened. We could gulp for air, wipe the sweat from our foreheads, and look about. We were all wounded, but we lived. We looked about, we looked up — oh, the wonder, the wonder of it!

The sky filled with airboats.

They slanted down from the east, so that I guessed Inch must have swung his fleet from the Blue Mountains around. And in that I was wrong. Gloriously wrong!

The fliers landed in the clearing and men poured out.

Such men!

I didn't believe it then. I just stood there, my mouth open, my rapier and dagger hanging limply, and any onker of a rast could have run me through as I gaped.

The very first man to hit the dusty rock of the clearing wore russet leathers, tasseled and fringed, with cunning pieces of armor strapped where they would protect the most. He wore a helmet, but I knew his hair was fair and bleached by the Suns of Antares. He swung an ax, double-bitted and daggered with six niches of flat-bladed steel. Belted at his side swung a great broadsword and a deadly shortsword. Over his back he carried, ready strung, a short reflex compound bow.

Hap Loder!

Running swiftly with him was a ferocious being all dun-colored hide and bristly bullet-head, massive shoulders, and short sinewy legs, clad in as brilliant a scarlet breech-clout as you will find on Kregen. He wore parts of armor, too, and carried a rapier and main-gauche. I smiled, guessing he had been taking lessons.

Gloag!

With these two ran a young man clad all in powder blue, with an elegant and handsome appearance, his bronzed face keen and his black eyes alert. He wore cropped hair beneath his steel cap. He handled his rapier and main-gauche with superb authority, a true bravo-fighter of Zenicce.

Varden! Prince Varden Wanek of the House of Eward!

Following on rushed a great crowd of men clad in the russet leathers of my clansmen, the brave scarlet of Strombor, the powder blue of Eward — and there were even a few bravos wearing the silver and black of the Reinmans, and the crimson and gold of the Wickens.

I saw those old familiar faces — Loku, Rov Kovno, Ark Atvar, fierce merciless clansmen sworn in obi brotherhood to me. And — and by Diproo the Nimble-fingered! There ran Nath the Thief, dressed up in clansmen's russets and the scarlet of Strombor, with an empty lesten-hide bag flapping at his side ready to be filled with the loot his nimble fingers could close on!

How I stared!

My men — my ferocious Clansmen of Felschraung with their horrendous axes and broadswords, and my bravo-fighters of Strombor! I had not seen them for long and long; but they had not forgotten me, for as they smashed like a solid wall of iron and steel into the panic-stricken mob of Furtway's mercenaries, they were yelling and roaring it out: "Hai! Jikai! Dray Prescot! Jikai!"

My clansmen roared in a deep rolling thunder of noise: "Hai! Zorcander! Hai! Vovedeer!" With the last they exaggerated, as they always did.

My men of Strombor roared in a high fierce screeching: "Hai! Strombor! Strombor!"

Furtway's men had little chance — hell! — they had no chance at all!

My clansmen, the most ferocious and brave warriors in all Kregen, simply smashed over the rapiers and daggers like a single wave blots out a fragile bridge. A few Undurkers let fly with their arrows, and from the rear ranks of the clansmen rose a sheeting storm from the cruel reflex bone and horn bows, and the Undurkers fled. They had recognized clansmen, and however impossible it was for clansmen to be here in the heart of Vallia — they were here, in iron and steel and blood!

The axes rose and fell. The great broadswords scythed. The shortswords stabbed, in and out, very deadly.

Then Vomanus, who had been staring with the eyes goggling in his head, shouted and pointed.

A second aerial armada settled down in the space cleared of dinosaur bones. The first man out was Inch, waving his huge Saxon-pattern ax, roaring into action to chop at an angle into the crazed mob of Furtway's mercenaries. I did not see the Kov Furtway, or his nephew Jenbar, or the wounded Trylon Larghos, but word was brought to me they had managed to escape. And I was willing they should go, for the score between us lay on a personal basis. Much more important, though, was the fact that the Star Lords wanted Furtway alive for their own schemes. I had been prepared to balk them and see the man slain for what he had tried to do, but I own I felt a certain relief, a cowardly relief, if you will, that the Star Lords would not have reason to toss me back to Earth.

Following Inch and his Saxon ax raced Korf Aighos at the head of the Blue Mountain Boys. I saw the way many swung the great sword of war of the Blue Mountains, even Ob-eye, and the flash and glitter from sharp-honed edges before they stained a more sinister hue.

After that it was all over. Then — I did shout.

"Majister! You may come out of the bones, now. You are safe."

He crawled out. He tried to arrange his robes, but they were torn and bedraggled. The sacred emblem strung around his neck winked blindingly in a flash of gold as he lifted his head. He did not look frightened, of that he cannot stand accused. But there was about him an air of shrunken pride and tawdry magnificence, the arrogance shredded away to a reality he had never had to face before. He walked slowly toward me followed by his retinue of old men. Among them I could not see Kov Vektor.

And then, for me at least, came the greatest wonder of all.

My men had fashioned a litter of dinosaur bones and over it flung a great scarlet silk, very grand in the suns-light. Golden cushions bestrewed the scarlet silk. They had lifted the litter high, proudly. Reclining there, warm and vibrant and altogether magnificent against the gold and scarlet, holding in her left hand the staff of Old Superb, my old flag with the yellow cross on the red field — *Delia!*

They carried her, those men of mine, they carried her proudly as befitted a princess. And no princess in two worlds ever had so proud or gallant a party so to carry her. My men! They carried my Princess in triumph before me, and over all waved the old flag of mine, Old Superb, as men called that flag, waving in the streaming mingled light from the twin Suns of Scorpio.

I heard Vomanus smother an exclamation. Then he and Seg were running, and in a twinkling they, too, were carrying that precious burden high before the Emperor of Vallia.

That Emperor, that proud man, looked at me most uncertainly.

"They shout a name, I think," he said. "Do you not hear the name they shout, Strom Drak?"

"Oh, aye, Majister, I hear." I would not take my eyes off my Delia to stare at him.

His voice reached me, whispering. "I am the Emperor, the Emperor of Vallia, the greatest power in Kregen." He might believe that; I did not, not when Havilfar provided airboats and those mysterious ships raided up from the southern oceans. "I keep my word," said Delia's father. "And, in truth, I believed myself already dead, and the promise of no great value."

Delia was smiling at me. I stared back, entranced.

"What promise was that?"

"I said that if you rescued me I would make you Prince Majister, Strom Drak."

"Oh, yes, I remember." I lifted my voice. I shouted to my men as they drew near bearing the dear form of my Princess. "Hai! Jikai!" And I hailed them, High Jikai, every one, by name.

The High Jikai is not lightly given on Kregen.

It came to me then in those tumultuous moments that nothing is purely perfect. There were two more faces I would fain have seen in that throng bearing so high and proudly my Delia, my Delia of Delphond. I would dearly have loved to see Nath and Zolta, my two oar-comrades, from far Sanurkazz. But that could not be, and I doubted not but that the Star Lords by their prior designs had thwarted that accomplishment, which would have been very great and wonderful indeed.

The dinosaur-bone litter lowered. Then I saw how my Delia was dressed as the great yellow and red flag lofted away. She wore the scarlet breechclout of Strombor. And over her shoulders gleamed those magnificent silky white ling furs I had won for her on the Plains of Segesthes. Lithely, her long lissome legs very wonderful to behold, she stepped down from the litter and ran to me.

My Delia, my Delia of Delphond, my Delia of the Blue Mountains! She ran to me and threw herself into my arms and she was laughing, sobbing, and crying my name, over and over.

"Hush, hush, my darling," I said. "And tell me how you did it."

It was superbly simple. Her airboat had been driven by that westerly gale and sent wildly toward the east, so that any hopes of her summoning rescue from the Blue Mountains had vanished. So — she had flown on to Strombor! And in their regular visits during the season Hap Loder and my Clansmen of Felschraung and Longuelm had been there, also. They had scoured the whole of Zenicce for airboats, and by gold and thievery — and here Nath the Thief hopped about from leg to leg in his excitement — they had drummed up the great armada, and had flown here as though all the glaciers of the Ice Floes of Sicce were calving around their necks. They hadn't bothered overmuch with food or drink, so as to cram every last fighting-man in, and now they were about to raid the rebels' camp. "And, Dray, my puissant Lord of Strombor, I have been paying regular visits to Zenicce season by season. Great-Aunt Shusha and all the others send you their love."

"Sink me!" I said, laughing. "I have a managing female to contend with!" And I hugged her close.

My men swaggered around us, for they knew the great Jikai they had performed, and as the song whose title I will not tell you says, great was the performance thereof.

Then I stood her off from me and said: "Your father—"

"I will treat him gently, Dray."

And I had feared and hesitated all this time!

We stood before the Emperor of Vallia in his ragged robes, and at my back bristled the weapons and the colors of my men, victorious in battle. I said softly, "Kiss him, Delia, embrace him."

She did so. And, watching them, I saw the real affection there. Delia looked back at me from the crook of her father's arm.

"I heard a name, Strom Drak — Strom of Valka — a name…" the Emperor said.

"Aye," I said. "You ordered my head chopped off. Do you think that a great jest now, Majister?"

He licked his lips. I believe that many men there expected me to order his head off, on the instant. That would have been the justice Kregen understands. Crude, violent; something I, not only for my own sins but for the purposes of the Savanti, wished to change.

He walked with his daughter toward me. He slid a great ring from his finger. He held it out. His hand did not tremble.

"By this ring you are now legally and heritably Prince of Vallia, Drak—"

And Delia said with her brilliant laugh: "Call him by his name, Father dear. For this is Pur Dray Prescot, Krozair of Zy, Lord of Strombor, Zorcander of Felschraung and Longuelm, Strom of Valka — and what else besides I shouldn't wonder. And, my father, know also that he is the man I shall marry, no matter if the whole of Kregen, let alone Vallia, stands in the way!"

She had placed Krozair of Zy in the prime position. I know my Delia understood.

"I am plain Dray Prescot," I said. I took Delia's hand. "And this is the woman who is my wife. We belong to each other."

He braced up. He was, after all, the Emperor.

"Dray Prescot. Dray. You are, as far as I and Vallia are concerned, Prince Majister Dray. And" — he swallowed and his hand closed on the sacred emblem strung on a golden chain about his neck — "and you have my blessing, both of you."

The hullabaloo racketed skyward, enormous, booming, uproarious. "Hai! Jikai!" The swords flashed skyward, glittering, shining, a forest of flashing blades. "Hai, Dray Prescot, Prince Majister of Vallia!"

Yes, they know how to do things with style in Kregen.

The sacred ring, emblem of the Majister, flashed and scintillated on my finger. I detest rings; this would go with the ring of Valka, safely sealed away to perform its duties on the days set apart. I held my Delia and I could not let her go.

Quietly, I spoke to the Emperor. "The third party has set Vallians against Vallians. But now that you are safe we can set about repairing the damage. I think Kov Furtway and Jenbar, no less than Trylon Larghos and the others, will fly for safety overseas. We can put Vallia back to rights."

And, I promised myself, with Delia's help we'd eradicate the obscenity of slavery from the place. That would take time. But we would do it. Had that been the reason for the Star Lords' manipulations of me?

I looked up, but I could see neither the scarlet and golden raptor of the Star Lords, nor the white dove of the Savanti. They would make further appearances, this I knew, during my life on Kregen. The Savanti might have thrown me out of paradise, and I would now prosecute diligent inquiries to find the scarlet-roped Todalpheme who might show me the way back to Aphrasöe; they had also thrown me upon the mercy of the Star Lords. For how long would I remain a Prince of Vallia at the side of my Princess?

I held her close. The wedding ceremony would be performed very soon. Korf Aighos whispered to me, and I laughed, and said to Delia: "Certain friends of ours discovered a king's ransom in wedding presents hidden in a gorge in the Blue Mountains. They think it proper they should be given to you, my Princess."

We felt a stroke of sadness that Vektor, Kov of Aduimbrev, had died of heart failure occasioned through fear as he ran for the palisade of bones; but death is cheap on Kregen, and life is for the living. Those wedding presents were fit for a princess, so a princess should receive them.

There was great feasting and great drinking beneath the Suns of Scorpio. Then we all took the airboats and flew for Vondium. I stood very close to Delia. How to believe that, at last, we had won each other? I was hers as much as she was mine. She looked up into my eyes and searched my ugly old face, and she sighed, and snuggled closer to me.

From the airboat floated the flags of Vallia and Prescot; the yellow saltire on the red ground, and the yellow cross on the red ground, and I saw what must be done with those.

"Are you content, Dray, my darling?"

"With you by my side, how could I not be?"

"With all these old comrades, Hap Loder, Gloag, Prince Varden, with Inch and dear Seg and all the others, I believe you think of your two rascals, Nath and Zolta."

Delia had never met those two unlikely specimens, but she understood. "Aye," I said. "And of Zorg, who is dead."

"Do not speak of death, Dray, not now! Now we have everything to live for! All of Vallia!"

"Yes." I hugged her and then said, "You did not mention Vomanus."

"No?" She looked around. "There should be no secrets between us. But this is a high state secret, so mind it! I think you believed Vomanus would marry me, was a rival, as those fool racters thought—"

"Well, woman?"

She chuckled, a silver tinkle of merriment against the swift passage of the flier.

"Vomanus is the son of my mother, before she married my father. He is my half-brother."

"No wonder," was all I could say. "He said Kovs were Kovs and Kovs to him!"

She laughed again, and so we stood there, together, with my fighting-men at my back, sailing under the twin yellow and red flags, as we sailed beneath the twin Suns of Scorpio casting down their mingled opaz radiance, sailing for Vondium and marriage and happiness.

I, Dray Prescot, of Earth, had found my home.

A Note on Prescot's Map of Part of Kregen

The map of a part of Kregen, that cruel and beautiful planet four hundred light-years away under the Suns of Scorpio, appearing in this volume, number five, of the Saga of Prescot of Antares, presents a new and strange turn of events in the fascinating story of Dray Prescot. The paper appears to be a completely ordinary white bond, the outlines are drawn with a blue felt-nibbed pen, apparently free-hand, and names and features are inserted in pencil. There is a red-lined border, and towns and cities are indicated by small red dots.

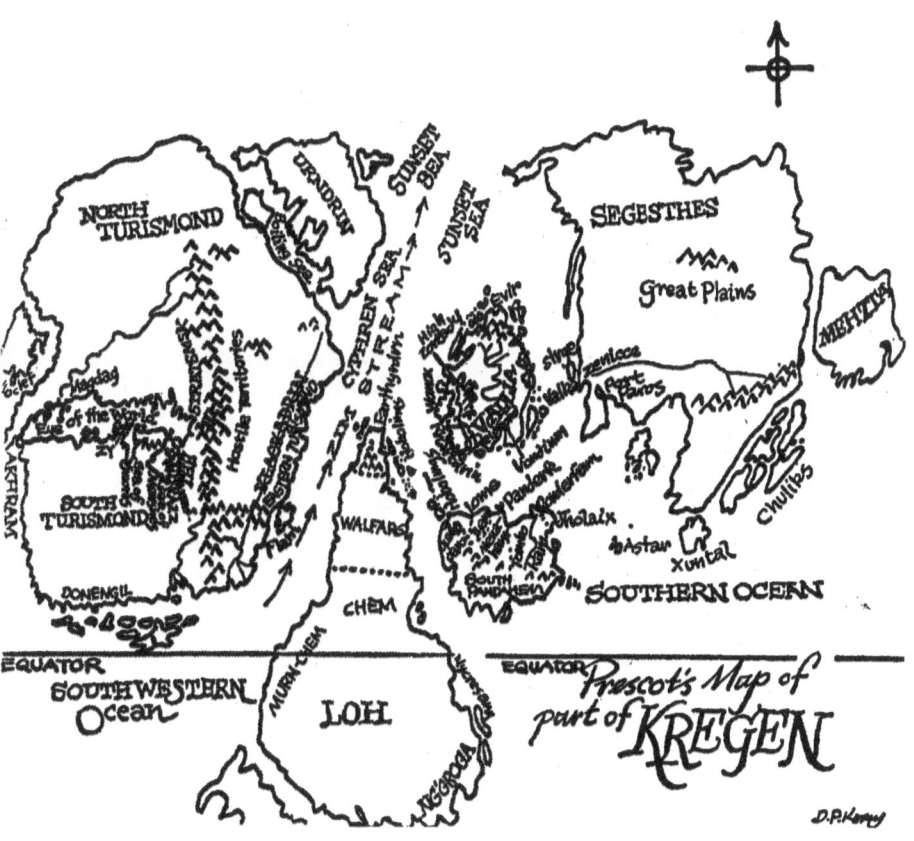

Various distances and bearings Prescot has mentioned from time to time in his story are now supported by this map, and we are now able to grasp more fully at an understanding of the topography of this savage world and where his adventures have taken him. In the bottom right-hand corner appear the letters *D. P. Krzy* faintly written in pencil in an old-fashioned script.

Dray Prescot is a man above medium height, with straight brown hair and brown eyes that are level and oddly dominating. His shoulders are immensely wide and there is about him an abrasive honesty, and a fearless courage. He moves like a great hunting cat, quiet and deadly. Born in 1775, he presents a picture of himself that, the more we learn of him, grows no less enigmatic.

Through the machinations of the Savanti nal Aphrasöe, mortal but superhuman men dedicated to the aid of humanity, and of the Star Lords, he has been taken to Kregen many times. In his early years he rose to become Zorcander among the Clansmen of Segesthes, and Lord of Strombor in Zenicce, and then a member of the mystic and martial Order of Krozairs of Zy. During this period he was guided by the single purpose of making his way to Vallia and there claiming his beloved, Delia of Delphond, Delia of the Blue Mountains. Able to afford assistance to Pando, boy Kov of Bormark in Pandahem, Prescot was abruptly flung back to Earth in the moment of triumph. He passes over that stay on Earth with a few brief sentences and welcomes wholeheartedly the summons of the Scorpion once more. His thoughts are clearly fixed on Kregen, that savage and beautiful, marvelous and terrible world of headlong adventure. He takes up the story when he is once more summoned to plunge at once into new and chilling danger, and that is where *Prince of Scorpio* begins.

This volume, *Prince of Scorpio,* then, brings to a satisfying conclusion the story contained in the first five books of the Saga of Prescot of Antares. The forthcoming volume, tentatively entitled *Manhounds of Antares,* begins a new cycle. I have taken the liberty of calling the first five books "The Delian Cycle," and with the next volume we are launched on "The Havilfar Cycle."

I have worked up a glossary which, through the kindness of the Publisher, Donald A. Wollheim, who suggested it, is appended to this volume. This should prove of great value to all those who have — as I have myself — followed with such thrilling fascination the Saga of Prescot of Antares.

Alan Burt Akers

648

A Glossary of Persons, Places, and Things in the Delian Cycle

References to the previous Scorpio books are given as:
TT: Transit to Scorpio
SU: The Suns of Scorpio
WA: Warrior of Scorpio
SS: Swordships of Scorpio

A

Aduimbrev: A province of Vallia, of which Vektor was Kov.

Aighos: A chieftain of the Blue Mountain Boys, nicknamed Korf.

Akhram: A castle and observatory at the eastern end of the Grand Canal in which the Todalpheme of Akhram carry on their work.

Angia, Kotera: Mother of Anko the Chisel.

Anko the Chisel: Cabinet-maker rescued from the bagnio in Vondium.

Aph, River: Great river down which Prescot sailed on his first visit to Kregen (TT).

Aphrasöe: The Swinging City. Built among giant plant-forms in a lake on the River Aph and inhabited by the Savanti (TT).

aragorn: Mercenary reavers and slavers.

Archbold: A leader of any of the Orders of Chivalry dedicated to Zair.

argenter: An oceangoing ship of Pandahem, broad and comfortable.

Arkasson: A city in the Hostile Territories.

Arkhebi, Hikdar: Captain of Katrin Rashumin's airboat.

Armipand: One of the devils in the pantheon of Pandahem.

Askinard: A land famed for its spices.

Atvar, Ark: A Jiktar of the Clan of Felschraung (TT).

B

balass: A wood similar to ebony, from which is made the balass stick, the title of authority of the petty overseers of the workers of Magdag.

Bargom: Young Bargom, son of Old Bargom, a Valkan, proprietor of *The Rose of Valka,* an inn and posting house in Vondium.

barynth: A large monster of great sinuousness and length, a hideous head, and four forward-grasping limbs.

beng: A saint.

benga: A female saint.

Benga Deste: Hot springs and a place of pilgrimage in West Segesthes.

Beng-Kishi: These famous bells are said to ring in the skull of anyone hit on the head. This happens frequently on Kregen.

Berran: The Vadvar of Rifuji, an estate in Vallia.

Black Chunkrah, By the: A clansman's oath.

Black Mountains: A range of lesser heights extending northward from the Blue Mountains.

bloin: A cultivated crop plant with a tall brittle green stem from which the fruits hang like golden bells.

Bloody Menaham, The: Name given by the Tomboramin to their neighbors of Menaham on Pandahem.

Blue Mountain Boys: Ruffians, bandits, mountain men, dedicated to Delia, the Princess Majestrix.

Blue Mountains: A small though lofty amphitheater-shaped mass of mountains in Western Vallia. The foothills and plain forming part of the province are famous for zorcamen and zorca-breeding. Delia's inheritance.

bokkertu: Legal business.

Bold: A Krozair Brother, generally one serving permanently in any of the fortresses of the Orders.

Borg, Ven, nal Ogier: A canalman of Vallia.

Bormark: A Kovnate on the western border of Tomboram.

bosk: A smaller form of vosk, a specialty of Valka.

Bowmen of Loh, The: A notorious song.

box: Small spined animal of the Segesthan plains.

Brokelsh: A squat-bodied people with much black bristle body hair. bur: The Kregan hour, approximately forty Terrestrial minutes.

C

calsany: A beast of burden.

Can-thirda: Large island to the east of Vallia.

Canticles of the Rose City, The: A myth-cycle at least three thousand years old concerning a half-legendary, half-historical man-god named Drak.

Careless Repose: Renders' hideout in the Hoboling Islands.

cham: A juicy rubbery fruit much chewed by workers.

chanks: Sharks of the inner sea.

Chem: The central tropical rain forests of Loh.

chemzite: A precious stone of great value.

Chersonang: A city of the Hostile Territories in opposition to Hiclantung.

Cherwangtung: Area of the Hostile Territories from which nocturnal primitives raid.

Chuktar: Commander of ten thousand. Military ranks have become nonspecific on Kregen now and do not denote the actual number of men commanded. There are many and various subdivisions of the four main ranks.

Chuliks: An extremely fierce and manlike race of people with oily yellow skin, the head shaved so as to leave a long pigtail, two three-inch-long tusks thrusting upward from the corners of the cruel mouth, and round black eyes. The training of the males from birth is designed to produce high-quality mercenary soldiers; they are employed all over Kregen and they generally command higher fees than other races.

chunkrah: A very large cattle animal, deep-chested, horned, fierce, with a russet coat, the mainstay of the clansmen of Segesthes.

clerketer: Leather harness attaching the rider to impiters or corths or other flying birds or animals of Turismond.

Company of Friends: Organizations of nobles and businessmen for trade in Vallia.

corth: Large saddle bird, splendidly marked in a variety of colors.

cramph: Term of abuse.

crested-korf: Large iridescent-blue-feathered bird of the Blue Mountains.

crofermen: Men-beasts — savage, untamed, cruel, and suspicious — inhabiting the outer portions of The Stratemsk.

Cyphren Sea: The sea separating Turismond from Loh.

D

Dam of Days: Colossal dam controlling the tides through the strait connecting the Eye of the World with the outer ocean.

Dancing Talu: A narrow boat owned by Ven Yelker nal Ogier.

Dean, Geoffrey: Recipient of *The Tapes from Africa* from Dan Fraser, passing them on to A.B.A.

Deldar: Commander of ten. The petty officers in charge of the drum, whips, and helm aboard ship commonly hold this rank.

Delia: Princess Majestrix of Vallia, Delia of the Blue Mountains, Delia of Delphond.

Delian Cycle, The: The first five books of the Saga of Prescot of Antares.

Delka Dwa: A one-time fortress town of Vindelka on the border of the Ocher Limits.

Delka Ob: Capital of the Kovnate province of Vindelka in Vallia.

Delphond: A province of Vallia situated on the southern coast, a rich, lazy, carefree, happy land. Dedicated to Delia.

dhem: Silver coin of Pandahem.

Diproo the Nimble-fingered, By: A thieves' oath.

dom: Kregish equivalent of English "mate" or American "pal."

Donengil: Coastal lands and islands of South Turismond.

dopa: A fiendish drink guaranteed to make a man fighting drunk.

Doty: Name of a personage or spirit used in invective by the aragorn and slave-masters of Vallia.

Dragon's Bones, The: A giant crater in the Ocher Limits filled with fossilized risslaca and mammal bones where Prescot was created Prince Majister of Vallia.

Drak: Name used on occasion by Dray Prescot.

Drak's Seat: Mountain peak in the form of a throne to the northeast of Vondium.

drin: Suffix in Kregish denoting "land."

dromviler: Vessel of the inner sea propelled partly by sail and partly by oar, used mainly by the Sorzarts.

dwa: Two.

dwabur: Measurement of length, approximately five miles.

dwbrs: Abbreviation of dwaburs.

E

Eling, Pallan: Minister (Secretary) of State of Vallia responsible for the canals.

Empire of Loh: More properly, the Empire of Walfarg. Empire carved out by Walfarg taking in all of Loh, Pandahem, Eastern Turismond, the Hoboling Islands, and other areas. Now completely fallen, although there are traces left in various countries — roads, religions, culture, fashions.

Encar of the Fields: Elder, appointed by Prescot, responsible for agriculture in Valka.

Erdgar the Shipwright: Elder, appointed by Prescot, responsible for dock-yards and shipping in Valka.

Erithor of Valkanium: A bard and song-maker of Valka held in high renown throughout Vallia.

Erthyrdrin: Land of mountains and valleys in the northernmost tip of Loh, famed for its Bowmen, the finest of Loh. Birthplace of Seg Segutorio.

Erthyr the Bow: The Supreme Being of Erthyrdrin.

Erstveheim, High Kov of: Councillor of the Presidio of Vallia.

Esser Rarioch: The high fortress overlooking Valkanium.

Esztercari: A noble house of Zenicce. Cydones was Prince of the House of Esztercari during Prescot's sojourn there (TT).

Everoinye: The Star Lords.

Evir: Northernmost province of Vallia.

Eward: A noble house of Zenicce. Wanek was Prince of the House of Eward during Prescot's sojourn there (TT).

Eye of the World: The inner sea of the continent of Turismond.

F

Falinur: A Kovnate province of Vallia.

fallimy: A little blue flower made into a paste to scour cisterns clean. Applied as a poultice to Prescot's chest by Thelda (WA).

Farris, Lord of Vomansoir: A Chuktar in the Vallian Air Service.

Fatal Love of Vela na Valka, The: A music drama known over most of Kregen.

Faygar, Strom of Vorgan: A member of the Racter party, owing allegiance to the Kov of Vomansoir. In his Stromnate Prescot first saw the headless zorcamen.

Felschraung: A clan of nomads roving the Great Plains of Segesthes. Prescot took obi of them and rose to be Zorcander (TT).

Felteraz: A harbor, town, fortress, and estate a few dwaburs east of Sanurkazz. A spot of exceptional beauty. Home of Mayfwy.

Fetching of Drak na Valka, The: Song made by Erithor of Valkanium commemorating Prescot's fetching freedom to Valka, by fetching the people to resist, and of their fetching of him, as Drak, to be their Strom. Runs to seven hundred and seventy-eight stanzas.

Flahi: An island group off the coast of Eastern Turismond.

Flahians: People of remarkable physical structure living on Flahi.

flick-flick: A plant with orange cone-shaped flowers and six-foot-long tendrils expert at fly-catching; kept in Kregan houses and kitchens for that purpose.

Foke the Ob-handed: A render who perpetrated atrocities in Valka.

Forpacheng: A treacherous councillor of Hiclantung who sold out to Umgar Stro (WA).

Fraser, Dan: In West Africa he afforded Prescot the opportunity to tell his story, resulting in *The Tapes from Africa*.

Fristle: Furred and bewhiskered cat-people, fierce and treacherous, often employed as mercenaries. Their racial weapon is the scimitar.

Furtway, Naghan, Kov of Falinur: A great lord of Vallia, rescued by Prescot from the Mountains of the North on orders from the Star Lords.

Fwymay: Daughter of Zorg and Mayfwy of Felteraz.

G

Gansk: A city of the northern shore of the inner sea.

Gdoinye: A giant scarlet and gold raptor, messenger and spy of the Star Lords.

Genal the Ice: An iceman of the Mountains of the North.

Genodras: The green sun of Antares.

Glittering Caves: Quarries and catacombs in jeweled mountains just outside Arkasson (SS).

Gloag: A Mehzta, slave of the Esztercaris, freed by Prescot to become a good comrade (TT).

Glycas: A prince of Magdag (SU).

Goforeng: A fortress city of the green north coast of the inner sea.

Golda: A great lady of Aphrasöe (TT).

Gons: A race who, ashamed of their white hair, habitually shave their heads bald.

Grace of Grodno: A swifter of Magdag (SU).

graint: A stubborn beast resembling a bear, but with eight legs and crocodile-like jaws extending for over eighteen inches.

Grakki-Grodno: Magdaggian sky-god of draft beasts.

Grand Archbold: Spiritual and temporal head of the Krozairs of Zy.

Grand Canal: Five miles wide, connects the inner sea with the outer oceans.

Great Northern Cut: A main canal of Vallia beginning in Vondium.

Great River: The major river of Vallia, winding from the Mountains of the North to the south coast where stands Vondium. Also known as Mother of Waters, and She of Fecundity.

green sun: Besides Genodras it has many thousands of names; Kokimur, Ryufraison, He of the Green Spear, Havil, are four.

gregarians: A Kregan fruit.

grint: A small creature like a six-legged opossum of the Owlarh Waste.

Grodno: The green-sun deity.

Grodno-Gasta: A blasphemously insulting epithet used against the people of Grodno.

grundal: Rock-ape of the inner sea, with six spiderish limbs and a gray pelt; large mouth closing in folds of flesh, opening to a round, and armed with concentric rows of needlelike teeth. Vicious, cowardly, and deadly when hunting in packs.

Gurush of the Bottomless Marsh, By: A canalman's oath.

Gyphimedes: The immortal mistress of the beloved of Grodno.

H

halflings: General term for the beast-men, man-beasts of Kregen.

Hall na Priags: A sacred chamber within one of the colossal megaliths of Magdag (SU).

Happy Swinging: Parting salutation in Aphrasöe.

Harfnars: Half-men of Chersonang, with flat noses across their faces wide as their lips, brilliant lemur-like eyes, squared-off chins and foreheads. Hereditary foemen of Hiclantung, they are well-armed and armored after the decadent fashion of Loh.

Havilfar: A continent of Kregen.

Havilfar Cycle, The: The second cycle in the Saga of Prescot of Antares.

Havilfarese: The people of any nation of Havilfar.

Heart Heights: Mountains and massif central in the center of Valka.

hibisum flour: Used in the Blue Mountains for baking ponsho tender.

Hiclantung: A city of the Hostile Territories ruled by Queen Lilah.

High Zorcady: Capital of the province of the Blue Mountains in Vallia.

Hikdar: Commander of a hundred.

Hlabro, Mount: A peak in Erthyrdrin.

Hlo-Hli: A spirit of Loh, appealed to and sworn by.

Hobolings: A race very squat of body and long of arm and leg, excellent topmen, inhabitants of the Hoboling Islands.

Hoboling Islands: Chain of islands stretching from Erthyrdrin to Northwest Pandahem off the northeast coast of Loh.

Hostile Territories: Area of central East Turismond between The Stratemsk and the Klackadrin, cut off from the outside world since the collapse of the Empire of Loh.

Hrunchuk: Idol in the temple gardens across the forbidden canal in Zenicce. Has three enormously valuable eyes.

humespack: Cloth used for clothing.

Hunter, Alex: Earthman sent by the Savanti on a mission to Valka.

Hurtado, Don, de Oquendo: Spaniard who taught Prescot rapier fighting.

I

ib: Spirit of the dead.

Ice Floes of Sicce: One of the versions of a Kregan hell.

impiter: Gigantic coal-black flying animal of Turismond, the mainstay of various races' aerial cavalry, as a saddle animal.

Inch: From Ng'groga. Seven feet tall, extraordinarily thin, with long fair hair. Wields an ax of the Saxon pattern. Obsessed with his taboos. A good comrade to Prescot.

Invisible Twins: see Opaz.

Isteria: Small island a comfortable day's pull from Sanurkazz.

J

Jenbar, Tyr: Nephew to Naghan Furtway, Kov of Falinur.

Jeniu: Old panval shipwrecked in Valka on the way to Penal islands.

Jholaix: Nation in the northeast of Pandahem famed for her wines.

Jikai!: A word of complex meaning; used in different forms means: "Kill!" "Warrior." "A noble feat of arms." "Bravo!" Many other related concepts to do with honor, pride, and warrior-status.

Jikaida: A board game combining chess, checkers, and Halma-like moves on a checkerboard of a rectangular shape: a war-game.

jikaider: To flog crisscross.

Jiktar: Commander of a thousand.

K

kalasbrune: A building material of great value.

king korf: Larger than the crested-korf; found in Erthyrdrin; its feathers are prized for fletching.

Klackadrin: A long narrow fault in the crust of Kregen running from the Boiling Sea in the north to the Lesser Stratemsk in the south of Eastern Turismond. Gives off hallucinogenic gases.

kleesh: Violently unpleasant, repulsive, stinking — an insult.

knuckle: Approximately 4.2 inches.

Kodifex: Leader of the Assembly in Zenicce, elected from among the Princes and the chiefs of the Houses of Zenicce.

Korer, Captain: Captain of a Valkan galleon.

Koter: A Vallian gentleman. Kr. is the abbreviation.

Kotera: A Vallian lady. Kta. is the abbreviated form.

Kothmir: Once a part of the Empire of Loh.

Kov: Title of Kregan nobility, approximating to "Duke."

Kovneva: Duchess.

Kovnate: An estate or province of a Kov.

Kovno, Rov: A Jiktar of the clan of Longuelm (TT).

Kregen: Planet circling Antares. Kregan is the adjective. Kregish is the language in universal use. There are many local tongues.

Krozair: Member of an Order dedicated to Zair.

Krz. Abbreviation for Krozair.

Krzy. Abbreviation for the Krozairs of Zy.

Kutven: Leader of the Vens of the canalfolk.

L

Lahal: Universal greeting for friend or acquaintance.

Larghos, Nath, Trylon of the Black Mountains: A Vallian nobleman.

Lashenda: Once a part of the Empire of Loh.

laypom: Fruit like a peach of a pale subtle yellow color, exquisite.

leem: A feral beast found in one form or another over most of Kregen. Eight-legged, it is furred, feline, and vicious, with a wedge-shaped head armed with fangs that can strike through oak. It is weasel-shaped but leopard-sized. Its paws can smash a man's head. There are various forms, as sea-leem, snow-leem, marsh-leem, desert-leem, and mountain-leem, each suitably camouflaged.

leepitix: A reptilian twelve-legged wriggler about a foot long infesting the canals. Has a nasty bite but can be frightened off by splashing.

lenk: A very hard wood similar to oak.

Lesser Stratemsk: Spur of The Stratemsk running due east to the coast of Eastern Turismond opposite Flahi.

lesten: A high-class hide used for belts, moneybags, etc.

Likshu the Treacherous: A Chulik divine spirit appealed to and sworn by.

Lilac Bird: Swifter commanded by Pur Zenkiren (SU).

Lilah: Queen of Hiclantung (WA).

ling: Animal as large as a collie dog, with six legs, and claws it can extend to four inches in length and open a rip in chunkrah bide. Lives among the bushes and rocks of the small prairie of Segesthes. Possesses a magnificent lightweight, long and silky white fur.

Llahal: Universal greeting for stranger.

Loder, Hap: Was Jiktar of the Clan of Felschraung when he gave obi to Prescot. Appointed Zorcander in Prescot's absence but remains intensely loyal and devoted to Prescot. A good comrade (TT).

Loguetter cheese: A first-quality cheese.

Loh: A continent of Kregen.

Loku: A Hikdar of the Clan of Felschraung (TT).

Lome: A nation in the northwest of Pandahem.

longsword, the Krozair: A perfectly balanced two-handed longsword with wide-spaced handgrips, able to be used one-handed, subject of rigorous and demanding training and mystical exercises. A terrible weapon of destruction.

Longuelm: A clan of the Great Plains of Segesthes, allied with the Clan of Felschraung under Prescot as Zorcander.

loomins: Mauve and white flowers.

Lord of Strombor: Dray Prescot.

Lorenztone: A Vallian Air Service flier.

lupu: A trance state induced by the Wizards of Loh.

lurfings: Low-bellied, lean-flanked, gray-furred scavengers of the plains with probing snout-like faces.

Lu-si-Yuong: A Wizard of Loh (WA).

M

ma faril: Translates out as "my dear."

magbird: Black carrion-eating bird of Magdag.

Magdag: Chief city of Grodno on the northern shore of the inner sea.

Maiden with the Many Smiles: The largest of Kregen's seven moons.

main-gauche: The left-handed dagger is often called the Hikdar.

Makki-Grodno: The base for a large and colorful variety of obscene oaths used by the followers of *Zair*.

Makku-Grodno: An evil spirit of Magdag.

Malar Marshes: Marshy area of Erthyrdrin.

Marble Quarries of Zenicce: It was in the infamous Black Marble Quarries that Prescot labored as a slave (TT).

Marlimor: A reasonably civilized city famed for beautiful legends.

Marshes of Buranaccl: Swampy area to the north of the Hostile Territories.

Marsilus, Marker: Son of the Kov of Bormark, husband of Tilda and father of Pando. Died as a soldier in East Turismond.

Marsilus, Murlock: Nephew of the Kov of Bormark, usurped the Kovnate.

mashcera: Material used for awnings.

Maspero: A citizen of Aphrasöe, one of the Savanti, Prescot's Tutor (TT).

Mayfwy: Widow of Zorg. Lively and beautiful, the great lady of Felteraz (SU).

Mazak, Pur, Lord of Frentozz: A Krozair of Zy and swifter captain (WA).

Mehzta: One of the Nine Islands. Lies off the east coast of Segesthes.

Mehztas: A race of very strong people with bristle bullet-heads, heavy muscles, thick dun-colored hides, and short sinewy legs. Inhabitants of Mehzta.

Memis: A province of Tomboram.

Men of the Sunrise: An ancient people of whom now only their monuments remain, constructors of the Dam of Days and the Grand Canal. Also referred to as the Men of the Sunset.

Menaham: Nation of central North Pandahem.

miscils: Tiny, fragile cakes that melt on the tongue.

missal: A tree with white and pink blossoms.

momolams: Small round yellow tubers eaten with roast ponsho.

moon-blooms: Flowers with a double ring of petals, both opening during the day, and the outer at night when moons are in the sky.

moons: Kregen has seven moons. The largest, the Maiden with the Many Smiles, is almost twice the size of Earth's moon. The next two, the twins, revolve around each other. The fourth is She of the Veils. The three smallest moons hurtle rapidly across the sky close to the surface of Kregen.

morfangs: Monsters of the Hostile Territories, squat, ovoid, with two arched coat-hanger-like shoulders each sprouting five long whip-like tendrils, which, if cut off, grow into new monsters. Quasi-intelligent, quick, treacherous, and incredibly strong.

Mother Zinzu the Blessed, By: A favorite oath of the drinking classes of Sanurkazz.

Mountains of the North: The mountain range in the north of Vallia from which flows the Great River and much of the canal headwaters.

muldavy: Small boat of the inner sea, generally clinker-built and with a dipping lug.

mur: The Kregan minute, fifty to a bur.

Murn-Chem: An area of western Loh.

muschafs: Cultivated bushes yielding crops.

mushk: A scented yellow plant used as a windbreak, attractive to bees.

N

na: "Of." Usually used to denote a person's land or province of origin. Sometimes rendered as *nal*.

nactrix: Close cousin of the sectrix.

Naghan the Paunch: An overseer of caravan guards between Pa Mejab and Pa Weinob (SS).

Natema: The Princess Natema Cydones of the Noble House of Esztercari of Zenicce. Married Prince Varden Wanek (TT).

Nath: Sometimes Nath of Sanurkazz, sometimes Nath ti Zullia, from his birthplace. Oar-comrade to Prescot, Zorg, and Zolta. Son of an illiterate ponsho farmer. Big, a drinking man, intensely loyal to Prescot. Eventually a member of the Zimen.

Nath the Needle, Doctor: Gave medical attention to Prescot in Vondium.

Nath the Thief: Assisted the clansmen in Zenicce (TT).

nathium: Precious metal used in trinkets and objects of art.

Nemo: King of Tomboram (SS).

Nemo Zhantil Faril Opaz: A King's Swordship of Tomboram (SS).

Ng'groga: Land in the southeast of Loh.

Ngrangi: Spirit of Ng'groga appealed to and sworn by.

Nicomeyn, Pallan: Councillor of State to King Nemo (SS).

Nycresand: Islands off the east coast of Loh.

O

oars: Silver and copper coins of Magdag.

ob: One.

Ob-eye: A Blue Mountain Boy.

obi: Among the clansmen it is given and taken, at first meeting, with or without combat as necessary, to determine social order. Carries implications of responsibility for the taker as obligations of the giver. Less violent systems occur elsewhere on Kregen.

obs: Copper coins. In Pandahem, eighty obs to a dhem.

Ocher Limits: Badlands northwest of Vindelka.

Ochs: A halfling people not above four feet tall, with six limbs, the central pair used indiscriminately as legs or arms. Lemon-shaped heads with puffy jaws and lolling chops. Found as mercenaries over most of Kregen.

Ogier Cut: An east-west canal system in Vallia.

Old Superb: Nickname given to Prescot's personal flag.

onker: Term of abuse.

Oolie Opaz: Words of a continuous hypnotic chant.

Opaz: Name given to the dual-spirit, the Invisible Twins, who are visibly represented in the sky by Zim and Genodras.

Overlords: The Overlords of Magdag, masters of the north shore of the inner sea (SU).

Owlarh Waste: Eastern section of the Hostile Territories leading to the Klackadrin.

P

paline: Yellow cherry-like fruit with the taste of old port grows almost everywhere on Kregen. Sovereign cure for hangovers.

Pallan: Equates with Councillor, Minister, or Secretary of State.

Pa Mejab: Colonial port city of Tomboram in Eastern Turismond.

Pandahem: One of the Nine Islands, off the east coast of Loh. People known as Pandaheem.

Panderk: Bay and Islands of North Pandahem.

Pandrite: A beneficent spirit of Pandahem.

Pando: Son of Tilda the Beautiful, inheritor of title of Kov of Bormark (SS).

Panifer, Paline: Young servant girl in Vondium.

Panvals: Vallian political party opposed to racters.

papishin: Leaves used as roof-coverings.

pappattu: Introduction.

Pass of Trampled Leaves: In Segesthes where Prescot's clansmen fired the wagons of their foemen (TT).

Pattelonia: Chief city of Proconia.

Pa Weinob: Frontier town of Tomboram in Eastern Turismond.

Pela: Lady-in-waiting to Katrin Rashumin.

Perithia: An area inland at the eastern end of the inner sea.

Phokaym: Intelligent and cruel reptilian race of risslaca ancestry inhabiting area to the immediate west of the Klackadrin.

Plains of Mist: Happy Hunting Grounds of the clansmen.

Plicla: Rapa city of the Hostile Territories.

Pomdermam: Capital of Tomboram.

ponsho: Domesticated animal providing meat and wool.

ponsho-trag: A Kregan sheep dog.

Ponthieu: A House of Zenicce.

Pool of Baptism: On the River Zelph in Aphrasöe.

Port Marsilus: Port of Bormark.

Port Paros: Small port in Segesthes southeast of Zenicce.

Port Tavetus: Colonial city of Vallia in Eastern Turismond.

Pracek, Prince: Of Ponthieu, presumed to the hand of Delia (TT).

Presidio: Government of Vallia under the Emperor.

preysany: A superior calsany used as a saddle animal.

Proconia: Land at the eastern end of the inner sea with people distinct from the north and south shore peoples.

Procul: A wine rich and dark red.

Prophet: Inspirational leader in the warrens of Magdag (TT).

Pugnarses: Overseer of the balass in the warrens of Magdag (TT).

Pur: Not a rank or a title (although apparently used as such), a badge of chivalry and honor, a pledge that the holder is a true Krozair. Prefixed to the holder's name, as: *Pur Dray.*

Q

Quanscott: Port of the Blue Mountains on the west coast of Vallia.

Queens of Pain: Infamous rulers of Loh.

Quest of Tyr Nath, The: A rollicking tale of mythical adventure at least two thousand years old and known all over Kregen.

R

racter: Member of the most powerful political party in Vallia.

Rahartdrin: Island and Kovnate off the southwest coast of Vallia.

Rapa: Gray vulturine-headed halflings living over most of Kregen as slaves, workers, or mercenary guards, or in their own cities.

rapier: Often called the Jiktar. "A rapier to sharpen" equates with "an ax to grind."

rark: Powerful hunting dog of Segesthes.

rashoon: Sudden and violent local gale on the inner sea.

Rashumin, Katrin: Kovneva of Rahartdrin.

rast: A disgusting six-legged rodent infesting dunghills.

Red Brethren of Lizz: A Fighting Order of Sanurkazz, devoted to Zair.

Relts: More gentle cousins of the Rapas.

Remberee: Universal salutation on parting.

Render: Pirate.

risslaca: Dinosaur.

River of Shining Spears: Flows from the Blue Mountains into the Great River.

Rodway, Pallan: In charge of the Treasury of Vallia.

Rojica Passage: Channel between Vallia and Can-thirda.

Rose of Valka, The:An inn and posting house in Vondium.

S

sah-lah: Cultivated bush with pink and white sweet blossoms.

San: An ancient title for master, dominie, sage.

samphron: Cultivated bush, the fruits yielding oil.

Sanurkazz: Chief city of the men of Zair.

Savanti: Mortal but superhuman people of Aphrasöe.

Sea-Barynth: Huge serpentine monster with oval body, long dorsal fin, an immense head, and fang-filled mouth above two paddle-fins.

Sea of Marshes: Southerly extension of the inner sea past Sanurkazz.

Sea of Swords: Smaller extension of the inner sea past Zy.

sectrix: Six-legged saddle animal, blunt-headed, wicked-eyed, pricked of ear, slate-blue hide covered with scanty coarse hair.

Segesthes: A continent of Kregen.

Segutorio, Seg: Bowman of Loh from Erthyrdrin. Ran away to be a mercenary. Intensely loyal to Prescot and a good comrade.

Selnix: Vad of Thadelm.

Shallan: Prescot's agent in Sanurkazz (SU/WA).

Shattered targes in Mount Hlabro, By all the: An Erthyr oath.

She of the Veils: Fourth moon of Kregen.

shorgortz: Giant reptilian monster with four eyes, in the Blue Mountains.

Shusha, Great-Aunt: The Lady of Strombor, married into the Ewards, from whom Prescot received Strombor.

shush-chiff: Sarong-like garment worn by girls on holiday.

silver trumpets of Loh: Famed trumpets that led on the armies of Walfarg.

So: Three.

Sooten and her Twelve Suitors: Theatrical tragedy well known on Kregen.

Sorzarts: Lizard-men of a group of islands in northeastern inner sea.

Sosie: Wife of Ven Yelker nal Vomansoir, a canalwoman.

Sosie na Arkasson: Young lady rescued by Prescot in the Hostile Territories (SS).

Spitz: A Bowman of Loh (SS).

squishes: Tiny and delicious fruit.

Star Lords: The Everoinye.

Stentors: 1. Chunkrah-horn blowers in swifters; 2. Spiral-brass-horn blowers in Emperor's canal boats.

Storr, Mount: Vineyards near Hiclantung.

Stovang, Hikdar: Vektor's officer in charge of wedding presents.

Stratemsk, The: Enormous mountain chain of Turismond.

Strigicaw: Powerful fast-running, six-legged carnivore, with striped foreparts and double-spotted rear, in red and brown.

Strigicaw: A zenzile swordship commanded by Prescot for Viridia (SS).

Strom: Title of Kregan nobility approximating to "count."

Strombor: A noble House of Zenicce.

Strye: Island northwest of Zenicce which provides cheap grass for mastodons.

sturm: Wood of many uses on Kregen.

Stylor: Name given to Prescot in the warrens of Magdag (SU).

Sunset Sea: Ocean stretching between Segesthes and Turismond.

Susheeng: Princess of Magdag (SU).

swifter: Multi-banked galley of the inner sea.

swingers: Platforms attached to plant tendrils used for transportation in Aphrasöe.

Swinging City: Aphrasöe.

Sword of Genodras: Magdaggian swifter captured by Prescot and Seg (WA).

swordship: Single-banked, broadside-armed galleass of the outer oceans.

Swordship and Barynth, The: An inn of Therminsax.

T

talens: Gold coins of Vallia.

Talu: Eight-armed dancer (possibly mythical).

Ta'temsk: Guardian spirit of the inner sea.

taylynes: Pea-sized scarlet and orange vegetables. Good with vosk.

terchick: Throwing-knife, often called the Deldar.

Thadelm: A province of Vallia northwest of Delphond.

Tharu of Vindelka: Kov sent by Delia to find Prescot on inner sea (SU).

Tharu ti Valkanium: Leader of the high assembly of Valka.

Theirson: Koter of Valka who helped Prescot during his canal sickness.

Thelda: Lady-in-waiting to Delia (WA).

Therminsax: Market town of central north Vallia.

Thisi the Fair: Wife to Theirson.

thorn-ivy: Unpleasant sharp-spined bush.

thyrrix: Nimble mountain-animal of Erthyrdrin.

ti: "Of." Usually used to denote a person's town or city of origin.

tikos: Little green and brown lizards.

Tilda: Mother of Pando. A famous theatrical entertainer, known as Tilda the Beautiful or Tilda of the Many Veils (SS).

Todalpheme: Astronomers and mathematicians.

Tom of Vulheim: Young Koter of Valka.

Tomboram: Nation of eastern North Pandahem.

toonon: Shortsword mounted on bamboo shaft, aerial weapon of Ullars.

Tremzo: A city of Zair.

Trylon: Title of Kregan nobility intermediate between Vad and Strom.

tuffa: A thin willowy tree.

Turismond: A continent of Kregen.

Tyr: Title equivalent to "Sir."

U

Ullardrin: Land of Northern Turismond.

Ullars: Barbarians from Ullardrin, with narrow-set eyes, square clamped mouths, blunt heads, hair dyed indigo. Whole tribes habitually travel by air astride saddle impiters.

Ullgishoa: Horrific monster belonging to Ullars (WA).

Umgar Stro: Leader of Ullars (WA).

Undurkers: Supercilious race of canine-headed halfling archers.

Undurkor: Group of islands of southwest coast of Segesthes.

Upalion: A rich estate of Proconia. The Lady Pulvia and her son were rescued by Prescot on orders from the Star Lords (WA).

V

Vad: Title of Kregan nobility intermediate between Kov and Trylon.

Valka: Island off the east coast of Can-thirda off Vallia.

Valkanium: Capital city of Valka.

Vallia: One of the Nine Islands situated between Segesthes and Loh.

Vandayha: City of Valka famed for its silversmiths.

Vangar ti Valkanium: A Deldar in the Vallian Air Service.

Vanki, Naghan: Lord of an island off Vallia.

Vaosh: Patron spirit of the canalfolk.

varter: Flat-trajectory ballista throwing rocks and darts.

Veiled Froyvil: Spirit appealed to and sworn by, of Erthyrdrin.

Vela's Tears: Strong red wine of southern Valka.

Vektor, Kov of Aduimbrev: Selected by the Emperor to marry Delia.

Ven: Courtesy title of canalmen. Feminine is Vena.

Venus: Swordship of Viridia's render maidens (SS).

Viktrik: A clan of the Great Plains of Segesthes.

vilmy: Blue flower with silver heart-shape on each petal; the paste makes a soothing ointment.

Vindelka: Province and Kovnate northwest of Vondium.

Violet offal of the snow-blind feister-feelt, By the: An Ullar oath.

Viridia the Render: A lady pirate of the Hoboling Islands (SS).

Vomansoir: Province and Kovnate of central Vallia.

Vomanus: Became Kov of Vindelka. Good comrade to Prescot (SU).

Vomer the Vile, By: Oath of the slave-masters of Vallia.

Vondium: Capital of Vallia.

voryasen: A risslaca, part crocodile, part tylosaurus.

Vorgan: A Stromnate owning allegiance to the Kov of Vomansoir.

vosk: A fat pig-like six-legged animal with a smooth oily skin of a whitish-yellow, with atrophied tusks, standing six feet at the shoulder. A beast of burden; more often a food animal.

vosk-skulls, or vosk-helmets: The workers and slaves of the warrens of Magdag trained up by Prescot into a phalanx received either of these names because they wore thick vosk skulls as helmets.

vove: Large and exceptionally ferocious eight-legged saddle-animal of the Great Plains of Segesthes, equipped with fangs and horns, russet-colored. Smaller and without the fangs and horns is called a half-vove.

Vovedeer: Leader of clans in Segesthes.

Vox, By: A Vallian oath.

Vulheim: Port city of western Valka.

W

Walfarg: Nation of Loh, now sunk in apathy, once the center of a great empire.

Wanek, Prince Varden: Of the House of Eward. A good comrade to Prescot

Wardens: Provided by all the Houses of Zenicce for police work and seaward defense.

wersting: A vicious black and white stripped four-legged hunting dog.

Wickens: A House of Zenicce.

Wil: Young boy of *Dancing Talu*.

Wizards of Loh: Sorcerers and magicians of great and apparently supernatural powers.

Wloclef: Large island off the west coast of Turismond, famed for its thick-fleeced curly-ponshos.

woflo: Small animal fond of cheese.

Womox: An island off the west coast of Vallia.

Womoxes: A strong, bull-necked people who carry their heads forward with two stumpy but formidable horns on their foreheads. Fierce, independent, not overly original.

Wulk: A barbarian of the northern hills, a friend to Prescot.

Wyndhai: An area of The Stratemsk, home of yellow eagles.

X

xi: Iridescent-scaled winged lizards of humid jungle-valleys of The Stratemsk.

Xoltemb: A caravan-master of Segesthes from Xuntal (TT).

Xuntal: An island off the southern promontory of Segesthes.

Y

Yelker, Ven, nal Vomansoir: A canalman, owner of the *Dancing Talu*.

Yerthyr: Very dark-green poisonous tree of Erthyrdrin from which are cut the finest-quality longbow staves.

yulshi: A draft bird of the Hostile Territories. Plural: yuelshi.

Yumapan: Nation of the west coast of Pandahem.

Z

Zair: The red-sun deity.

Zamu: A city dedicated to Zair, base of the Krozairs of Zamu.

Zantristar the Merciful, By: A Sanurkazzian oath.

Zazz, Pur: Grand Archbold of the Krozairs of Zy (SU).

Zelph, River: Joins the River Aph at Aphrasöe.

Zenicce: Great enclave city of a million souls on west coast of Segesthes.

Zenkiren, Pur: Krozair of Zy, Grand Archbold elect (SU/WA).

zhantil: A magnificent wild animal larger than a leem, massively built in the foreparts, banded in tiger-stripes of umber and ruby, with a rich golden mane.

zhantil to saddle, a: A secret and difficult purpose.

Zim: The red sun of Antares. Has many other names.

Zimen: Lay brothers of the Krozairs of Zy.

Zim Stream: Warm water flowing northward through the Cyphren Sea.

Zim-Zair, By: A Krozair oath.

zizils: Giant flying animals of The Stratemsk.

Zo, King: King of Sanurkazz (SU).

Zolta: Oar-comrade to Prescot, Zorg, and Nath. Took the apostis seat. Gives no details of his history, is a man for the ladies. Eventually a member of the Zimen.

Zond: Produces the finest wine of the southern shore of the inner sea.

Zora: Name usually given by Prescot to swifters he commanded.

zorca: Swift riding animal, short-coupled, four extremely long and thin legs, hoofed. A single curled horn rises from its forehead.

Zorcander: Leader of clans.

Zorg: Son of Zorg and Mayfwy (SU).

Zorg of Felteraz: Oar-comrade of Prescot, Zolta, and Nath. Krozair of Zy. Died under the lash on the slave-benches of the Magdaggian swifter *Grace of Grodno*.

Zulfiria: A city of the southern shore of the inner sea.

Zullia: Village to the south of Sanurkazz devoted to ponsho fanning. Birth-place of Nath, oar-comrade to Prescot.

Zy: Island formed from an extinct volcano, in the mouth of the Sea of Swords. Headquarters of the Krozairs of Zy.

Zyna: Daughter of Ven Yelker and Vena Sosie, of the *Dancing Talu*.

Notes

i: A bur is the Kregan hour, some forty Earth minutes long. It is divided into fifty murs, the Kregan minute. Discrepancies in the year caused by the orbit of Kregan about a binary are ironed out at festival times. There are forty-eight burs in the Kregan day and night cycle. I have omitted much of what Dray Prescot says of mensuration on Kregan and have considerably amended his account of the technical activities of the tide-watchers, the Todalpheme. *A.B.A.*

ii: I have left Prescot's use of the Kregish "dwabur" here. A dwabur is one of the standard units of measurement and is approximately five Terrestrial miles. Its origin, according to Prescot, comes from the sunset people's army marching disciplines: they would continue for two of their hours, that is, burs (the Kregish word for two is dwa), with a halt. Their speed must therefore have been something over three and a half miles an hour. More usual are the local lesser fractions of the dwabur. *A.B.A.*

iii: This is the point where at least one cassette is missing, as I have written in A Note on the Tapes from Africa at the beginning of this volume. It is clear from internal evidence that Prescot achieved command of a four-sixtyswifter and the next consecutive cassette picks up his story when he had spent probably three, at the least, seasons as a galley captain on the inner sea. What is lost we do not know, but from our knowledge of Dray Prescot I think it evident it was lurid, violent, and vividly colored in the extreme. *A.B.A.*

iv: Clearly, here, Prescot is referring to passages in the lost cassettes. This is a great pity, for any light he can shed on galley propulsion and crewing is of the greatest academic interest to scholars. *A.B.A.*

v: Further information lost to us from Prescot's narrative in the missing cassettes. *A.B.A.*

vi: Idem. *A.B.A.*

vii: *Transit to Scorpio* and *The Suns of Scorpio.*

viii: A further reference to the missing cassettes' information we do not have, as related in *The Suns of Scorpio. A.B.A.*

ix: Prescot spells out Lu-si-Yuong, and is meticulous about getting the name and pronunciation right. He also elaborates on these famous Wizards, and is careful to use the title San. Jikai, here, clearly is being used in a titular role, and must be assumed to be the general for "warrior". *A.B.A.*

x: The Word "Kyr" has been used by Prescot many times in his narrative but I have generally changed it to "Lord." It begins to look as though this usage may be incorrect, and the honorific "sir" is a better translation. As part of the title of a book its use here is perfectly justified. Also we have here, I suspect, the root reason why there are so many Naths on Kregen.

xi: Here is another example of a reference to incidents in Dray Prescot's life on Kregen during the period he spent on the inner sea and in Sanurkazz lost to us with those missing cassettes, as related in "A note on the tapes from Africa" in *The Suns of Scorpio. A.B.A.*

xii: Prescot spells out this name, Phokaym, giving it the "Ph" and the "Y," although he nowhere tells us where he learned that these were the correct spellings, in place of the "F" and the "I". *A.B.A.*

xiii: I think it worth pointing out that the suffix "A" clearly does not invariably denote the feminine gender in Kregish, as Prescot suggested in "Beng" and "Benga," the Kregish for male and female "Saint." We have also the example of Zolta — a man if ever there was one. *A.B.A.*

xiv: Elsewhere Prescot says that *Koter* is usually abbreviated to *Kr,* as is "Mister" on Earth abbreviated to "Mr." Also, he says that *Krozair* is often abbreviated to *Krz.* The Kregans, like the ancient Romans and modern men, are fond of abbreviations. *A.B.A.*

xv: *Kta., Kotera*, the female equivalent of *Koter*, of *Kr. A.B.A.*

Kenneth Bulmer

Alan Burt Akers was a pen name of the prolific British author Kenneth Bulmer, who died in December 2005 aged eighty-four.

Bulmer wrote over 160 novels and countless short stories, predominantly science fiction, both under his real name and numerous pseudonyms, including Alan Burt Akers, Frank Brandon, Rupert Clinton, Ernest Corley, Peter Green, Adam Hardy, Philip Kent, Bruno Krauss, Karl Maras, Manning Norvil, Chesman Scot, Nelson Sherwood, Richard Silver, H. Philip Stratford, and Tully Zetford. Kenneth Johns was a collective pseudonym used for a collaboration with author John Newman. Some of Bulmer's works were published along with the works of other authors under "house names" (collective pseudonyms) such as Ken Blake (for a series of tie-ins with the 1970s television programme The Professionals), Arthur Frazier, Neil Langholm, Charles R. Pike, and Andrew Quiller.

Bulmer was also active in science fiction fandom, and in the 1970s he edited nine issues of the New Writings in Science Fiction anthology series in succession to John Carnell, who originated the series.

More details about the author, and current links to other sources of information, can be found at wikipedia.org.